GOLDFISCH

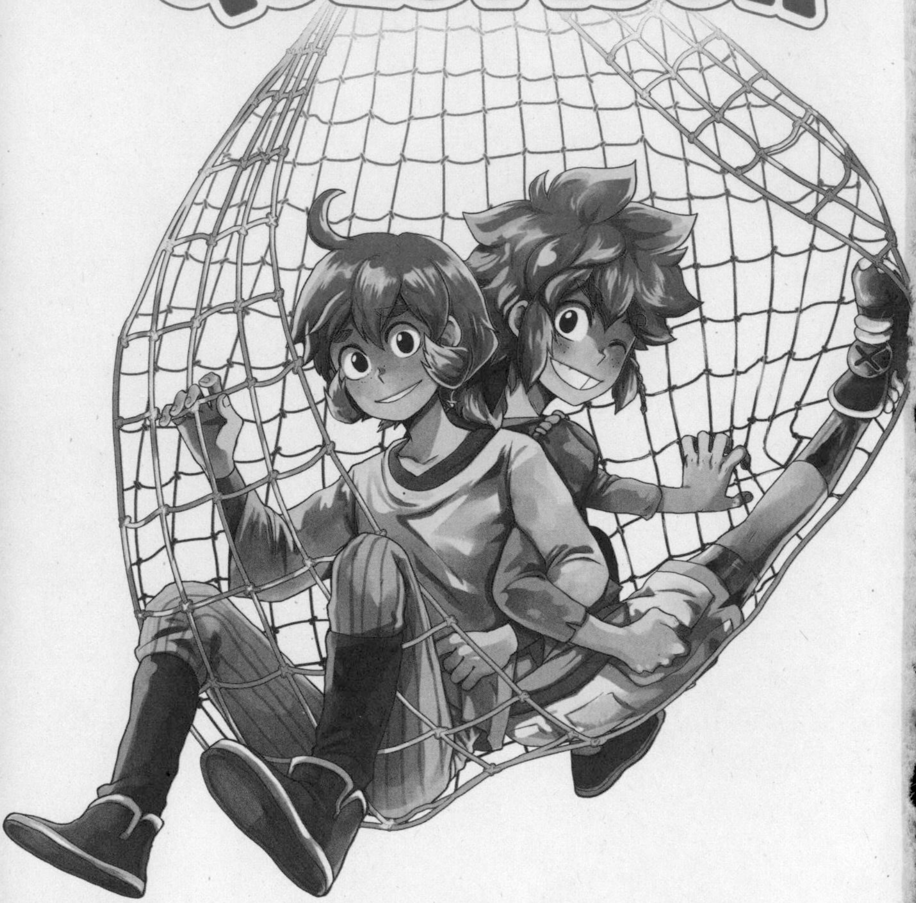

2

Nana Yaa

TOKYOPOP

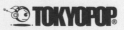

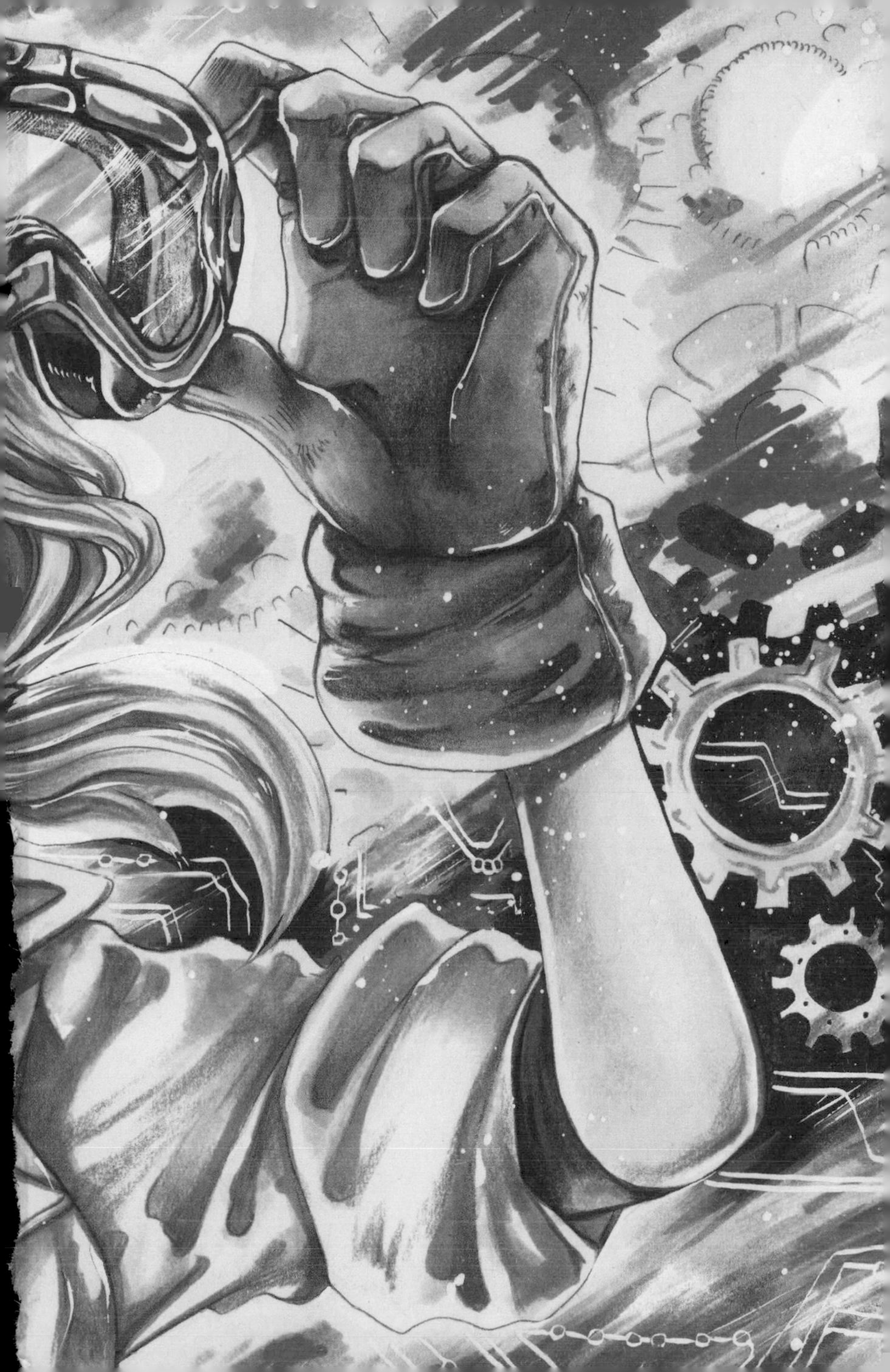

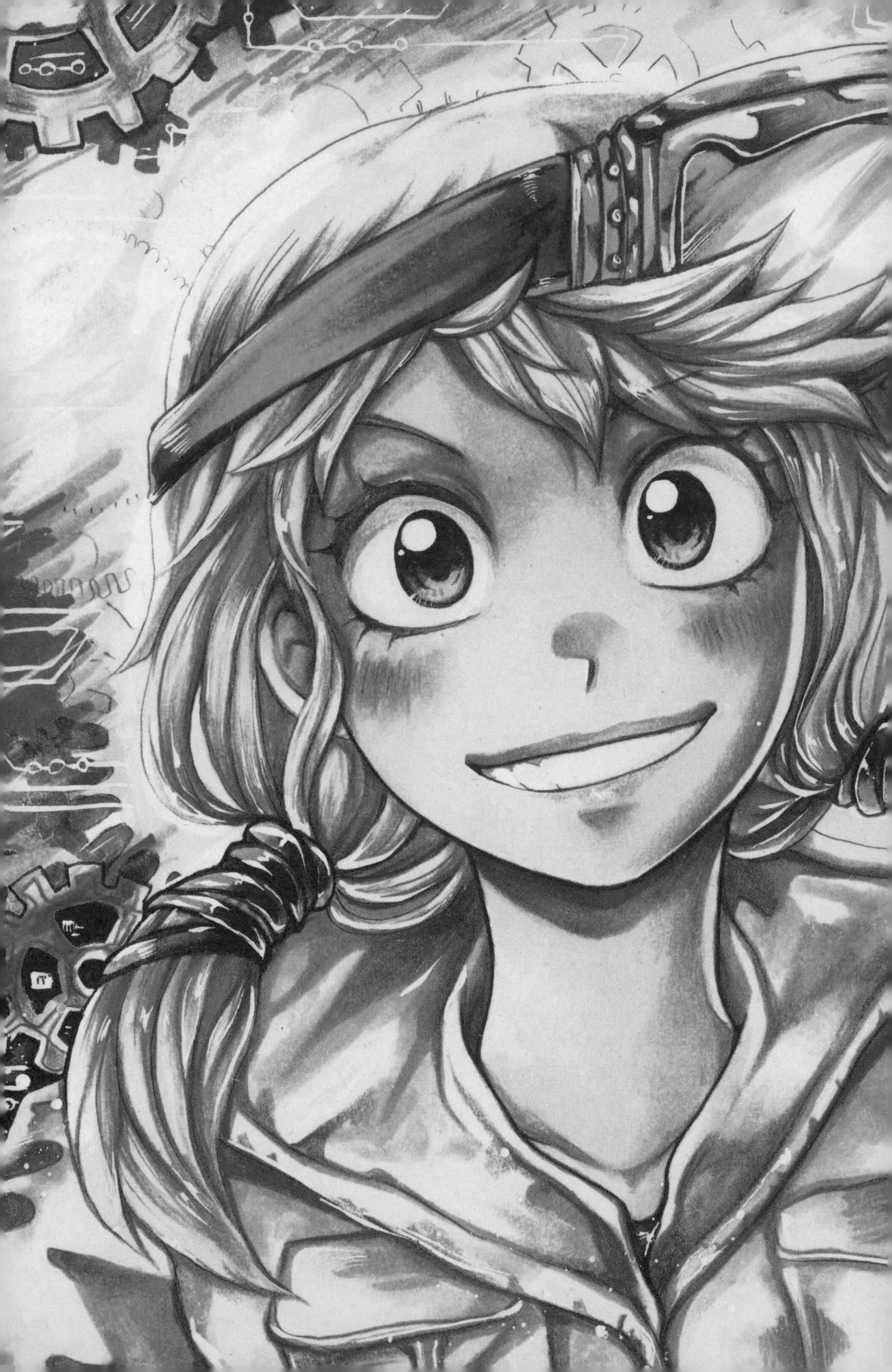

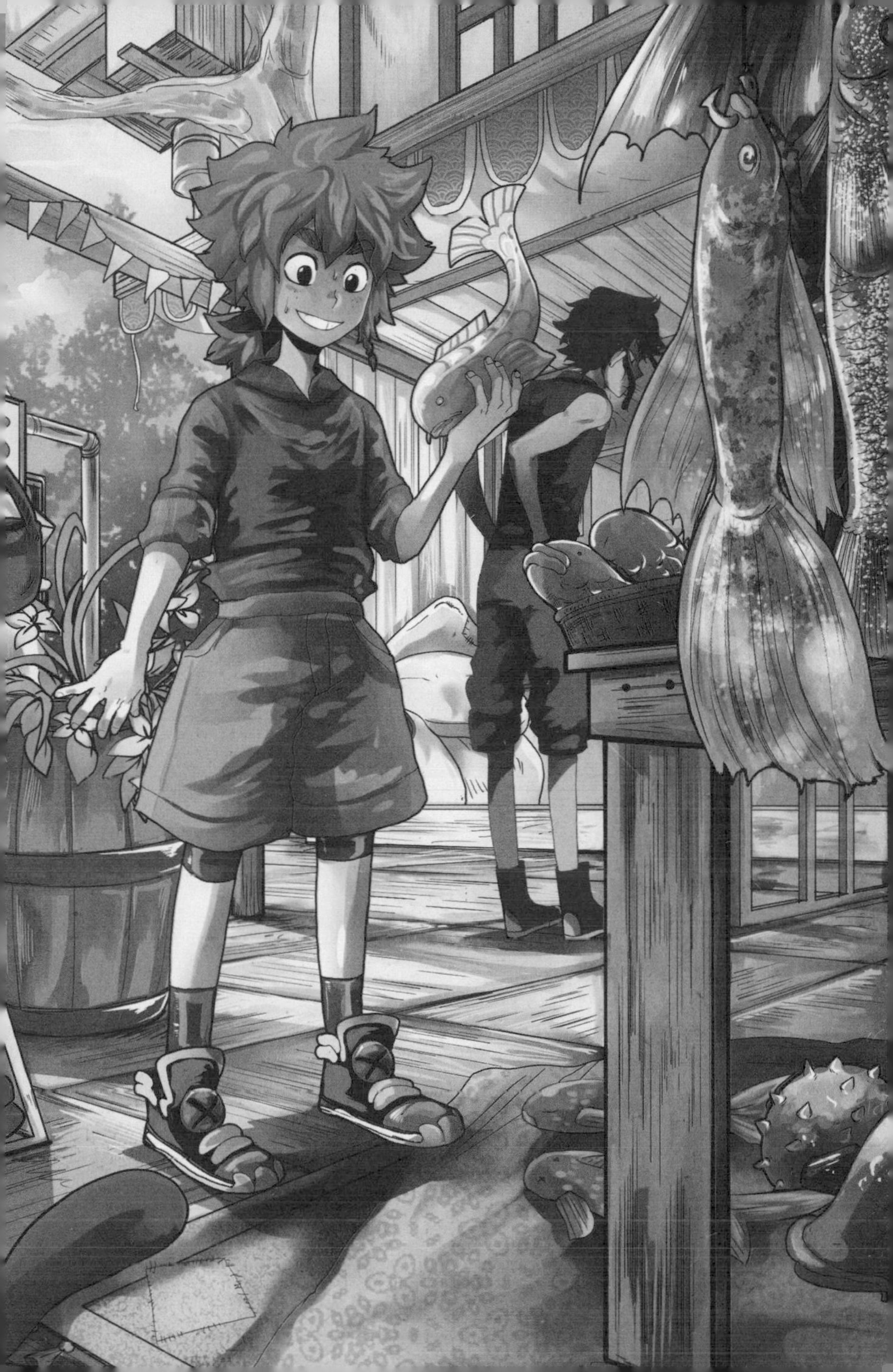

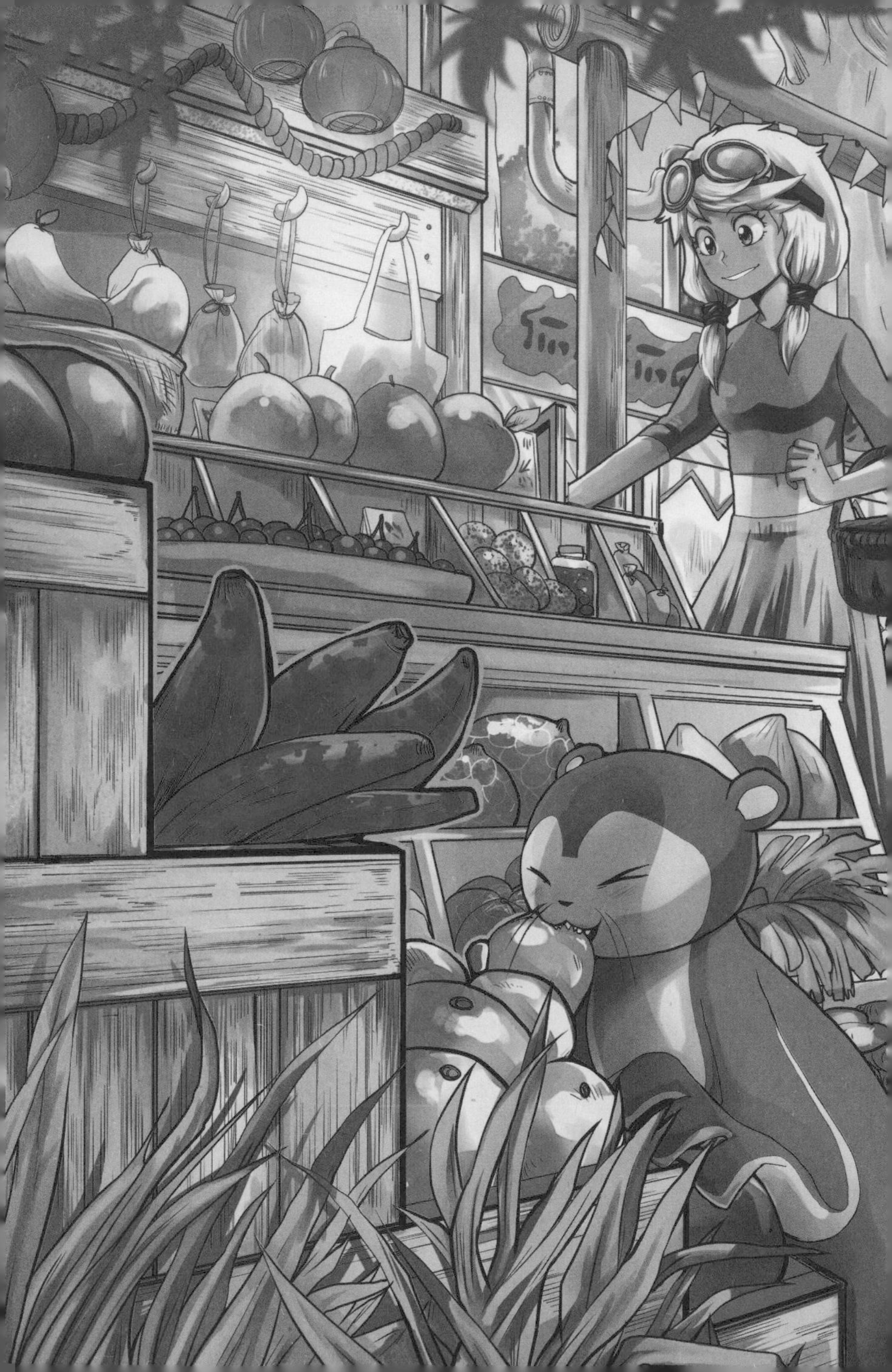

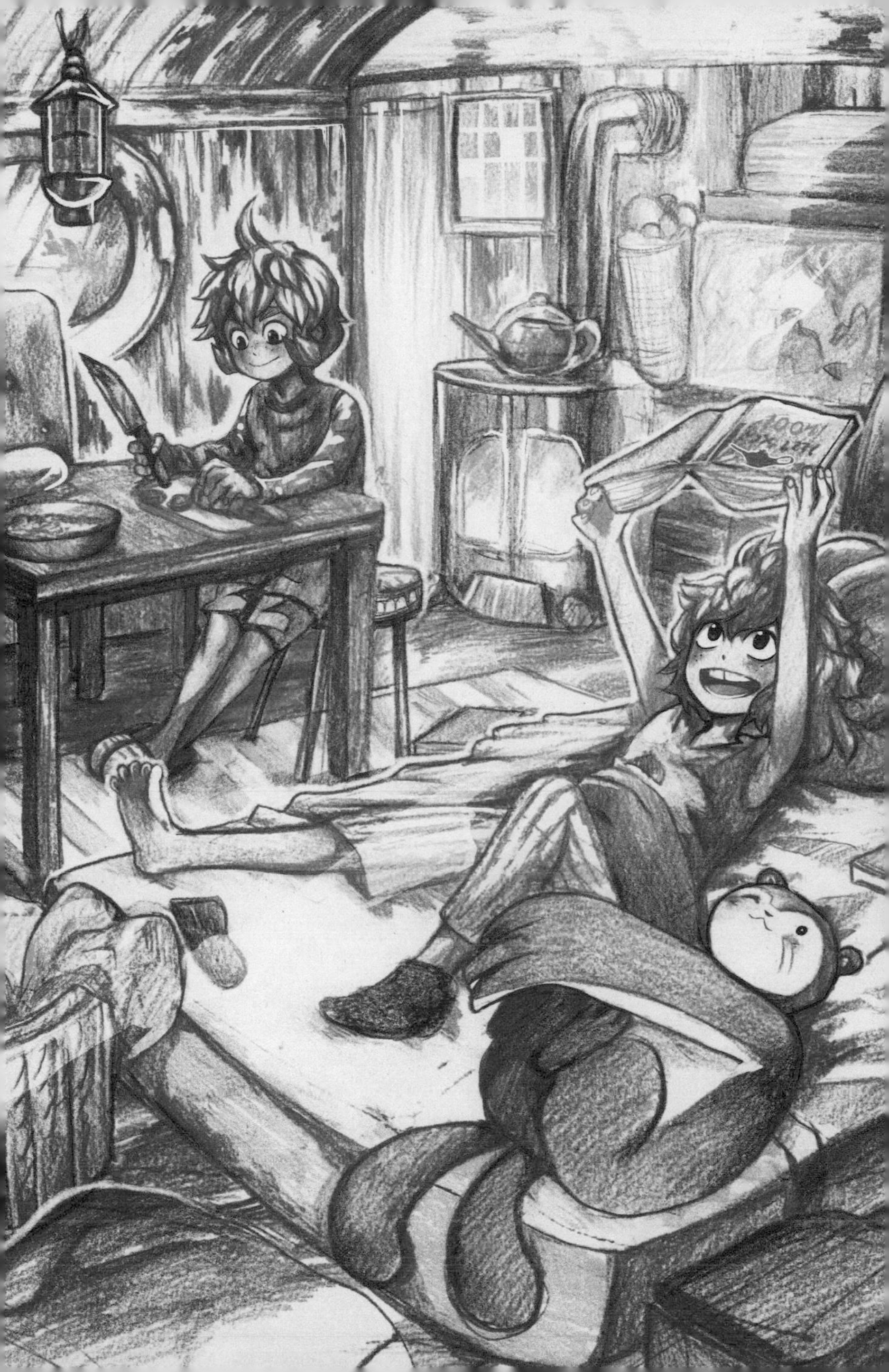

GOLDFISCH

2

Nana Yaa

TOKYOPOP®

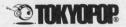

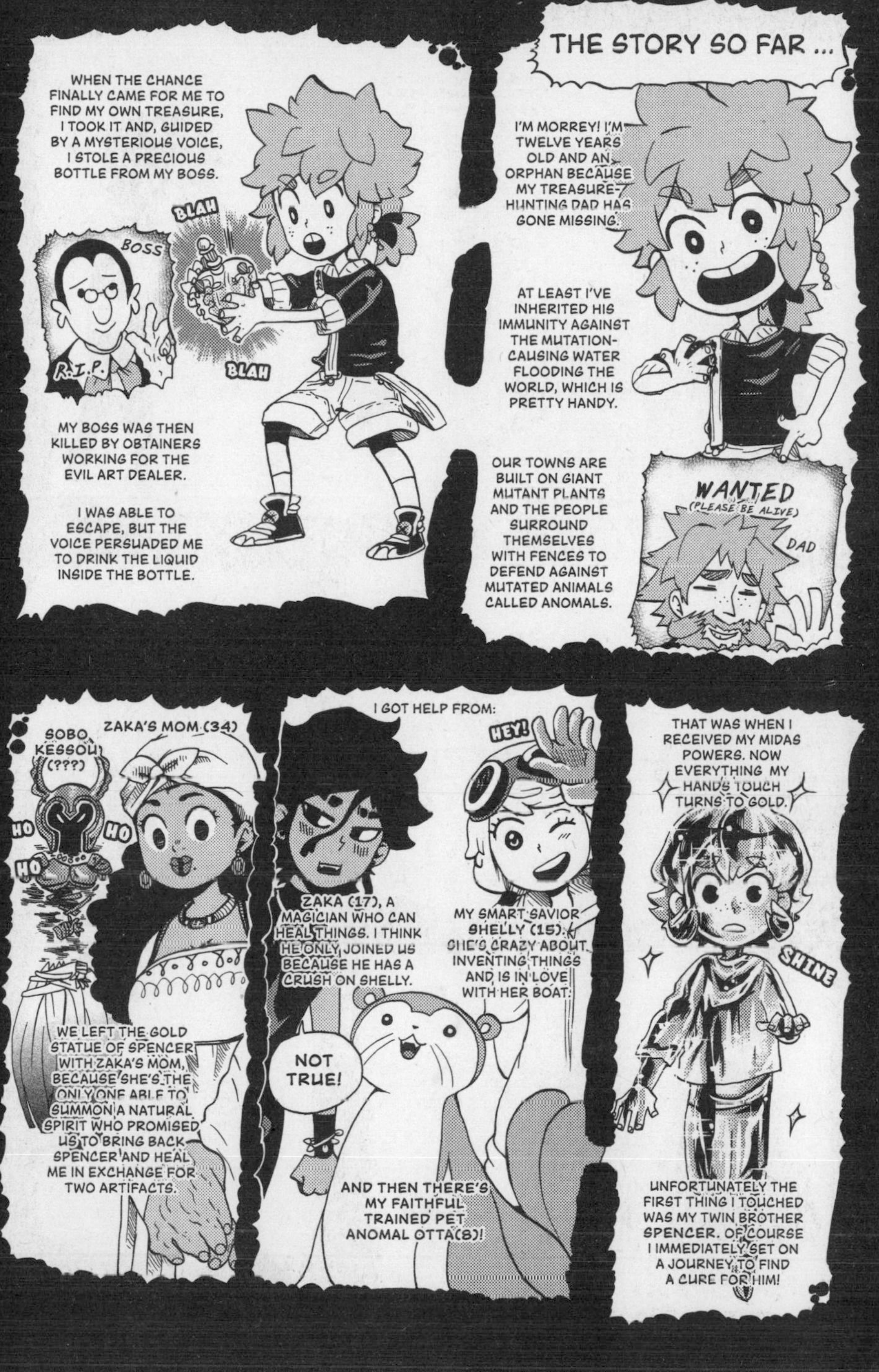
THE STORY SO FAR ...
I'M MORREY! I'M TWELVE YEARS OLD AND AN ORPHAN BECAUSE MY TREASURE-HUNTING DAD HAS GONE MISSING.
AT LEAST I'VE INHERITED HIS IMMUNITY AGAINST THE MUTATION-CAUSING WATER FLOODING THE WORLD, WHICH IS PRETTY HANDY.
OUR TOWNS ARE BUILT ON GIANT MUTANT PLANTS AND THE PEOPLE SURROUND THEMSELVES WITH FENCES TO DEFEND AGAINST MUTATED ANIMALS CALLED ANOMALS.
WANTED
(PLEASE BE ALIVE)
DAD
WHEN THE CHANCE FINALLY CAME FOR ME TO FIND MY OWN TREASURE, I TOOK IT AND, GUIDED BY A MYSTERIOUS VOICE, I STOLE A PRECIOUS BOTTLE FROM MY BOSS.
BLAH
BOSS
BLAH
R.I.P.
MY BOSS WAS THEN KILLED BY OBTAINERS WORKING FOR THE EVIL ART DEALER.
I WAS ABLE TO ESCAPE, BUT THE VOICE PERSUADED ME TO DRINK THE LIQUID INSIDE THE BOTTLE.
THAT WAS WHEN I RECEIVED MY MIDAS POWERS. NOW EVERYTHING MY HANDS TOUCH TURNS TO GOLD.
SHINE
UNFORTUNATELY THE FIRST THING I TOUCHED WAS MY TWIN BROTHER SPENCER. OF COURSE I IMMEDIATELY SET ON A JOURNEY TO FIND A CURE FOR HIM!
I GOT HELP FROM:
HEY!
MY SMART SAVIOR SHELLY (15). SHE'S CRAZY ABOUT INVENTING THINGS AND IS IN LOVE WITH HER BOAT.
ZAKA (17), A MAGICIAN WHO CAN HEAL THINGS. I THINK HE ONLY JOINED US BECAUSE HE HAS A CRUSH ON SHELLY.
NOT TRUE!
AND THEN THERE'S MY FAITHFUL TRAINED PET ANOMAL OTTA(8)!
ZAKA'S MOM (34)
SOBO KESSOU (???)
HO
HO
HO
WE LEFT THE GOLD STATUE OF SPENCER WITH ZAKA'S MOM, BECAUSE SHE'S THE ONLY ONE ABLE TO SUMMON A NATURAL SPIRIT WHO PROMISED US TO BRING BACK SPENCER AND HEAL ME IN EXCHANGE FOR TWO ARTIFACTS.

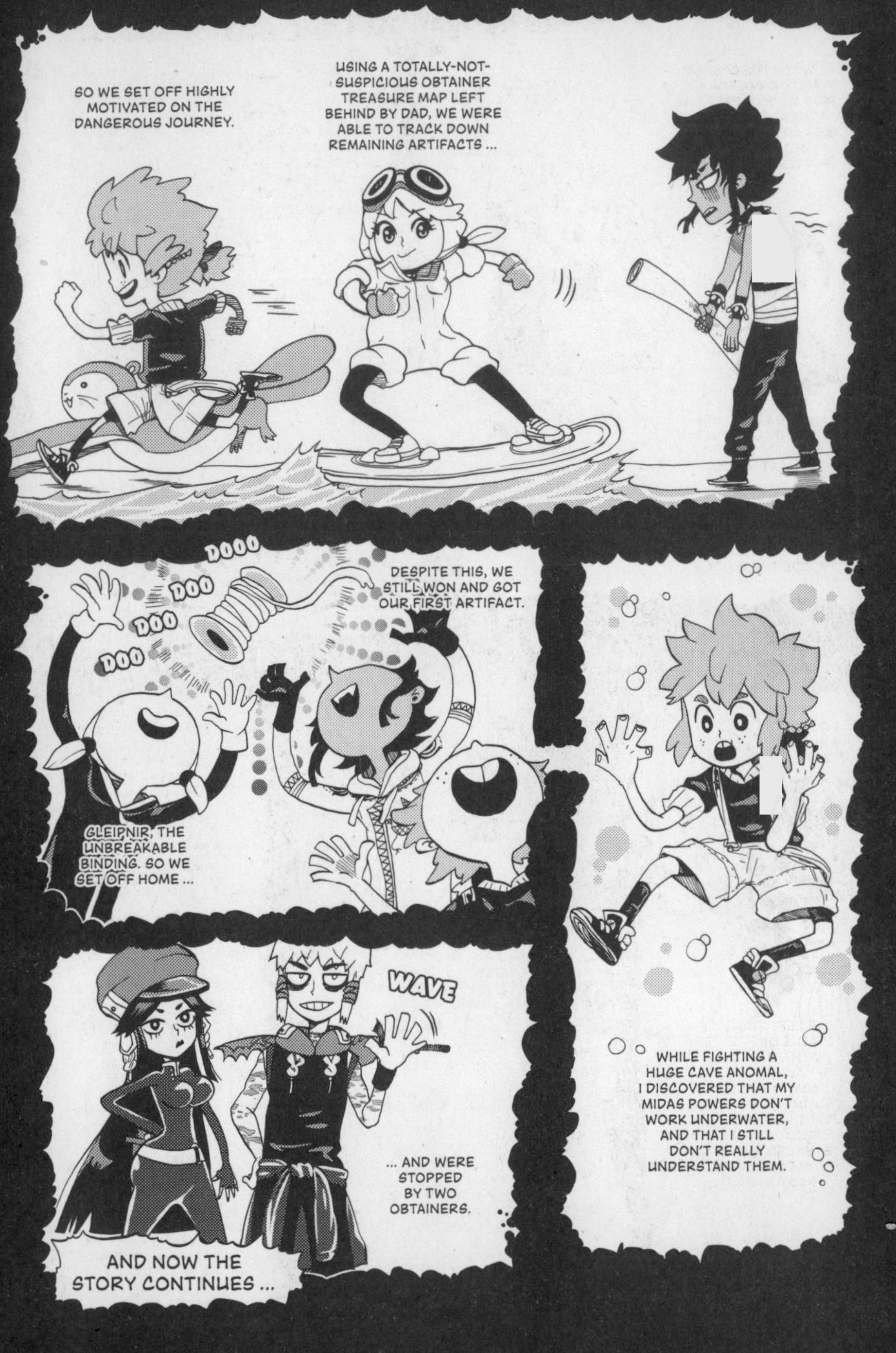
USING A TOTALLY-NOT-SUSPICIOUS OBTAINER TREASURE MAP LEFT BEHIND BY DAD, WE WERE ABLE TO TRACK DOWN REMAINING ARTIFACTS ...
SO WE SET OFF HIGHLY MOTIVATED ON THE DANGEROUS JOURNEY.
WHILE FIGHTING A HUGE CAVE ANOMAL, I DISCOVERED THAT MY MIDAS POWERS DON'T WORK UNDERWATER, AND THAT I STILL DON'T REALLY UNDERSTAND THEM.
DESPITE THIS, WE STILL WON AND GOT OUR FIRST ARTIFACT.
DOOOO
DOO
DOO
DOO
GLEIPNIR, THE UNBREAKABLE BINDING. SO WE SET OFF HOME ...
WAVE
... AND WERE STOPPED BY TWO OBTAINERS.
AND NOW THE STORY CONTINUES ...

CONTENTS

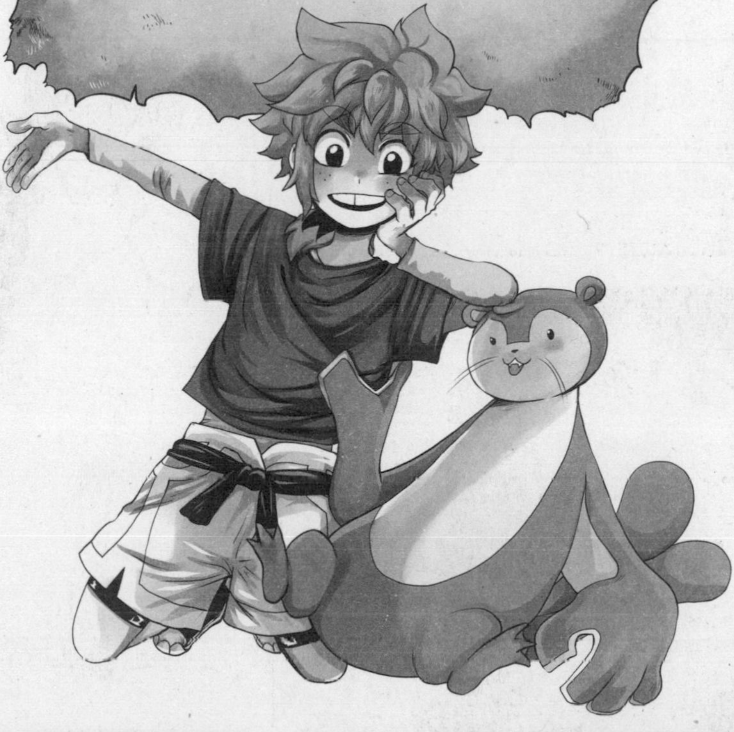

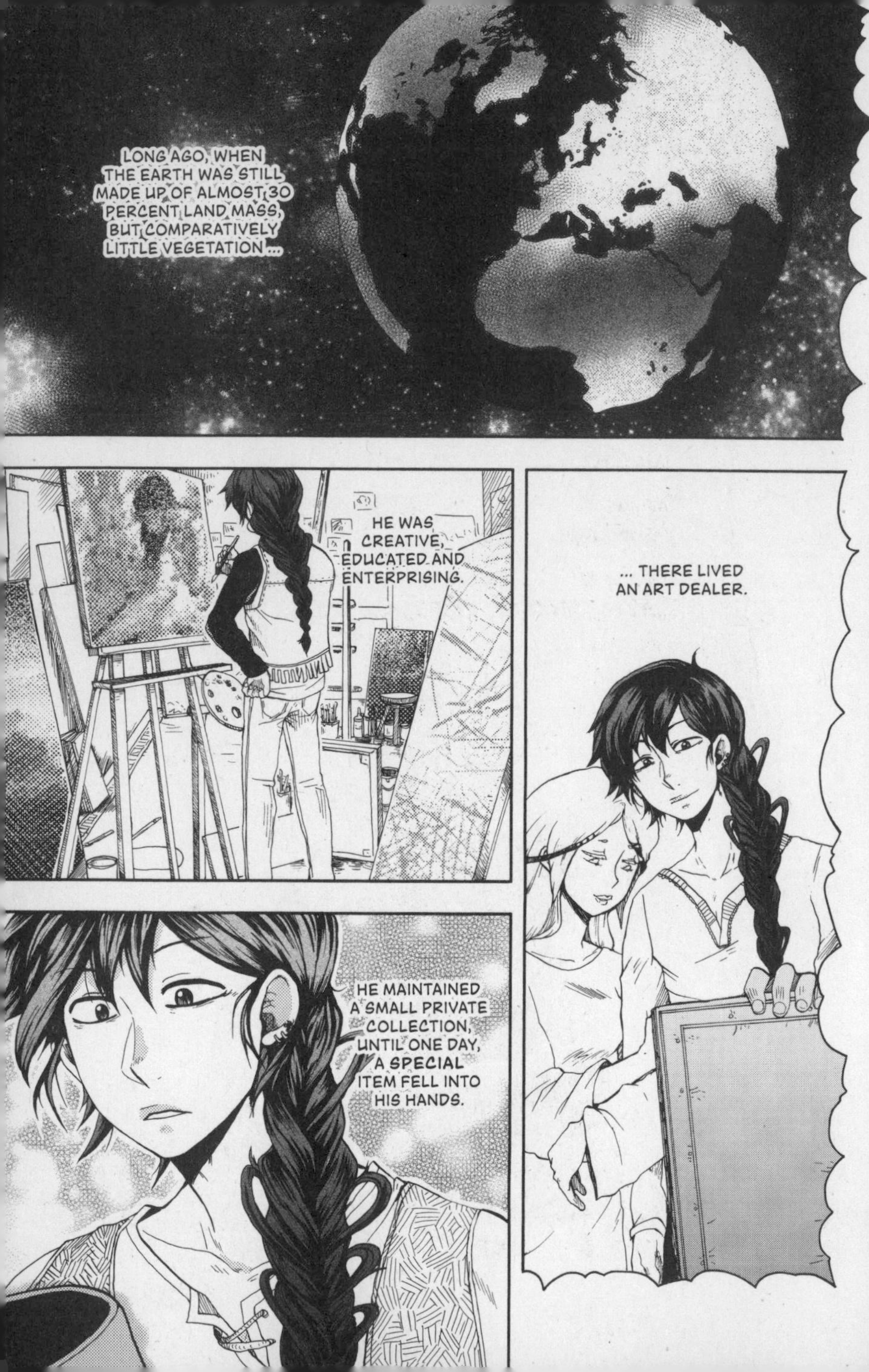
LONG AGO, WHEN THE EARTH WAS STILL MADE UP OF ALMOST 30 PERCENT LAND MASS, BUT COMPARATIVELY LITTLE VEGETATION ...
... THERE LIVED AN ART DEALER.
HE WAS CREATIVE, EDUCATED AND ENTERPRISING.
HE MAINTAINED A SMALL PRIVATE COLLECTION, UNTIL ONE DAY, A SPECIAL ITEM FELL INTO HIS HANDS.

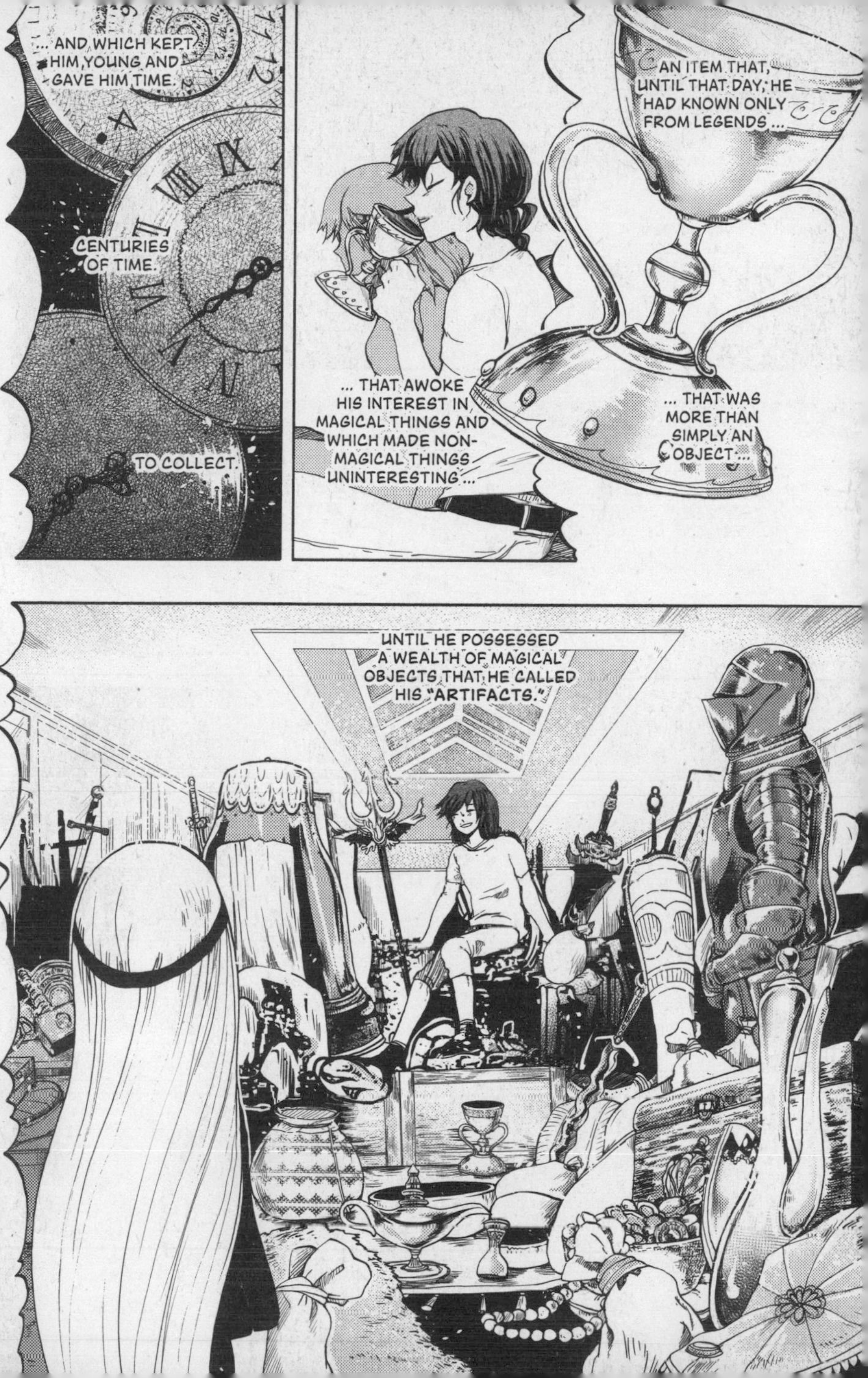
AN ITEM THAT, UNTIL THAT DAY, HE HAD KNOWN ONLY FROM LEGENDS ...
... THAT WAS MORE THAN SIMPLY AN OBJECT ...
... THAT AWOKE HIS INTEREST IN MAGICAL THINGS AND WHICH MADE NON-MAGICAL THINGS UNINTERESTING ...
... AND WHICH KEPT HIM YOUNG AND GAVE HIM TIME.
CENTURIES OF TIME.
TO COLLECT.
UNTIL HE POSSESSED A WEALTH OF MAGICAL OBJECTS THAT HE CALLED HIS "ARTIFACTS."

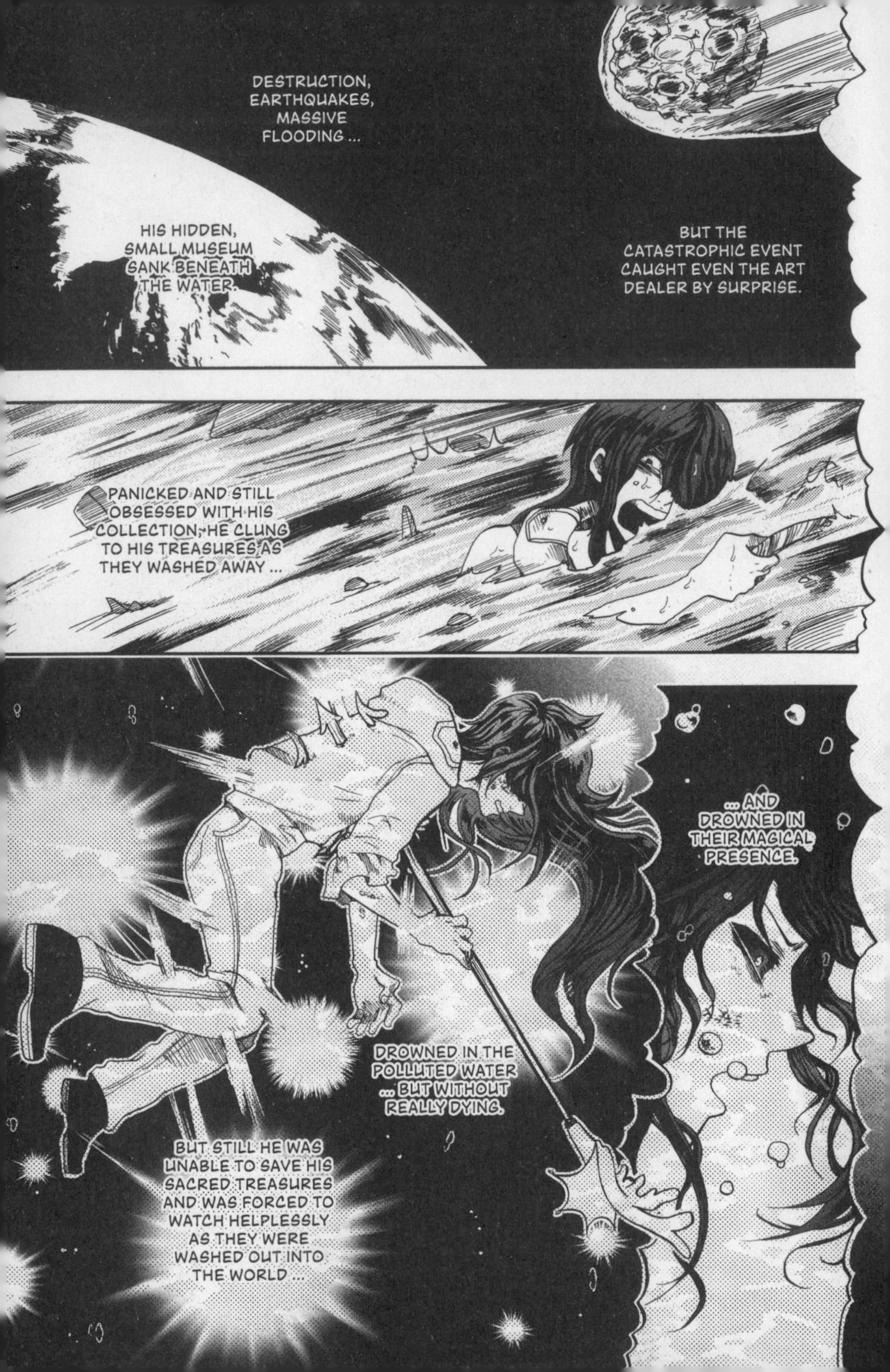
BUT THE CATASTROPHIC EVENT CAUGHT EVEN THE ART DEALER BY SURPRISE.
DESTRUCTION, EARTHQUAKES, MASSIVE FLOODING ...
HIS HIDDEN, SMALL MUSEUM SANK BENEATH THE WATER.
PANICKED AND STILL OBSESSED WITH HIS COLLECTION, HE CLUNG TO HIS TREASURES AS THEY WASHED AWAY ...
... AND DROWNED IN THEIR MAGICAL PRESENCE.
DROWNED IN THE POLLUTED WATER ... BUT WITHOUT REALLY DYING.
BUT STILL HE WAS UNABLE TO SAVE HIS SACRED TREASURES AND WAS FORCED TO WATCH HELPLESSLY AS THEY WERE WASHED OUT INTO THE WORLD ...

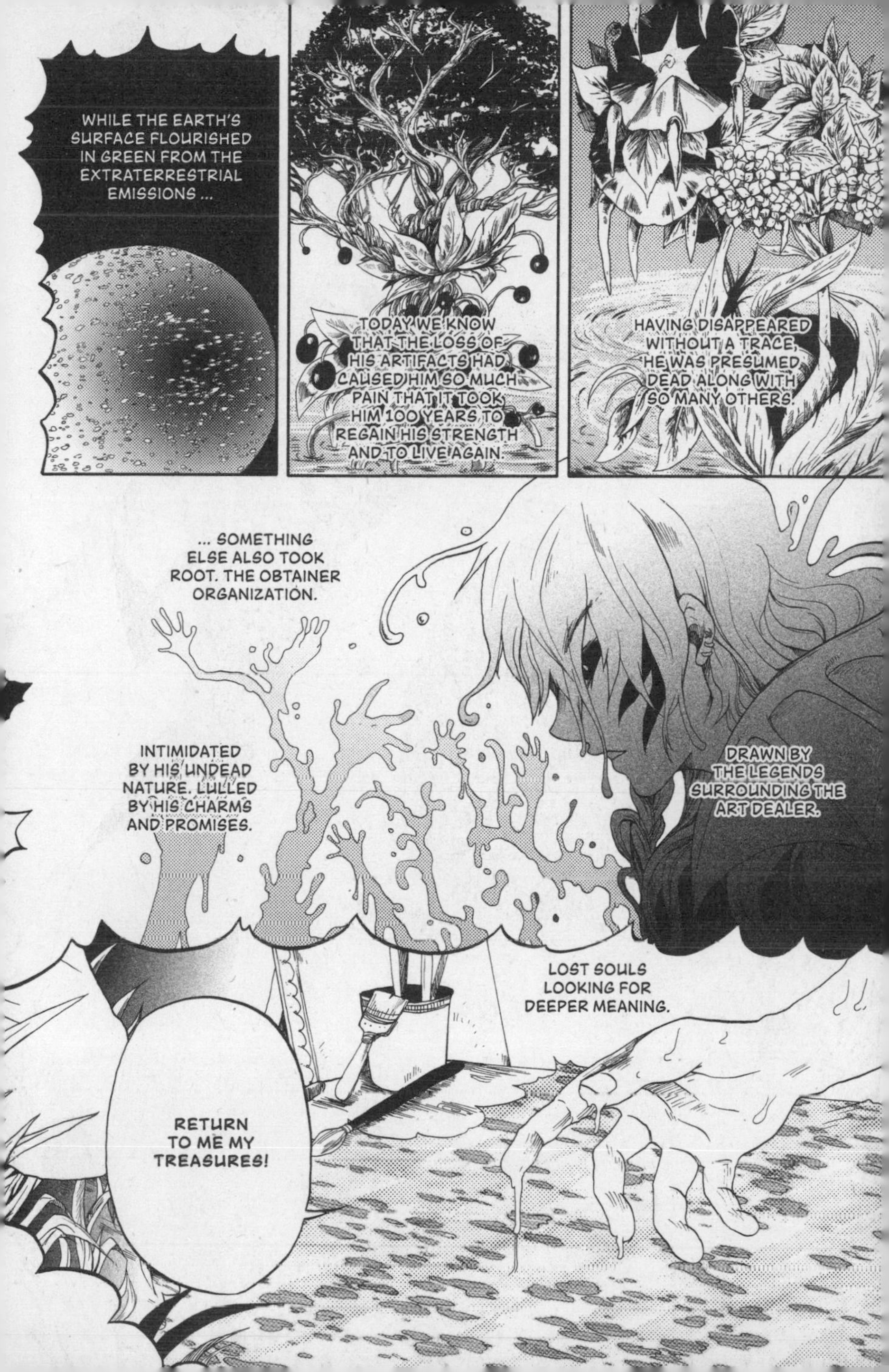
HAVING DISAPPEARED WITHOUT A TRACE, HE WAS PRESUMED DEAD ALONG WITH SO MANY OTHERS.
TODAY WE KNOW THAT THE LOSS OF HIS ARTIFACTS HAD CAUSED HIM SO MUCH PAIN THAT IT TOOK HIM 100 YEARS TO REGAIN HIS STRENGTH AND TO LIVE AGAIN.
WHILE THE EARTH'S SURFACE FLOURISHED IN GREEN FROM THE EXTRATERRESTRIAL EMISSIONS ...
... SOMETHING ELSE ALSO TOOK ROOT. THE OBTAINER ORGANIZATION.
DRAWN BY THE LEGENDS SURROUNDING THE ART DEALER.
INTIMIDATED BY HIS UNDEAD NATURE. LULLED BY HIS CHARMS AND PROMISES.
LOST SOULS LOOKING FOR DEEPER MEANING.
RETURN TO ME MY TREASURES!

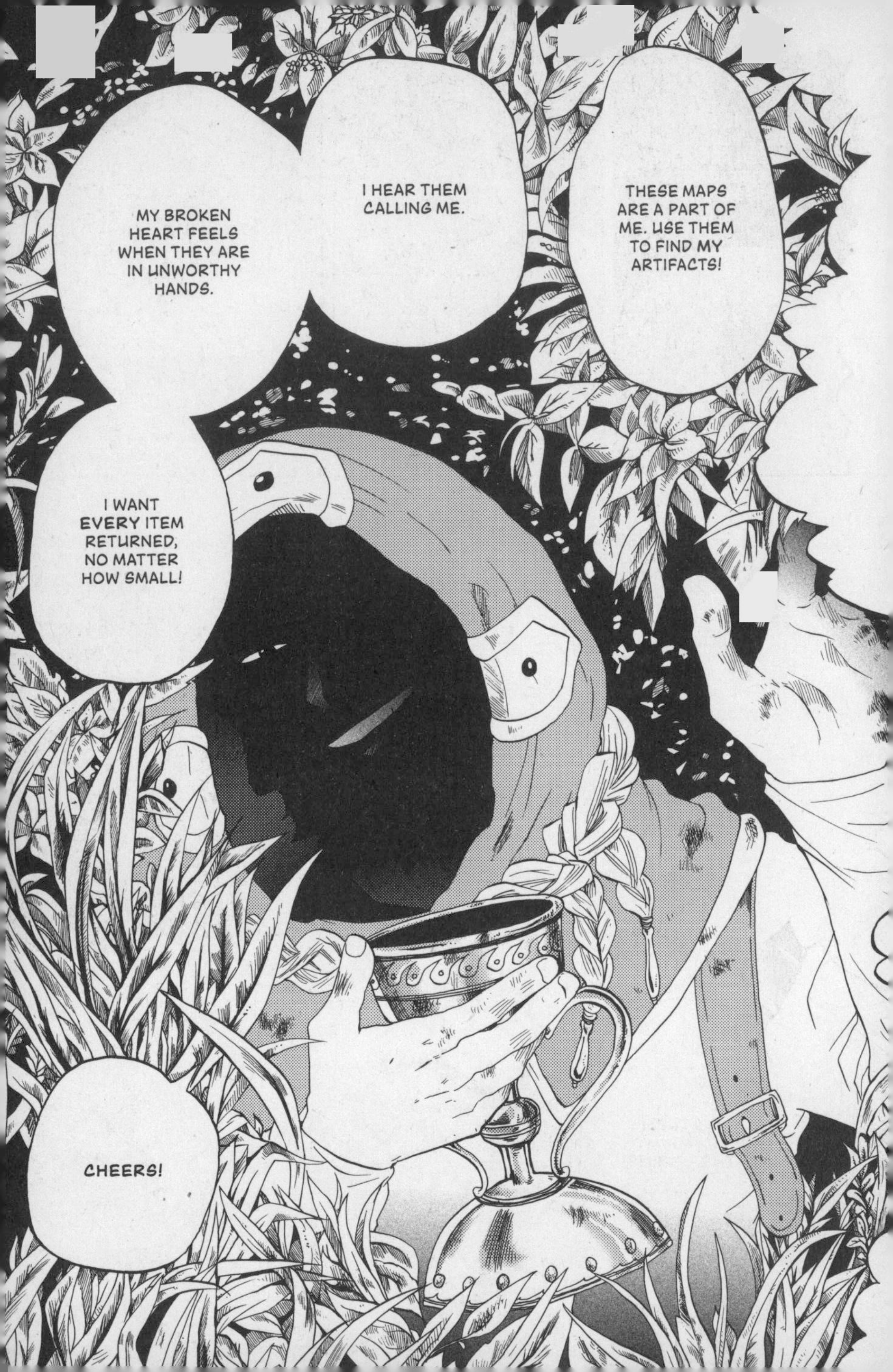
THESE MAPS ARE A PART OF ME. USE THEM TO FIND MY ARTIFACTS!
I HEAR THEM CALLING ME.
MY BROKEN HEART FEELS WHEN THEY ARE IN UNWORTHY HANDS.
I WANT EVERY ITEM RETURNED, NO MATTER HOW SMALL!
CHEERS!

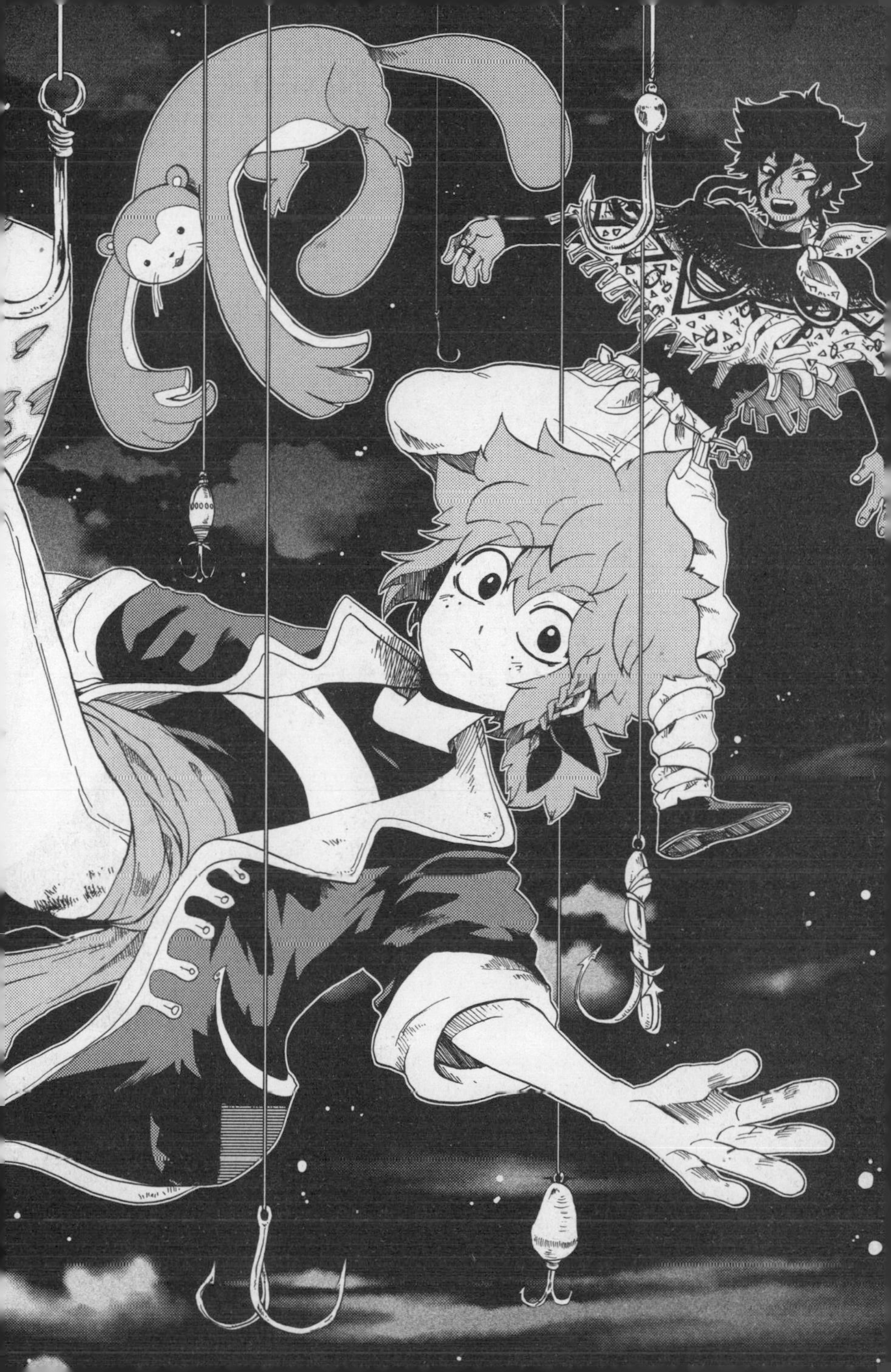

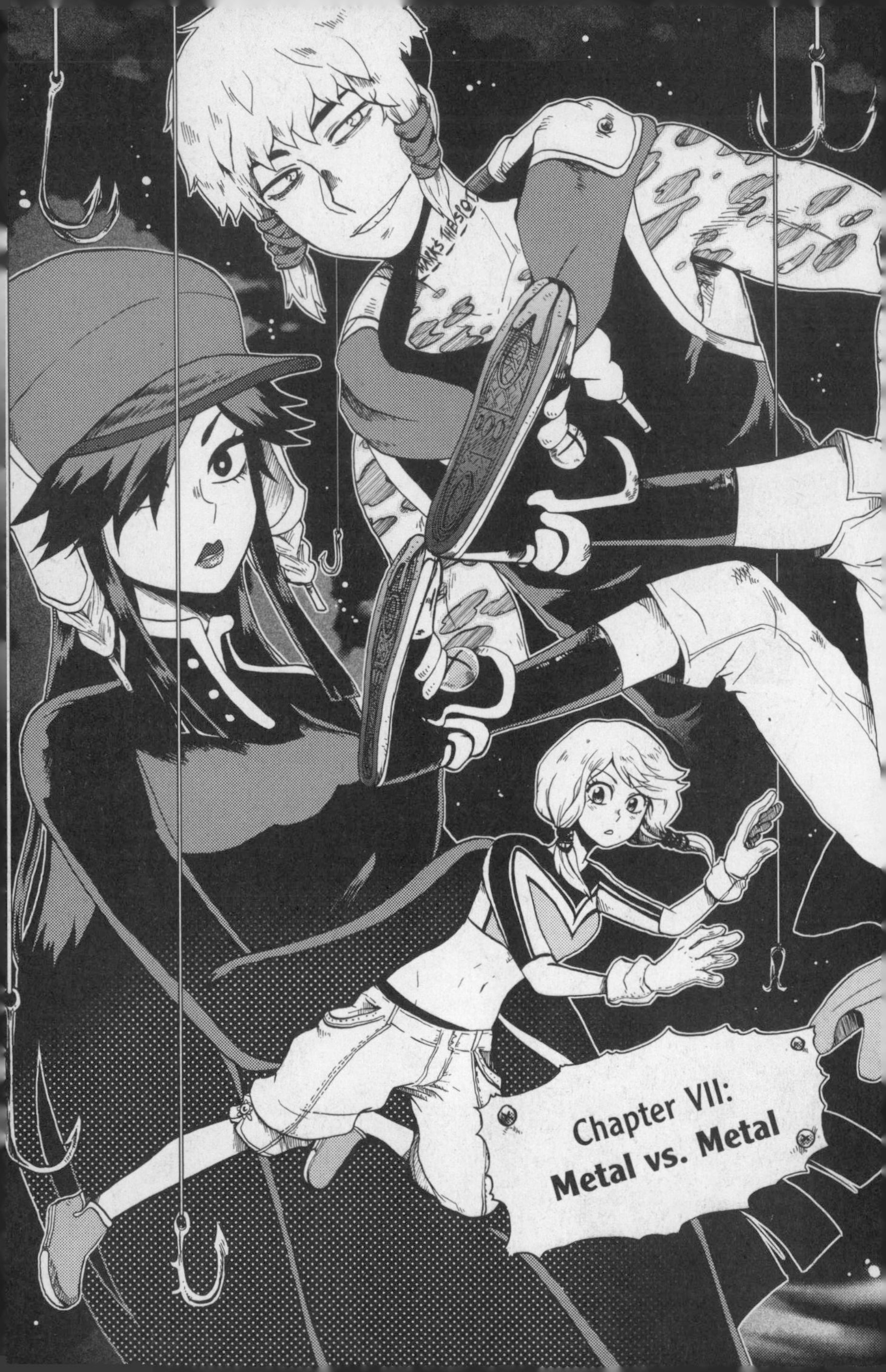
Chapter VII:
Metal vs. Metal

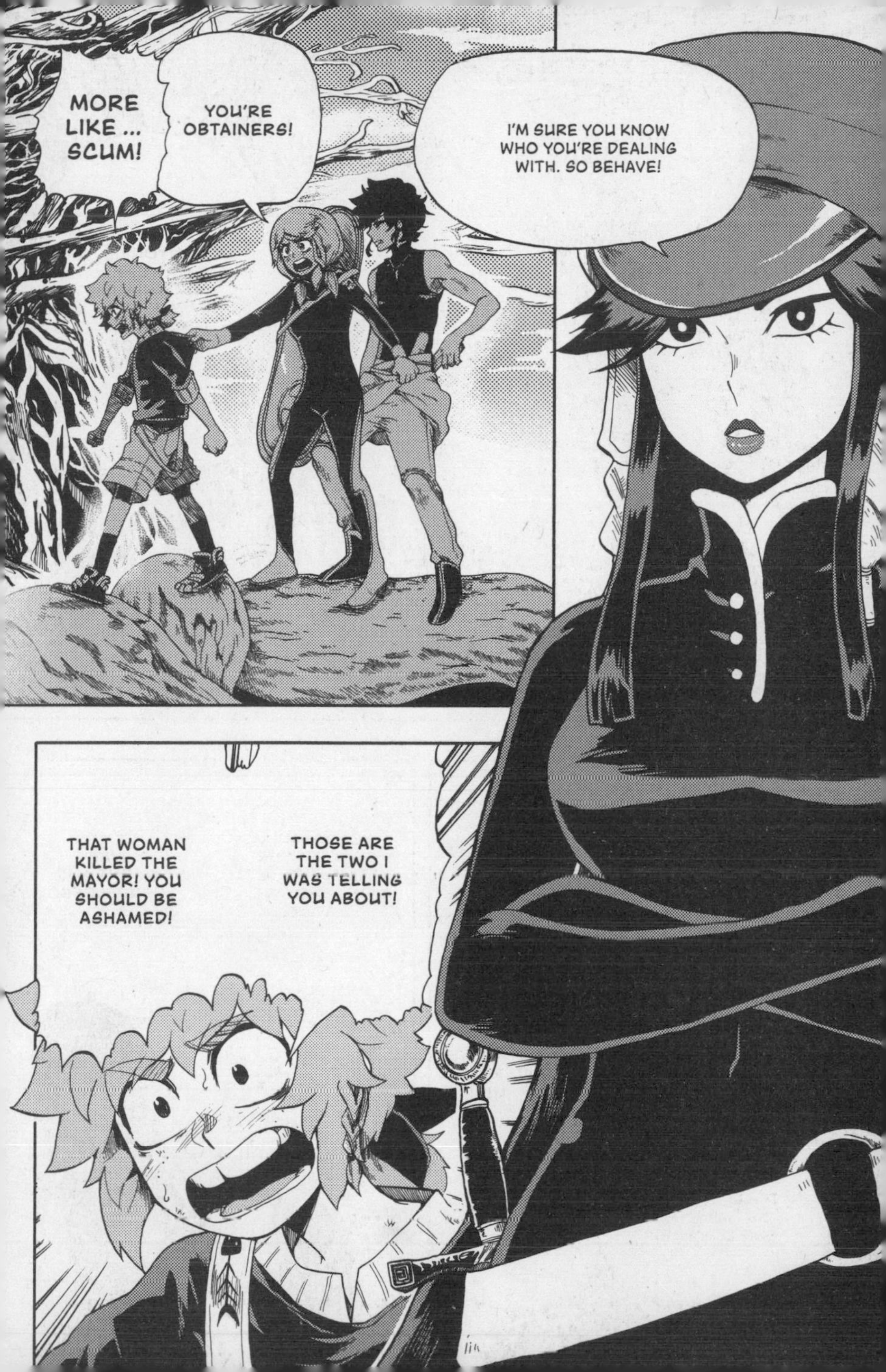
I'M SURE YOU KNOW WHO YOU'RE DEALING WITH. SO BEHAVE!
YOU'RE OBTAINERS!
MORE LIKE ... SCUM!
THOSE ARE THE TWO I WAS TELLING YOU ABOUT!
THAT WOMAN KILLED THE MAYOR! YOU SHOULD BE ASHAMED!

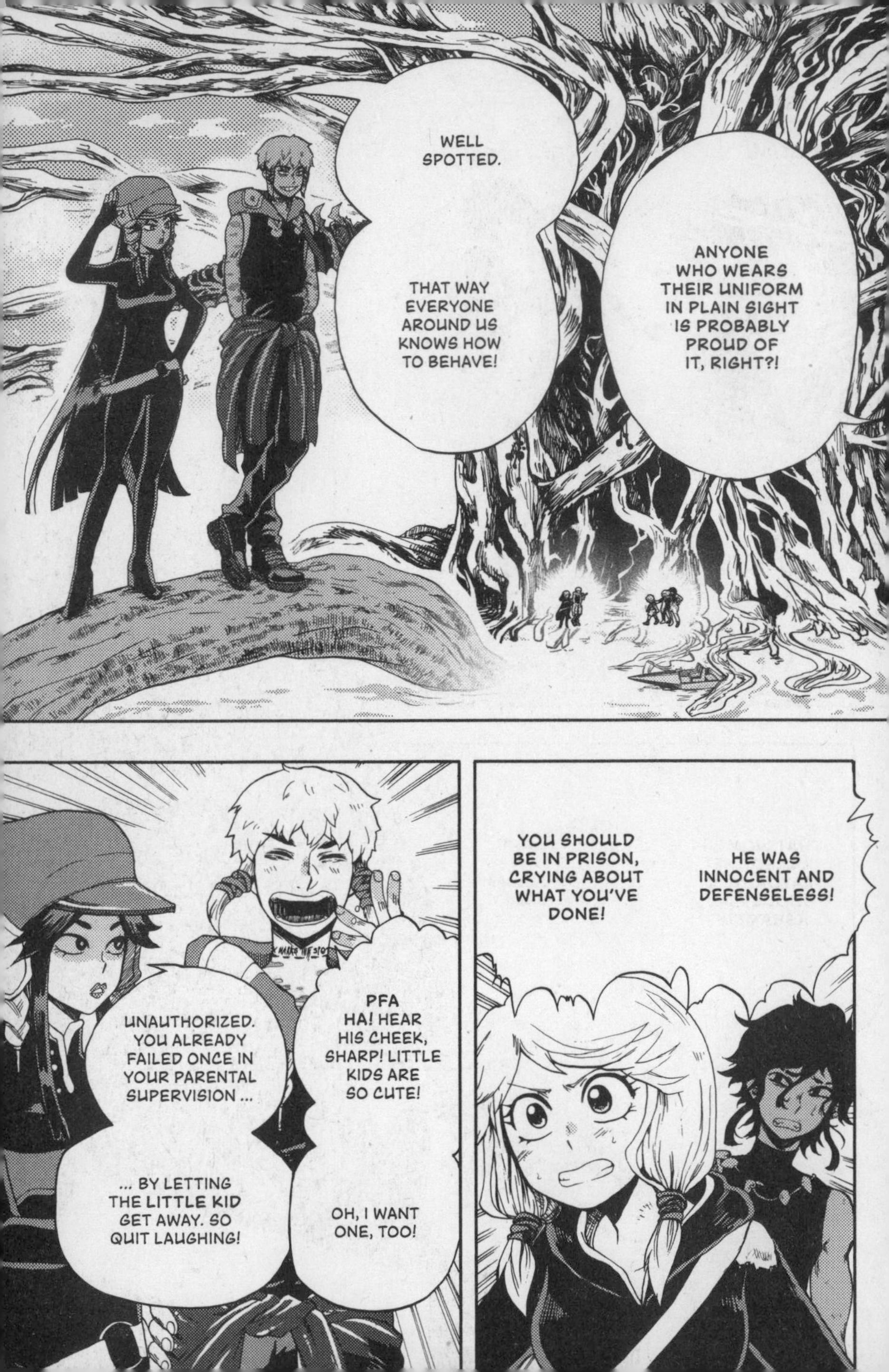
ANYONE WHO WEARS THEIR UNIFORM IN PLAIN SIGHT IS PROBABLY PROUD OF IT, RIGHT?!
WELL SPOTTED.
THAT WAY EVERYONE AROUND US KNOWS HOW TO BEHAVE!
HE WAS INNOCENT AND DEFENSELESS!
YOU SHOULD BE IN PRISON, CRYING ABOUT WHAT YOU'VE DONE!
PFA HA! HEAR HIS CHEEK, SHARP! LITTLE KIDS ARE SO CUTE!
OH, I WANT ONE, TOO!
UNAUTHORIZED. YOU ALREADY FAILED ONCE IN YOUR PARENTAL SUPERVISION ...
... BY LETTING THE LITTLE KID GET AWAY. SO QUIT LAUGHING!

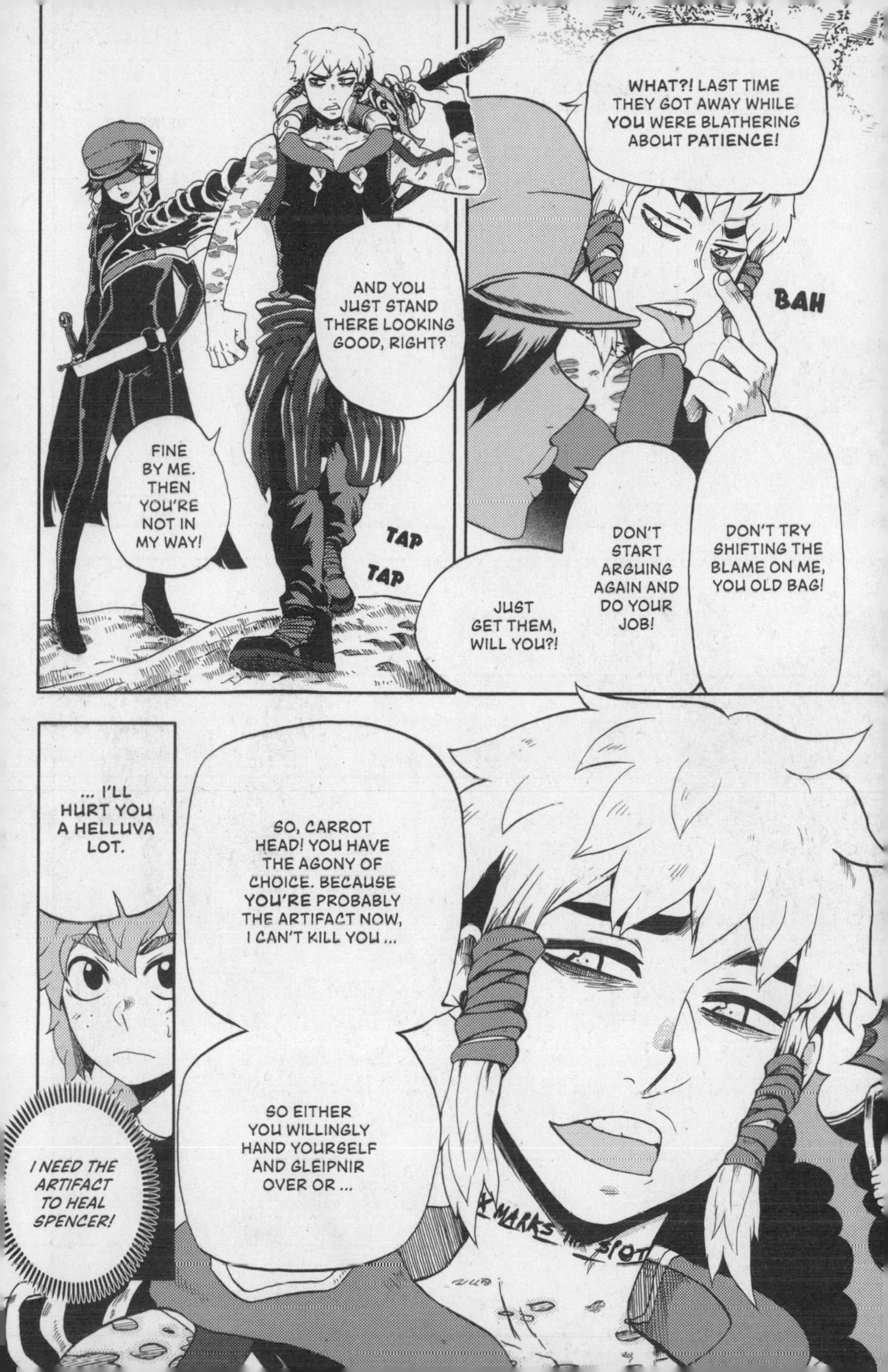
WHAT?! LAST TIME THEY GOT AWAY WHILE YOU WERE BLATHERING ABOUT PATIENCE!
BAH
DON'T TRY SHIFTING THE BLAME ON ME, YOU OLD BAG!
DON'T START ARGUING AGAIN AND DO YOUR JOB!
JUST GET THEM, WILL YOU?!
AND YOU JUST STAND THERE LOOKING GOOD, RIGHT?
FINE BY ME. THEN YOU'RE NOT IN MY WAY!
TAP
TAP
SO, CARROT HEAD! YOU HAVE THE AGONY OF CHOICE. BECAUSE YOU'RE PROBABLY THE ARTIFACT NOW, I CAN'T KILL YOU ...
SO EITHER YOU WILLINGLY HAND YOURSELF AND GLEIPNIR OVER OR ...
... I'LL HURT YOU A HELLUVA LOT.
I NEED THE ARTIFACT TO HEAL SPENCER!

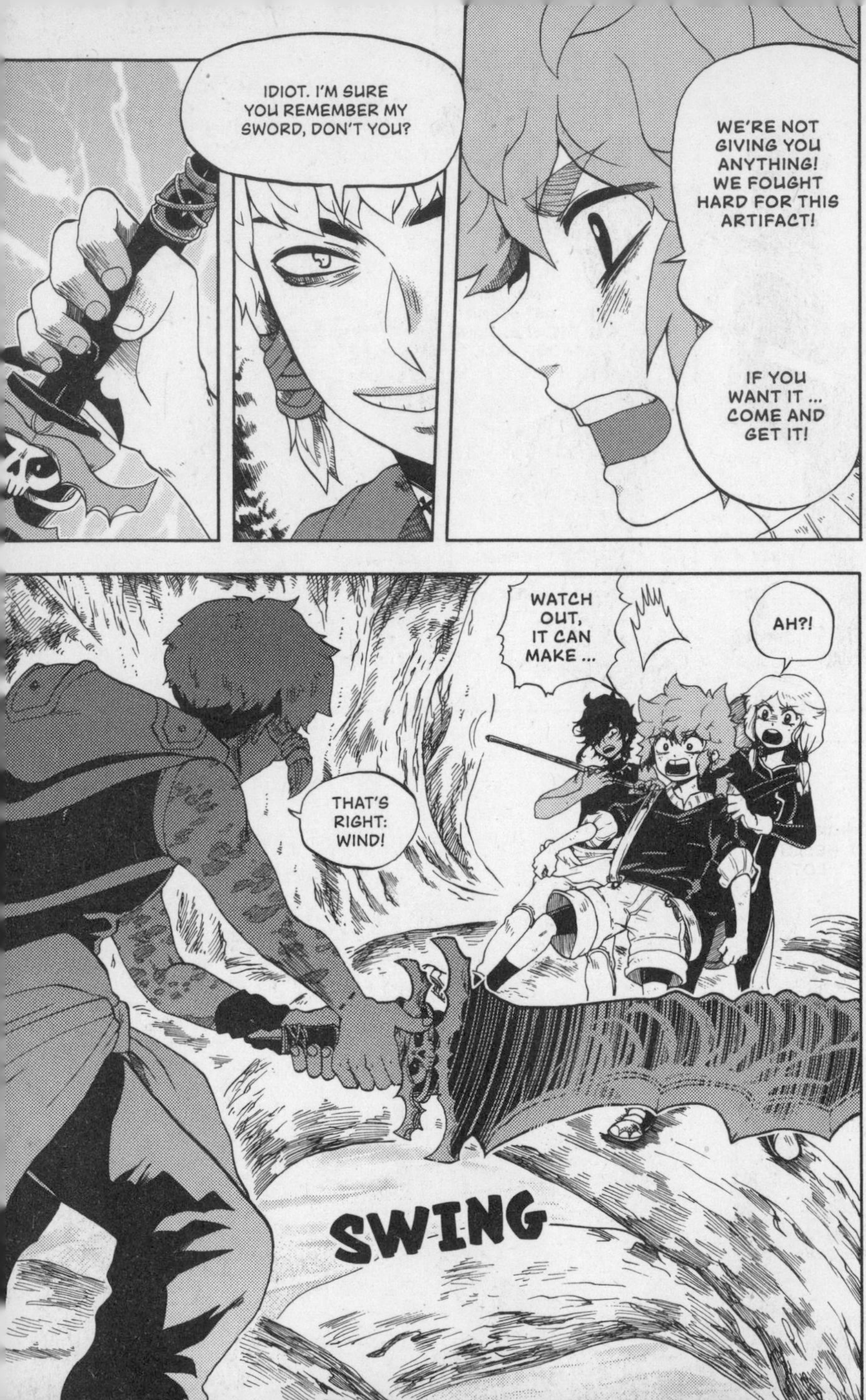
WE'RE NOT GIVING YOU ANYTHING! WE FOUGHT HARD FOR THIS ARTIFACT!
IF YOU WANT IT ... COME AND GET IT!
IDIOT. I'M SURE YOU REMEMBER MY SWORD, DON'T YOU?
AH?!
WATCH OUT, IT CAN MAKE ...
THAT'S RIGHT: WIND!
SWING

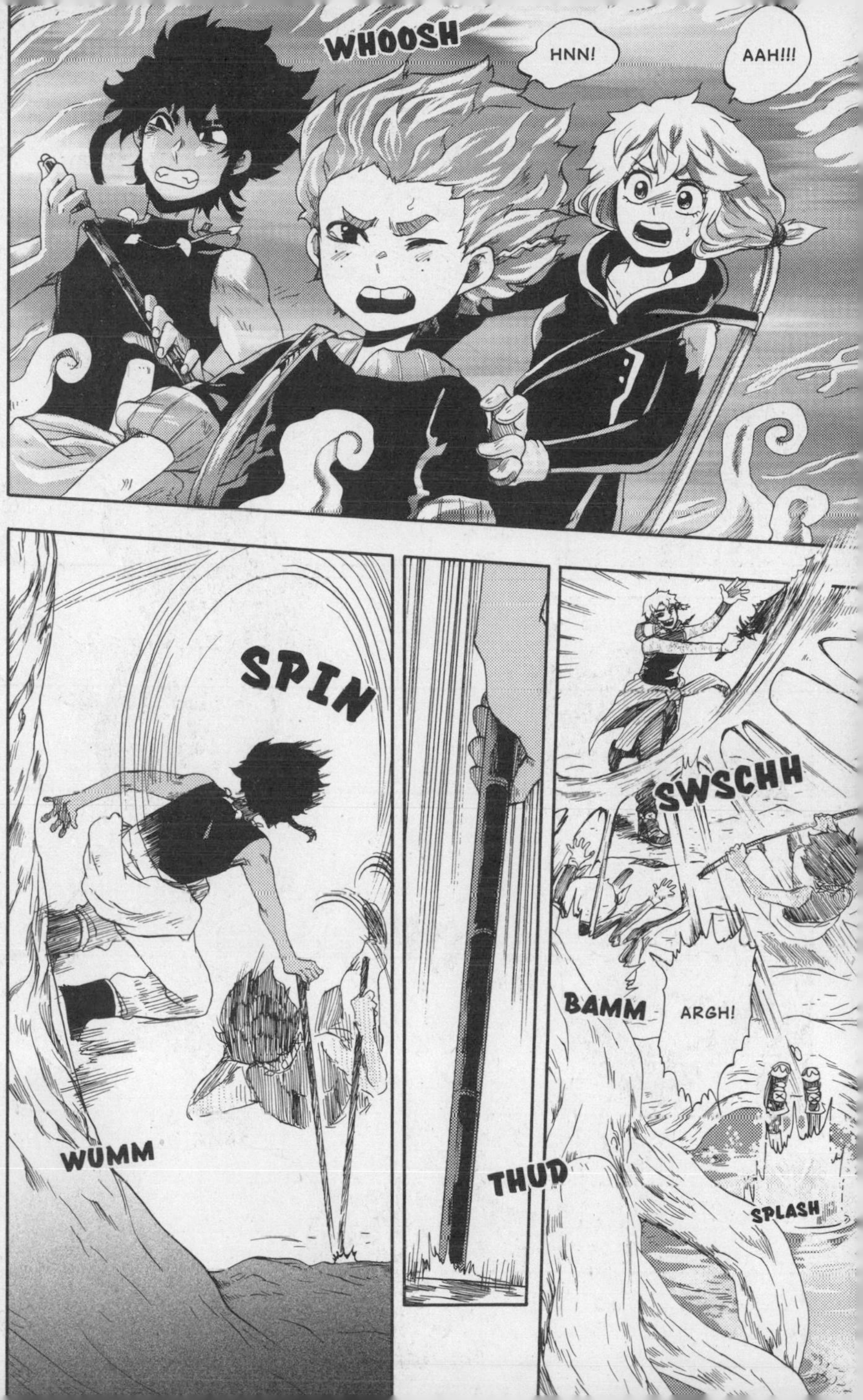
AAH!!!
HNN!
WHOOSH
SWSCHH
ARGH!
BAMM
SPLASH
THUD
SPIN
WUMM

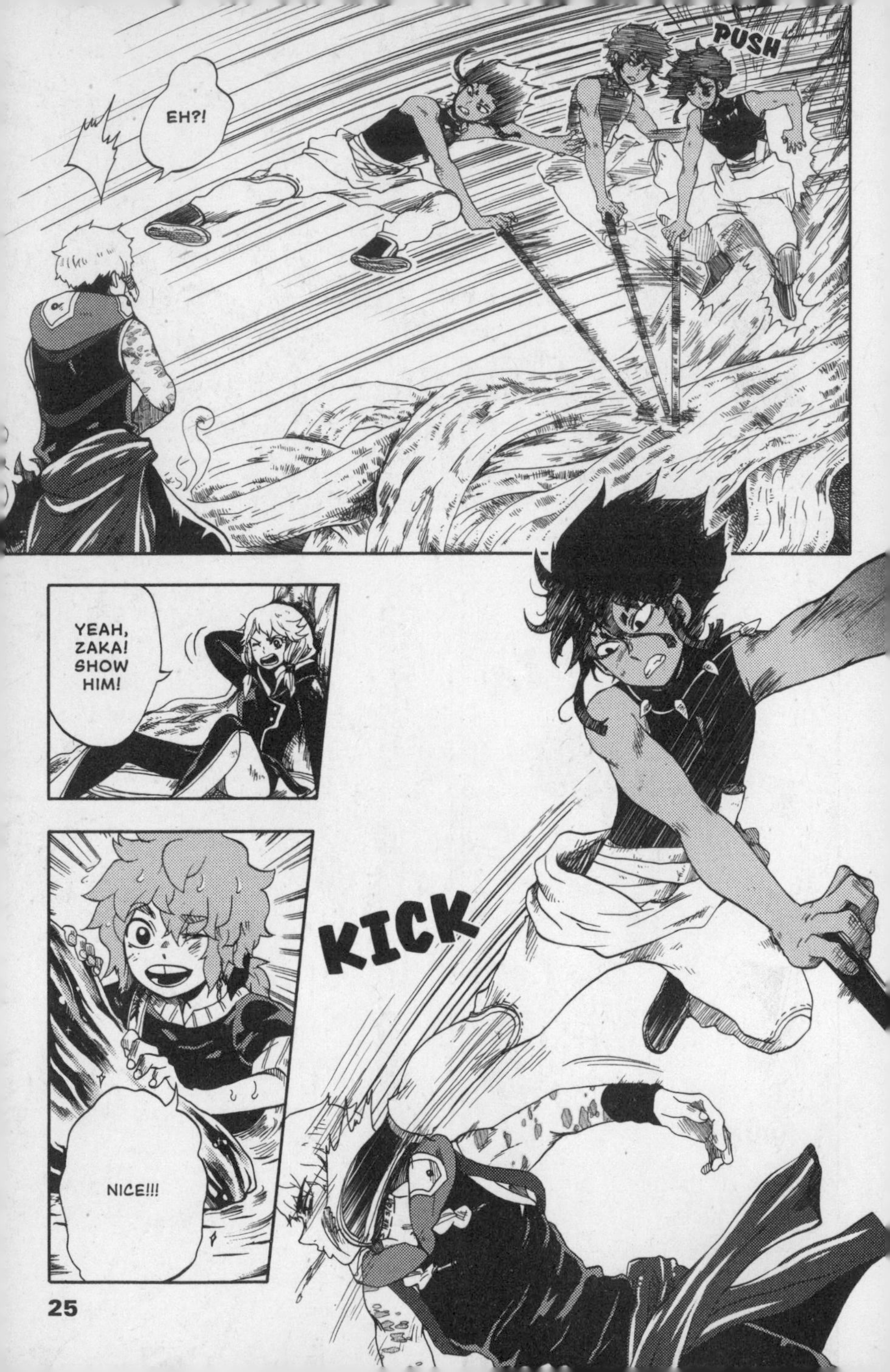
PUSH
EH?!
KICK
YEAH, ZAKA! SHOW HIM!
NICE!!!

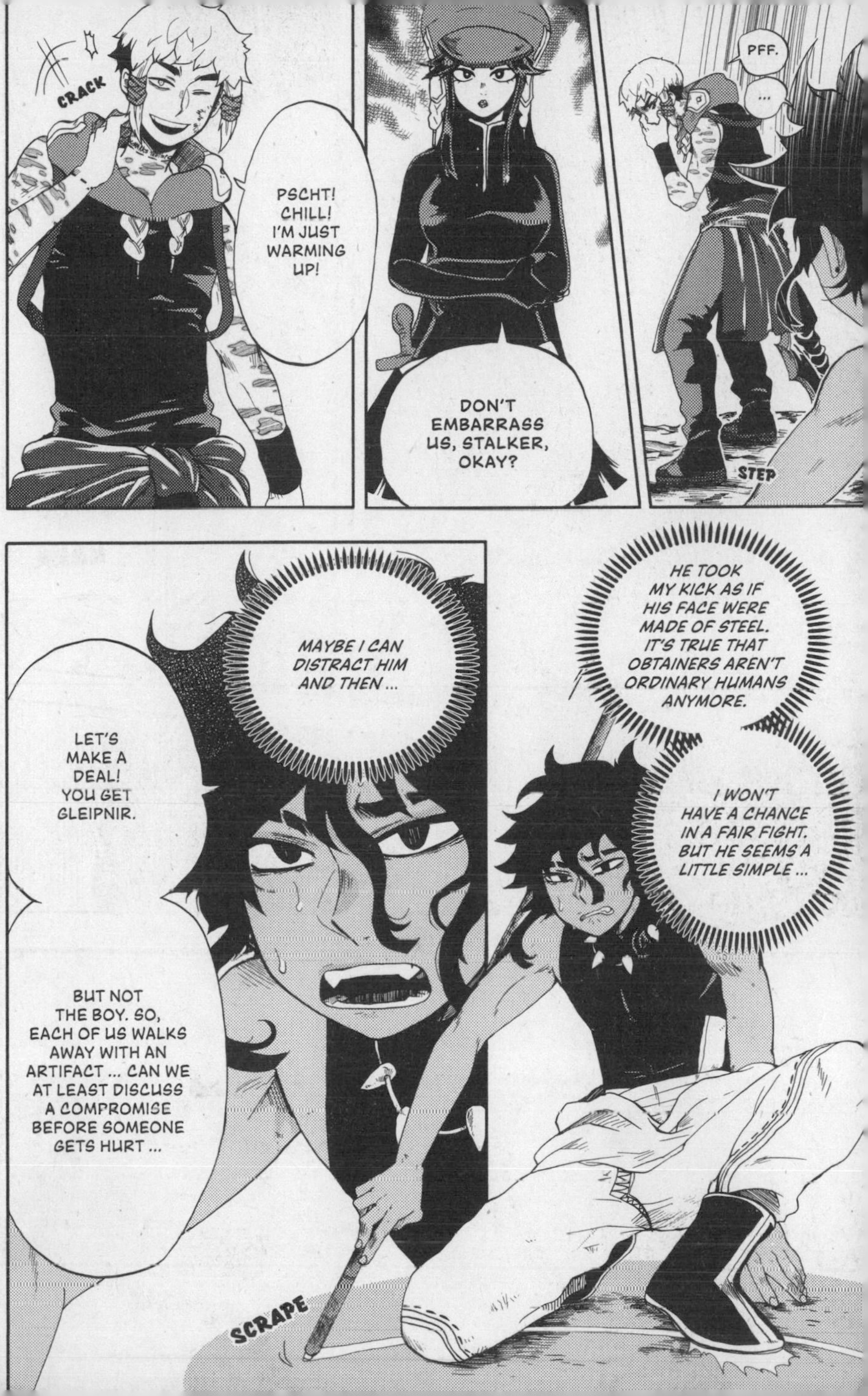
PFF.
...
STEP
DON'T EMBARRASS US, STALKER, OKAY?
CRACK
PSCHT! CHILL! I'M JUST WARMING UP!
HE TOOK MY KICK AS IF HIS FACE WERE MADE OF STEEL. IT'S TRUE THAT OBTAINERS AREN'T ORDINARY HUMANS ANYMORE.
I WON'T HAVE A CHANCE IN A FAIR FIGHT. BUT HE SEEMS A LITTLE SIMPLE ...
MAYBE I CAN DISTRACT HIM AND THEN ...
LET'S MAKE A DEAL! YOU GET GLEIPNIR.
BUT NOT THE BOY. SO, EACH OF US WALKS AWAY WITH AN ARTIFACT ... CAN WE AT LEAST DISCUSS A COMPROMISE BEFORE SOMEONE GETS HURT ...
SCRAPE

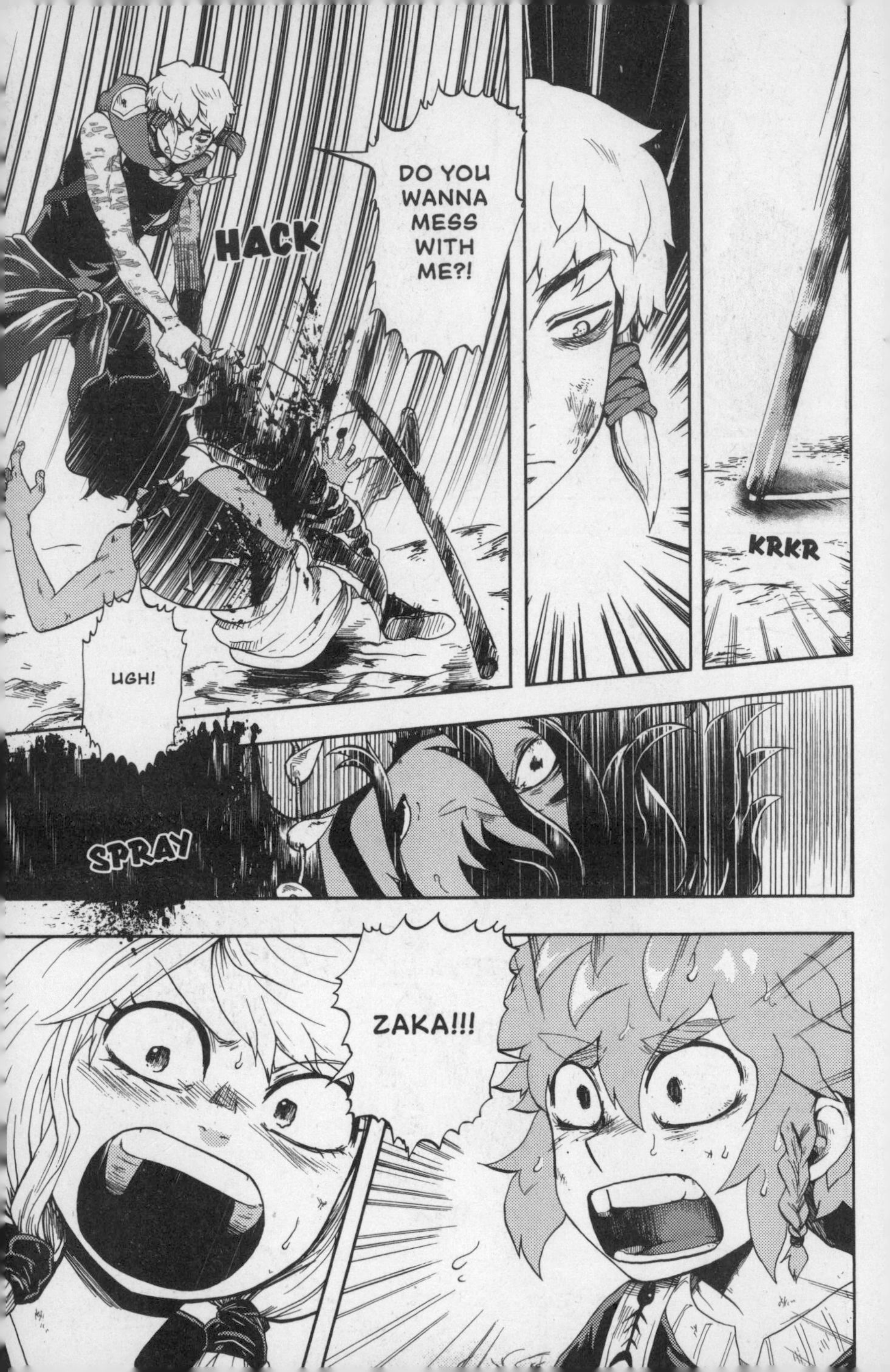
KRKR
DO YOU WANNA MESS WITH ME?!
HACK
UGH!
SPRAY
ZAKA!!!

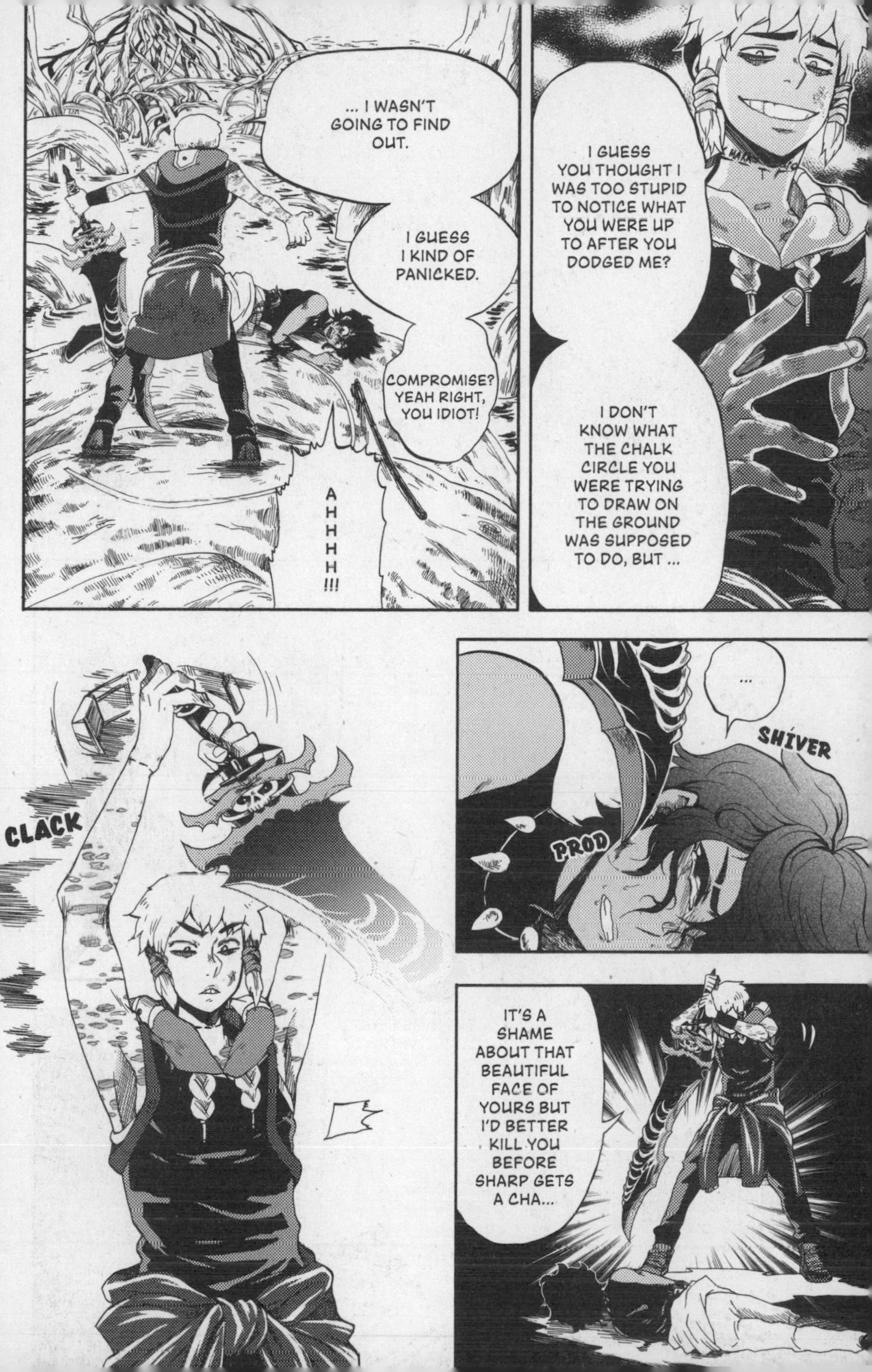
I GUESS YOU THOUGHT I WAS TOO STUPID TO NOTICE WHAT YOU WERE UP TO AFTER YOU DODGED ME?
I DON'T KNOW WHAT THE CHALK CIRCLE YOU WERE TRYING TO DRAW ON THE GROUND WAS SUPPOSED TO DO, BUT ...
... I WASN'T GOING TO FIND OUT.
I GUESS I KIND OF PANICKED.
COMPROMISE? YEAH RIGHT, YOU IDIOT!
AHHHH!!!
...
SHIVER
PROD
IT'S A SHAME ABOUT THAT BEAUTIFUL FACE OF YOURS BUT I'D BETTER KILL YOU BEFORE SHARP GETS A CHA...
CLACK

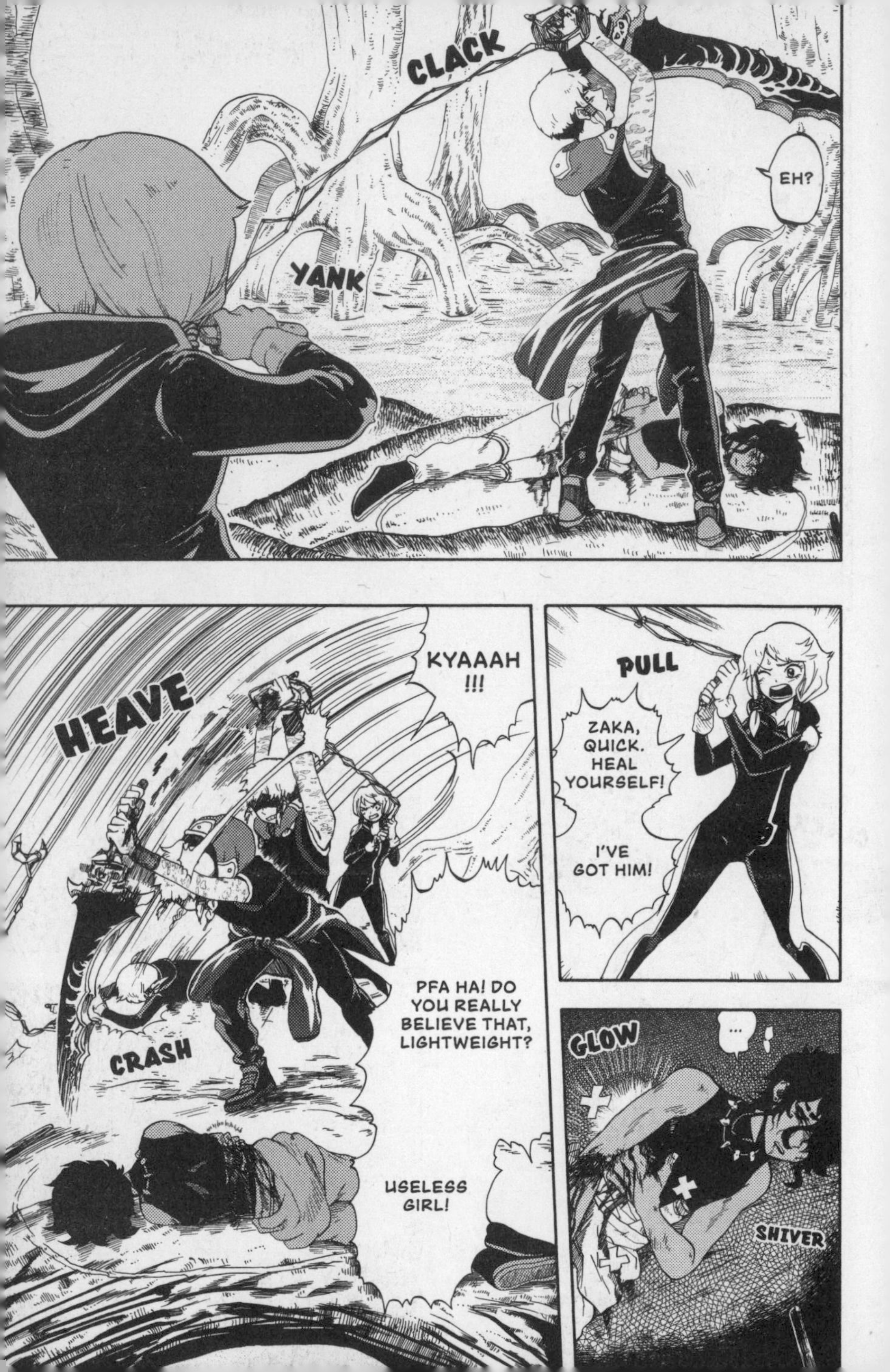
EH?
CLACK
YANK
PULL
ZAKA, QUICK. HEAL YOURSELF!
I'VE GOT HIM!
GLOW
...
!
SHIVER
KYAAAH!!!
HEAVE
PFA HA! DO YOU REALLY BELIEVE THAT, LIGHTWEIGHT?
CRASH
USELESS GIRL!

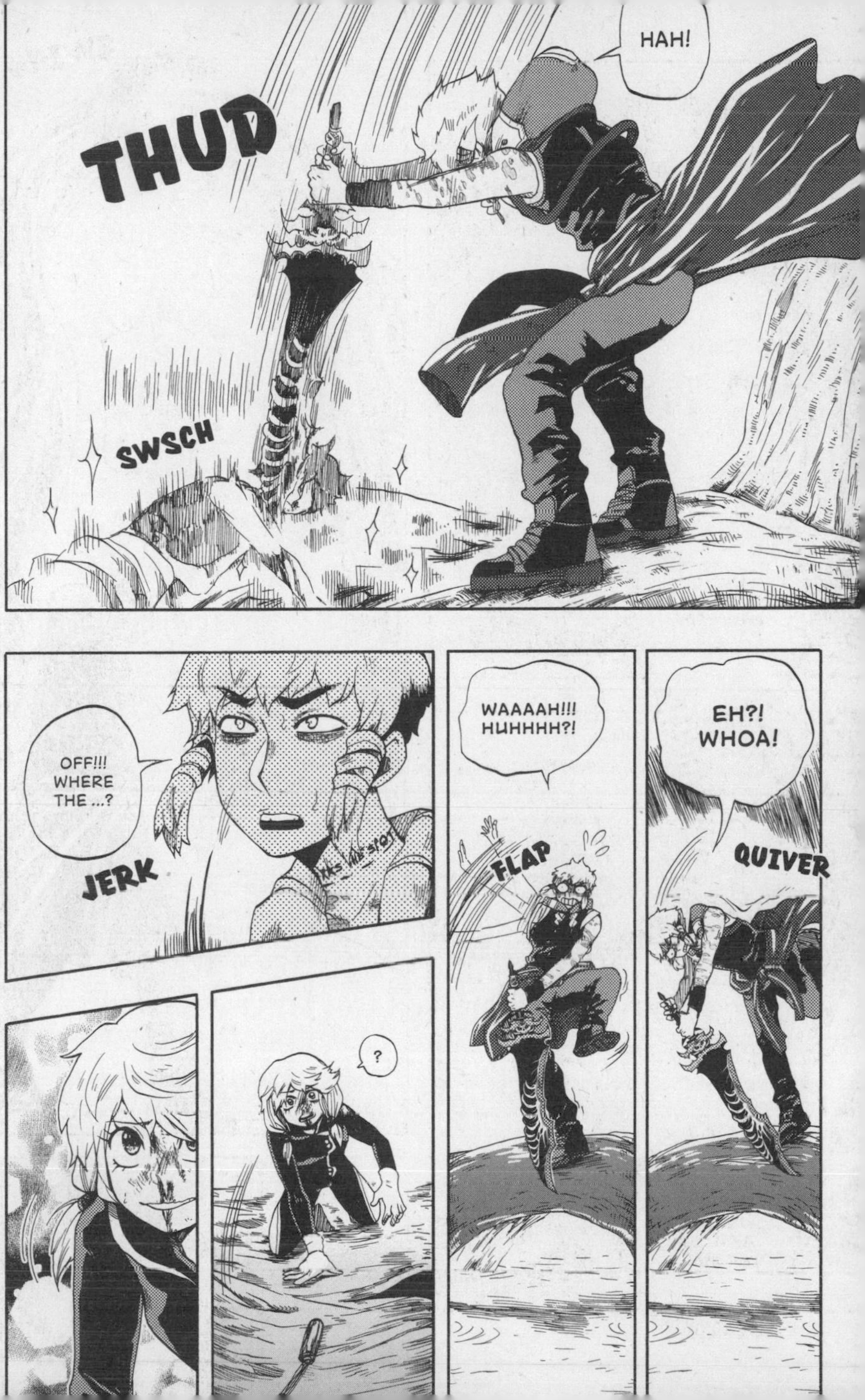
HAH!
THUD
SWSCH
EH?! WHOA!
QUIVER
WAAAAH!!! HUHHHH?!
FLAP
OFF!!! WHERE THE ...?
JERK
?

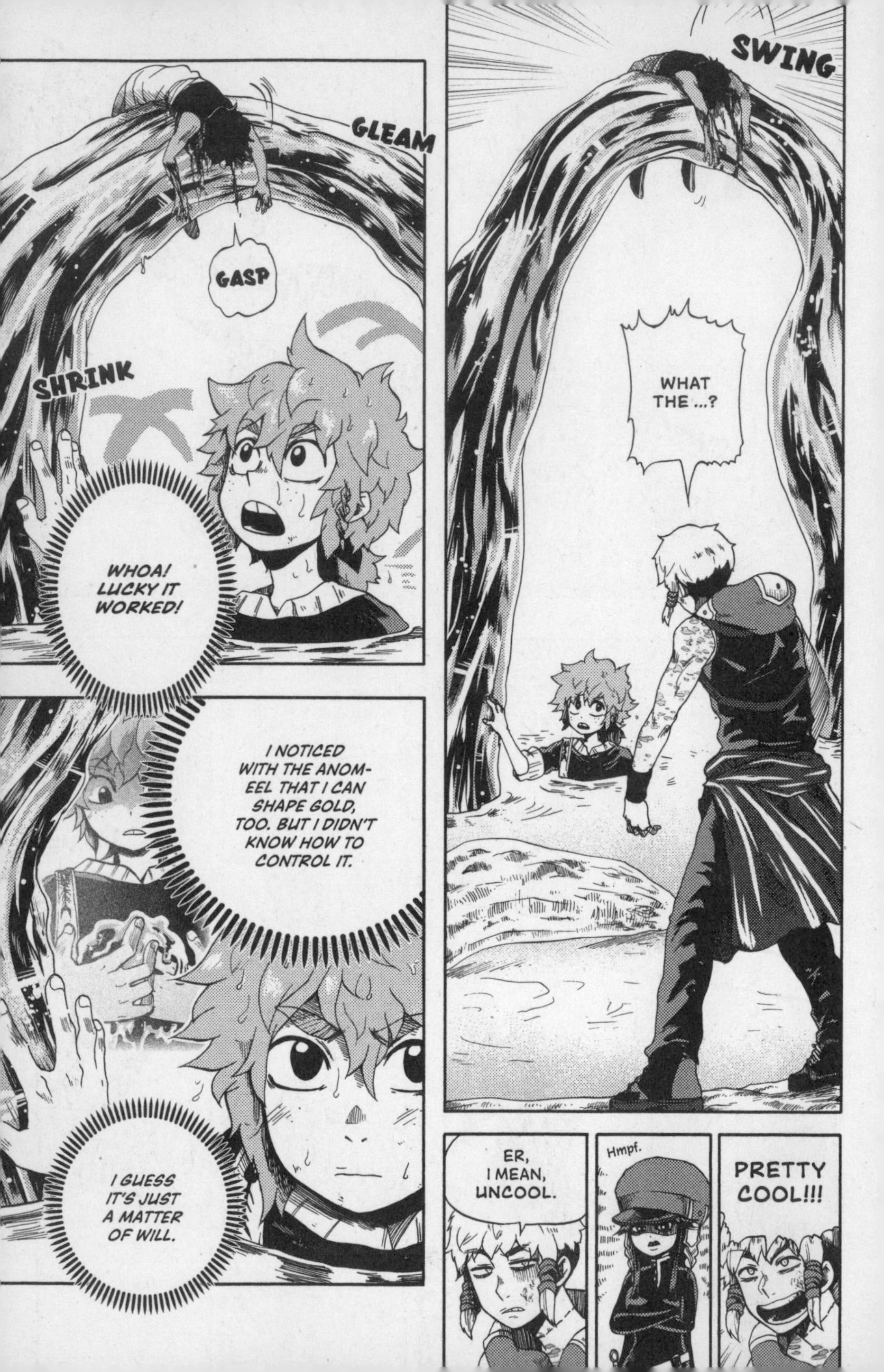
SWING
WHAT THE ...?
PRETTY COOL!!!
Hmpf.
ER, I MEAN, UNCOOL.
GLEAM
GASP
SHRINK
WHOA! LUCKY IT WORKED!
I NOTICED WITH THE ANOMEEL THAT I CAN SHAPE GOLD, TOO. BUT I DIDN'T KNOW HOW TO CONTROL IT.
I GUESS IT'S JUST A MATTER OF WILL.

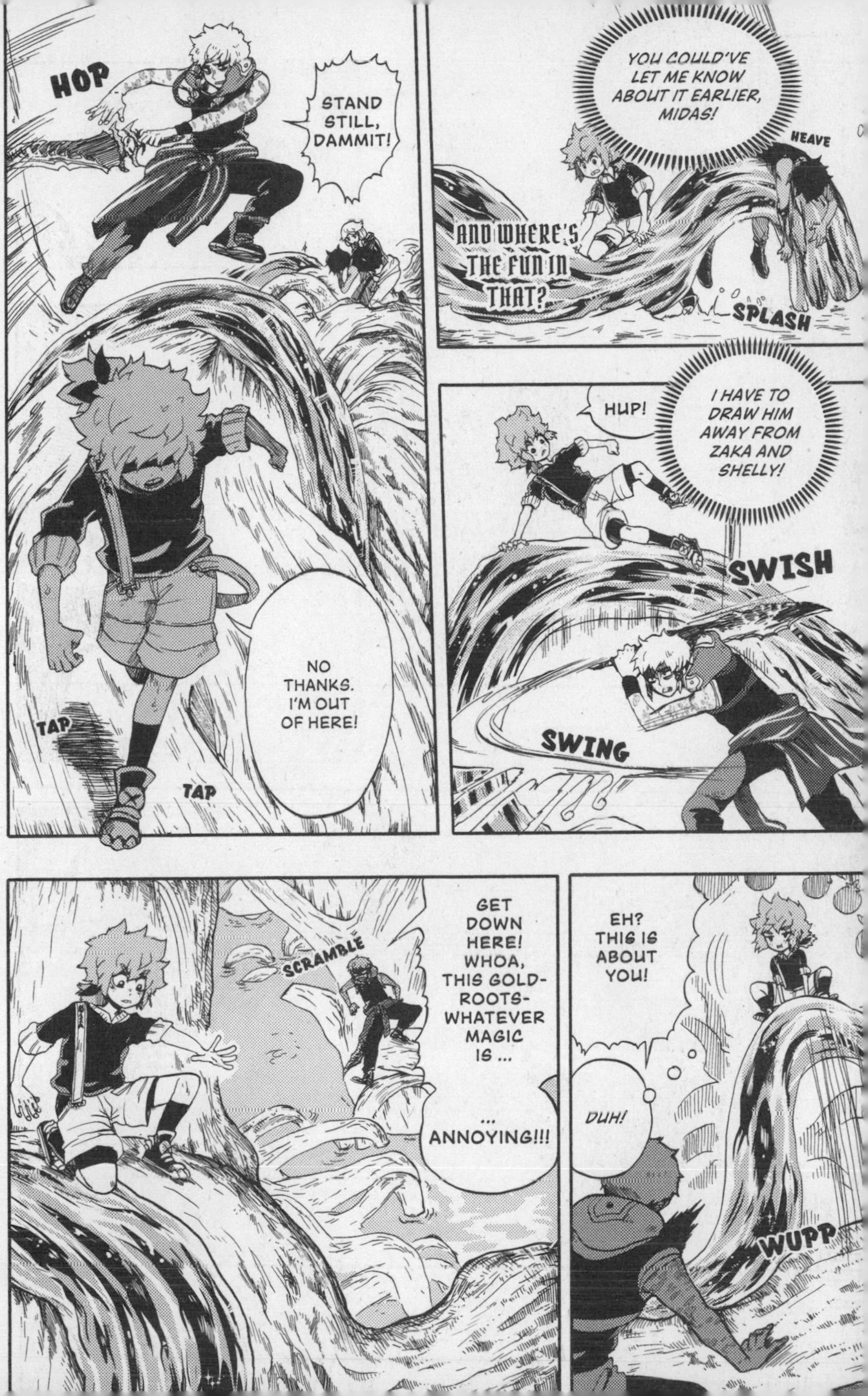
YOU COULD'VE LET ME KNOW ABOUT IT EARLIER, MIDAS!
HEAVE
AND WHERE'S THE FUN IN THAT?
SPLASH
I HAVE TO DRAW HIM AWAY FROM ZAKA AND SHELLY!
HUP!
SWISH
SWING
STAND STILL, DAMMIT!
HOP
NO THANKS. I'M OUT OF HERE!
TAP
TAP
EH? THIS IS ABOUT YOU!
DUH!
WUPP
GET DOWN HERE! WHOA, THIS GOLD-ROOTS-WHATEVER MAGIC IS ...
SCRAMBLE
... ANNOYING!!!

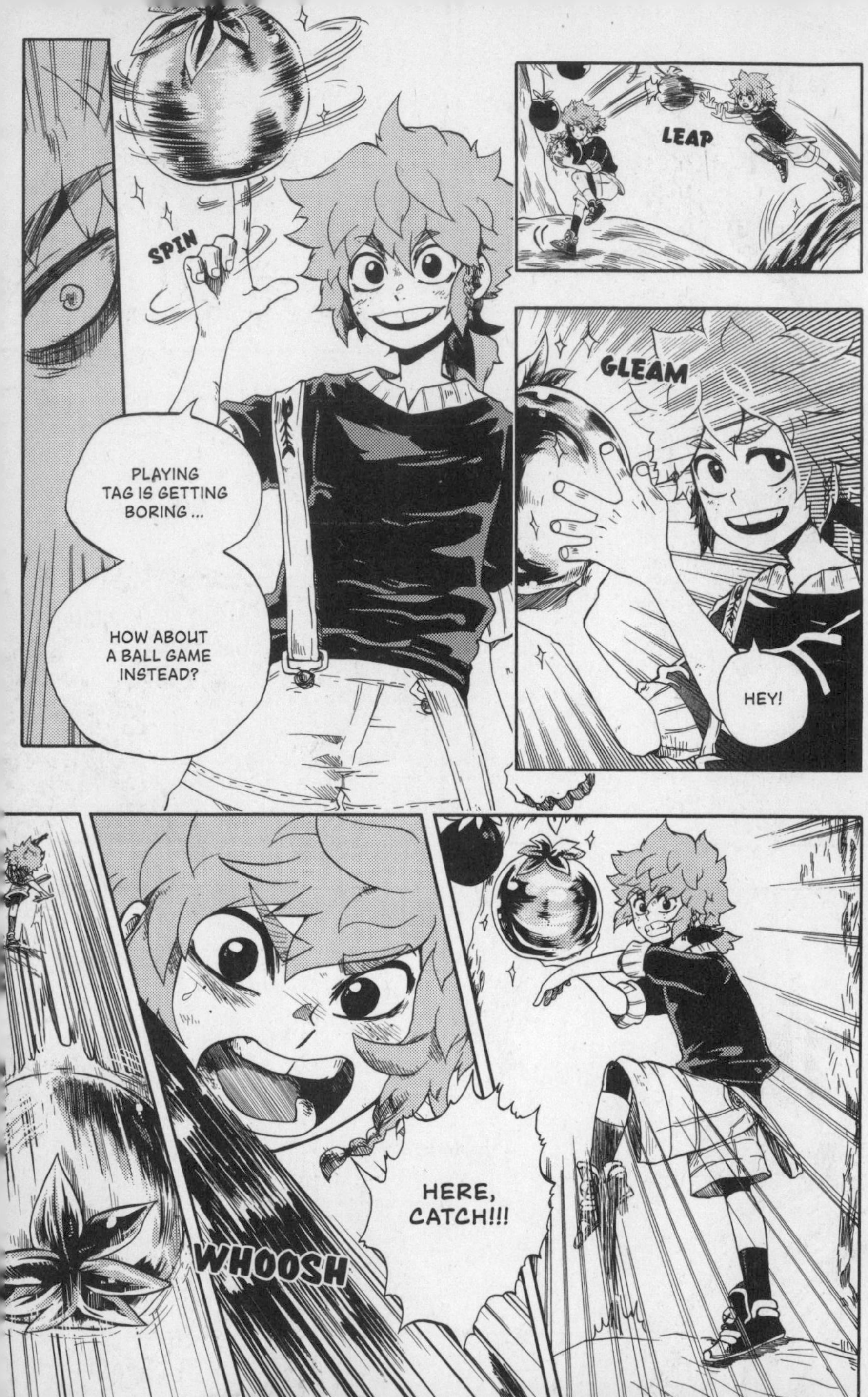
LEAP
GLEAM
HEY!
SPIN
PLAYING TAG IS GETTING BORING ...
HOW ABOUT A BALL GAME INSTEAD?
HERE, CATCH!!!
WHOOSH

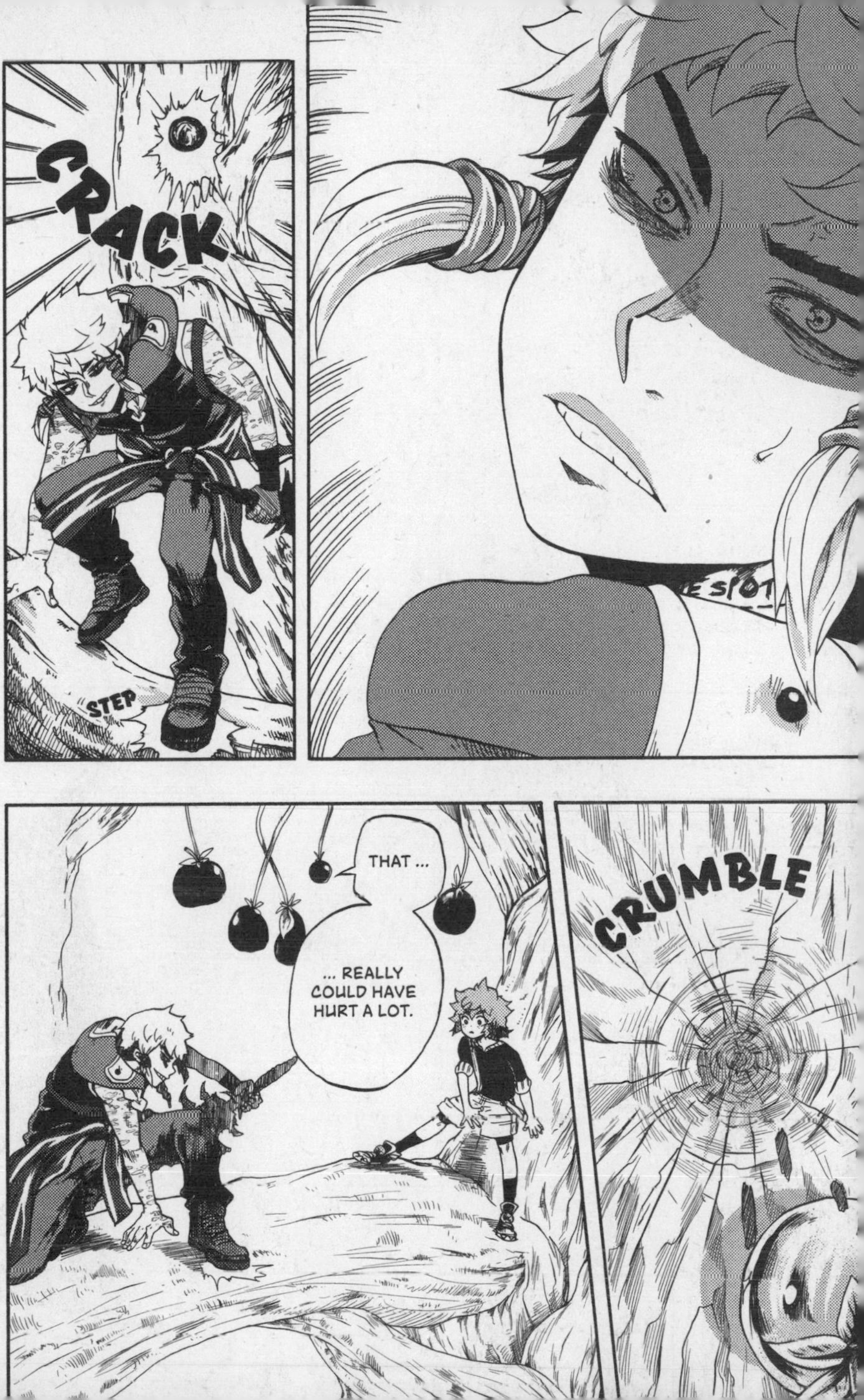
CRACK
STEP
CRUMBLE
THAT ...
... REALLY COULD HAVE HURT A LOT.

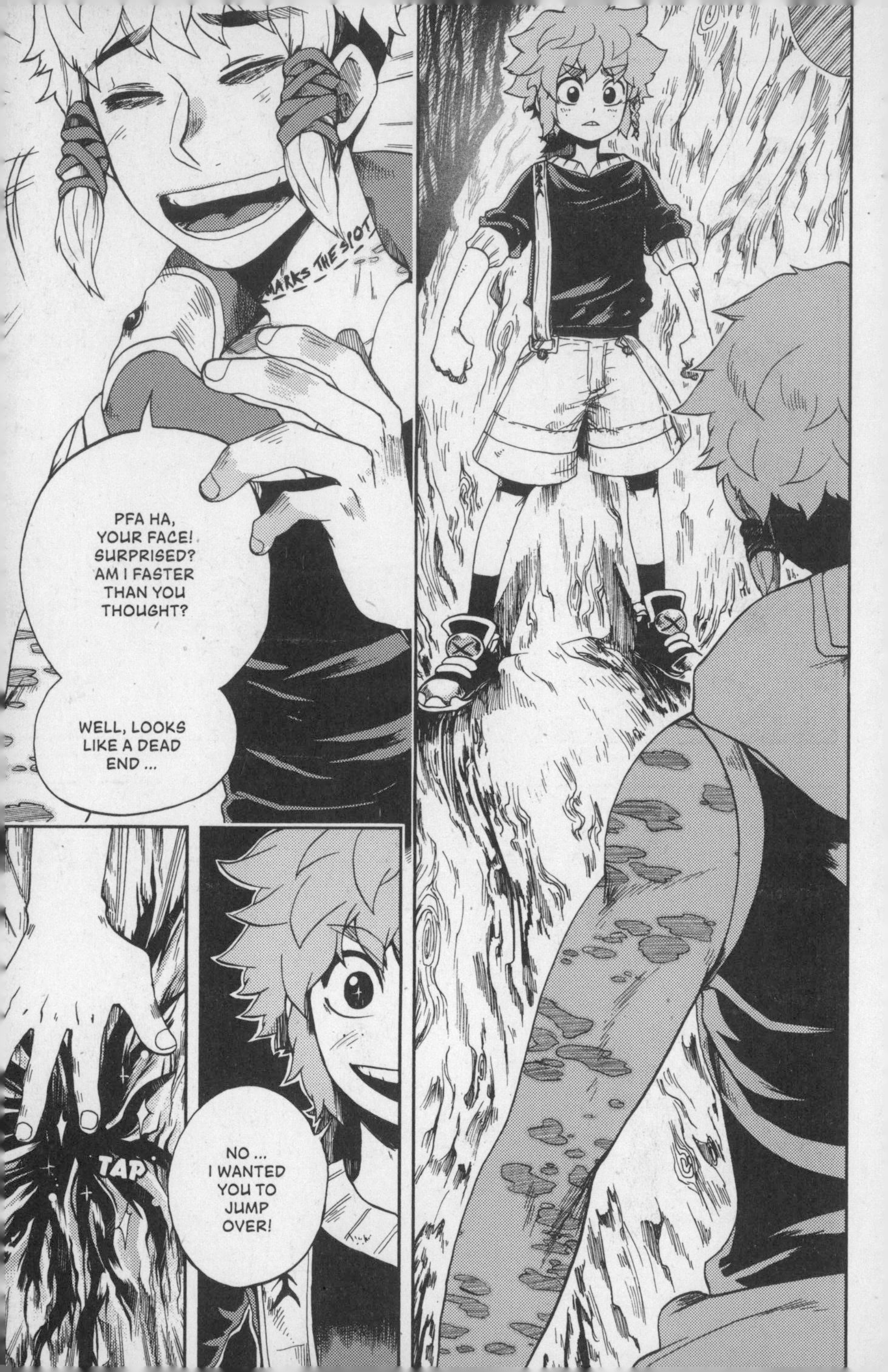
MARKS THE SPOT
PFA HA, YOUR FACE! SURPRISED? AM I FASTER THAN YOU THOUGHT?
WELL, LOOKS LIKE A DEAD END ...
NO ... I WANTED YOU TO JUMP OVER!
TAP

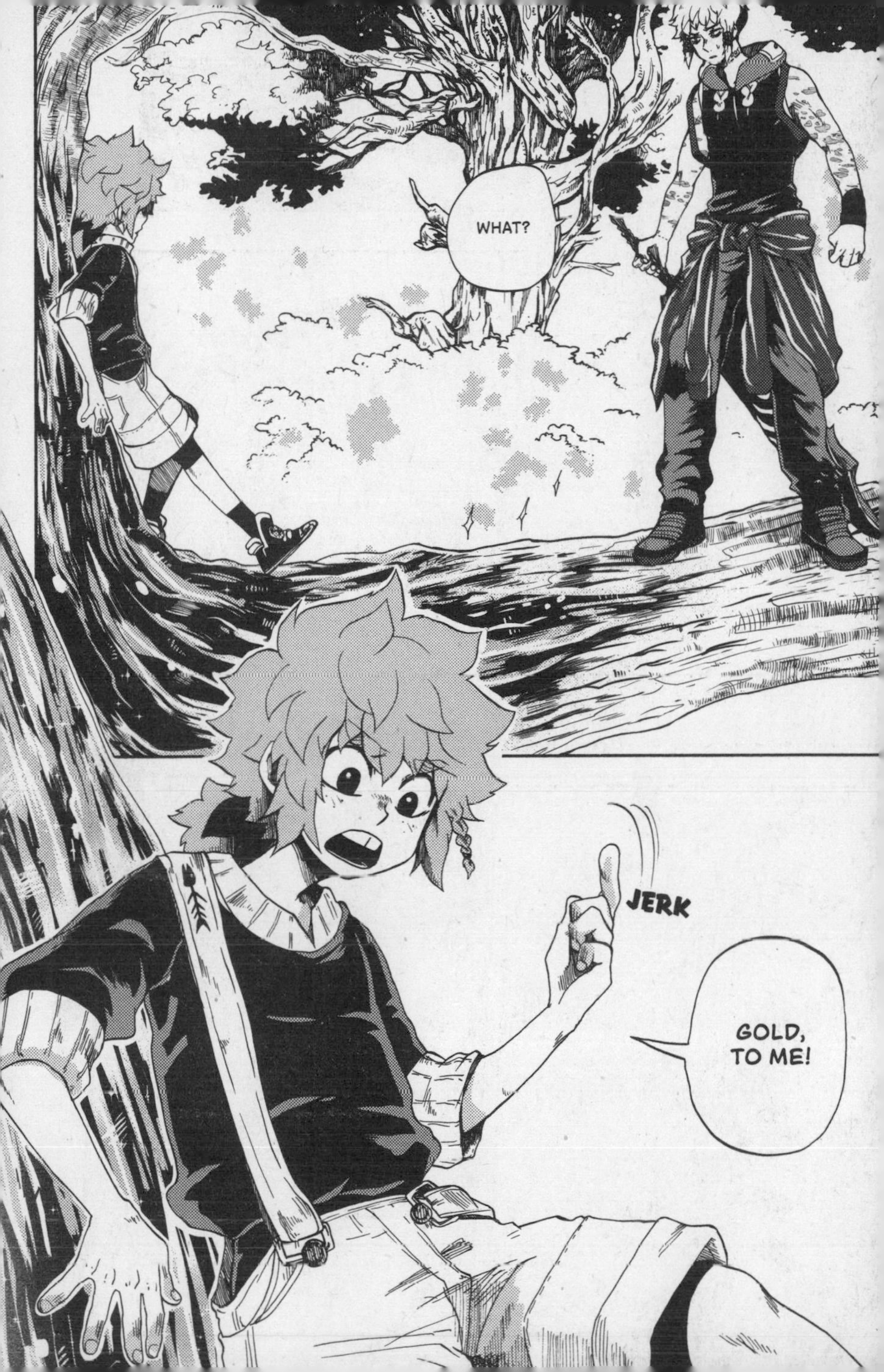
WHAT?
GOLD, TO ME!
JERK

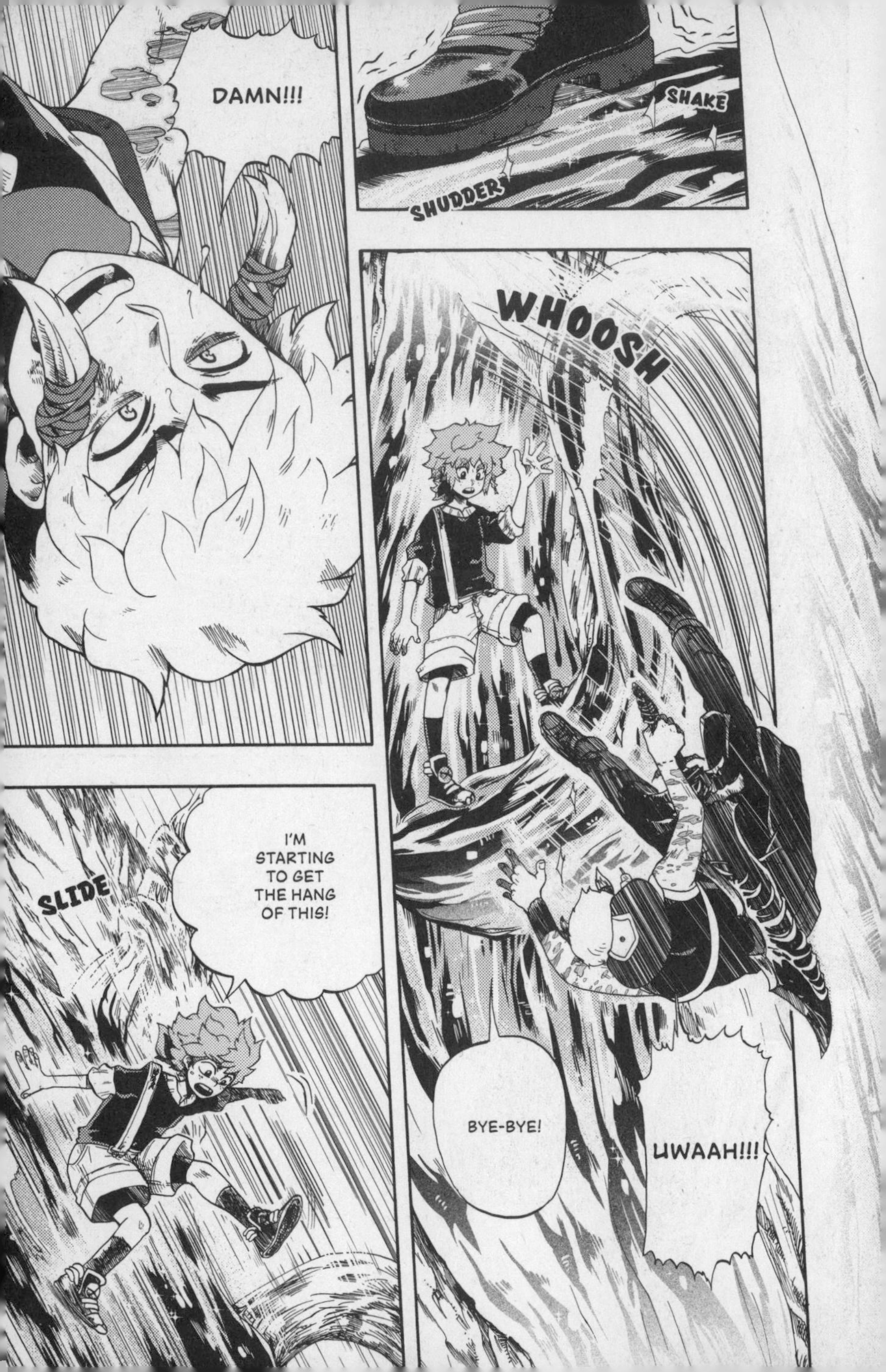
SHAKE
SHUDDER
DAMN!!!
WHOOSH
BYE-BYE!
UWAAH!!!
SLIDE
I'M STARTING TO GET THE HANG OF THIS!

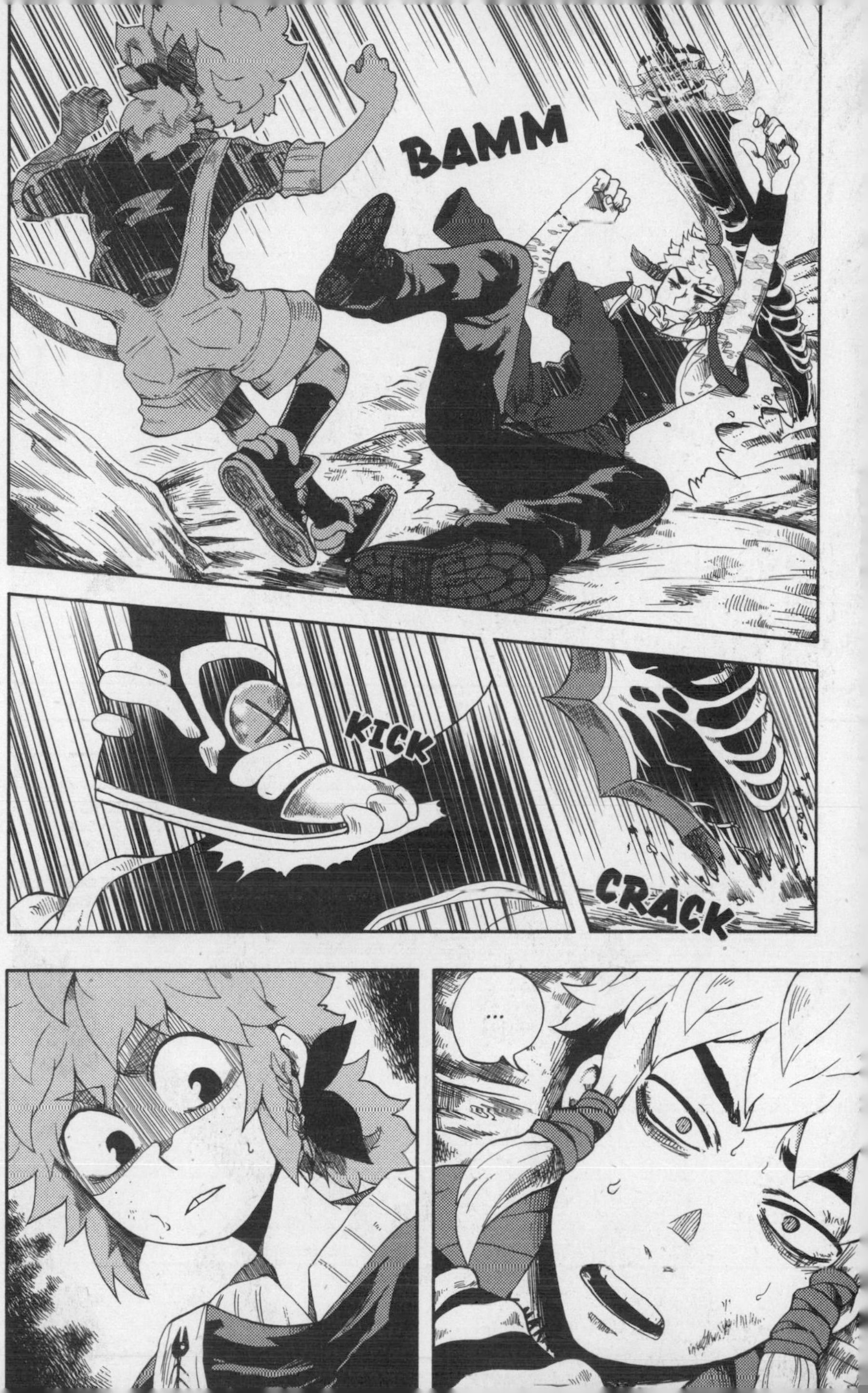
BAMM
CRACK
KICK
...

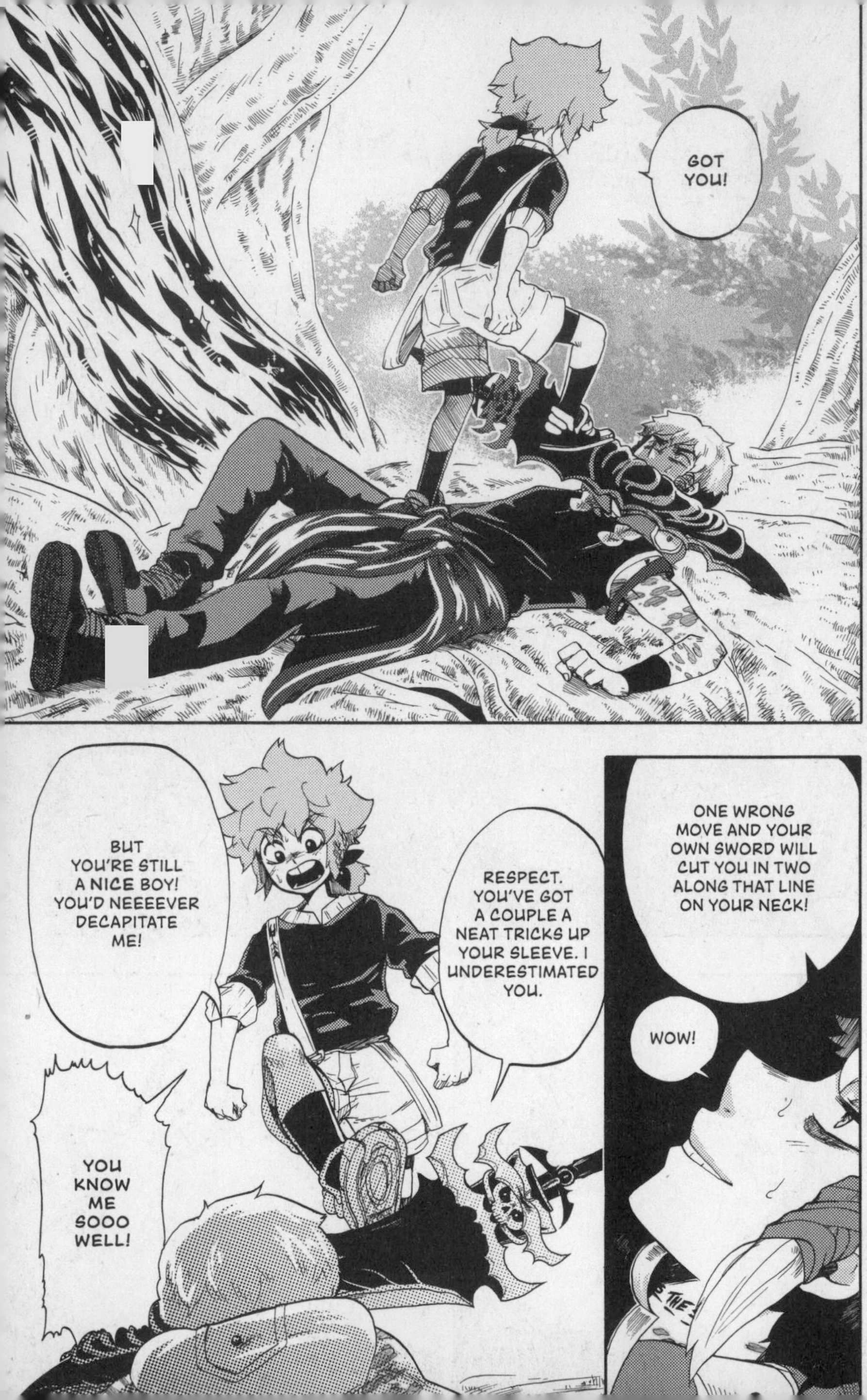
GOT YOU!
ONE WRONG MOVE AND YOUR OWN SWORD WILL CUT YOU IN TWO ALONG THAT LINE ON YOUR NECK!
WOW!
RESPECT. YOU'VE GOT A COUPLE A NEAT TRICKS UP YOUR SLEEVE. I UNDERESTIMATED YOU.
BUT YOU'RE STILL A NICE BOY! YOU'D NEEEEVER DECAPITATE ME!
YOU KNOW ME SOOO WELL!

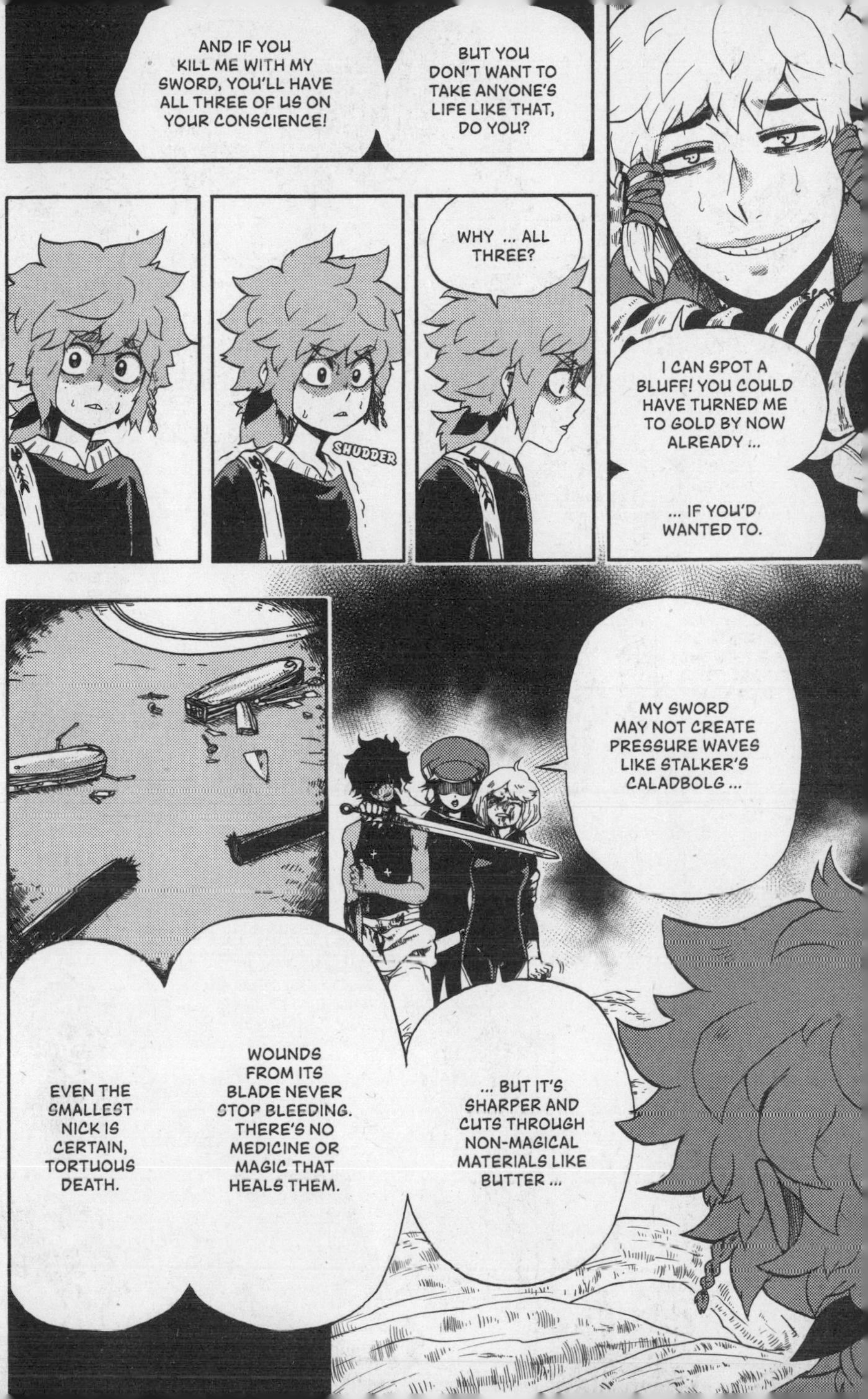
I CAN SPOT A BLUFF! YOU COULD HAVE TURNED ME TO GOLD BY NOW ALREADY ...
... IF YOU'D WANTED TO.
BUT YOU DON'T WANT TO TAKE ANYONE'S LIFE LIKE THAT, DO YOU?
AND IF YOU KILL ME WITH MY SWORD, YOU'LL HAVE ALL THREE OF US ON YOUR CONSCIENCE!
WHY ... ALL THREE?
SHUDDER
MY SWORD MAY NOT CREATE PRESSURE WAVES LIKE STALKER'S CALADBOLG ...
... BUT IT'S SHARPER AND CUTS THROUGH NON-MAGICAL MATERIALS LIKE BUTTER ...
WOUNDS FROM ITS BLADE NEVER STOP BLEEDING. THERE'S NO MEDICINE OR MAGIC THAT HEALS THEM.
EVEN THE SMALLEST NICK IS CERTAIN, TORTUOUS DEATH.

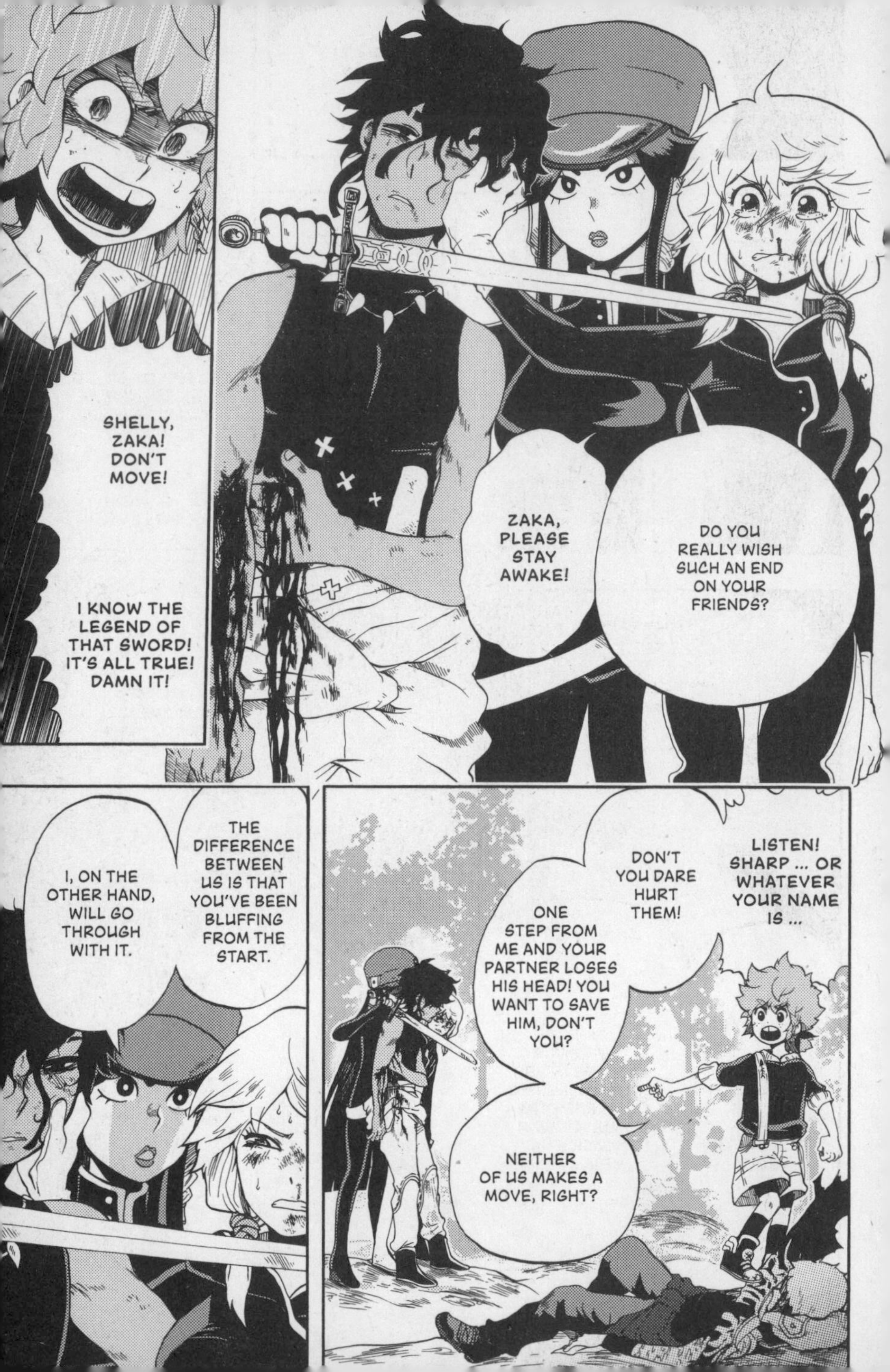
DO YOU REALLY WISH SUCH AN END ON YOUR FRIENDS?
ZAKA, PLEASE STAY AWAKE!
SHELLY, ZAKA! DON'T MOVE!
I KNOW THE LEGEND OF THAT SWORD! IT'S ALL TRUE! DAMN IT!
LISTEN! SHARP ... OR WHATEVER YOUR NAME IS ...
DON'T YOU DARE HURT THEM!
ONE STEP FROM ME AND YOUR PARTNER LOSES HIS HEAD! YOU WANT TO SAVE HIM, DON'T YOU?
NEITHER OF US MAKES A MOVE, RIGHT?
THE DIFFERENCE BETWEEN US IS THAT YOU'VE BEEN BLUFFING FROM THE START.
I, ON THE OTHER HAND, WILL GO THROUGH WITH IT.

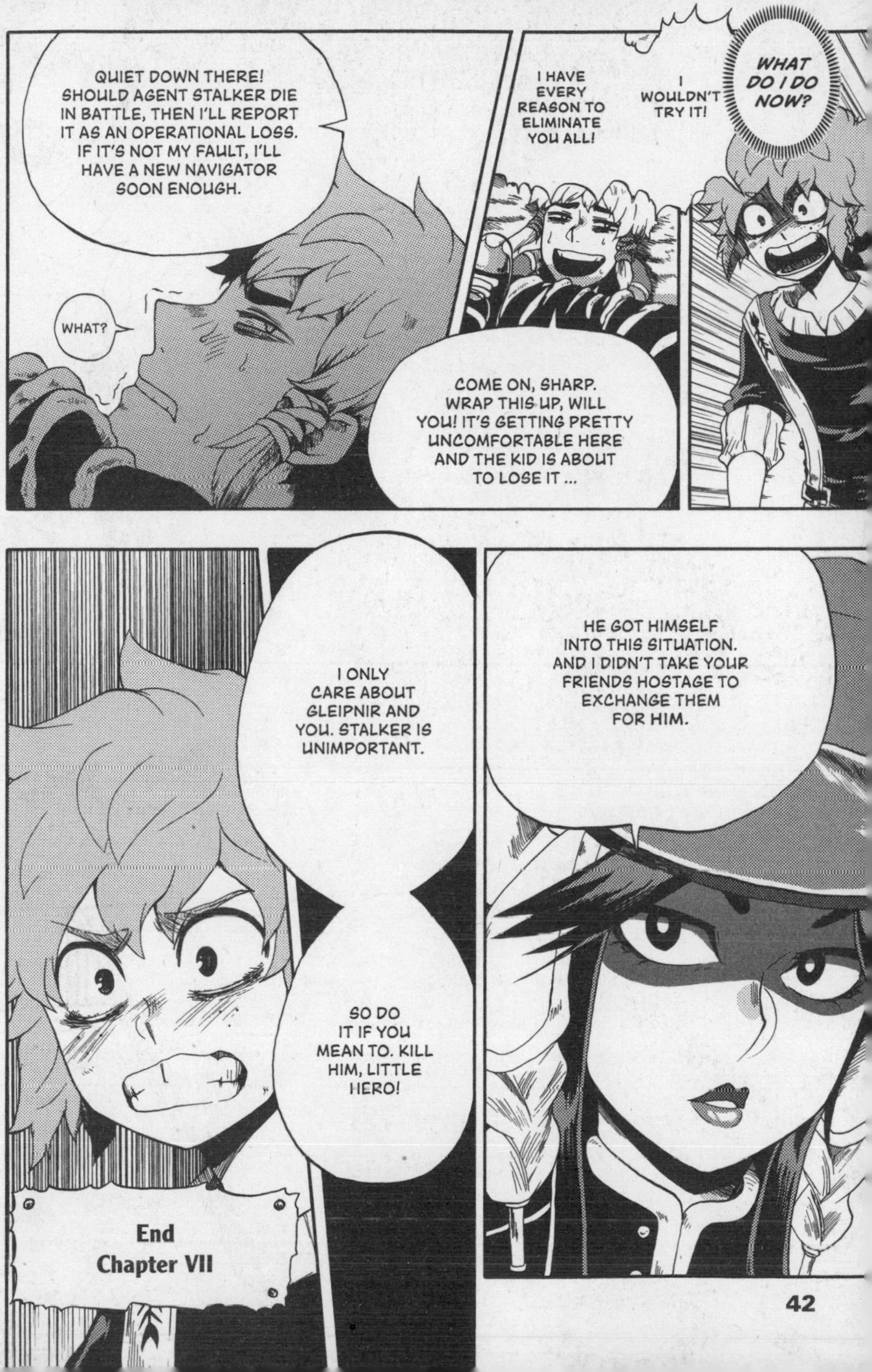
WHAT DO I DO NOW?
I WOULDN'T TRY IT!
I HAVE EVERY REASON TO ELIMINATE YOU ALL!
COME ON, SHARP. WRAP THIS UP, WILL YOU! IT'S GETTING PRETTY UNCOMFORTABLE HERE AND THE KID IS ABOUT TO LOSE IT ...
QUIET DOWN THERE! SHOULD AGENT STALKER DIE IN BATTLE, THEN I'LL REPORT IT AS AN OPERATIONAL LOSS. IF IT'S NOT MY FAULT, I'LL HAVE A NEW NAVIGATOR SOON ENOUGH.
WHAT?
HE GOT HIMSELF INTO THIS SITUATION. AND I DIDN'T TAKE YOUR FRIENDS HOSTAGE TO EXCHANGE THEM FOR HIM.
I ONLY CARE ABOUT GLEIPNIR AND YOU. STALKER IS UNIMPORTANT.
SO DO IT IF YOU MEAN TO. KILL HIM, LITTLE HERO!
End
Chapter VII

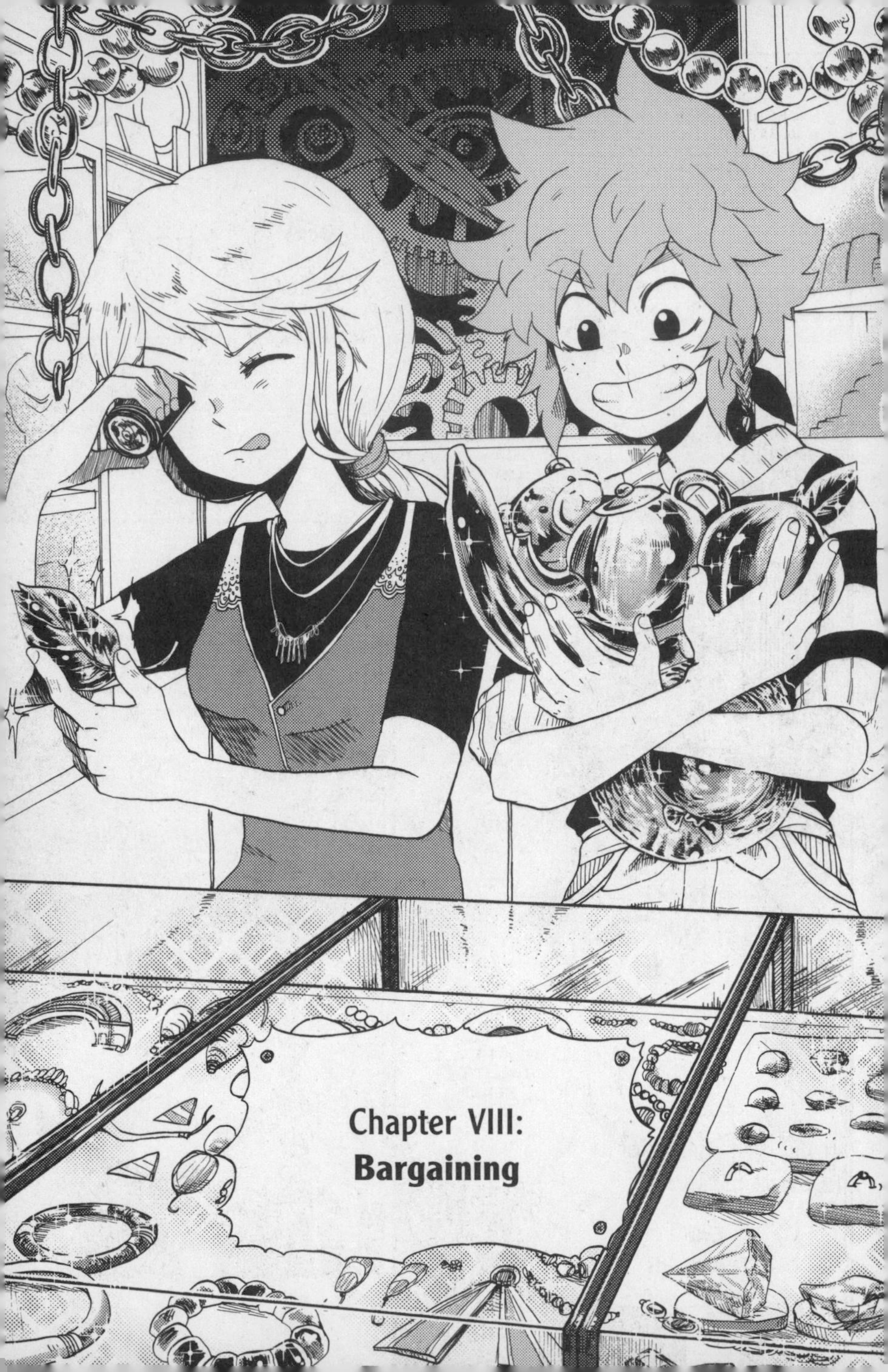
Chapter VIII:
Bargaining

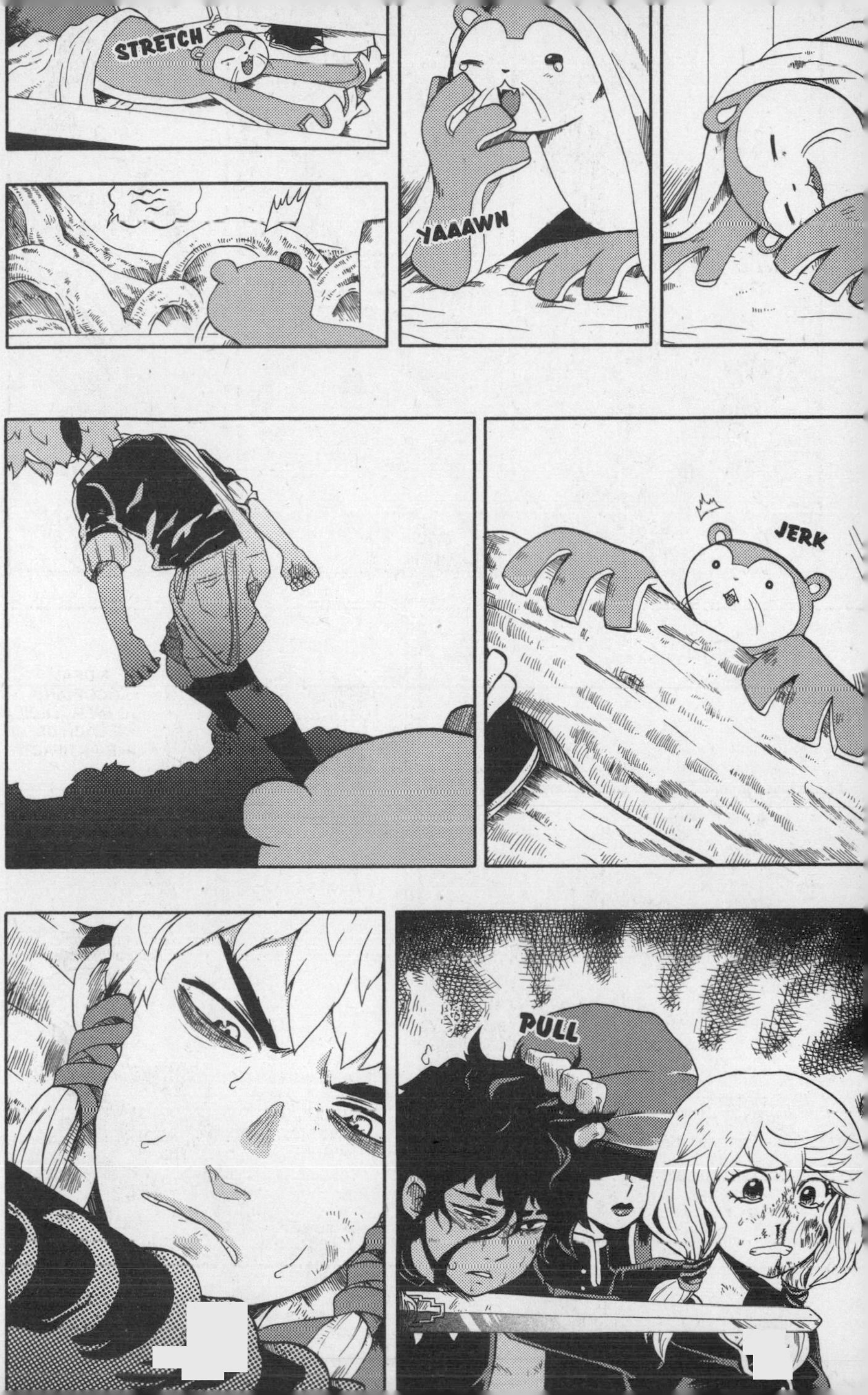
YAAAWN
STRETCH
JERK
PULL

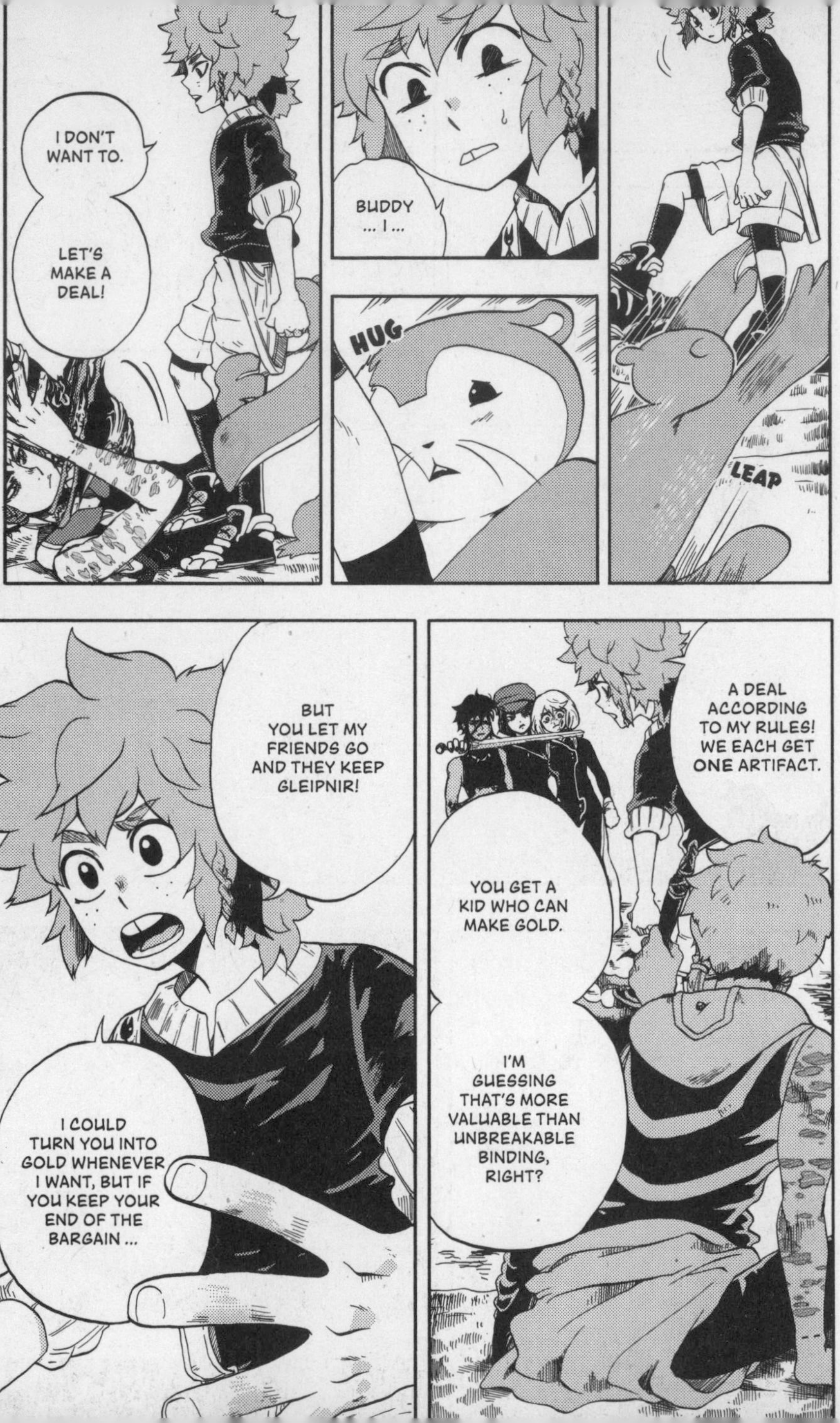
LEAP
BUDDY ... I ...
HUG
I DON'T WANT TO.
LET'S MAKE A DEAL!
A DEAL ACCORDING TO MY RULES! WE EACH GET ONE ARTIFACT.
YOU GET A KID WHO CAN MAKE GOLD.
I'M GUESSING THAT'S MORE VALUABLE THAN UNBREAKABLE BINDING, RIGHT?
BUT YOU LET MY FRIENDS GO AND THEY KEEP GLEIPNIR!
I COULD TURN YOU INTO GOLD WHENEVER I WANT, BUT IF YOU KEEP YOUR END OF THE BARGAIN ...

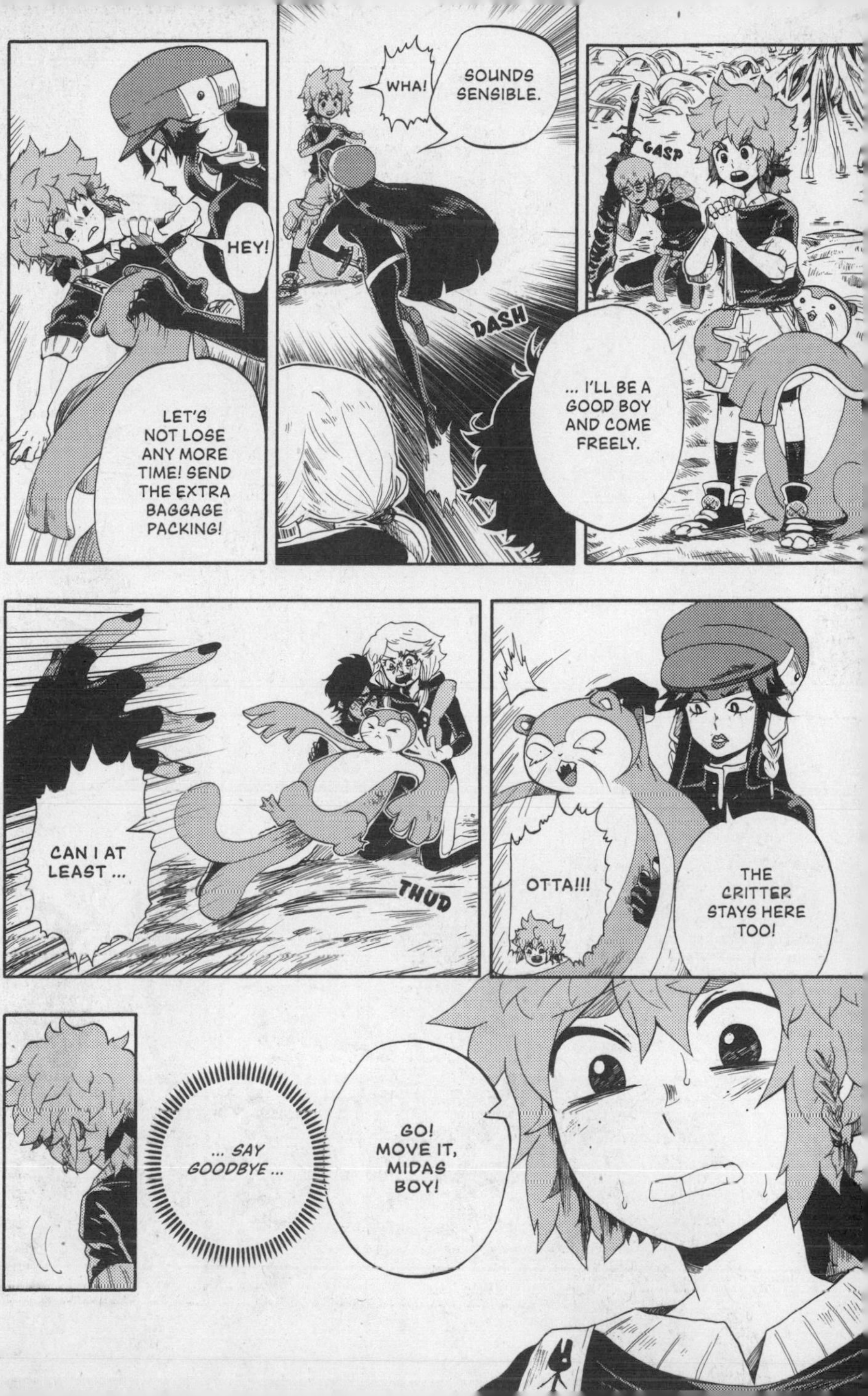
GASP
... I'LL BE A GOOD BOY AND COME FREELY.
SOUNDS SENSIBLE.
WHA!
DASH
HEY!
LET'S NOT LOSE ANY MORE TIME! SEND THE EXTRA BAGGAGE PACKING!
THE CRITTER STAYS HERE TOO!
OTTA!!!
CAN I AT LEAST ...
THUD
GO! MOVE IT, MIDAS BOY!
... SAY GOODBYE ...

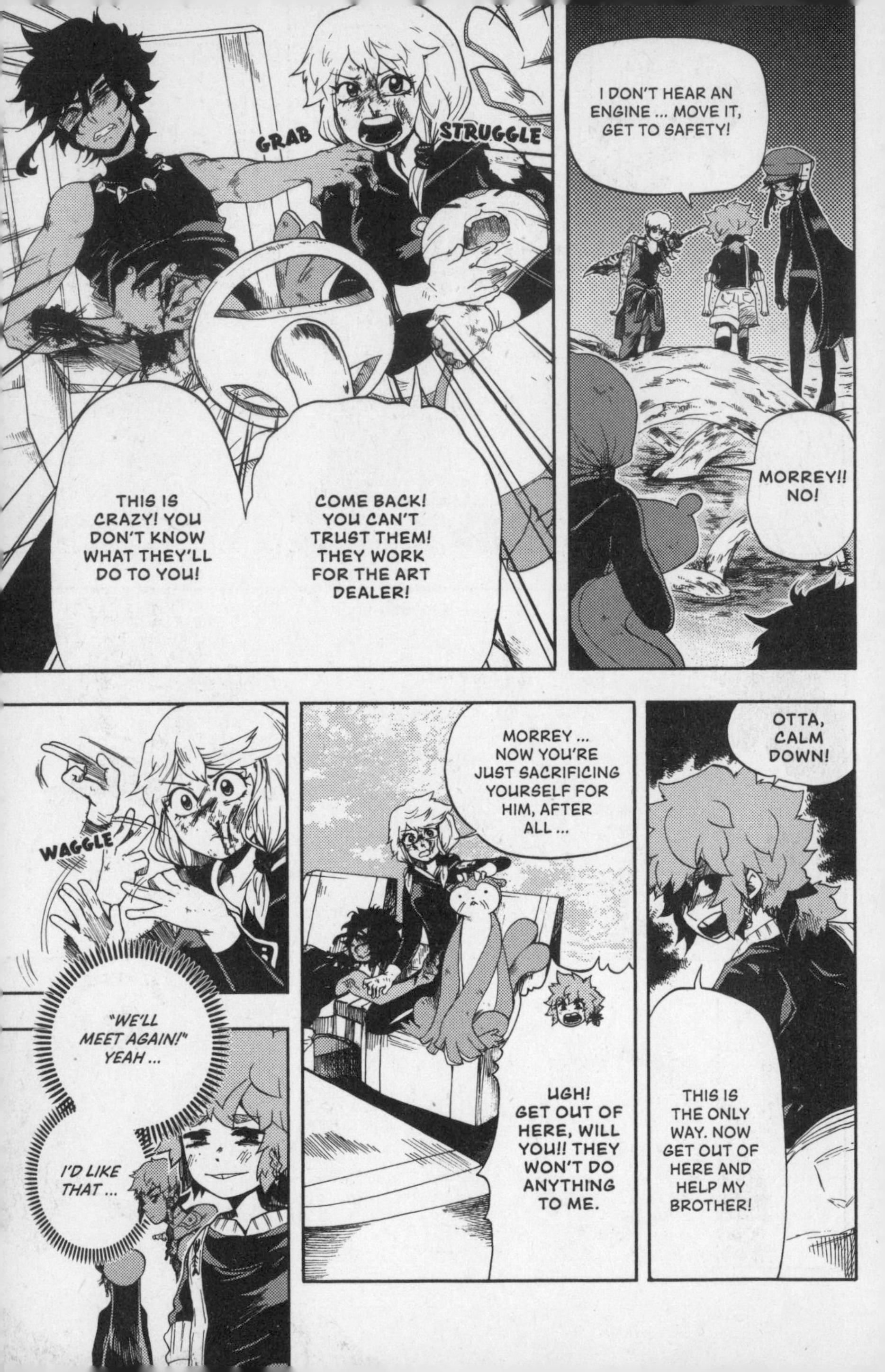
I DON'T HEAR AN ENGINE ... MOVE IT, GET TO SAFETY!
MORREY!! NO!
STRUGGLE
GRAB
COME BACK! YOU CAN'T TRUST THEM! THEY WORK FOR THE ART DEALER!
THIS IS CRAZY! YOU DON'T KNOW WHAT THEY'LL DO TO YOU!
OTTA, CALM DOWN!
THIS IS THE ONLY WAY. NOW GET OUT OF HERE AND HELP MY BROTHER!
MORREY ... NOW YOU'RE JUST SACRIFICING YOURSELF FOR HIM, AFTER ALL ...
UGH! GET OUT OF HERE, WILL YOU!! THEY WON'T DO ANYTHING TO ME.
WAGGLE
"WE'LL MEET AGAIN!" YEAH ...
I'D LIKE THAT ...

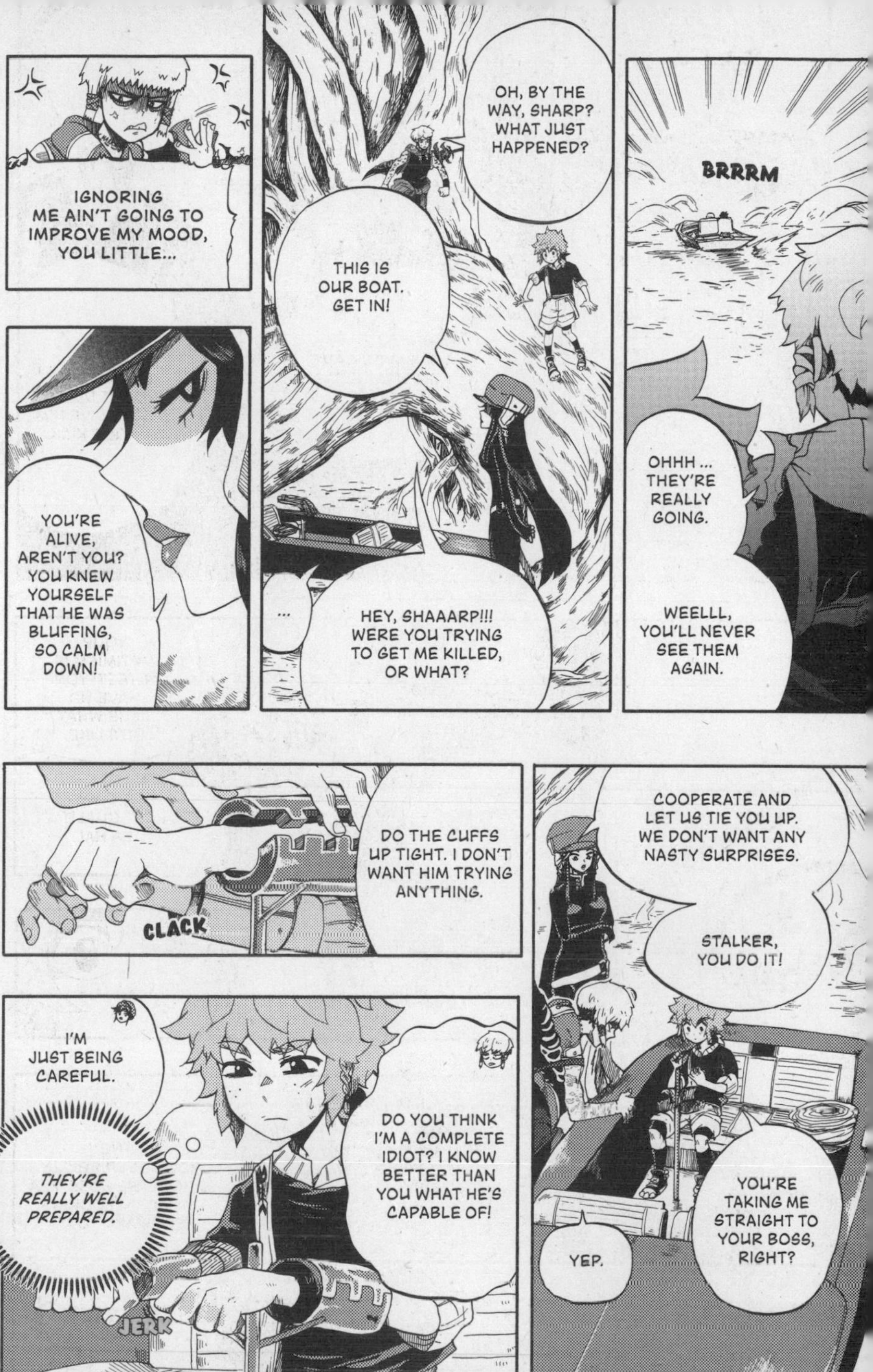
BRRRM
OHHH ... THEY'RE REALLY GOING.
WEELLL, YOU'LL NEVER SEE THEM AGAIN.
OH, BY THE WAY, SHARP? WHAT JUST HAPPENED?
THIS IS OUR BOAT. GET IN!
HEY, SHAAARP!!! WERE YOU TRYING TO GET ME KILLED, OR WHAT?
...
IGNORING ME AIN'T GOING TO IMPROVE MY MOOD, YOU LITTLE...
YOU'RE ALIVE, AREN'T YOU? YOU KNEW YOURSELF THAT HE WAS BLUFFING, SO CALM DOWN!
COOPERATE AND LET US TIE YOU UP. WE DON'T WANT ANY NASTY SURPRISES.
STALKER, YOU DO IT!
YOU'RE TAKING ME STRAIGHT TO YOUR BOSS, RIGHT?
YEP.
DO THE CUFFS UP TIGHT. I DON'T WANT HIM TRYING ANYTHING.
CLACK
DO YOU THINK I'M A COMPLETE IDIOT? I KNOW BETTER THAN YOU WHAT HE'S CAPABLE OF!
I'M JUST BEING CAREFUL.
THEY'RE REALLY WELL PREPARED.
JERK

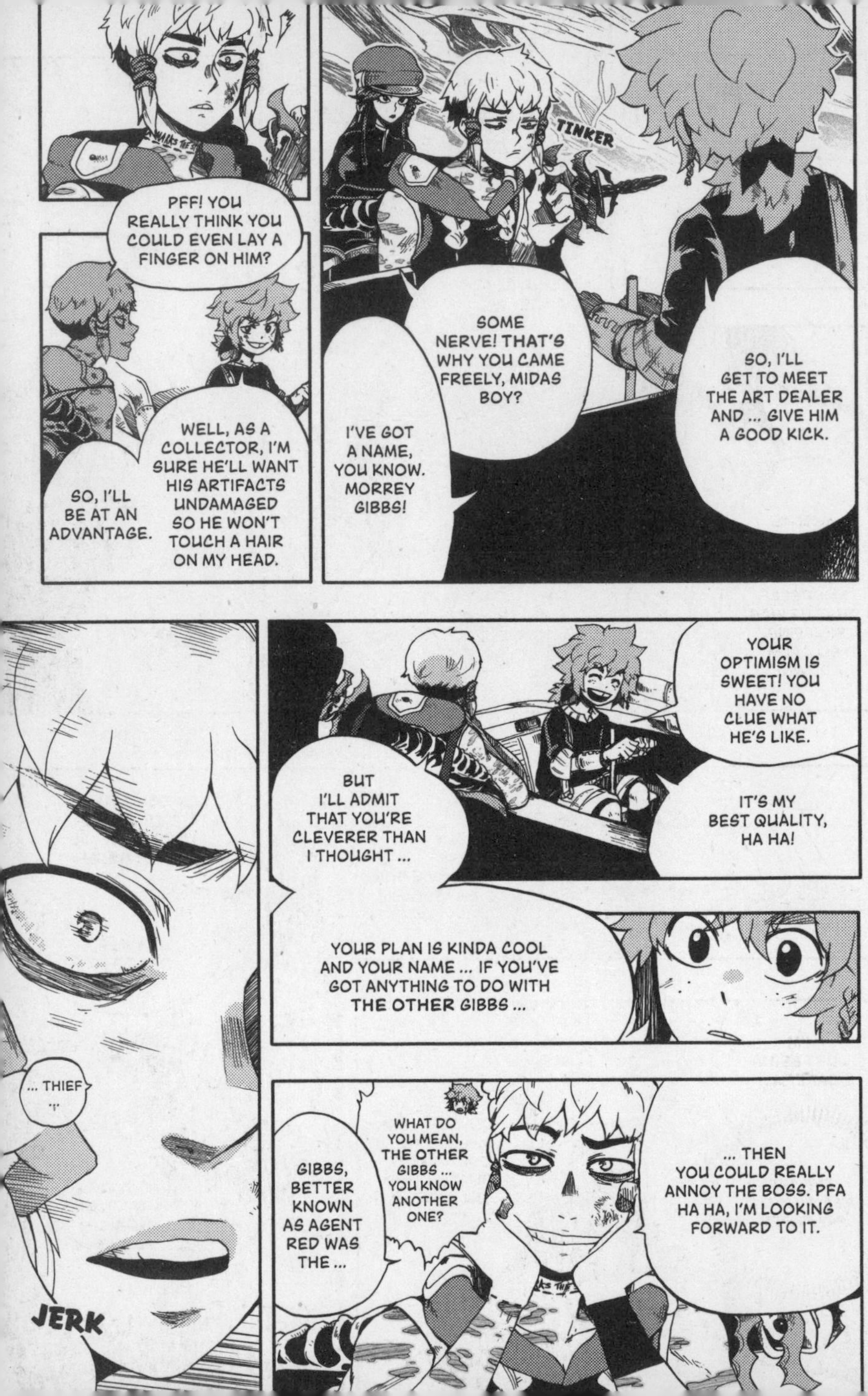
TINKER
SO, I'LL GET TO MEET THE ART DEALER AND ... GIVE HIM A GOOD KICK.
SOME NERVE! THAT'S WHY YOU CAME FREELY, MIDAS BOY?
I'VE GOT A NAME, YOU KNOW. MORREY GIBBS!
PFF! YOU REALLY THINK YOU COULD EVEN LAY A FINGER ON HIM?
WELL, AS A COLLECTOR, I'M SURE HE'LL WANT HIS ARTIFACTS UNDAMAGED SO HE WON'T TOUCH A HAIR ON MY HEAD.
SO, I'LL BE AT AN ADVANTAGE.
YOUR OPTIMISM IS SWEET! YOU HAVE NO CLUE WHAT HE'S LIKE.
IT'S MY BEST QUALITY, HA HA!
BUT I'LL ADMIT THAT YOU'RE CLEVERER THAN I THOUGHT ...
YOUR PLAN IS KINDA COOL AND YOUR NAME ... IF YOU'VE GOT ANYTHING TO DO WITH THE OTHER GIBBS ...
... THEN YOU COULD REALLY ANNOY THE BOSS. PFA HA HA, I'M LOOKING FORWARD TO IT.
WHAT DO YOU MEAN, THE OTHER GIBBS ... YOU KNOW ANOTHER ONE?
GIBBS, BETTER KNOWN AS AGENT RED WAS THE ...
... THIEF
JERK

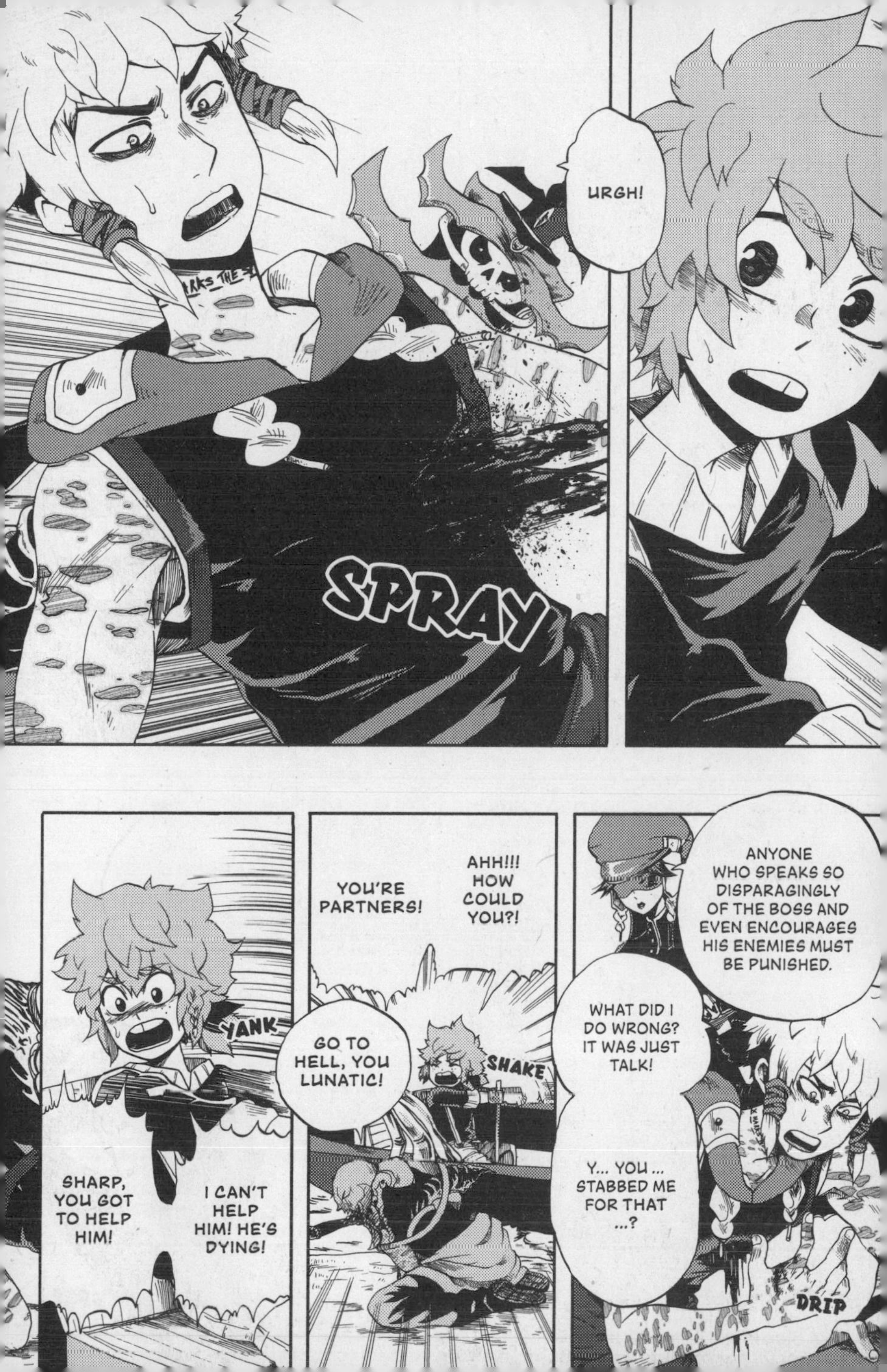
URGH!
SPRAY
ANYONE WHO SPEAKS SO DISPARAGINGLY OF THE BOSS AND EVEN ENCOURAGES HIS ENEMIES MUST BE PUNISHED.
WHAT DID I DO WRONG? IT WAS JUST TALK!
Y... YOU ... STABBED ME FOR THAT ...?
DRIP
AHH!!! HOW COULD YOU?!
YOU'RE PARTNERS!
GO TO HELL, YOU LUNATIC!
SHAKE
YANK
SHARP, YOU GOT TO HELP HIM!
I CAN'T HELP HIM! HE'S DYING!

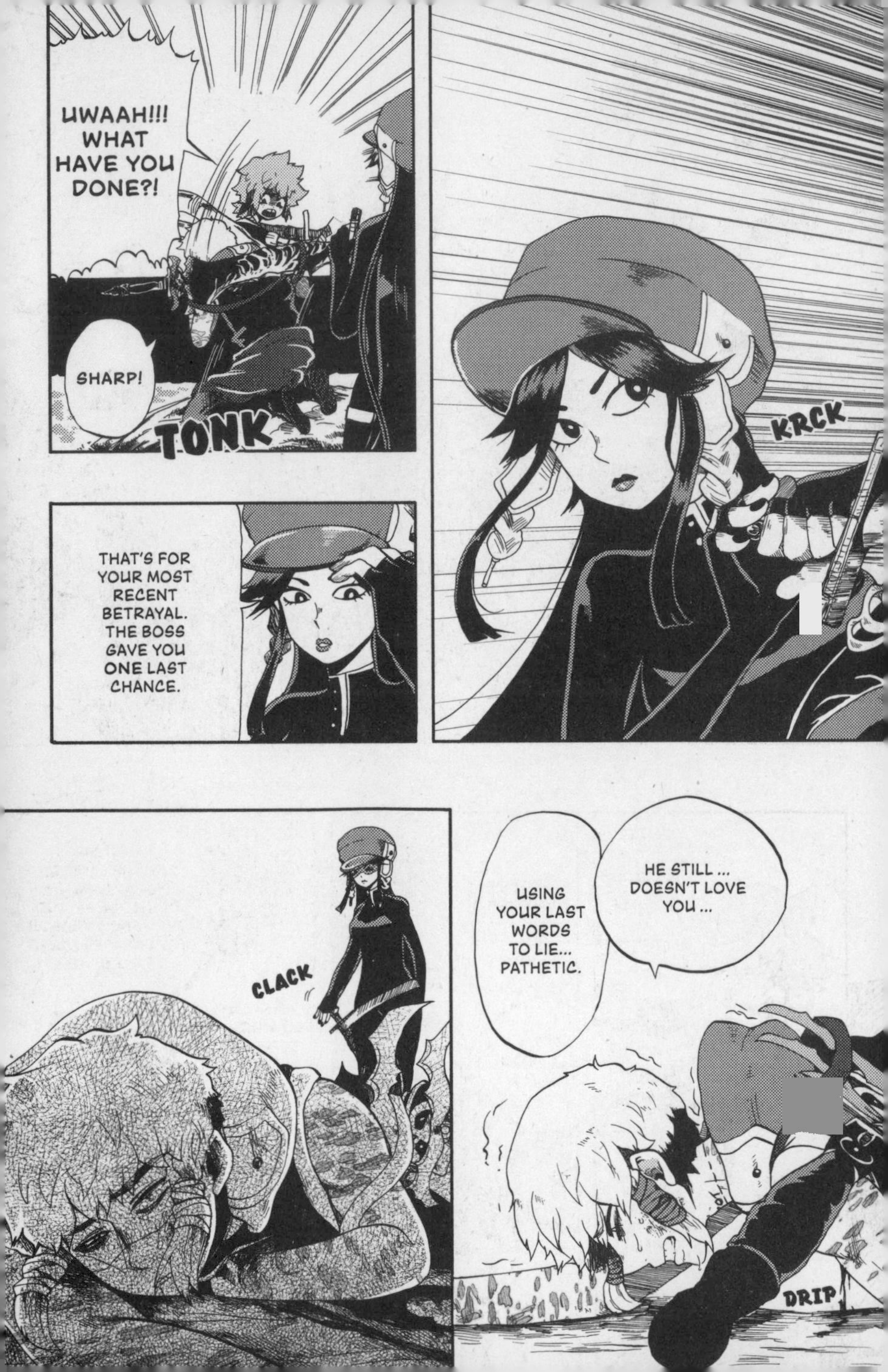
KRCK
UWAAH!!! WHAT HAVE YOU DONE?!
SHARP!
TONK
THAT'S FOR YOUR MOST RECENT BETRAYAL. THE BOSS GAVE YOU ONE LAST CHANCE.
HE STILL ... DOESN'T LOVE YOU ...
USING YOUR LAST WORDS TO LIE... PATHETIC.
DRIP
CLACK

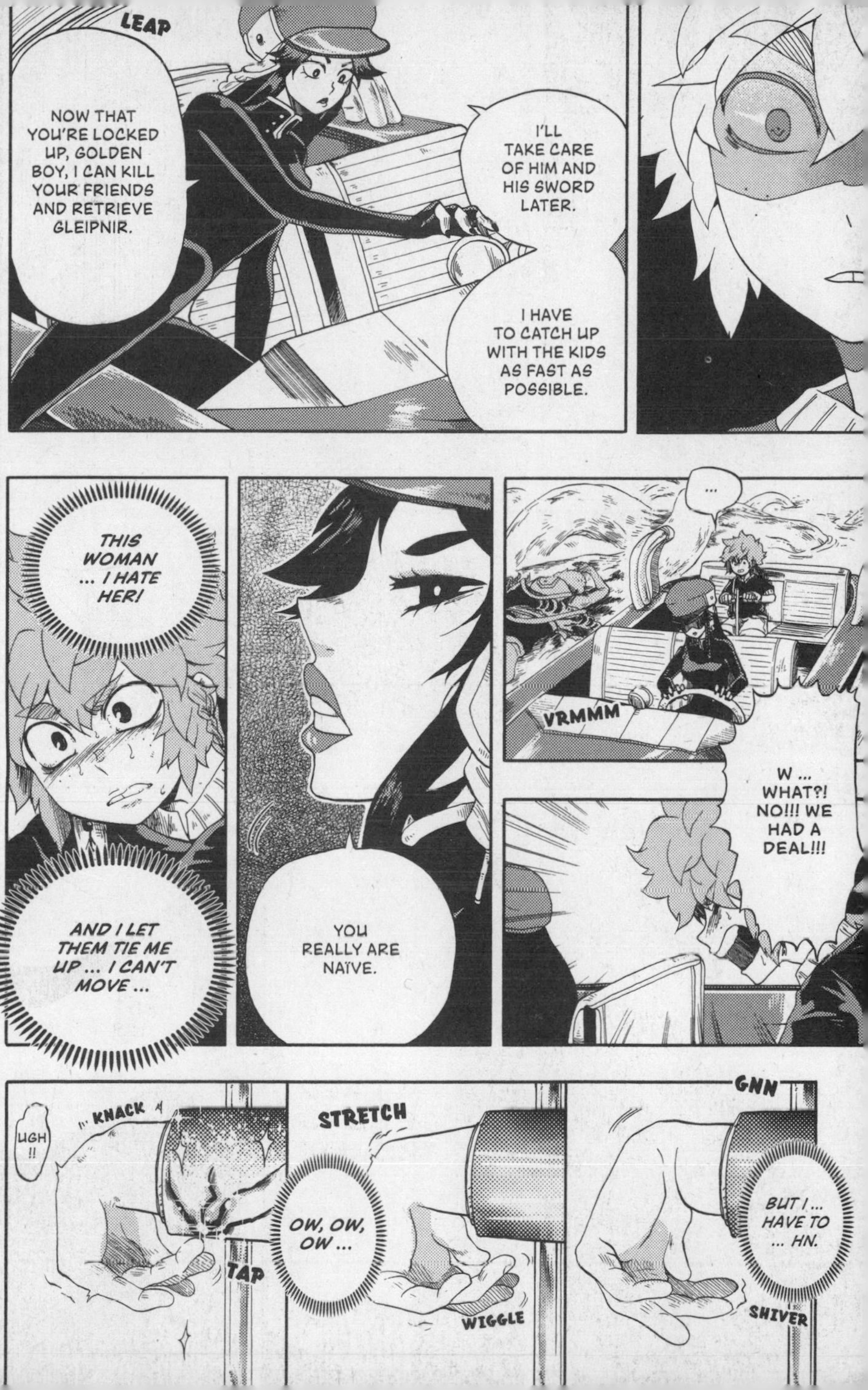
LEAP
NOW THAT YOU'RE LOCKED UP, GOLDEN BOY, I CAN KILL YOUR FRIENDS AND RETRIEVE GLEIPNIR.
I'LL TAKE CARE OF HIM AND HIS SWORD LATER.
I HAVE TO CATCH UP WITH THE KIDS AS FAST AS POSSIBLE.
...
VRMMM
W ... WHAT?! NO!!! WE HAD A DEAL!!!
YOU REALLY ARE NAÏVE.
THIS WOMAN ... I HATE HER!
AND I LET THEM TIE ME UP ... I CAN'T MOVE ...
GNN
BUT I ... HAVE TO ... HN.
SHIVER
STRETCH
OW, OW, OW ...
WIGGLE
KNACK
UGH !!
TAP

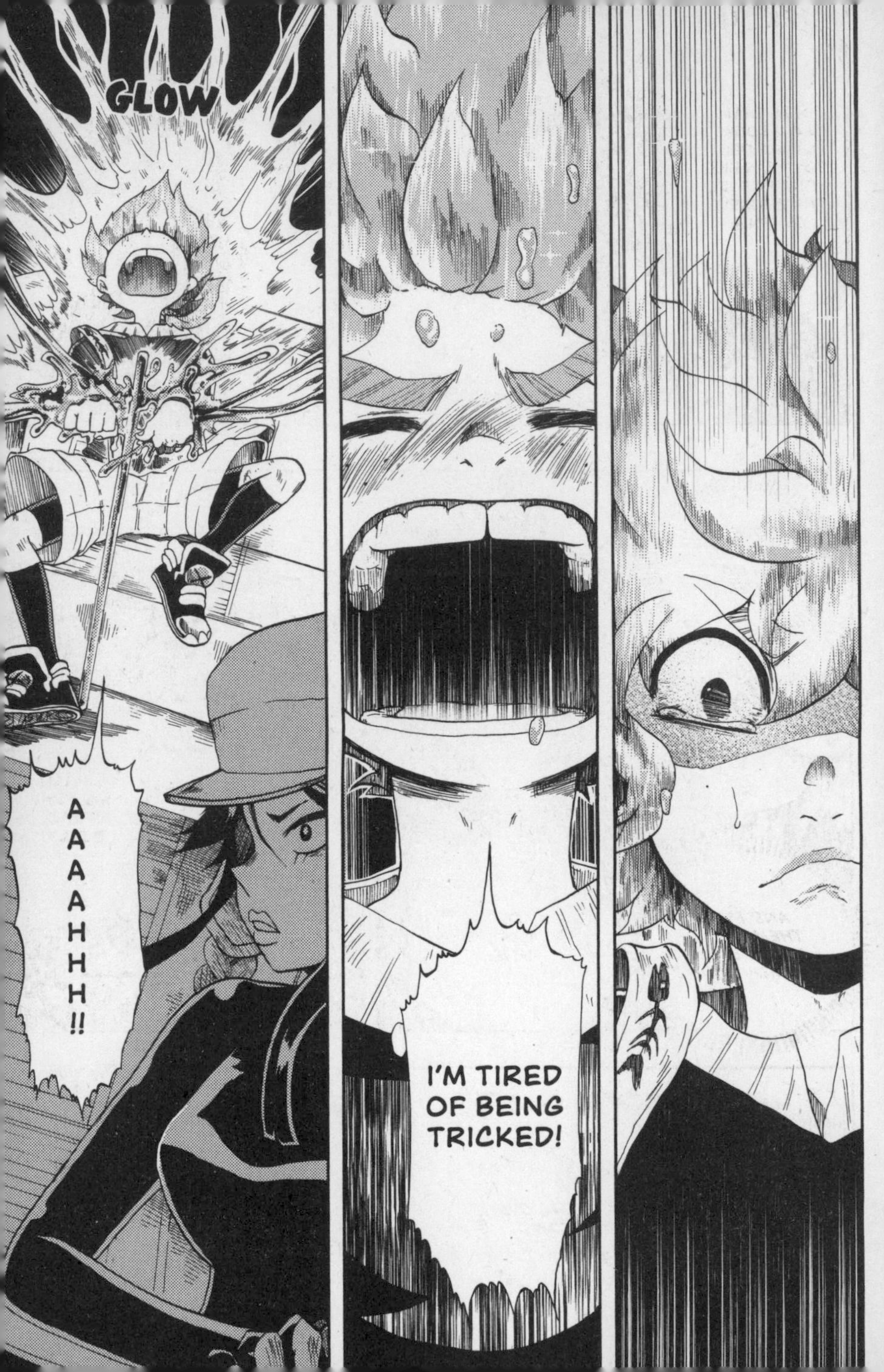
I'M TIRED OF BEING TRICKED!
GLOW
AAAAHHH!!

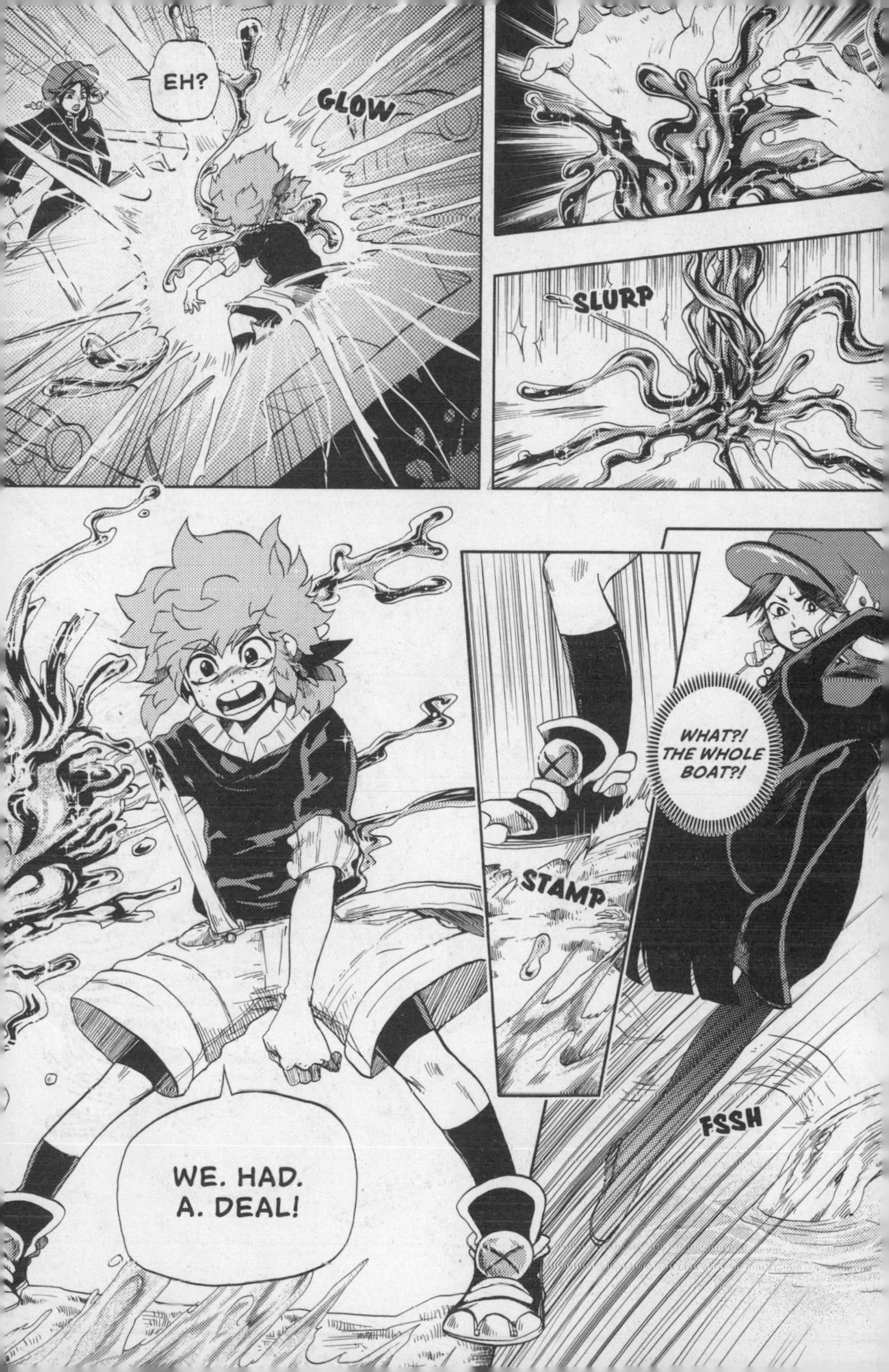
SLURP
EH?
GLOW
WHAT?! THE WHOLE BOAT?!
FSSH
STAMP
WE. HAD. A. DEAL!

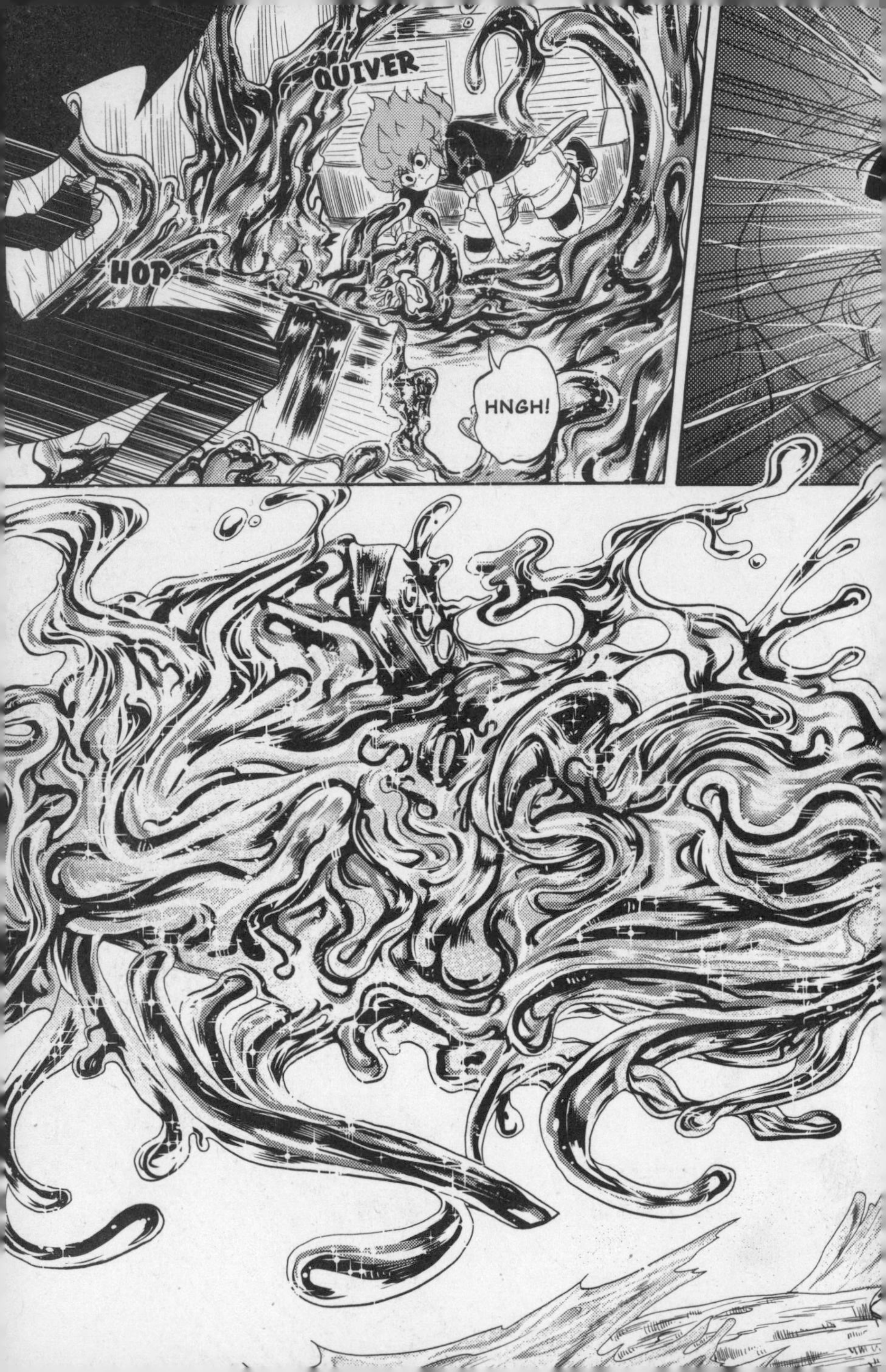
QUIVER
HOP
HNGH!

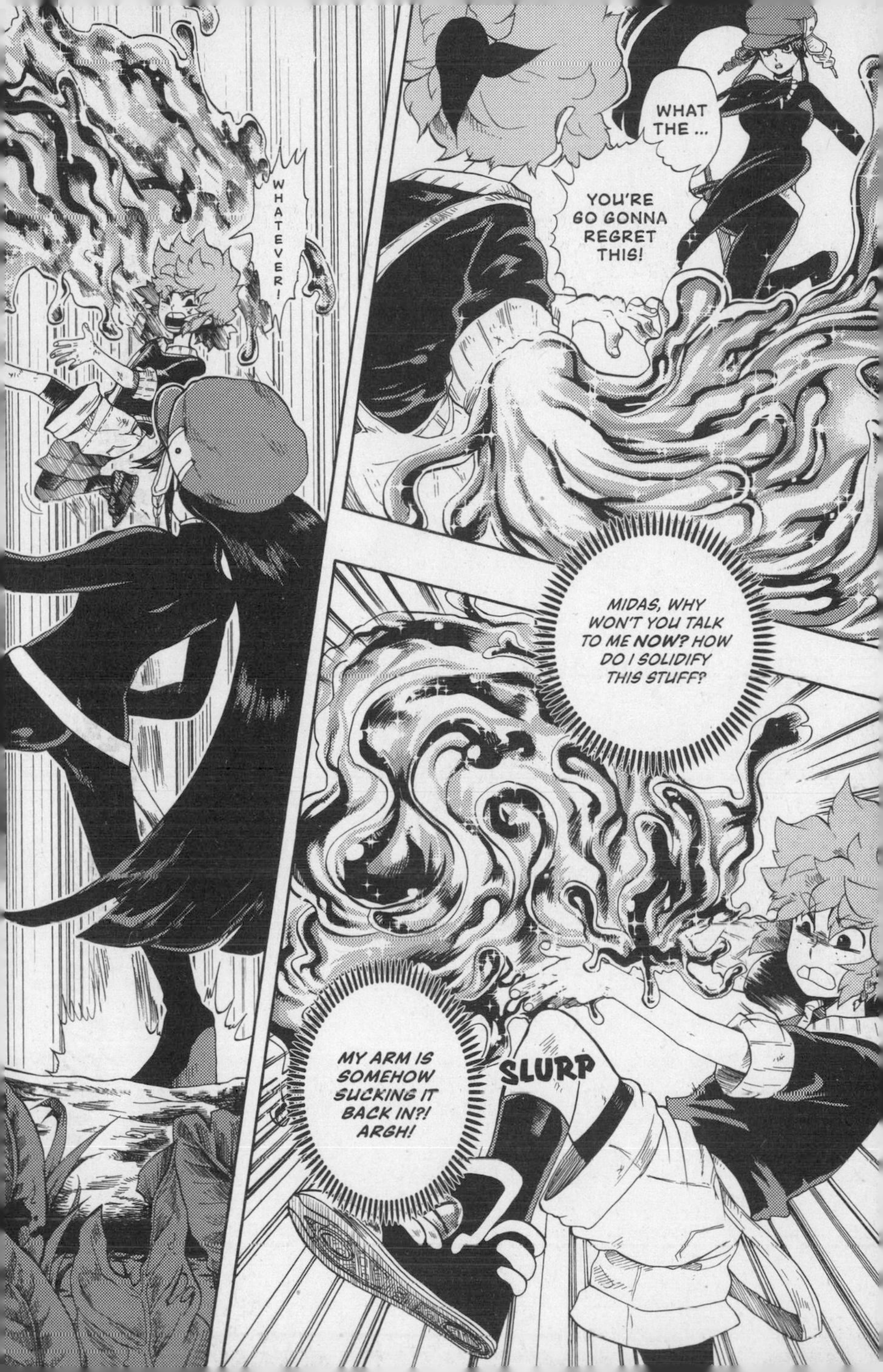
WHAT THE ...
YOU'RE SO GONNA REGRET THIS!
MIDAS, WHY WON'T YOU TALK TO ME NOW? HOW DO I SOLIDIFY THIS STUFF?
MY ARM IS SOMEHOW SUCKING IT BACK IN?! ARGH!
SLURP
WHATEVER!

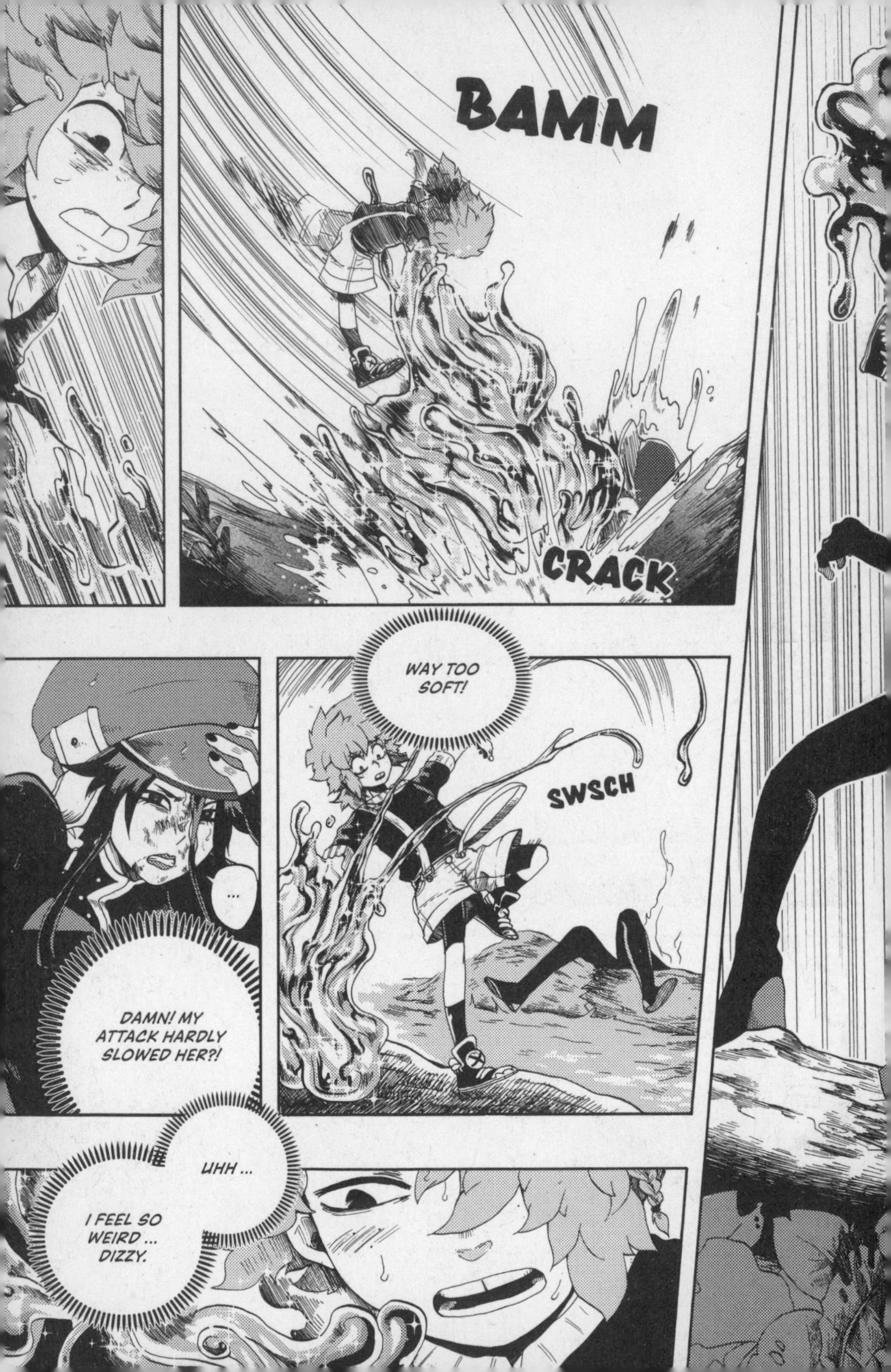
BAMM
CRACK
WAY TOO SOFT!
SWSCH
...
DAMN! MY ATTACK HARDLY SLOWED HER?!
UHH ...
I FEEL SO WEIRD ... DIZZY.

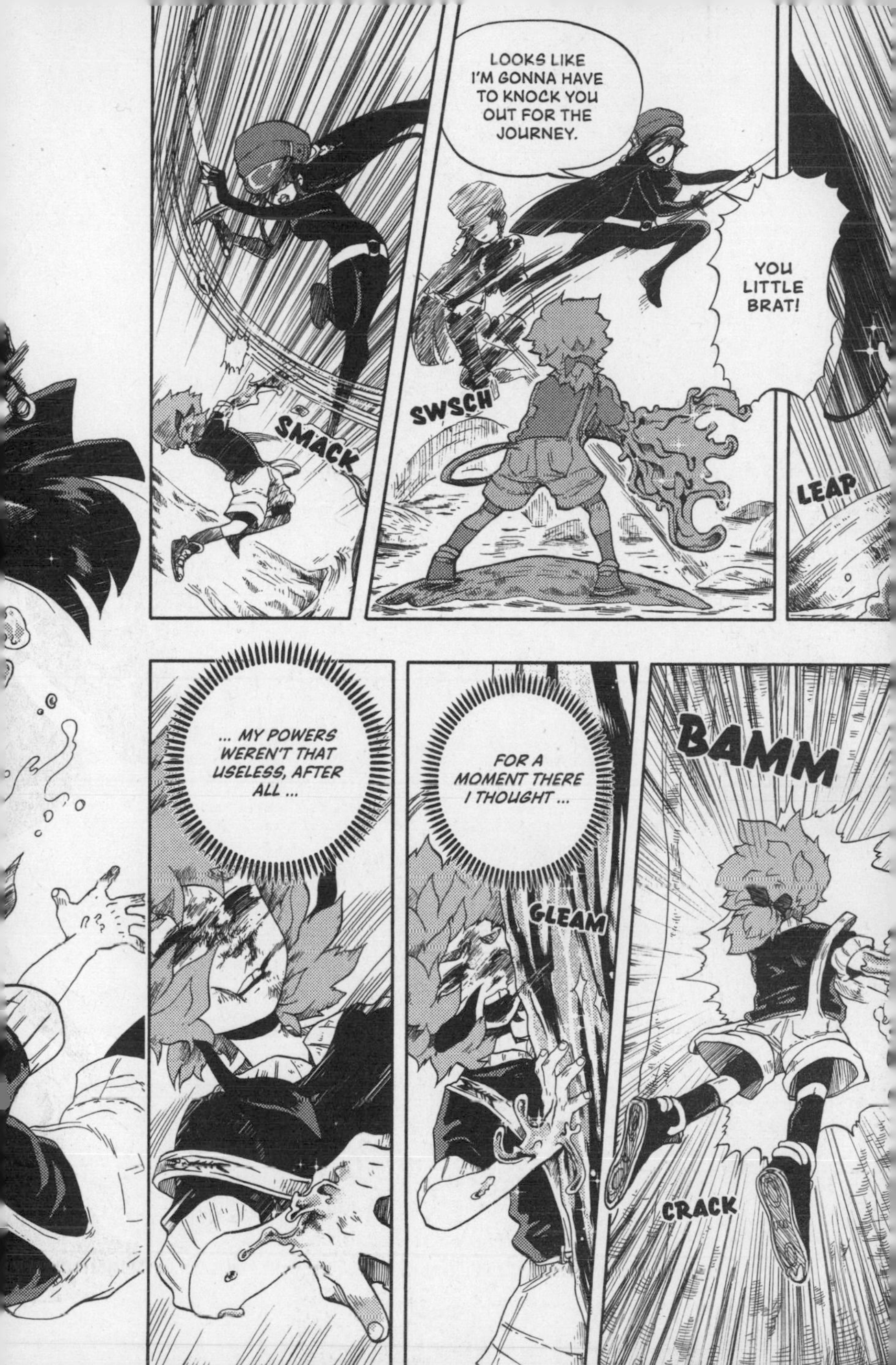
YOU LITTLE BRAT!
LEAP
LOOKS LIKE I'M GONNA HAVE TO KNOCK YOU OUT FOR THE JOURNEY.
SWSCH
SMACK
BAMM
CRACK
FOR A MOMENT THERE I THOUGHT ...
GLEAM
... MY POWERS WEREN'T THAT USELESS, AFTER ALL ...

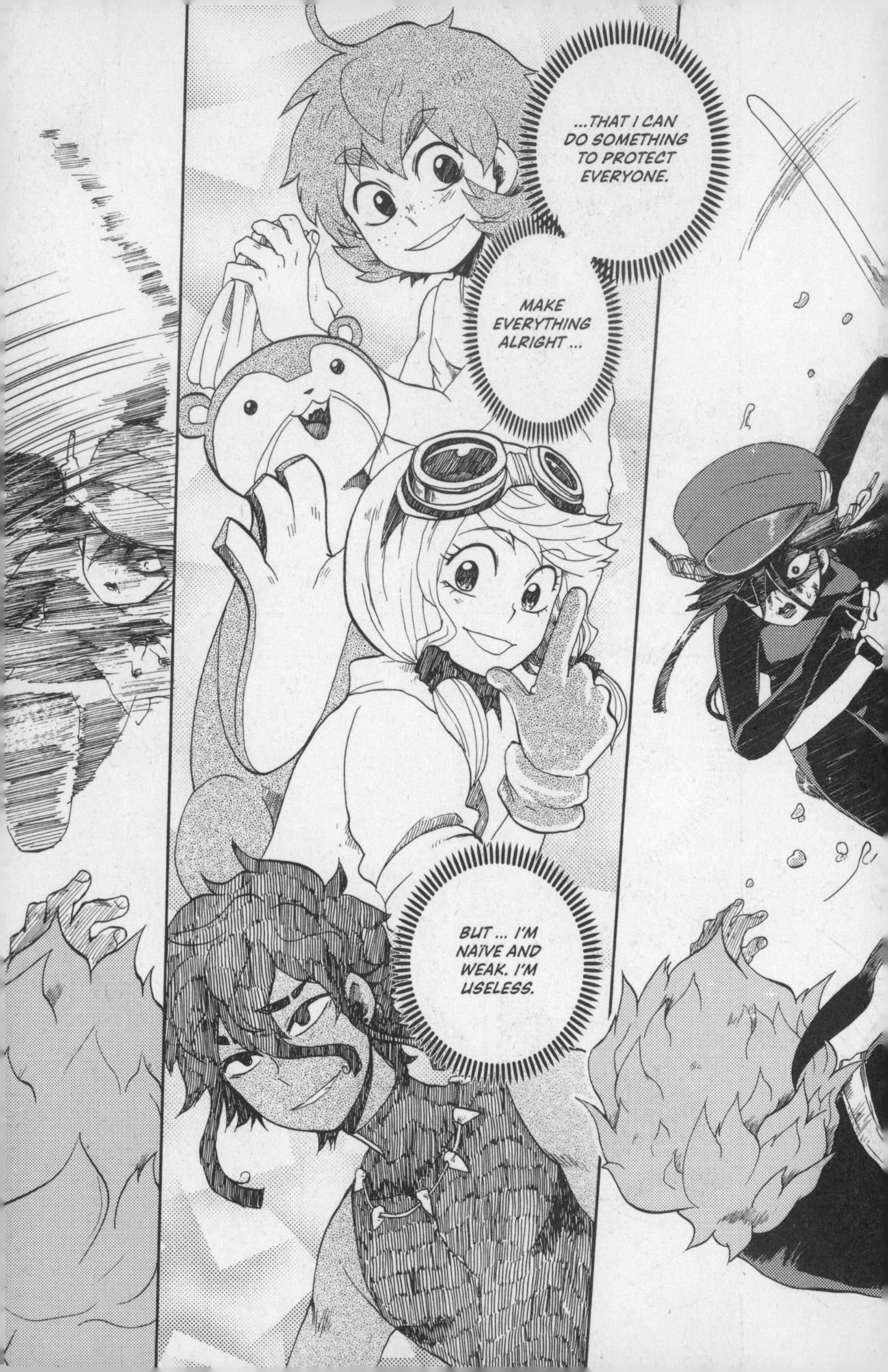
...THAT I CAN DO SOMETHING TO PROTECT EVERYONE.
MAKE EVERYTHING ALRIGHT ...
BUT ... I'M NAÏVE AND WEAK. I'M USELESS.

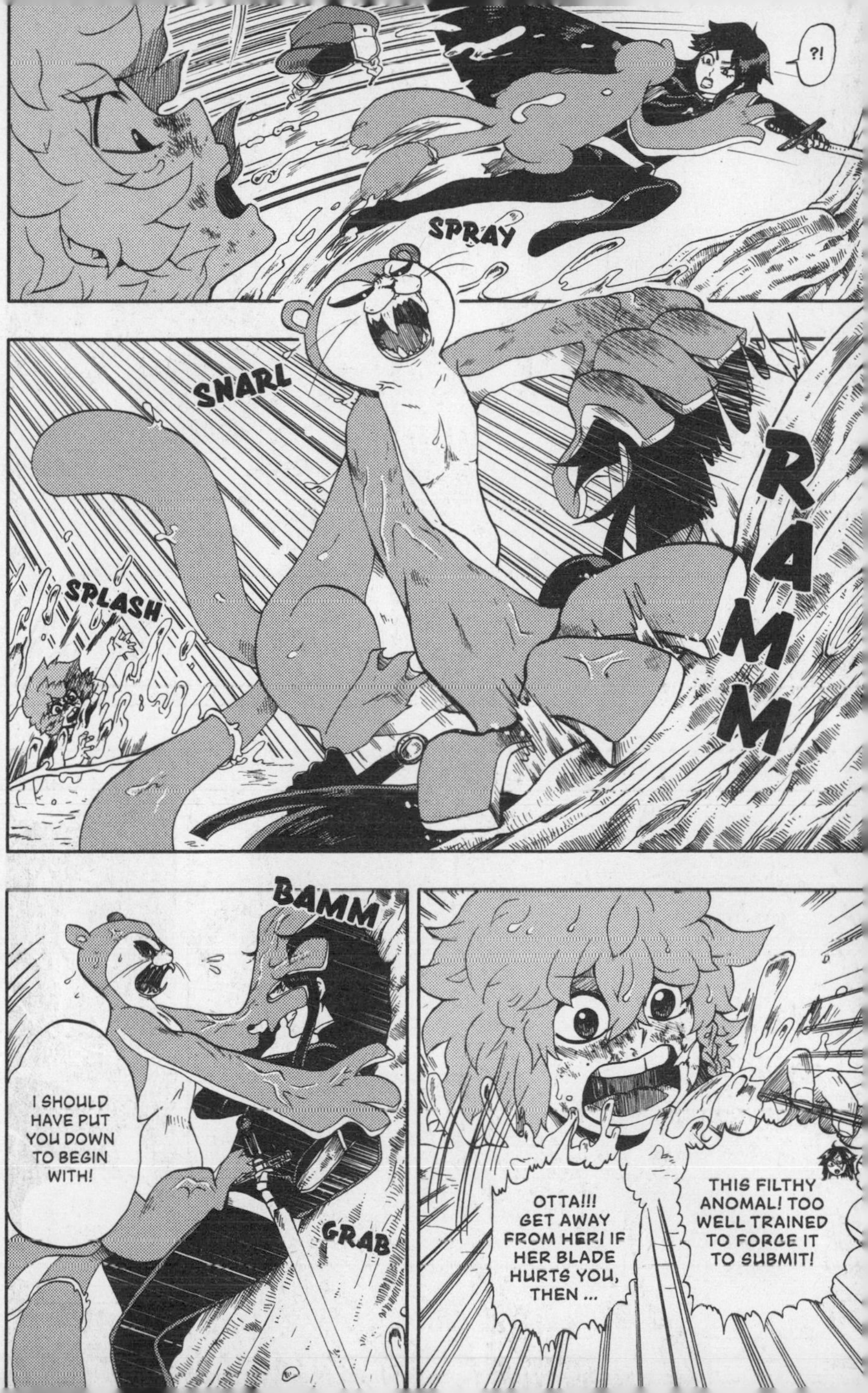
?!
SPRAY
RAMMM
SNARL
SPLASH
THIS FILTHY ANOMAL! TOO WELL TRAINED TO FORCE IT TO SUBMIT!
OTTA!!! GET AWAY FROM HER! IF HER BLADE HURTS YOU, THEN ...
BAMM
I SHOULD HAVE PUT YOU DOWN TO BEGIN WITH!
GRAB

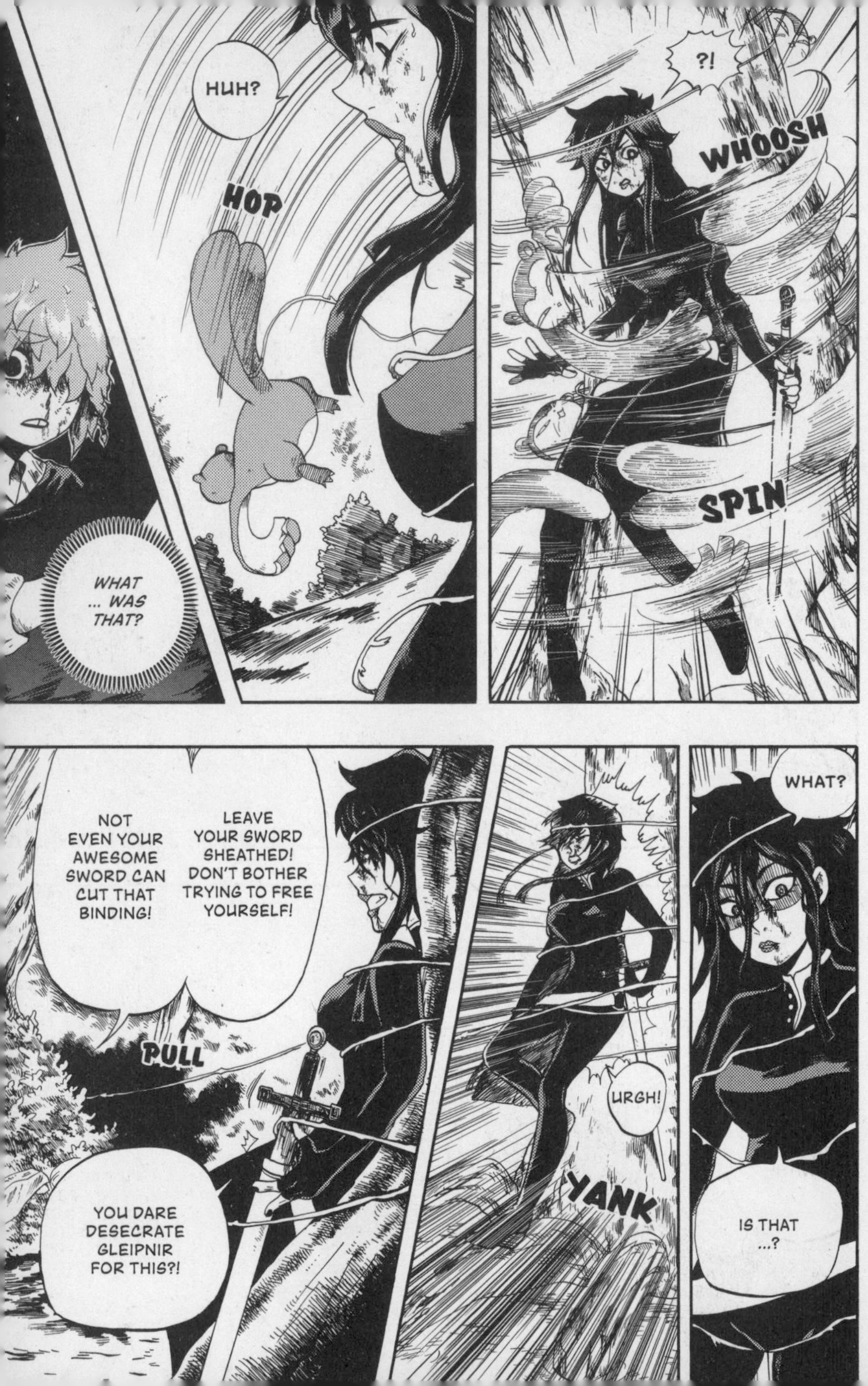
?!
WHOOSH
SPIN
HUH?
HOP
WHAT ... WAS THAT?
WHAT?
IS THAT ...?
URGH!
YANK
LEAVE YOUR SWORD SHEATHED! DON'T BOTHER TRYING TO FREE YOURSELF!
NOT EVEN YOUR AWESOME SWORD CAN CUT THAT BINDING!
PULL
YOU DARE DESECRATE GLEIPNIR FOR THIS?!

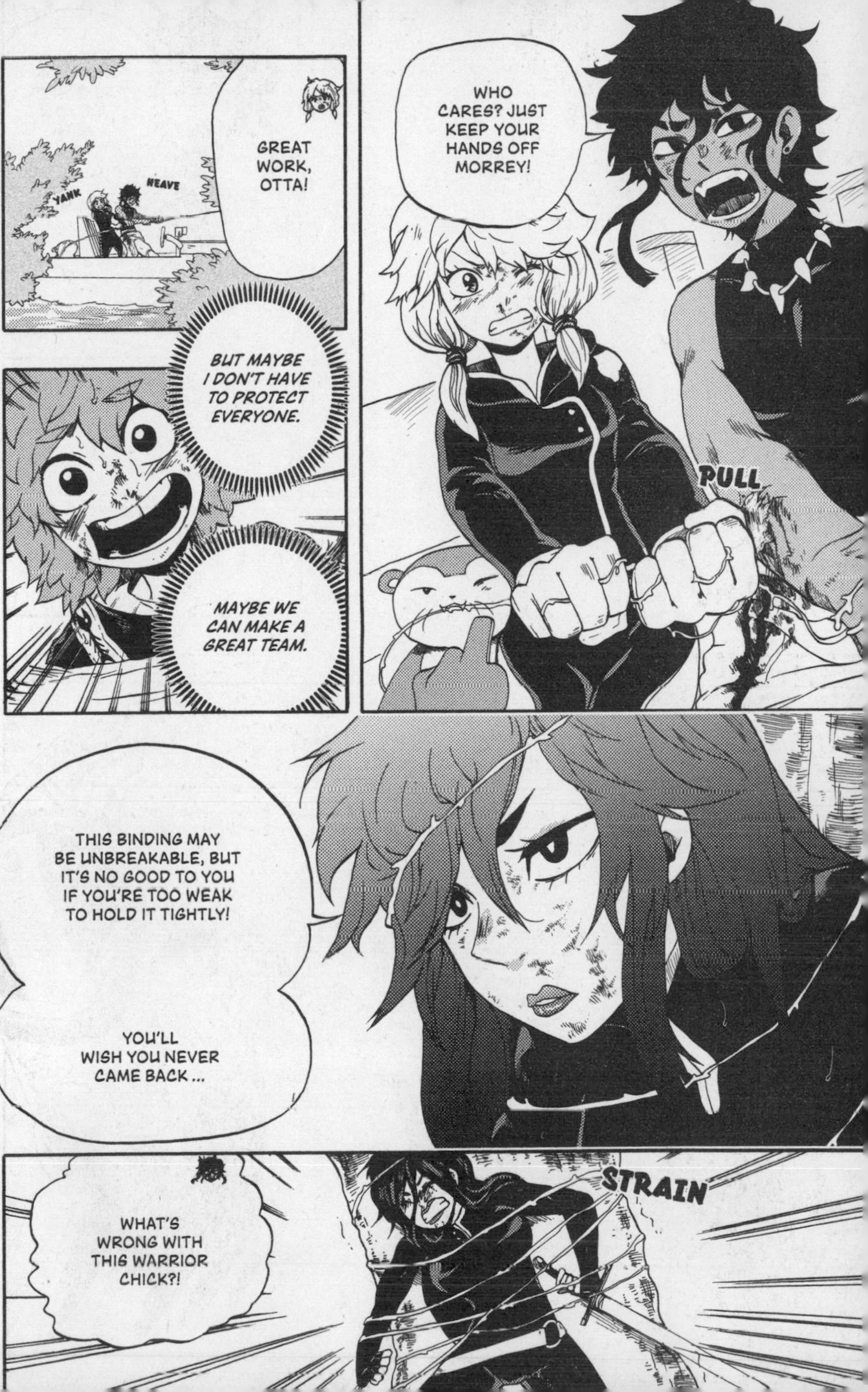
WHO CARES? JUST KEEP YOUR HANDS OFF MORREY!
PULL
GREAT WORK, OTTA!
HEAVE
YANK
BUT MAYBE I DON'T HAVE TO PROTECT EVERYONE.
MAYBE WE CAN MAKE A GREAT TEAM.
THIS BINDING MAY BE UNBREAKABLE, BUT IT'S NO GOOD TO YOU IF YOU'RE TOO WEAK TO HOLD IT TIGHTLY!
YOU'LL WISH YOU NEVER CAME BACK ...
STRAIN
WHAT'S WRONG WITH THIS WARRIOR CHICK?!

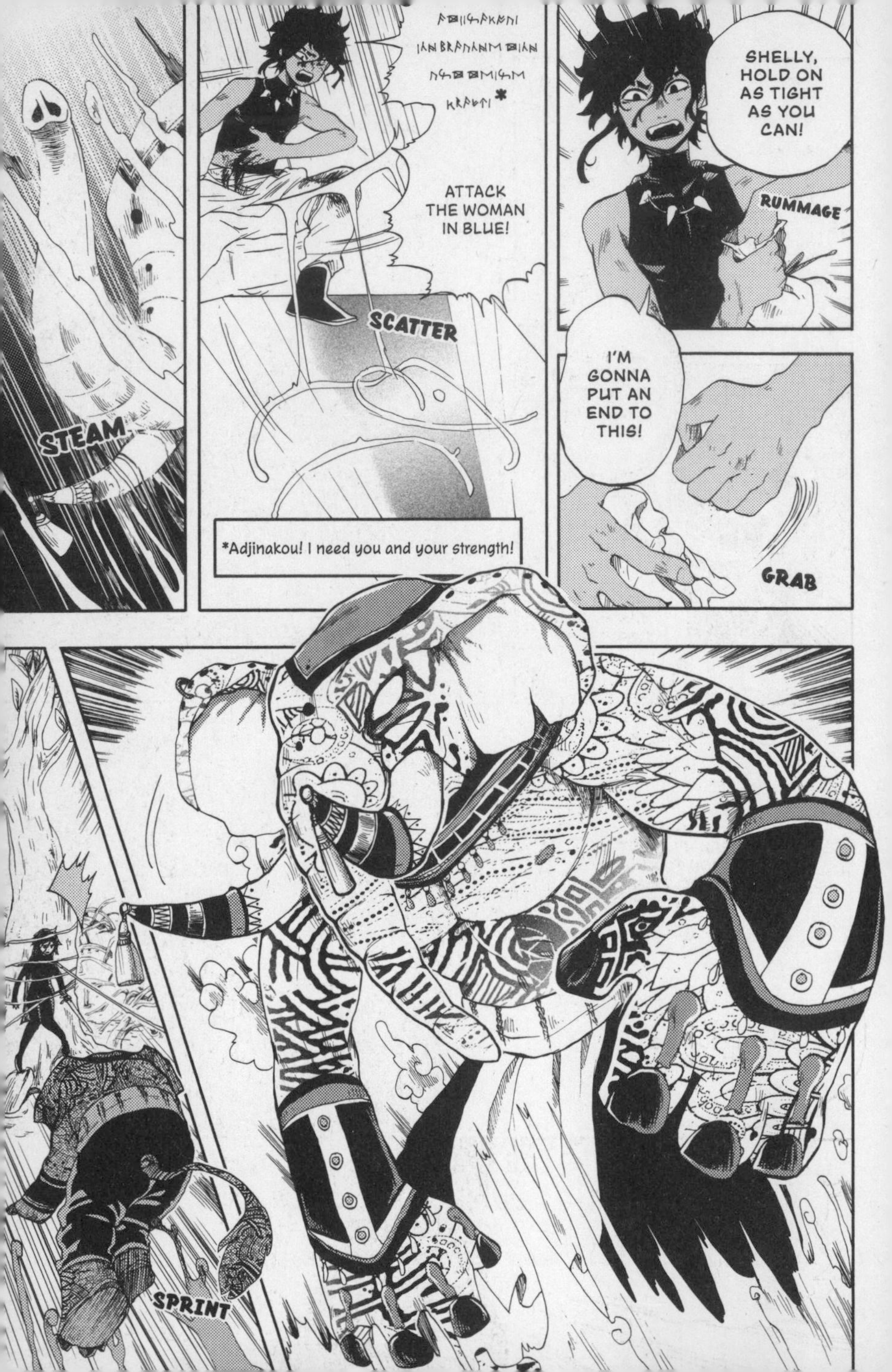
SHELLY, HOLD ON AS TIGHT AS YOU CAN!
RUMMAGE
I'M GONNA PUT AN END TO THIS!
GRAB
ATTACK THE WOMAN IN BLUE!
SCATTER
*Adjinakou! I need you and your strength!
STEAM
SPRINT

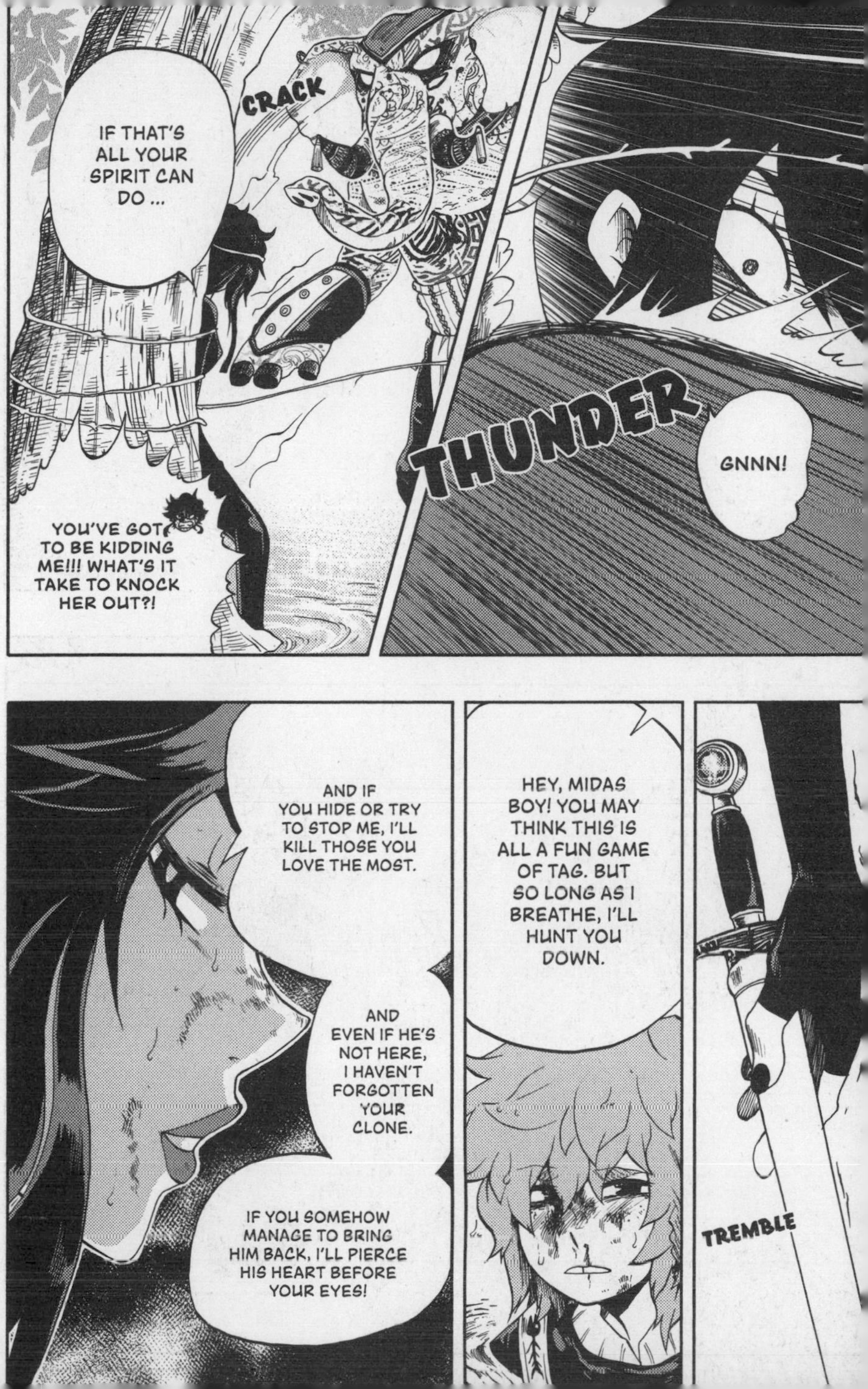
THUNDER
GNNN!
CRACK
IF THAT'S ALL YOUR SPIRIT CAN DO ...
YOU'VE GOT TO BE KIDDING ME!!! WHAT'S IT TAKE TO KNOCK HER OUT?!
TREMBLE
HEY, MIDAS BOY! YOU MAY THINK THIS IS ALL A FUN GAME OF TAG. BUT SO LONG AS I BREATHE, I'LL HUNT YOU DOWN.
AND IF YOU HIDE OR TRY TO STOP ME, I'LL KILL THOSE YOU LOVE THE MOST.
AND EVEN IF HE'S NOT HERE, I HAVEN'T FORGOTTEN YOUR CLONE.
IF YOU SOMEHOW MANAGE TO BRING HIM BACK, I'LL PIERCE HIS HEART BEFORE YOUR EYES!

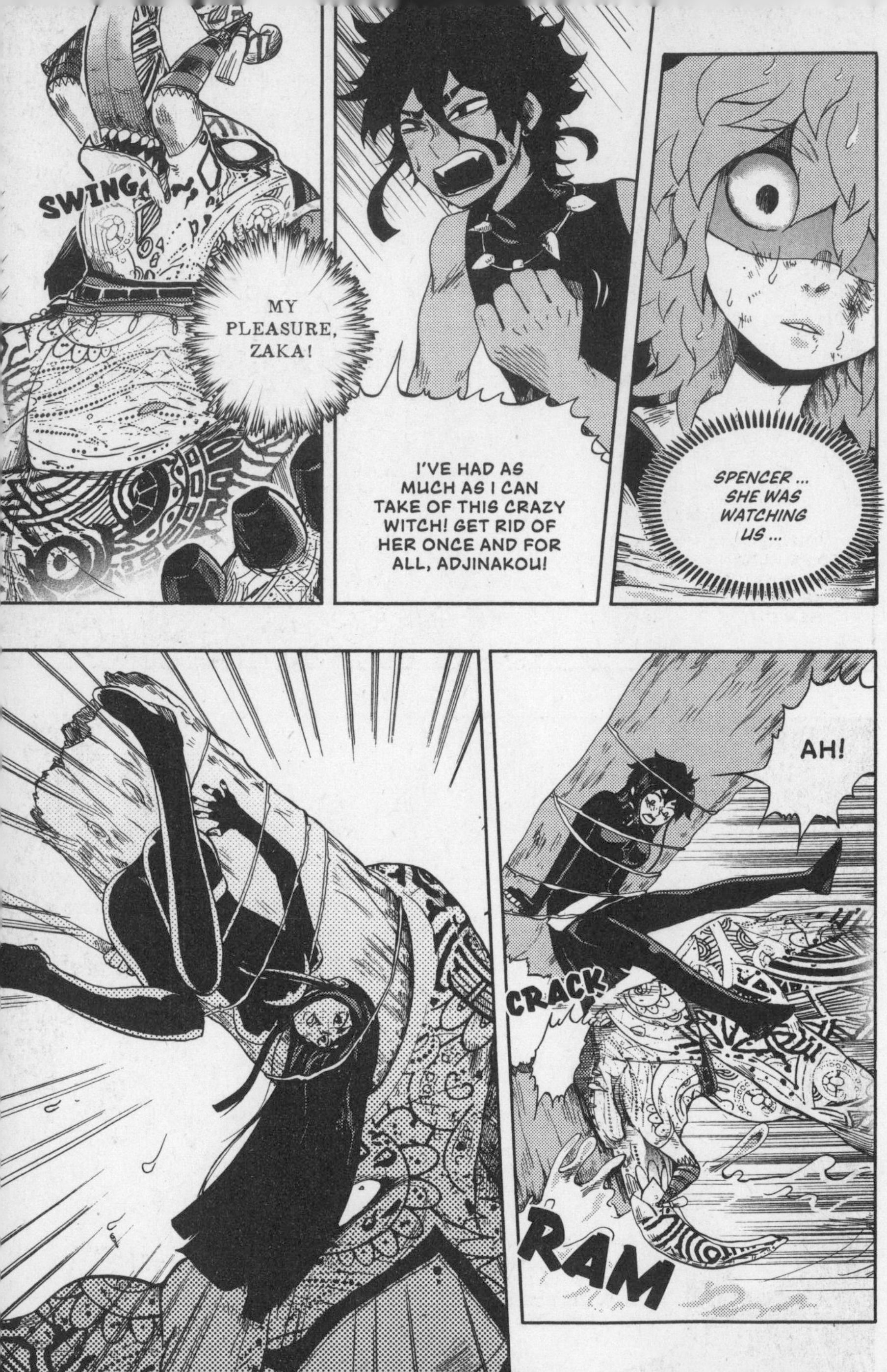
SPENCER ... SHE WAS WATCHING US ...
I'VE HAD AS MUCH AS I CAN TAKE OF THIS CRAZY WITCH! GET RID OF HER ONCE AND FOR ALL, ADJINAKOU!
SWING
MY PLEASURE, ZAKA!
AH!
CRACK
RAM

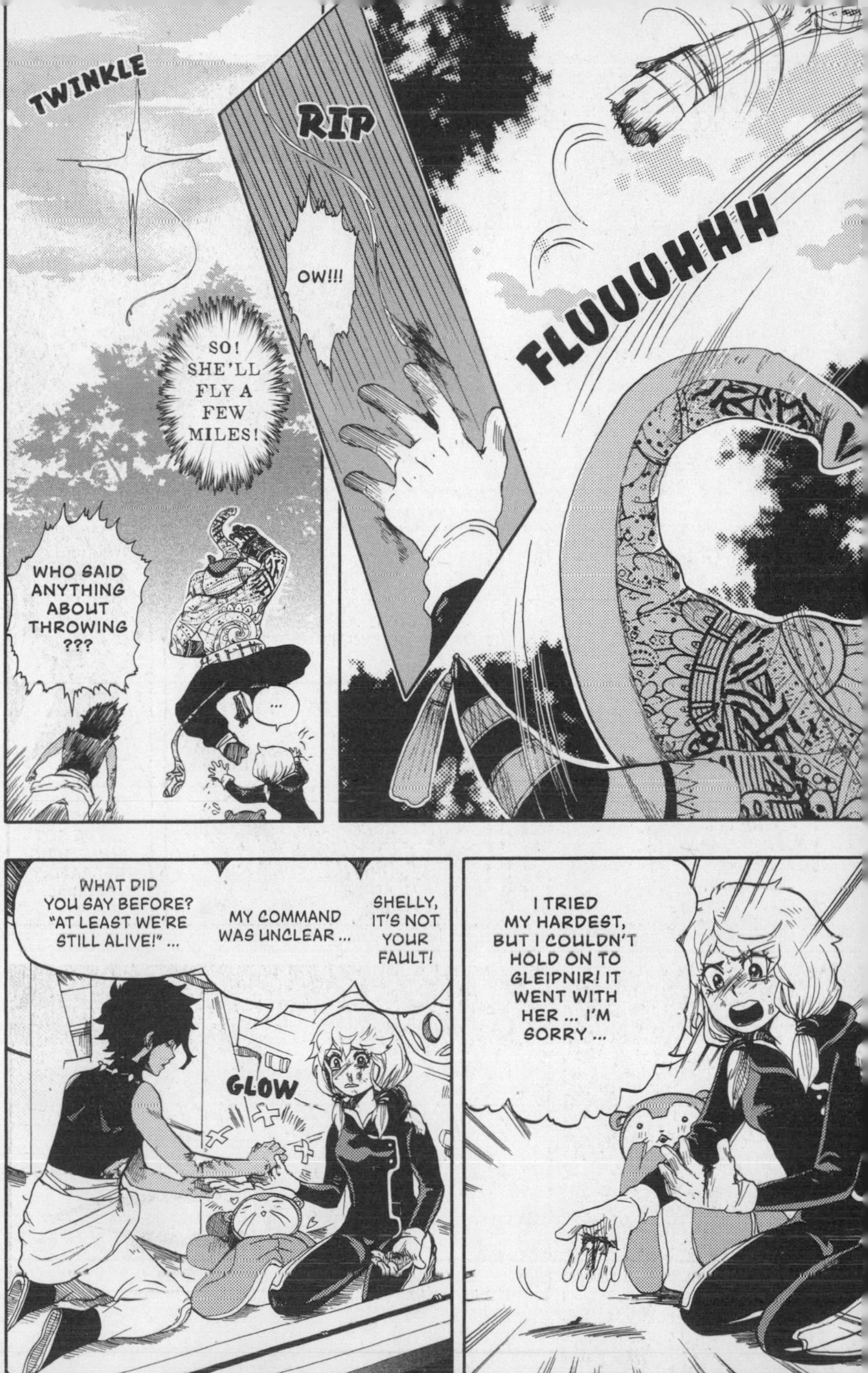
FLUUUHHH
RIP
OW!!!
TWINKLE
SO! SHE'LL FLY A FEW MILES!
WHO SAID ANYTHING ABOUT THROWING???
...
I TRIED MY HARDEST, BUT I COULDN'T HOLD ON TO GLEIPNIR! IT WENT WITH HER ... I'M SORRY ...
SHELLY, IT'S NOT YOUR FAULT!
MY COMMAND WAS UNCLEAR ...
WHAT DID YOU SAY BEFORE? "AT LEAST WE'RE STILL ALIVE!" ...
GLOW

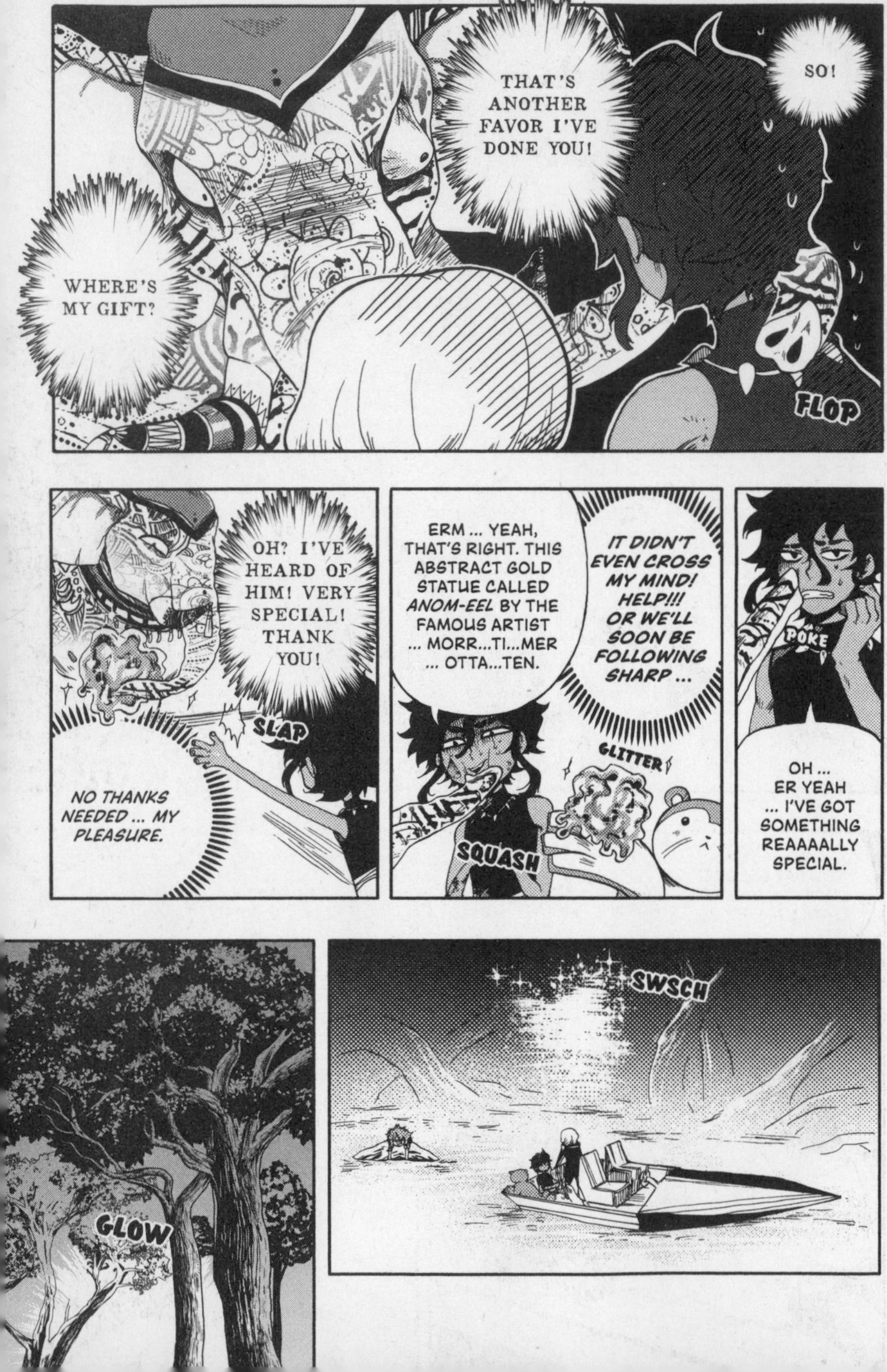
SO!
THAT'S ANOTHER FAVOR I'VE DONE YOU!
FLOP
WHERE'S MY GIFT?
POKE
OH ... ER YEAH ... I'VE GOT SOMETHING REAAAALLY SPECIAL.
IT DIDN'T EVEN CROSS MY MIND! HELP!!! OR WE'LL SOON BE FOLLOWING SHARP ...
ERM ... YEAH, THAT'S RIGHT. THIS ABSTRACT GOLD STATUE CALLED ANOM-EEL BY THE FAMOUS ARTIST ... MORR...TI...MER ... OTTA...TEN.
GLITTER
SQUASH
OH? I'VE HEARD OF HIM! VERY SPECIAL! THANK YOU!
SLAP
NO THANKS NEEDED ... MY PLEASURE.
SWSCH
GLOW

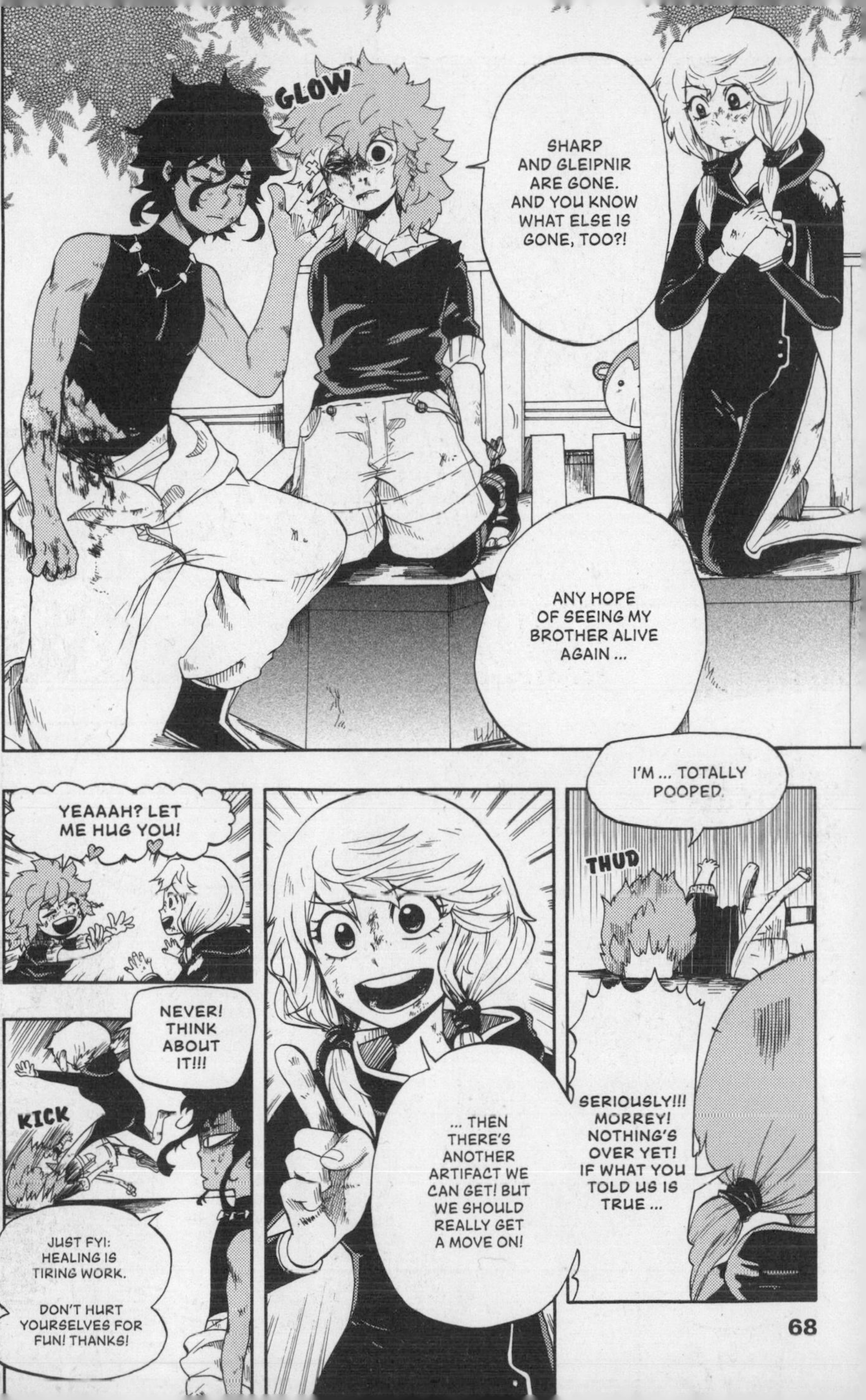
SHARP AND GLEIPNIR ARE GONE. AND YOU KNOW WHAT ELSE IS GONE, TOO?!
GLOW
ANY HOPE OF SEEING MY BROTHER ALIVE AGAIN ...
I'M ... TOTALLY POOPED.
THUD
SERIOUSLY!!! MORREY! NOTHING'S OVER YET! IF WHAT YOU TOLD US IS TRUE ...
... THEN THERE'S ANOTHER ARTIFACT WE CAN GET! BUT WE SHOULD REALLY GET A MOVE ON!
YEAAAH? LET ME HUG YOU!
NEVER! THINK ABOUT IT!!!
KICK
JUST FYI: HEALING IS TIRING WORK.
DON'T HURT YOURSELVES FOR FUN! THANKS!

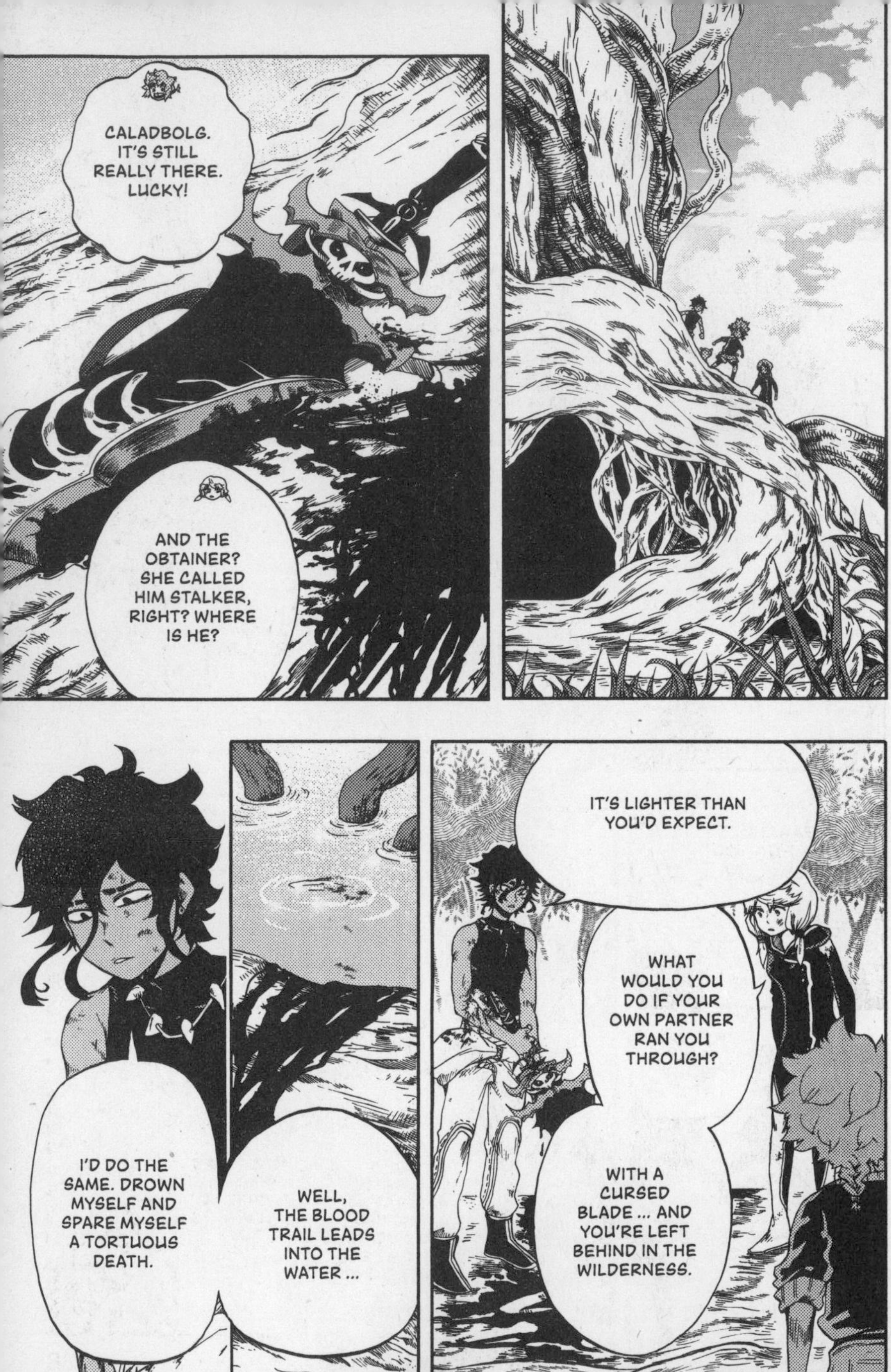
CALADBOLG. IT'S STILL REALLY THERE. LUCKY!
AND THE OBTAINER? SHE CALLED HIM STALKER, RIGHT? WHERE IS HE?
IT'S LIGHTER THAN YOU'D EXPECT.
WHAT WOULD YOU DO IF YOUR OWN PARTNER RAN YOU THROUGH?
WITH A CURSED BLADE ... AND YOU'RE LEFT BEHIND IN THE WILDERNESS.
WELL, THE BLOOD TRAIL LEADS INTO THE WATER ...
I'D DO THE SAME. DROWN MYSELF AND SPARE MYSELF A TORTUOUS DEATH.

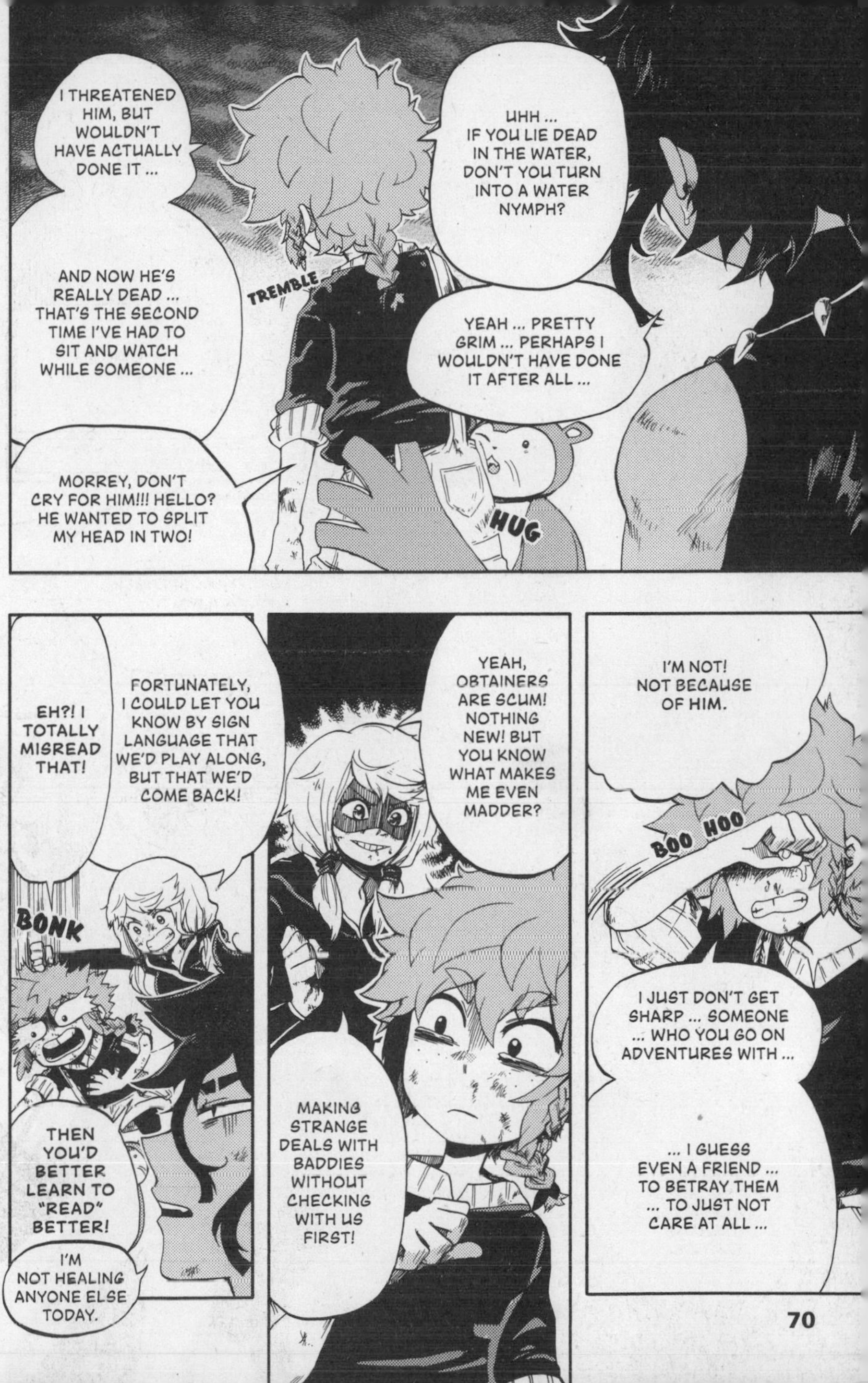
UHH ... IF YOU LIE DEAD IN THE WATER, DON'T YOU TURN INTO A WATER NYMPH?
I THREATENED HIM, BUT WOULDN'T HAVE ACTUALLY DONE IT ...
TREMBLE
YEAH ... PRETTY GRIM ... PERHAPS I WOULDN'T HAVE DONE IT AFTER ALL ...
AND NOW HE'S REALLY DEAD ... THAT'S THE SECOND TIME I'VE HAD TO SIT AND WATCH WHILE SOMEONE ...
HUG
MORREY, DON'T CRY FOR HIM!!! HELLO? HE WANTED TO SPLIT MY HEAD IN TWO!
I'M NOT! NOT BECAUSE OF HIM.
BOO HOO
I JUST DON'T GET SHARP ... SOMEONE ... WHO YOU GO ON ADVENTURES WITH ...
... I GUESS EVEN A FRIEND ... TO BETRAY THEM ... TO JUST NOT CARE AT ALL ...
YEAH, OBTAINERS ARE SCUM! NOTHING NEW! BUT YOU KNOW WHAT MAKES ME EVEN MADDER?
MAKING STRANGE DEALS WITH BADDIES WITHOUT CHECKING WITH US FIRST!
FORTUNATELY, I COULD LET YOU KNOW BY SIGN LANGUAGE THAT WE'D PLAY ALONG, BUT THAT WE'D COME BACK!
EH?! I TOTALLY MISREAD THAT!
BONK
THEN YOU'D BETTER LEARN TO "READ" BETTER!
I'M NOT HEALING ANYONE ELSE TODAY.

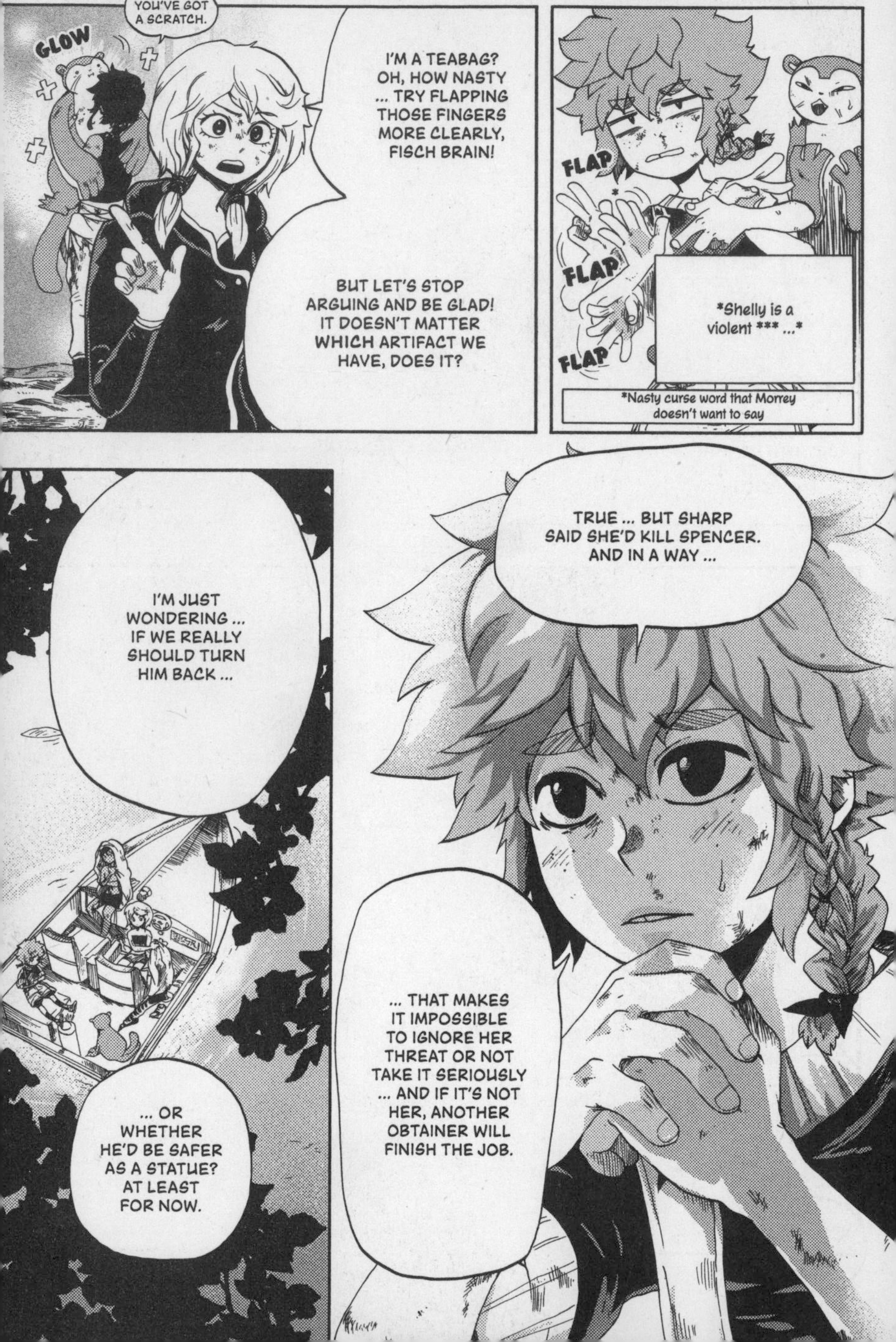
FLAP
FLAP
FLAP
*Shelly is a violent *** ...*
*Nasty curse word that Morrey doesn't want to say
I'M A TEABAG? OH, HOW NASTY ... TRY FLAPPING THOSE FINGERS MORE CLEARLY, FISCH BRAIN!
OH, YOU'VE GOT A SCRATCH.
GLOW
BUT LET'S STOP ARGUING AND BE GLAD! IT DOESN'T MATTER WHICH ARTIFACT WE HAVE, DOES IT?
TRUE ... BUT SHARP SAID SHE'D KILL SPENCER. AND IN A WAY ...
... THAT MAKES IT IMPOSSIBLE TO IGNORE HER THREAT OR NOT TAKE IT SERIOUSLY ... AND IF IT'S NOT HER, ANOTHER OBTAINER WILL FINISH THE JOB.
I'M JUST WONDERING ... IF WE REALLY SHOULD TURN HIM BACK ...
... OR WHETHER HE'D BE SAFER AS A STATUE? AT LEAST FOR NOW.

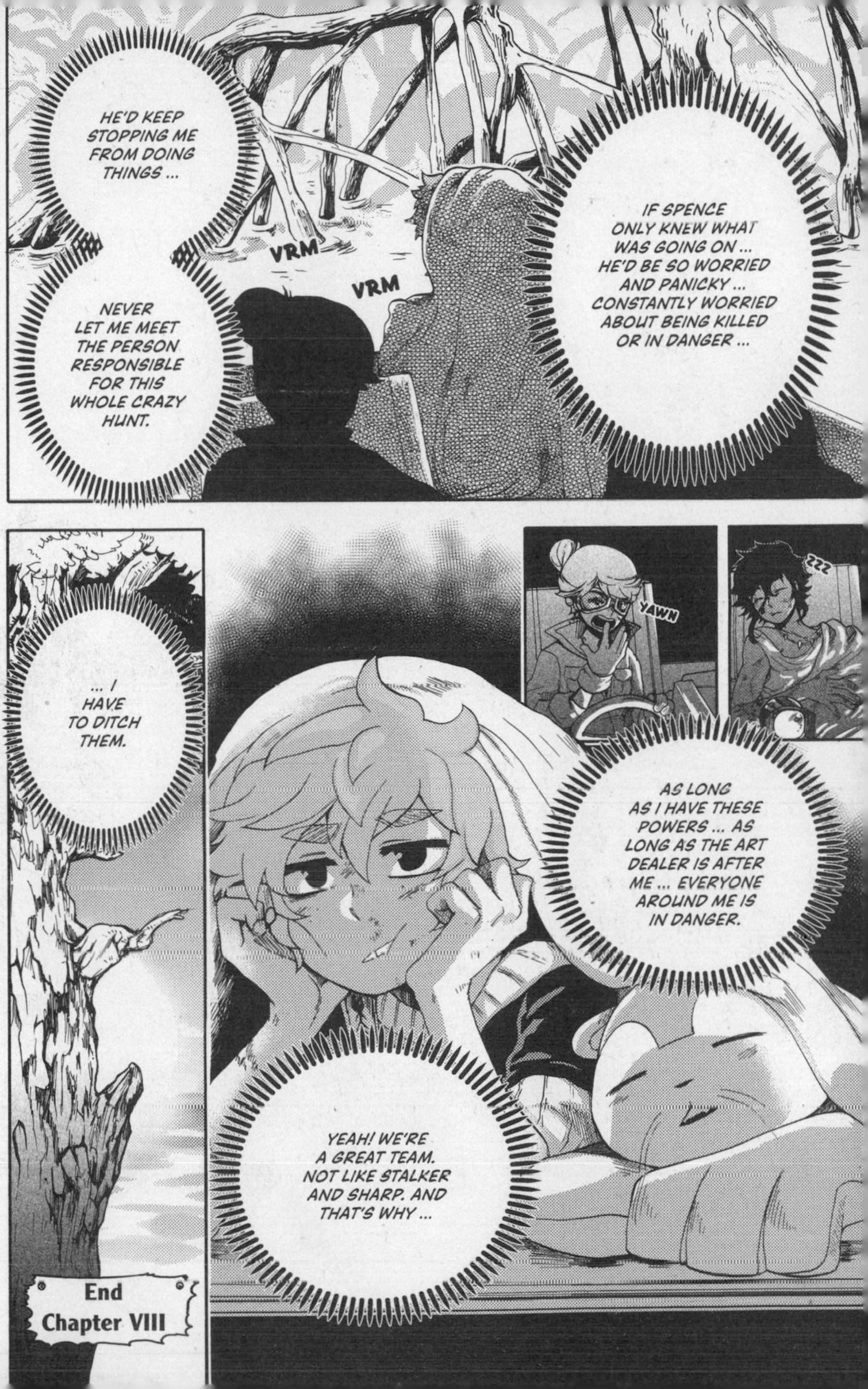
IF SPENCE ONLY KNEW WHAT WAS GOING ON ... HE'D BE SO WORRIED AND PANICKY ... CONSTANTLY WORRIED ABOUT BEING KILLED OR IN DANGER ...
HE'D KEEP STOPPING ME FROM DOING THINGS ...
VRM
VRM
NEVER LET ME MEET THE PERSON RESPONSIBLE FOR THIS WHOLE CRAZY HUNT.
ZZZ
YAWN
AS LONG AS I HAVE THESE POWERS ... AS LONG AS THE ART DEALER IS AFTER ME ... EVERYONE AROUND ME IS IN DANGER.
YEAH! WE'RE A GREAT TEAM. NOT LIKE STALKER AND SHARP. AND THAT'S WHY ...
... I HAVE TO DITCH THEM.
End Chapter VIII

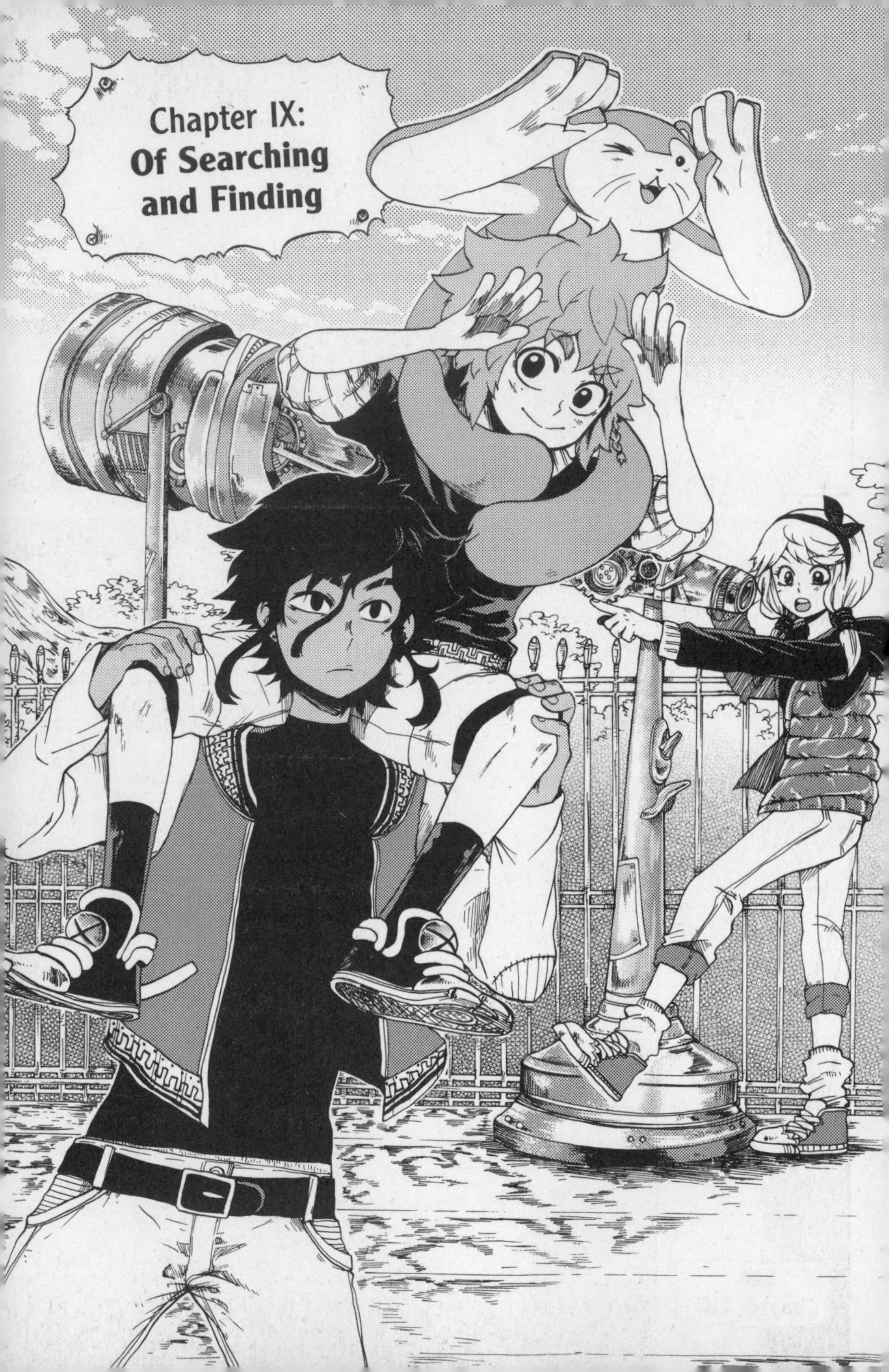
Chapter IX:
Of Searching and Finding

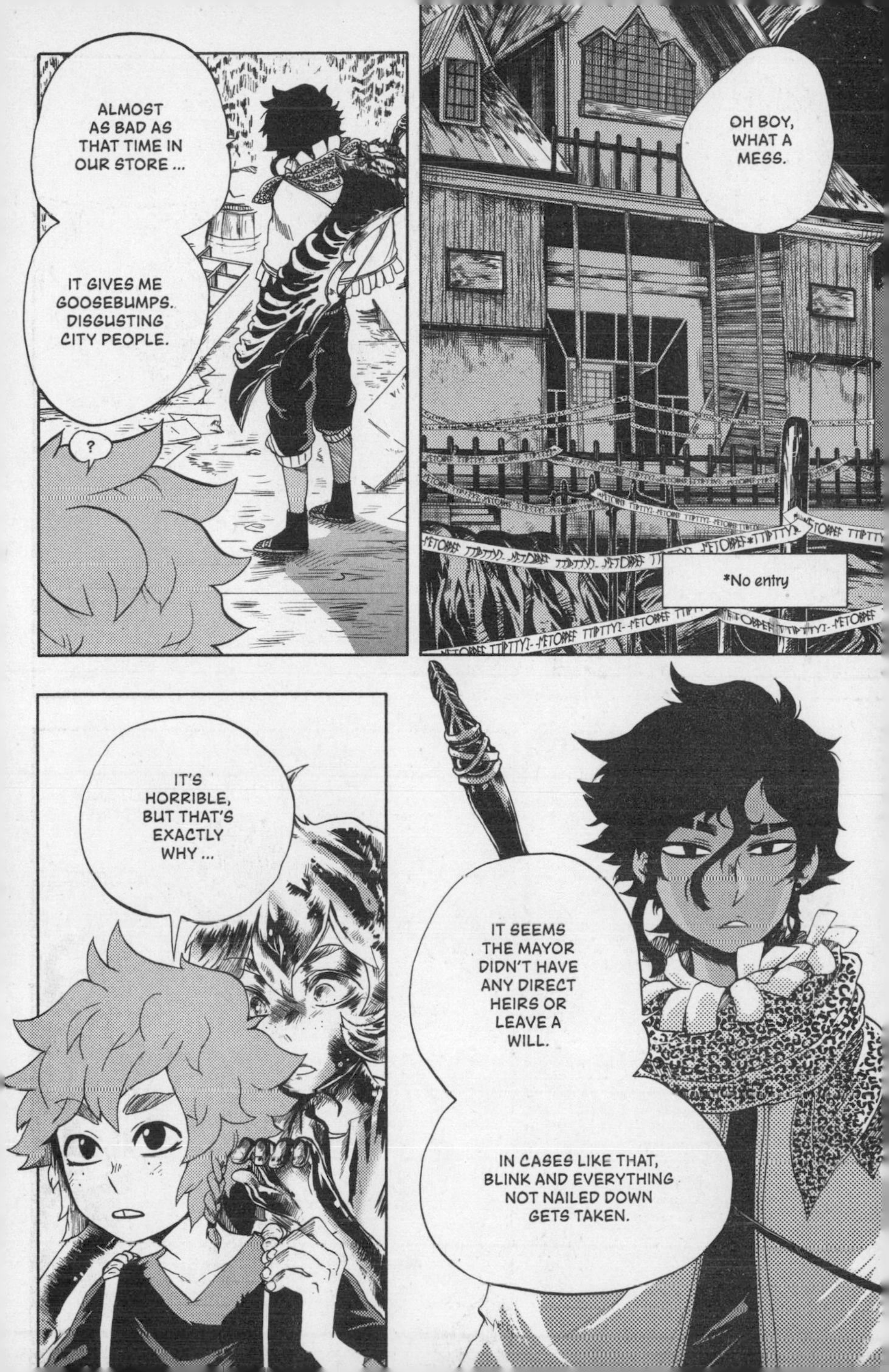
OH BOY, WHAT A MESS.
*No entry
ALMOST AS BAD AS THAT TIME IN OUR STORE ...
IT GIVES ME GOOSEBUMPS. DISGUSTING CITY PEOPLE.
?
IT SEEMS THE MAYOR DIDN'T HAVE ANY DIRECT HEIRS OR LEAVE A WILL.
IN CASES LIKE THAT, BLINK AND EVERYTHING NOT NAILED DOWN GETS TAKEN.
IT'S HORRIBLE, BUT THAT'S EXACTLY WHY ...

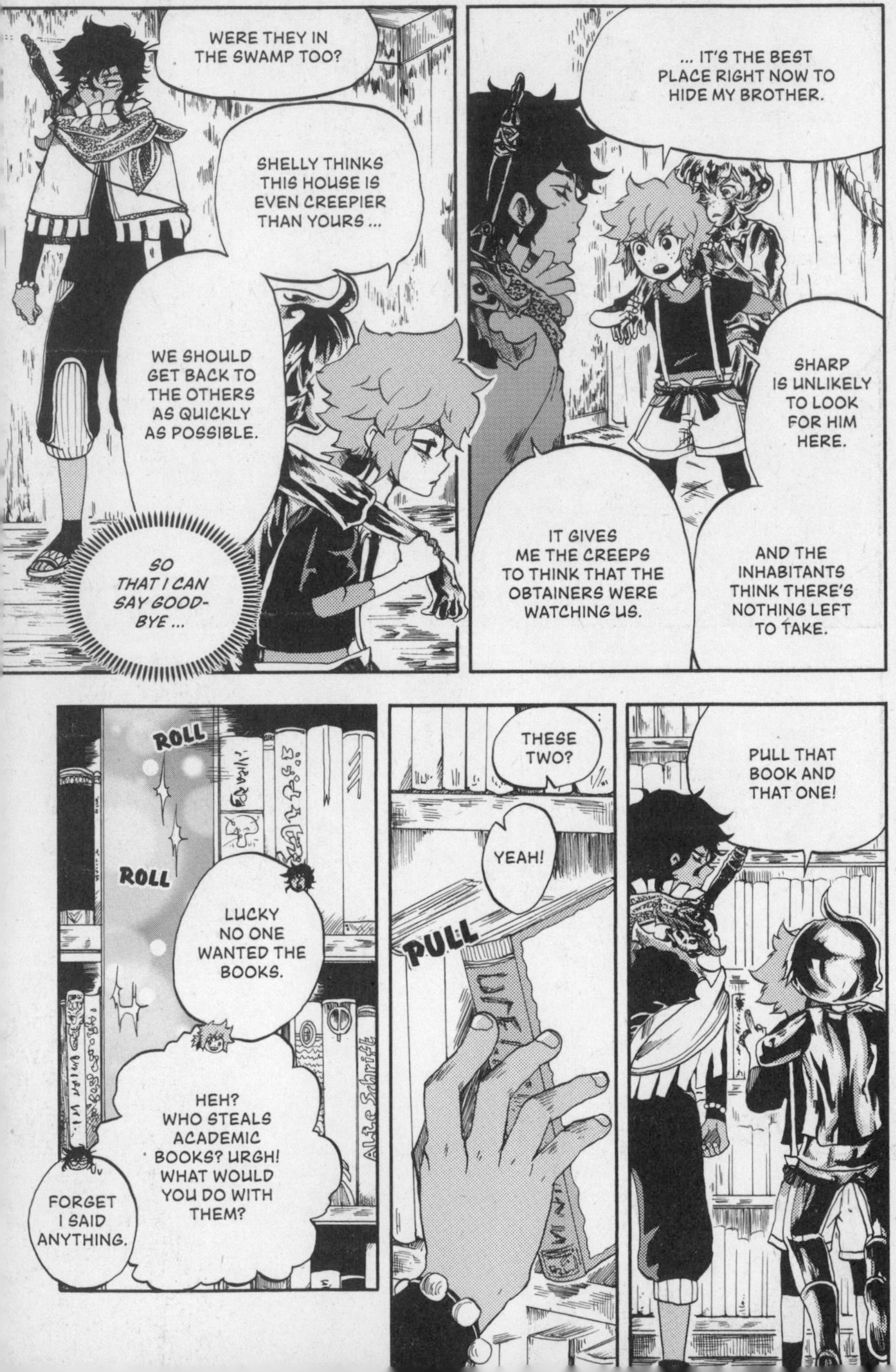
... IT'S THE BEST PLACE RIGHT NOW TO HIDE MY BROTHER.
SHARP IS UNLIKELY TO LOOK FOR HIM HERE.
AND THE INHABITANTS THINK THERE'S NOTHING LEFT TO TAKE.
IT GIVES ME THE CREEPS TO THINK THAT THE OBTAINERS WERE WATCHING US.
WERE THEY IN THE SWAMP TOO?
SHELLY THINKS THIS HOUSE IS EVEN CREEPIER THAN YOURS ...
WE SHOULD GET BACK TO THE OTHERS AS QUICKLY AS POSSIBLE.
SO THAT I CAN SAY GOOD-BYE ...
PULL THAT BOOK AND THAT ONE!
THESE TWO?
YEAH!
PULL
ROLL
ROLL
LUCKY NO ONE WANTED THE BOOKS.
HEH? WHO STEALS ACADEMIC BOOKS? URGH! WHAT WOULD YOU DO WITH THEM?
FORGET I SAID ANYTHING.
Alte Schrift

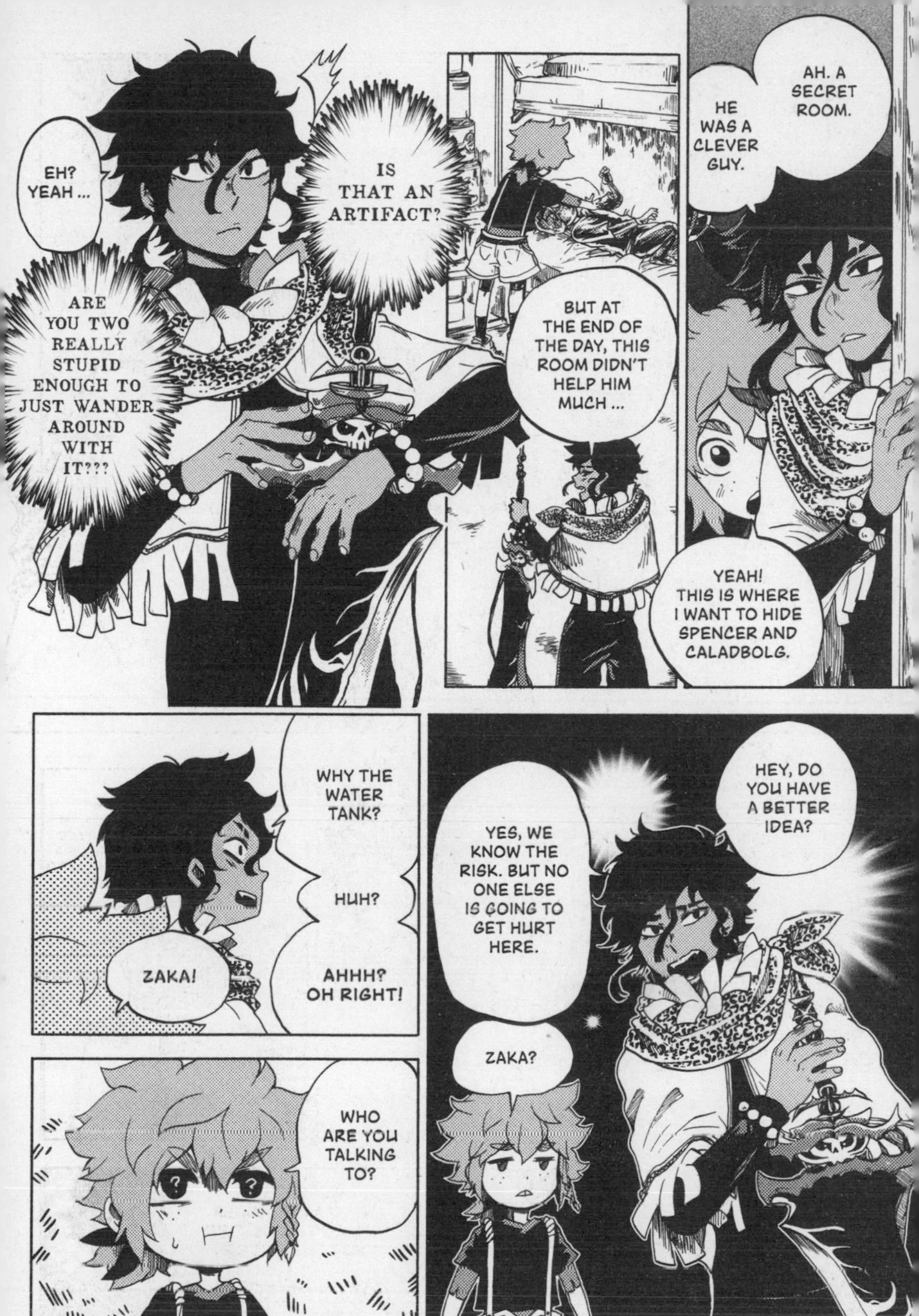
AH. A SECRET ROOM.
HE WAS A CLEVER GUY.
YEAH! THIS IS WHERE I WANT TO HIDE SPENCER AND CALADBOLG.
BUT AT THE END OF THE DAY, THIS ROOM DIDN'T HELP HIM MUCH ...
IS THAT AN ARTIFACT?
EH? YEAH ...
ARE YOU TWO REALLY STUPID ENOUGH TO JUST WANDER AROUND WITH IT???
HEY, DO YOU HAVE A BETTER IDEA?
YES, WE KNOW THE RISK. BUT NO ONE ELSE IS GOING TO GET HURT HERE.
ZAKA?
WHY THE WATER TANK?
HUH?
AHHH? OH RIGHT!
ZAKA!
WHO ARE YOU TALKING TO?

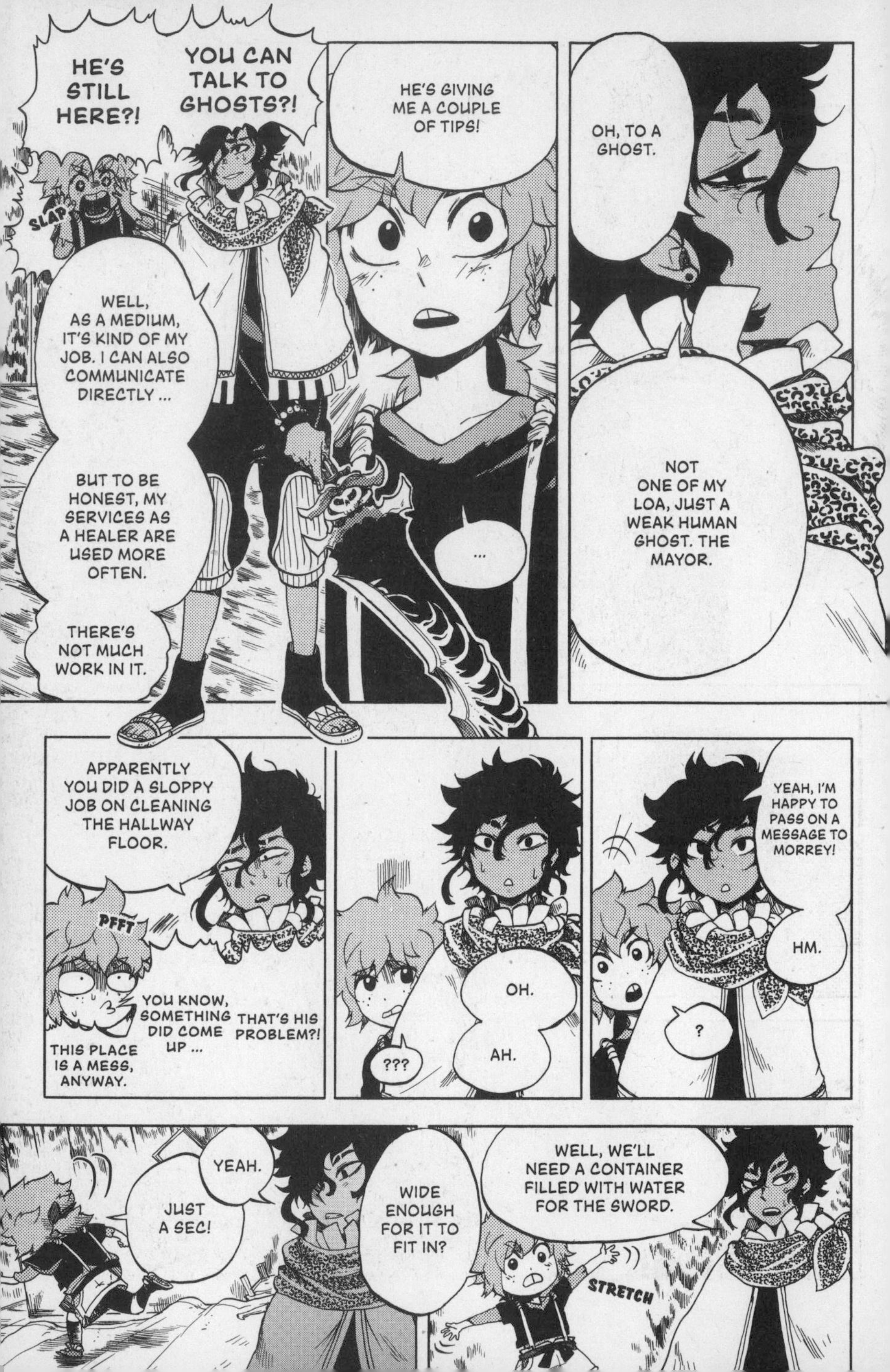
OH, TO A GHOST.
NOT ONE OF MY LOA, JUST A WEAK HUMAN GHOST. THE MAYOR.
HE'S GIVING ME A COUPLE OF TIPS!
...
YOU CAN TALK TO GHOSTS?!
HE'S STILL HERE?!
SLAP
WELL, AS A MEDIUM, IT'S KIND OF MY JOB. I CAN ALSO COMMUNICATE DIRECTLY ...
BUT TO BE HONEST, MY SERVICES AS A HEALER ARE USED MORE OFTEN.
THERE'S NOT MUCH WORK IN IT.
YEAH, I'M HAPPY TO PASS ON A MESSAGE TO MORREY!
HM.
?
OH.
AH.
???
APPARENTLY YOU DID A SLOPPY JOB ON CLEANING THE HALLWAY FLOOR.
PFFT
THAT'S HIS PROBLEM?!
YOU KNOW, SOMETHING DID COME UP ...
THIS PLACE IS A MESS, ANYWAY.
WELL, WE'LL NEED A CONTAINER FILLED WITH WATER FOR THE SWORD.
STRETCH
WIDE ENOUGH FOR IT TO FIT IN?
YEAH.
JUST A SEC!

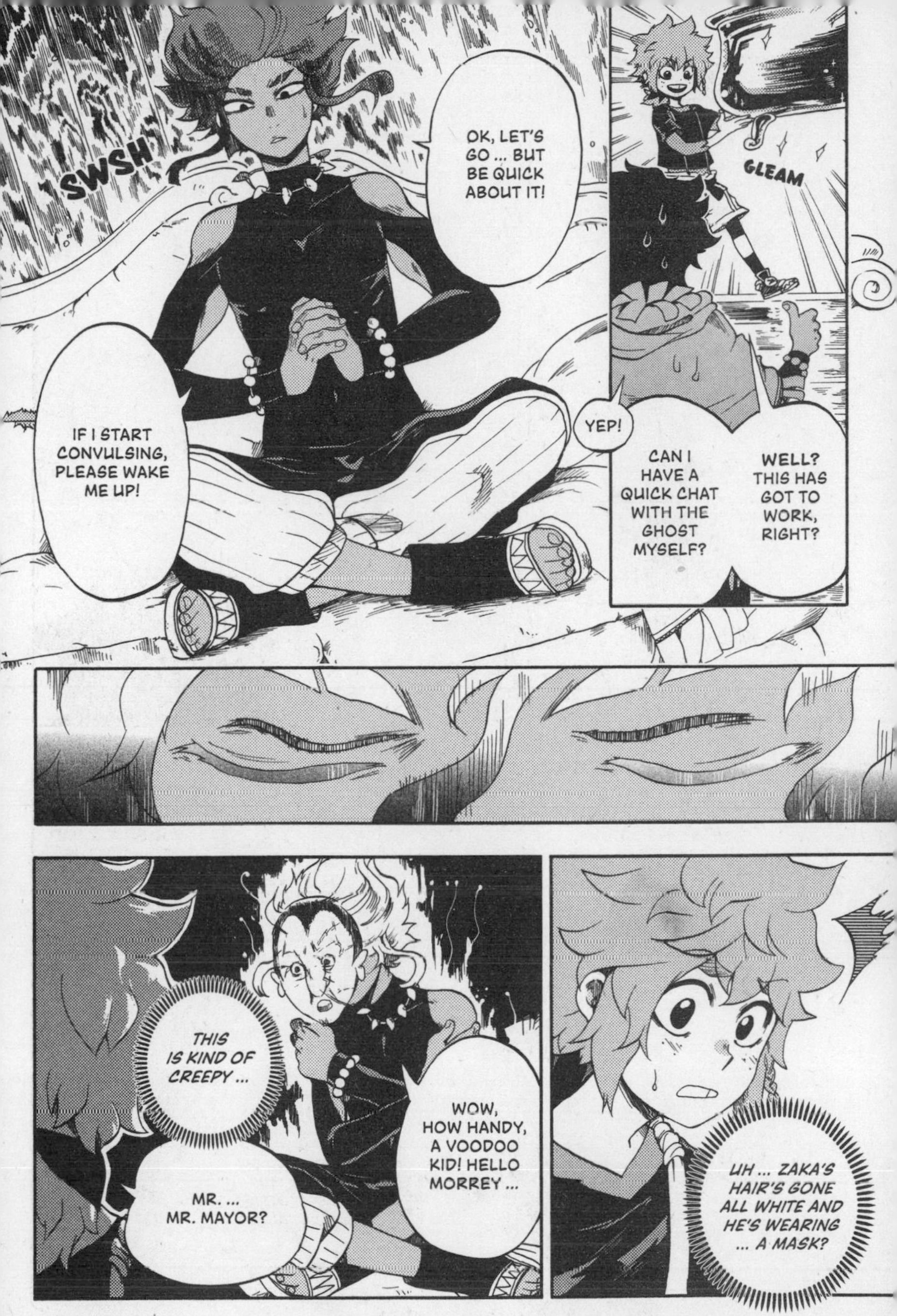
GLEAM
WELL? THIS HAS GOT TO WORK, RIGHT?
CAN I HAVE A QUICK CHAT WITH THE GHOST MYSELF?
YEP!
SWSH
OK, LET'S GO ... BUT BE QUICK ABOUT IT!
IF I START CONVULSING, PLEASE WAKE ME UP!
UH ... ZAKA'S HAIR'S GONE ALL WHITE AND HE'S WEARING ... A MASK?
WOW, HOW HANDY, A VOODOO KID! HELLO MORREY ...
THIS IS KIND OF CREEPY ...
MR. ... MR. MAYOR?

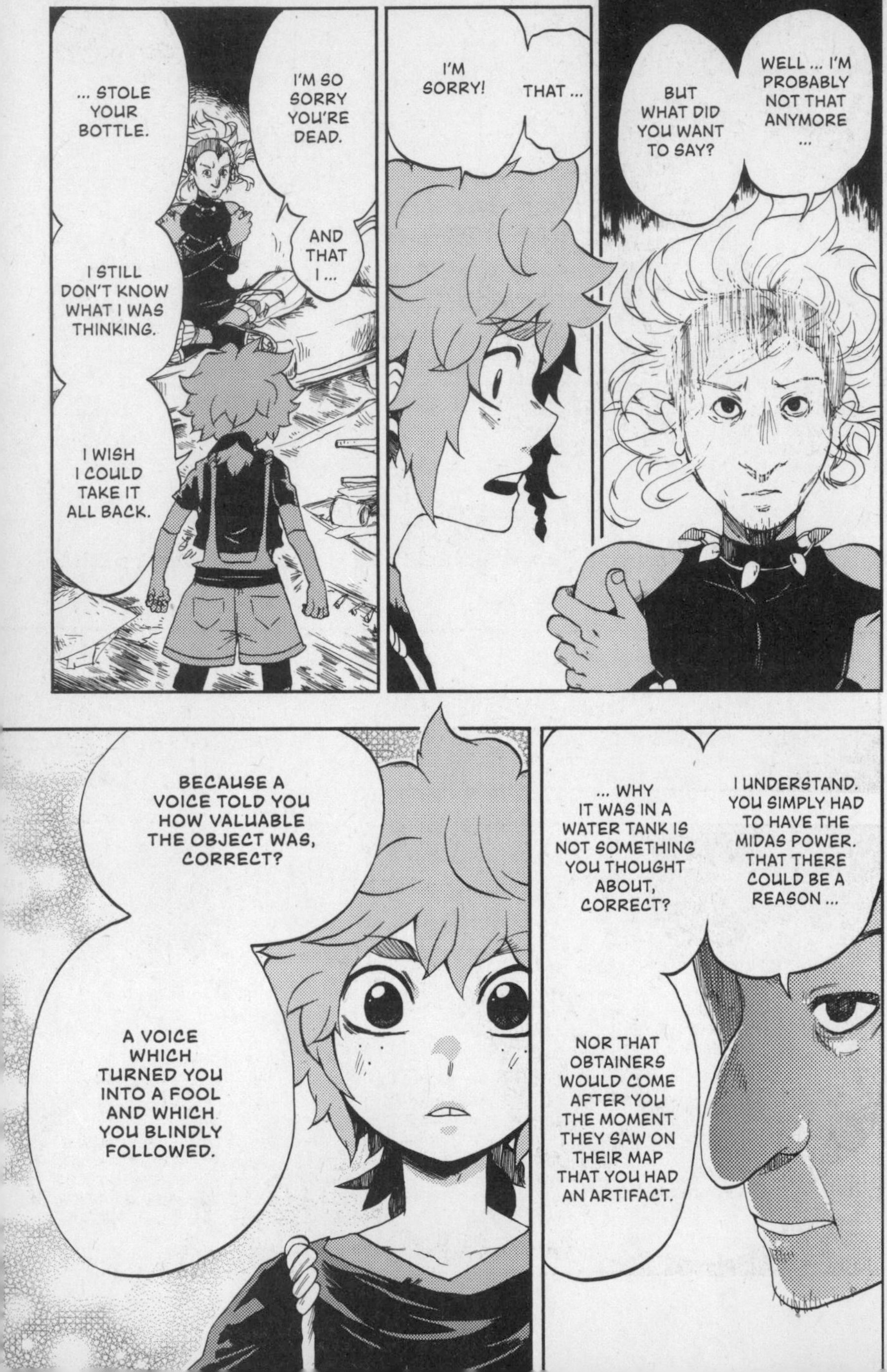
WELL ... I'M PROBABLY NOT THAT ANYMORE ...
BUT WHAT DID YOU WANT TO SAY?
THAT ...
I'M SORRY!
I'M SO SORRY YOU'RE DEAD.
AND THAT I ...
... STOLE YOUR BOTTLE.
I STILL DON'T KNOW WHAT I WAS THINKING.
I WISH I COULD TAKE IT ALL BACK.
I UNDERSTAND. YOU SIMPLY HAD TO HAVE THE MIDAS POWER. THAT THERE COULD BE A REASON ...
... WHY IT WAS IN A WATER TANK IS NOT SOMETHING YOU THOUGHT ABOUT, CORRECT?
NOR THAT OBTAINERS WOULD COME AFTER YOU THE MOMENT THEY SAW ON THEIR MAP THAT YOU HAD AN ARTIFACT.
BECAUSE A VOICE TOLD YOU HOW VALUABLE THE OBJECT WAS, CORRECT?
A VOICE WHICH TURNED YOU INTO A FOOL AND WHICH YOU BLINDLY FOLLOWED.

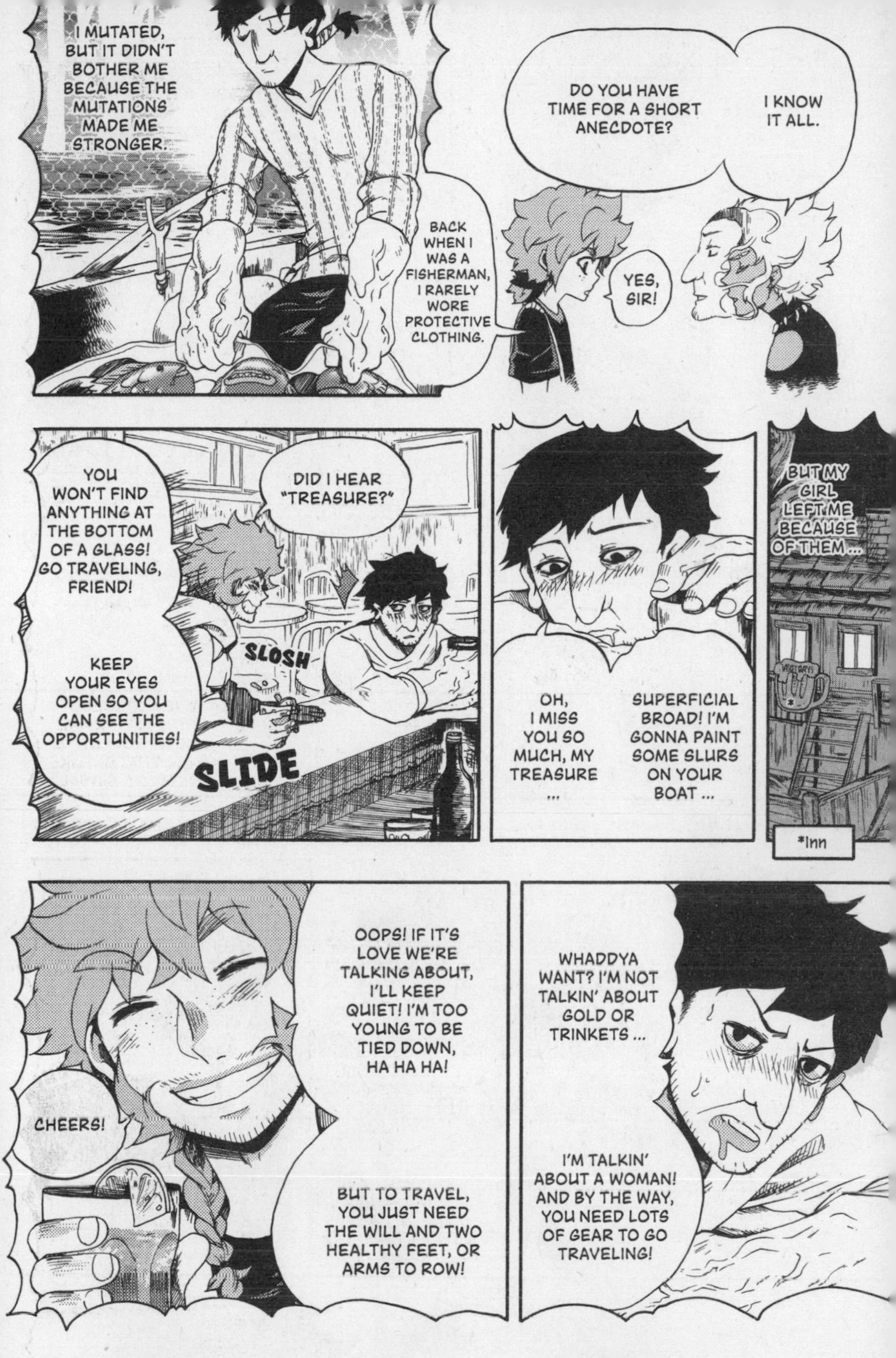
I KNOW IT ALL.
DO YOU HAVE TIME FOR A SHORT ANECDOTE?
YES, SIR!
BACK WHEN I WAS A FISHERMAN, I RARELY WORE PROTECTIVE CLOTHING.
I MUTATED, BUT IT DIDN'T BOTHER ME BECAUSE THE MUTATIONS MADE ME STRONGER.
BUT MY GIRL LEFT ME BECAUSE OF THEM ...
*Inn
SUPERFICIAL BROAD! I'M GONNA PAINT SOME SLURS ON YOUR BOAT ...
OH, I MISS YOU SO MUCH, MY TREASURE ...
DID I HEAR "TREASURE?"
YOU WON'T FIND ANYTHING AT THE BOTTOM OF A GLASS! GO TRAVELING, FRIEND!
SLOSH
KEEP YOUR EYES OPEN SO YOU CAN SEE THE OPPORTUNITIES!
SLIDE
WHADDYA WANT? I'M NOT TALKIN' ABOUT GOLD OR TRINKETS ...
I'M TALKIN' ABOUT A WOMAN! AND BY THE WAY, YOU NEED LOTS OF GEAR TO GO TRAVELING!
OOPS! IF IT'S LOVE WE'RE TALKING ABOUT, I'LL KEEP QUIET! I'M TOO YOUNG TO BE TIED DOWN, HA HA HA!
CHEERS!
BUT TO TRAVEL, YOU JUST NEED THE WILL AND TWO HEALTHY FEET, OR ARMS TO ROW!

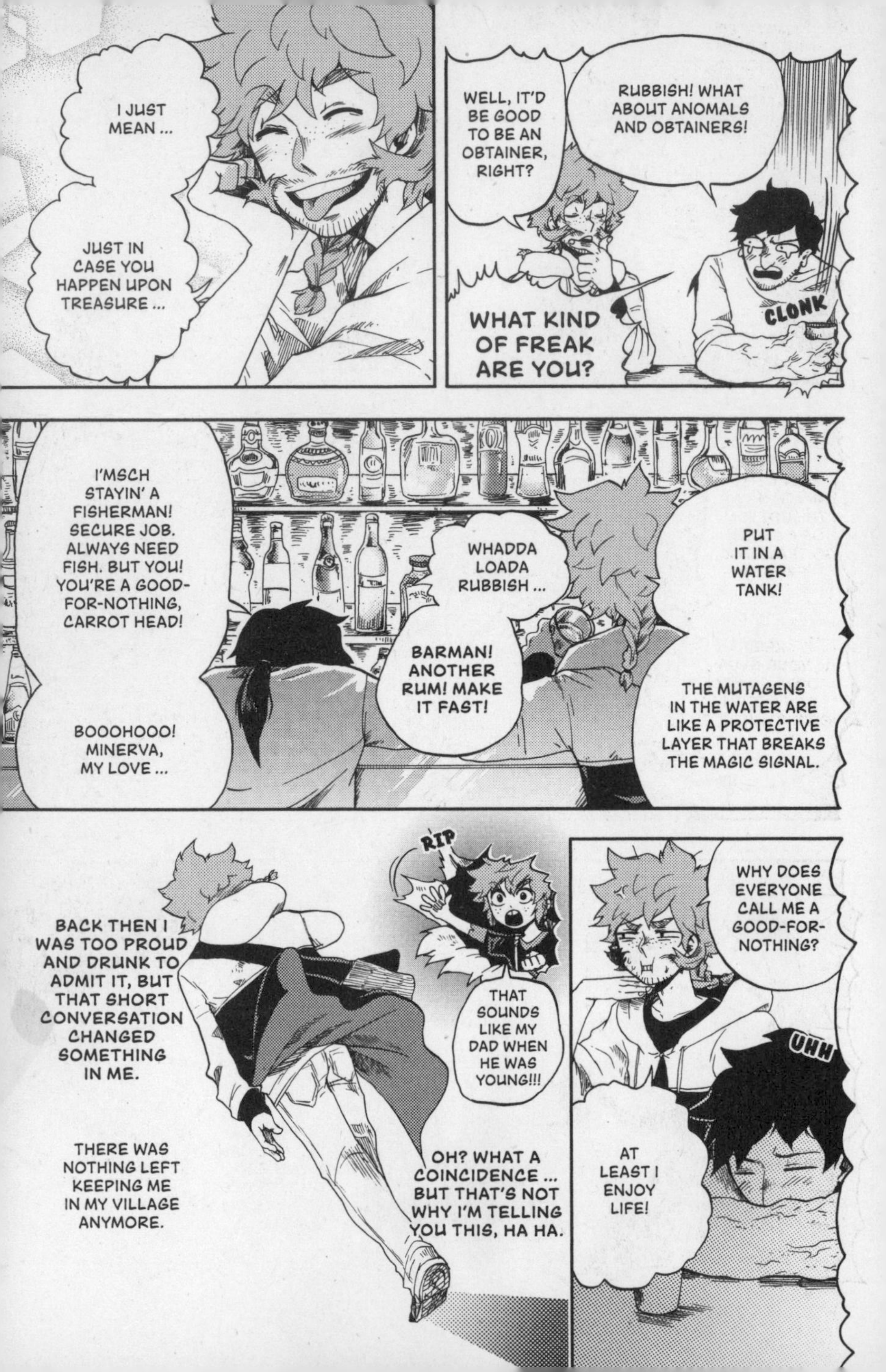
RUBBISH! WHAT ABOUT ANOMALS AND OBTAINERS!
WELL, IT'D BE GOOD TO BE AN OBTAINER, RIGHT?
CLONK
WHAT KIND OF FREAK ARE YOU?
I JUST MEAN ...
JUST IN CASE YOU HAPPEN UPON TREASURE ...
PUT IT IN A WATER TANK!
THE MUTAGENS IN THE WATER ARE LIKE A PROTECTIVE LAYER THAT BREAKS THE MAGIC SIGNAL.
WHADDA LOADA RUBBISH ...
BARMAN! ANOTHER RUM! MAKE IT FAST!
I'MSCH STAYIN' A FISHERMAN! SECURE JOB. ALWAYS NEED FISH. BUT YOU! YOU'RE A GOOD-FOR-NOTHING, CARROT HEAD!
BOOOHOOO! MINERVA, MY LOVE ...
WHY DOES EVERYONE CALL ME A GOOD-FOR-NOTHING?
UHH
AT LEAST I ENJOY LIFE!
RIP
THAT SOUNDS LIKE MY DAD WHEN HE WAS YOUNG!!!
OH? WHAT A COINCIDENCE ... BUT THAT'S NOT WHY I'M TELLING YOU THIS, HA HA.
BACK THEN I WAS TOO PROUD AND DRUNK TO ADMIT IT, BUT THAT SHORT CONVERSATION CHANGED SOMETHING IN ME.
THERE WAS NOTHING LEFT KEEPING ME IN MY VILLAGE ANYMORE.

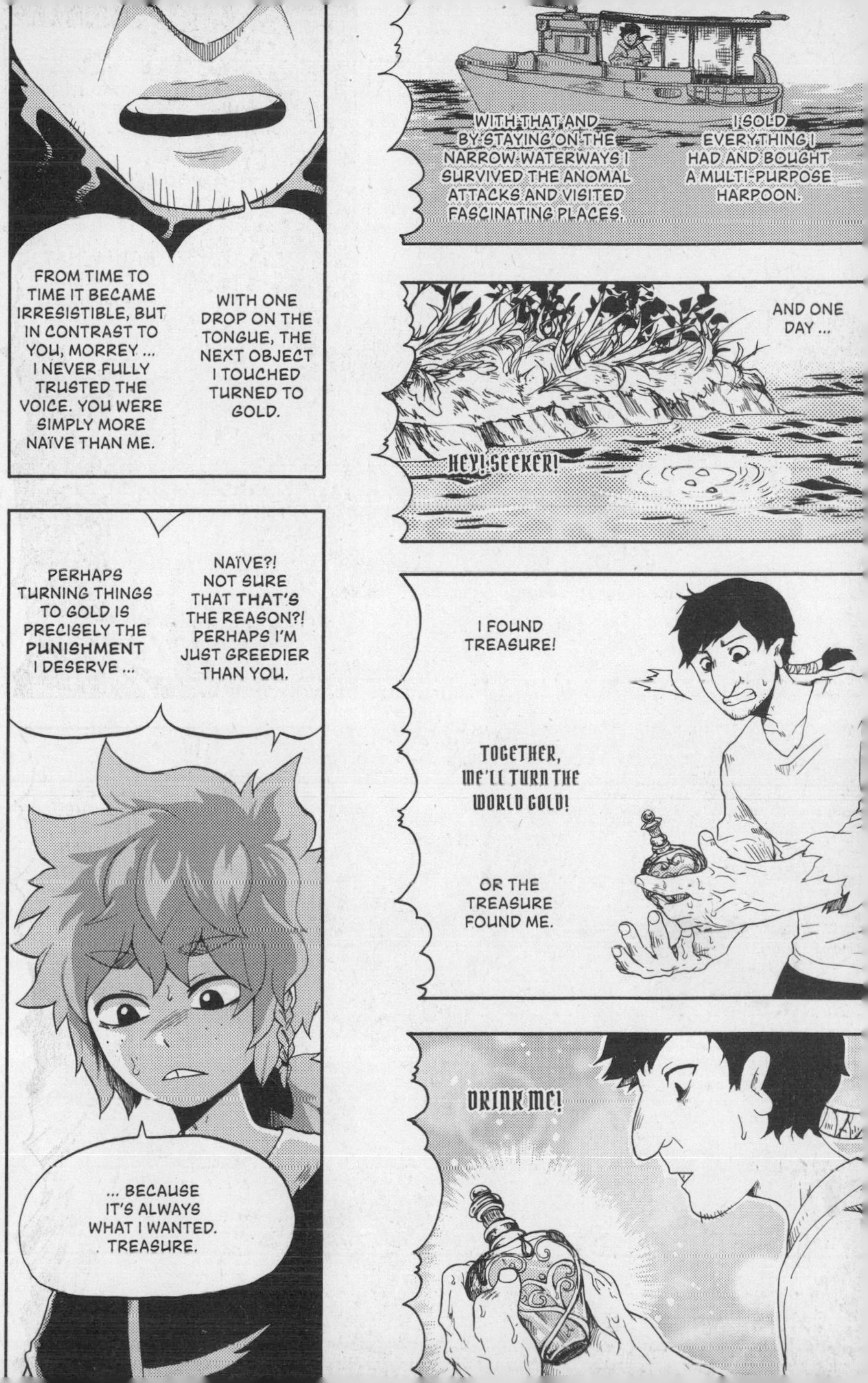
I SOLD EVERYTHING I HAD AND BOUGHT A MULTI-PURPOSE HARPOON.
WITH THAT AND BY STAYING ON THE NARROW WATERWAYS I SURVIVED THE ANOMAL ATTACKS AND VISITED FASCINATING PLACES.
AND ONE DAY ...
HEY! SEEKER!
I FOUND TREASURE!
TOGETHER, WE'LL TURN THE WORLD GOLD!
OR THE TREASURE FOUND ME.
DRINK ME!
WITH ONE DROP ON THE TONGUE, THE NEXT OBJECT I TOUCHED TURNED TO GOLD.
FROM TIME TO TIME IT BECAME IRRESISTIBLE, BUT IN CONTRAST TO YOU, MORREY ... I NEVER FULLY TRUSTED THE VOICE. YOU WERE SIMPLY MORE NAÏVE THAN ME.
NAÏVE?! NOT SURE THAT THAT'S THE REASON?! PERHAPS I'M JUST GREEDIER THAN YOU.
PERHAPS TURNING THINGS TO GOLD IS PRECISELY THE PUNISHMENT I DESERVE ...
... BECAUSE IT'S ALWAYS WHAT I WANTED. TREASURE.

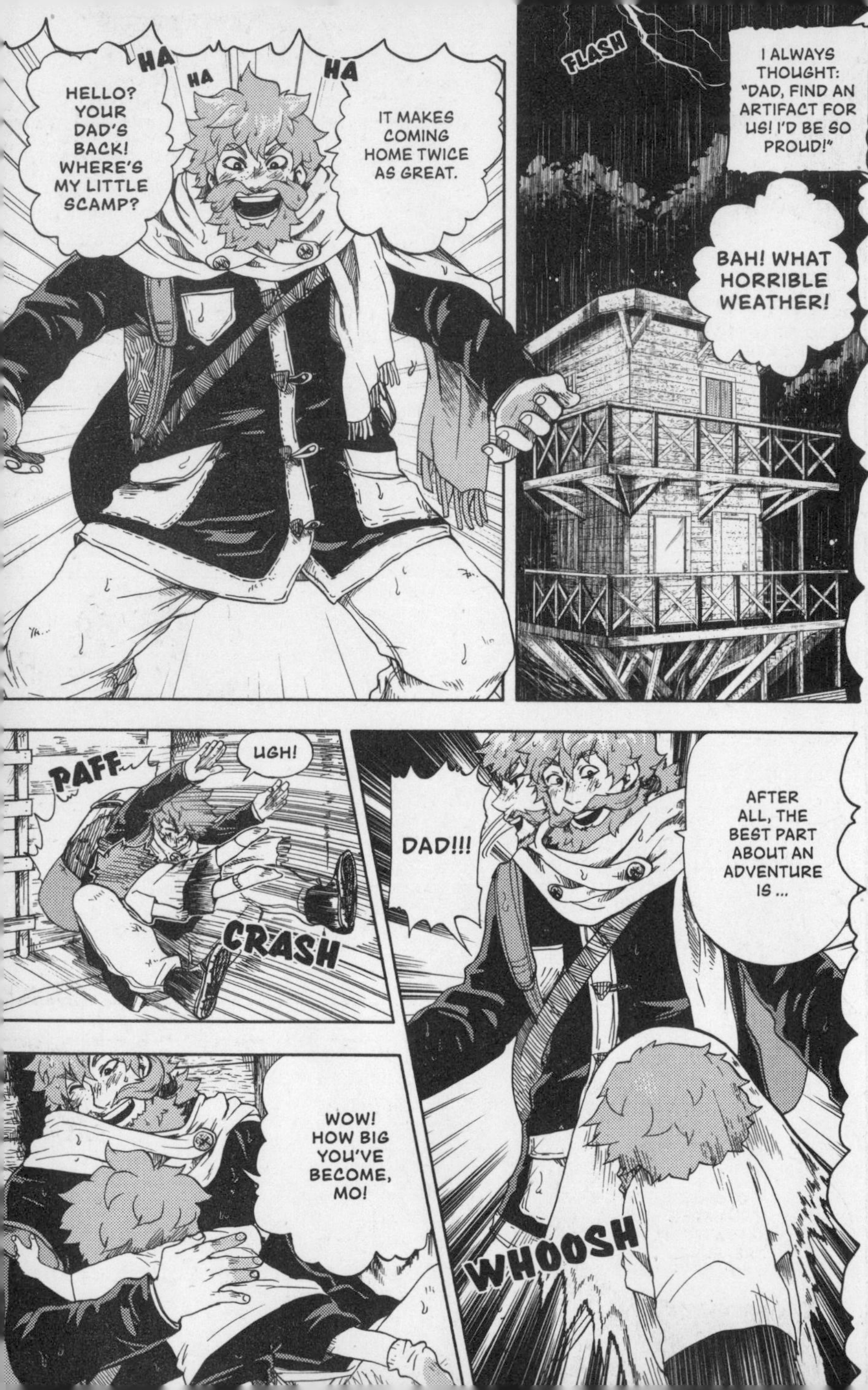
FLASH
I ALWAYS THOUGHT: "DAD, FIND AN ARTIFACT FOR US! I'D BE SO PROUD!"
BAH! WHAT HORRIBLE WEATHER!
HA HA HA
HELLO? YOUR DAD'S BACK! WHERE'S MY LITTLE SCAMP?
IT MAKES COMING HOME TWICE AS GREAT.
AFTER ALL, THE BEST PART ABOUT AN ADVENTURE IS ...
DAD!!!
WHOOSH
UGH!
PAFF
CRASH
WOW! HOW BIG YOU'VE BECOME, MO!

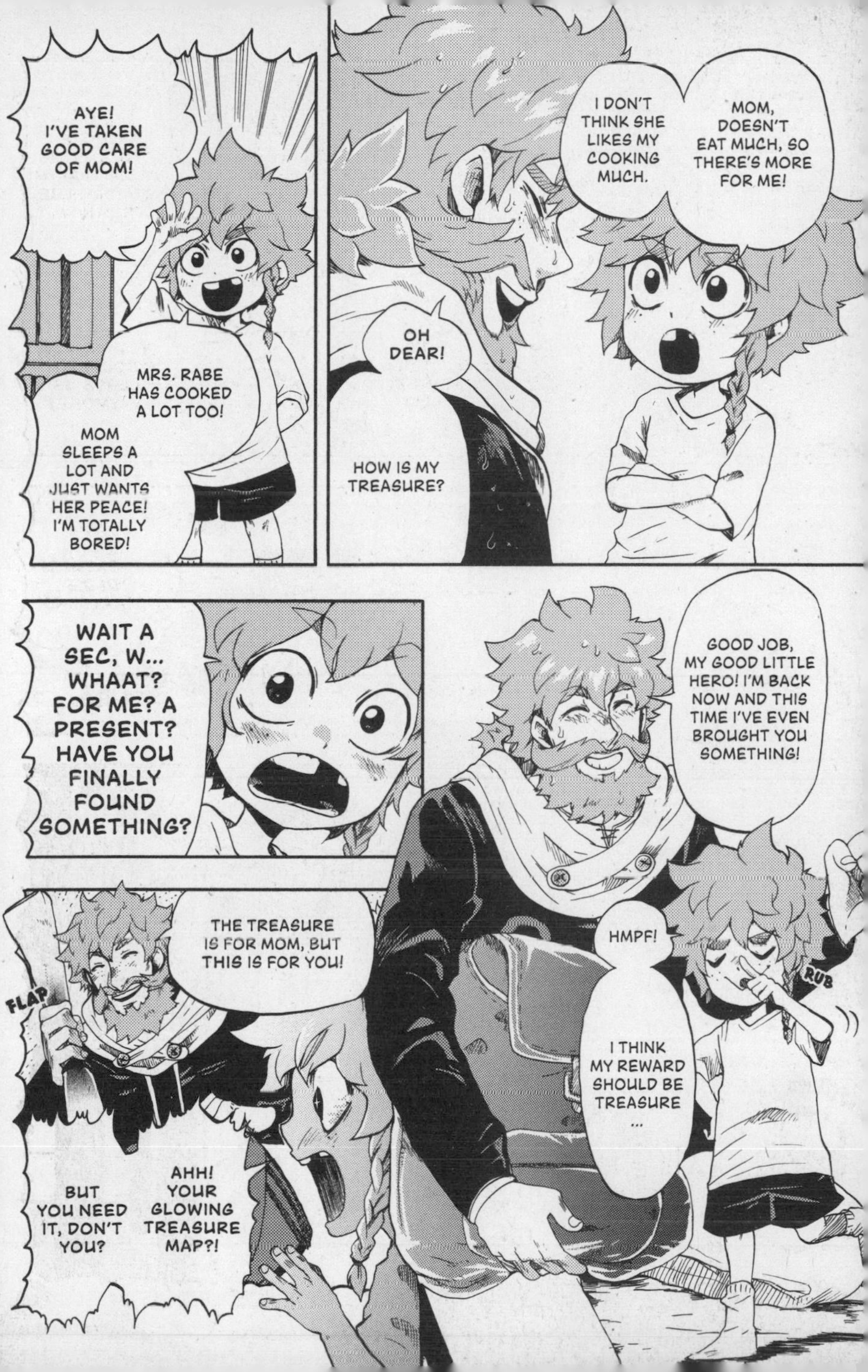
AYE! I'VE TAKEN GOOD CARE OF MOM!
MRS. RABE HAS COOKED A LOT TOO!
MOM SLEEPS A LOT AND JUST WANTS HER PEACE! I'M TOTALLY BORED!
OH DEAR!
HOW IS MY TREASURE?
I DON'T THINK SHE LIKES MY COOKING MUCH.
MOM, DOESN'T EAT MUCH, SO THERE'S MORE FOR ME!
GOOD JOB, MY GOOD LITTLE HERO! I'M BACK NOW AND THIS TIME I'VE EVEN BROUGHT YOU SOMETHING!
HMPF!
RUB
I THINK MY REWARD SHOULD BE TREASURE ...
WAIT A SEC, W... WHAAT? FOR ME? A PRESENT? HAVE YOU FINALLY FOUND SOMETHING?
THE TREASURE IS FOR MOM, BUT THIS IS FOR YOU!
FLAP
AHH! YOUR GLOWING TREASURE MAP?!
BUT YOU NEED IT, DON'T YOU?

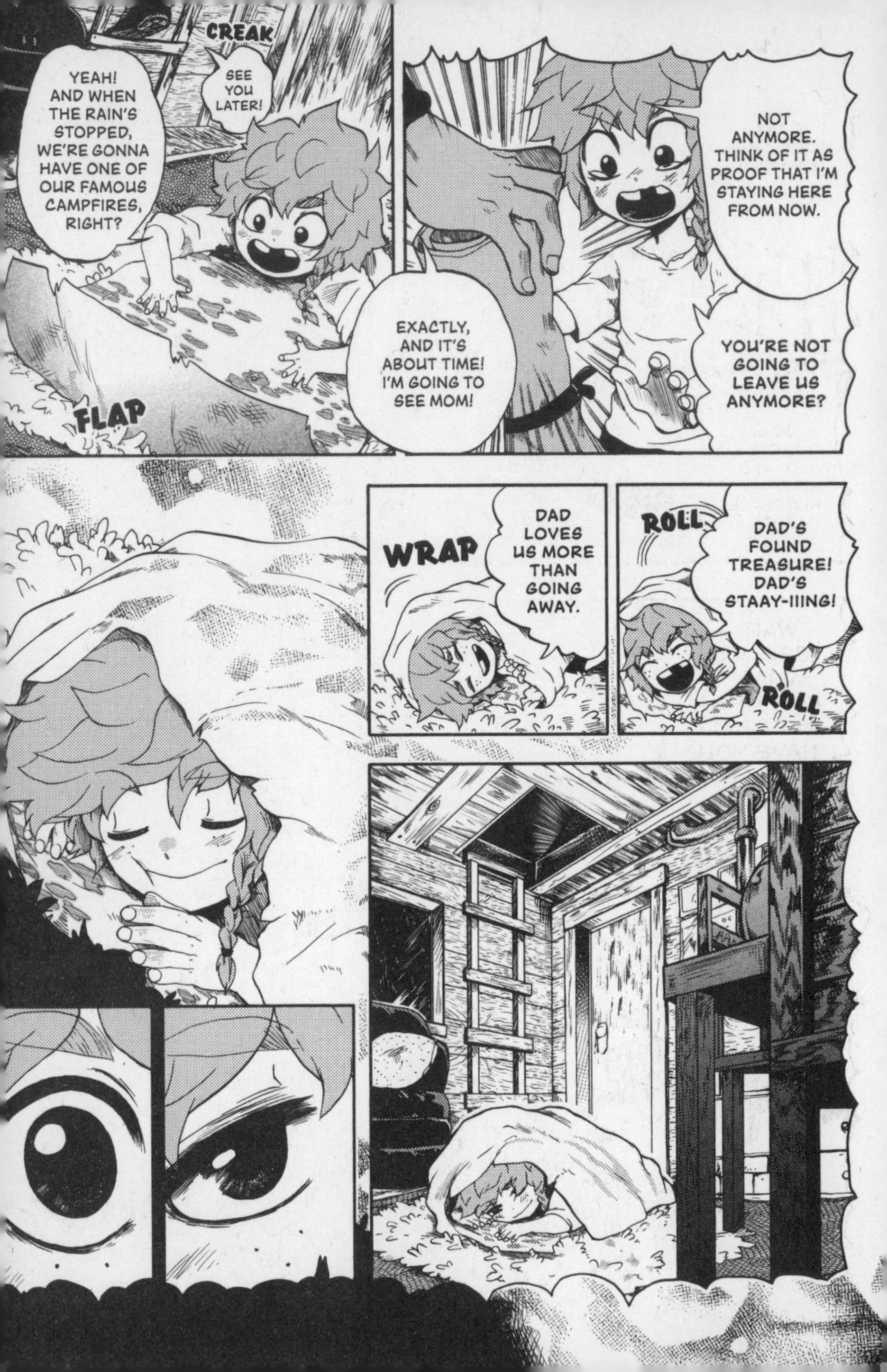
NOT ANYMORE. THINK OF IT AS PROOF THAT I'M STAYING HERE FROM NOW.
YOU'RE NOT GOING TO LEAVE US ANYMORE?
EXACTLY, AND IT'S ABOUT TIME! I'M GOING TO SEE MOM!
CREAK
SEE YOU LATER!
YEAH! AND WHEN THE RAIN'S STOPPED, WE'RE GONNA HAVE ONE OF OUR FAMOUS CAMPFIRES, RIGHT?
FLAP
ROLL
DAD'S FOUND TREASURE! DAD'S STAAY-IIING!
ROLL
WRAP
DAD LOVES US MORE THAN GOING AWAY.

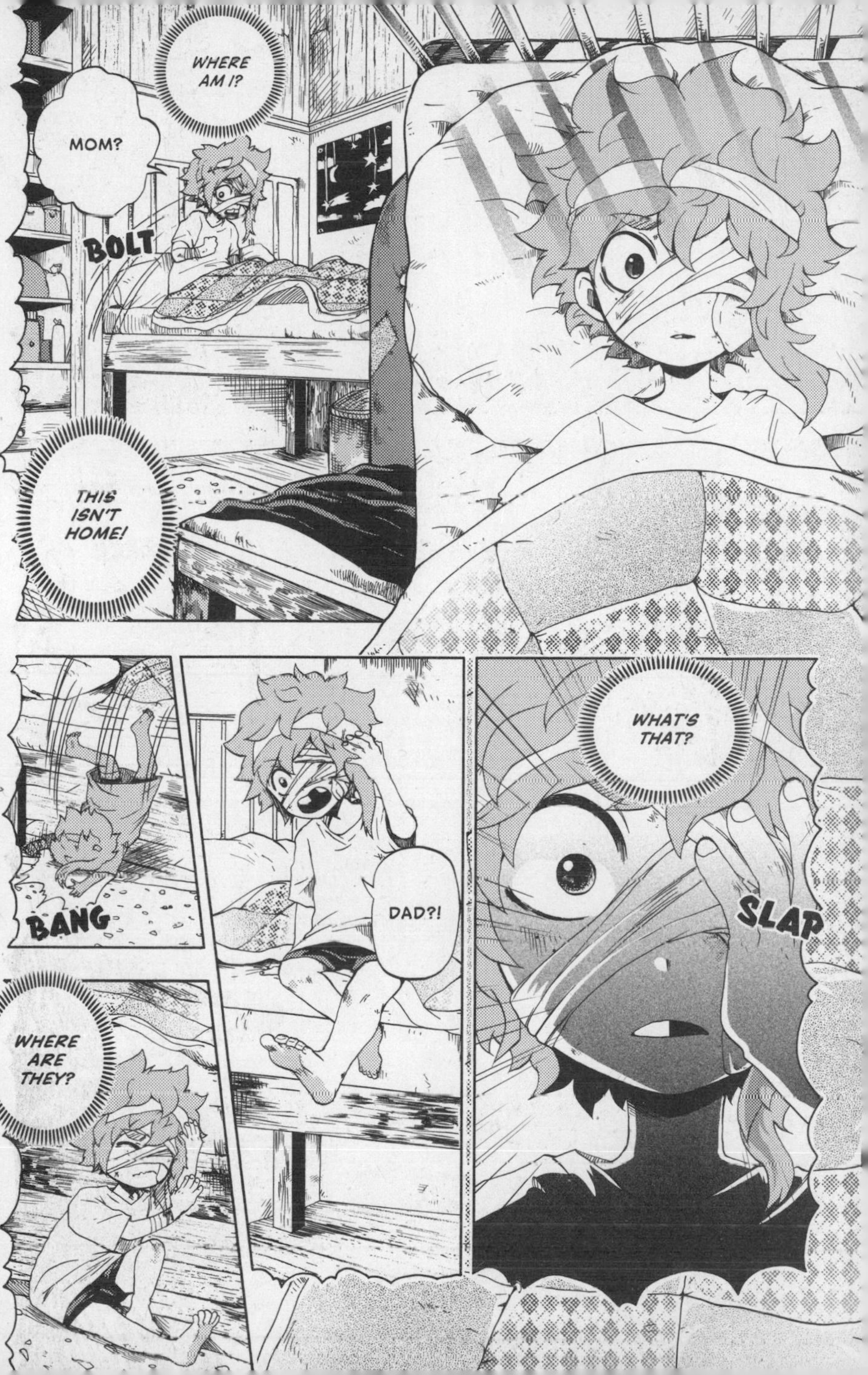
WHERE AM I?
MOM?
BOLT
THIS ISN'T HOME!
WHAT'S THAT?
SLAP
DAD?!
BANG
WHERE ARE THEY?

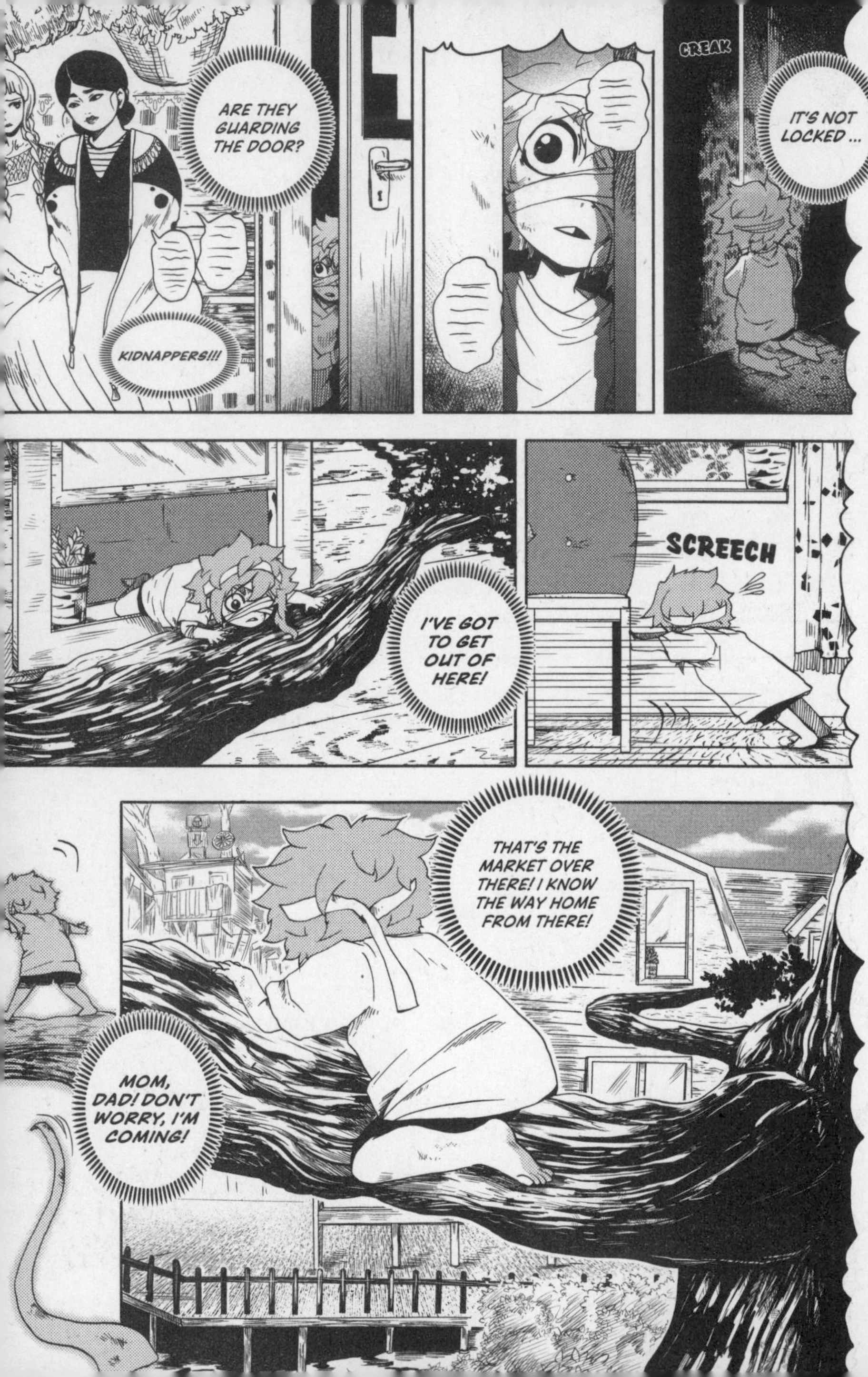
CREAK
IT'S NOT LOCKED ...
ARE THEY GUARDING THE DOOR?
KIDNAPPERS!!!
SCREECH
I'VE GOT TO GET OUT OF HERE!
THAT'S THE MARKET OVER THERE! I KNOW THE WAY HOME FROM THERE!
MOM, DAD! DON'T WORRY, I'M COMING!

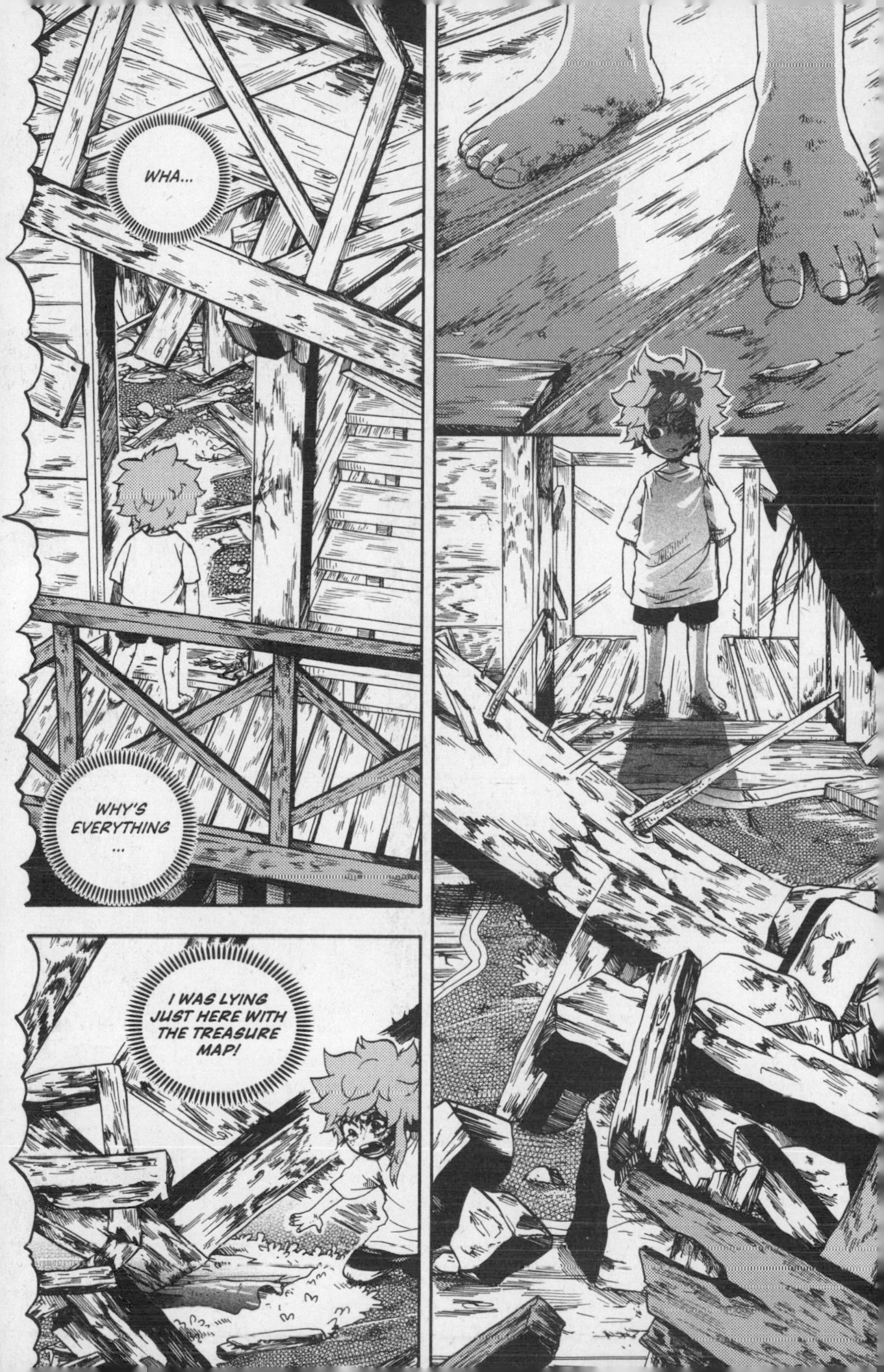
WHA...
WHY'S EVERYTHING ...
I WAS LYING JUST HERE WITH THE TREASURE MAP!

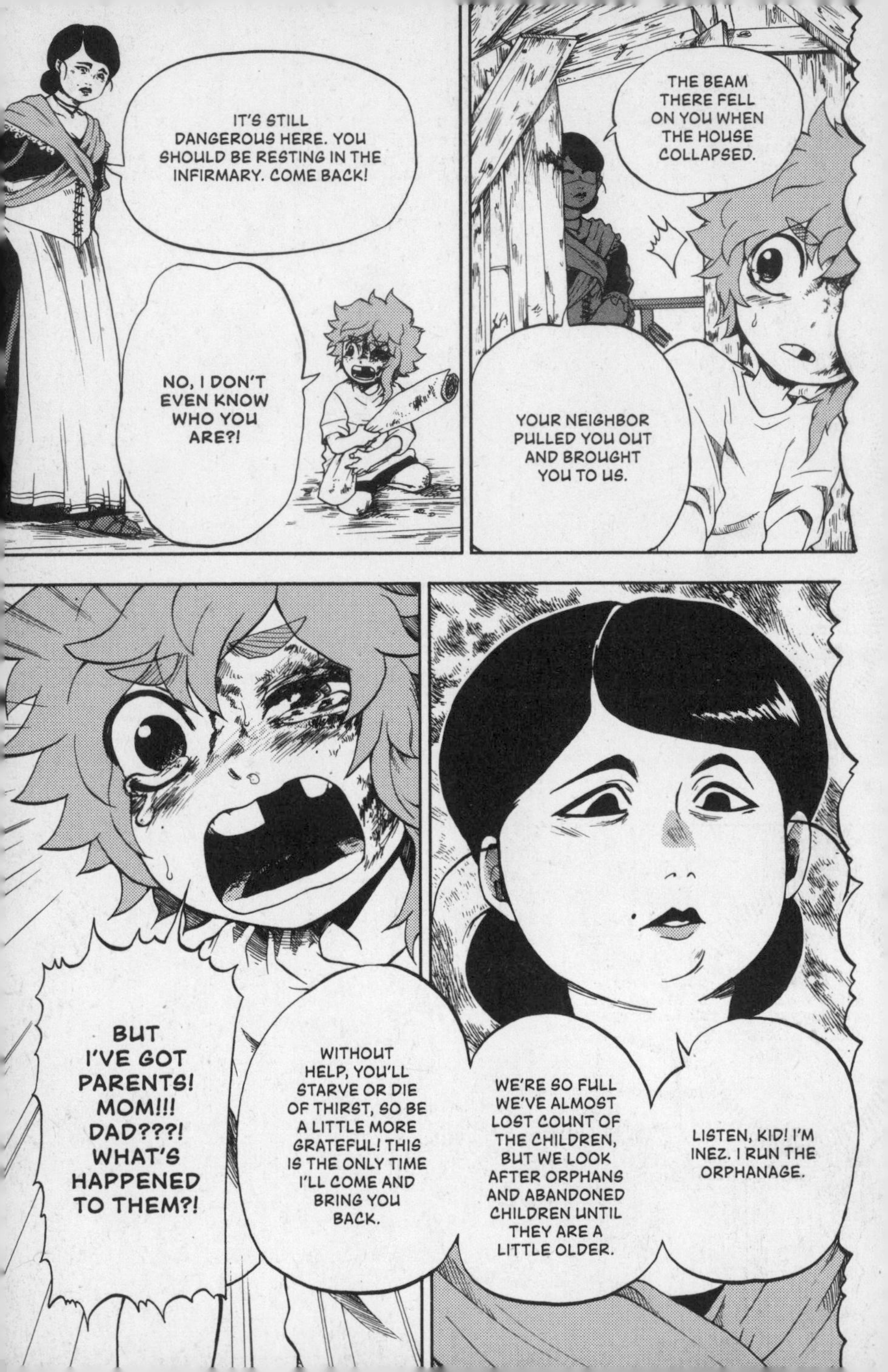
THE BEAM THERE FELL ON YOU WHEN THE HOUSE COLLAPSED.
YOUR NEIGHBOR PULLED YOU OUT AND BROUGHT YOU TO US.
IT'S STILL DANGEROUS HERE. YOU SHOULD BE RESTING IN THE INFIRMARY. COME BACK!
NO, I DON'T EVEN KNOW WHO YOU ARE?!
LISTEN, KID! I'M INEZ. I RUN THE ORPHANAGE.
WE'RE SO FULL WE'VE ALMOST LOST COUNT OF THE CHILDREN, BUT WE LOOK AFTER ORPHANS AND ABANDONED CHILDREN UNTIL THEY ARE A LITTLE OLDER.
WITHOUT HELP, YOU'LL STARVE OR DIE OF THIRST, SO BE A LITTLE MORE GRATEFUL! THIS IS THE ONLY TIME I'LL COME AND BRING YOU BACK.
BUT I'VE GOT PARENTS! MOM!!! DAD???! WHAT'S HAPPENED TO THEM?!

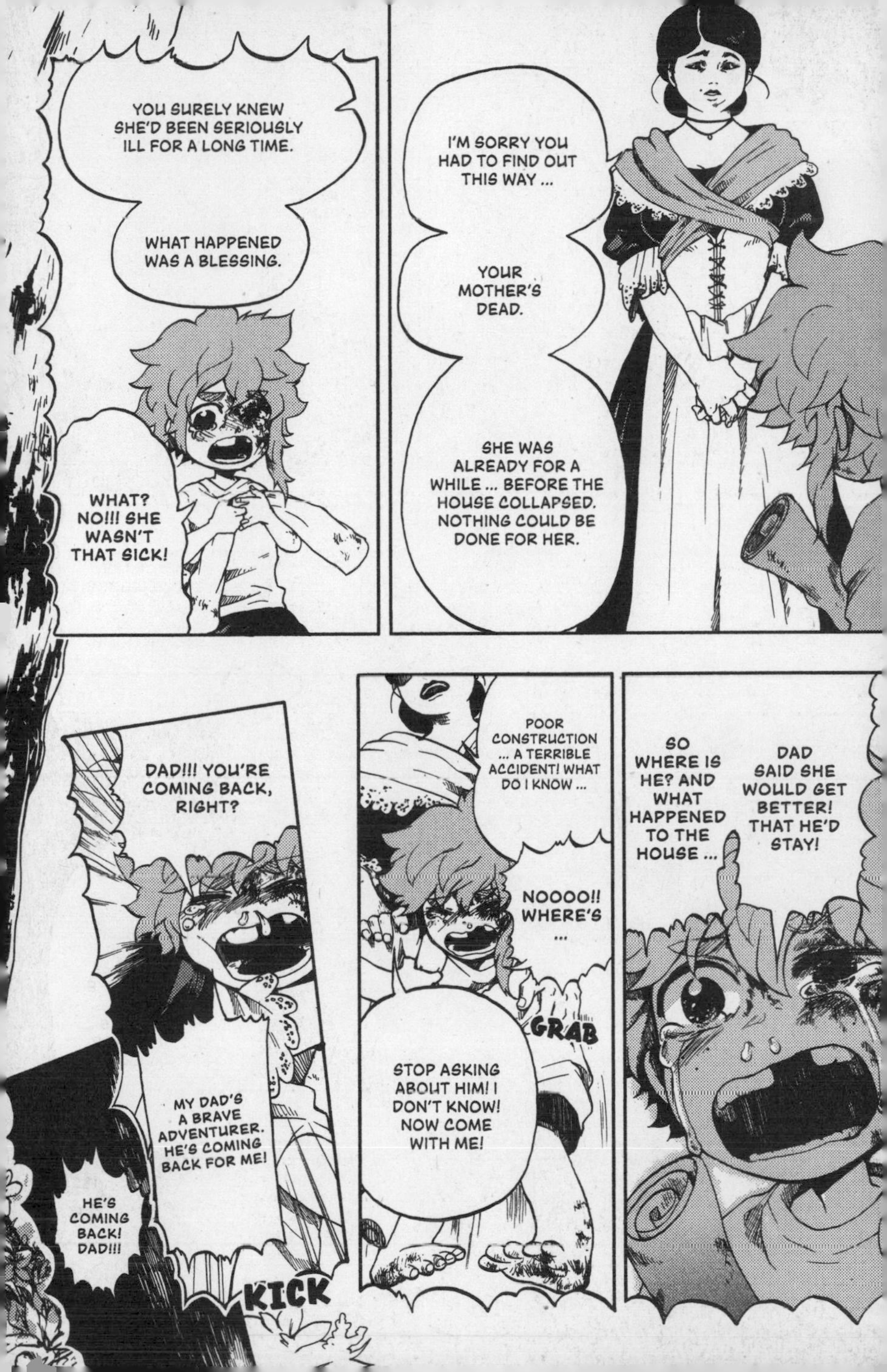
I'M SORRY YOU HAD TO FIND OUT THIS WAY ...
YOUR MOTHER'S DEAD.
SHE WAS ALREADY FOR A WHILE ... BEFORE THE HOUSE COLLAPSED. NOTHING COULD BE DONE FOR HER.
YOU SURELY KNEW SHE'D BEEN SERIOUSLY ILL FOR A LONG TIME.
WHAT HAPPENED WAS A BLESSING.
WHAT? NO!!! SHE WASN'T THAT SICK!
DAD SAID SHE WOULD GET BETTER! THAT HE'D STAY!
SO WHERE IS HE? AND WHAT HAPPENED TO THE HOUSE ...
POOR CONSTRUCTION ... A TERRIBLE ACCIDENT! WHAT DO I KNOW ...
NOOOO!! WHERE'S ...
GRAB
STOP ASKING ABOUT HIM! I DON'T KNOW! NOW COME WITH ME!
DAD!!! YOU'RE COMING BACK, RIGHT?
MY DAD'S A BRAVE ADVENTURER. HE'S COMING BACK FOR ME!
HE'S COMING BACK! DAD!!!
KICK

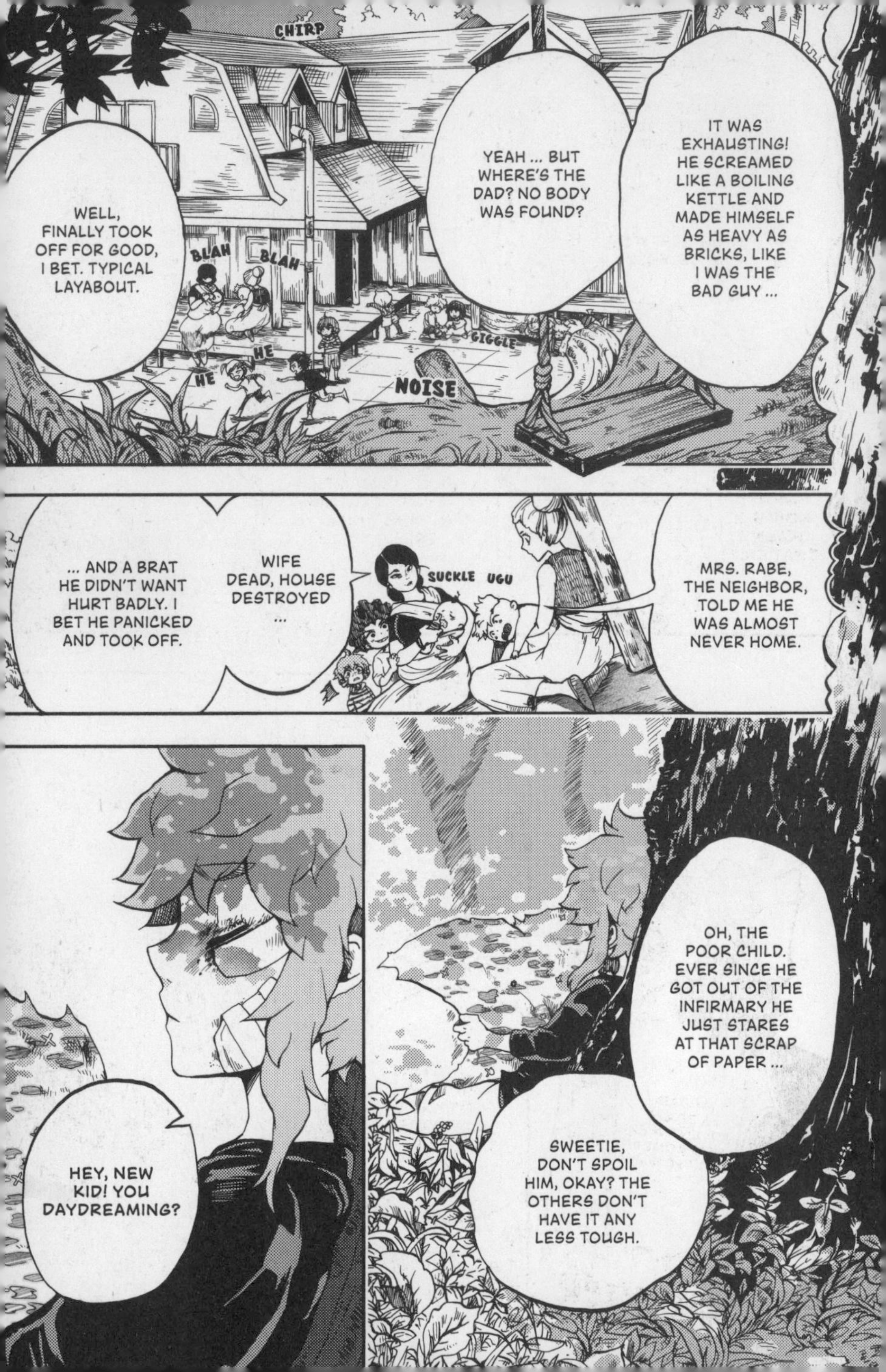
CHIRP
IT WAS EXHAUSTING! HE SCREAMED LIKE A BOILING KETTLE AND MADE HIMSELF AS HEAVY AS BRICKS, LIKE I WAS THE BAD GUY ...
YEAH ... BUT WHERE'S THE DAD? NO BODY WAS FOUND?
WELL, FINALLY TOOK OFF FOR GOOD, I BET. TYPICAL LAYABOUT.
BLAH
BLAH
GIGGLE
HE
HE
NOISE
MRS. RABE, THE NEIGHBOR, TOLD ME HE WAS ALMOST NEVER HOME.
UGU
SUCKLE
WIFE DEAD, HOUSE DESTROYED ...
... AND A BRAT HE DIDN'T WANT HURT BADLY. I BET HE PANICKED AND TOOK OFF.
OH, THE POOR CHILD. EVER SINCE HE GOT OUT OF THE INFIRMARY HE JUST STARES AT THAT SCRAP OF PAPER ...
SWEETIE, DON'T SPOIL HIM, OKAY? THE OTHERS DON'T HAVE IT ANY LESS TOUGH.
HEY, NEW KID! YOU DAYDREAMING?

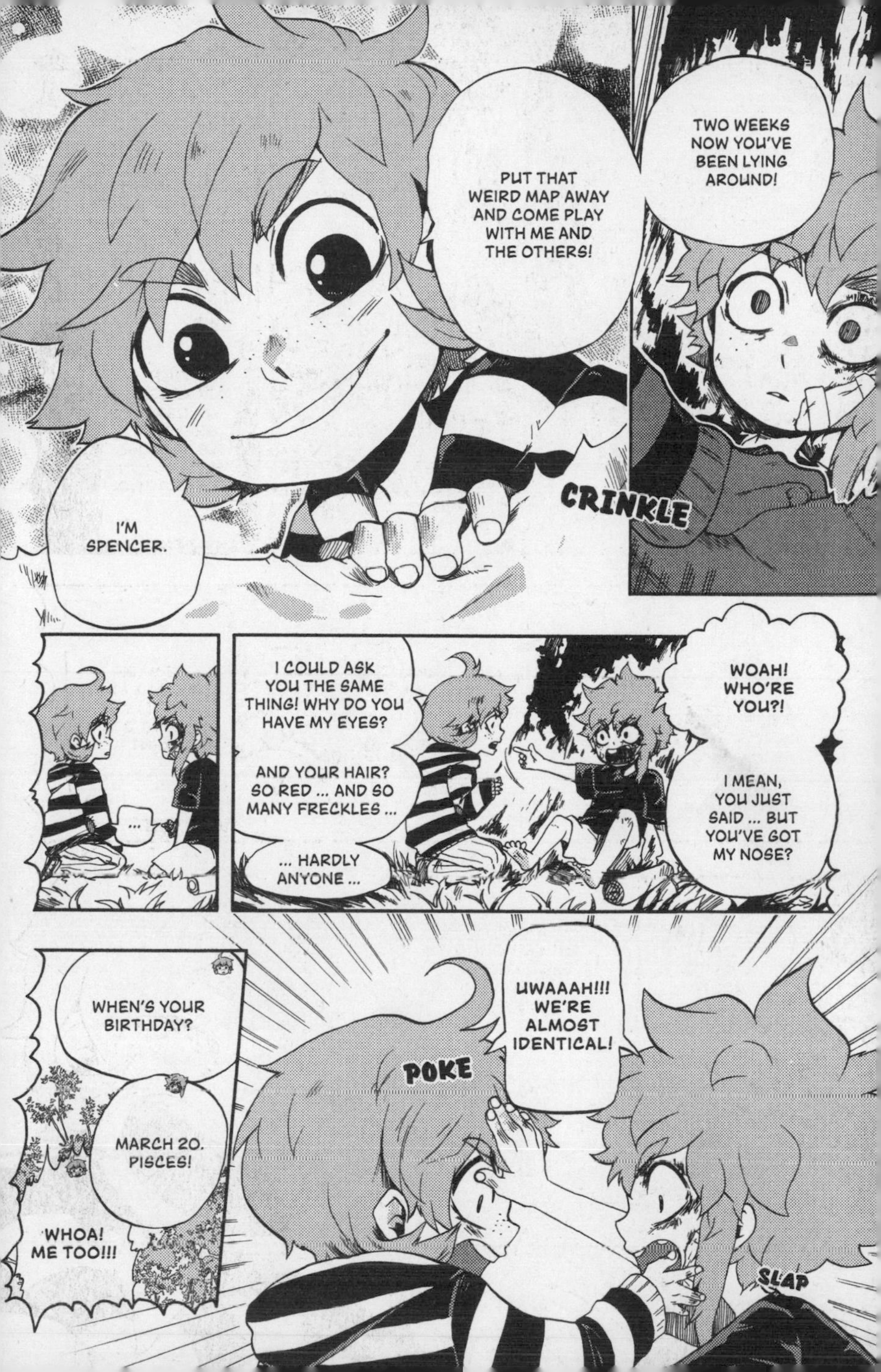
TWO WEEKS NOW YOU'VE BEEN LYING AROUND!
CRINKLE
PUT THAT WEIRD MAP AWAY AND COME PLAY WITH ME AND THE OTHERS!
I'M SPENCER.
WOAH! WHO'RE YOU?!
I MEAN, YOU JUST SAID ... BUT YOU'VE GOT MY NOSE?
I COULD ASK YOU THE SAME THING! WHY DO YOU HAVE MY EYES?
AND YOUR HAIR? SO RED ... AND SO MANY FRECKLES ...
... HARDLY ANYONE ...
...
UWAAAH!!! WE'RE ALMOST IDENTICAL!
POKE
SLAP
WHEN'S YOUR BIRTHDAY?
MARCH 20. PISCES!
WHOA! ME TOO!!!

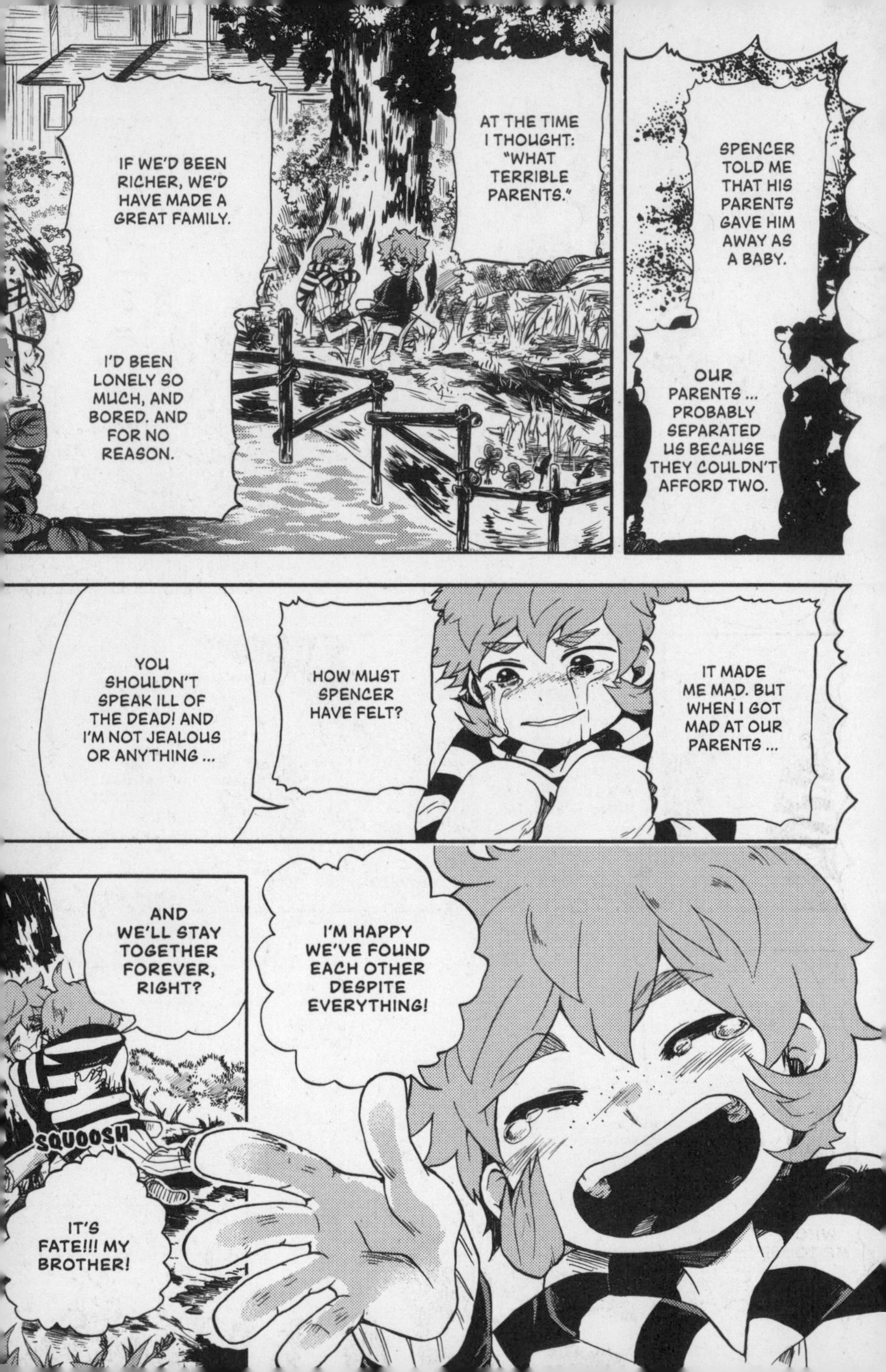
SPENCER TOLD ME THAT HIS PARENTS GAVE HIM AWAY AS A BABY.
OUR PARENTS ... PROBABLY SEPARATED US BECAUSE THEY COULDN'T AFFORD TWO.
AT THE TIME I THOUGHT: "WHAT TERRIBLE PARENTS."
IF WE'D BEEN RICHER, WE'D HAVE MADE A GREAT FAMILY.
I'D BEEN LONELY SO MUCH, AND BORED. AND FOR NO REASON.
IT MADE ME MAD. BUT WHEN I GOT MAD AT OUR PARENTS ...
HOW MUST SPENCER HAVE FELT?
YOU SHOULDN'T SPEAK ILL OF THE DEAD! AND I'M NOT JEALOUS OR ANYTHING ...
I'M HAPPY WE'VE FOUND EACH OTHER DESPITE EVERYTHING!
AND WE'LL STAY TOGETHER FOREVER, RIGHT?
SQUOOSH
IT'S FATE!!! MY BROTHER!

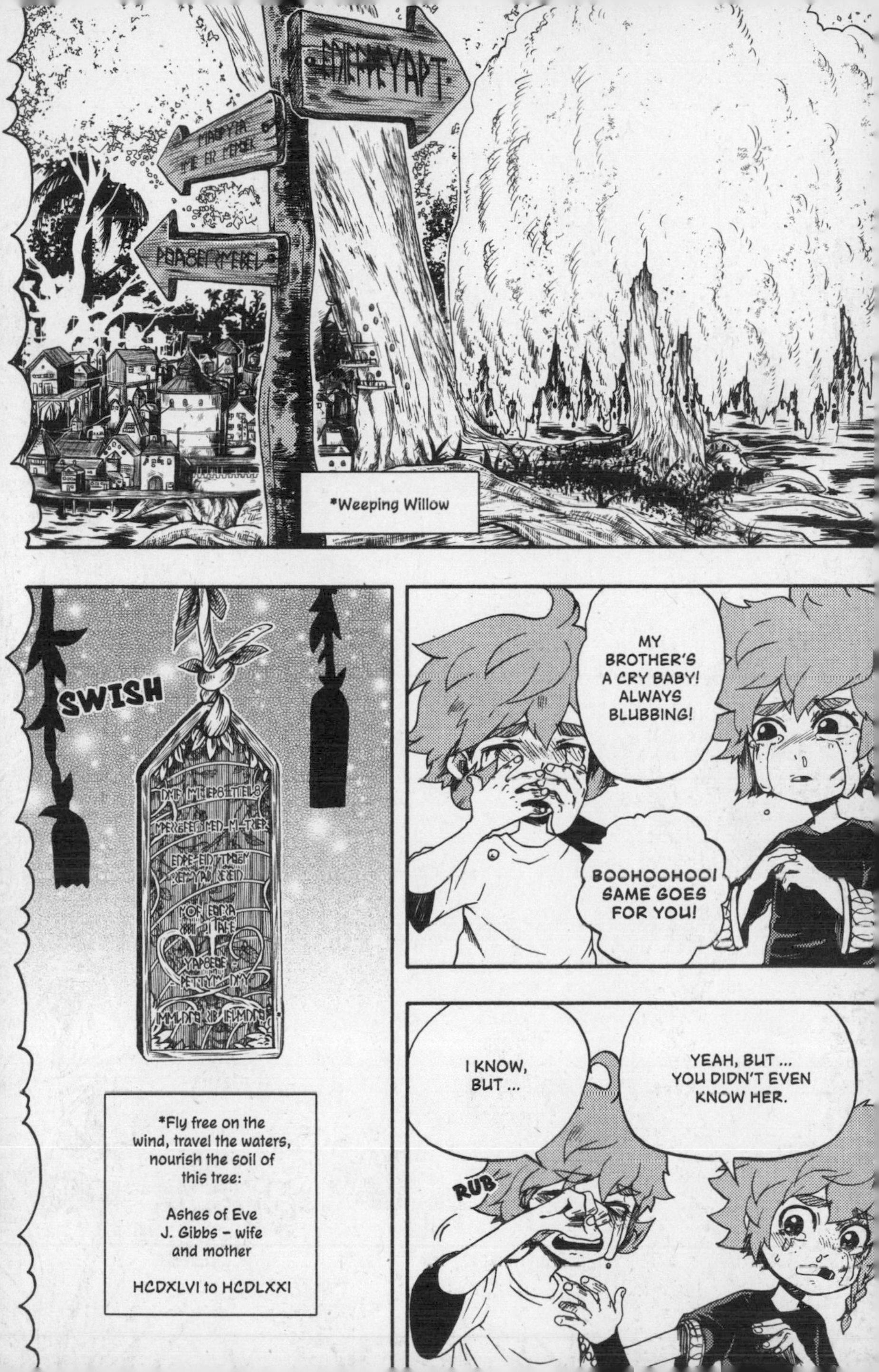
*Weeping Willow
MY BROTHER'S A CRY BABY! ALWAYS BLUBBING!
BOOHOOHOO! SAME GOES FOR YOU!
YEAH, BUT ... YOU DIDN'T EVEN KNOW HER.
I KNOW, BUT ...
RUB
SWISH
*Fly free on the wind, travel the waters, nourish the soil of this tree:
Ashes of Eve J. Gibbs – wife and mother
HCDXLVI to HCDLXXI

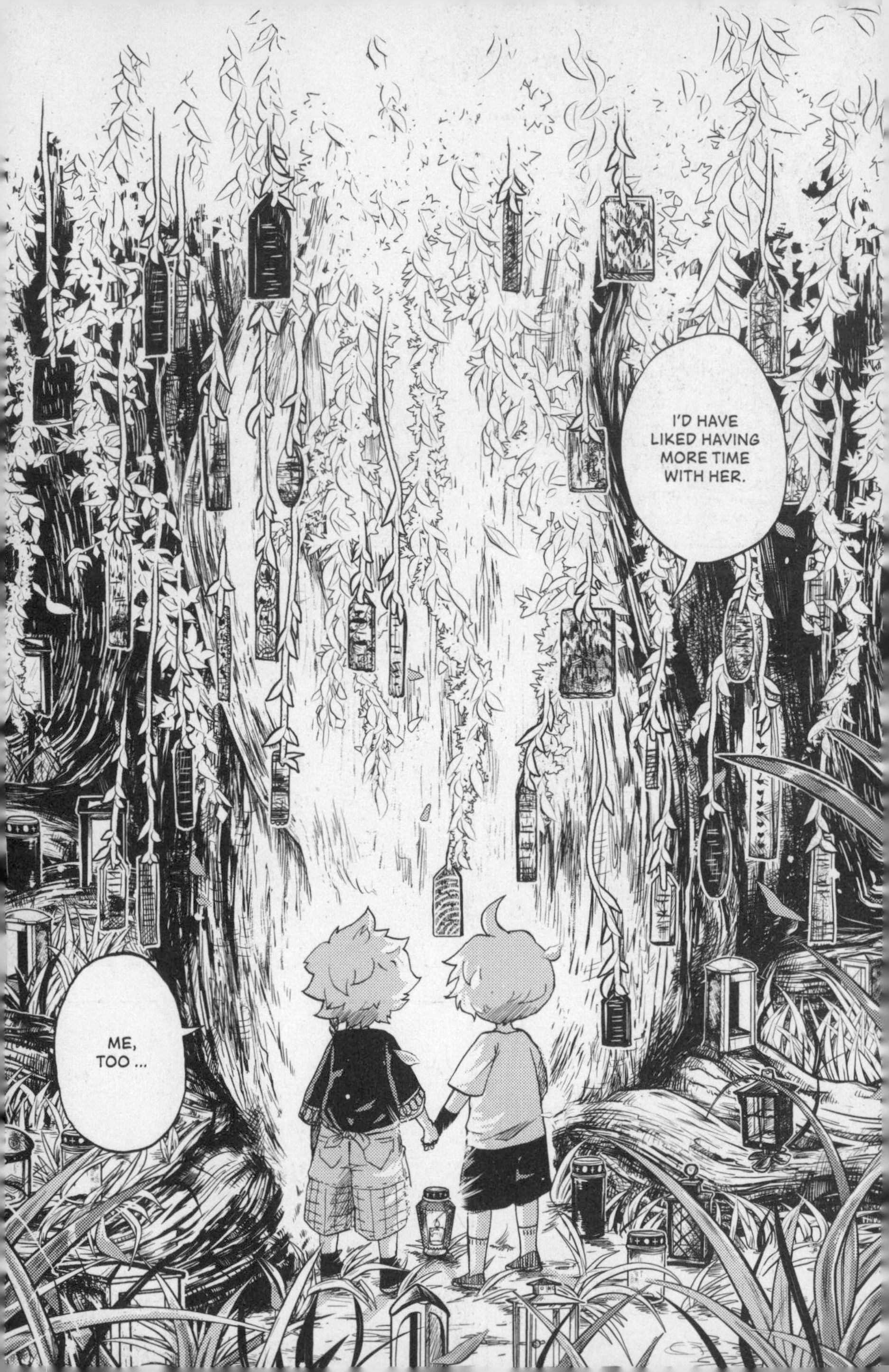
I'D HAVE LIKED HAVING MORE TIME WITH HER.
ME, TOO ...

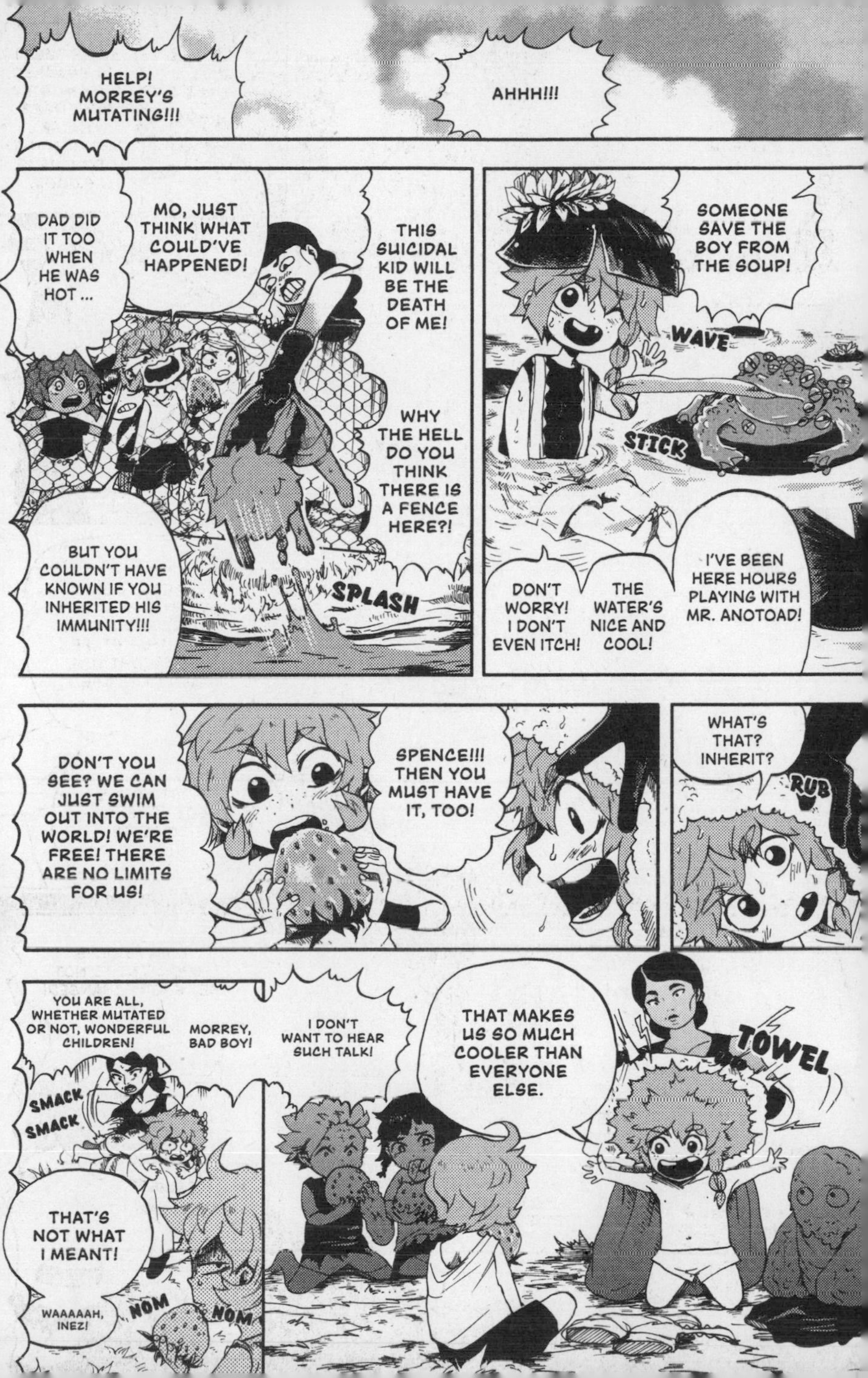
AHHH!!!
HELP! MORREY'S MUTATING!!!
SOMEONE SAVE THE BOY FROM THE SOUP!
WAVE
STICK
I'VE BEEN HERE HOURS PLAYING WITH MR. ANOTOAD!
THE WATER'S NICE AND COOL!
DON'T WORRY! I DON'T EVEN ITCH!
THIS SUICIDAL KID WILL BE THE DEATH OF ME!
WHY THE HELL DO YOU THINK THERE IS A FENCE HERE?!
MO, JUST THINK WHAT COULD'VE HAPPENED!
DAD DID IT TOO WHEN HE WAS HOT ...
SPLASH
BUT YOU COULDN'T HAVE KNOWN IF YOU INHERITED HIS IMMUNITY!!!
WHAT'S THAT? INHERIT?
RUB
SPENCE!!! THEN YOU MUST HAVE IT, TOO!
DON'T YOU SEE? WE CAN JUST SWIM OUT INTO THE WORLD! WE'RE FREE! THERE ARE NO LIMITS FOR US!
TOWEL
THAT MAKES US SO MUCH COOLER THAN EVERYONE ELSE.
I DON'T WANT TO HEAR SUCH TALK!
MORREY, BAD BOY!
YOU ARE ALL, WHETHER MUTATED OR NOT, WONDERFUL CHILDREN!
SMACK
SMACK
THAT'S NOT WHAT I MEANT!
NOM
NOM
WAAAAAH, INEZ!

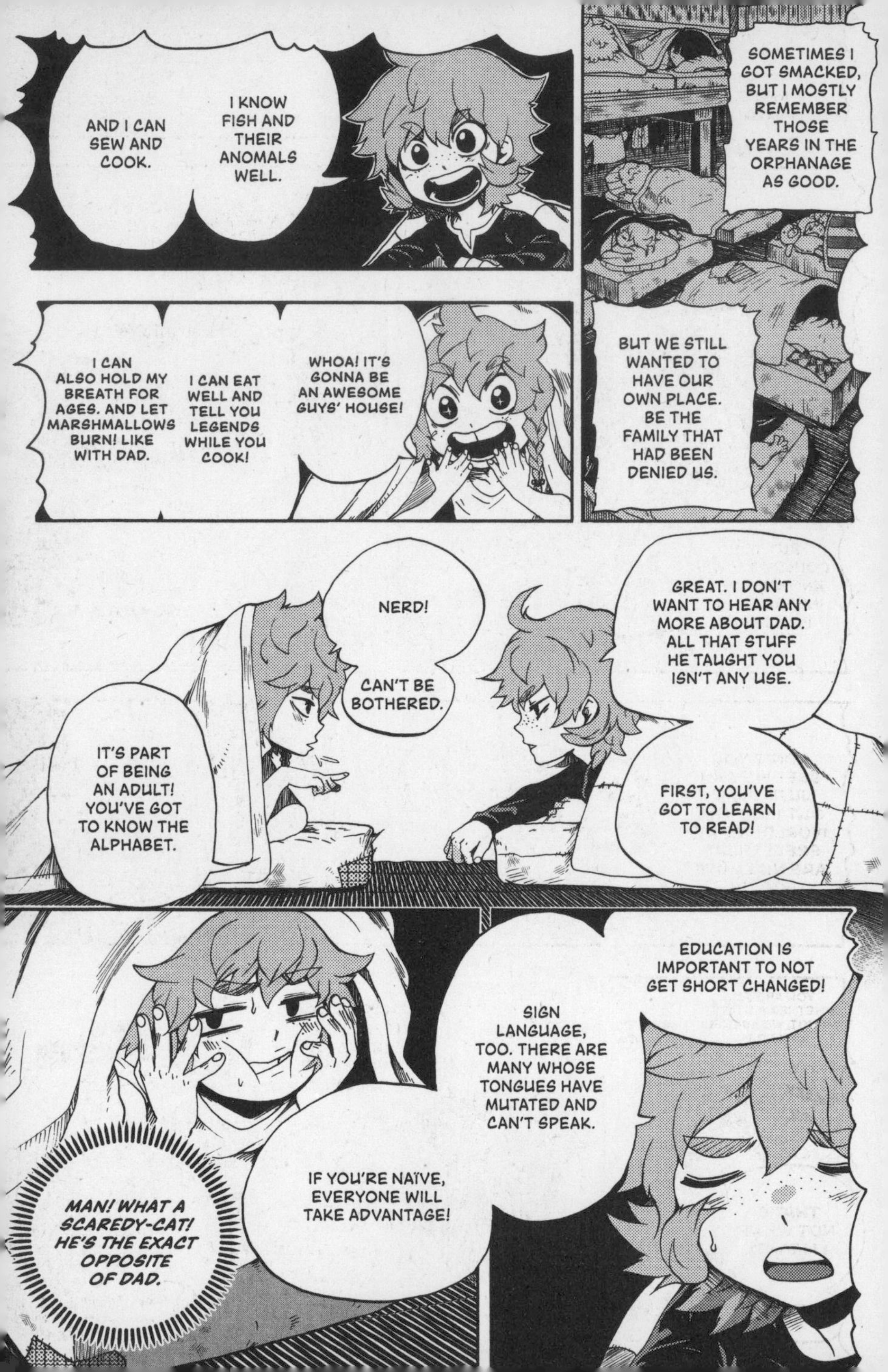
SOMETIMES I GOT SMACKED, BUT I MOSTLY REMEMBER THOSE YEARS IN THE ORPHANAGE AS GOOD.
BUT WE STILL WANTED TO HAVE OUR OWN PLACE. BE THE FAMILY THAT HAD BEEN DENIED US.
I KNOW FISH AND THEIR ANOMALS WELL.
AND I CAN SEW AND COOK.
WHOA! IT'S GONNA BE AN AWESOME GUYS' HOUSE!
I CAN EAT WELL AND TELL YOU LEGENDS WHILE YOU COOK!
I CAN ALSO HOLD MY BREATH FOR AGES. AND LET MARSHMALLOWS BURN! LIKE WITH DAD.
GREAT. I DON'T WANT TO HEAR ANY MORE ABOUT DAD. ALL THAT STUFF HE TAUGHT YOU ISN'T ANY USE.
FIRST, YOU'VE GOT TO LEARN TO READ!
NERD!
CAN'T BE BOTHERED.
IT'S PART OF BEING AN ADULT! YOU'VE GOT TO KNOW THE ALPHABET.
EDUCATION IS IMPORTANT TO NOT GET SHORT CHANGED!
SIGN LANGUAGE, TOO. THERE ARE MANY WHOSE TONGUES HAVE MUTATED AND CAN'T SPEAK.
IF YOU'RE NAÏVE, EVERYONE WILL TAKE ADVANTAGE!
MAN! WHAT A SCAREDY-CAT! HE'S THE EXACT OPPOSITE OF DAD.

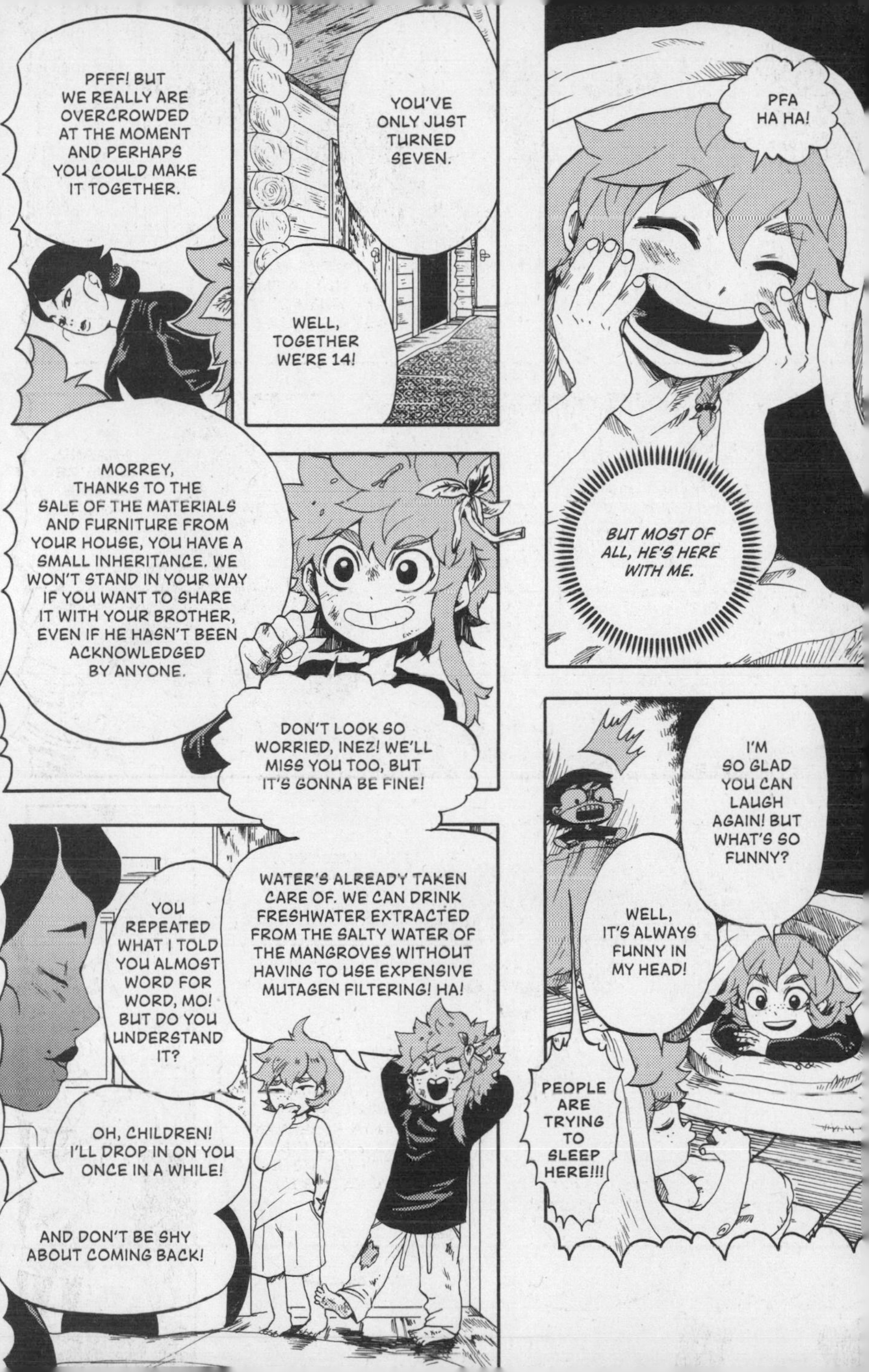
PFFF! BUT WE REALLY ARE OVERCROWDED AT THE MOMENT AND PERHAPS YOU COULD MAKE IT TOGETHER.
YOU'VE ONLY JUST TURNED SEVEN.
WELL, TOGETHER WE'RE 14!
MORREY, THANKS TO THE SALE OF THE MATERIALS AND FURNITURE FROM YOUR HOUSE, YOU HAVE A SMALL INHERITANCE. WE WON'T STAND IN YOUR WAY IF YOU WANT TO SHARE IT WITH YOUR BROTHER, EVEN IF HE HASN'T BEEN ACKNOWLEDGED BY ANYONE.
DON'T LOOK SO WORRIED, INEZ! WE'LL MISS YOU TOO, BUT IT'S GONNA BE FINE!
WATER'S ALREADY TAKEN CARE OF. WE CAN DRINK FRESHWATER EXTRACTED FROM THE SALTY WATER OF THE MANGROVES WITHOUT HAVING TO USE EXPENSIVE MUTAGEN FILTERING! HA!
YOU REPEATED WHAT I TOLD YOU ALMOST WORD FOR WORD, MO! BUT DO YOU UNDERSTAND IT?
OH, CHILDREN! I'LL DROP IN ON YOU ONCE IN A WHILE!
AND DON'T BE SHY ABOUT COMING BACK!
PFA HA HA!
BUT MOST OF ALL, HE'S HERE WITH ME.
I'M SO GLAD YOU CAN LAUGH AGAIN! BUT WHAT'S SO FUNNY?
WELL, IT'S ALWAYS FUNNY IN MY HEAD!
PEOPLE ARE TRYING TO SLEEP HERE!!!

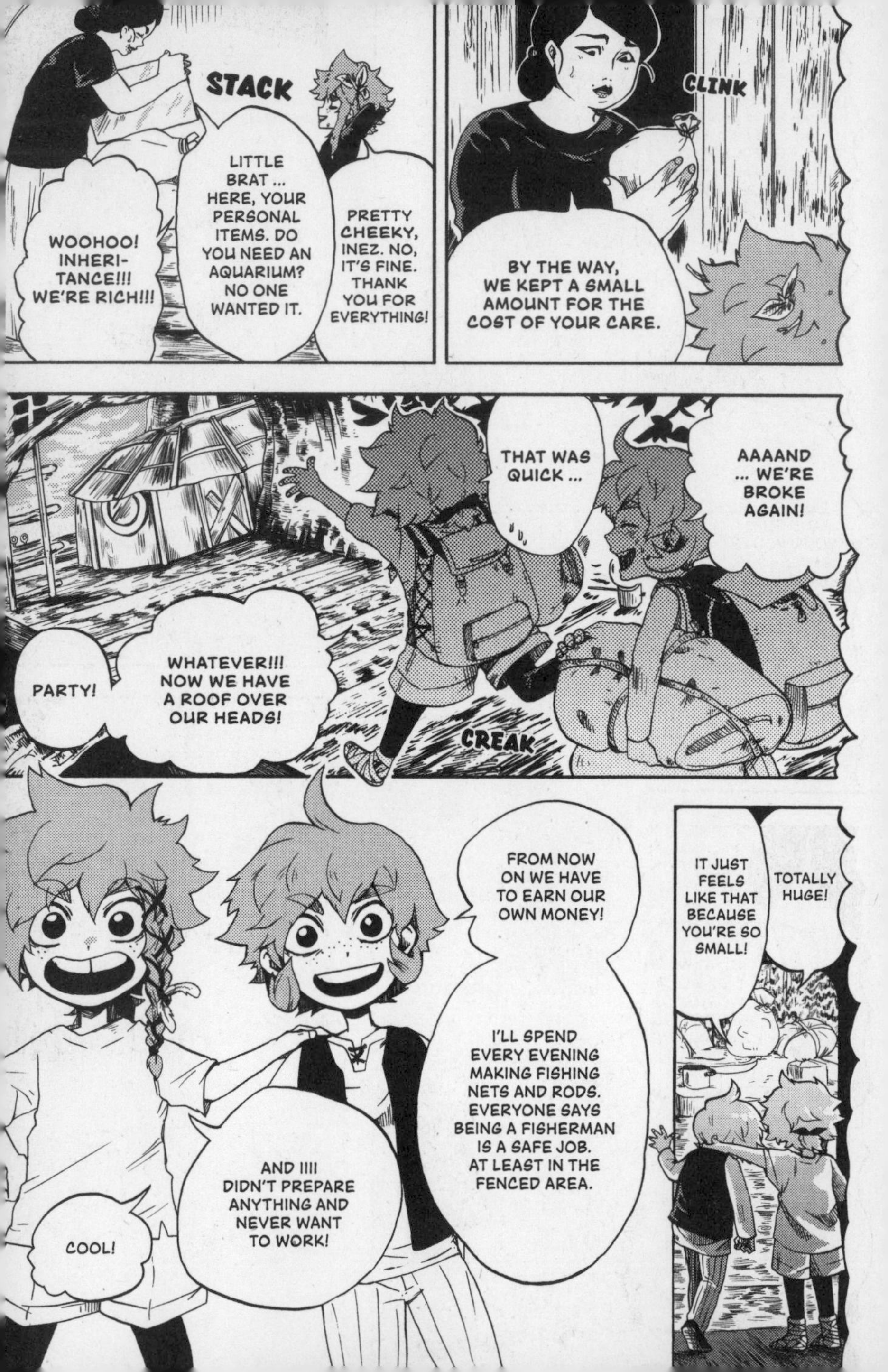
CLINK
BY THE WAY, WE KEPT A SMALL AMOUNT FOR THE COST OF YOUR CARE.
STACK
LITTLE BRAT ... HERE, YOUR PERSONAL ITEMS. DO YOU NEED AN AQUARIUM? NO ONE WANTED IT.
PRETTY CHEEKY, INEZ. NO, IT'S FINE. THANK YOU FOR EVERYTHING!
WOOHOO! INHERI-TANCE!!! WE'RE RICH!!!
AAAAND ... WE'RE BROKE AGAIN!
THAT WAS QUICK ...
WHATEVER!!! NOW WE HAVE A ROOF OVER OUR HEADS!
PARTY!
CREAK
TOTALLY HUGE!
IT JUST FEELS LIKE THAT BECAUSE YOU'RE SO SMALL!
FROM NOW ON WE HAVE TO EARN OUR OWN MONEY!
I'LL SPEND EVERY EVENING MAKING FISHING NETS AND RODS. EVERYONE SAYS BEING A FISHERMAN IS A SAFE JOB. AT LEAST IN THE FENCED AREA.
AND IIII DIDN'T PREPARE ANYTHING AND NEVER WANT TO WORK!
COOL!

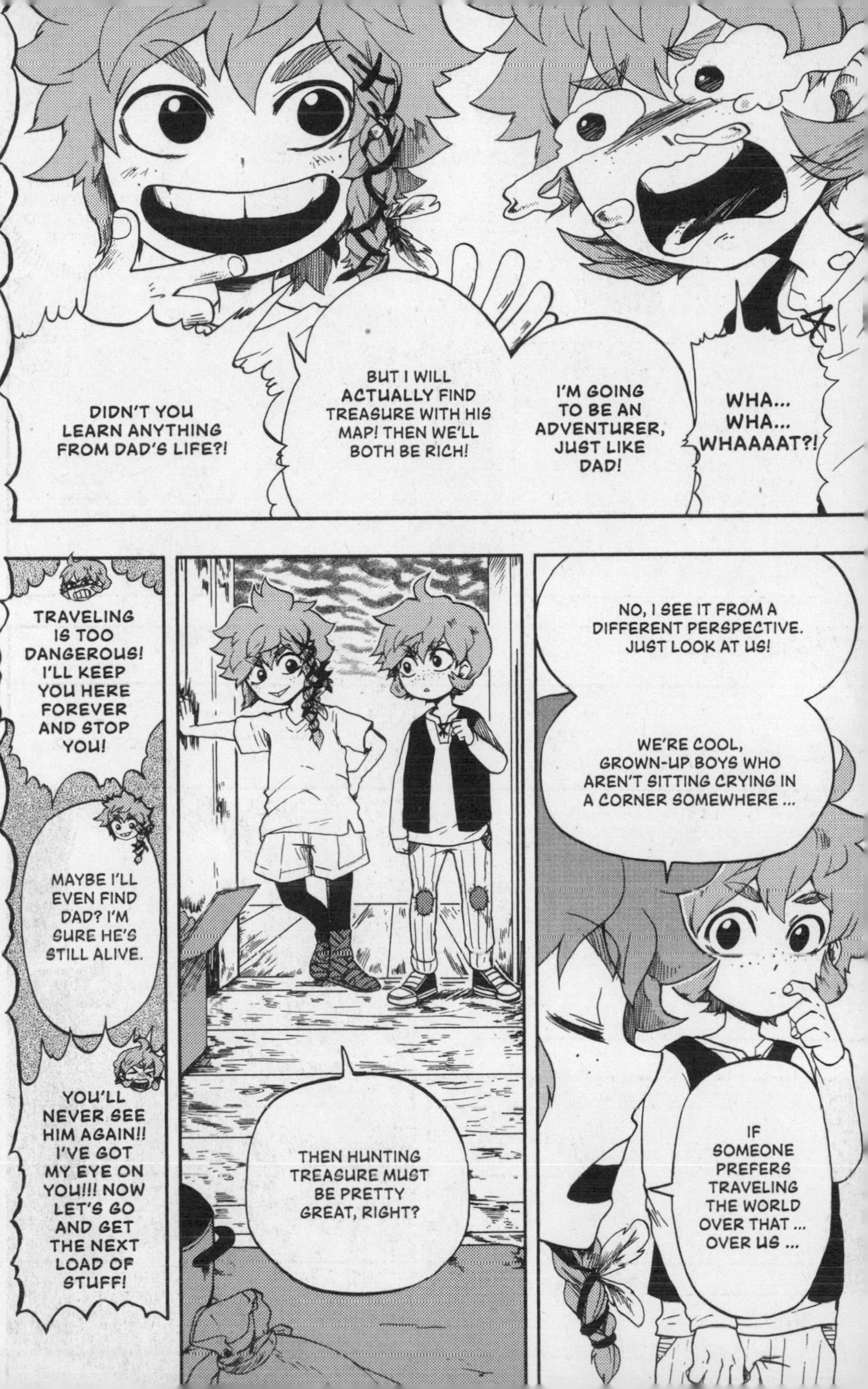
WHA... WHA... WHAAAAT?!
I'M GOING TO BE AN ADVENTURER, JUST LIKE DAD!
BUT I WILL ACTUALLY FIND TREASURE WITH HIS MAP! THEN WE'LL BOTH BE RICH!
DIDN'T YOU LEARN ANYTHING FROM DAD'S LIFE?!
NO, I SEE IT FROM A DIFFERENT PERSPECTIVE. JUST LOOK AT US!
WE'RE COOL, GROWN-UP BOYS WHO AREN'T SITTING CRYING IN A CORNER SOMEWHERE ...
IF SOMEONE PREFERS TRAVELING THE WORLD OVER THAT ... OVER US ...
THEN HUNTING TREASURE MUST BE PRETTY GREAT, RIGHT?
TRAVELING IS TOO DANGEROUS! I'LL KEEP YOU HERE FOREVER AND STOP YOU!
MAYBE I'LL EVEN FIND DAD? I'M SURE HE'S STILL ALIVE.
YOU'LL NEVER SEE HIM AGAIN!! I'VE GOT MY EYE ON YOU!!! NOW LET'S GO AND GET THE NEXT LOAD OF STUFF!

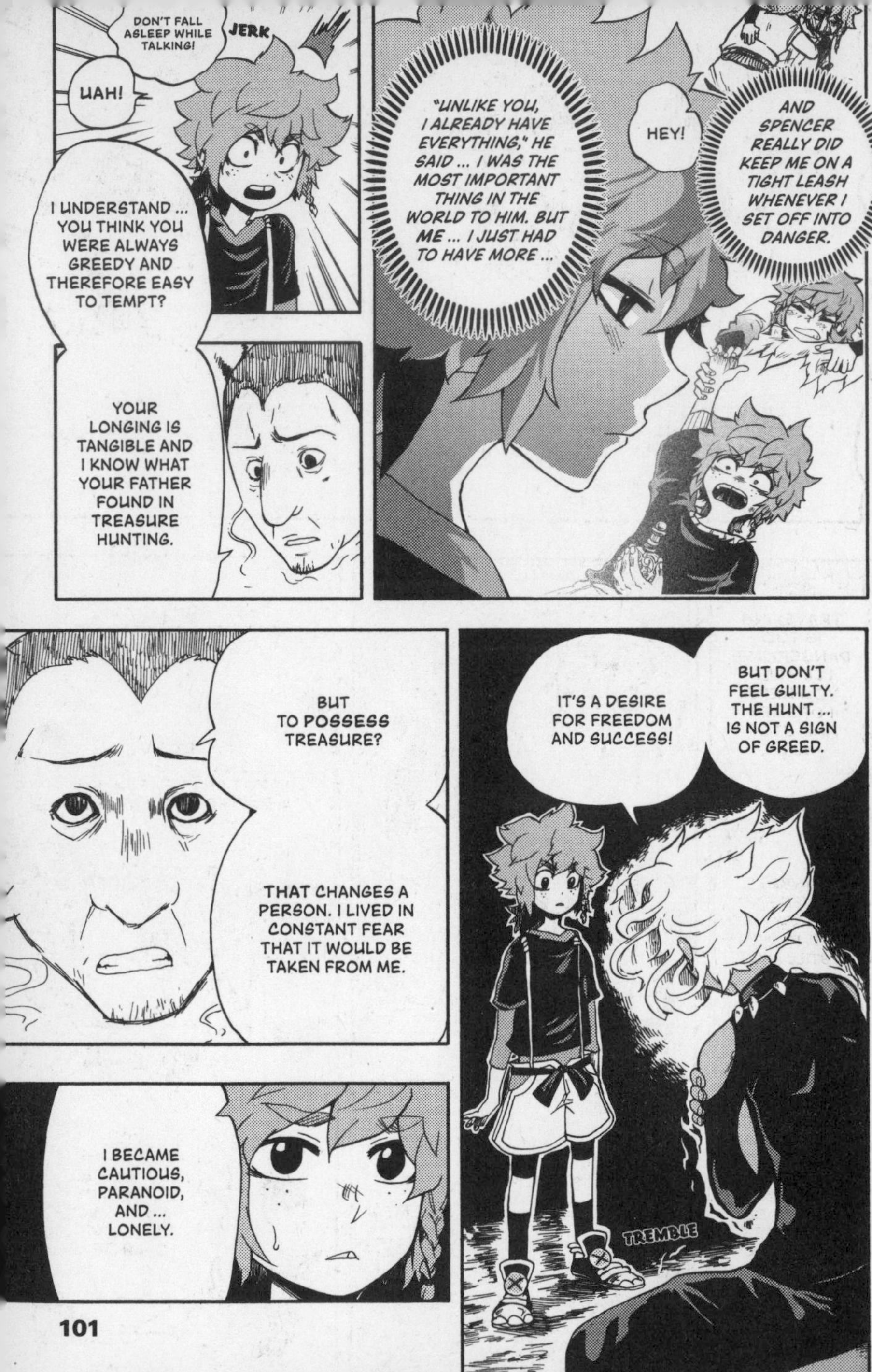
AND SPENCER REALLY DID KEEP ME ON A TIGHT LEASH WHENEVER I SET OFF INTO DANGER.
HEY!
"UNLIKE YOU, I ALREADY HAVE EVERYTHING," HE SAID ... I WAS THE MOST IMPORTANT THING IN THE WORLD TO HIM. BUT ME ... I JUST HAD TO HAVE MORE ...
DON'T FALL ASLEEP WHILE TALKING!
JERK
UAH!
I UNDERSTAND ... YOU THINK YOU WERE ALWAYS GREEDY AND THEREFORE EASY TO TEMPT?
YOUR LONGING IS TANGIBLE AND I KNOW WHAT YOUR FATHER FOUND IN TREASURE HUNTING.
BUT DON'T FEEL GUILTY. THE HUNT ... IS NOT A SIGN OF GREED.
IT'S A DESIRE FOR FREEDOM AND SUCCESS!
TREMBLE
BUT TO POSSESS TREASURE?
THAT CHANGES A PERSON. I LIVED IN CONSTANT FEAR THAT IT WOULD BE TAKEN FROM ME.
I BECAME CAUTIOUS, PARANOID, AND ... LONELY.

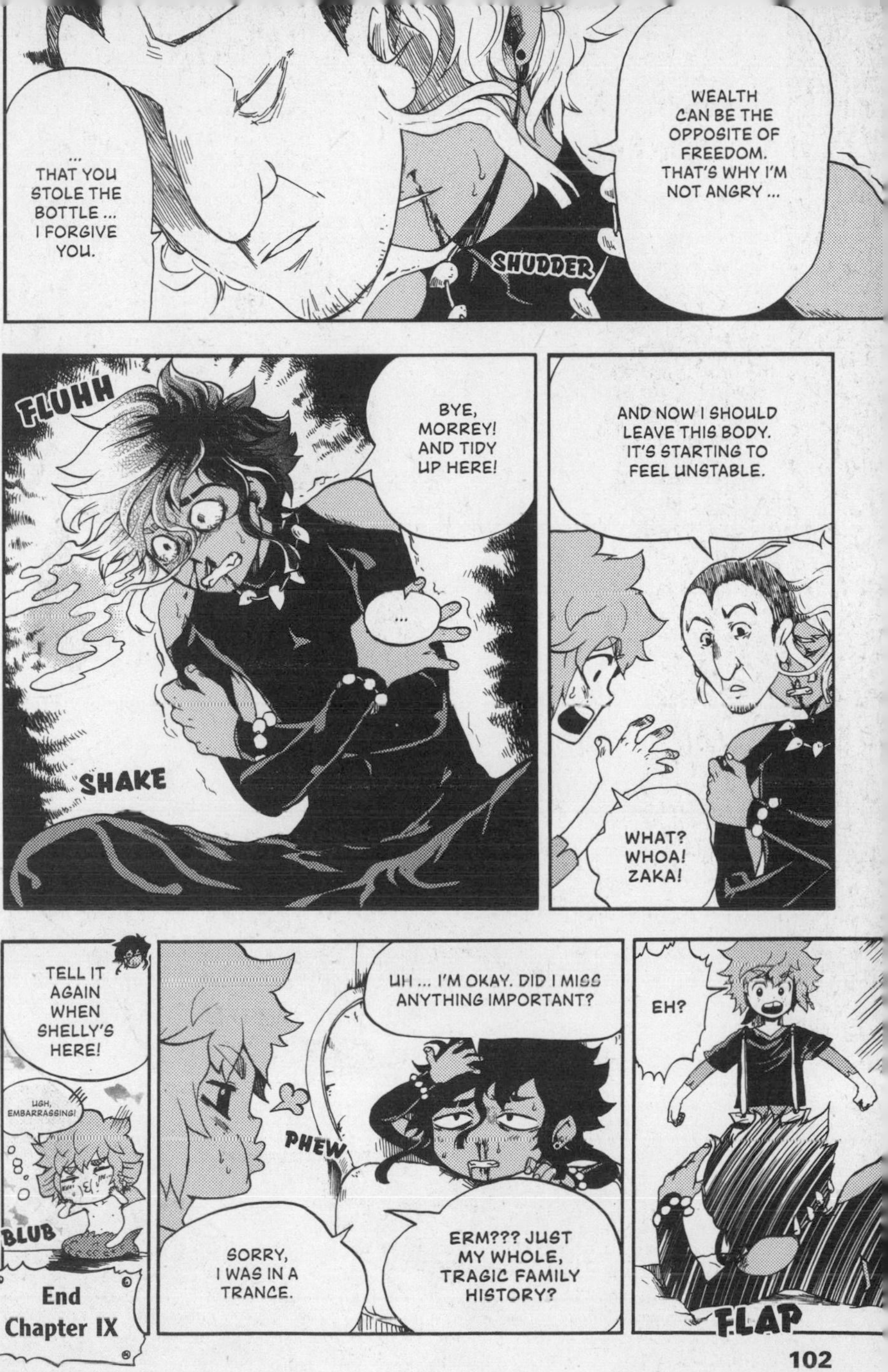
WEALTH CAN BE THE OPPOSITE OF FREEDOM. THAT'S WHY I'M NOT ANGRY ...
SHUDDER
... THAT YOU STOLE THE BOTTLE ... I FORGIVE YOU.
AND NOW I SHOULD LEAVE THIS BODY. IT'S STARTING TO FEEL UNSTABLE.
WHAT? WHOA! ZAKA!
BYE, MORREY! AND TIDY UP HERE!
FLUHH
...
SHAKE
EH?
F.LAP
UH ... I'M OKAY. DID I MISS ANYTHING IMPORTANT?
PHEW
ERM??? JUST MY WHOLE, TRAGIC FAMILY HISTORY?
SORRY, I WAS IN A TRANCE.
TELL IT AGAIN WHEN SHELLY'S HERE!
UGH, EMBARRASSING!
BLUB
End Chapter IX

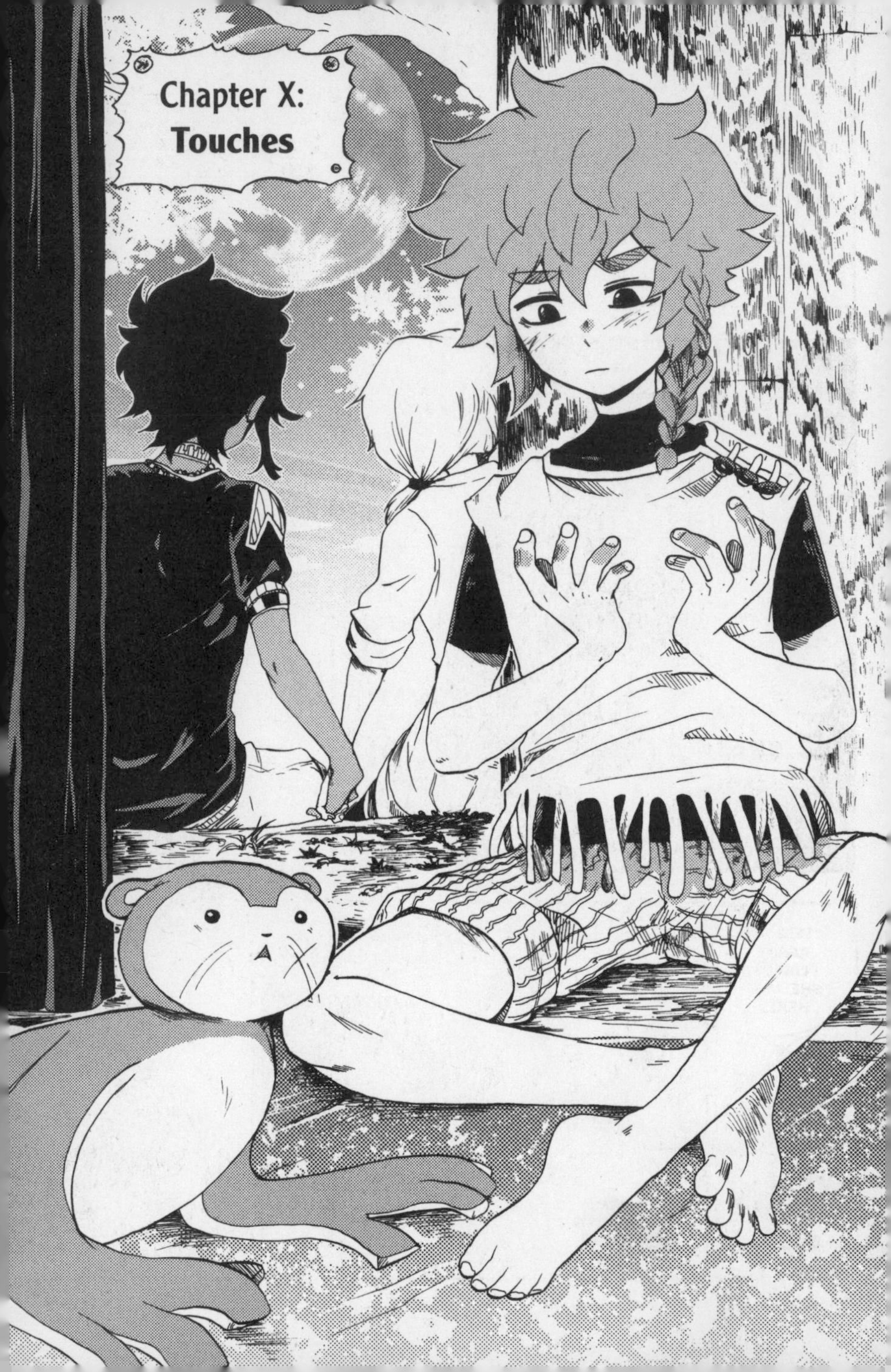
Chapter X:
Touches

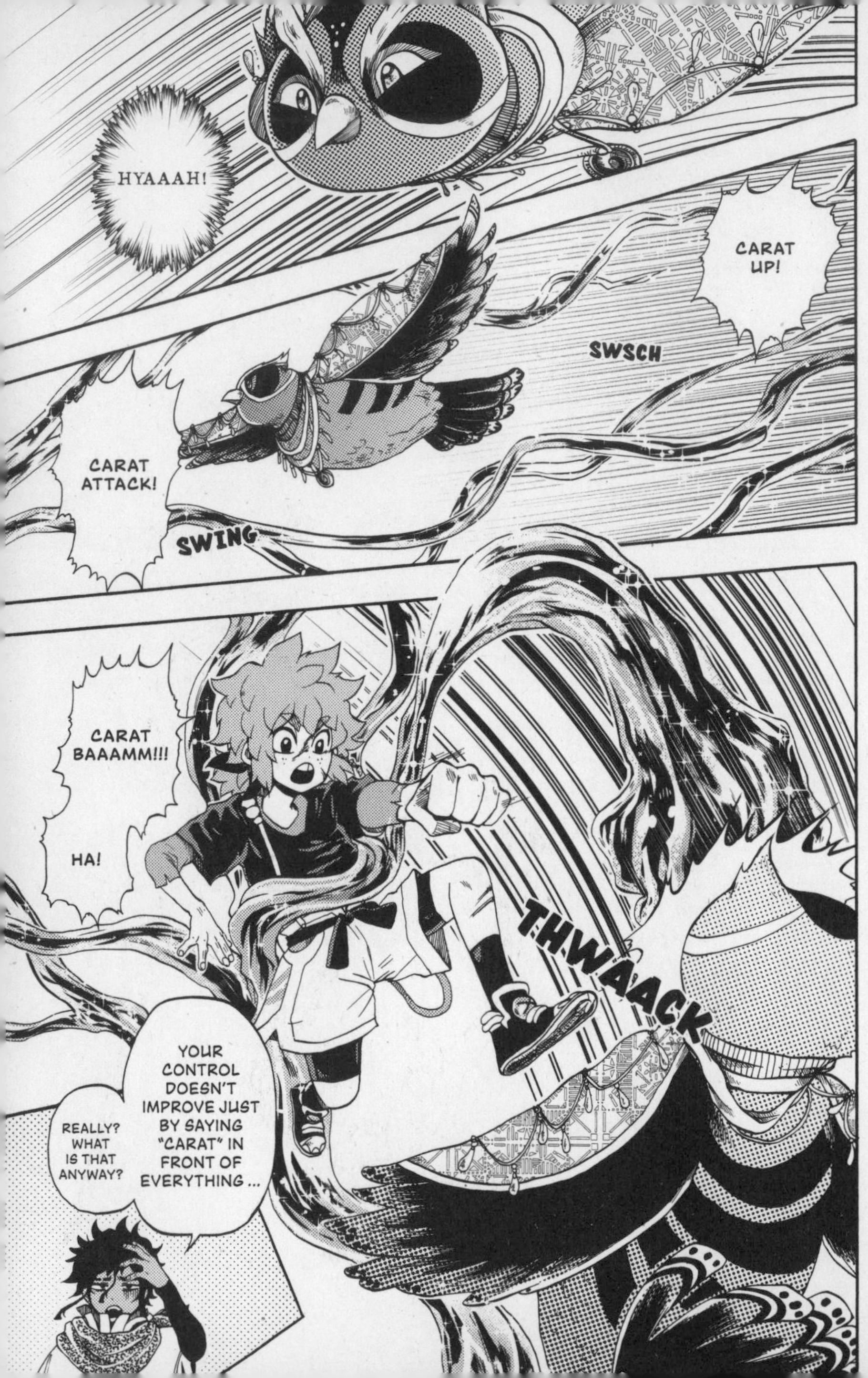
HYAAAH!
CARAT UP!
SWSCH
CARAT ATTACK!
SWING
CARAT BAAAMM!!!
HA!
THWAAACK
YOUR CONTROL DOESN'T IMPROVE JUST BY SAYING "CARAT" IN FRONT OF EVERYTHING ...
REALLY? WHAT IS THAT ANYWAY?

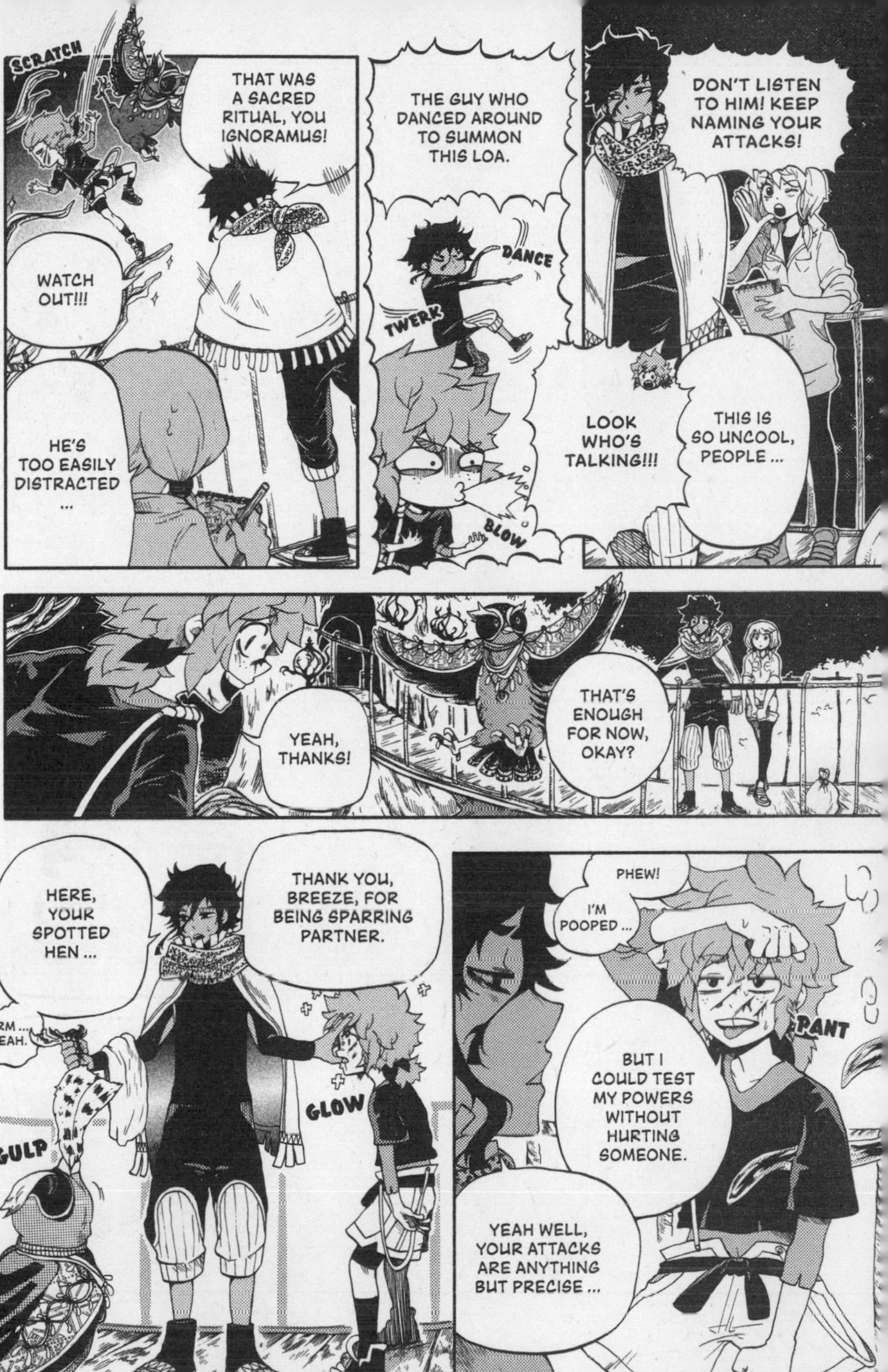
DON'T LISTEN TO HIM! KEEP NAMING YOUR ATTACKS!
THIS IS SO UNCOOL, PEOPLE ...
LOOK WHO'S TALKING!!!
THE GUY WHO DANCED AROUND TO SUMMON THIS LOA.
DANCE
TWERK
BLOW
THAT WAS A SACRED RITUAL, YOU IGNORAMUS!
SCRATCH
WATCH OUT!!!
HE'S TOO EASILY DISTRACTED ...
THAT'S ENOUGH FOR NOW, OKAY?
YEAH, THANKS!
PHEW!
I'M POOPED ...
PANT
BUT I COULD TEST MY POWERS WITHOUT HURTING SOMEONE.
YEAH WELL, YOUR ATTACKS ARE ANYTHING BUT PRECISE ...
THANK YOU, BREEZE, FOR BEING SPARRING PARTNER.
HERE, YOUR SPOTTED HEN ...
ERM ... YEAH.
GLOW
GULP

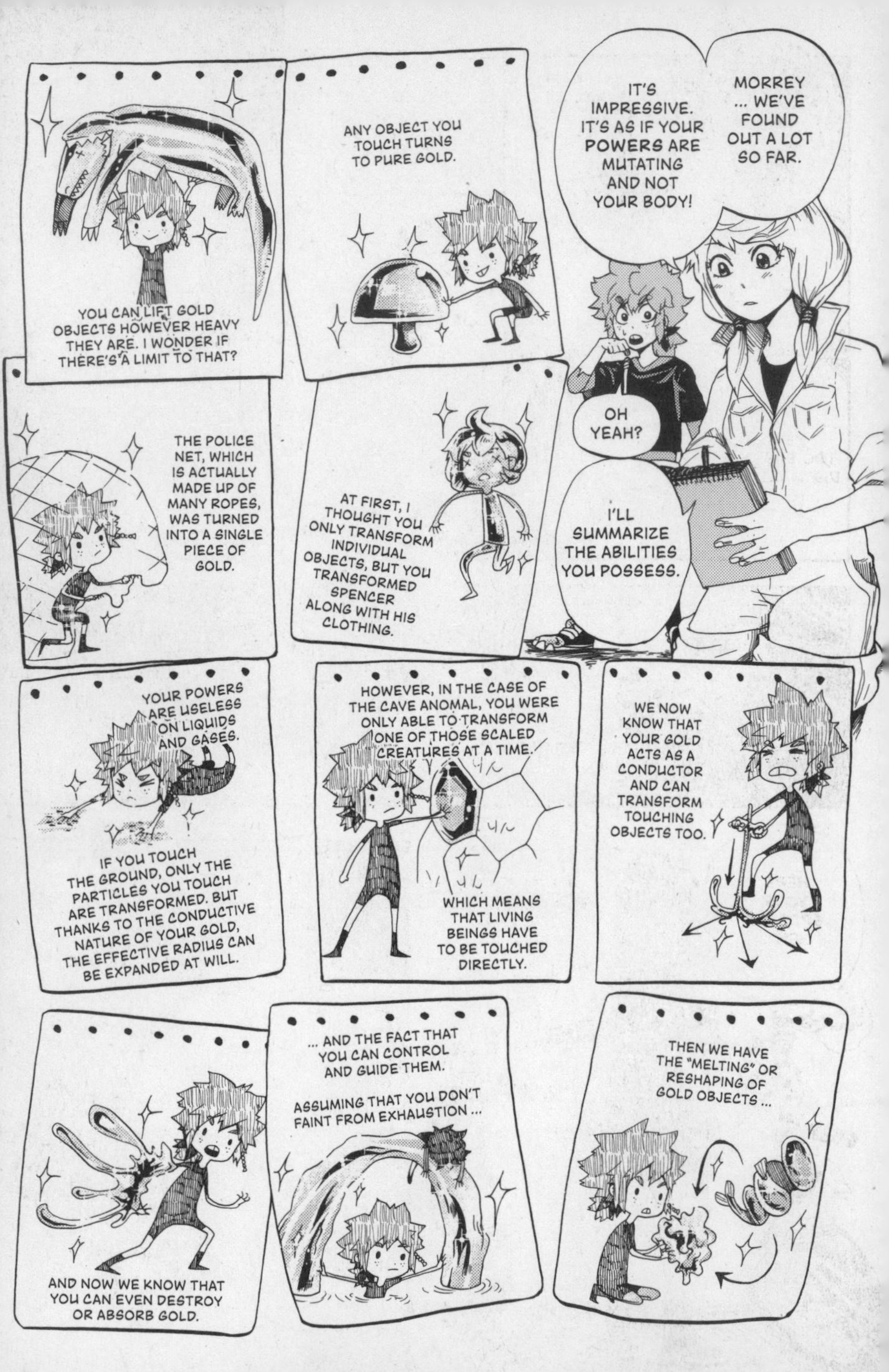
MORREY ... WE'VE FOUND OUT A LOT SO FAR.
IT'S IMPRESSIVE. IT'S AS IF YOUR POWERS ARE MUTATING AND NOT YOUR BODY!
OH YEAH?
I'LL SUMMARIZE THE ABILITIES YOU POSSESS.
ANY OBJECT YOU TOUCH TURNS TO PURE GOLD.
YOU CAN LIFT GOLD OBJECTS HOWEVER HEAVY THEY ARE. I WONDER IF THERE'S A LIMIT TO THAT?
AT FIRST, I THOUGHT YOU ONLY TRANSFORM INDIVIDUAL OBJECTS, BUT YOU TRANSFORMED SPENCER ALONG WITH HIS CLOTHING.
THE POLICE NET, WHICH IS ACTUALLY MADE UP OF MANY ROPES, WAS TURNED INTO A SINGLE PIECE OF GOLD.
WE NOW KNOW THAT YOUR GOLD ACTS AS A CONDUCTOR AND CAN TRANSFORM TOUCHING OBJECTS TOO.
HOWEVER, IN THE CASE OF THE CAVE ANOMAL, YOU WERE ONLY ABLE TO TRANSFORM ONE OF THOSE SCALED CREATURES AT A TIME.
WHICH MEANS THAT LIVING BEINGS HAVE TO BE TOUCHED DIRECTLY.
YOUR POWERS ARE USELESS ON LIQUIDS AND GASES.
IF YOU TOUCH THE GROUND, ONLY THE PARTICLES YOU TOUCH ARE TRANSFORMED. BUT THANKS TO THE CONDUCTIVE NATURE OF YOUR GOLD, THE EFFECTIVE RADIUS CAN BE EXPANDED AT WILL.
THEN WE HAVE THE "MELTING" OR RESHAPING OF GOLD OBJECTS ...
... AND THE FACT THAT YOU CAN CONTROL AND GUIDE THEM.
ASSUMING THAT YOU DON'T FAINT FROM EXHAUSTION ...
AND NOW WE KNOW THAT YOU CAN EVEN DESTROY OR ABSORB GOLD.

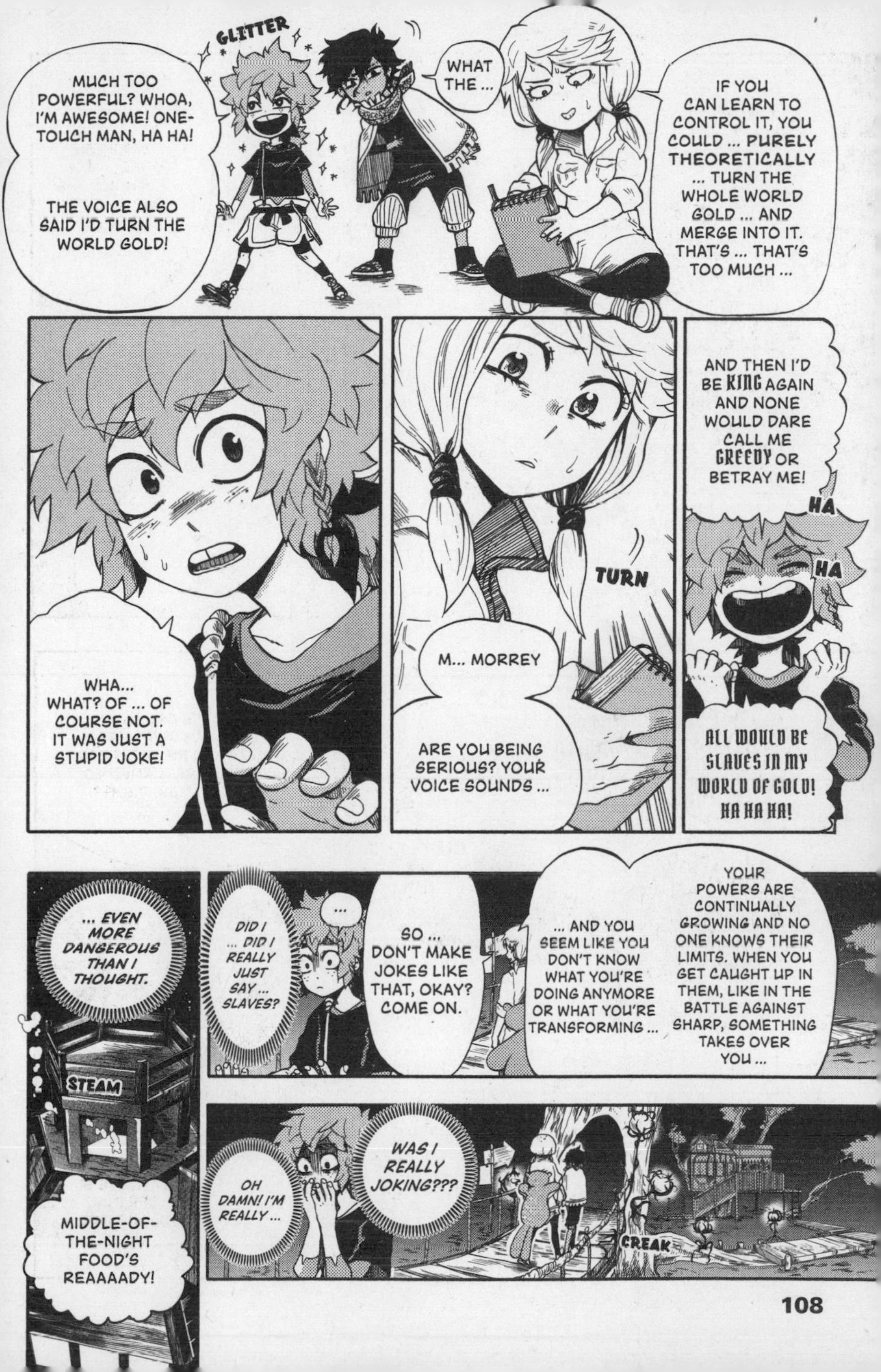
IF YOU CAN LEARN TO CONTROL IT, YOU COULD ... PURELY THEORETICALLY ... TURN THE WHOLE WORLD GOLD ... AND MERGE INTO IT. THAT'S ... THAT'S TOO MUCH ...
WHAT THE ...
GLITTER
MUCH TOO POWERFUL? WHOA, I'M AWESOME! ONE-TOUCH MAN, HA HA!
THE VOICE ALSO SAID I'D TURN THE WORLD GOLD!
AND THEN I'D BE KING AGAIN AND NONE WOULD DARE CALL ME GREEDY OR BETRAY ME!
HA
HA
ALL WOULD BE SLAVES IN MY WORLD OF GOLD! HA HA HA!
TURN
M... MORREY
ARE YOU BEING SERIOUS? YOUR VOICE SOUNDS ...
WHA... WHAT? OF ... OF COURSE NOT. IT WAS JUST A STUPID JOKE!
YOUR POWERS ARE CONTINUALLY GROWING AND NO ONE KNOWS THEIR LIMITS. WHEN YOU GET CAUGHT UP IN THEM, LIKE IN THE BATTLE AGAINST SHARP, SOMETHING TAKES OVER YOU ...
... AND YOU SEEM LIKE YOU DON'T KNOW WHAT YOU'RE DOING ANYMORE OR WHAT YOU'RE TRANSFORMING ...
SO ... DON'T MAKE JOKES LIKE THAT, OKAY? COME ON.
...
DID I ... DID I REALLY JUST SAY ... SLAVES?
WAS I REALLY JOKING???
OH DAMN! I'M REALLY ...
CREAK
... EVEN MORE DANGEROUS THAN I THOUGHT.
STEAM
MIDDLE-OF-THE-NIGHT FOOD'S REAAAADY!

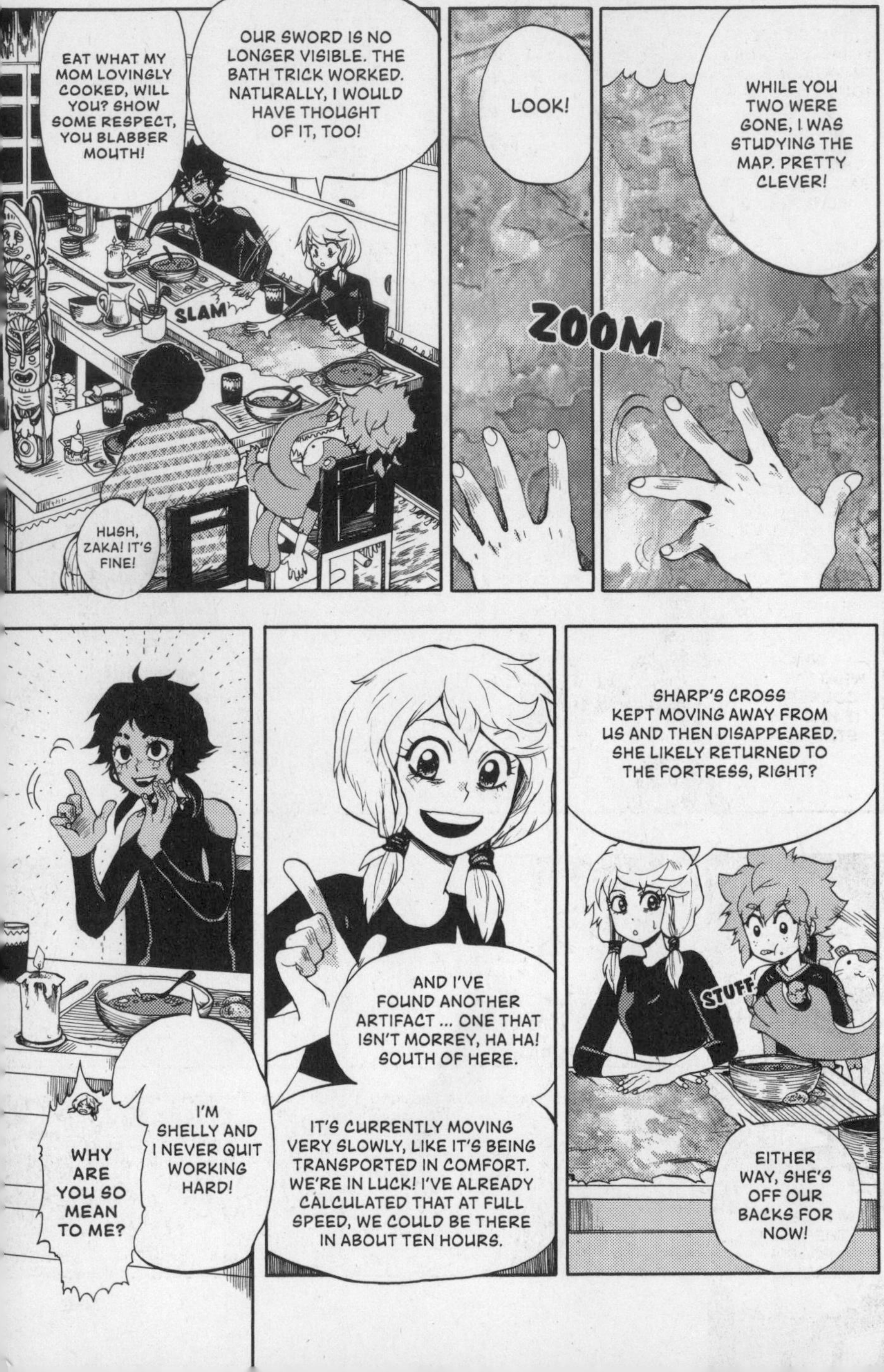
WHILE YOU TWO WERE GONE, I WAS STUDYING THE MAP. PRETTY CLEVER!
LOOK!
ZOOM
OUR SWORD IS NO LONGER VISIBLE. THE BATH TRICK WORKED. NATURALLY, I WOULD HAVE THOUGHT OF IT, TOO!
EAT WHAT MY MOM LOVINGLY COOKED, WILL YOU? SHOW SOME RESPECT, YOU BLABBER MOUTH!
SLAM
HUSH, ZAKA! IT'S FINE!
SHARP'S CROSS KEPT MOVING AWAY FROM US AND THEN DISAPPEARED. SHE LIKELY RETURNED TO THE FORTRESS, RIGHT?
STUFF
EITHER WAY, SHE'S OFF OUR BACKS FOR NOW!
AND I'VE FOUND ANOTHER ARTIFACT ... ONE THAT ISN'T MORREY, HA HA! SOUTH OF HERE.
IT'S CURRENTLY MOVING VERY SLOWLY, LIKE IT'S BEING TRANSPORTED IN COMFORT. WE'RE IN LUCK! I'VE ALREADY CALCULATED THAT AT FULL SPEED, WE COULD BE THERE IN ABOUT TEN HOURS.
I'M SHELLY AND I NEVER QUIT WORKING HARD!
WHY ARE YOU SO MEAN TO ME?

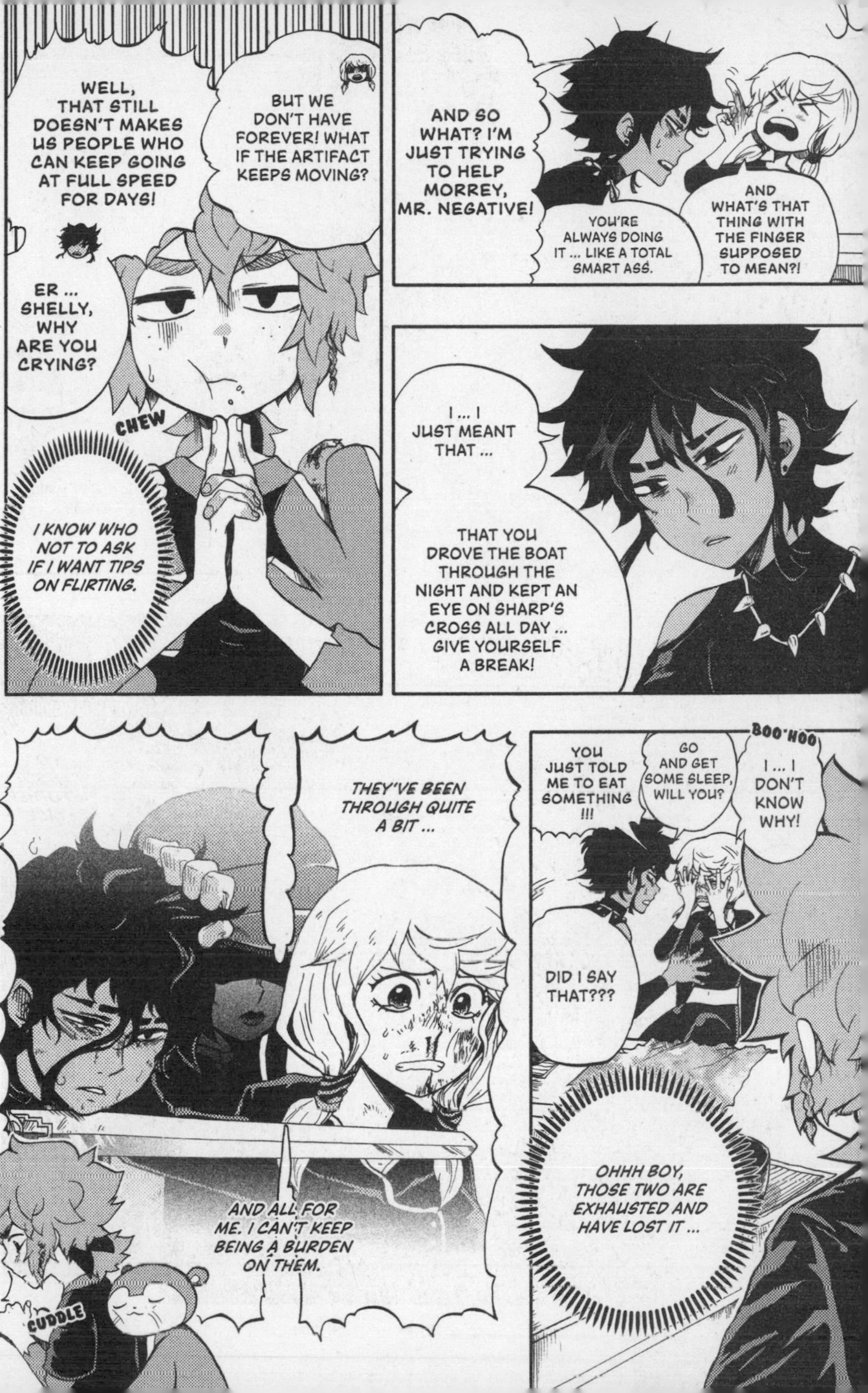
AND SO WHAT? I'M JUST TRYING TO HELP MORREY, MR. NEGATIVE!
AND WHAT'S THAT THING WITH THE FINGER SUPPOSED TO MEAN?!
YOU'RE ALWAYS DOING IT ... LIKE A TOTAL SMART ASS.
I ... I JUST MEANT THAT ...
THAT YOU DROVE THE BOAT THROUGH THE NIGHT AND KEPT AN EYE ON SHARP'S CROSS ALL DAY ... GIVE YOURSELF A BREAK!
BUT WE DON'T HAVE FOREVER! WHAT IF THE ARTIFACT KEEPS MOVING?
WELL, THAT STILL DOESN'T MAKES US PEOPLE WHO CAN KEEP GOING AT FULL SPEED FOR DAYS!
ER ... SHELLY, WHY ARE YOU CRYING?
CHEW
I KNOW WHO NOT TO ASK IF I WANT TIPS ON FLIRTING.
BOO-HOO
I ... I DON'T KNOW WHY!
GO AND GET SOME SLEEP, WILL YOU?
YOU JUST TOLD ME TO EAT SOMETHING !!!
DID I SAY THAT???
OHHH BOY, THOSE TWO ARE EXHAUSTED AND HAVE LOST IT ...
THEY'VE BEEN THROUGH QUITE A BIT ...
AND ALL FOR ME. I CAN'T KEEP BEING A BURDEN ON THEM.
CUDDLE

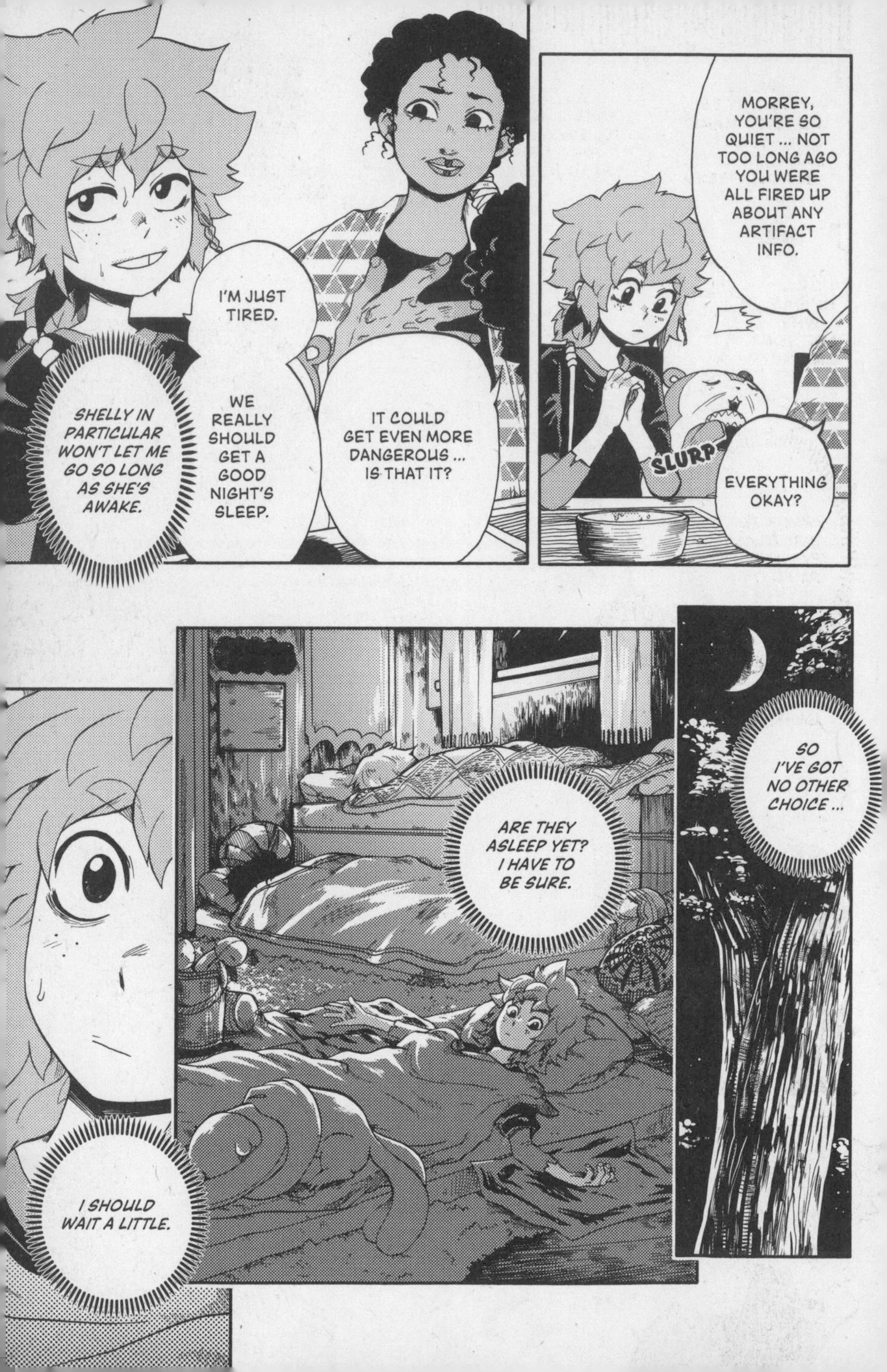
MORREY, YOU'RE SO QUIET ... NOT TOO LONG AGO YOU WERE ALL FIRED UP ABOUT ANY ARTIFACT INFO.
SLURP
EVERYTHING OKAY?
I'M JUST TIRED.
IT COULD GET EVEN MORE DANGEROUS ... IS THAT IT?
WE REALLY SHOULD GET A GOOD NIGHT'S SLEEP.
SHELLY IN PARTICULAR WON'T LET ME GO SO LONG AS SHE'S AWAKE.
SO I'VE GOT NO OTHER CHOICE ...
ARE THEY ASLEEP YET? I HAVE TO BE SURE.
I SHOULD WAIT A LITTLE.

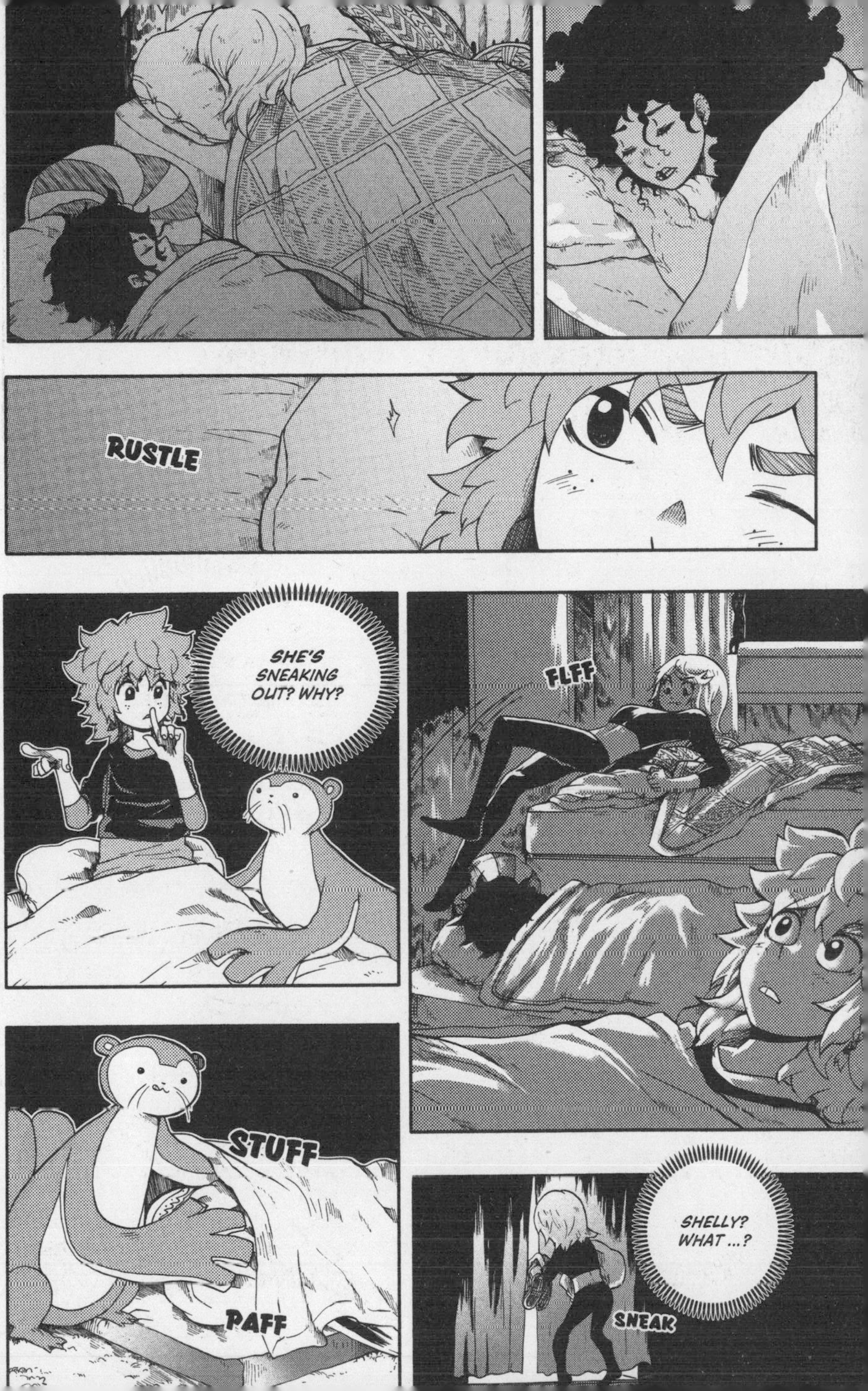
RUSTLE
FLFF
SHE'S SNEAKING OUT? WHY?
SHELLY? WHAT ...?
SNEAK
STUFF
PAFF

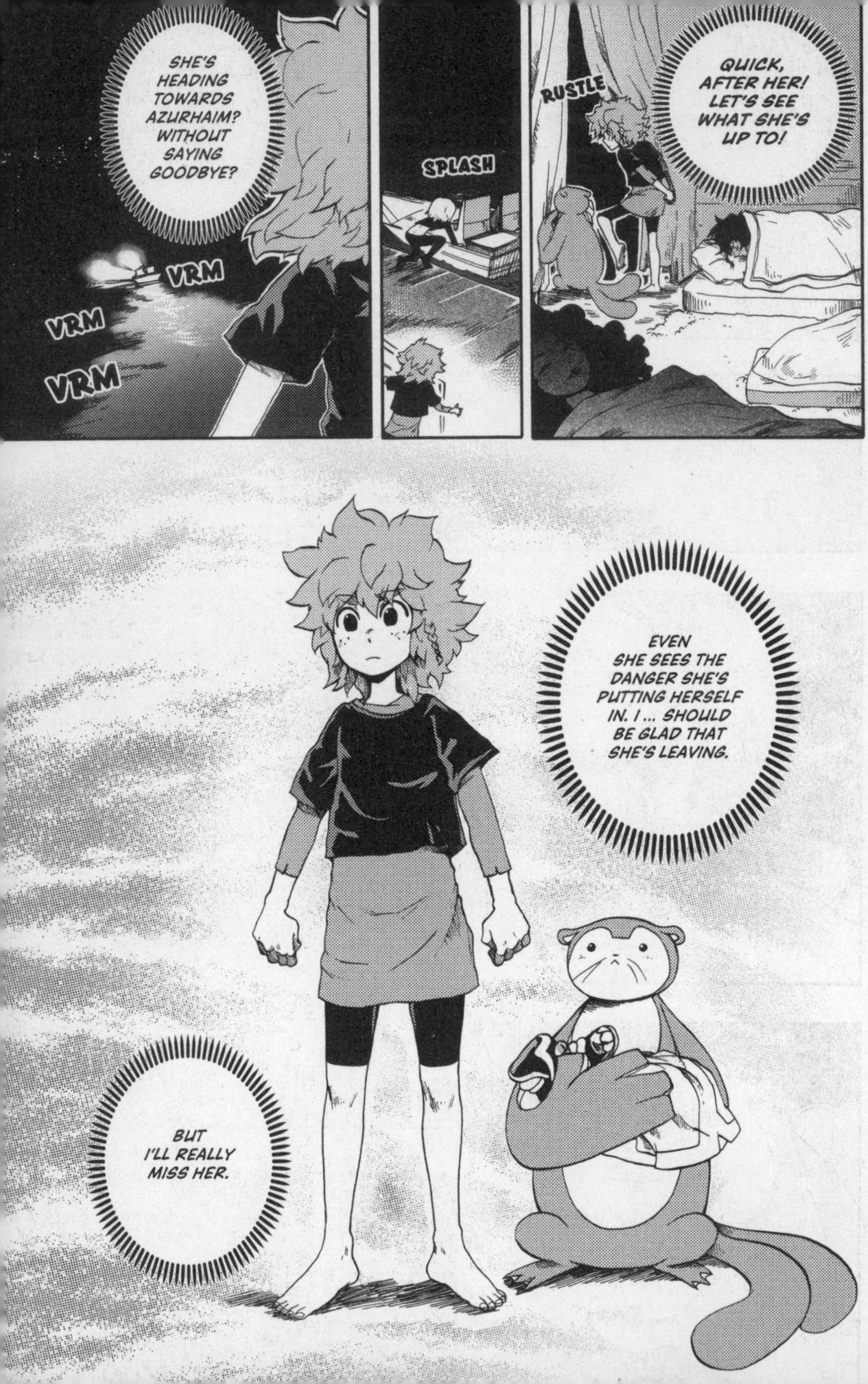
QUICK, AFTER HER! LET'S SEE WHAT SHE'S UP TO!
RUSTLE
SPLASH
SHE'S HEADING TOWARDS AZURHAIM? WITHOUT SAYING GOODBYE?
VRM
VRM
VRM
EVEN SHE SEES THE DANGER SHE'S PUTTING HERSELF IN. I ... SHOULD BE GLAD THAT SHE'S LEAVING.
BUT I'LL REALLY MISS HER.

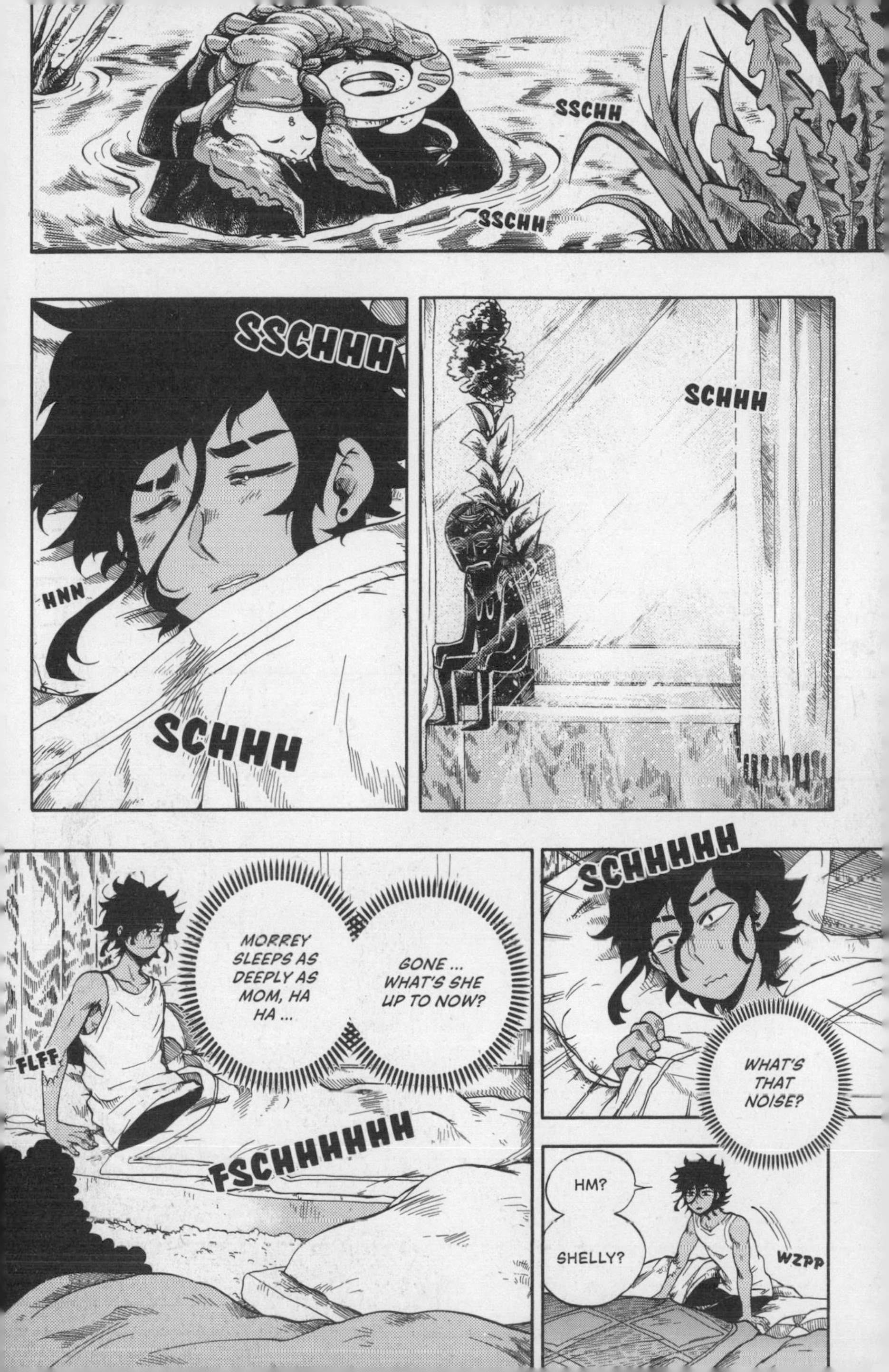
SSCHH
SSCHH
SCHHH
SSCHHH
HNN
SCHHH
SCHHHHH
WHAT'S THAT NOISE?
HM?
SHELLY?
WZPP
GONE ... WHAT'S SHE UP TO NOW?
MORREY SLEEPS AS DEEPLY AS MOM, HA HA ...
FLFF
FSCHHHHHH

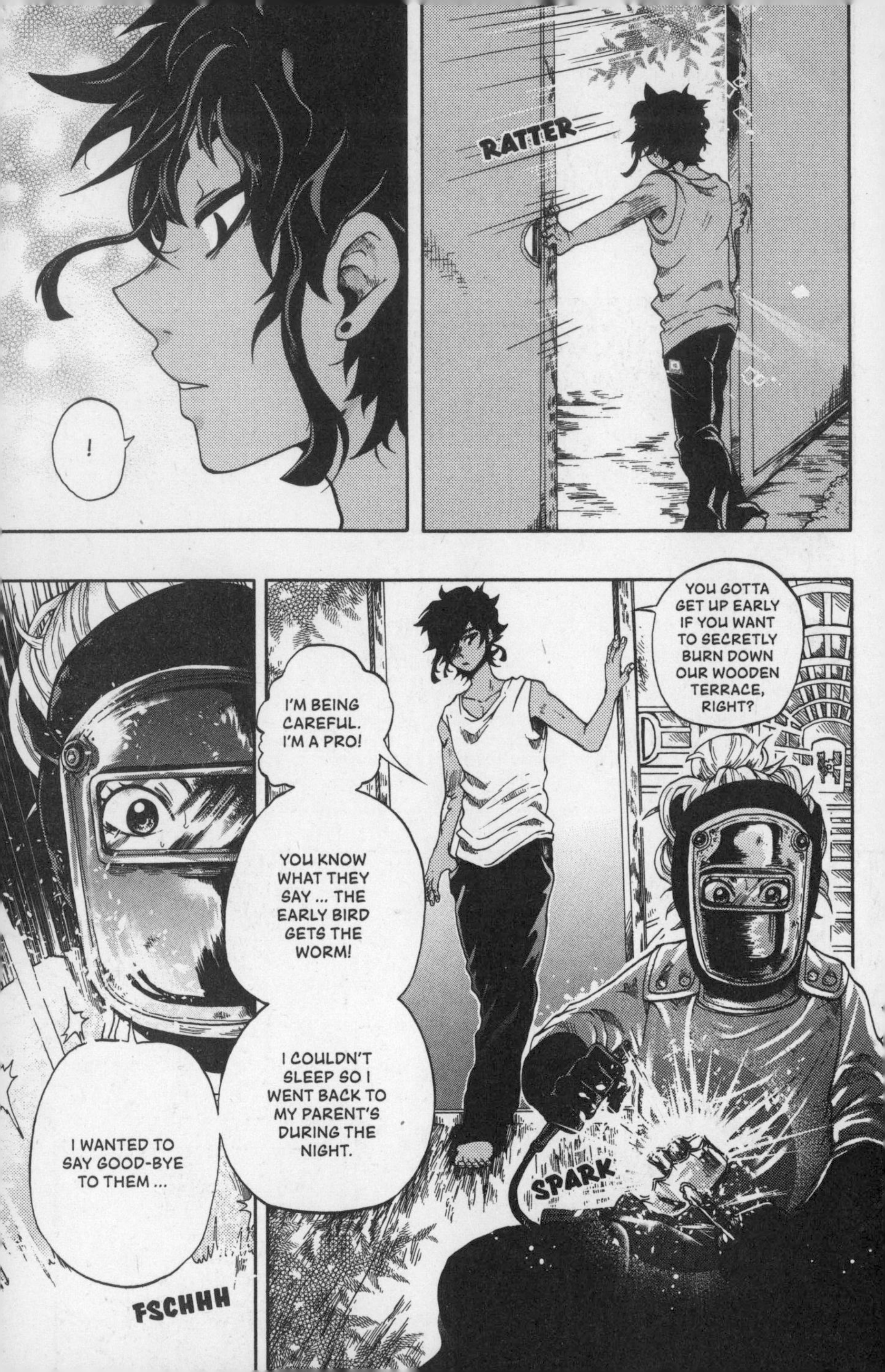
RATTER
!
YOU GOTTA GET UP EARLY IF YOU WANT TO SECRETLY BURN DOWN OUR WOODEN TERRACE, RIGHT?
I'M BEING CAREFUL. I'M A PRO!
YOU KNOW WHAT THEY SAY ... THE EARLY BIRD GETS THE WORM!
I COULDN'T SLEEP SO I WENT BACK TO MY PARENT'S DURING THE NIGHT.
SPARK
I WANTED TO SAY GOOD-BYE TO THEM ...
FSCHHH

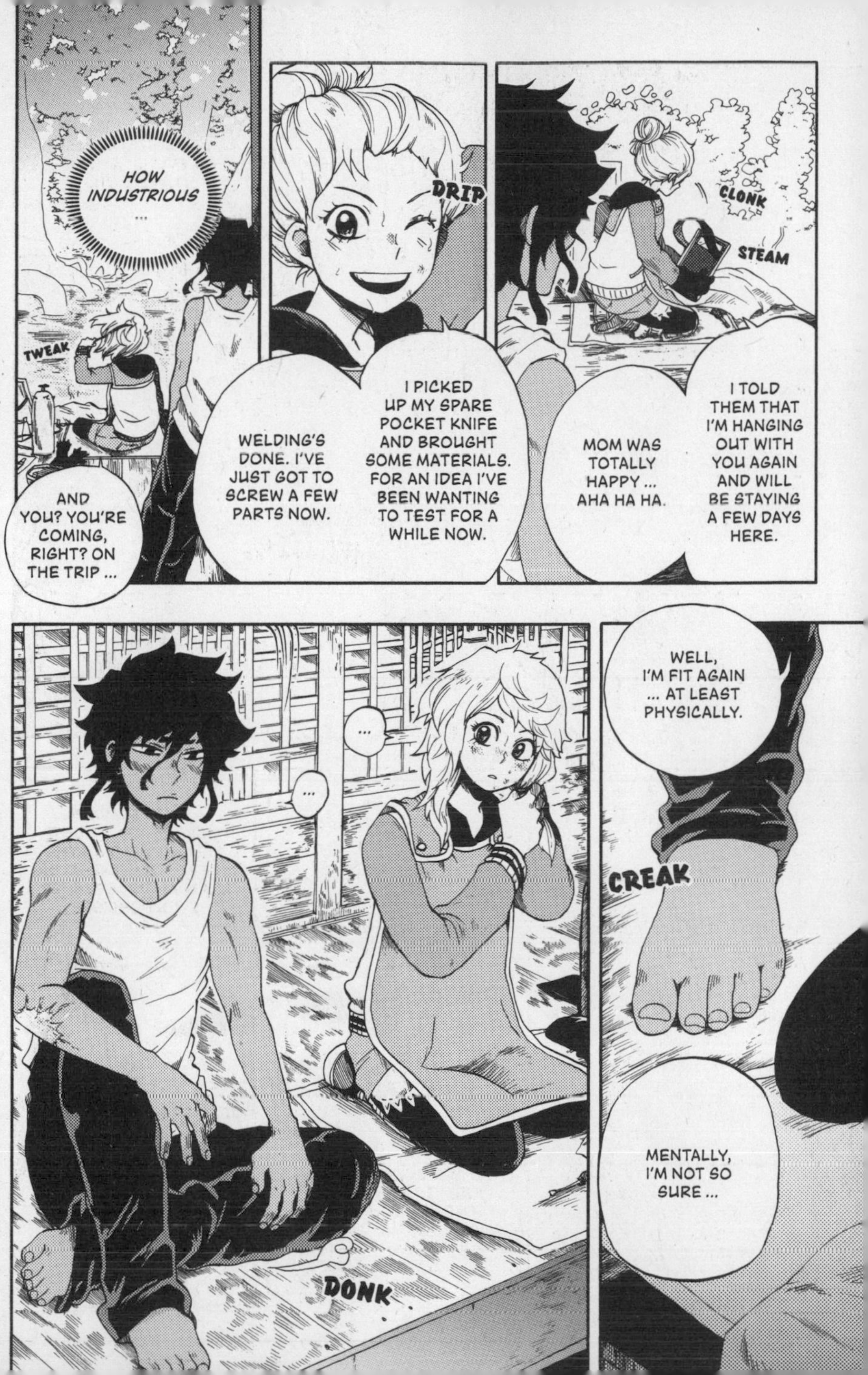
CLONK
STEAM
I TOLD THEM THAT I'M HANGING OUT WITH YOU AGAIN AND WILL BE STAYING A FEW DAYS HERE.
MOM WAS TOTALLY HAPPY ... AHA HA HA.
DRIP
I PICKED UP MY SPARE POCKET KNIFE AND BROUGHT SOME MATERIALS. FOR AN IDEA I'VE BEEN WANTING TO TEST FOR A WHILE NOW.
WELDING'S DONE. I'VE JUST GOT TO SCREW A FEW PARTS NOW.
HOW INDUSTRIOUS ...
TWEAK
AND YOU? YOU'RE COMING, RIGHT? ON THE TRIP ...
WELL, I'M FIT AGAIN ... AT LEAST PHYSICALLY.
CREAK
MENTALLY, I'M NOT SO SURE ...
...
...
DONK

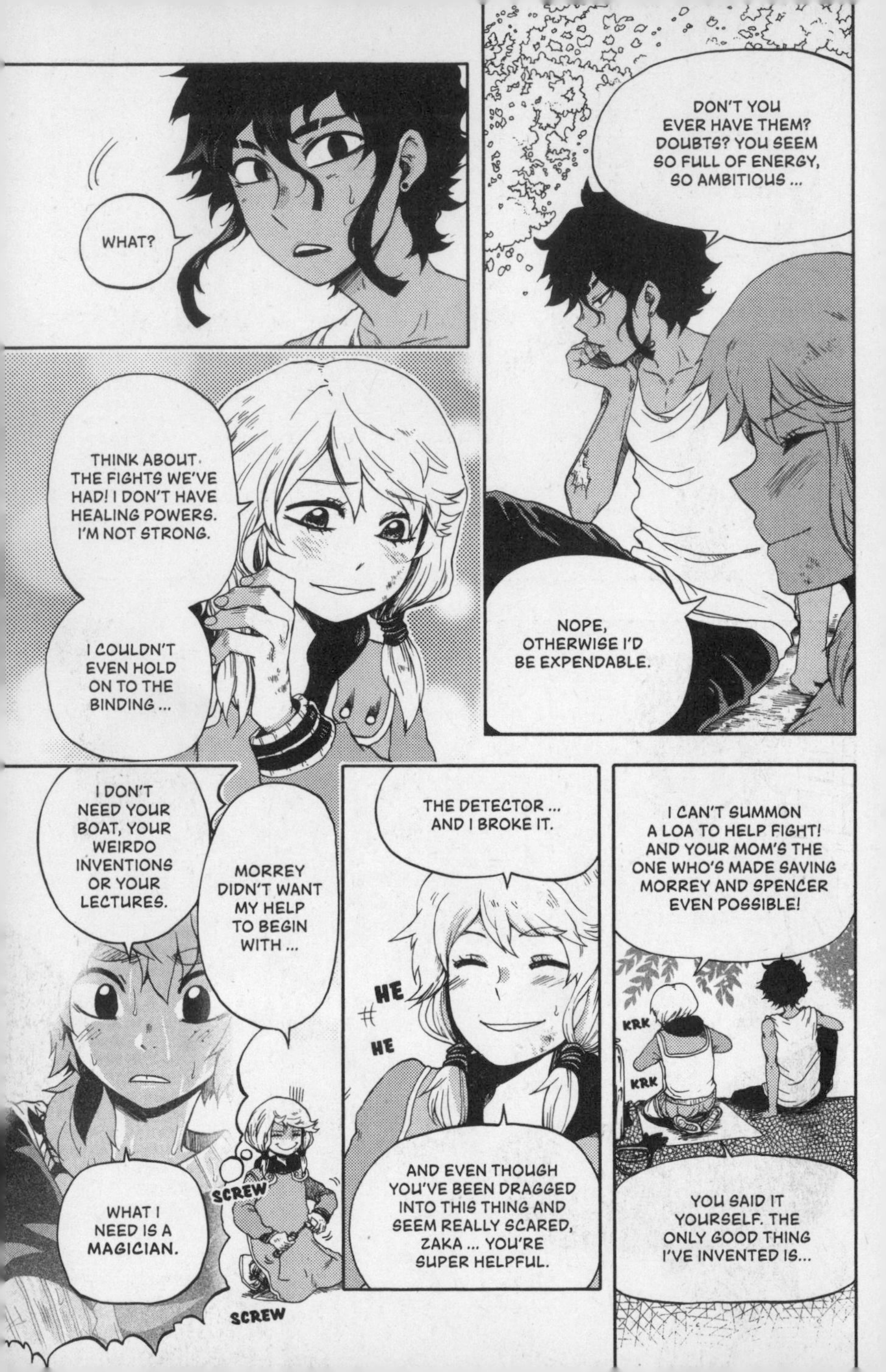
DON'T YOU EVER HAVE THEM? DOUBTS? YOU SEEM SO FULL OF ENERGY, SO AMBITIOUS ...
NOPE, OTHERWISE I'D BE EXPENDABLE.
WHAT?
THINK ABOUT THE FIGHTS WE'VE HAD! I DON'T HAVE HEALING POWERS. I'M NOT STRONG.
I COULDN'T EVEN HOLD ON TO THE BINDING ...
I CAN'T SUMMON A LOA TO HELP FIGHT! AND YOUR MOM'S THE ONE WHO'S MADE SAVING MORREY AND SPENCER EVEN POSSIBLE!
KRK
KRK
YOU SAID IT YOURSELF. THE ONLY GOOD THING I'VE INVENTED IS...
THE DETECTOR ... AND I BROKE IT.
HE
HE
AND EVEN THOUGH YOU'VE BEEN DRAGGED INTO THIS THING AND SEEM REALLY SCARED, ZAKA ... YOU'RE SUPER HELPFUL.
MORREY DIDN'T WANT MY HELP TO BEGIN WITH ...
I DON'T NEED YOUR BOAT, YOUR WEIRDO INVENTIONS OR YOUR LECTURES.
SCREW
WHAT I NEED IS A MAGICIAN.
SCREW

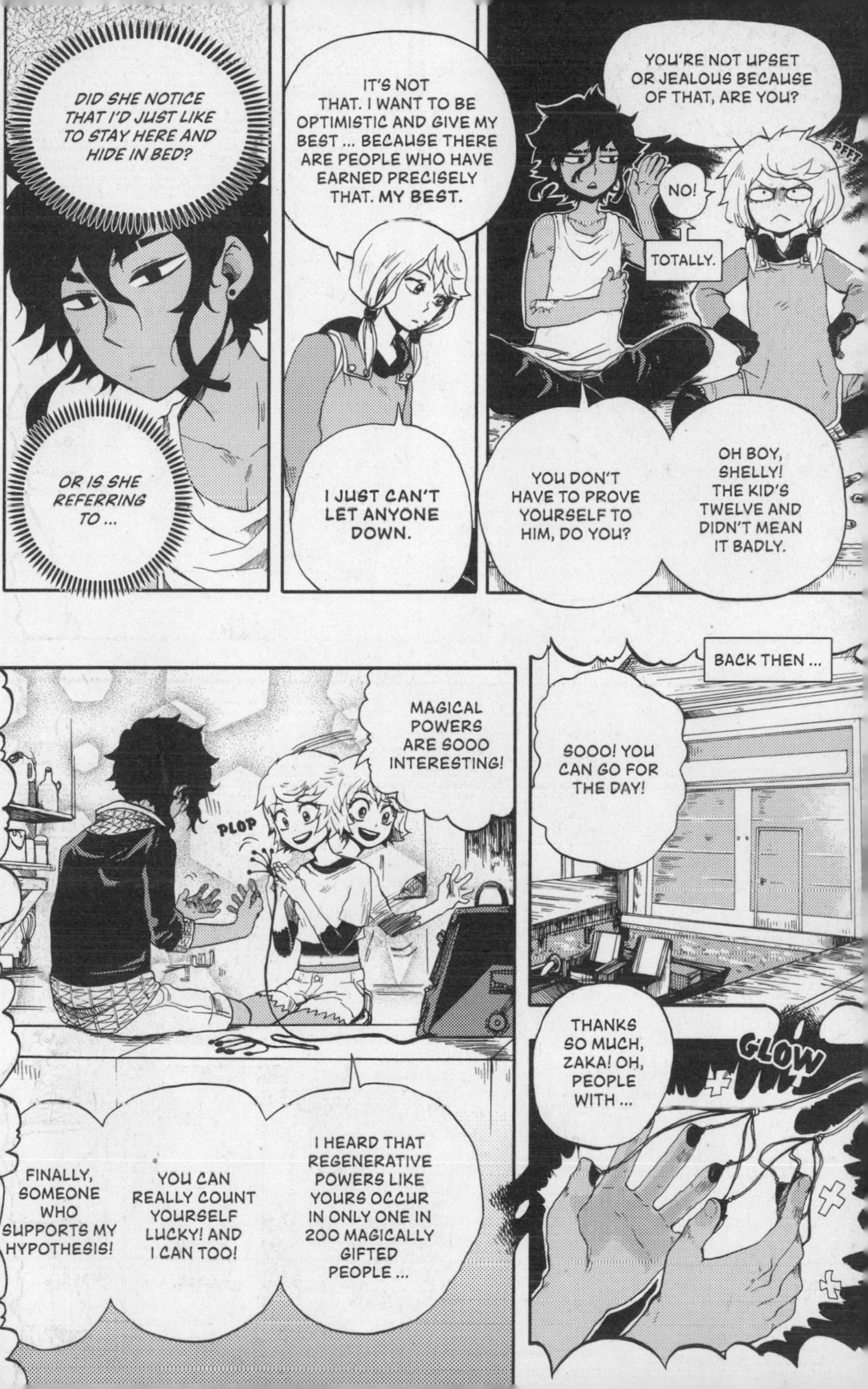

YOU'RE NOT UPSET OR JEALOUS BECAUSE OF THAT, ARE YOU?
PFFT
NO!
TOTALLY.
OH BOY, SHELLY! THE KID'S TWELVE AND DIDN'T MEAN IT BADLY.
YOU DON'T HAVE TO PROVE YOURSELF TO HIM, DO YOU?
IT'S NOT THAT. I WANT TO BE OPTIMISTIC AND GIVE MY BEST ... BECAUSE THERE ARE PEOPLE WHO HAVE EARNED PRECISELY THAT. MY BEST.
I JUST CAN'T LET ANYONE DOWN.
DID SHE NOTICE THAT I'D JUST LIKE TO STAY HERE AND HIDE IN BED?
OR IS SHE REFERRING TO ...
BACK THEN ...
SOOO! YOU CAN GO FOR THE DAY!
THANKS SO MUCH, ZAKA! OH, PEOPLE WITH ...
GLOW
MAGICAL POWERS ARE SOOO INTERESTING!
PLOP
I HEARD THAT REGENERATIVE POWERS LIKE YOURS OCCUR IN ONLY ONE IN 200 MAGICALLY GIFTED PEOPLE ...
YOU CAN REALLY COUNT YOURSELF LUCKY! AND I CAN TOO!
FINALLY, SOMEONE WHO SUPPORTS MY HYPOTHESIS!

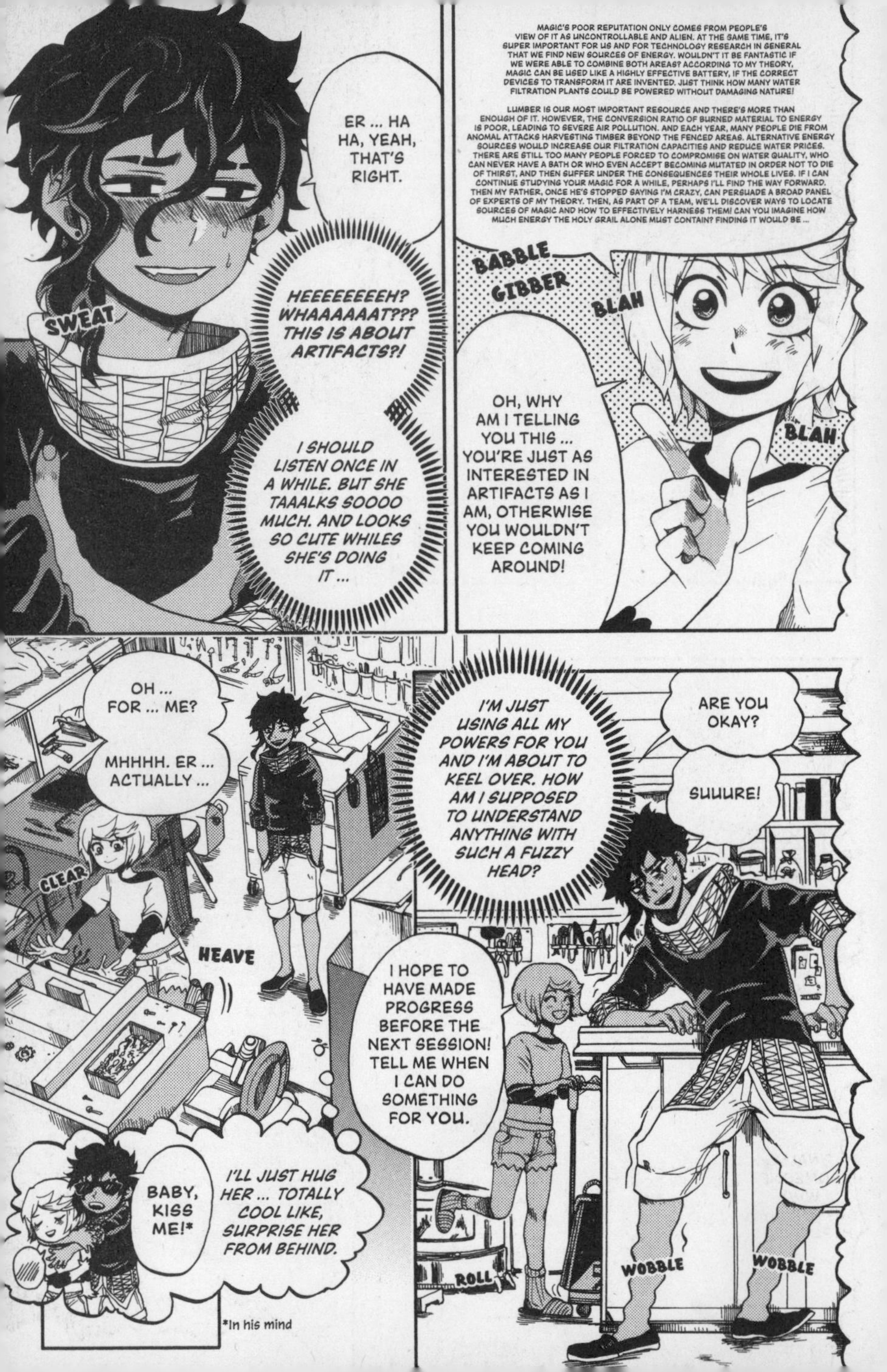
MAGIC'S POOR REPUTATION ONLY COMES FROM PEOPLE'S VIEW OF IT AS UNCONTROLLABLE AND ALIEN. AT THE SAME TIME, IT'S SUPER IMPORTANT FOR US AND FOR TECHNOLOGY RESEARCH IN GENERAL THAT WE FIND NEW SOURCES OF ENERGY. WOULDN'T IT BE FANTASTIC IF WE WERE ABLE TO COMBINE BOTH AREAS? ACCORDING TO MY THEORY, MAGIC CAN BE USED LIKE A HIGHLY EFFECTIVE BATTERY, IF THE CORRECT DEVICES TO TRANSFORM IT ARE INVENTED. JUST THINK HOW MANY WATER FILTRATION PLANTS COULD BE POWERED WITHOUT DAMAGING NATURE!
LUMBER IS OUR MOST IMPORTANT RESOURCE AND THERE'S MORE THAN ENOUGH OF IT. HOWEVER, THE CONVERSION RATIO OF BURNED MATERIAL TO ENERGY IS POOR, LEADING TO SEVERE AIR POLLUTION. AND EACH YEAR, MANY PEOPLE DIE FROM ANOMAL ATTACKS HARVESTING TIMBER BEYOND THE FENCED AREAS. ALTERNATIVE ENERGY SOURCES WOULD INCREASE OUR FILTRATION CAPACITIES AND REDUCE WATER PRICES. THERE ARE STILL TOO MANY PEOPLE FORCED TO COMPROMISE ON WATER QUALITY, WHO CAN NEVER HAVE A BATH OR WHO EVEN ACCEPT BECOMING MUTATED IN ORDER NOT TO DIE OF THIRST, AND THEN SUFFER UNDER THE CONSEQUENCES THEIR WHOLE LIVES. IF I CAN CONTINUE STUDYING YOUR MAGIC FOR A WHILE, PERHAPS I'LL FIND THE WAY FORWARD. THEN MY FATHER, ONCE HE'S STOPPED SAYING I'M CRAZY, CAN PERSUADE A BROAD PANEL OF EXPERTS OF MY THEORY. THEN, AS PART OF A TEAM, WE'LL DISCOVER WAYS TO LOCATE SOURCES OF MAGIC AND HOW TO EFFECTIVELY HARNESS THEM! CAN YOU IMAGINE HOW MUCH ENERGY THE HOLY GRAIL ALONE MUST CONTAIN? FINDING IT WOULD BE ...
BABBLE
GIBBER
BLAH
BLAH
OH, WHY AM I TELLING YOU THIS ... YOU'RE JUST AS INTERESTED IN ARTIFACTS AS I AM, OTHERWISE YOU WOULDN'T KEEP COMING AROUND!
ER ... HA HA, YEAH, THAT'S RIGHT.
SWEAT
HEEEEEEEEH? WHAAAAAAT??? THIS IS ABOUT ARTIFACTS?!
I SHOULD LISTEN ONCE IN A WHILE. BUT SHE TAAALKS SOOOO MUCH. AND LOOKS SO CUTE WHILES SHE'S DOING IT ...
ARE YOU OKAY?
SUUURE!
I'M JUST USING ALL MY POWERS FOR YOU AND I'M ABOUT TO KEEL OVER. HOW AM I SUPPOSED TO UNDERSTAND ANYTHING WITH SUCH A FUZZY HEAD?
I HOPE TO HAVE MADE PROGRESS BEFORE THE NEXT SESSION! TELL ME WHEN I CAN DO SOMETHING FOR YOU.
WOBBLE
WOBBLE
ROLL
OH ... FOR ... ME?
MHHHH. ER ... ACTUALLY ...
CLEAR
HEAVE
I'LL JUST HUG HER ... TOTALLY COOL LIKE, SURPRISE HER FROM BEHIND.
BABY, KISS ME!*
*In his mind

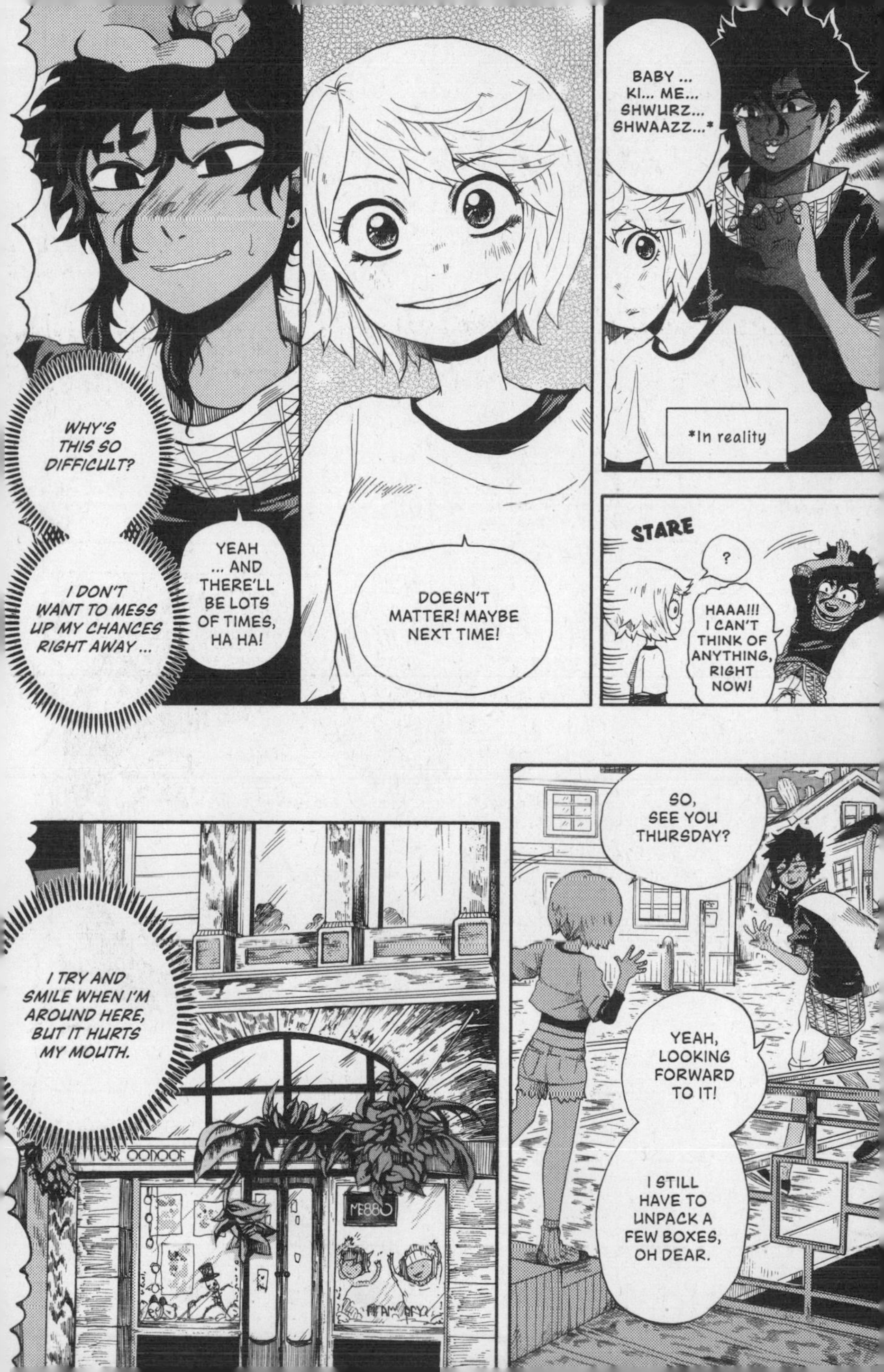
BABY ... KI... ME... SHWURZ... SHWAAZZ...*
*In reality
STARE
?
HAAA!!! I CAN'T THINK OF ANYTHING, RIGHT NOW!
DOESN'T MATTER! MAYBE NEXT TIME!
YEAH ... AND THERE'LL BE LOTS OF TIMES, HA HA!
WHY'S THIS SO DIFFICULT?
I DON'T WANT TO MESS UP MY CHANCES RIGHT AWAY ...
SO, SEE YOU THURSDAY?
YEAH, LOOKING FORWARD TO IT!
I STILL HAVE TO UNPACK A FEW BOXES, OH DEAR.
I TRY AND SMILE WHEN I'M AROUND HERE, BUT IT HURTS MY MOUTH.

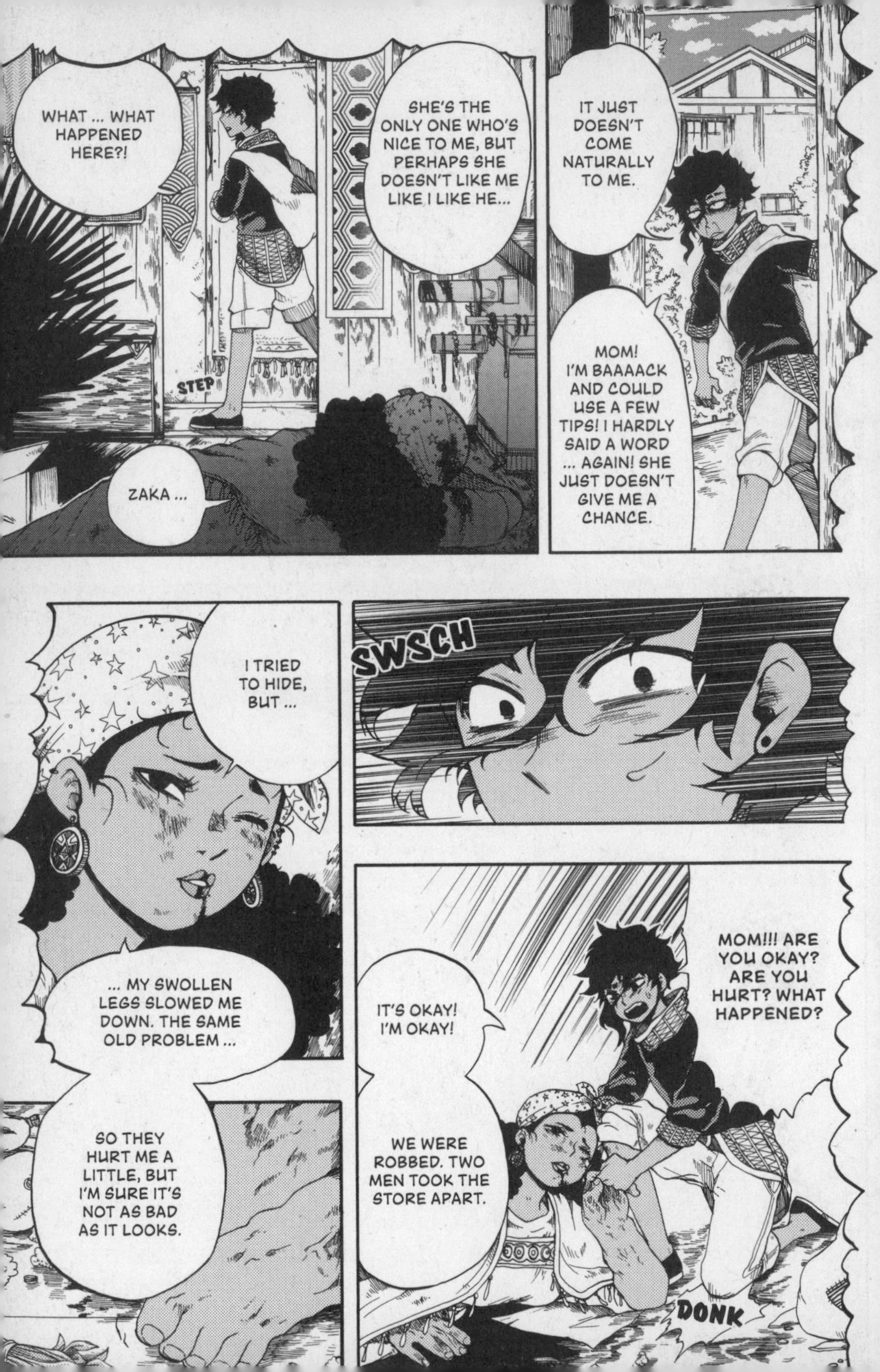
IT JUST DOESN'T COME NATURALLY TO ME.
MOM! I'M BAAAACK AND COULD USE A FEW TIPS! I HARDLY SAID A WORD ... AGAIN! SHE JUST DOESN'T GIVE ME A CHANCE.
SHE'S THE ONLY ONE WHO'S NICE TO ME, BUT PERHAPS SHE DOESN'T LIKE ME LIKE I LIKE HE...
WHAT ... WHAT HAPPENED HERE?!
STEP
ZAKA ...
SWSCH
MOM!!! ARE YOU OKAY? ARE YOU HURT? WHAT HAPPENED?
IT'S OKAY! I'M OKAY!
WE WERE ROBBED. TWO MEN TOOK THE STORE APART.
DONK
I TRIED TO HIDE, BUT ...
... MY SWOLLEN LEGS SLOWED ME DOWN. THE SAME OLD PROBLEM ...
SO THEY HURT ME A LITTLE, BUT I'M SURE IT'S NOT AS BAD AS IT LOOKS.

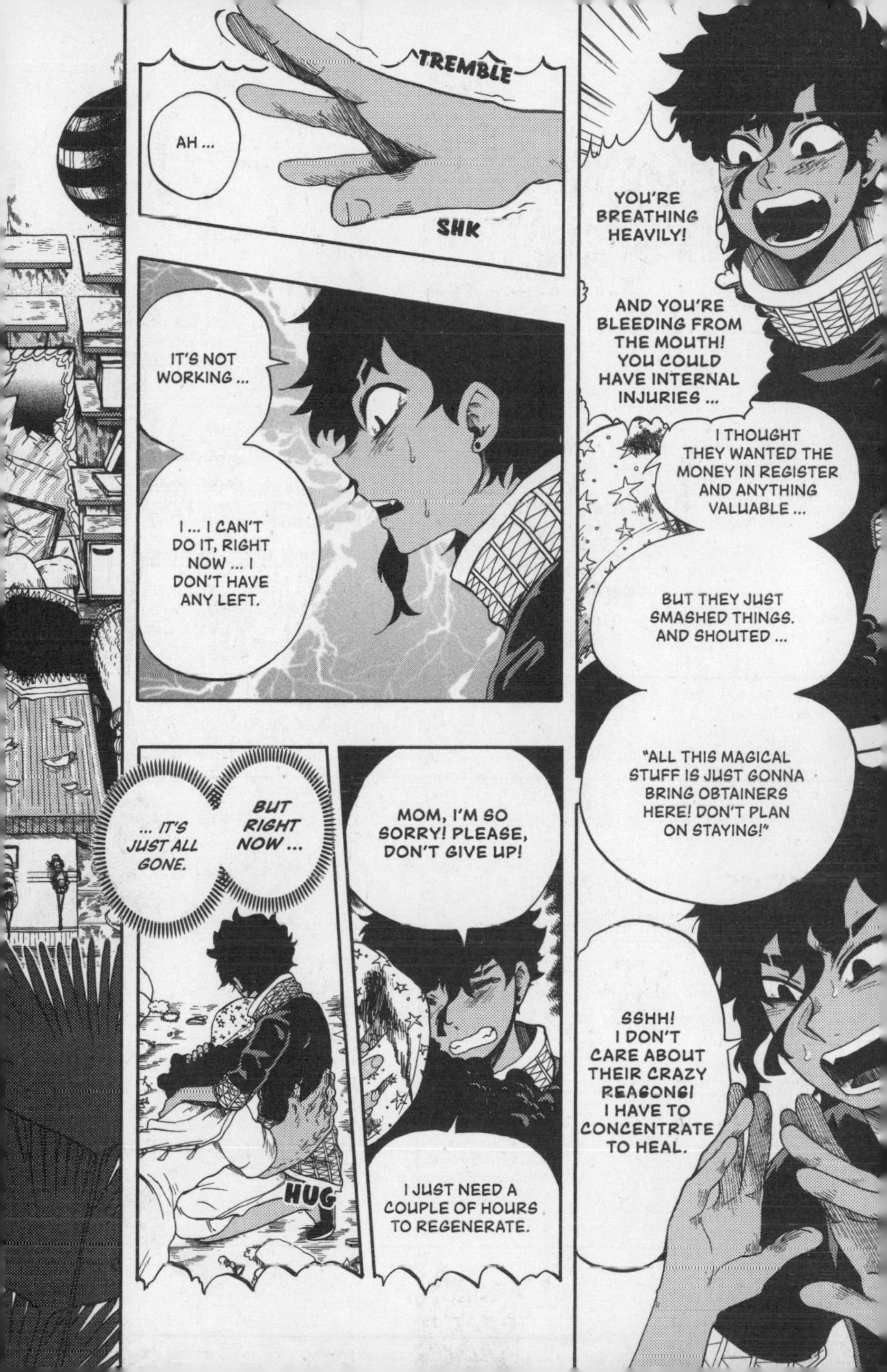
YOU'RE BREATHING HEAVILY!
AND YOU'RE BLEEDING FROM THE MOUTH! YOU COULD HAVE INTERNAL INJURIES ...
I THOUGHT THEY WANTED THE MONEY IN REGISTER AND ANYTHING VALUABLE ...
BUT THEY JUST SMASHED THINGS. AND SHOUTED ...
"ALL THIS MAGICAL STUFF IS JUST GONNA BRING OBTAINERS HERE! DON'T PLAN ON STAYING!"
SSHH! I DON'T CARE ABOUT THEIR CRAZY REASONS! I HAVE TO CONCENTRATE TO HEAL.
TREMBLE
AH ...
SHK
IT'S NOT WORKING ...
I ... I CAN'T DO IT, RIGHT NOW ... I DON'T HAVE ANY LEFT.
MOM, I'M SO SORRY! PLEASE, DON'T GIVE UP!
I JUST NEED A COUPLE OF HOURS TO REGENERATE.
BUT RIGHT NOW ...
... IT'S JUST ALL GONE.
HUG

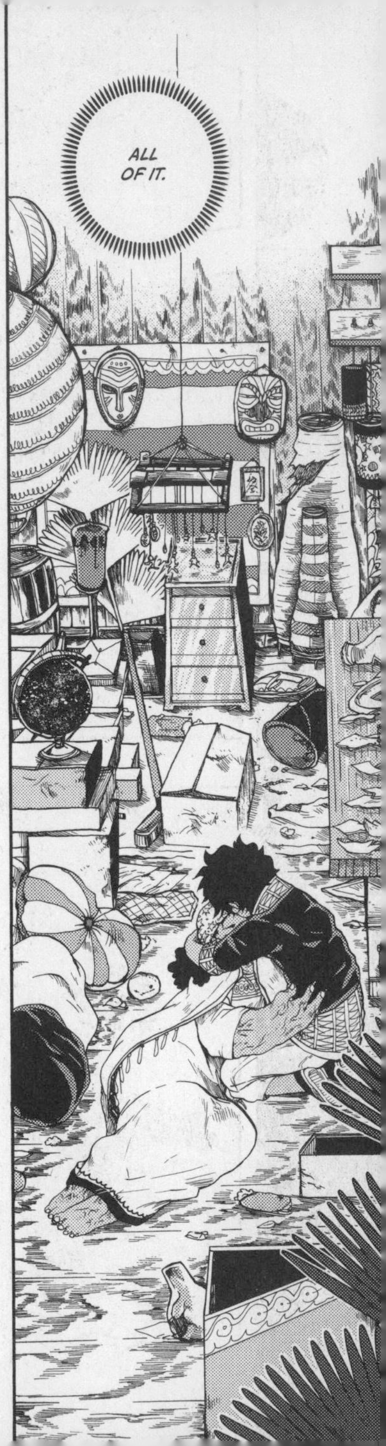
ALL OF IT.

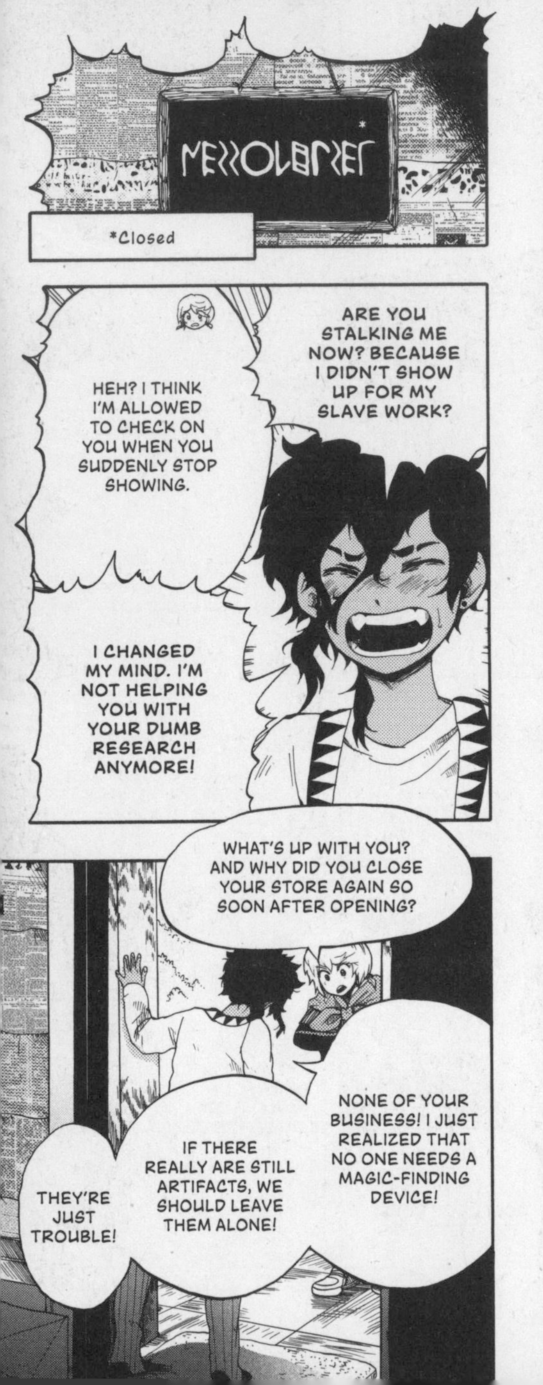
*Closed
ARE YOU STALKING ME NOW? BECAUSE I DIDN'T SHOW UP FOR MY SLAVE WORK?
HEH? I THINK I'M ALLOWED TO CHECK ON YOU WHEN YOU SUDDENLY STOP SHOWING.
I CHANGED MY MIND. I'M NOT HELPING YOU WITH YOUR DUMB RESEARCH ANYMORE!
WHAT'S UP WITH YOU? AND WHY DID YOU CLOSE YOUR STORE AGAIN SO SOON AFTER OPENING?
NONE OF YOUR BUSINESS! I JUST REALIZED THAT NO ONE NEEDS A MAGIC-FINDING DEVICE!
IF THERE REALLY ARE STILL ARTIFACTS, WE SHOULD LEAVE THEM ALONE!
THEY'RE JUST TROUBLE!

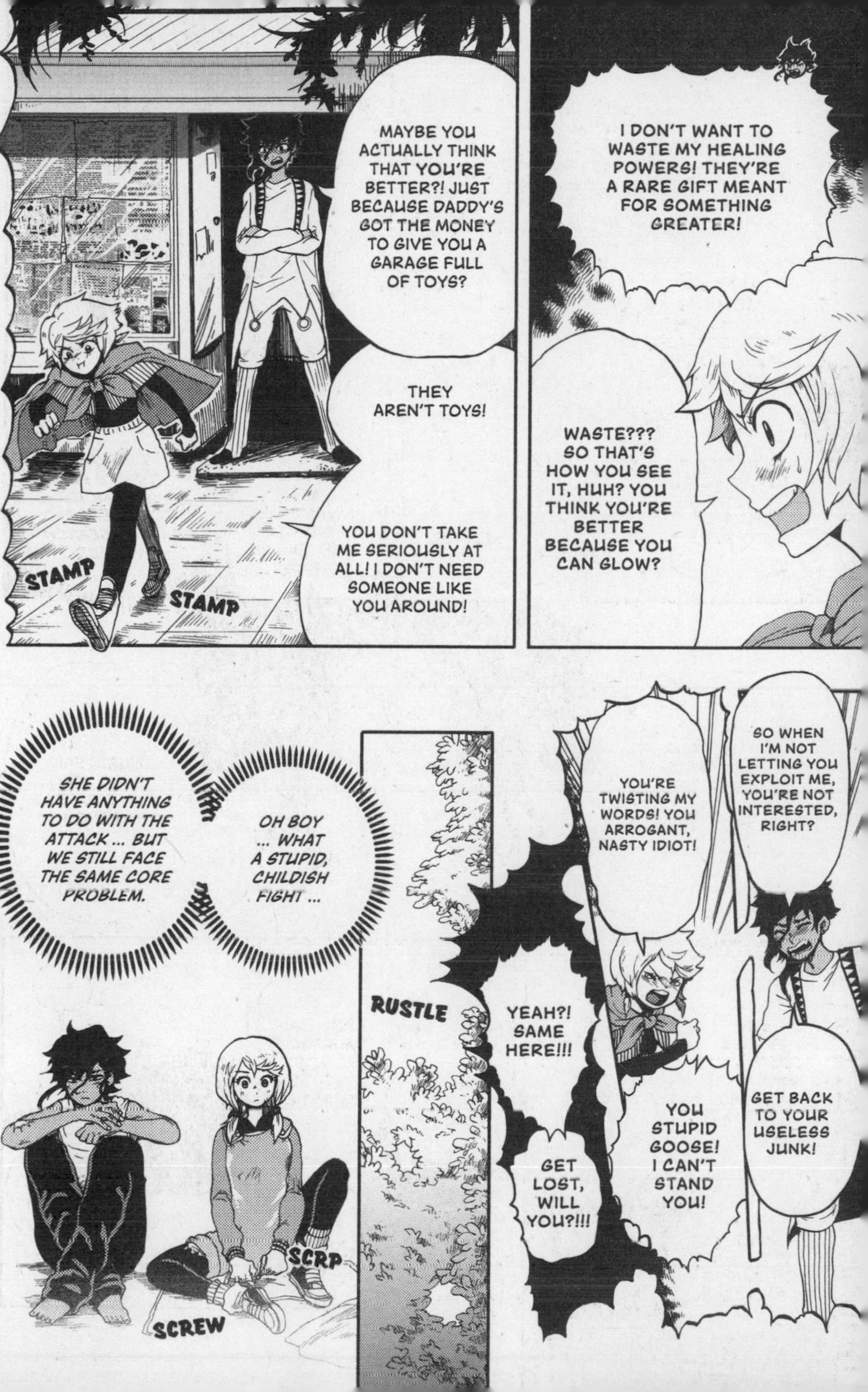
I DON'T WANT TO WASTE MY HEALING POWERS! THEY'RE A RARE GIFT MEANT FOR SOMETHING GREATER!
WASTE??? SO THAT'S HOW YOU SEE IT, HUH? YOU THINK YOU'RE BETTER BECAUSE YOU CAN GLOW?
MAYBE YOU ACTUALLY THINK THAT YOU'RE BETTER?! JUST BECAUSE DADDY'S GOT THE MONEY TO GIVE YOU A GARAGE FULL OF TOYS?
THEY AREN'T TOYS!
YOU DON'T TAKE ME SERIOUSLY AT ALL! I DON'T NEED SOMEONE LIKE YOU AROUND!
STAMP
STAMP
SO WHEN I'M NOT LETTING YOU EXPLOIT ME, YOU'RE NOT INTERESTED, RIGHT?
YOU'RE TWISTING MY WORDS! YOU ARROGANT, NASTY IDIOT!
GET BACK TO YOUR USELESS JUNK!
YEAH?! SAME HERE!!!
YOU STUPID GOOSE! I CAN'T STAND YOU!
GET LOST, WILL YOU?!!!
RUSTLE
OH BOY ... WHAT A STUPID, CHILDISH FIGHT ...
SHE DIDN'T HAVE ANYTHING TO DO WITH THE ATTACK ... BUT WE STILL FACE THE SAME CORE PROBLEM.
SCRP
SCREW

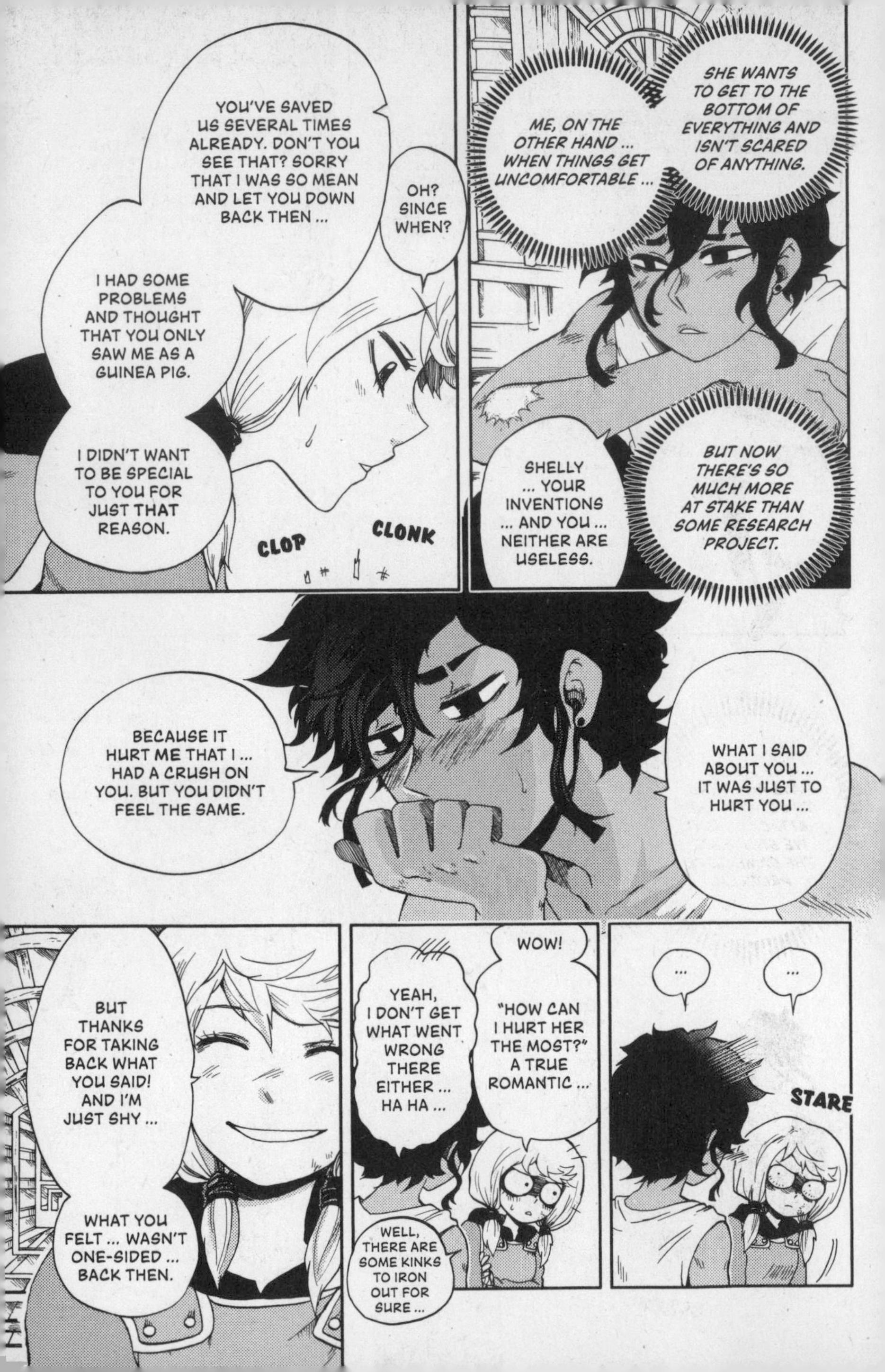
SHE WANTS TO GET TO THE BOTTOM OF EVERYTHING AND ISN'T SCARED OF ANYTHING.
ME, ON THE OTHER HAND ... WHEN THINGS GET UNCOMFORTABLE ...
BUT NOW THERE'S SO MUCH MORE AT STAKE THAN SOME RESEARCH PROJECT.
SHELLY ... YOUR INVENTIONS ... AND YOU ... NEITHER ARE USELESS.
OH? SINCE WHEN?
YOU'VE SAVED US SEVERAL TIMES ALREADY. DON'T YOU SEE THAT? SORRY THAT I WAS SO MEAN AND LET YOU DOWN BACK THEN ...
I HAD SOME PROBLEMS AND THOUGHT THAT YOU ONLY SAW ME AS A GUINEA PIG.
I DIDN'T WANT TO BE SPECIAL TO YOU FOR JUST THAT REASON.
CLONK
CLOP
WHAT I SAID ABOUT YOU ... IT WAS JUST TO HURT YOU ...
BECAUSE IT HURT ME THAT I ... HAD A CRUSH ON YOU. BUT YOU DIDN'T FEEL THE SAME.
...
...
STARE
WOW!
"HOW CAN I HURT HER THE MOST?" A TRUE ROMANTIC ...
YEAH, I DON'T GET WHAT WENT WRONG THERE EITHER ... HA HA ...
WELL, THERE ARE SOME KINKS TO IRON OUT FOR SURE ...
BUT THANKS FOR TAKING BACK WHAT YOU SAID! AND I'M JUST SHY ...
WHAT YOU FELT ... WASN'T ONE-SIDED ... BACK THEN.

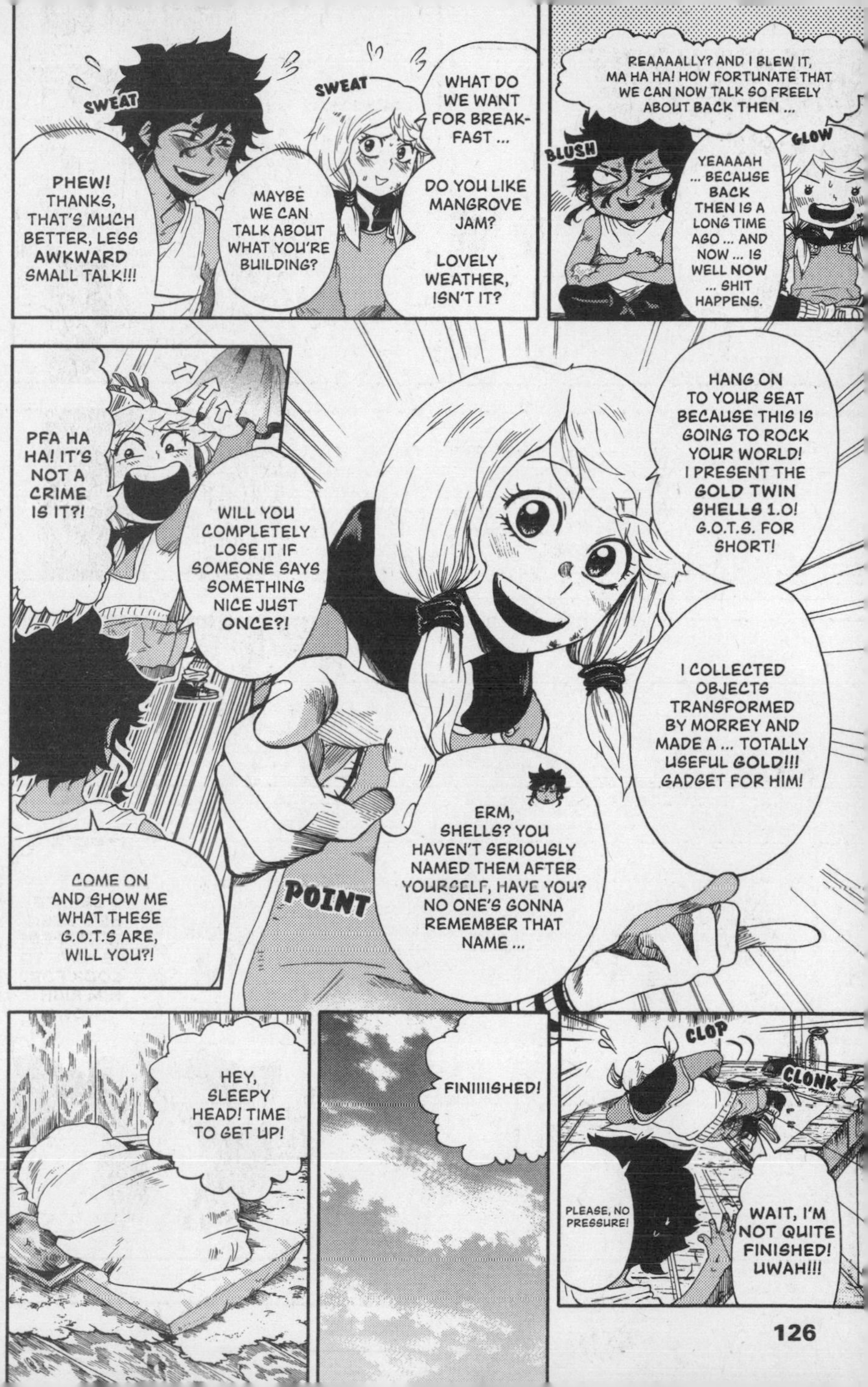
REAAAALLY? AND I BLEW IT, MA HA HA! HOW FORTUNATE THAT WE CAN NOW TALK SO FREELY ABOUT BACK THEN ...
GLOW
BLUSH
YEAAAAH ... BECAUSE BACK THEN IS A LONG TIME AGO ... AND NOW ... IS WELL NOW ... SHIT HAPPENS.
WHAT DO WE WANT FOR BREAK-FAST ...
DO YOU LIKE MANGROVE JAM?
LOVELY WEATHER, ISN'T IT?
SWEAT
MAYBE WE CAN TALK ABOUT WHAT YOU'RE BUILDING?
SWEAT
PHEW! THANKS, THAT'S MUCH BETTER, LESS AWKWARD SMALL TALK!!!
HANG ON TO YOUR SEAT BECAUSE THIS IS GOING TO ROCK YOUR WORLD! I PRESENT THE GOLD TWIN SHELLS 1.0! G.O.T.S. FOR SHORT!
I COLLECTED OBJECTS TRANSFORMED BY MORREY AND MADE A ... TOTALLY USEFUL GOLD!!! GADGET FOR HIM!
ERM, SHELLS? YOU HAVEN'T SERIOUSLY NAMED THEM AFTER YOURSELF, HAVE YOU? NO ONE'S GONNA REMEMBER THAT NAME ...
POINT
PFA HA HA! IT'S NOT A CRIME IS IT?!
WILL YOU COMPLETELY LOSE IT IF SOMEONE SAYS SOMETHING NICE JUST ONCE?!
COME ON AND SHOW ME WHAT THESE G.O.T.S ARE, WILL YOU?!
CLOP
CLONK
WAIT, I'M NOT QUITE FINISHED! UWAH!!!
PLEASE, NO PRESSURE!
FINIIIISHED!
HEY, SLEEPY HEAD! TIME TO GET UP!

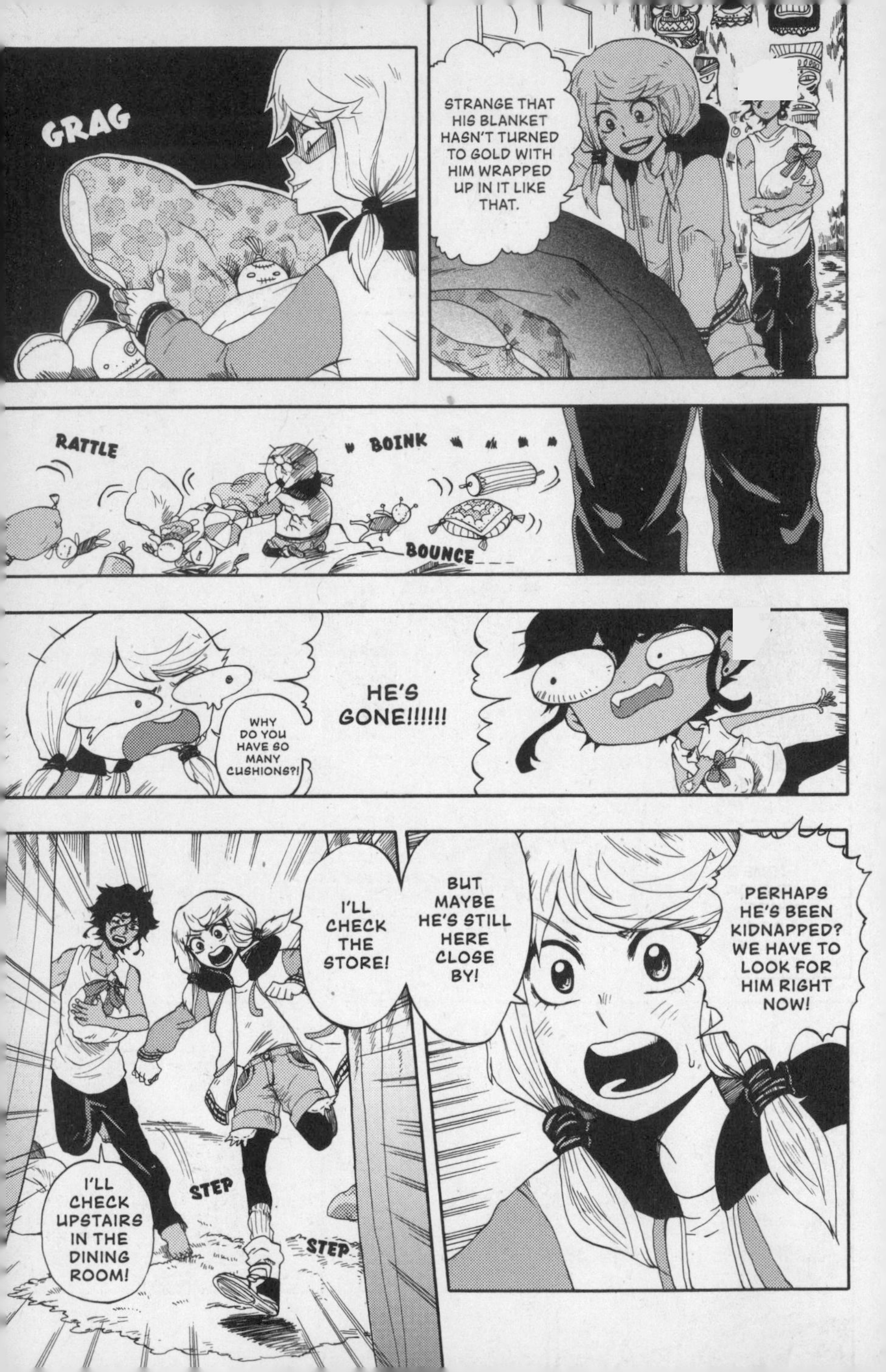
STRANGE THAT HIS BLANKET HASN'T TURNED TO GOLD WITH HIM WRAPPED UP IN IT LIKE THAT.
GRAG
BOINK
RATTLE
BOUNCE
HE'S GONE!!!!!!
WHY DO YOU HAVE SO MANY CUSHIONS?!
PERHAPS HE'S BEEN KIDNAPPED? WE HAVE TO LOOK FOR HIM RIGHT NOW!
BUT MAYBE HE'S STILL HERE CLOSE BY!
I'LL CHECK THE STORE!
I'LL CHECK UPSTAIRS IN THE DINING ROOM!
STEP
STEP

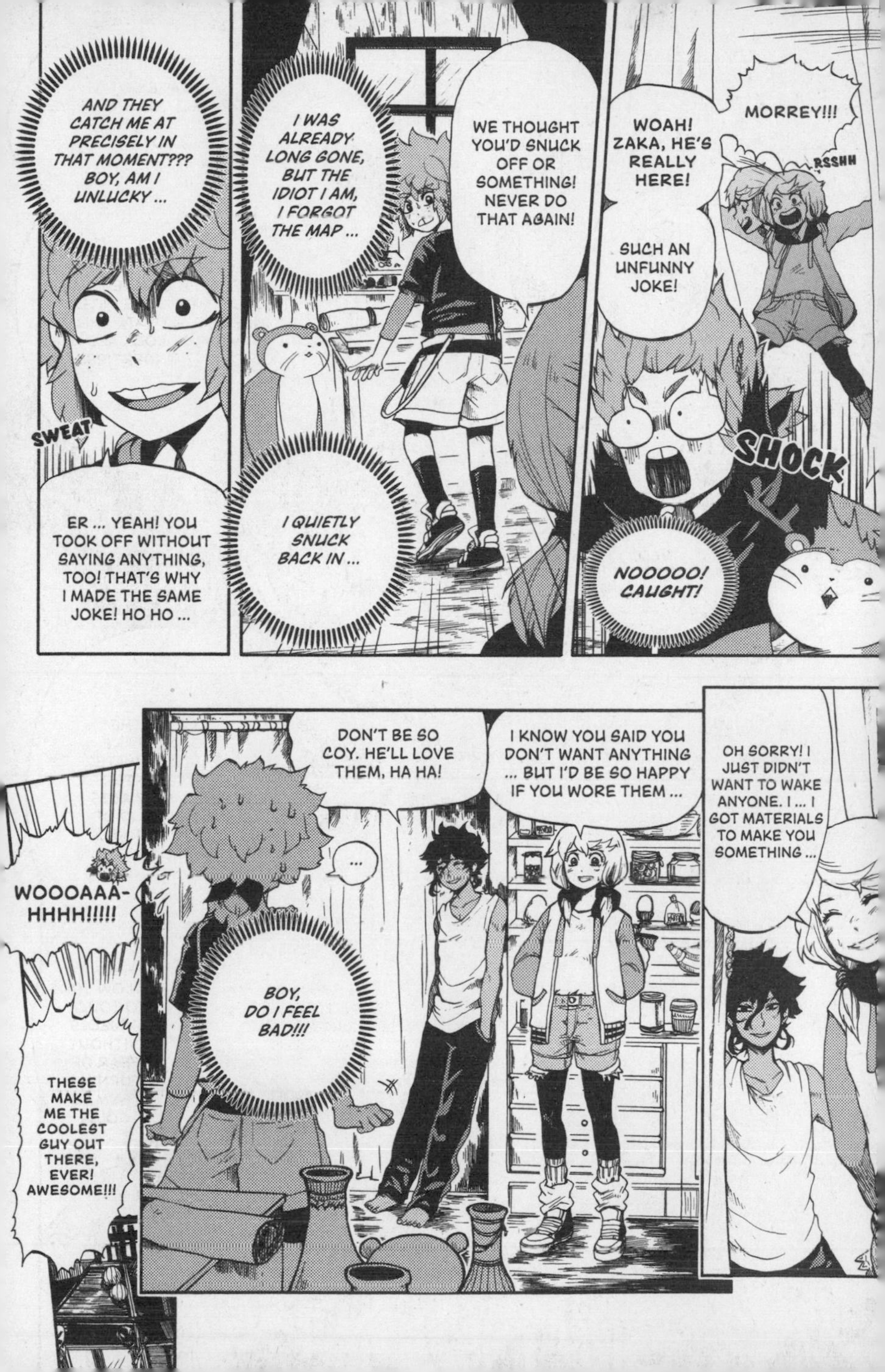
MORREY!!!
RSSHH
WOAH! ZAKA, HE'S REALLY HERE!
SUCH AN UNFUNNY JOKE!
SHOCK
NOOOOO! CAUGHT!
WE THOUGHT YOU'D SNUCK OFF OR SOMETHING! NEVER DO THAT AGAIN!
I WAS ALREADY LONG GONE, BUT THE IDIOT I AM, I FORGOT THE MAP ...
I QUIETLY SNUCK BACK IN ...
AND THEY CATCH ME AT PRECISELY IN THAT MOMENT??? BOY, AM I UNLUCKY ...
SWEAT
ER ... YEAH! YOU TOOK OFF WITHOUT SAYING ANYTHING, TOO! THAT'S WHY I MADE THE SAME JOKE! HO HO ...
OH SORRY! I JUST DIDN'T WANT TO WAKE ANYONE. I ... I GOT MATERIALS TO MAKE YOU SOMETHING ...
I KNOW YOU SAID YOU DON'T WANT ANYTHING ... BUT I'D BE SO HAPPY IF YOU WORE THEM ...
DON'T BE SO COY. HE'LL LOVE THEM, HA HA!
...
BOY, DO I FEEL BAD!!!
WOOOAAA-HHHH!!!!!
THESE MAKE ME THE COOLEST GUY OUT THERE, EVER! AWESOME!!!

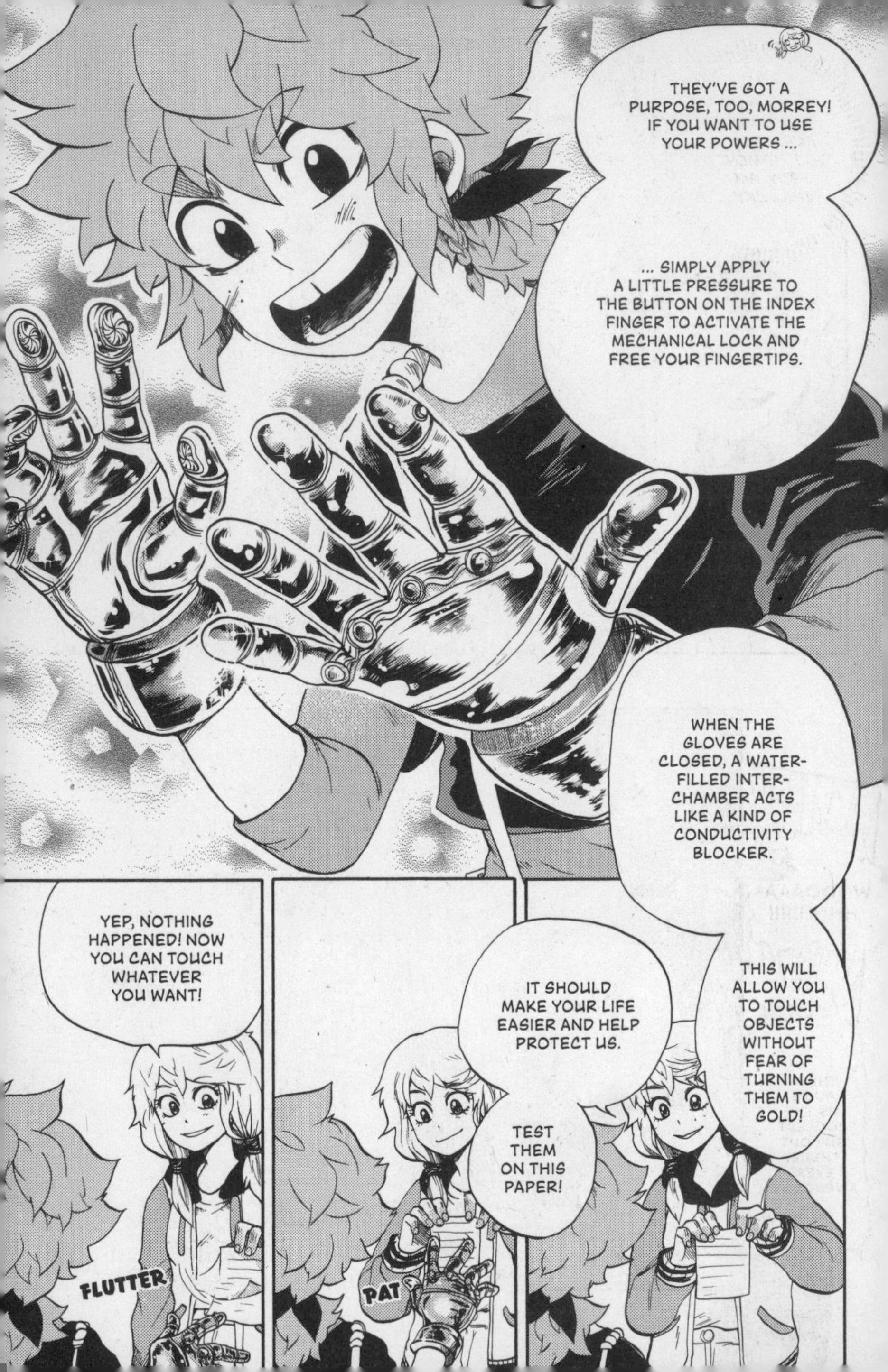
THEY'VE GOT A PURPOSE, TOO, MORREY! IF YOU WANT TO USE YOUR POWERS ...
... SIMPLY APPLY A LITTLE PRESSURE TO THE BUTTON ON THE INDEX FINGER TO ACTIVATE THE MECHANICAL LOCK AND FREE YOUR FINGERTIPS.
WHEN THE GLOVES ARE CLOSED, A WATER-FILLED INTER-CHAMBER ACTS LIKE A KIND OF CONDUCTIVITY BLOCKER.
THIS WILL ALLOW YOU TO TOUCH OBJECTS WITHOUT FEAR OF TURNING THEM TO GOLD!
IT SHOULD MAKE YOUR LIFE EASIER AND HELP PROTECT US.
TEST THEM ON THIS PAPER!
PAT
YEP, NOTHING HAPPENED! NOW YOU CAN TOUCH WHATEVER YOU WANT!
FLUTTER

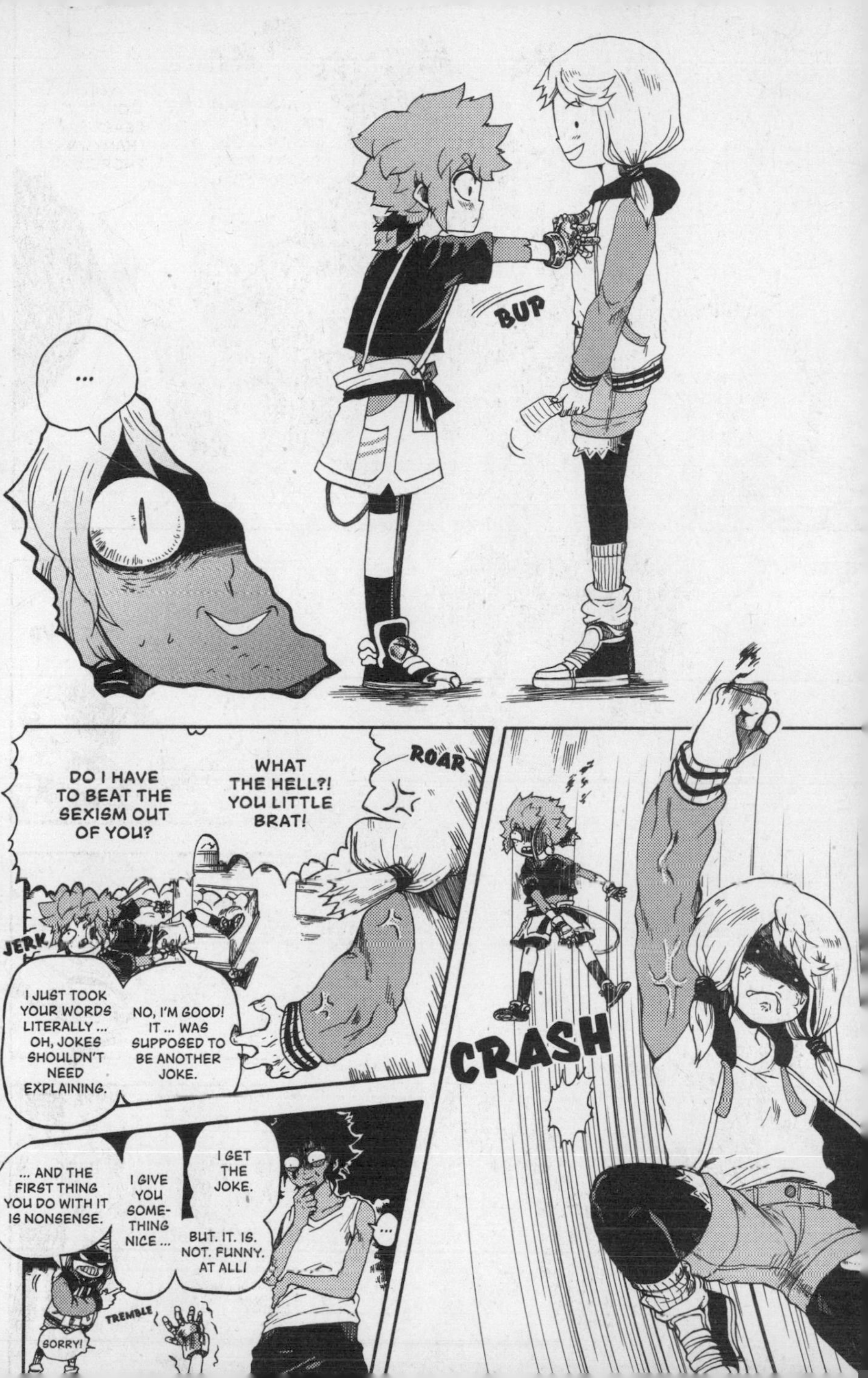
BUP
...
CRASH
ROAR
WHAT THE HELL?! YOU LITTLE BRAT!
DO I HAVE TO BEAT THE SEXISM OUT OF YOU?
JERK
NO, I'M GOOD! IT ... WAS SUPPOSED TO BE ANOTHER JOKE.
I JUST TOOK YOUR WORDS LITERALLY ... OH, JOKES SHOULDN'T NEED EXPLAINING.
I GET THE JOKE.
BUT. IT. IS. NOT. FUNNY. AT ALL!
I GIVE YOU SOME-THING NICE ...
... AND THE FIRST THING YOU DO WITH IT IS NONSENSE.
...
TREMBLE
SORRY!

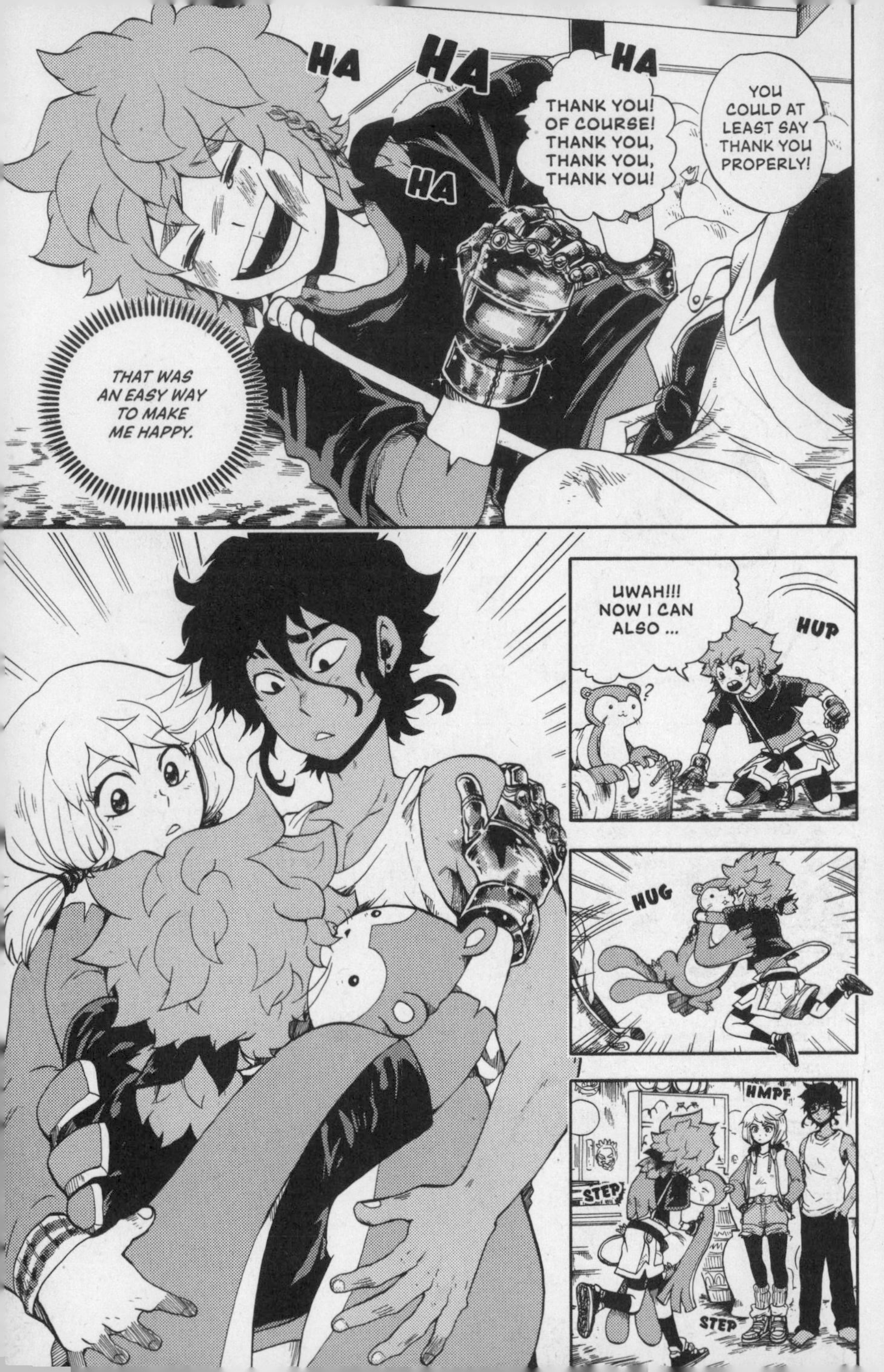
HA
YOU COULD AT LEAST SAY THANK YOU PROPERLY!
HA
HA
THANK YOU! OF COURSE! THANK YOU, THANK YOU, THANK YOU!
HA
THAT WAS AN EASY WAY TO MAKE ME HAPPY.
HUP
UWAH!!! NOW I CAN ALSO ...
?
HUG
HMPF
STEP
STEP

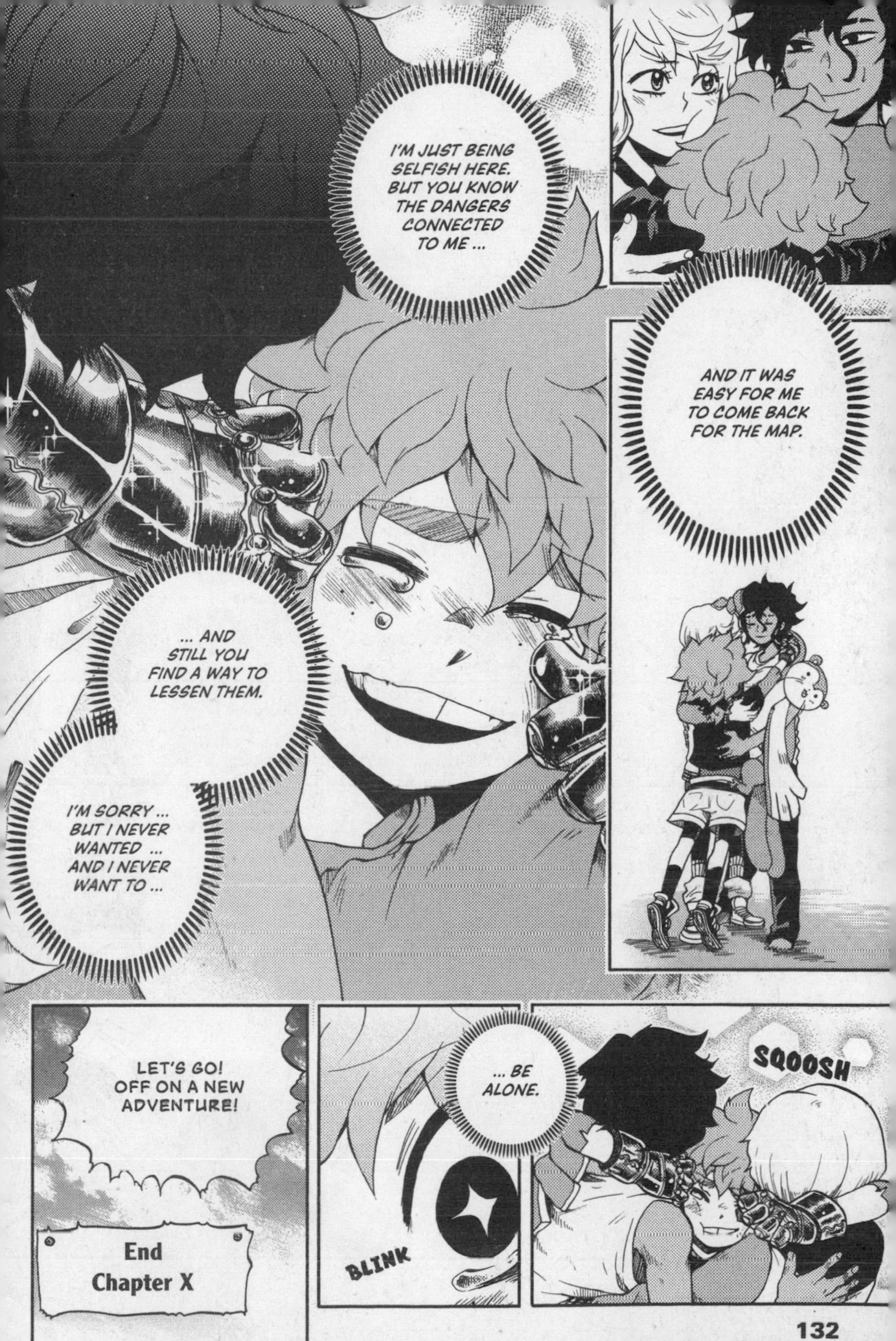
I'M JUST BEING SELFISH HERE. BUT YOU KNOW THE DANGERS CONNECTED TO ME ...
AND IT WAS EASY FOR ME TO COME BACK FOR THE MAP.
... AND STILL YOU FIND A WAY TO LESSEN THEM.
I'M SORRY ... BUT I NEVER WANTED ... AND I NEVER WANT TO ...
SQOOSH
... BE ALONE.
BLINK
LET'S GO! OFF ON A NEW ADVENTURE!
End
Chapter X

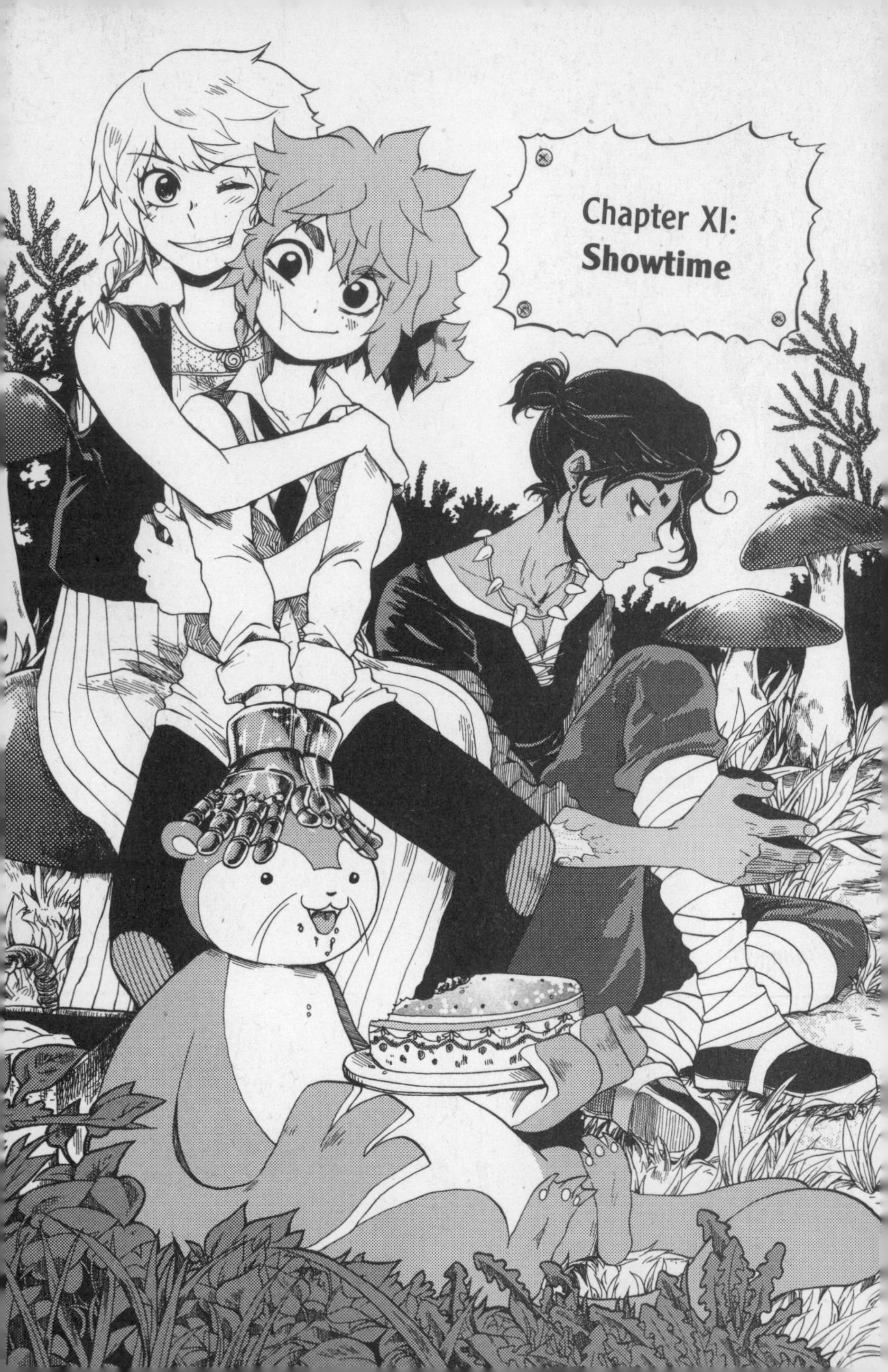
Chapter XI:
Showtime

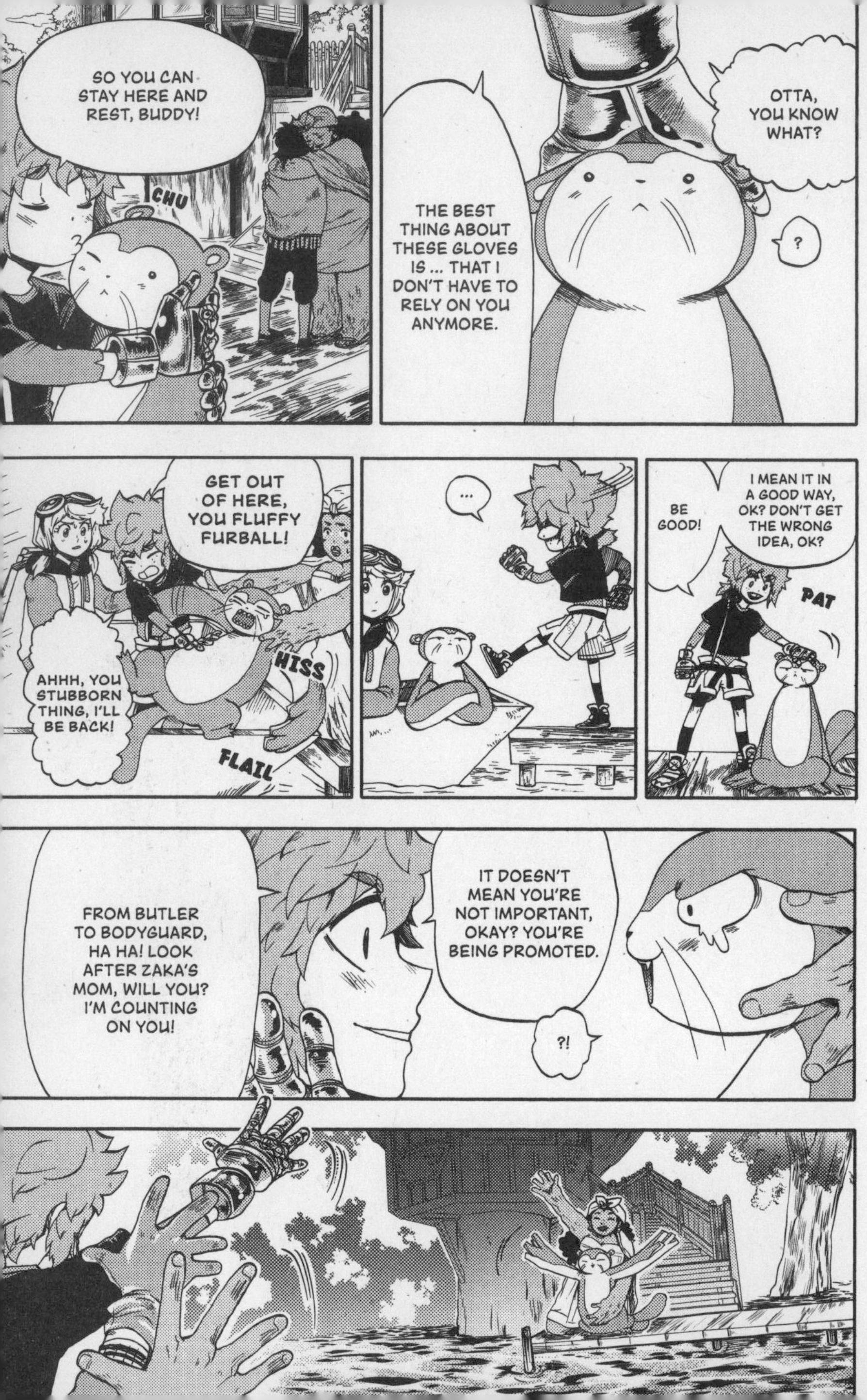
OTTA, YOU KNOW WHAT?
?
THE BEST THING ABOUT THESE GLOVES IS ... THAT I DON'T HAVE TO RELY ON YOU ANYMORE.
SO YOU CAN STAY HERE AND REST, BUDDY!
CHU
I MEAN IT IN A GOOD WAY, OK? DON'T GET THE WRONG IDEA, OK?
BE GOOD!
PAT
...
GET OUT OF HERE, YOU FLUFFY FURBALL!
HISS
AHHH, YOU STUBBORN THING, I'LL BE BACK!
FLAIL
IT DOESN'T MEAN YOU'RE NOT IMPORTANT, OKAY? YOU'RE BEING PROMOTED.
?!
FROM BUTLER TO BODYGUARD, HA HA! LOOK AFTER ZAKA'S MOM, WILL YOU? I'M COUNTING ON YOU!

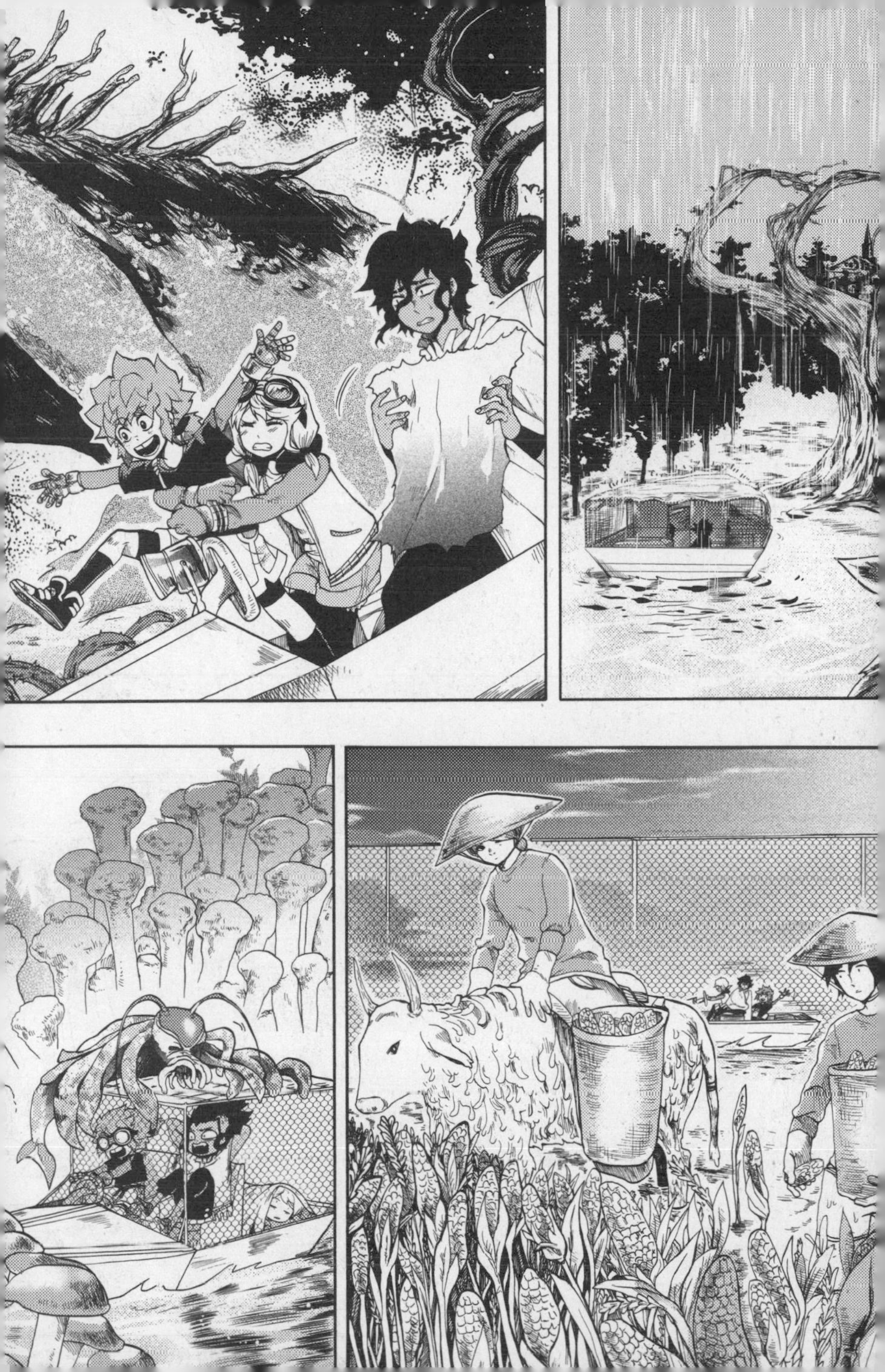

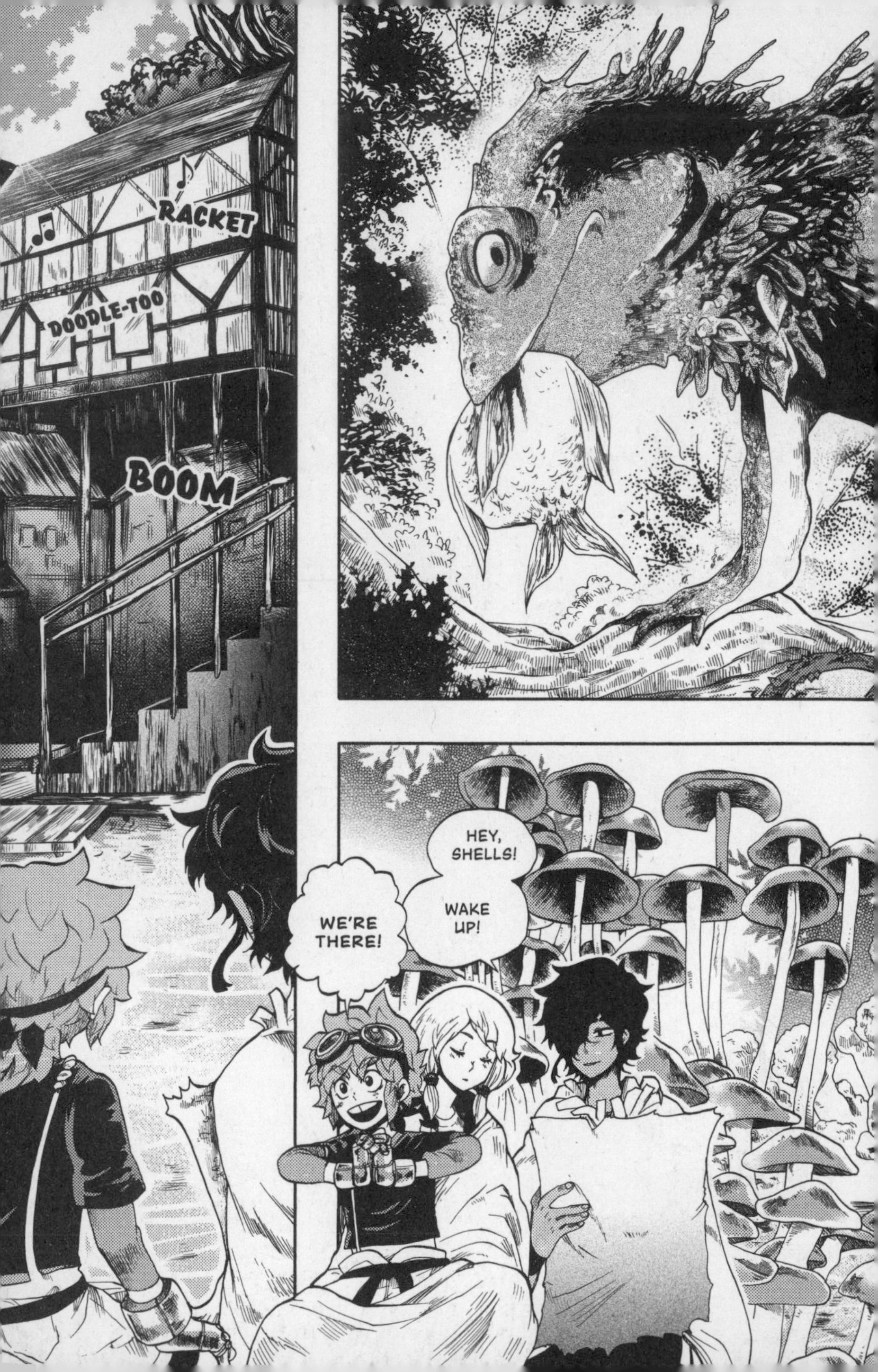
HEY, SHELLS!
WAKE UP!
WE'RE THERE!
RACKET
DOODLE-TOO
BOOM

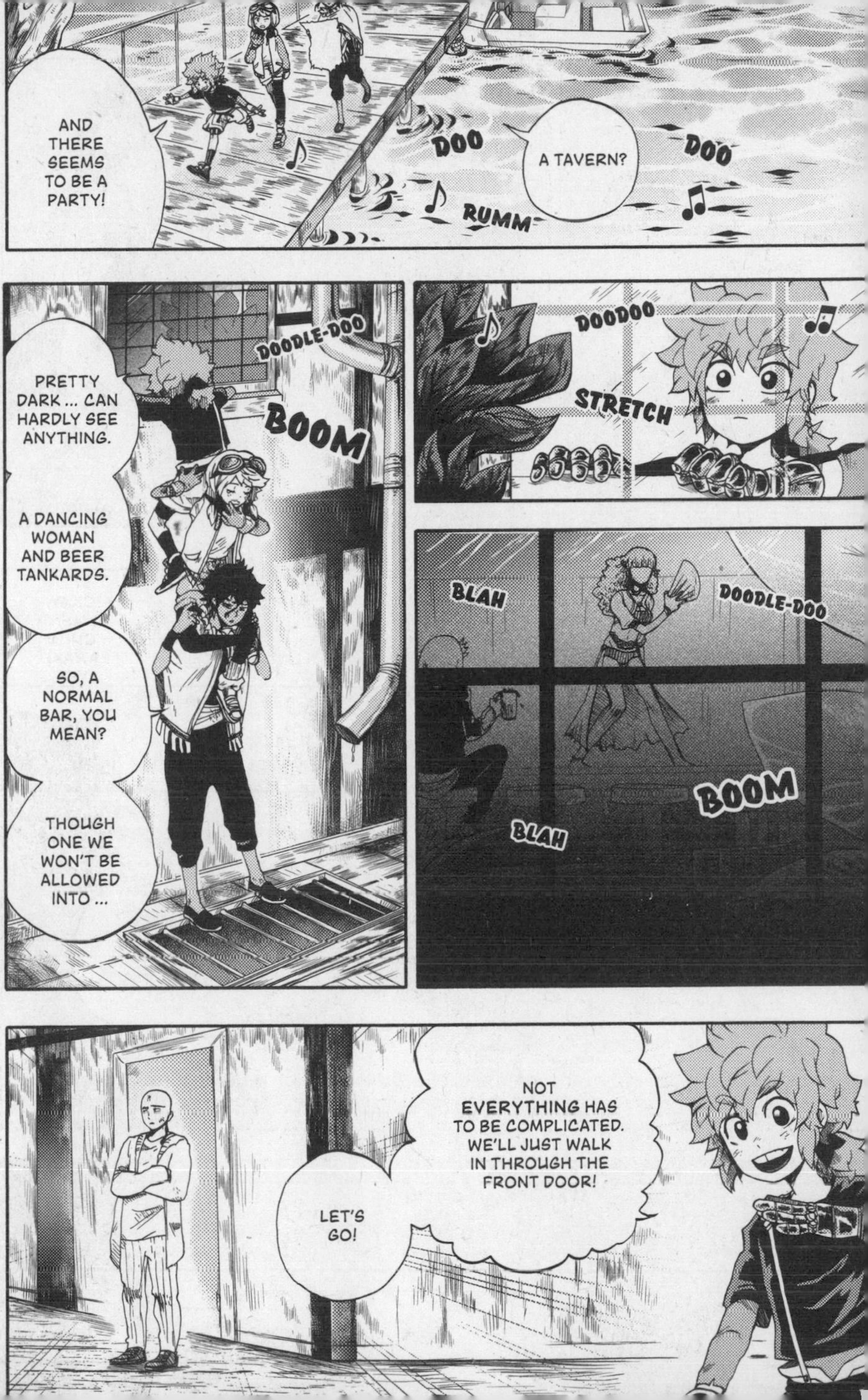
DOO
A TAVERN?
DOO
RUMM
AND THERE SEEMS TO BE A PARTY!
DOODOO
STRETCH
DOODLE-DOO
BLAH
BOOM
BLAH
DOODLE-DOO
BOOM
PRETTY DARK ... CAN HARDLY SEE ANYTHING.
A DANCING WOMAN AND BEER TANKARDS.
SO, A NORMAL BAR, YOU MEAN?
THOUGH ONE WE WON'T BE ALLOWED INTO ...
NOT EVERYTHING HAS TO BE COMPLICATED. WE'LL JUST WALK IN THROUGH THE FRONT DOOR!
LET'S GO!

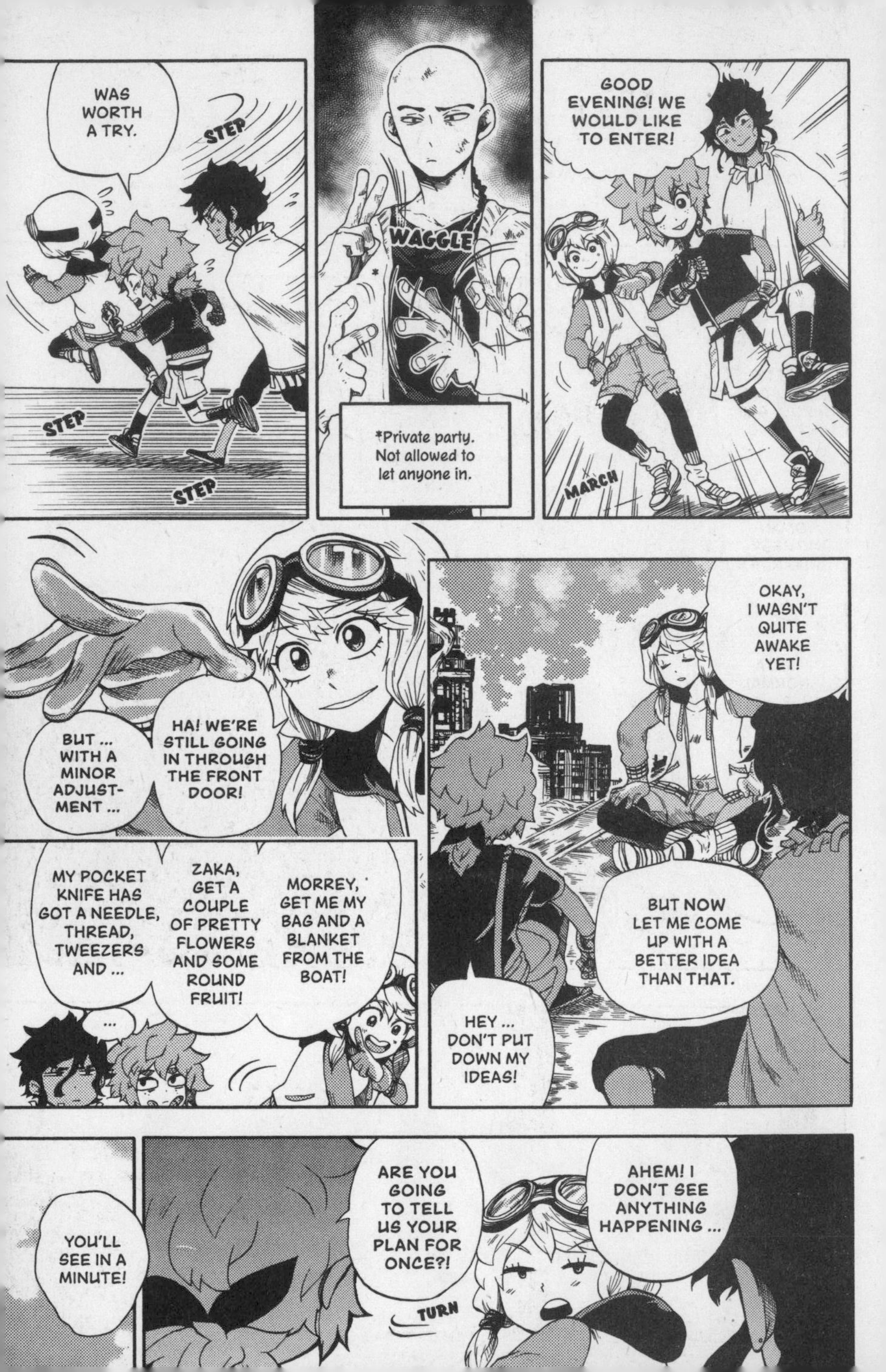
GOOD EVENING! WE WOULD LIKE TO ENTER!
MARCH
WAGGLE
*Private party. Not allowed to let anyone in.
WAS WORTH A TRY.
STEP
STEP
STEP
OKAY, I WASN'T QUITE AWAKE YET!
BUT NOW LET ME COME UP WITH A BETTER IDEA THAN THAT.
HEY ... DON'T PUT DOWN MY IDEAS!
HA! WE'RE STILL GOING IN THROUGH THE FRONT DOOR!
BUT ... WITH A MINOR ADJUSTMENT ...
MORREY, GET ME MY BAG AND A BLANKET FROM THE BOAT!
ZAKA, GET A COUPLE OF PRETTY FLOWERS AND SOME ROUND FRUIT!
MY POCKET KNIFE HAS GOT A NEEDLE, THREAD, TWEEZERS AND ...
...
AHEM! I DON'T SEE ANYTHING HAPPENING ...
ARE YOU GOING TO TELL US YOUR PLAN FOR ONCE?!
TURN
YOU'LL SEE IN A MINUTE!

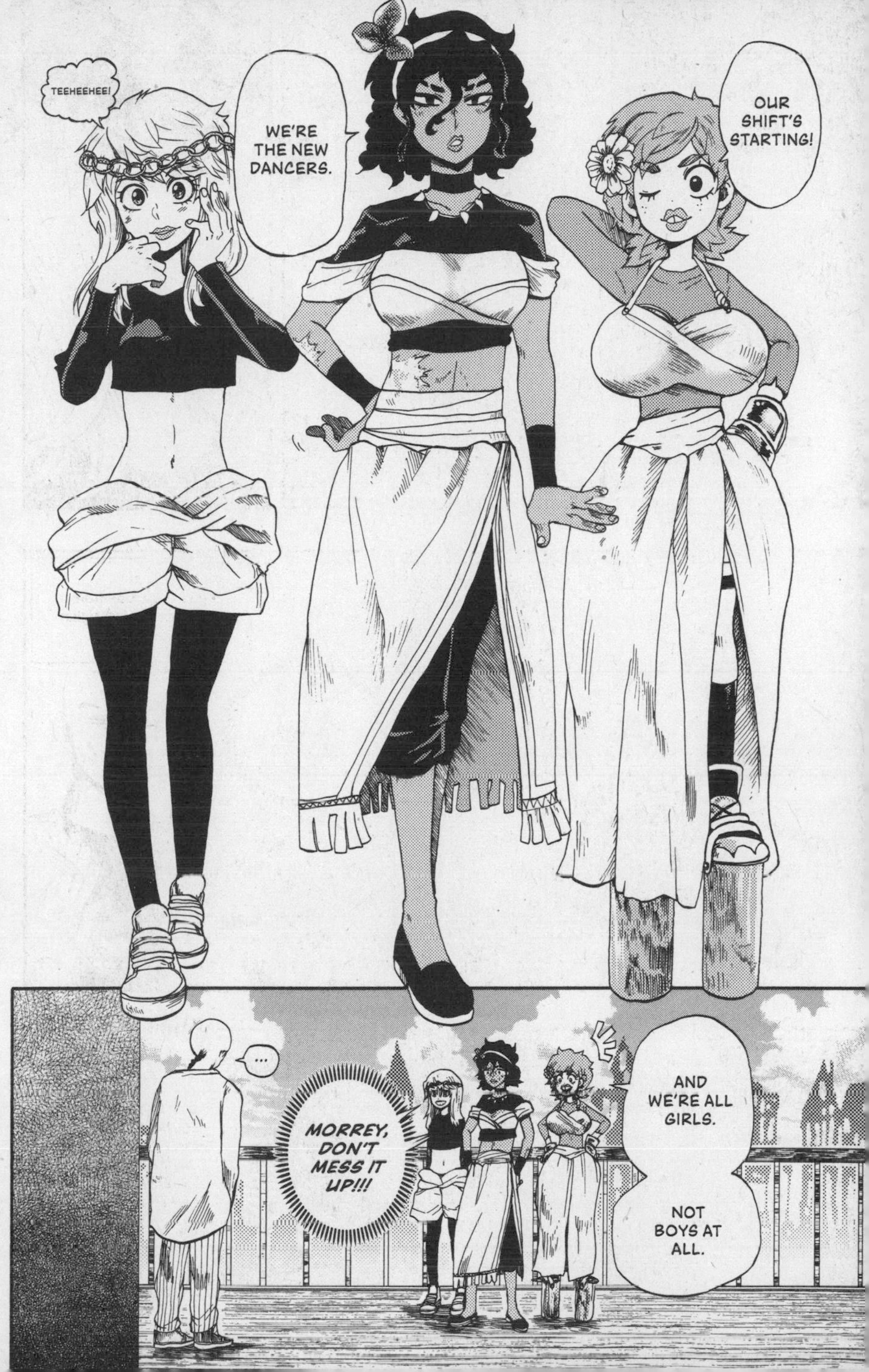
OUR SHIFT'S STARTING!
WE'RE THE NEW DANCERS.
TEEHEEHEE!
AND WE'RE ALL GIRLS.
NOT BOYS AT ALL.
MORREY, DON'T MESS IT UP!!!
...

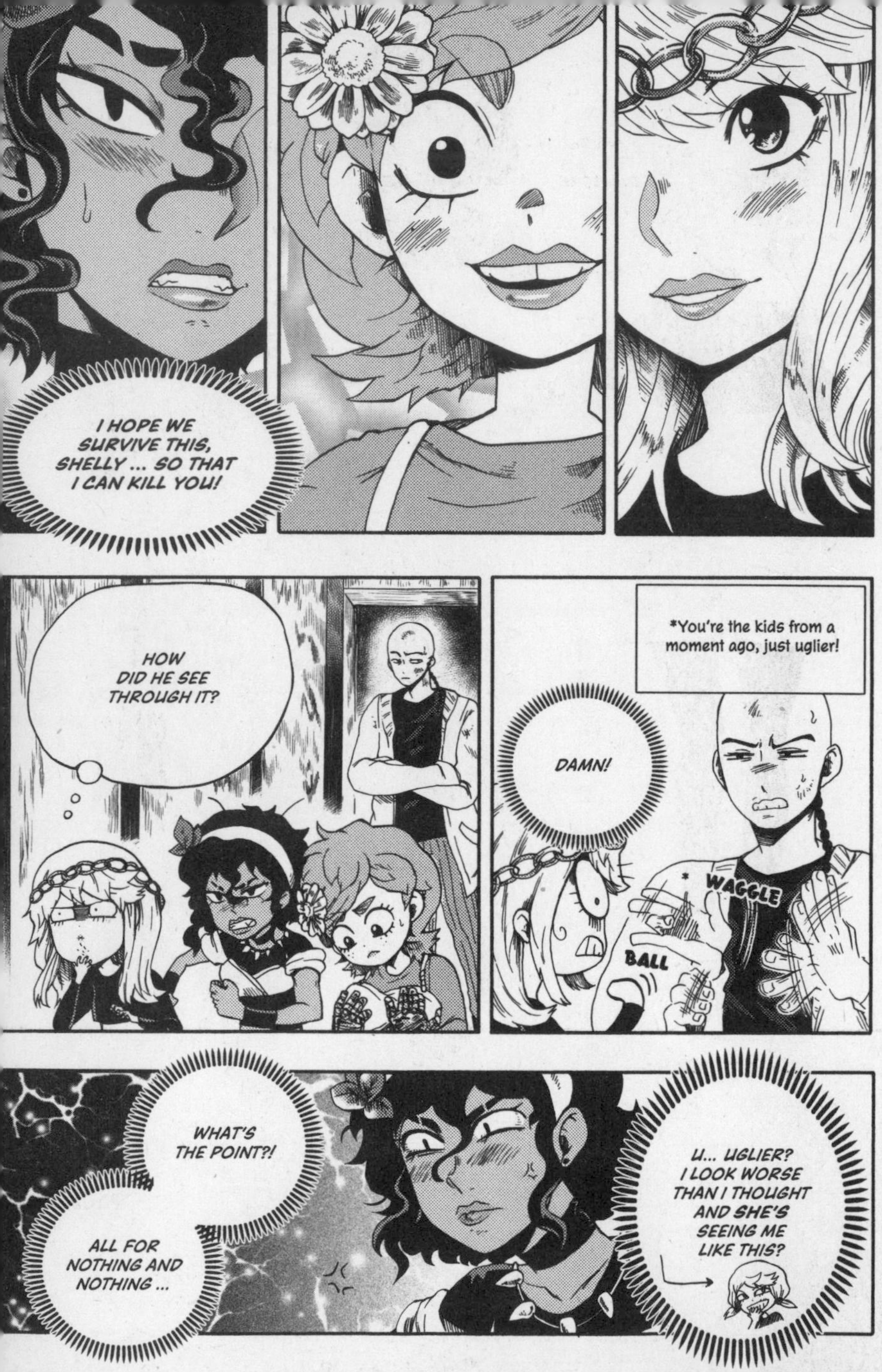
I HOPE WE SURVIVE THIS, SHELLY ... SO THAT I CAN KILL YOU!
*You're the kids from a moment ago, just uglier!
DAMN!
WAGGLE
BALL
HOW DID HE SEE THROUGH IT?
U... UGLIER? I LOOK WORSE THAN I THOUGHT AND SHE'S SEEING ME LIKE THIS?
WHAT'S THE POINT?!
ALL FOR NOTHING AND NOTHING ...

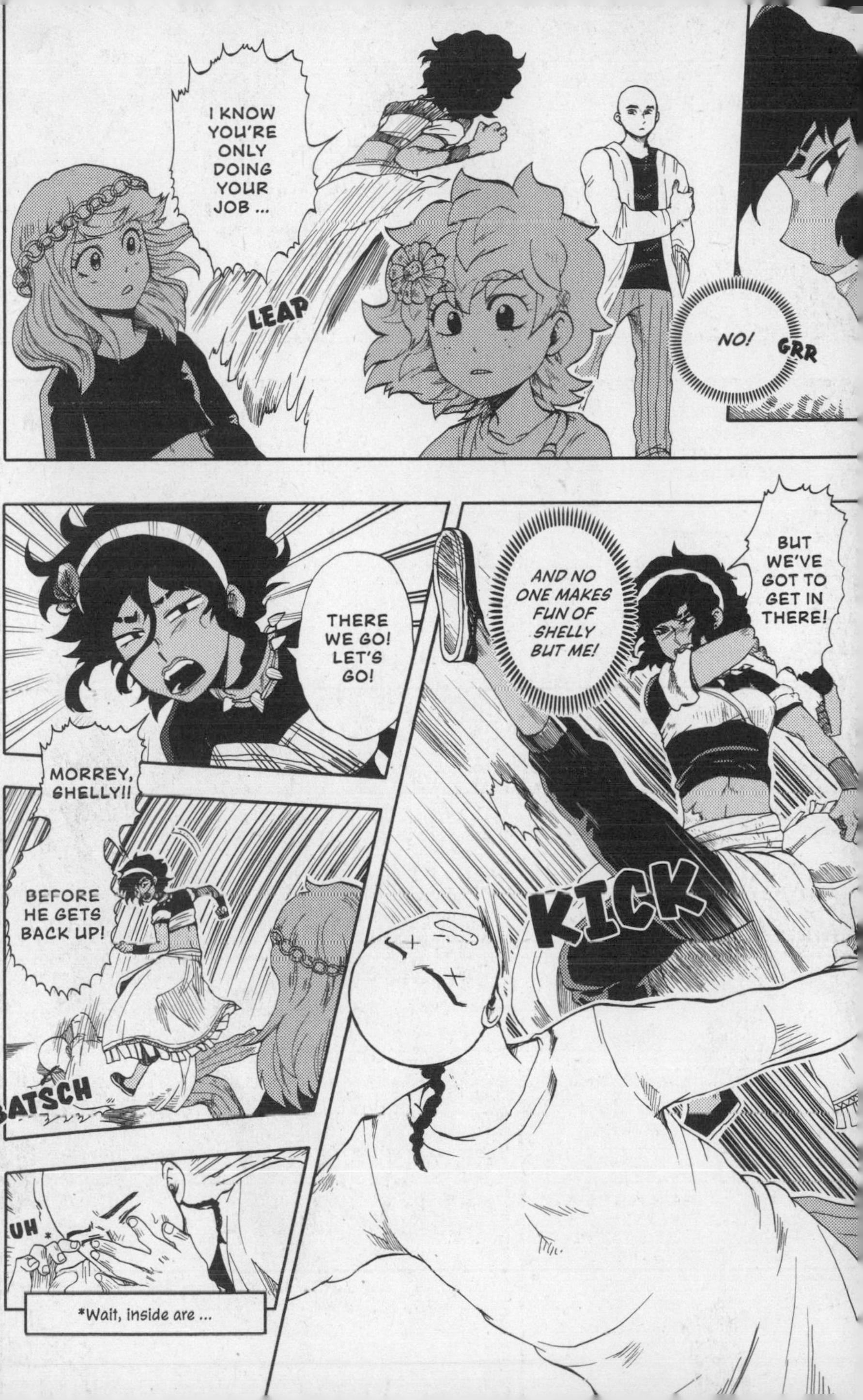
NO!
GRR
I KNOW YOU'RE ONLY DOING YOUR JOB ...
LEAP
BUT WE'VE GOT TO GET IN THERE!
AND NO ONE MAKES FUN OF SHELLY BUT ME!
KICK
THERE WE GO! LET'S GO!
MORREY, SHELLY!!
BEFORE HE GETS BACK UP!
BATSCH
UH *
*Wait, inside are ...

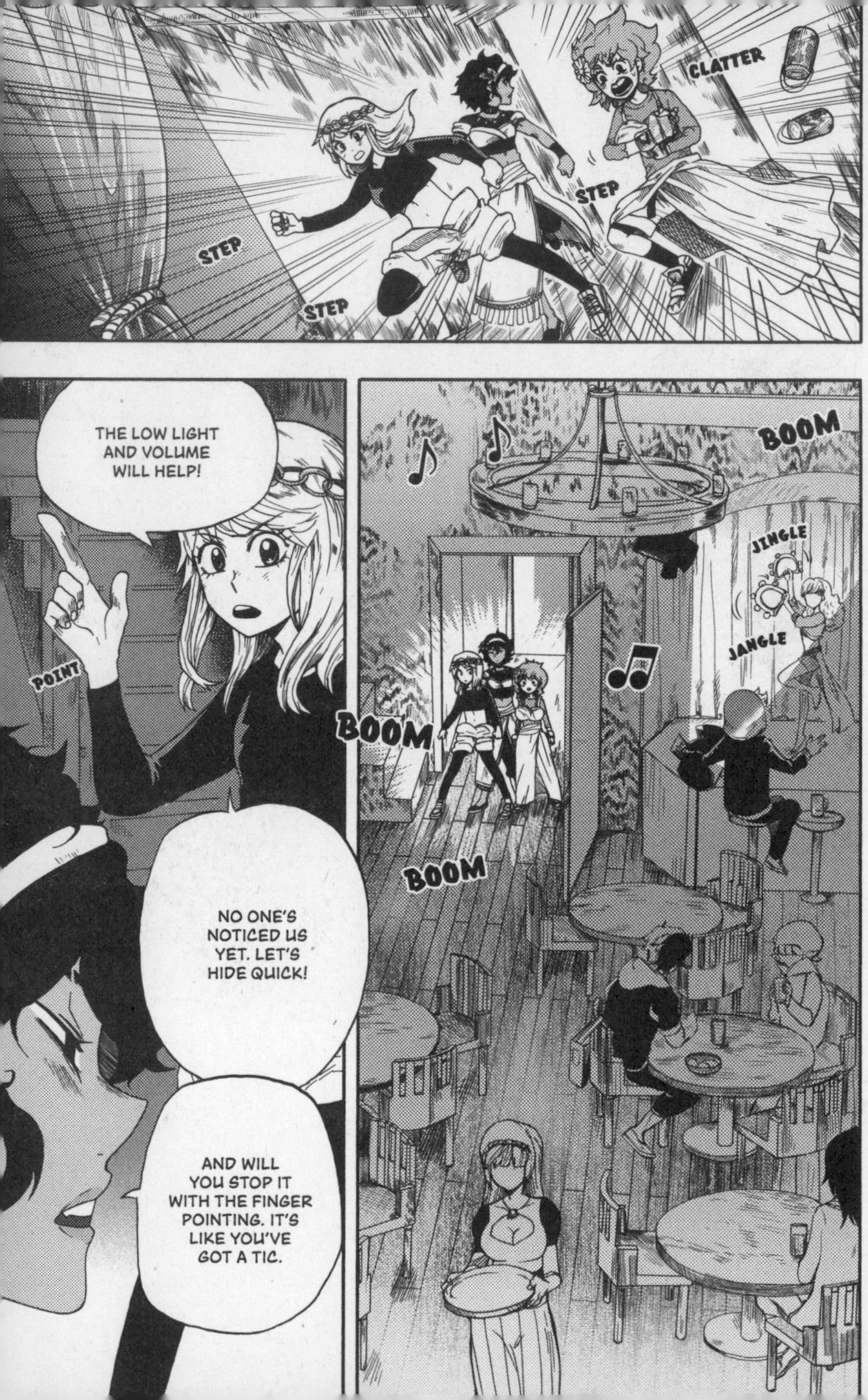
CLATTER
STEP
STEP
STEP
BOOM
JINGLE
JANGLE
BOOM
BOOM
THE LOW LIGHT AND VOLUME WILL HELP!
POINT
NO ONE'S NOTICED US YET. LET'S HIDE QUICK!
AND WILL YOU STOP IT WITH THE FINGER POINTING. IT'S LIKE YOU'VE GOT A TIC.

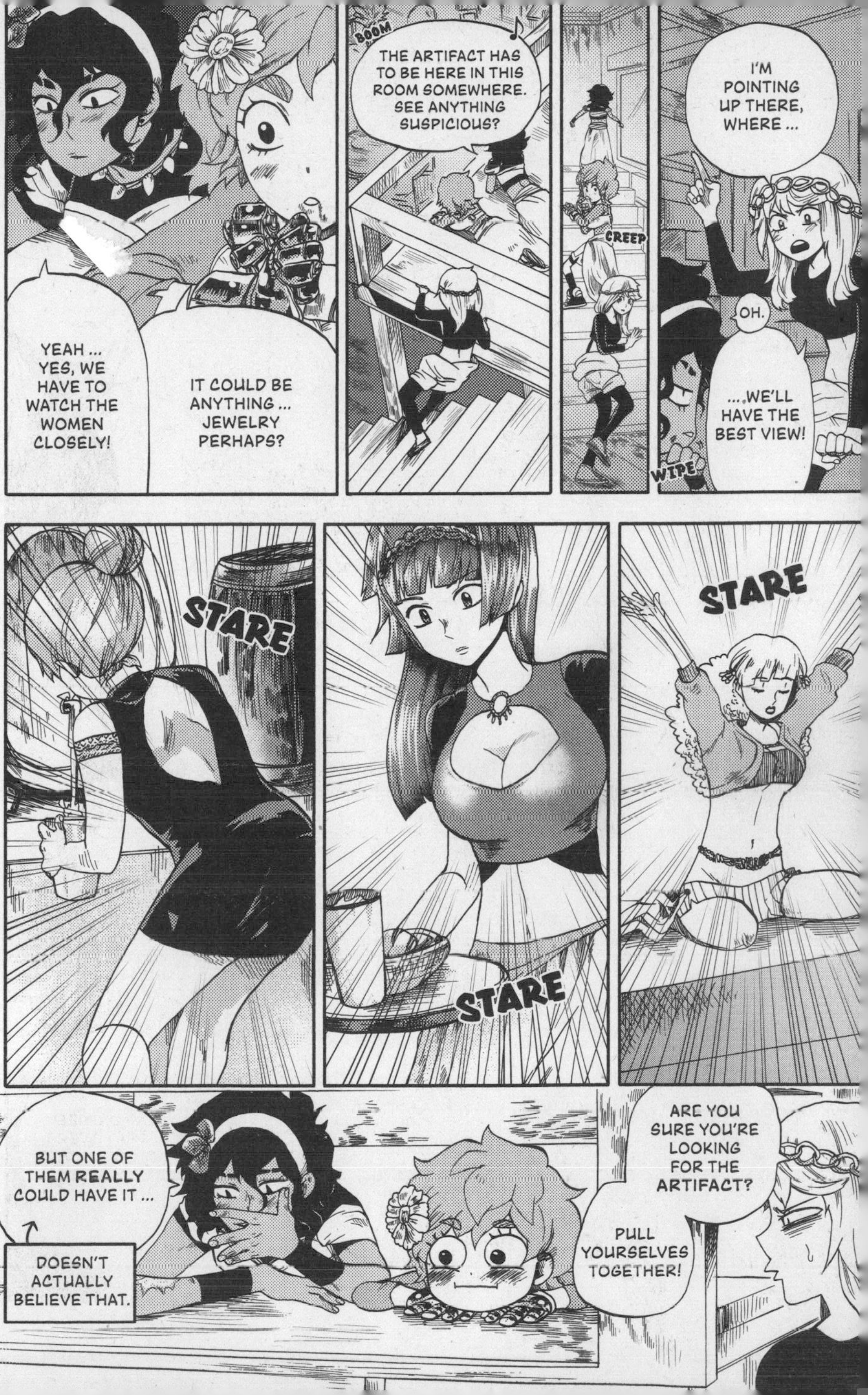
I'M POINTING UP THERE, WHERE ...
OH.
....WE'LL HAVE THE BEST VIEW!
WIPE
CREEP
BOOM
THE ARTIFACT HAS TO BE HERE IN THIS ROOM SOMEWHERE. SEE ANYTHING SUSPICIOUS?
IT COULD BE ANYTHING ... JEWELRY PERHAPS?
YEAH ... YES, WE HAVE TO WATCH THE WOMEN CLOSELY!
STARE
STARE
STARE
ARE YOU SURE YOU'RE LOOKING FOR THE ARTIFACT?
PULL YOURSELVES TOGETHER!
BUT ONE OF THEM REALLY COULD HAVE IT ...
DOESN'T ACTUALLY BELIEVE THAT.

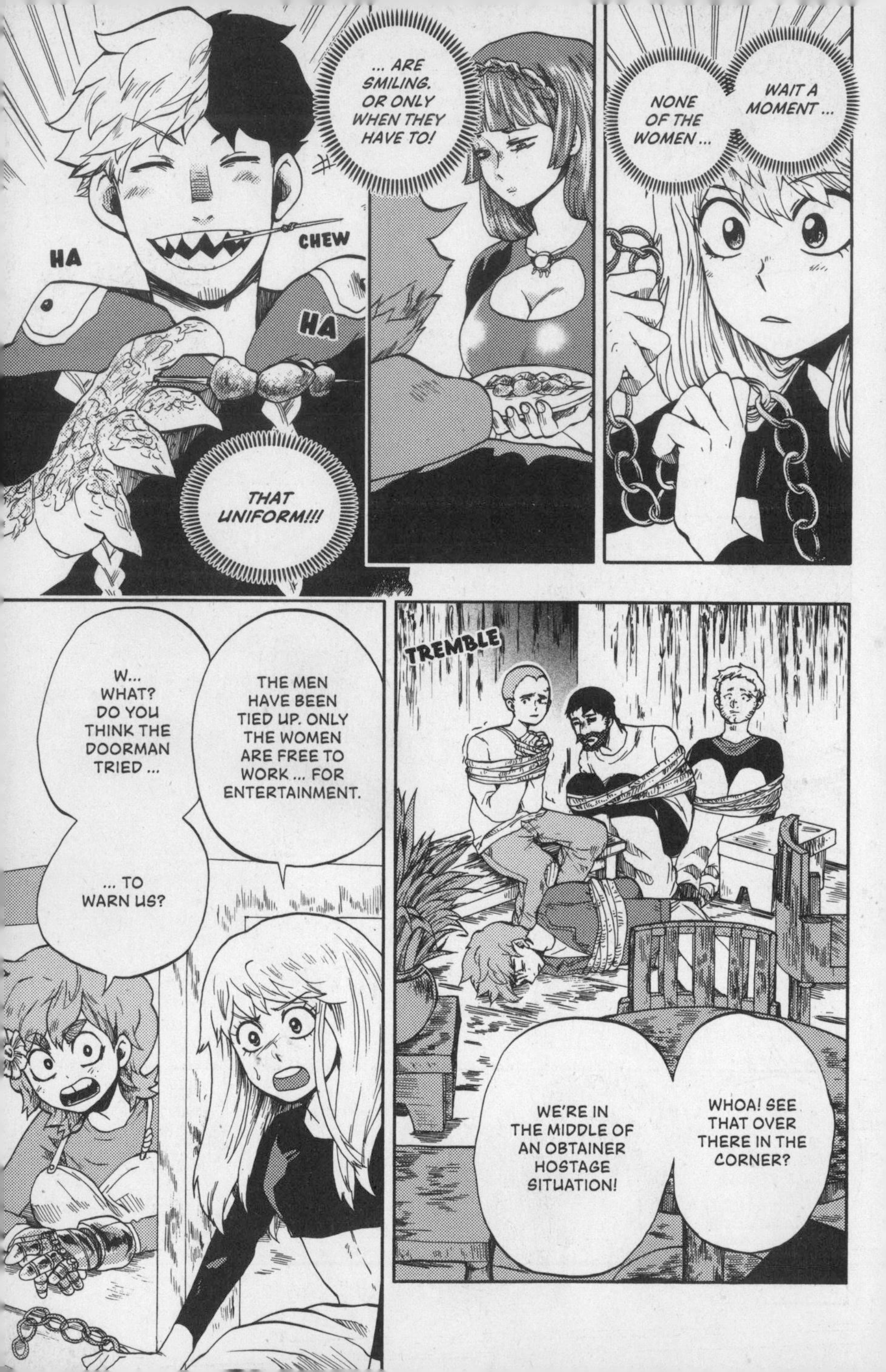
WAIT A MOMENT ...
NONE OF THE WOMEN ...
... ARE SMILING. OR ONLY WHEN THEY HAVE TO!
CHEW
HA
HA
THAT UNIFORM!!!
TREMBLE
WHOA! SEE THAT OVER THERE IN THE CORNER?
WE'RE IN THE MIDDLE OF AN OBTAINER HOSTAGE SITUATION!
THE MEN HAVE BEEN TIED UP. ONLY THE WOMEN ARE FREE TO WORK ... FOR ENTERTAINMENT.
W... WHAT? DO YOU THINK THE DOORMAN TRIED ...
... TO WARN US?

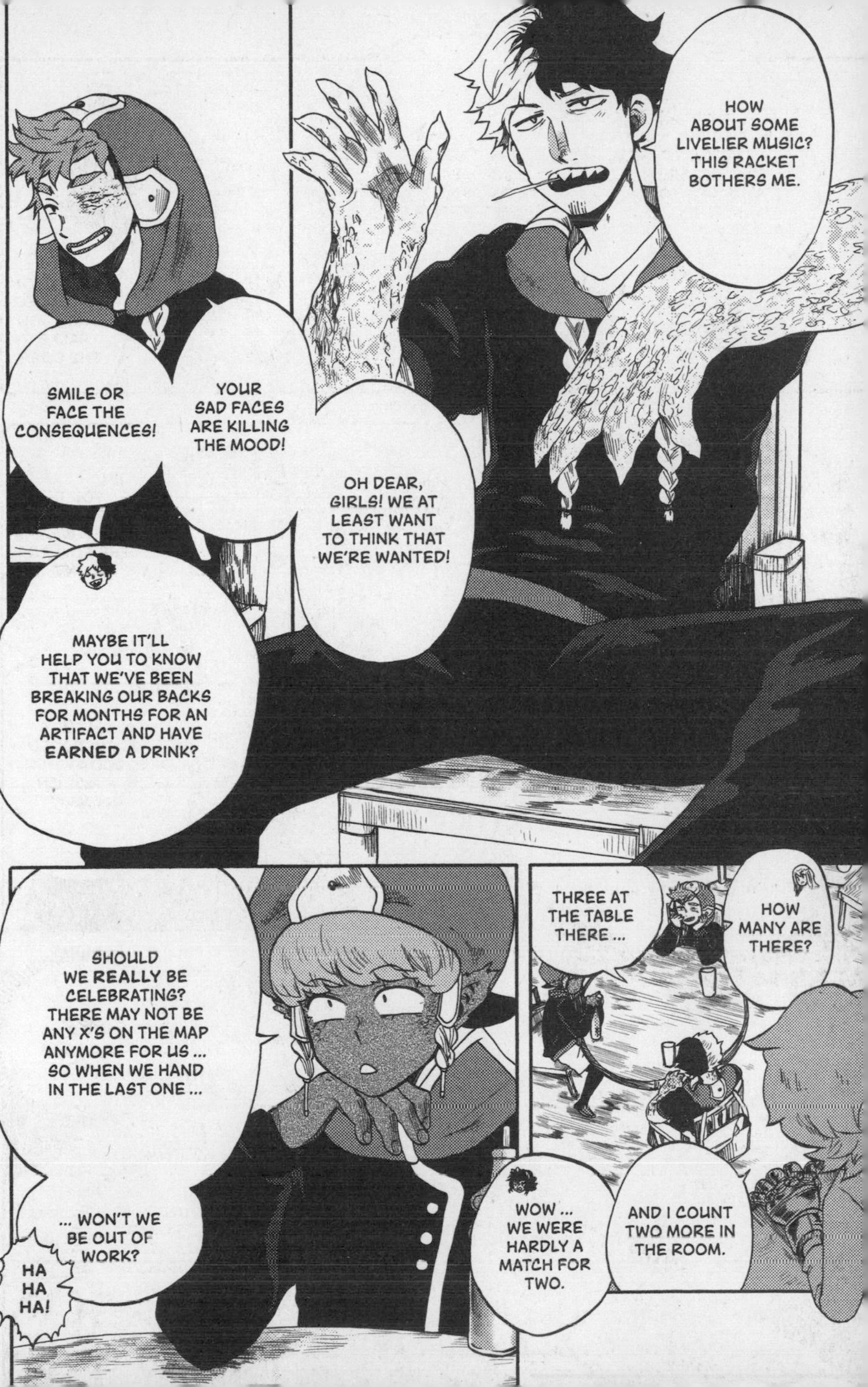
HOW ABOUT SOME LIVELIER MUSIC? THIS RACKET BOTHERS ME.
YOUR SAD FACES ARE KILLING THE MOOD!
SMILE OR FACE THE CONSEQUENCES!
OH DEAR, GIRLS! WE AT LEAST WANT TO THINK THAT WE'RE WANTED!
MAYBE IT'LL HELP YOU TO KNOW THAT WE'VE BEEN BREAKING OUR BACKS FOR MONTHS FOR AN ARTIFACT AND HAVE EARNED A DRINK?
HOW MANY ARE THERE?
THREE AT THE TABLE THERE ...
AND I COUNT TWO MORE IN THE ROOM.
WOW ... WE WERE HARDLY A MATCH FOR TWO.
SHOULD WE REALLY BE CELEBRATING? THERE MAY NOT BE ANY X'S ON THE MAP ANYMORE FOR US ... SO WHEN WE HAND IN THE LAST ONE ...
... WON'T WE BE OUT OF WORK?
HA HA HA!

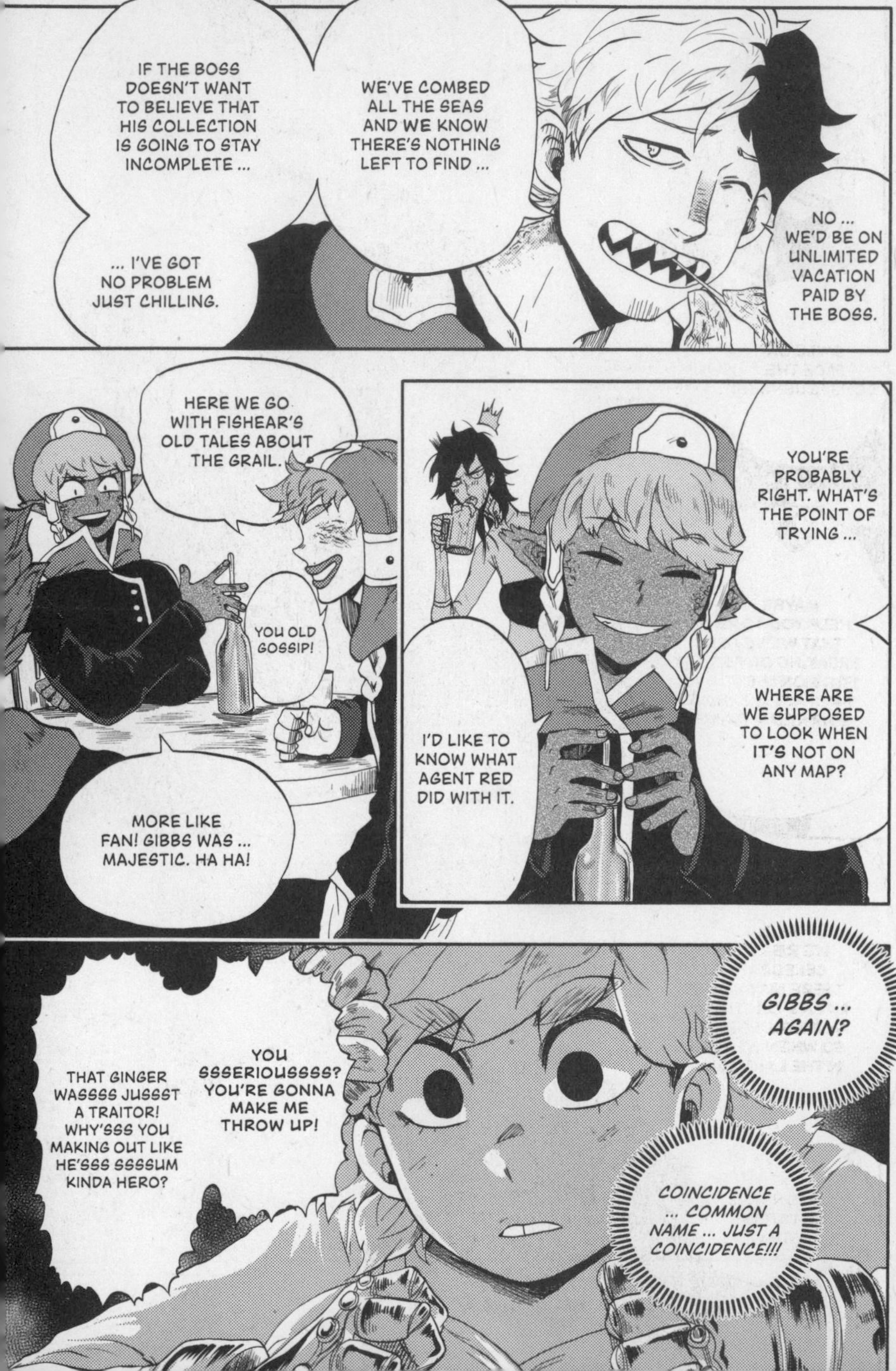
NO ... WE'D BE ON UNLIMITED VACATION PAID BY THE BOSS.
WE'VE COMBED ALL THE SEAS AND WE KNOW THERE'S NOTHING LEFT TO FIND ...
IF THE BOSS DOESN'T WANT TO BELIEVE THAT HIS COLLECTION IS GOING TO STAY INCOMPLETE ...
... I'VE GOT NO PROBLEM JUST CHILLING.
YOU'RE PROBABLY RIGHT. WHAT'S THE POINT OF TRYING ...
WHERE ARE WE SUPPOSED TO LOOK WHEN IT'S NOT ON ANY MAP?
I'D LIKE TO KNOW WHAT AGENT RED DID WITH IT.
HERE WE GO WITH FISHEAR'S OLD TALES ABOUT THE GRAIL.
YOU OLD GOSSIP!
MORE LIKE FAN! GIBBS WAS ... MAJESTIC. HA HA!
GIBBS ... AGAIN?
COINCIDENCE ... COMMON NAME ... JUST A COINCIDENCE!!!
YOU SSSERIOUSSSS? YOU'RE GONNA MAKE ME THROW UP!
THAT GINGER WASSSS JUSSST A TRAITOR! WHY'SSS YOU MAKING OUT LIKE HE'SSS SSSSUM KINDA HERO?

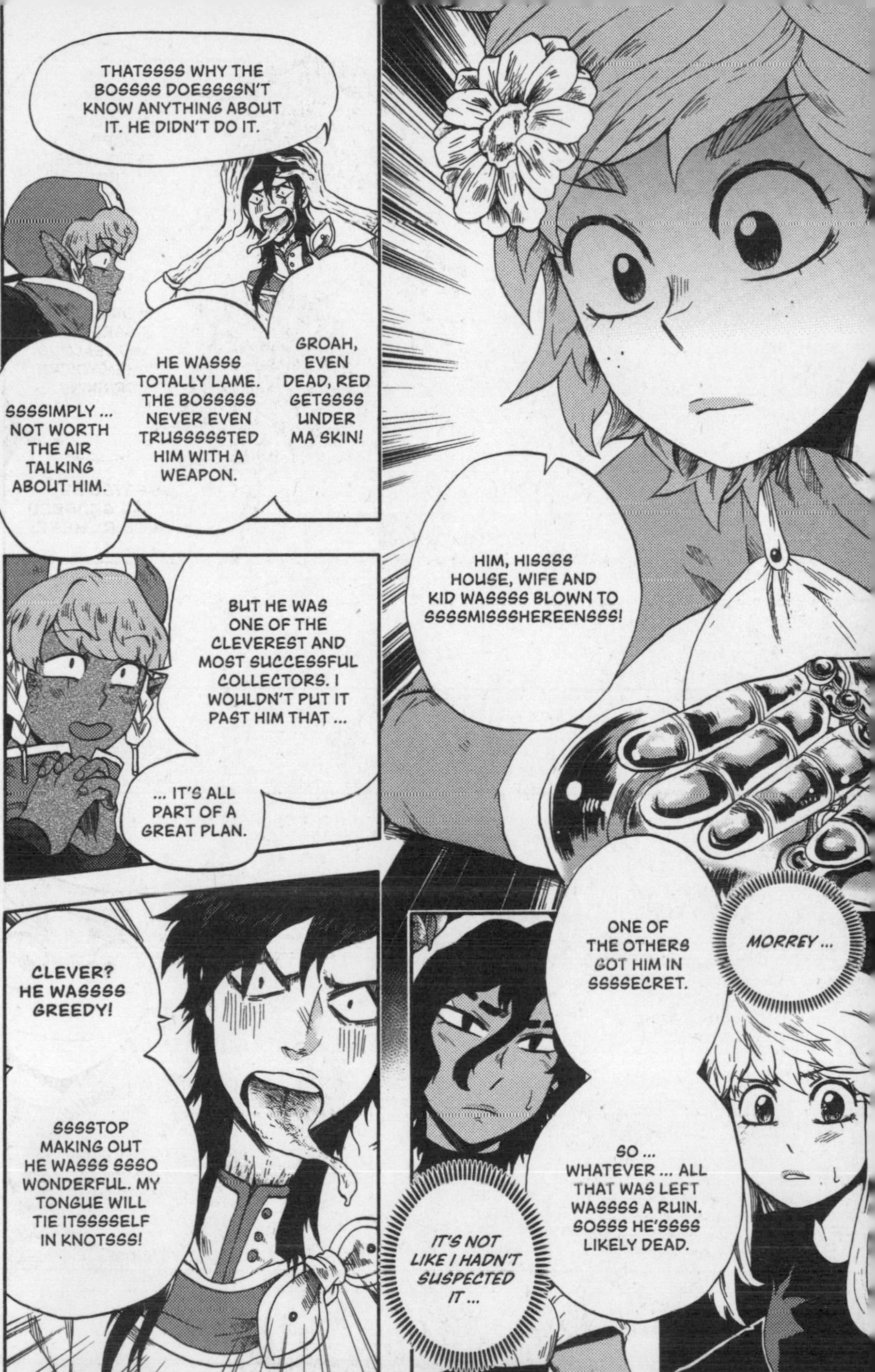
HIM, HISSSS HOUSE, WIFE AND KID WASSSS BLOWN TO SSSSMISSSHEREENSSS!
THATSSSS WHY THE BOSSSS DOESSSSN'T KNOW ANYTHING ABOUT IT. HE DIDN'T DO IT.
GROAH, EVEN DEAD, RED GETSSSS UNDER MA SKIN!
HE WASSS TOTALLY LAME. THE BOSSSSS NEVER EVEN TRUSSSSSTED HIM WITH A WEAPON.
SSSSIMPLY ... NOT WORTH THE AIR TALKING ABOUT HIM.
BUT HE WAS ONE OF THE CLEVEREST AND MOST SUCCESSFUL COLLECTORS. I WOULDN'T PUT IT PAST HIM THAT ...
... IT'S ALL PART OF A GREAT PLAN.
MORREY ...
ONE OF THE OTHERS GOT HIM IN SSSSECRET.
SO ... WHATEVER ... ALL THAT WAS LEFT WASSSS A RUIN. SOSSS HE'SSSS LIKELY DEAD.
IT'S NOT LIKE I HADN'T SUSPECTED IT ...
CLEVER? HE WASSSS GREEDY!
SSSSTOP MAKING OUT HE WASSS SSSO WONDERFUL. MY TONGUE WILL TIE ITSSSSELF IN KNOTSSS!

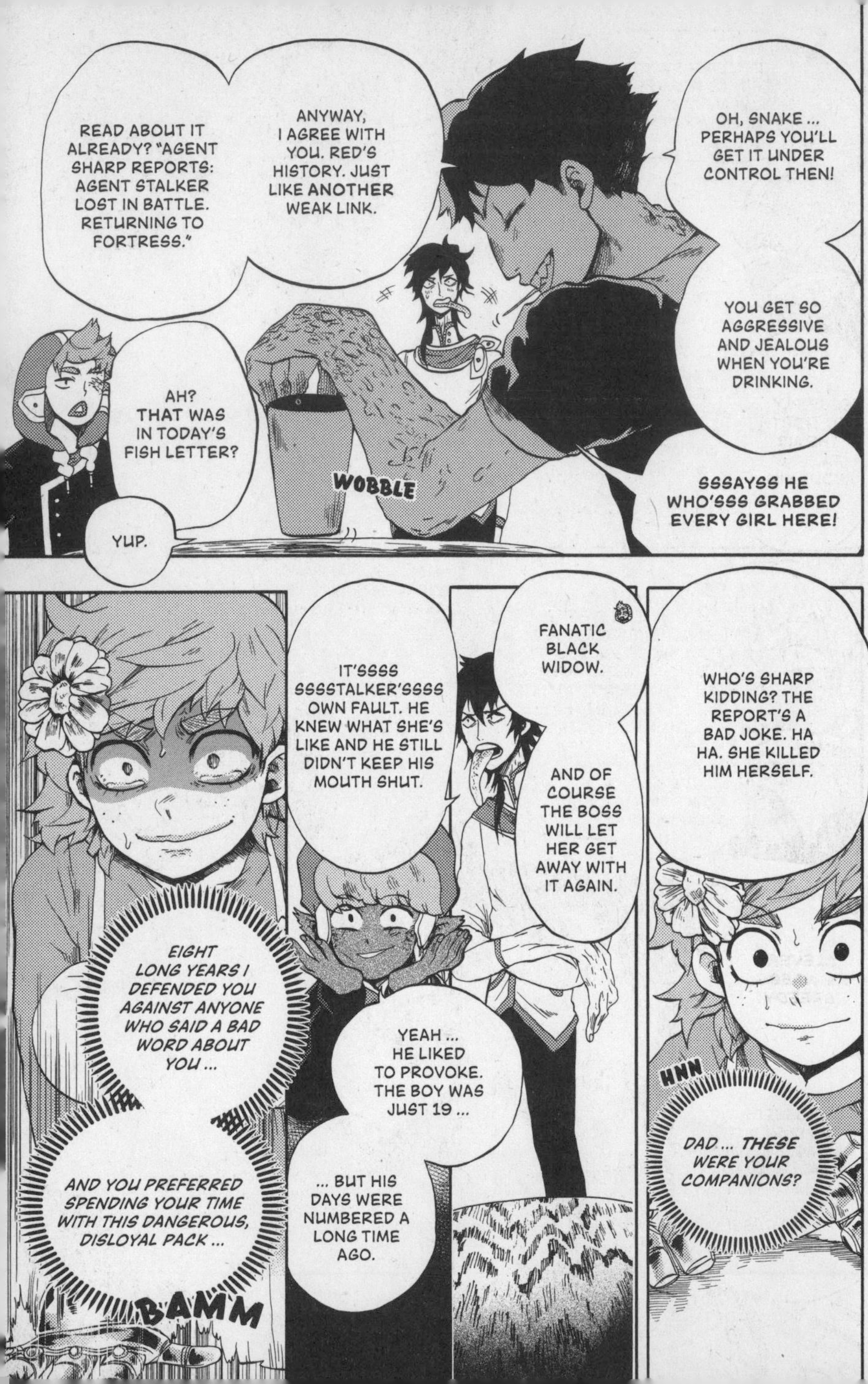
OH, SNAKE ... PERHAPS YOU'LL GET IT UNDER CONTROL THEN!
YOU GET SO AGGRESSIVE AND JEALOUS WHEN YOU'RE DRINKING.
SSSAYSS HE WHO'SSS GRABBED EVERY GIRL HERE!
ANYWAY, I AGREE WITH YOU. RED'S HISTORY. JUST LIKE ANOTHER WEAK LINK.
READ ABOUT IT ALREADY? "AGENT SHARP REPORTS: AGENT STALKER LOST IN BATTLE. RETURNING TO FORTRESS."
AH? THAT WAS IN TODAY'S FISH LETTER?
WOBBLE
YUP.
WHO'S SHARP KIDDING? THE REPORT'S A BAD JOKE. HA HA. SHE KILLED HIM HERSELF.
HNN
DAD ... THESE WERE YOUR COMPANIONS?
FANATIC BLACK WIDOW.
AND OF COURSE THE BOSS WILL LET HER GET AWAY WITH IT AGAIN.
IT'SSSS SSSSTALKER'SSSS OWN FAULT. HE KNEW WHAT SHE'S LIKE AND HE STILL DIDN'T KEEP HIS MOUTH SHUT.
YEAH ... HE LIKED TO PROVOKE. THE BOY WAS JUST 19 ...
... BUT HIS DAYS WERE NUMBERED A LONG TIME AGO.
EIGHT LONG YEARS I DEFENDED YOU AGAINST ANYONE WHO SAID A BAD WORD ABOUT YOU ...
AND YOU PREFERRED SPENDING YOUR TIME WITH THIS DANGEROUS, DISLOYAL PACK ...
BAMM

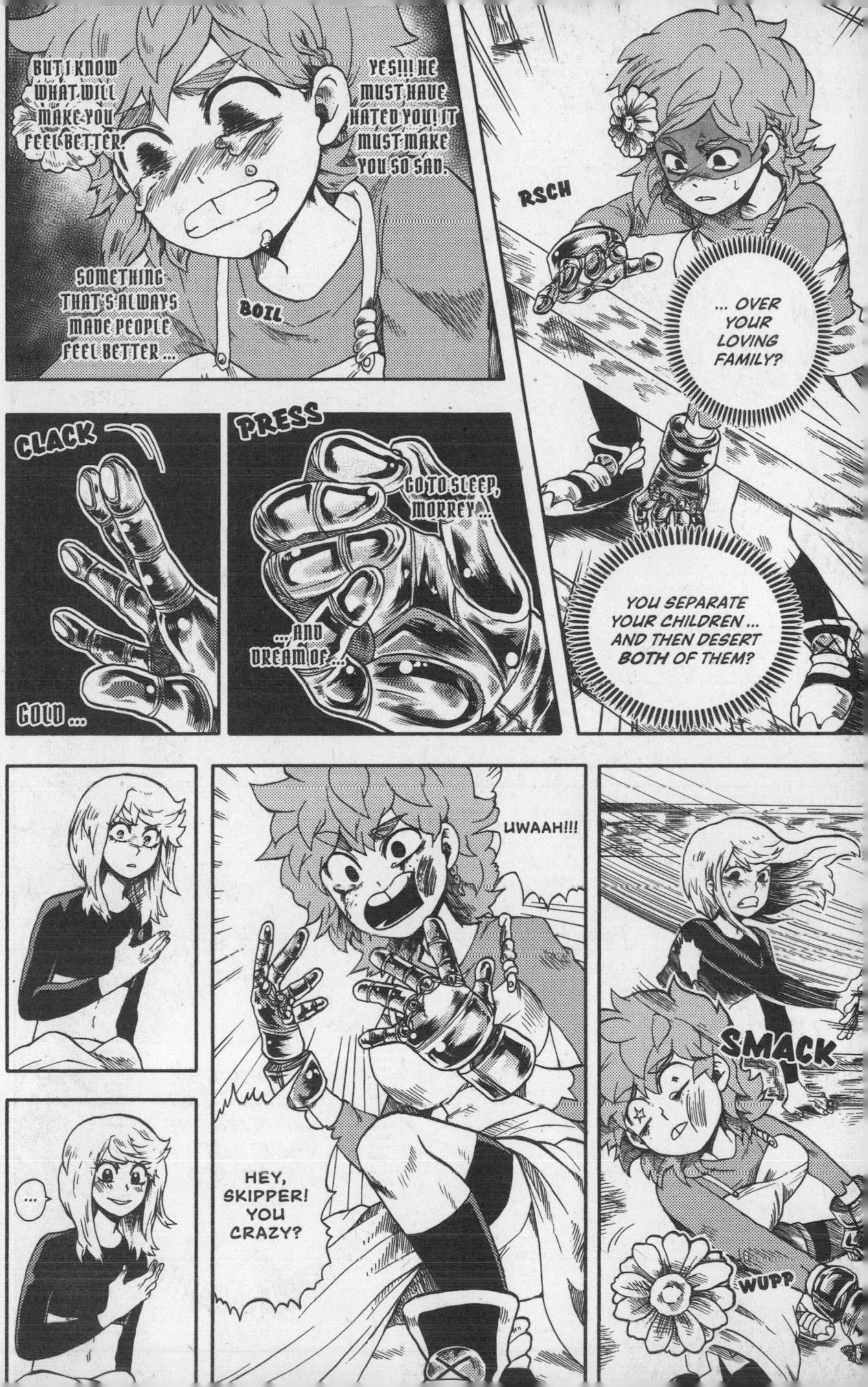
RSCH
... OVER YOUR LOVING FAMILY?
YOU SEPARATE YOUR CHILDREN ... AND THEN DESERT BOTH OF THEM?
YES!!! HE MUST HAVE HATED YOU! IT MUST MAKE YOU SO SAD.
BUT I KNOW WHAT WILL MAKE YOU FEEL BETTER.
SOMETHING THAT'S ALWAYS MADE PEOPLE FEEL BETTER ...
BOIL
PRESS
GO TO SLEEP, MORREY ...
... AND DREAM OF ...
CLACK
GOLD ...
SMACK
WUPP
UWAAH!!!
HEY, SKIPPER! YOU CRAZY?
...

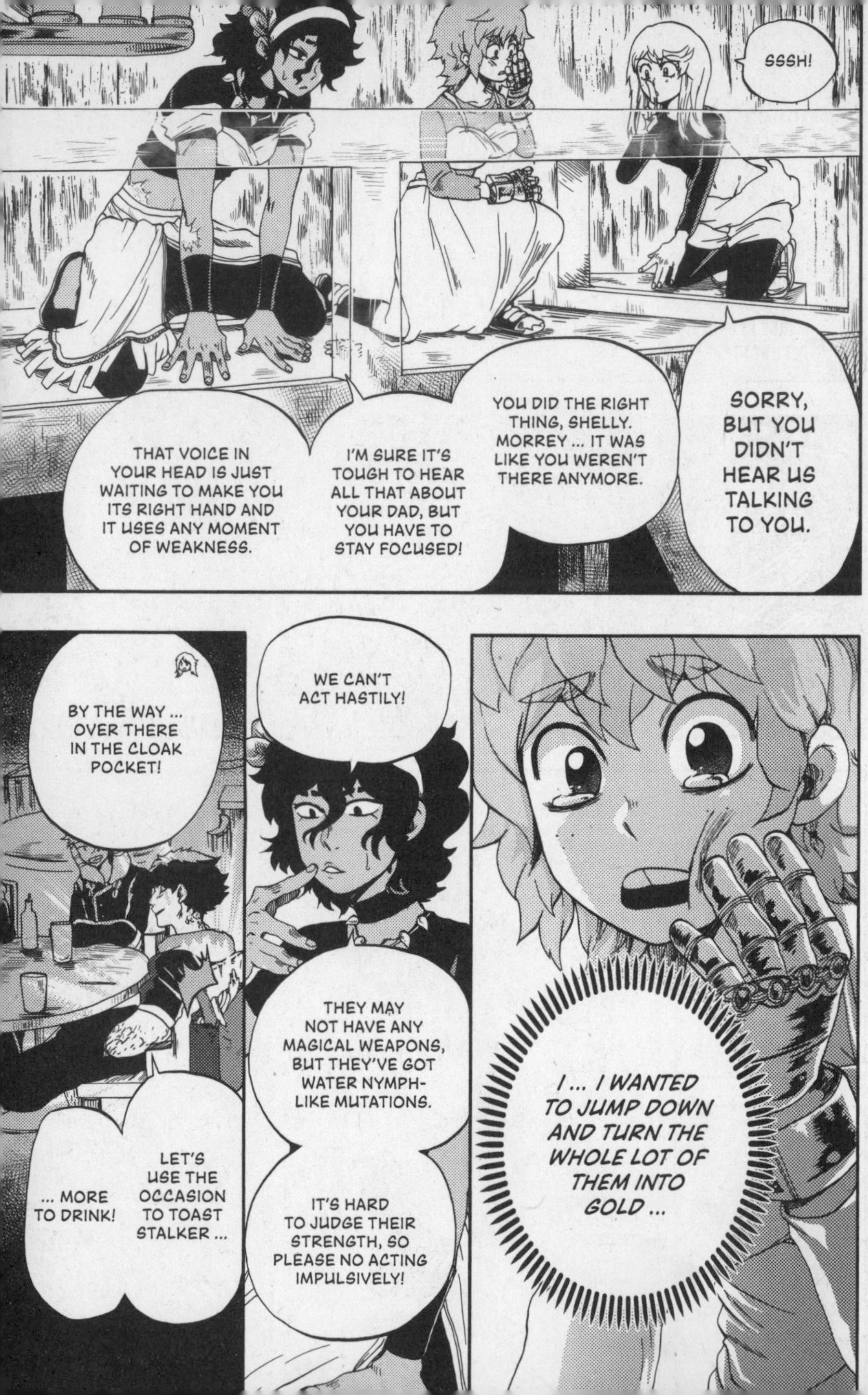
SSSH!
SORRY, BUT YOU DIDN'T HEAR US TALKING TO YOU.
YOU DID THE RIGHT THING, SHELLY. MORREY ... IT WAS LIKE YOU WEREN'T THERE ANYMORE.
I'M SURE IT'S TOUGH TO HEAR ALL THAT ABOUT YOUR DAD, BUT YOU HAVE TO STAY FOCUSED!
THAT VOICE IN YOUR HEAD IS JUST WAITING TO MAKE YOU ITS RIGHT HAND AND IT USES ANY MOMENT OF WEAKNESS.
I ... I WANTED TO JUMP DOWN AND TURN THE WHOLE LOT OF THEM INTO GOLD ...
WE CAN'T ACT HASTILY!
THEY MAY NOT HAVE ANY MAGICAL WEAPONS, BUT THEY'VE GOT WATER NYMPH-LIKE MUTATIONS.
IT'S HARD TO JUDGE THEIR STRENGTH, SO PLEASE NO ACTING IMPULSIVELY!
BY THE WAY ... OVER THERE IN THE CLOAK POCKET!
LET'S USE THE OCCASION TO TOAST STALKER ...
... MORE TO DRINK!

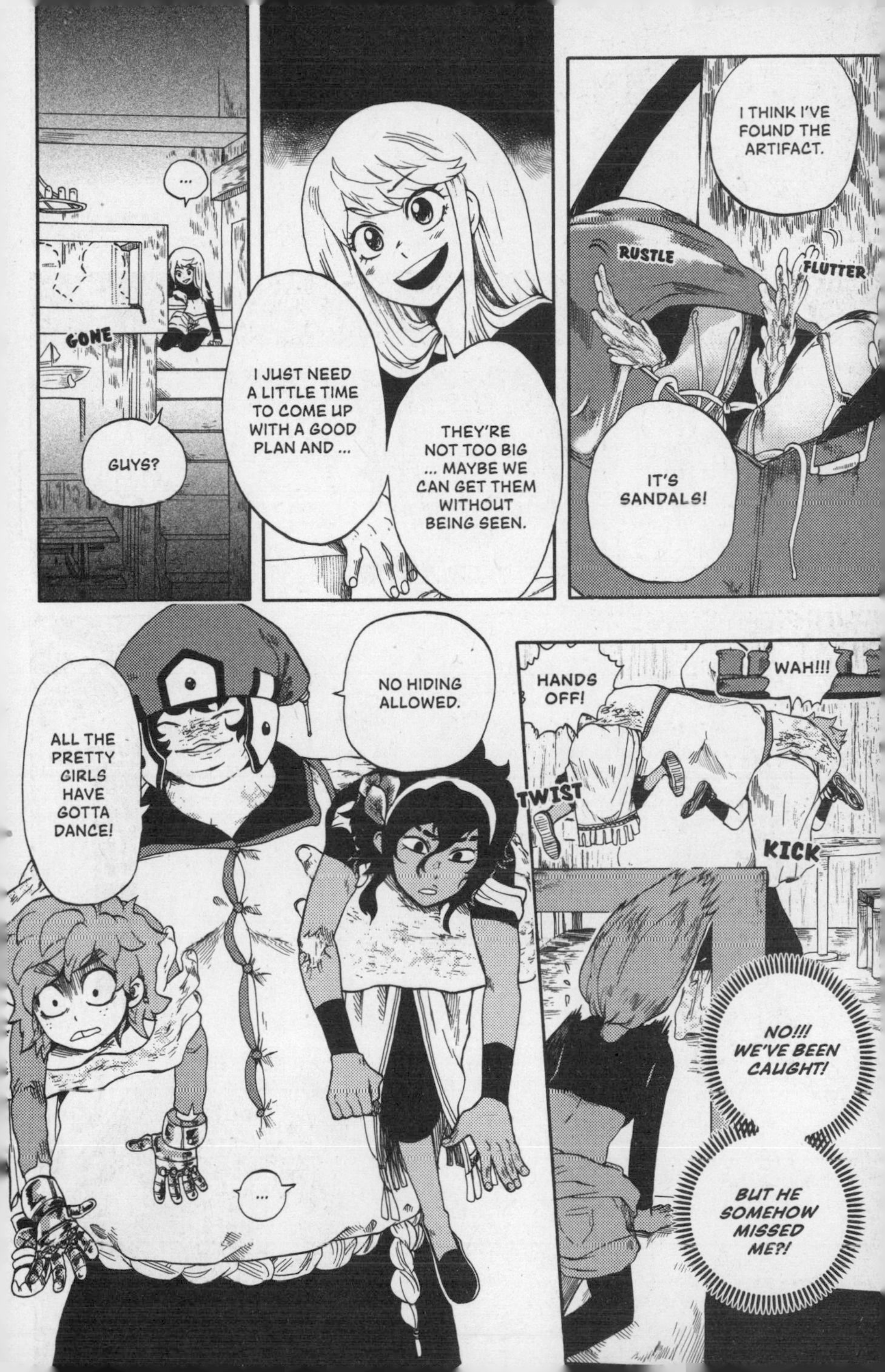
I THINK I'VE FOUND THE ARTIFACT.
RUSTLE
FLUTTER
IT'S SANDALS!
THEY'RE NOT TOO BIG ... MAYBE WE CAN GET THEM WITHOUT BEING SEEN.
I JUST NEED A LITTLE TIME TO COME UP WITH A GOOD PLAN AND ...
...
GONE
GUYS?
WAH!!!
HANDS OFF!
TWIST
KICK
NO!!! WE'VE BEEN CAUGHT!
BUT HE SOMEHOW MISSED ME?!
NO HIDING ALLOWED.
ALL THE PRETTY GIRLS HAVE GOTTA DANCE!
...

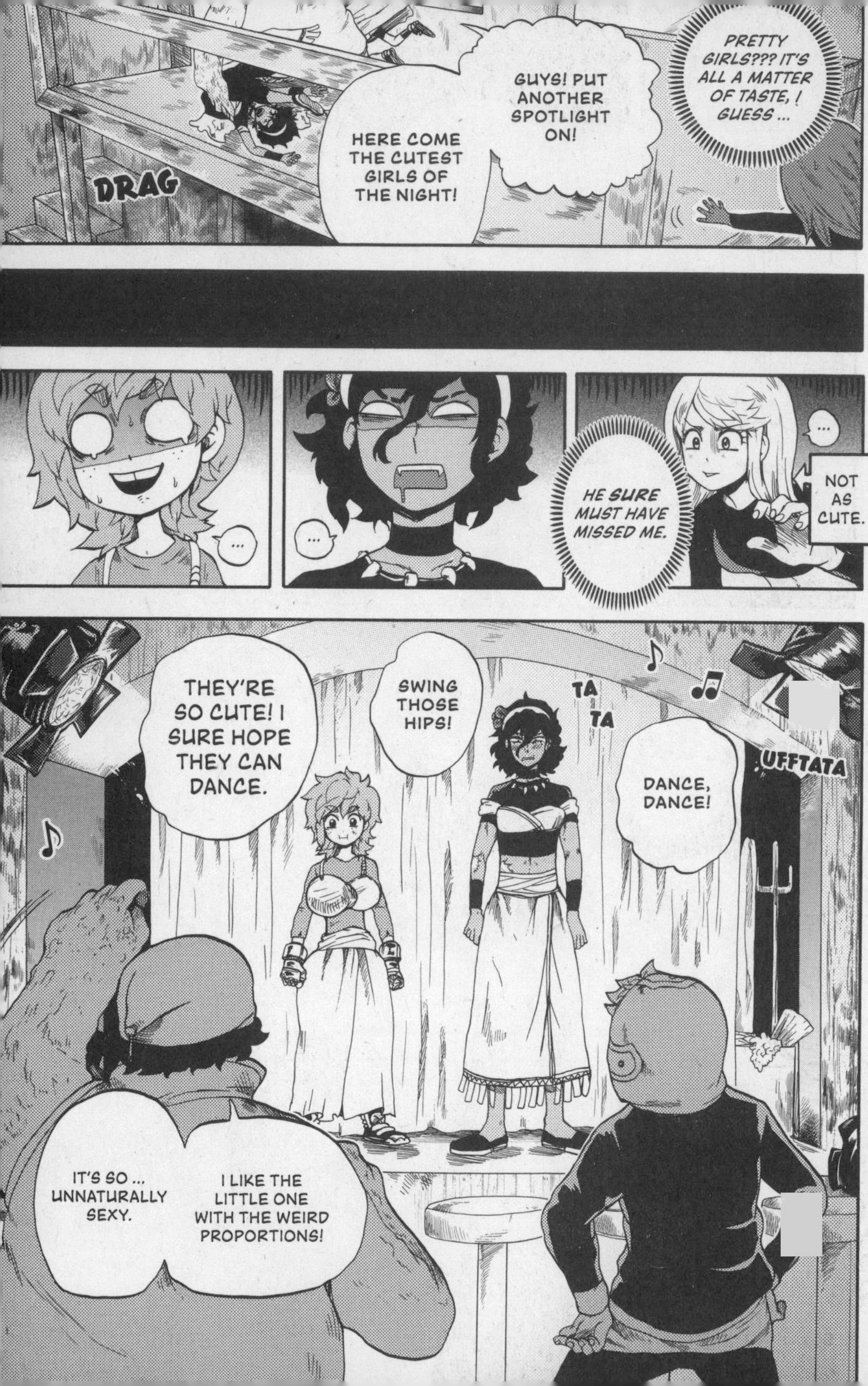
PRETTY GIRLS??? IT'S ALL A MATTER OF TASTE, I GUESS ...
GUYS! PUT ANOTHER SPOTLIGHT ON!
HERE COME THE CUTEST GIRLS OF THE NIGHT!
DRAG
...
NOT AS CUTE.
HE *SURE* MUST HAVE MISSED ME.
...
...
DANCE, DANCE!
UFFTATA
TA
TA
SWING THOSE HIPS!
THEY'RE SO CUTE! I SURE HOPE THEY CAN DANCE.
I LIKE THE LITTLE ONE WITH THE WEIRD PROPORTIONS!
IT'S SO ... UNNATURALLY SEXY.

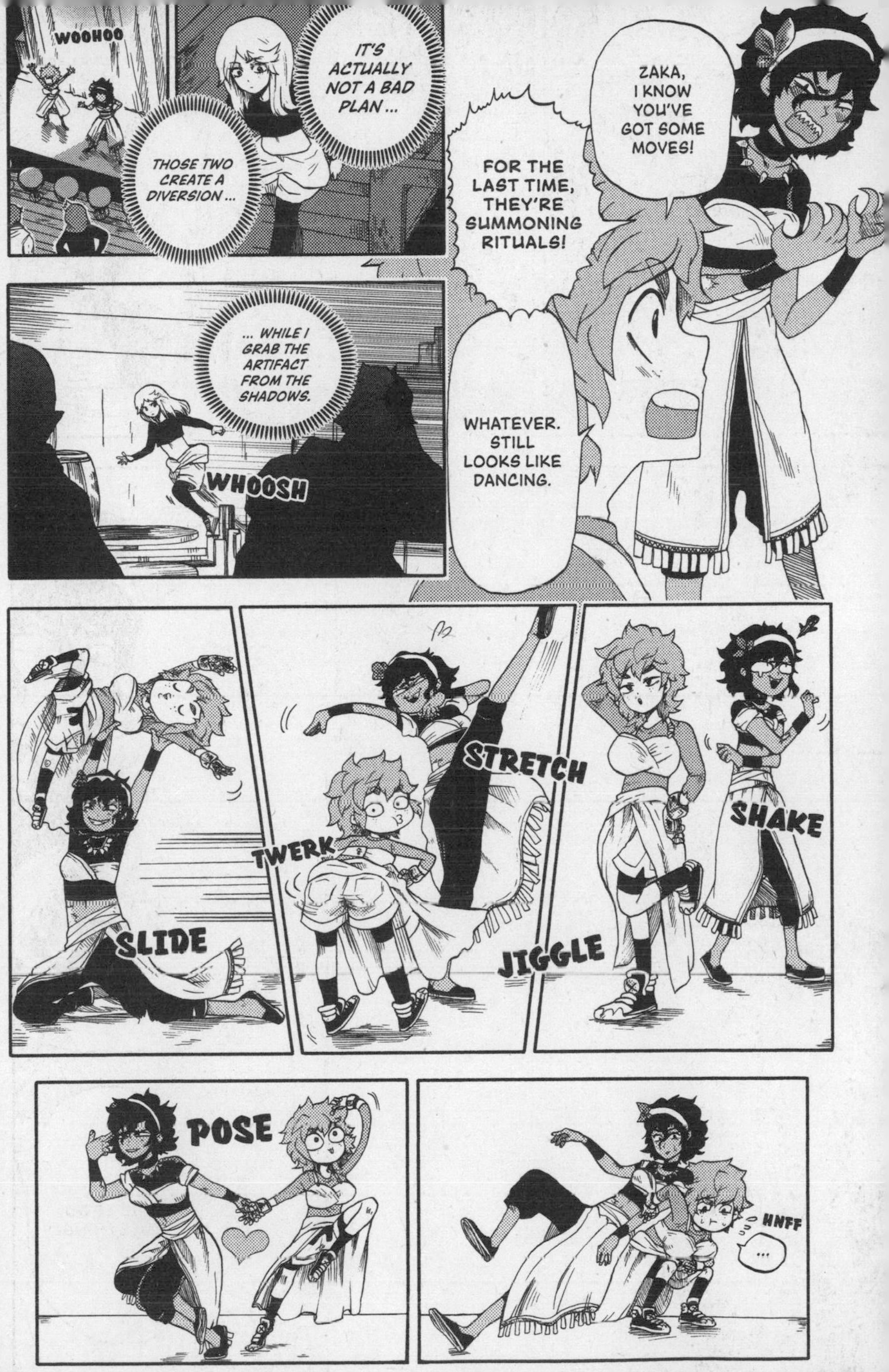
ZAKA, I KNOW YOU'VE GOT SOME MOVES!
FOR THE LAST TIME, THEY'RE SUMMONING RITUALS!
WHATEVER. STILL LOOKS LIKE DANCING.
WOOHOO
IT'S ACTUALLY NOT A BAD PLAN ...
THOSE TWO CREATE A DIVERSION ...
... WHILE I GRAB THE ARTIFACT FROM THE SHADOWS.
WHOOSH
SHAKE
JIGGLE
STRETCH
TWERK
SLIDE
HNFF
...
POSE

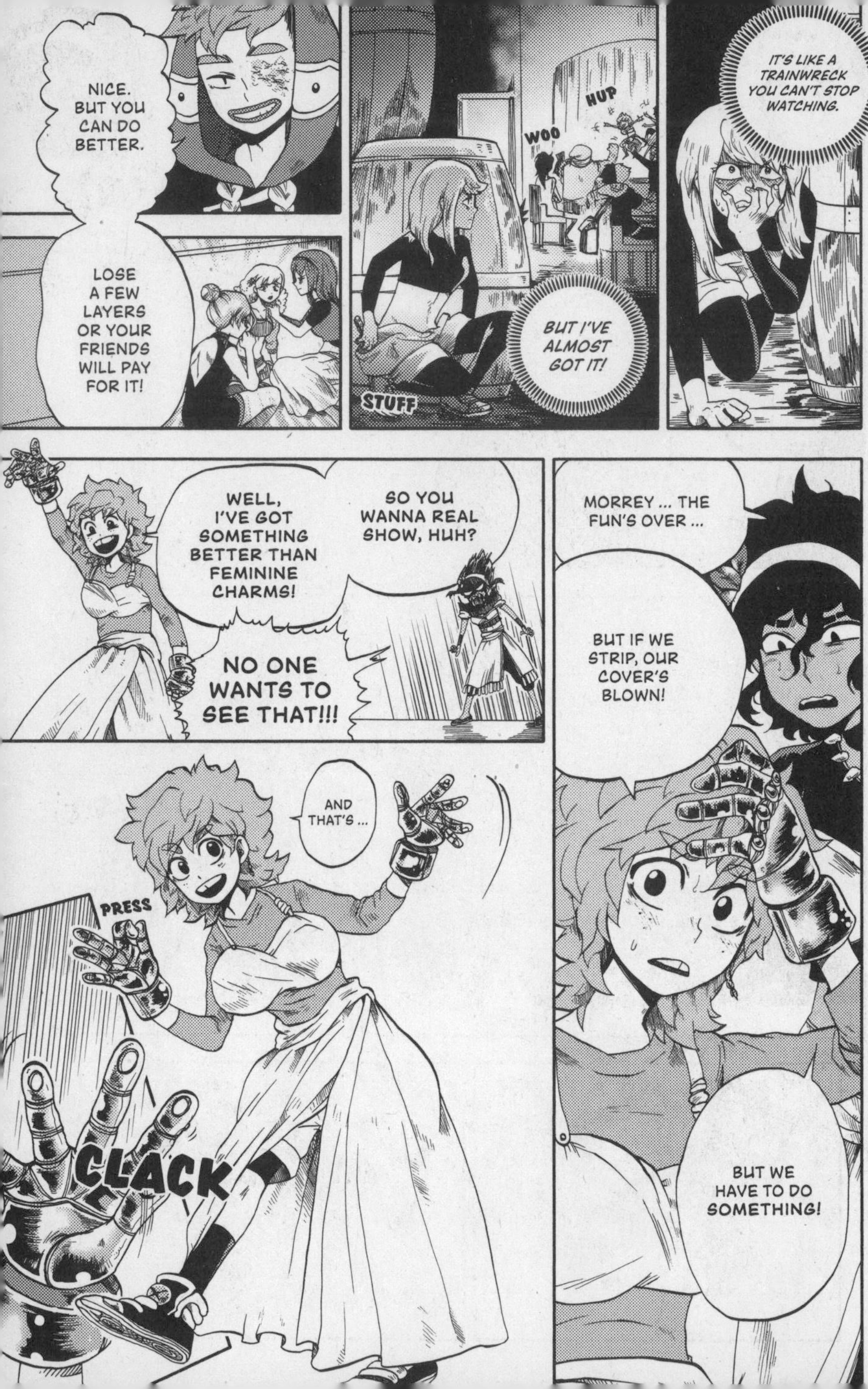
IT'S LIKE A TRAINWRECK YOU CAN'T STOP WATCHING.
HUP
WOO
BUT I'VE ALMOST GOT IT!
STUFF
NICE. BUT YOU CAN DO BETTER.
LOSE A FEW LAYERS OR YOUR FRIENDS WILL PAY FOR IT!
MORREY ... THE FUN'S OVER ...
BUT IF WE STRIP, OUR COVER'S BLOWN!
BUT WE HAVE TO DO SOMETHING!
SO YOU WANNA REAL SHOW, HUH?
WELL, I'VE GOT SOMETHING BETTER THAN FEMININE CHARMS!
NO ONE WANTS TO SEE THAT!!!
AND THAT'S ...
PRESS
CLACK

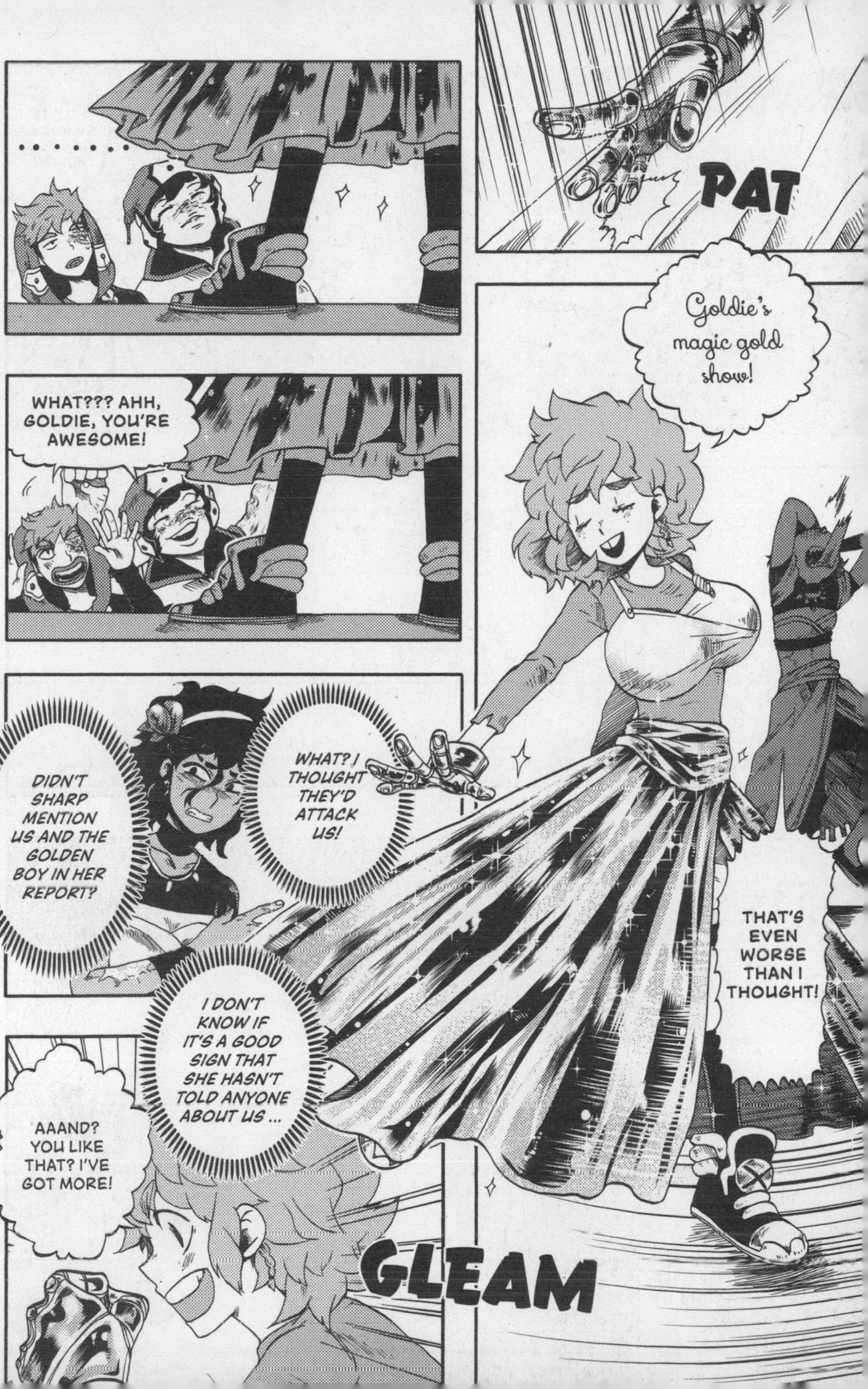
PAT
......
Goldie's magic gold show!
GLEAM
THAT'S EVEN WORSE THAN I THOUGHT!
WHAT??? AHH, GOLDIE, YOU'RE AWESOME!
WHAT? I THOUGHT THEY'D ATTACK US!
DIDN'T SHARP MENTION US AND THE GOLDEN BOY IN HER REPORT?
I DON'T KNOW IF IT'S A GOOD SIGN THAT SHE HASN'T TOLD ANYONE ABOUT US ...
AAAND? YOU LIKE THAT? I'VE GOT MORE!

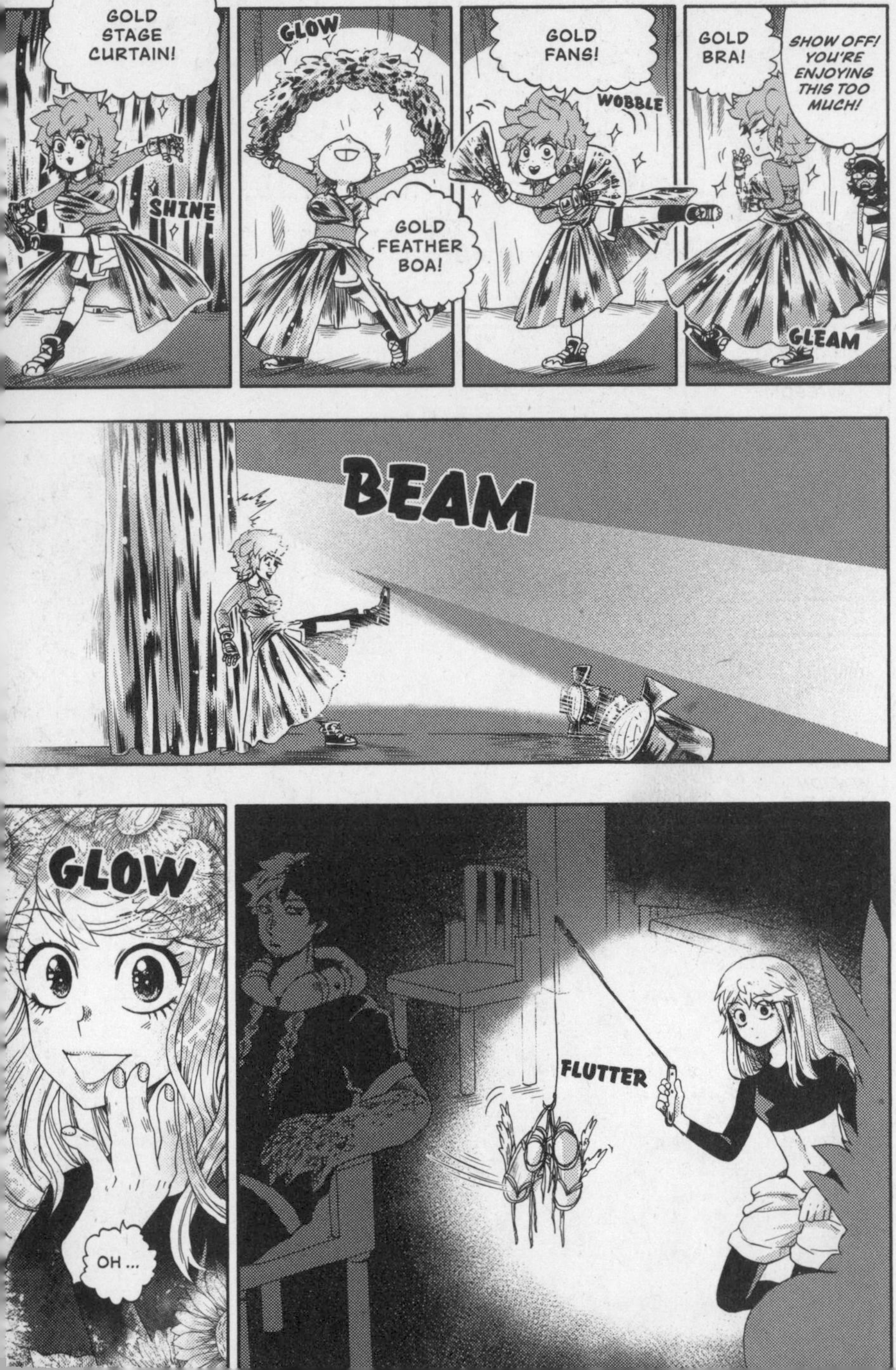
SHOW OFF! YOU'RE ENJOYING THIS TOO MUCH!
GOLD BRA!
GLEAM
GOLD FANS!
WOBBLE
GLOW
GOLD FEATHER BOA!
GOLD STAGE CURTAIN!
SHINE
BEAM
FLUTTER
GLOW
OH ...

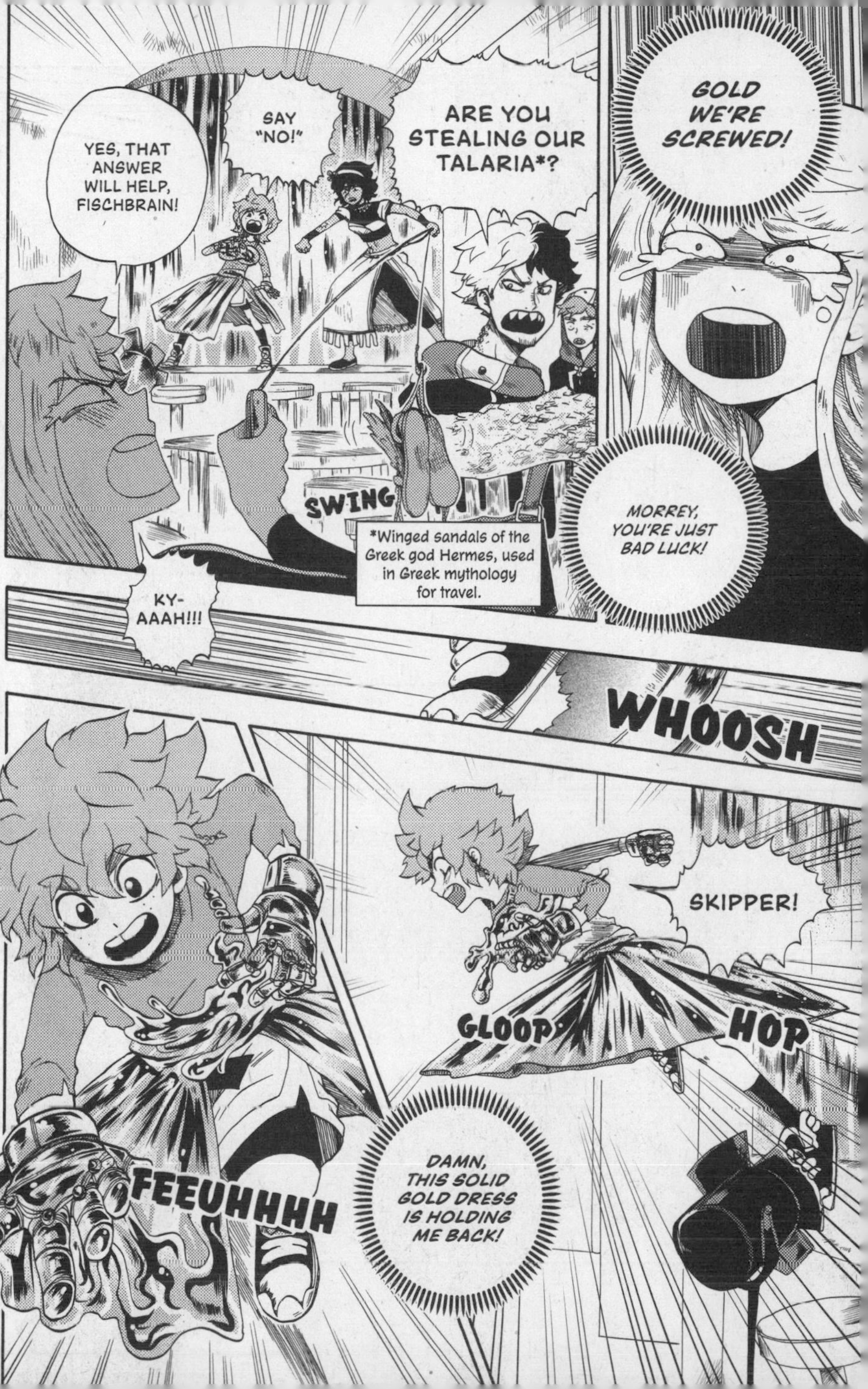
GOLD WE'RE SCREWED!
MORREY, YOU'RE JUST BAD LUCK!
ARE YOU STEALING OUR TALARIA*?
SAY "NO!"
YES, THAT ANSWER WILL HELP, FISCHBRAIN!
SWING
*Winged sandals of the Greek god Hermes, used in Greek mythology for travel.
KY-AAAH!!!
WHOOSH
SKIPPER!
HOP
GLOOP
DAMN, THIS SOLID GOLD DRESS IS HOLDING ME BACK!
FEEUHHHHH

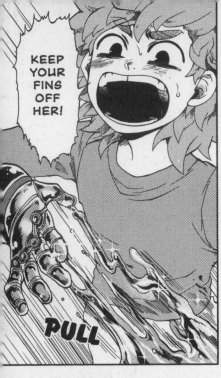

KEEP YOUR FINS OFF HER!

PULL

ZONK

CLACK

CLACK

HEY!!!

SWSCH

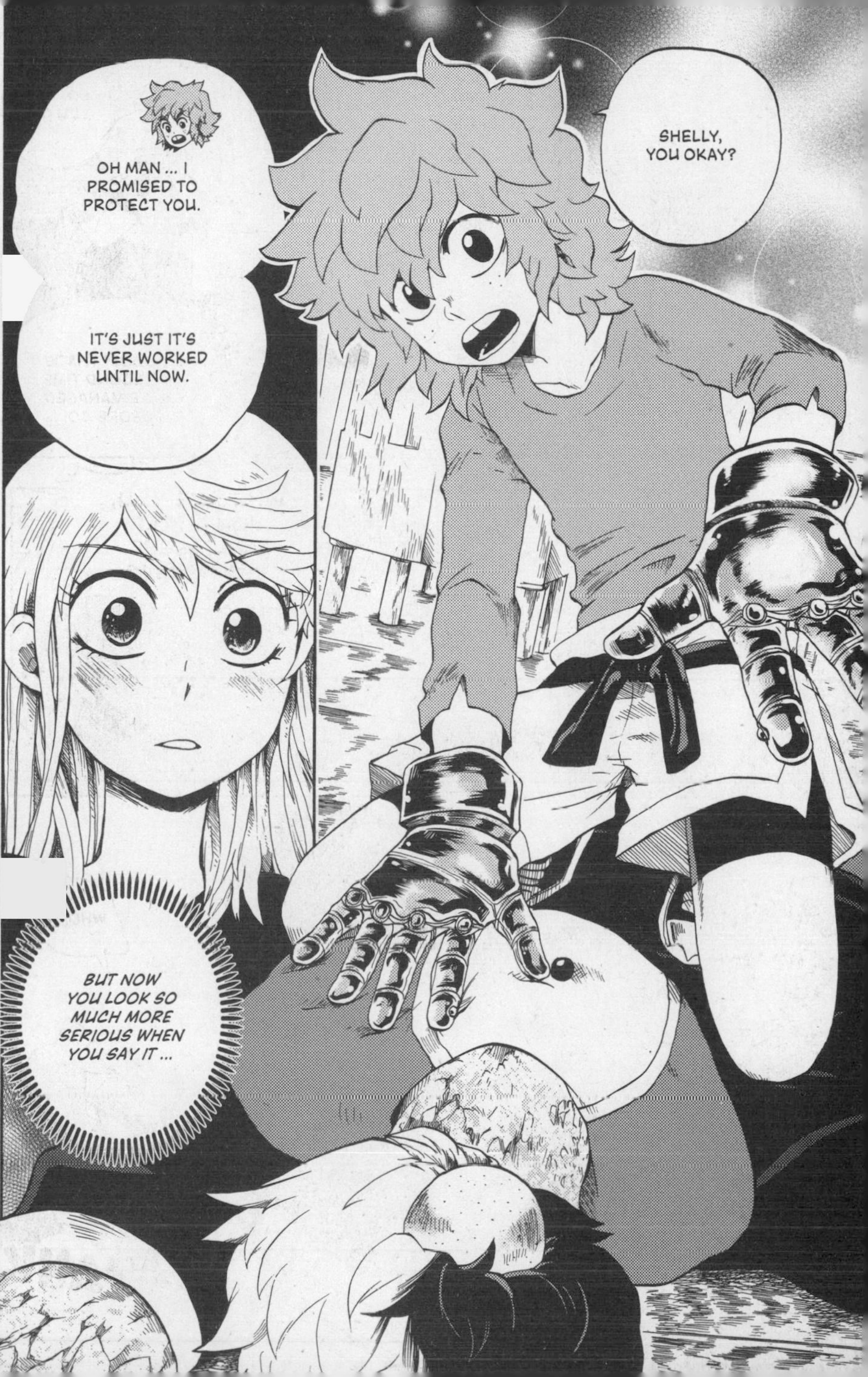
SHELLY, YOU OKAY?
OH MAN ... I PROMISED TO PROTECT YOU.
IT'S JUST IT'S NEVER WORKED UNTIL NOW.
BUT NOW YOU LOOK SO MUCH MORE SERIOUS WHEN YOU SAY IT ...

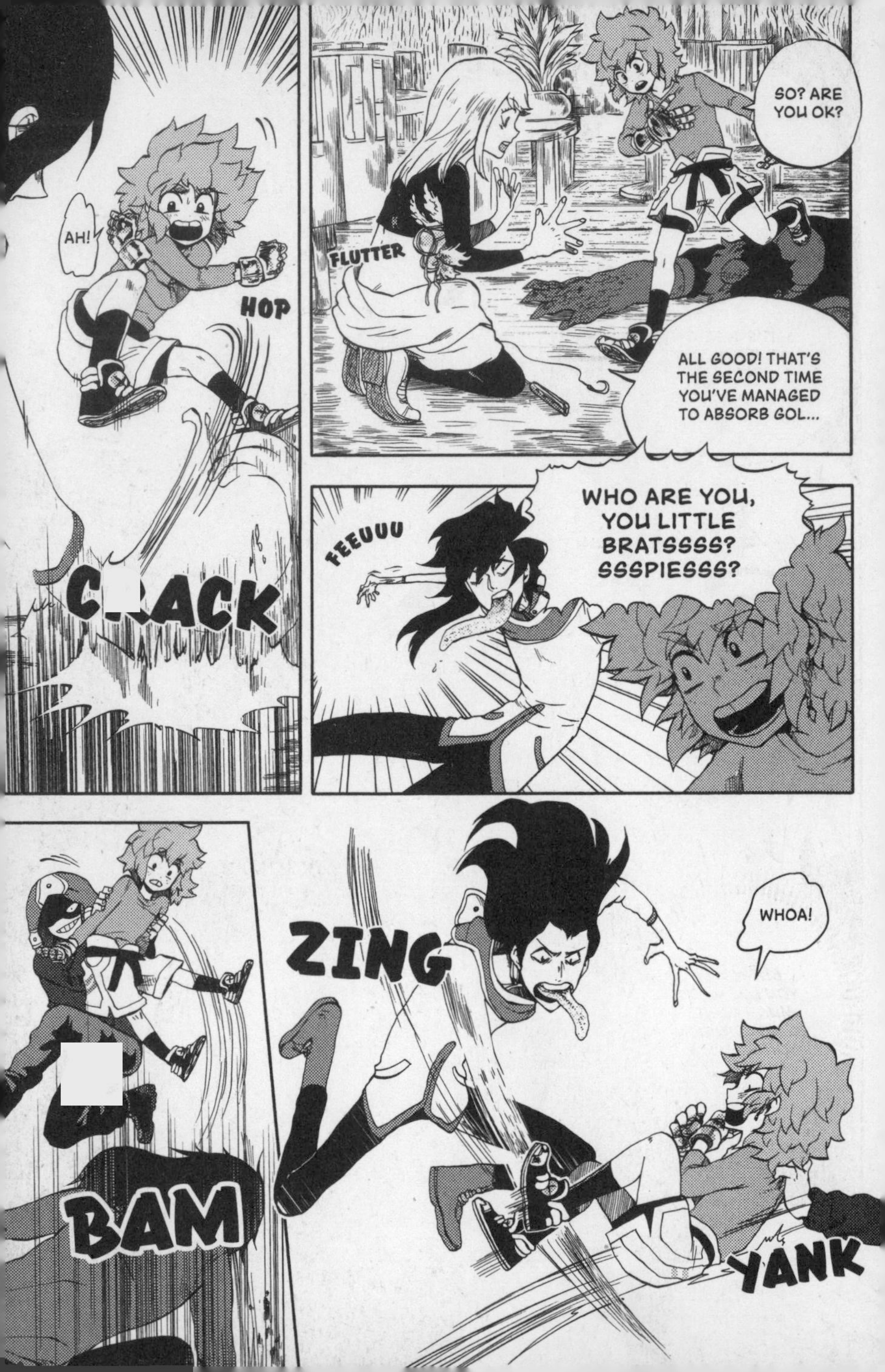
SO? ARE YOU OK?
FLUTTER
ALL GOOD! THAT'S THE SECOND TIME YOU'VE MANAGED TO ABSORB GOL...
WHO ARE YOU, YOU LITTLE BRATSSSS? SSSPIESSS?
FEEUUU
AH!
HOP
CRACK
WHOA!
ZING
YANK
BAM

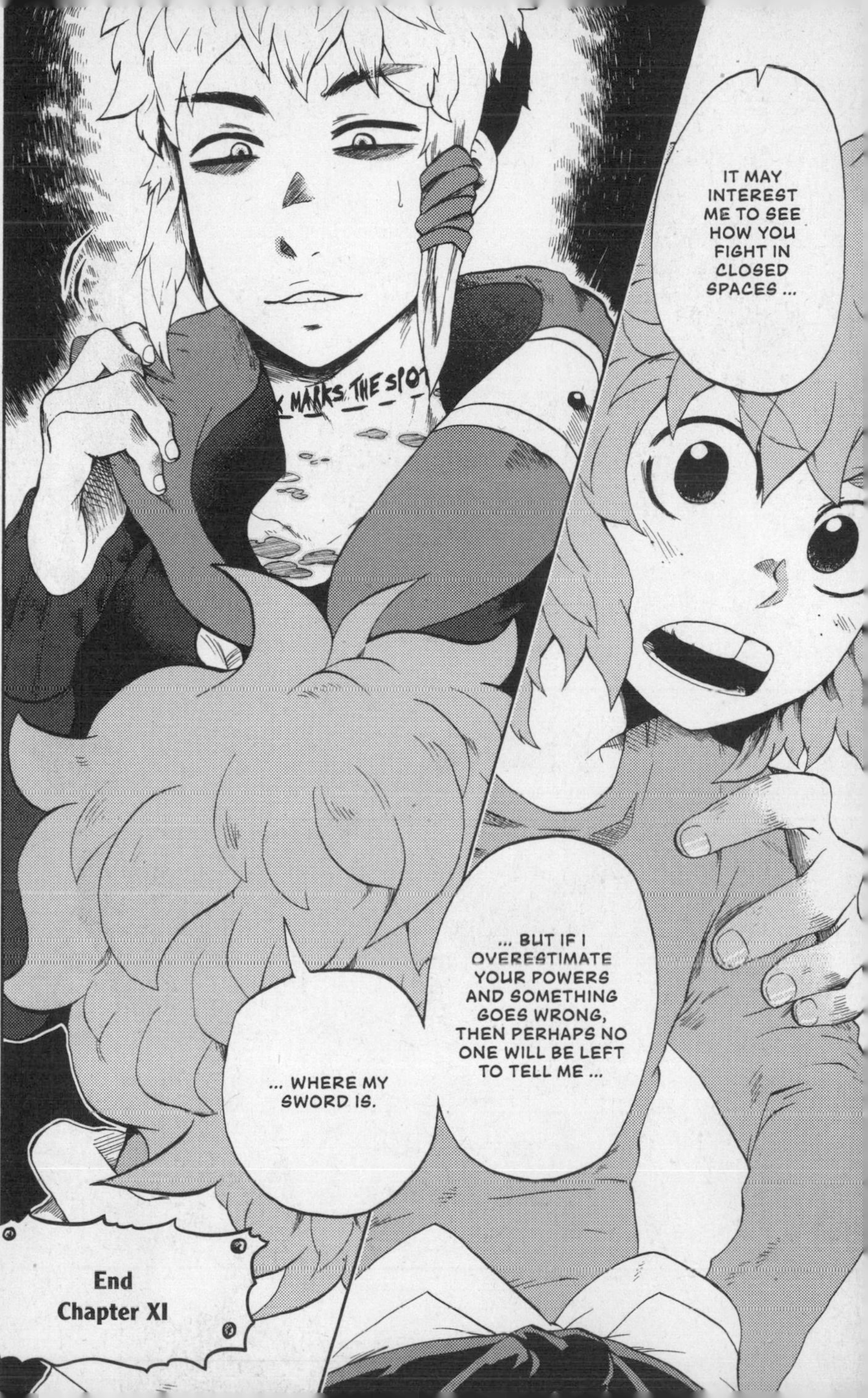
IT MAY INTEREST ME TO SEE HOW YOU FIGHT IN CLOSED SPACES ...
X MARKS THE SPO
... BUT IF I OVERESTIMATE YOUR POWERS AND SOMETHING GOES WRONG, THEN PERHAPS NO ONE WILL BE LEFT TO TELL ME ...
... WHERE MY SWORD IS.
End Chapter XI

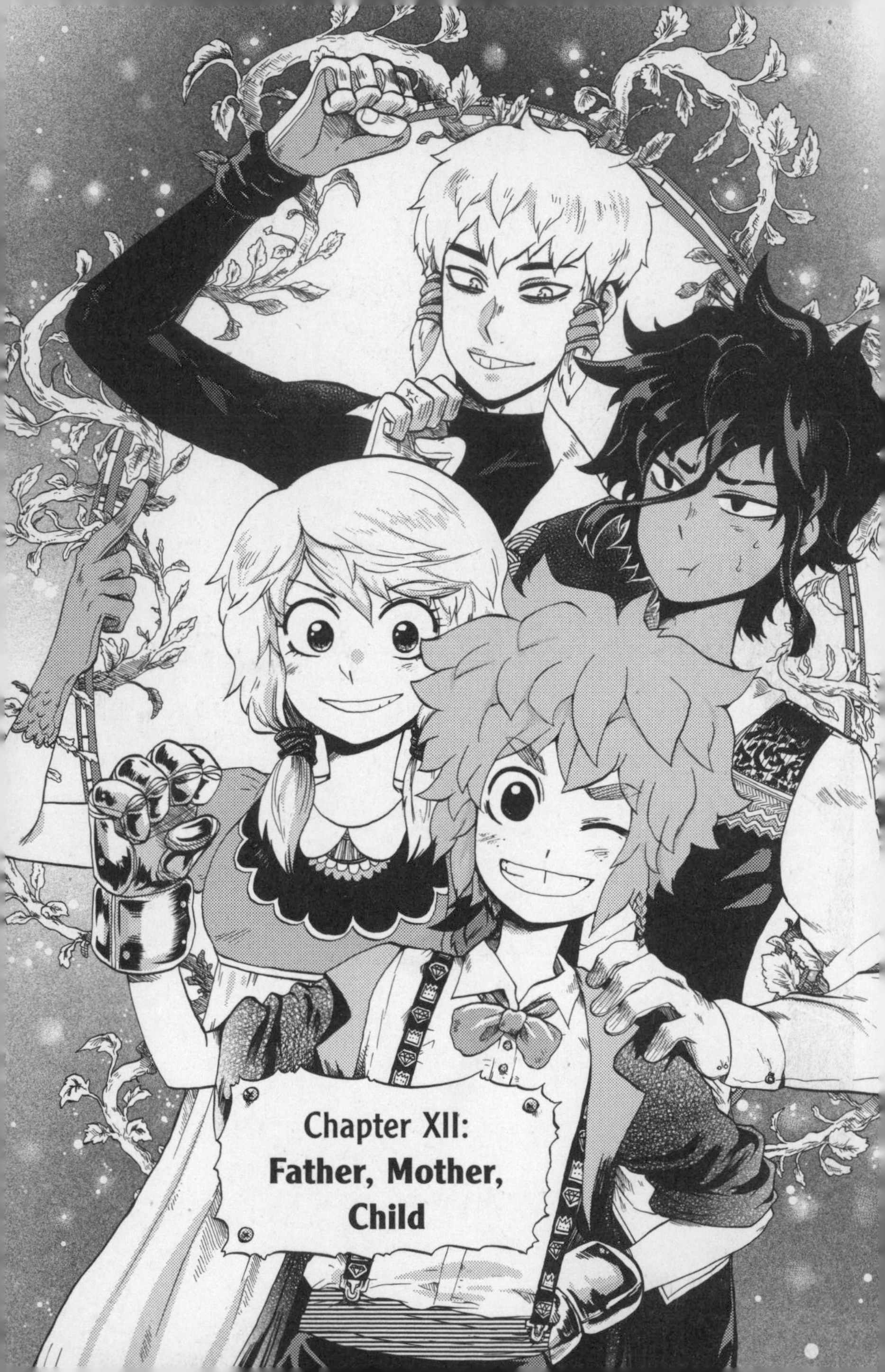
Chapter XII:
Father, Mother,
Child

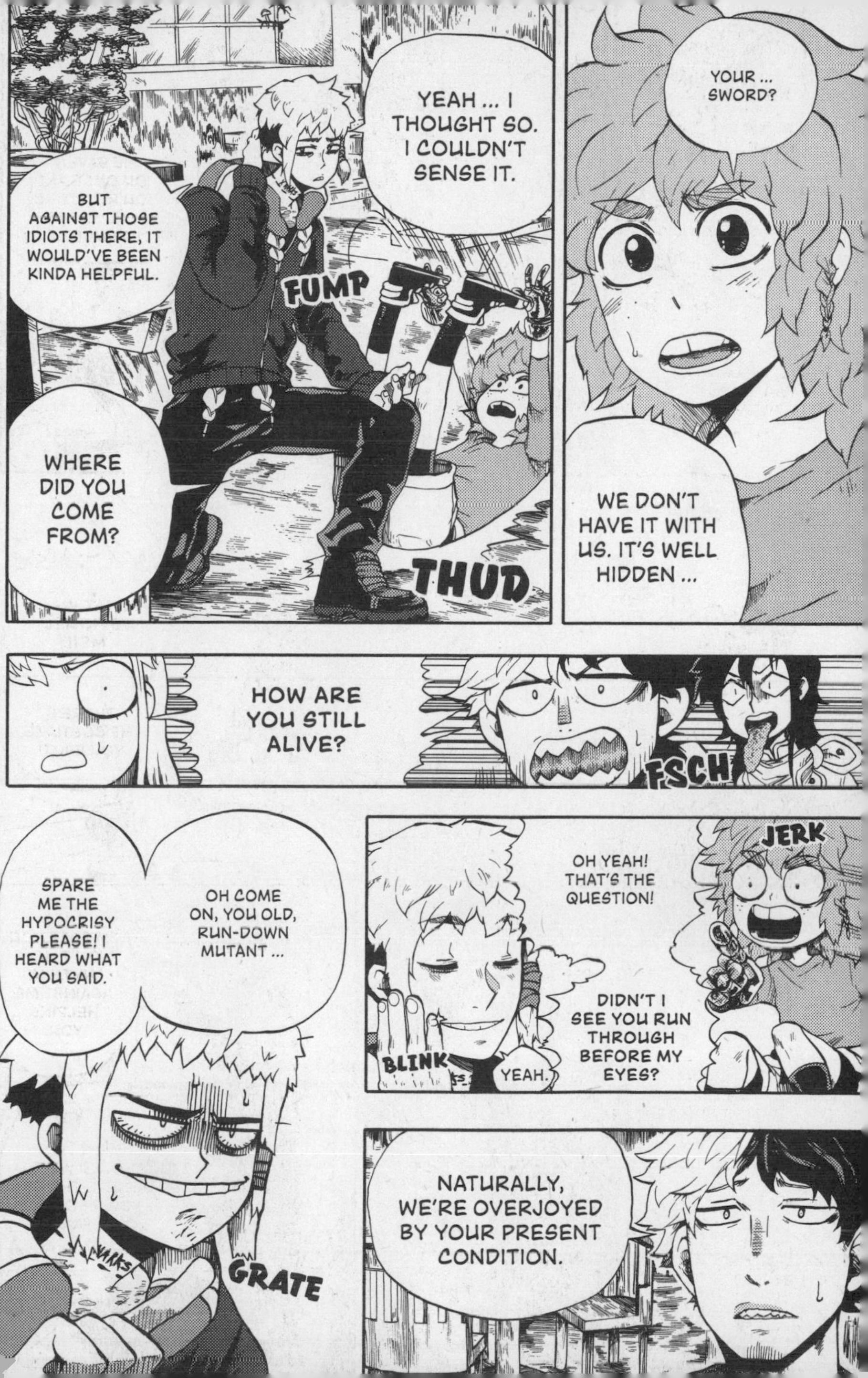
YOUR ... SWORD?
WE DON'T HAVE IT WITH US. IT'S WELL HIDDEN ...
YEAH ... I THOUGHT SO. I COULDN'T SENSE IT.
BUT AGAINST THOSE IDIOTS THERE, IT WOULD'VE BEEN KINDA HELPFUL.
FUMP
WHERE DID YOU COME FROM?
THUD
HOW ARE YOU STILL ALIVE?
FSCH
JERK
OH YEAH! THAT'S THE QUESTION!
DIDN'T I SEE YOU RUN THROUGH BEFORE MY EYES?
YEAH.
BLINK
NATURALLY, WE'RE OVERJOYED BY YOUR PRESENT CONDITION.
OH COME ON, YOU OLD, RUN-DOWN MUTANT ...
SPARE ME THE HYPOCRISY PLEASE! I HEARD WHAT YOU SAID.
GRATE

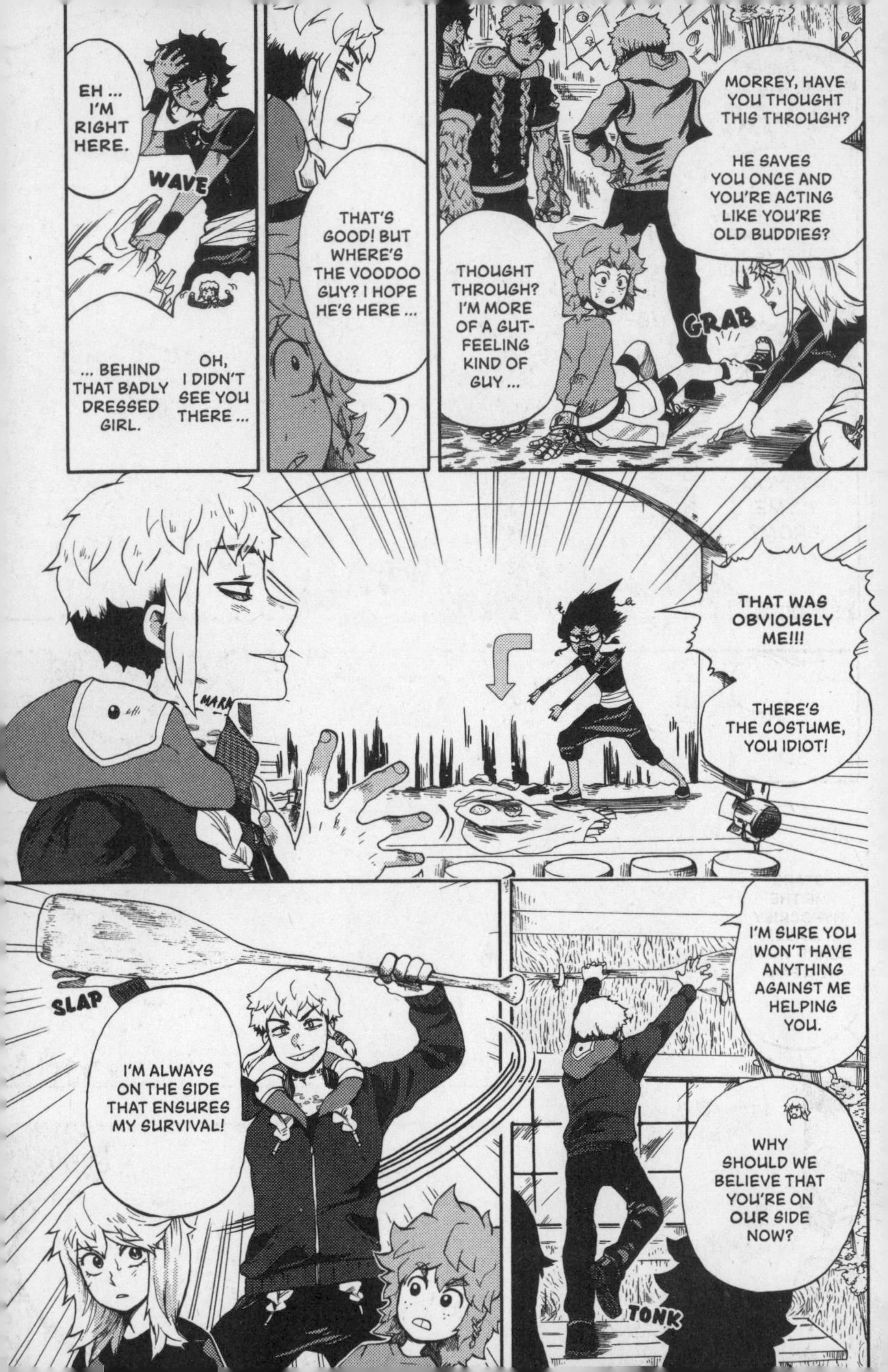
MORREY, HAVE YOU THOUGHT THIS THROUGH?
HE SAVES YOU ONCE AND YOU'RE ACTING LIKE YOU'RE OLD BUDDIES?
GRAB
THOUGHT THROUGH? I'M MORE OF A GUT-FEELING KIND OF GUY ...
THAT'S GOOD! BUT WHERE'S THE VOODOO GUY? I HOPE HE'S HERE ...
EH ... I'M RIGHT HERE.
WAVE
OH, I DIDN'T SEE YOU THERE ...
... BEHIND THAT BADLY DRESSED GIRL.
THAT WAS OBVIOUSLY ME!!!
THERE'S THE COSTUME, YOU IDIOT!
I'M SURE YOU WON'T HAVE ANYTHING AGAINST ME HELPING YOU.
WHY SHOULD WE BELIEVE THAT YOU'RE ON OUR SIDE NOW?
TONK
SLAP
I'M ALWAYS ON THE SIDE THAT ENSURES MY SURVIVAL!

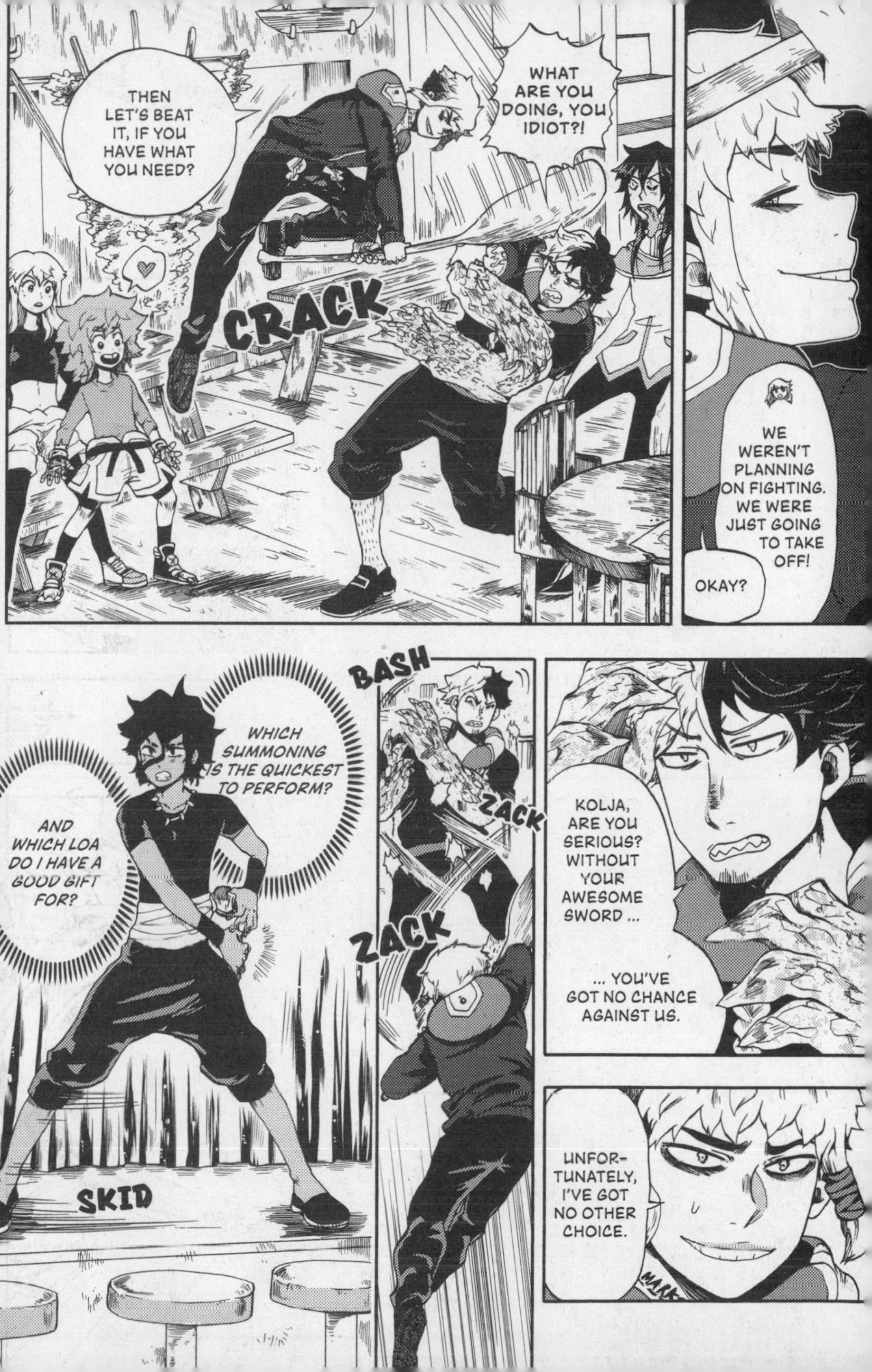
WE WEREN'T PLANNING ON FIGHTING. WE WERE JUST GOING TO TAKE OFF!
OKAY?
WHAT ARE YOU DOING, YOU IDIOT?!
THEN LET'S BEAT IT, IF YOU HAVE WHAT YOU NEED?
CRACK
KOLJA, ARE YOU SERIOUS? WITHOUT YOUR AWESOME SWORD ...
... YOU'VE GOT NO CHANCE AGAINST US.
UNFOR-TUNATELY, I'VE GOT NO OTHER CHOICE.
BASH
ZACK
ZACK
WHICH SUMMONING IS THE QUICKEST TO PERFORM?
AND WHICH LOA DO I HAVE A GOOD GIFT FOR?
SKID

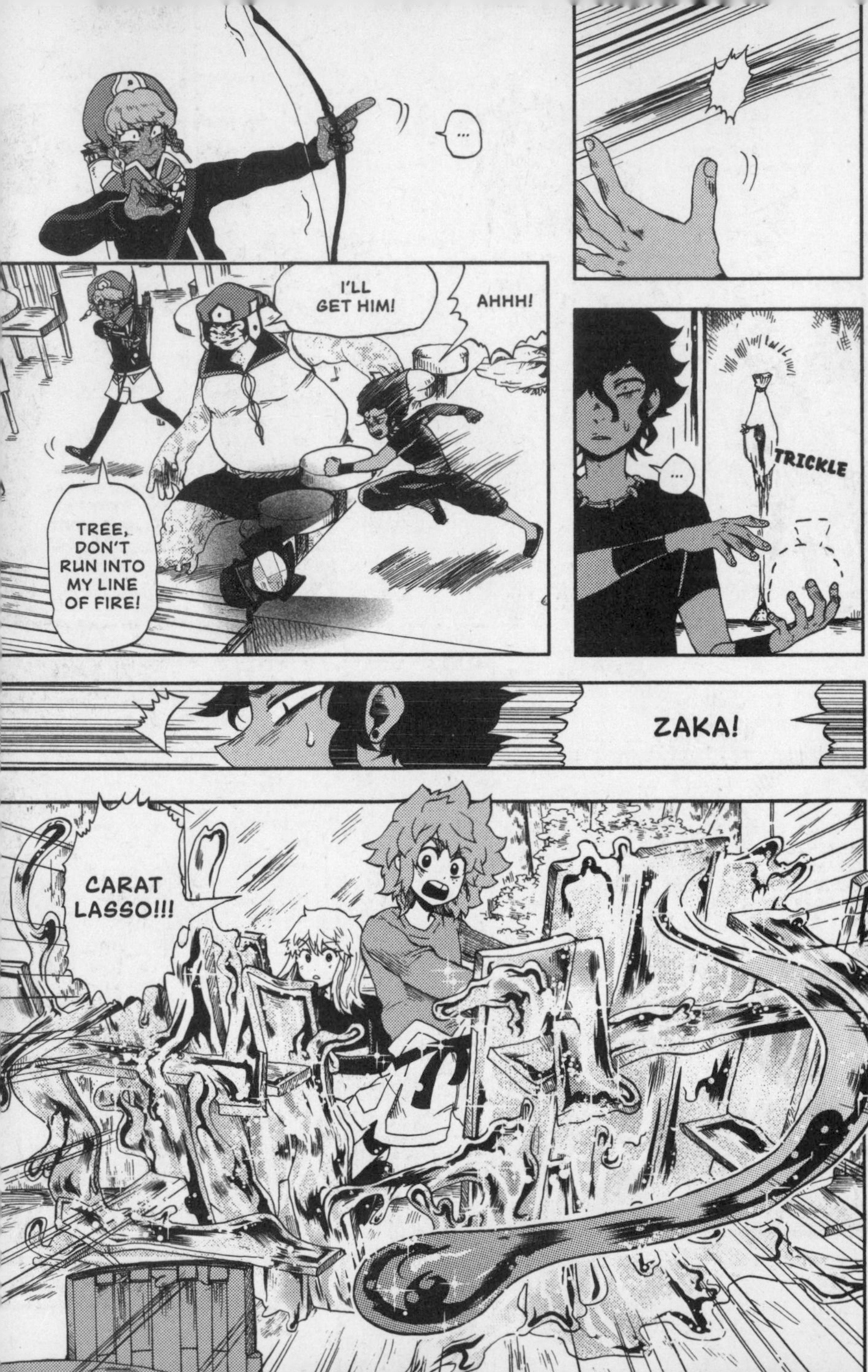
...
TRICKLE
...
I'LL GET HIM!
AHHH!
TREE, DON'T RUN INTO MY LINE OF FIRE!
ZAKA!
CARAT LASSO!!!

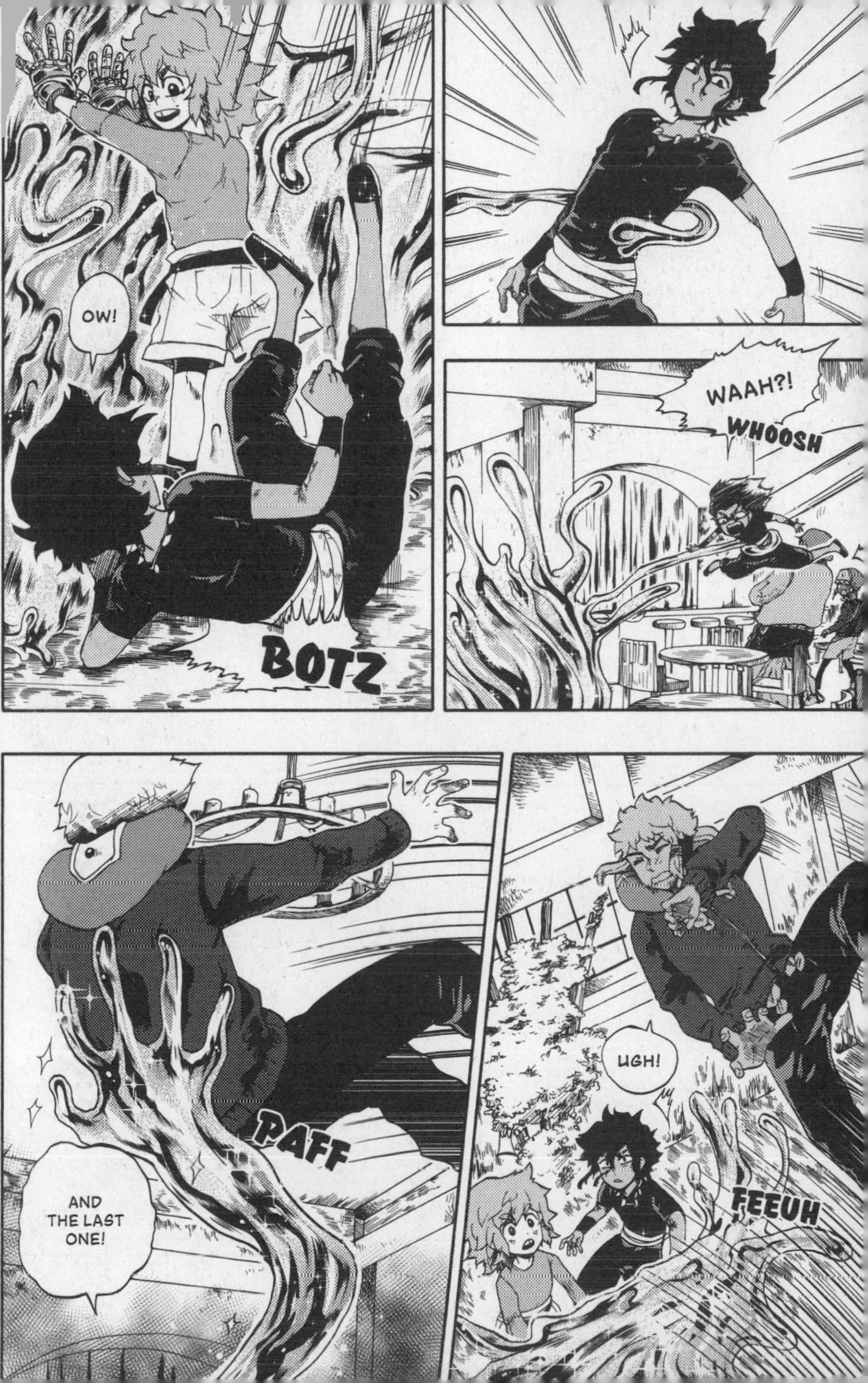
WAAH?!
WHOOSH
OW!
BOTZ
UGH!
FEEUH
PAFF
AND THE LAST ONE!

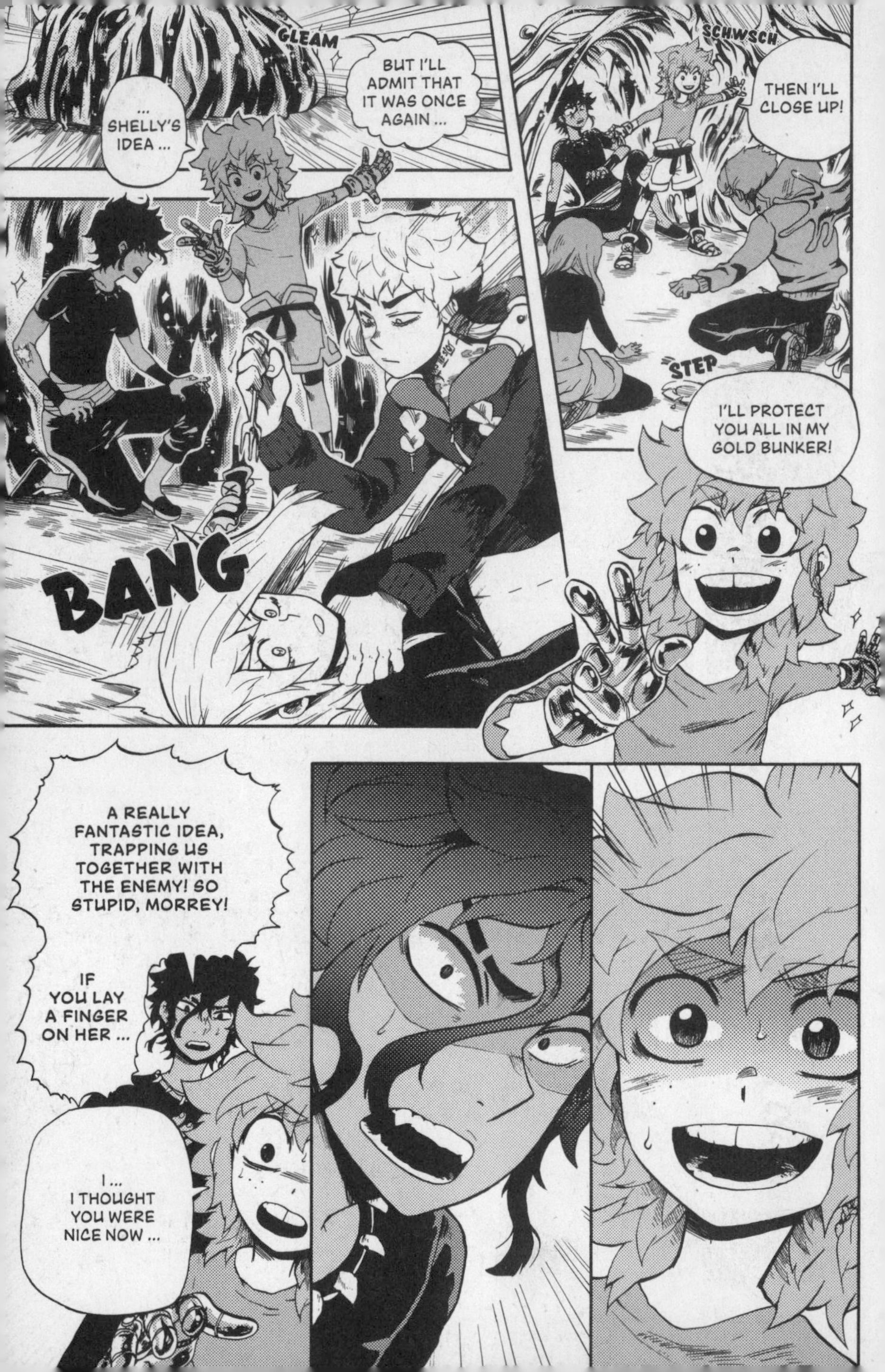
SCHWSCH
THEN I'LL CLOSE UP!
STEP
I'LL PROTECT YOU ALL IN MY GOLD BUNKER!
GLEAM
BUT I'LL ADMIT THAT IT WAS ONCE AGAIN ...
... SHELLY'S IDEA ...
BANG
A REALLY FANTASTIC IDEA, TRAPPING US TOGETHER WITH THE ENEMY! SO STUPID, MORREY!
IF YOU LAY A FINGER ON HER ...
I ... I THOUGHT YOU WERE NICE NOW ...

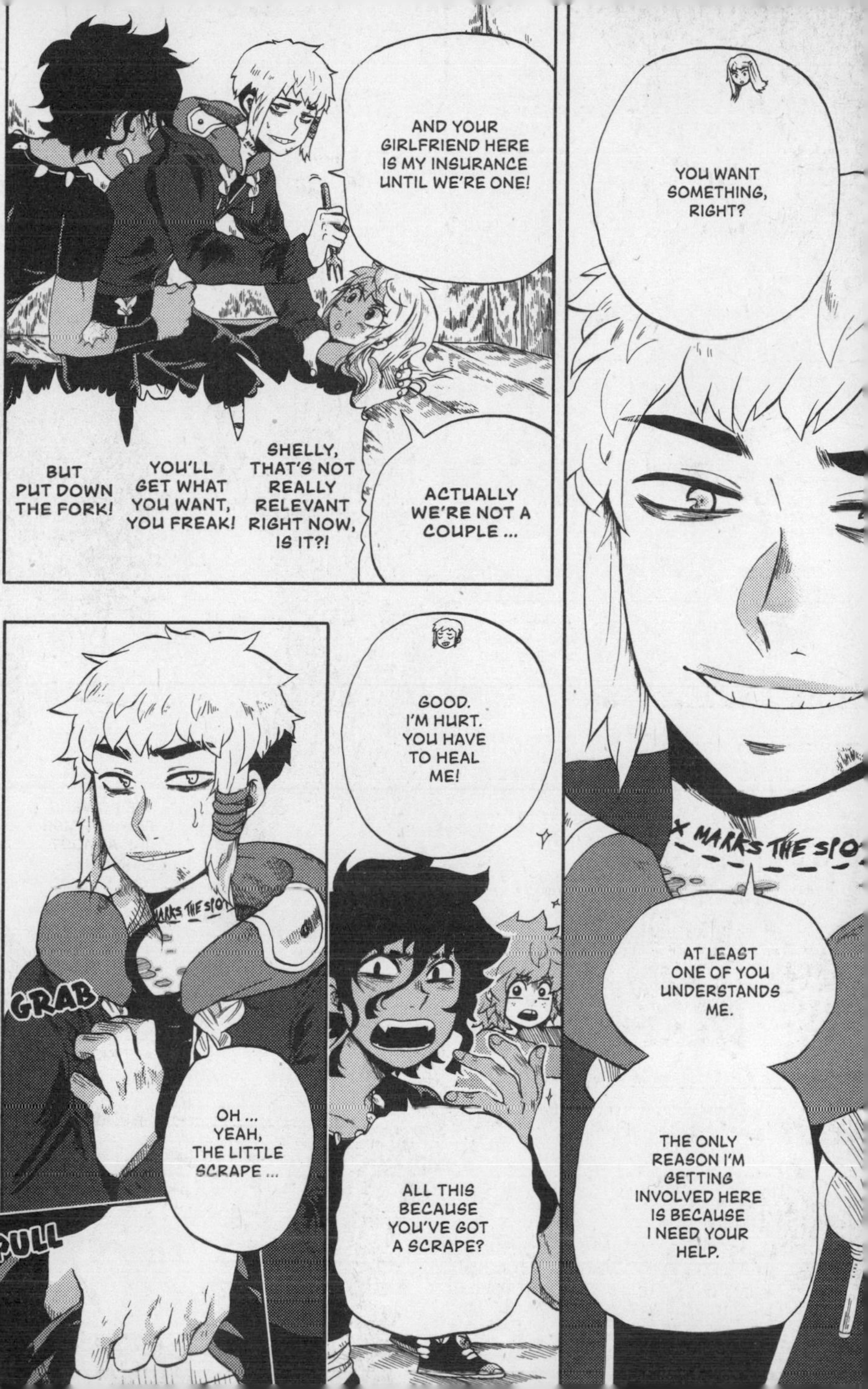
YOU WANT SOMETHING, RIGHT?
X MARKS THE SPO
AT LEAST ONE OF YOU UNDERSTANDS ME.
THE ONLY REASON I'M GETTING INVOLVED HERE IS BECAUSE I NEED YOUR HELP.
AND YOUR GIRLFRIEND HERE IS MY INSURANCE UNTIL WE'RE ONE!
ACTUALLY WE'RE NOT A COUPLE ...
SHELLY, THAT'S NOT REALLY RELEVANT RIGHT NOW, IS IT?!
YOU'LL GET WHAT YOU WANT, YOU FREAK!
BUT PUT DOWN THE FORK!
GOOD. I'M HURT. YOU HAVE TO HEAL ME!
ALL THIS BECAUSE YOU'VE GOT A SCRAPE?
MARKS THE SPOT
GRAB
OH ... YEAH, THE LITTLE SCRAPE ...
PULL

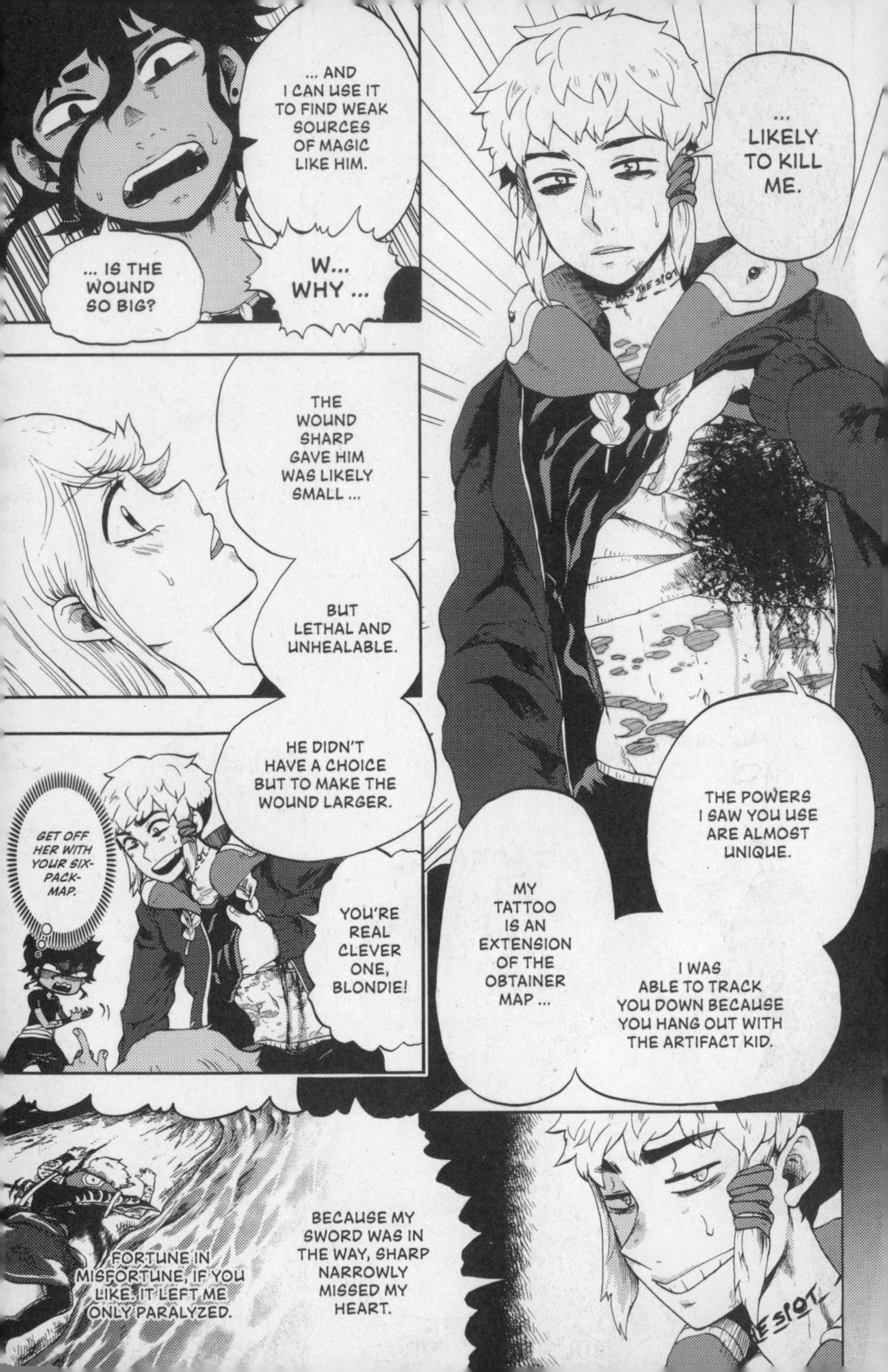
... LIKELY TO KILL ME.
THE POWERS I SAW YOU USE ARE ALMOST UNIQUE.
MY TATTOO IS AN EXTENSION OF THE OBTAINER MAP ...
I WAS ABLE TO TRACK YOU DOWN BECAUSE YOU HANG OUT WITH THE ARTIFACT KID.
... AND I CAN USE IT TO FIND WEAK SOURCES OF MAGIC LIKE HIM.
W... WHY ...
... IS THE WOUND SO BIG?
THE WOUND SHARP GAVE HIM WAS LIKELY SMALL ...
BUT LETHAL AND UNHEALABLE.
HE DIDN'T HAVE A CHOICE BUT TO MAKE THE WOUND LARGER.
YOU'RE REAL CLEVER ONE, BLONDIE!
GET OFF HER WITH YOUR SIX-PACK-MAP.
BECAUSE MY SWORD WAS IN THE WAY, SHARP NARROWLY MISSED MY HEART.
FORTUNE IN MISFORTUNE, IF YOU LIKE. IT LEFT ME ONLY PARALYZED.

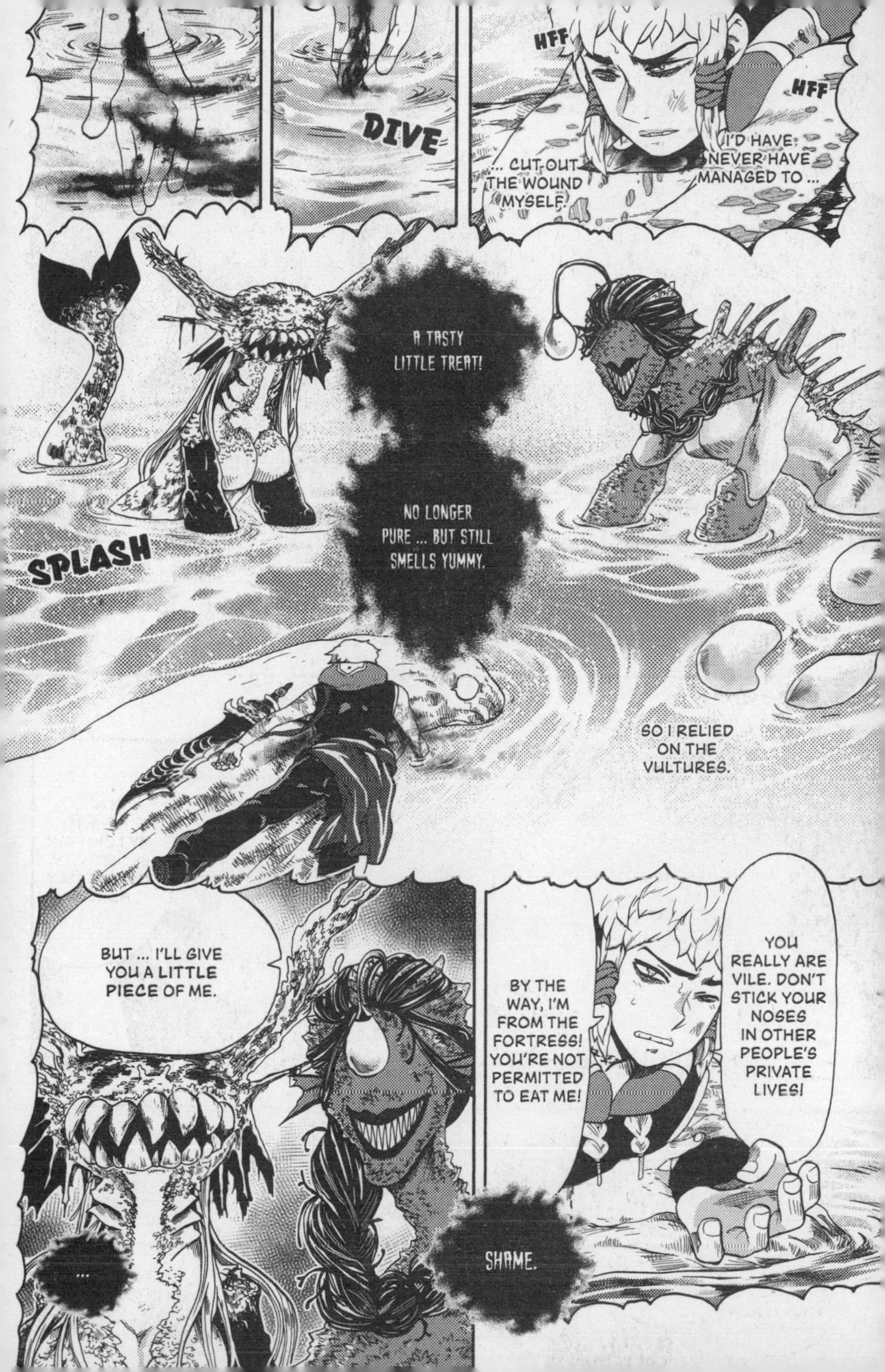
HFF
HFF
I'D HAVE NEVER HAVE MANAGED TO ...
... CUT OUT THE WOUND MYSELF.
DIVE
A TASTY LITTLE TREAT!
NO LONGER PURE ... BUT STILL SMELLS YUMMY.
SO I RELIED ON THE VULTURES.
SPLASH
YOU REALLY ARE VILE. DON'T STICK YOUR NOSES IN OTHER PEOPLE'S PRIVATE LIVES!
BY THE WAY, I'M FROM THE FORTRESS! YOU'RE NOT PERMITTED TO EAT ME!
SHAME.
BUT ... I'LL GIVE YOU A LITTLE PIECE OF ME.
...

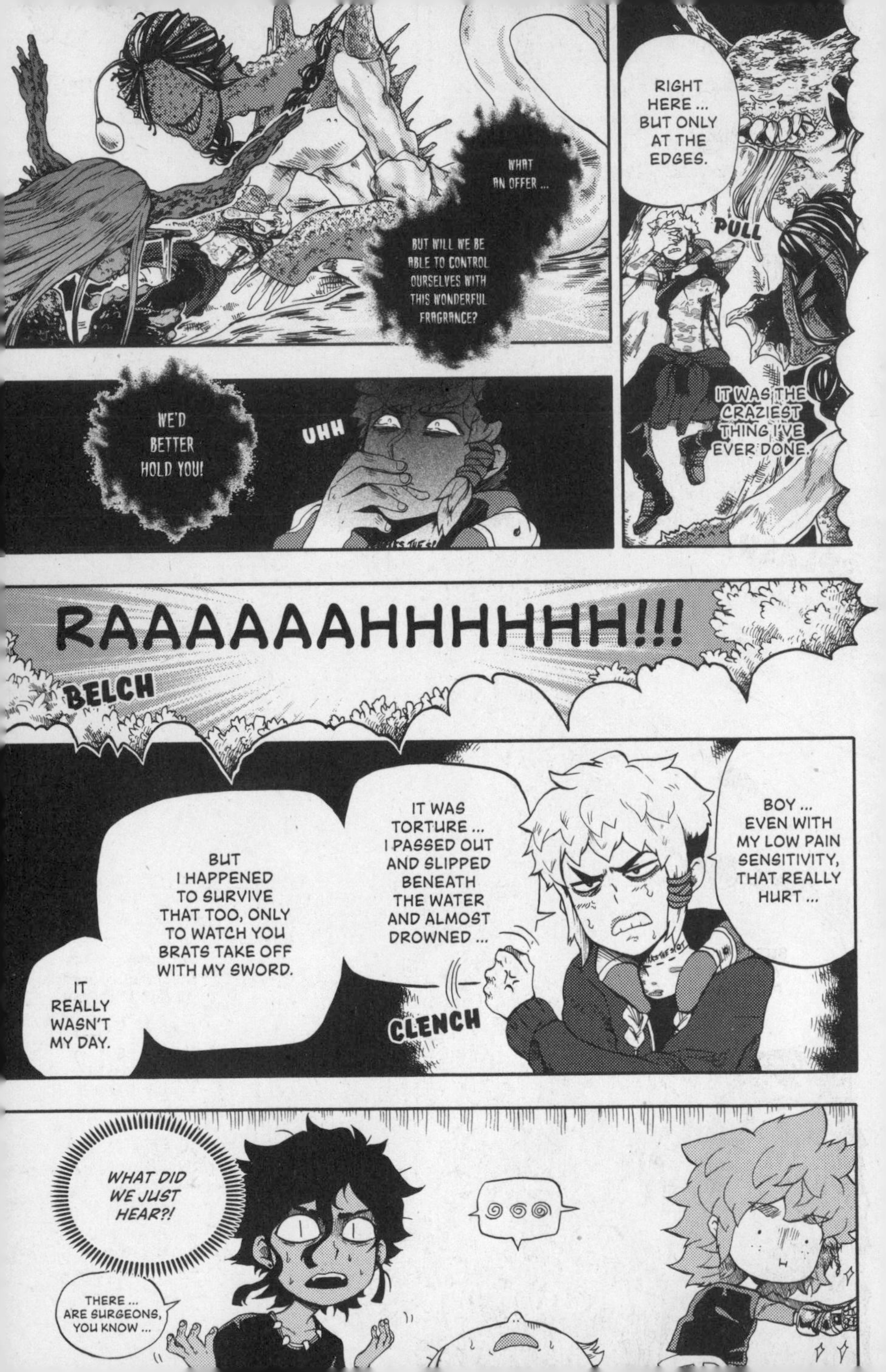
RIGHT HERE ... BUT ONLY AT THE EDGES.
PULL
IT WAS THE CRAZIEST THING I'VE EVER DONE.
WHAT AN OFFER ...
BUT WILL WE BE ABLE TO CONTROL OURSELVES WITH THIS WONDERFUL FRAGRANCE?
UHH
WE'D BETTER HOLD YOU!
RAAAAAAHHHHHH!!!
BELCH
BOY ... EVEN WITH MY LOW PAIN SENSITIVITY, THAT REALLY HURT ...
IT WAS TORTURE ... I PASSED OUT AND SLIPPED BENEATH THE WATER AND ALMOST DROWNED ...
CLENCH
BUT I HAPPENED TO SURVIVE THAT TOO, ONLY TO WATCH YOU BRATS TAKE OFF WITH MY SWORD.
IT REALLY WASN'T MY DAY.
WHAT DID WE JUST HEAR?!
THERE ... ARE SURGEONS, YOU KNOW ...

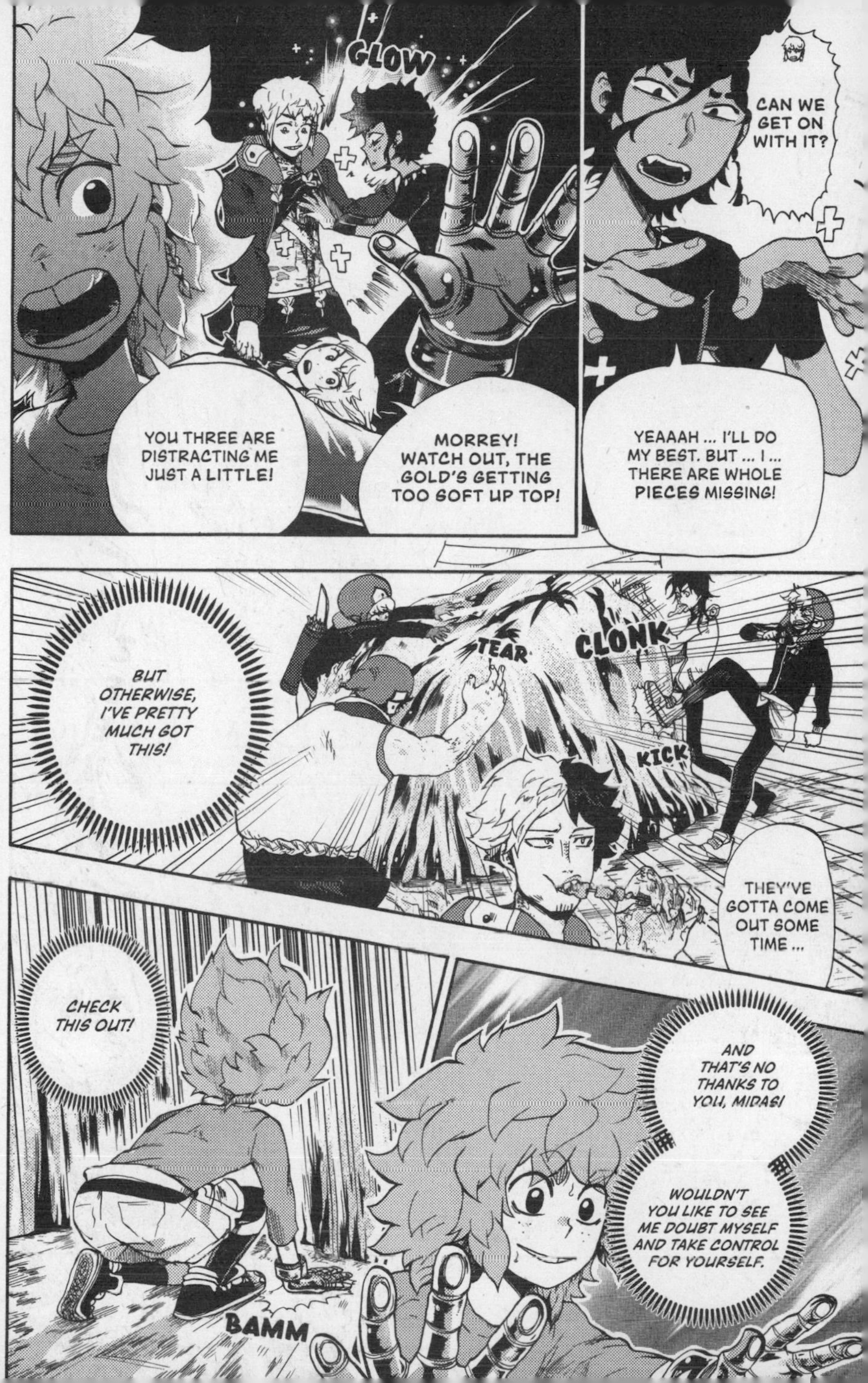
CAN WE GET ON WITH IT?
YEAAAH ... I'LL DO MY BEST. BUT ... I ... THERE ARE WHOLE PIECES MISSING!
GLOW
MORREY! WATCH OUT, THE GOLD'S GETTING TOO SOFT UP TOP!
YOU THREE ARE DISTRACTING ME JUST A LITTLE!
CLONK
TEAR
KICK
BUT OTHERWISE, I'VE PRETTY MUCH GOT THIS!
THEY'VE GOTTA COME OUT SOME TIME ...
AND THAT'S NO THANKS TO YOU, MIDAS!
WOULDN'T YOU LIKE TO SEE ME DOUBT MYSELF AND TAKE CONTROL FOR YOURSELF.
CHECK THIS OUT!
BAMM

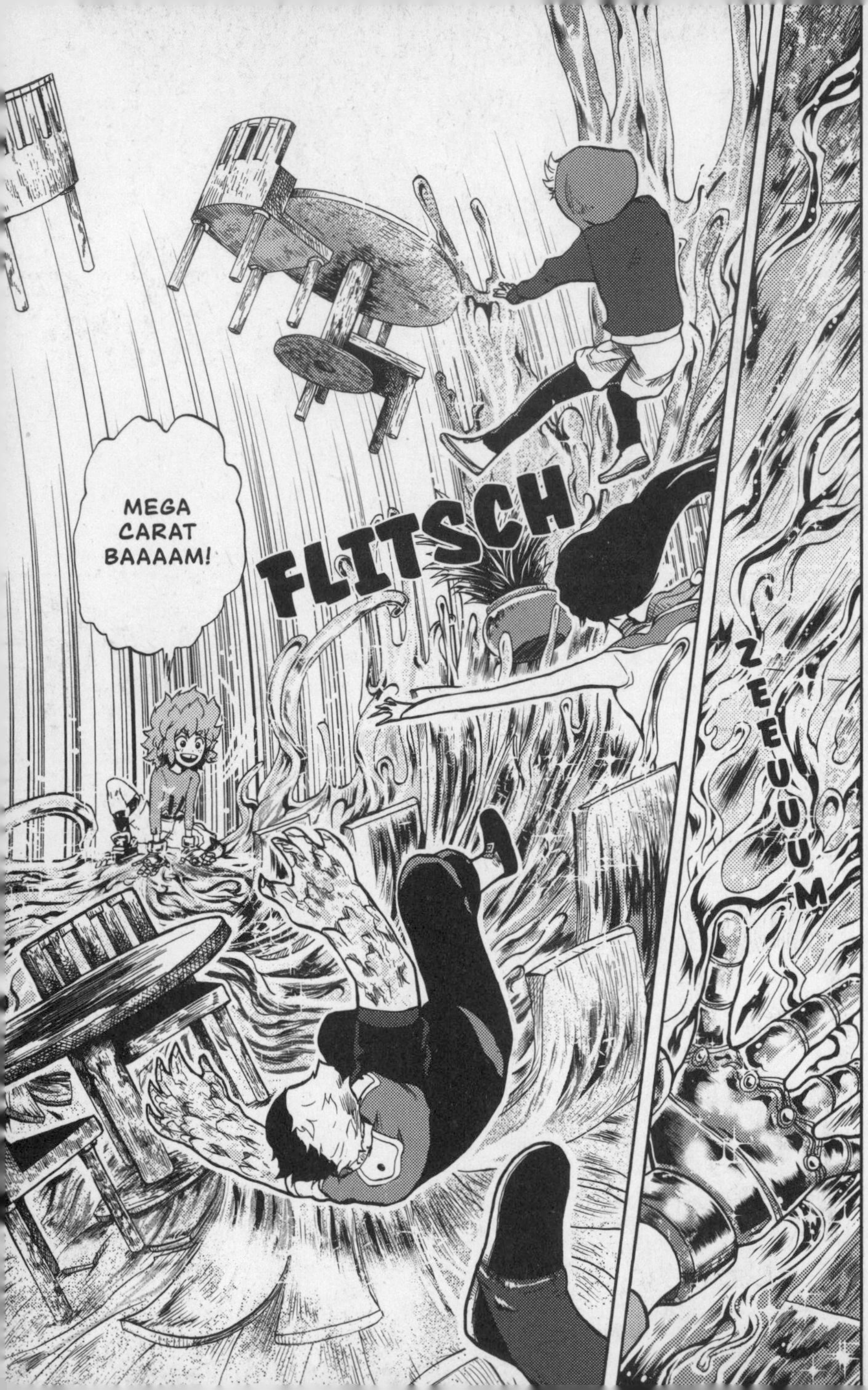
ZEEUUUM
FLITSCH
MEGA CARAT BAAAAM!

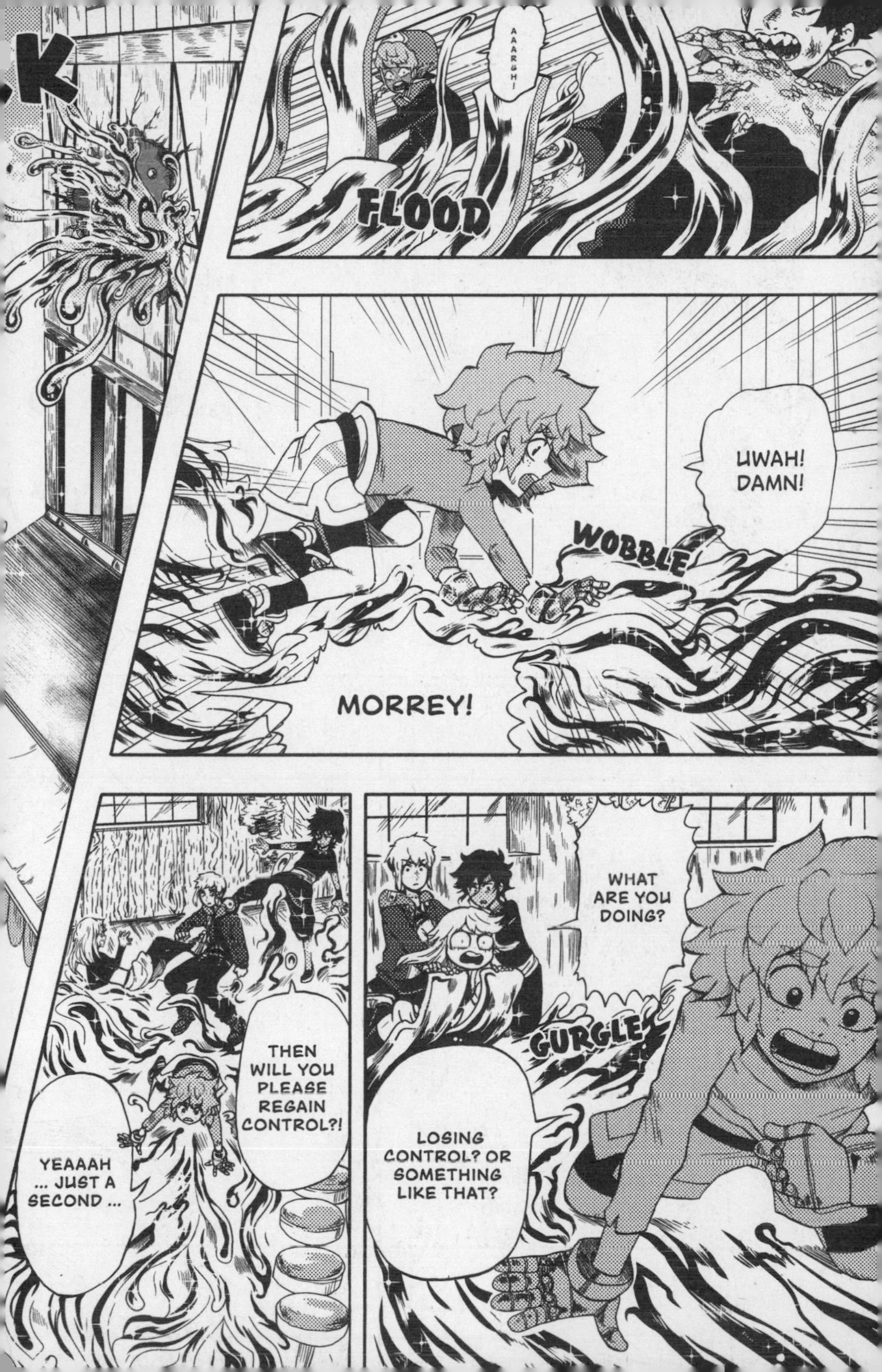
AAARGH!
FLOOD
UWAH! DAMN!
WOBBLE
MORREY!
WHAT ARE YOU DOING?
GURGLE
LOSING CONTROL? OR SOMETHING LIKE THAT?
THEN WILL YOU PLEASE REGAIN CONTROL?!
YEAAAH ... JUST A SECOND ...
K

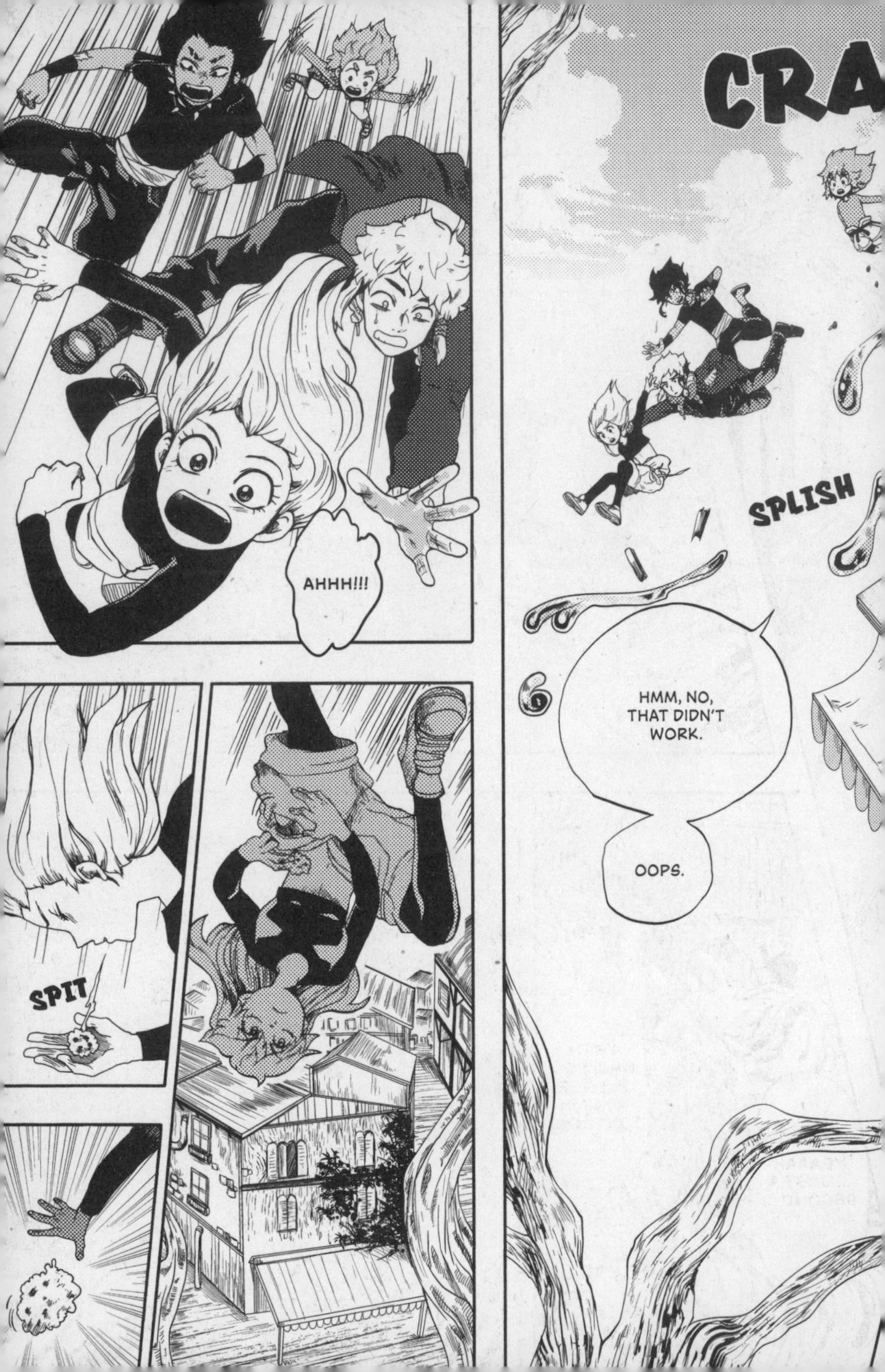
CRA
SPLISH
HMM, NO, THAT DIDN'T WORK.
OOPS.
AHHH!!!
SPIT

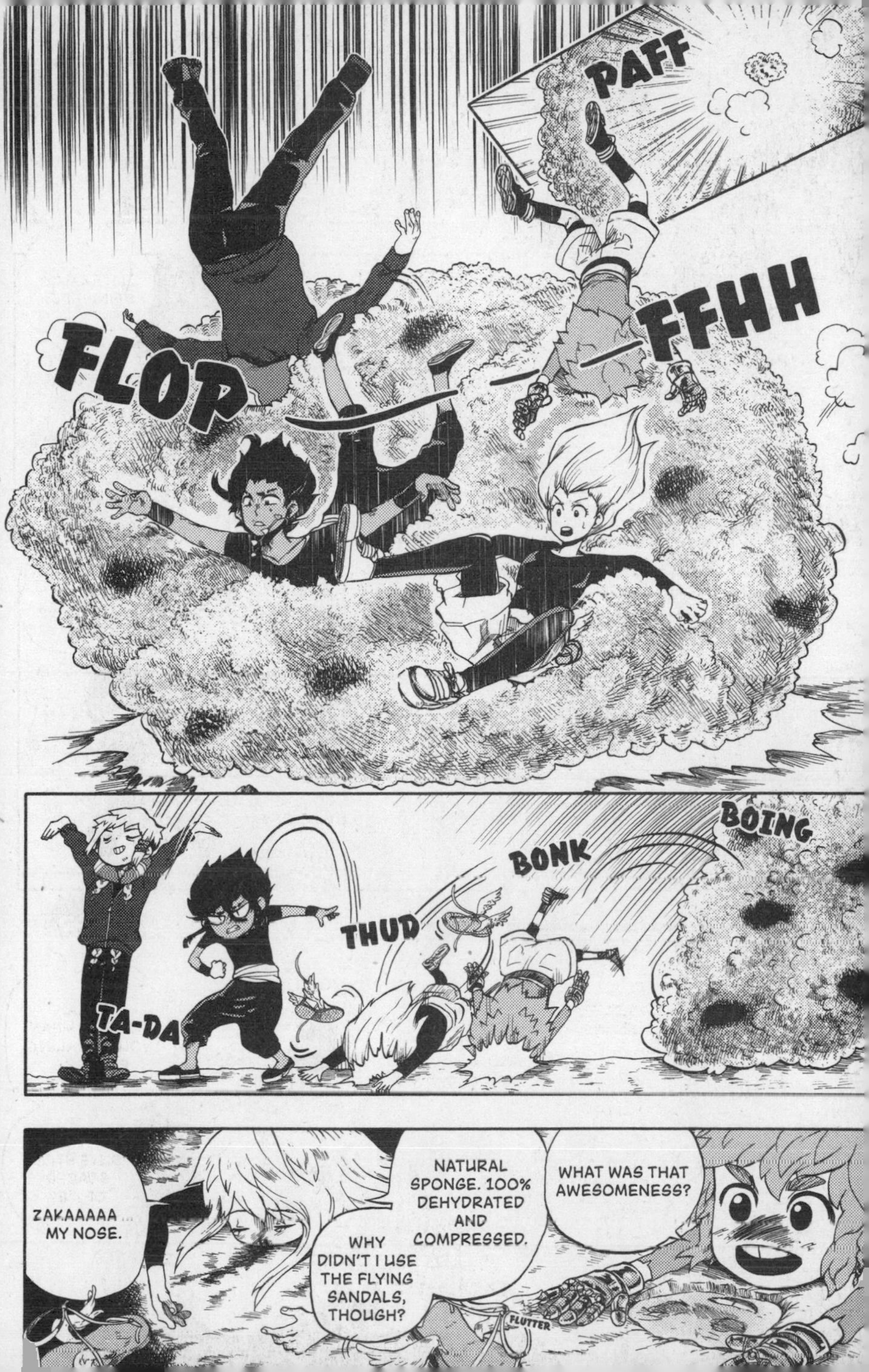
PAFF
FFHH
FLOP
BOING
BONK
THUD
TA-DA
WHAT WAS THAT AWESOMENESS?
NATURAL SPONGE. 100% DEHYDRATED AND COMPRESSED.
WHY DIDN'T I USE THE FLYING SANDALS, THOUGH?
FLUTTER
ZAKAAAAA... MY NOSE.

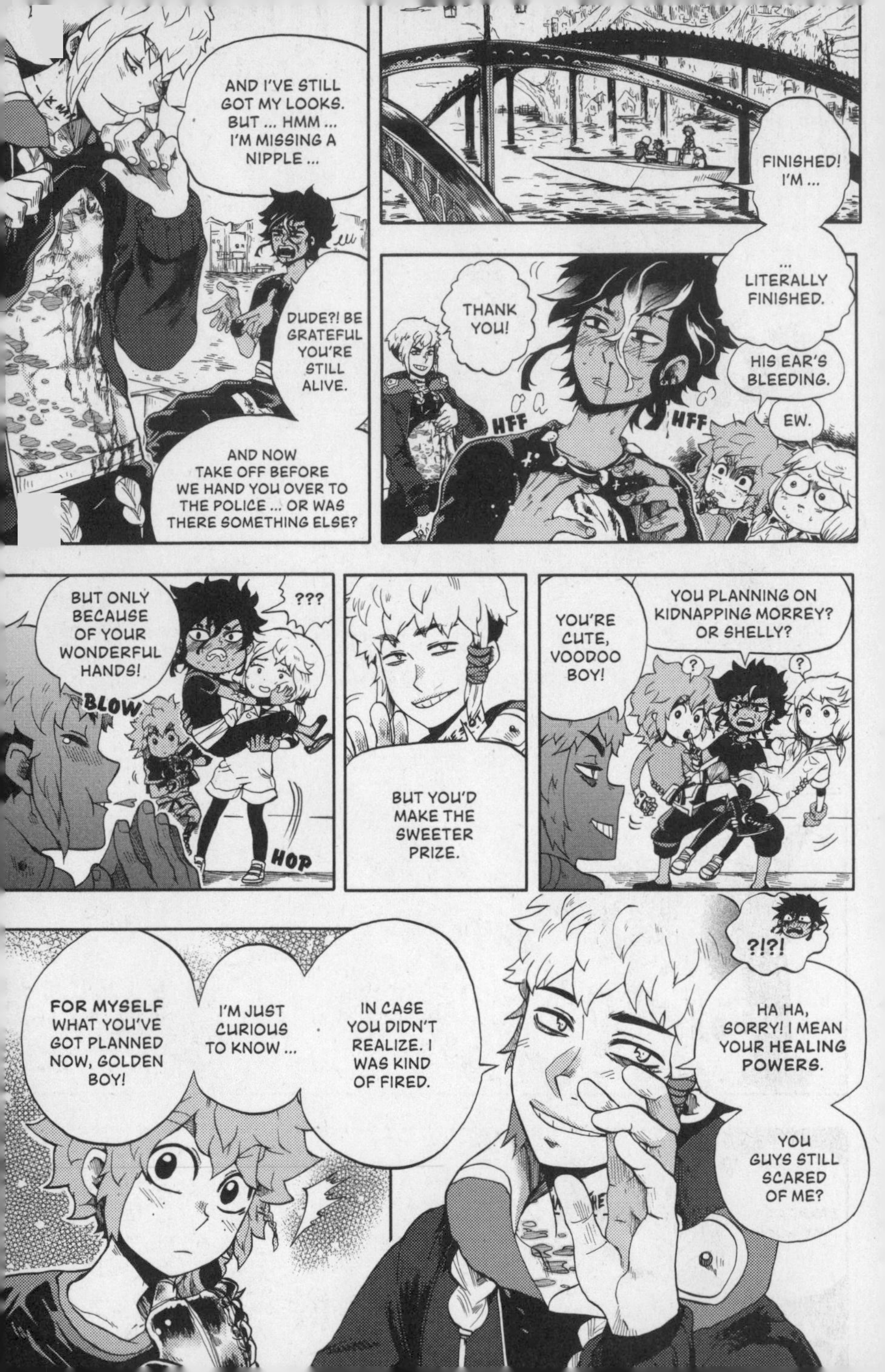
FINISHED! I'M ...
... LITERALLY FINISHED.
HIS EAR'S BLEEDING.
EW.
THANK YOU!
HFF
HFF
AND I'VE STILL GOT MY LOOKS. BUT ... HMM ... I'M MISSING A NIPPLE ...
DUDE?! BE GRATEFUL YOU'RE STILL ALIVE.
AND NOW TAKE OFF BEFORE WE HAND YOU OVER TO THE POLICE ... OR WAS THERE SOMETHING ELSE?
YOU PLANNING ON KIDNAPPING MORREY? OR SHELLY?
YOU'RE CUTE, VOODOO BOY!
BUT YOU'D MAKE THE SWEETER PRIZE.
???
BUT ONLY BECAUSE OF YOUR WONDERFUL HANDS!
BLOW
HOP
?!?!
HA HA, SORRY! I MEAN YOUR HEALING POWERS.
YOU GUYS STILL SCARED OF ME?
IN CASE YOU DIDN'T REALIZE. I WAS KIND OF FIRED.
I'M JUST CURIOUS TO KNOW ...
FOR MYSELF WHAT YOU'VE GOT PLANNED NOW, GOLDEN BOY!

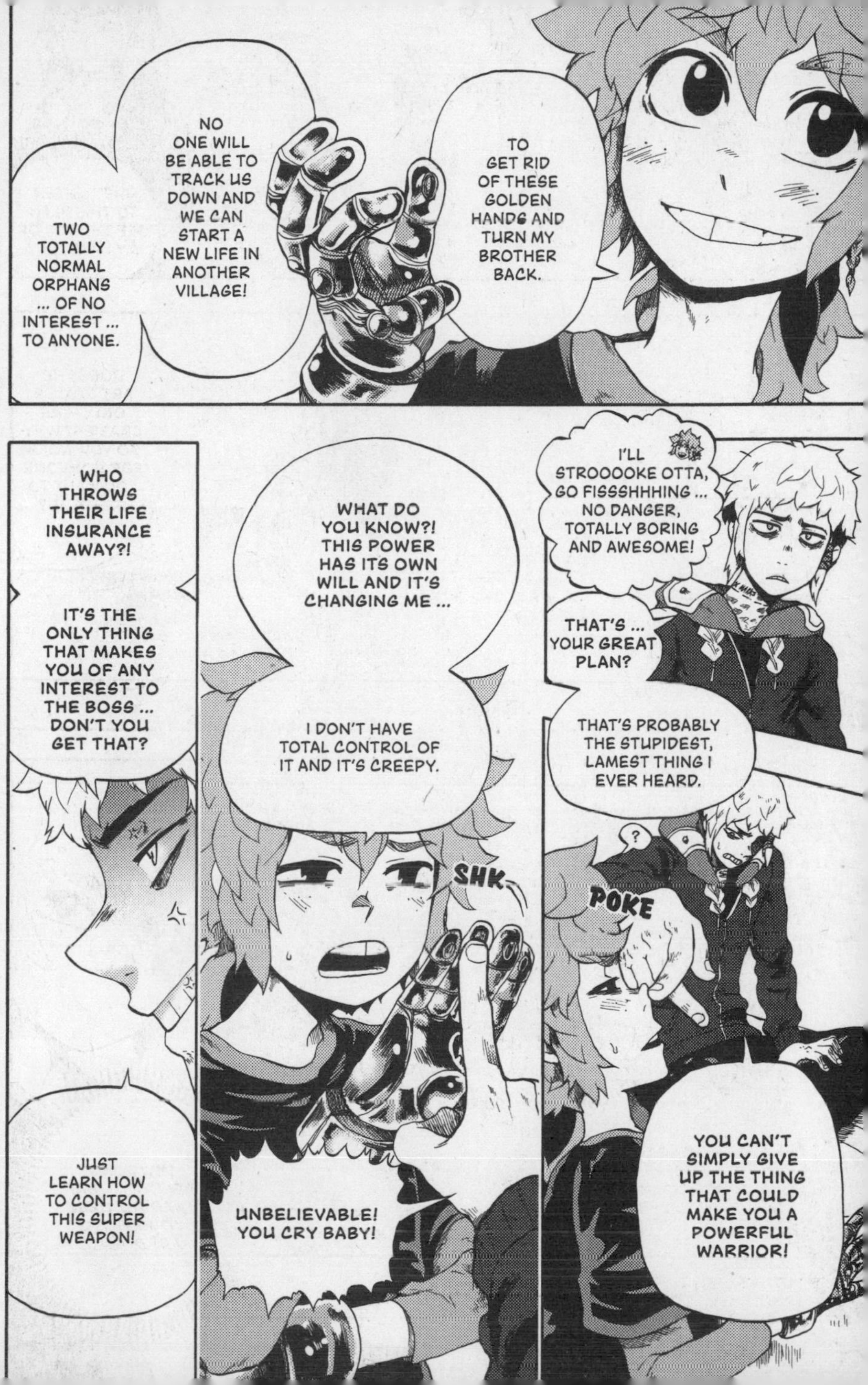

TO GET RID OF THESE GOLDEN HANDS AND TURN MY BROTHER BACK.
NO ONE WILL BE ABLE TO TRACK US DOWN AND WE CAN START A NEW LIFE IN ANOTHER VILLAGE!
TWO TOTALLY NORMAL ORPHANS ... OF NO INTEREST ... TO ANYONE.
I'LL STROOOOKE OTTA, GO FISSSHHHING ... NO DANGER, TOTALLY BORING AND AWESOME!
THAT'S ... YOUR GREAT PLAN?
THAT'S PROBABLY THE STUPIDEST, LAMEST THING I EVER HEARD.
?
POKE
YOU CAN'T SIMPLY GIVE UP THE THING THAT COULD MAKE YOU A POWERFUL WARRIOR!
WHAT DO YOU KNOW?! THIS POWER HAS ITS OWN WILL AND IT'S CHANGING ME ...
I DON'T HAVE TOTAL CONTROL OF IT AND IT'S CREEPY.
SHK
UNBELIEVABLE! YOU CRY BABY!
WHO THROWS THEIR LIFE INSURANCE AWAY?!
IT'S THE ONLY THING THAT MAKES YOU OF ANY INTEREST TO THE BOSS ... DON'T YOU GET THAT?
JUST LEARN HOW TO CONTROL THIS SUPER WEAPON!

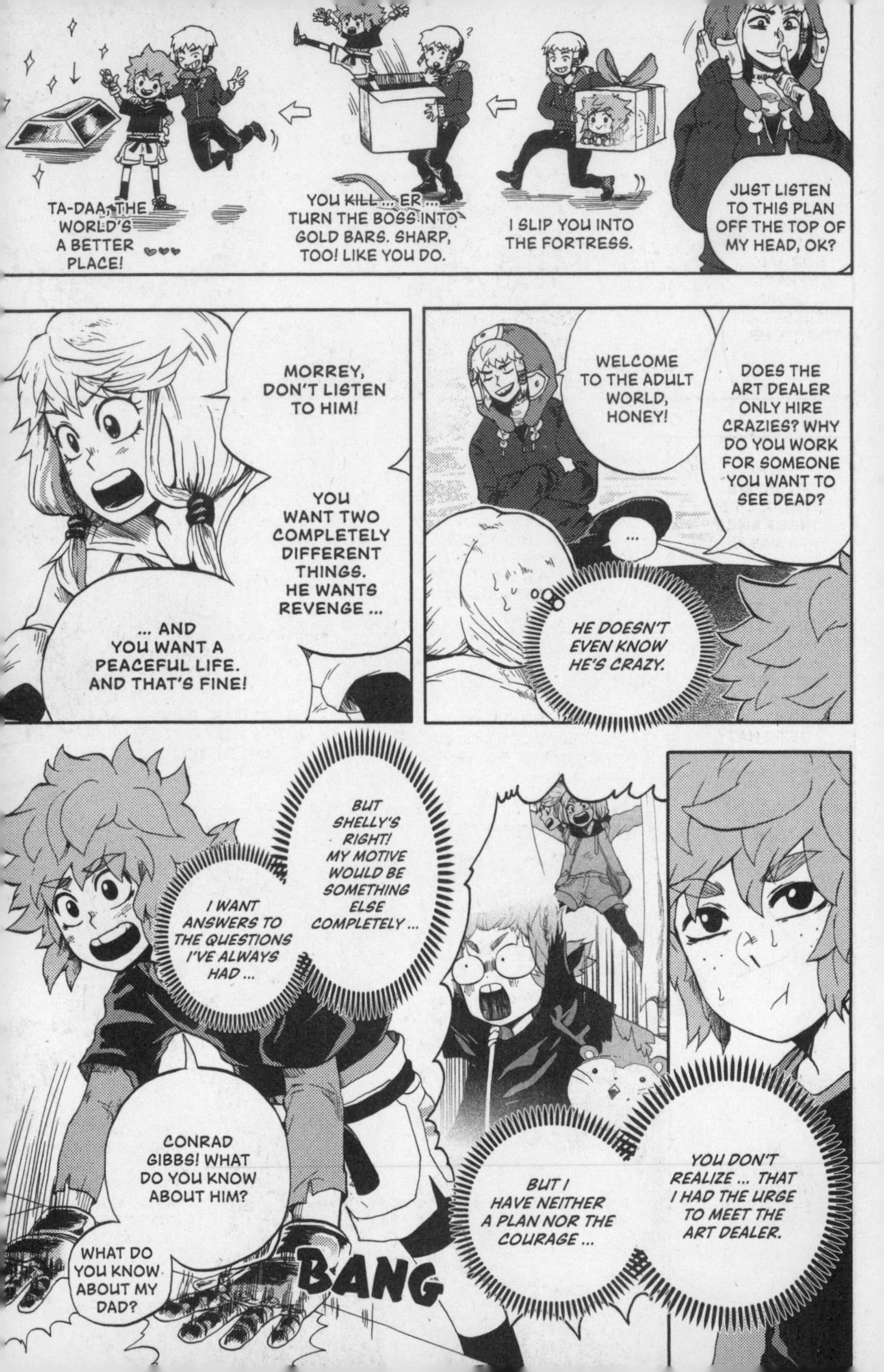
JUST LISTEN TO THIS PLAN OFF THE TOP OF MY HEAD, OK?
I SLIP YOU INTO THE FORTRESS.
YOU ~~KILL~~ ... ER ... TURN THE BOSS INTO GOLD BARS. SHARP, TOO! LIKE YOU DO.
TA-DAA, THE WORLD'S A BETTER PLACE!
DOES THE ART DEALER ONLY HIRE CRAZIES? WHY DO YOU WORK FOR SOMEONE YOU WANT TO SEE DEAD?
WELCOME TO THE ADULT WORLD, HONEY!
...
HE DOESN'T EVEN KNOW HE'S CRAZY.
MORREY, DON'T LISTEN TO HIM!
YOU WANT TWO COMPLETELY DIFFERENT THINGS. HE WANTS REVENGE ...
... AND YOU WANT A PEACEFUL LIFE. AND THAT'S FINE!
YOU DON'T REALIZE ... THAT I HAD THE URGE TO MEET THE ART DEALER.
BUT I HAVE NEITHER A PLAN NOR THE COURAGE ...
BUT SHELLY'S RIGHT! MY MOTIVE WOULD BE SOMETHING ELSE COMPLETELY ...
I WANT ANSWERS TO THE QUESTIONS I'VE ALWAYS HAD ...
BANG
CONRAD GIBBS! WHAT DO YOU KNOW ABOUT HIM?
WHAT DO YOU KNOW ABOUT MY DAD?

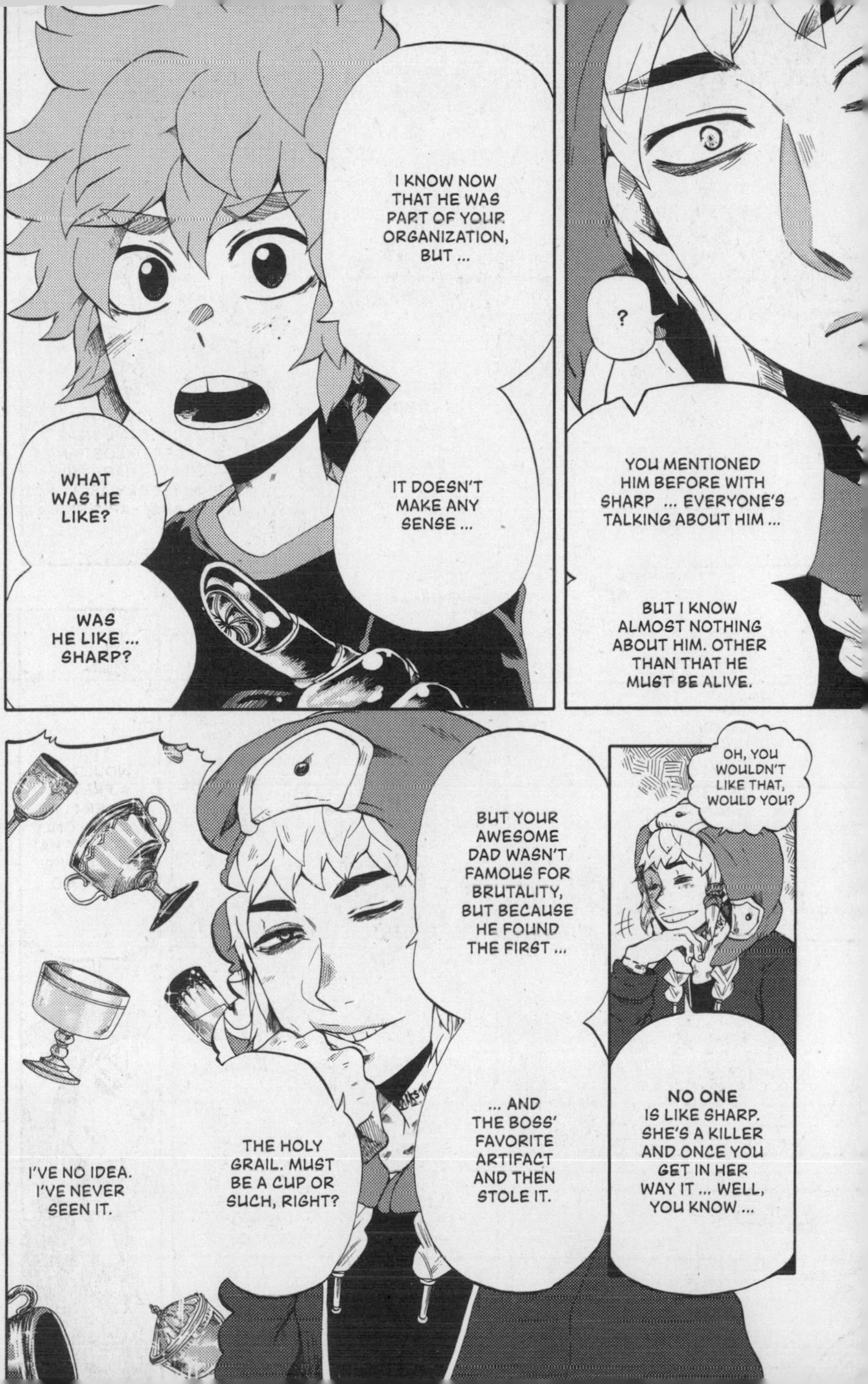
?
YOU MENTIONED HIM BEFORE WITH SHARP ... EVERYONE'S TALKING ABOUT HIM ...
BUT I KNOW ALMOST NOTHING ABOUT HIM. OTHER THAN THAT HE MUST BE ALIVE.
I KNOW NOW THAT HE WAS PART OF YOUR ORGANIZATION, BUT ...
IT DOESN'T MAKE ANY SENSE ...
WHAT WAS HE LIKE?
WAS HE LIKE ... SHARP?
OH, YOU WOULDN'T LIKE THAT, WOULD YOU?
NO ONE IS LIKE SHARP. SHE'S A KILLER AND ONCE YOU GET IN HER WAY IT ... WELL, YOU KNOW ...
BUT YOUR AWESOME DAD WASN'T FAMOUS FOR BRUTALITY, BUT BECAUSE HE FOUND THE FIRST ...
... AND THE BOSS' FAVORITE ARTIFACT AND THEN STOLE IT.
THE HOLY GRAIL. MUST BE A CUP OR SUCH, RIGHT?
I'VE NO IDEA. I'VE NEVER SEEN IT.

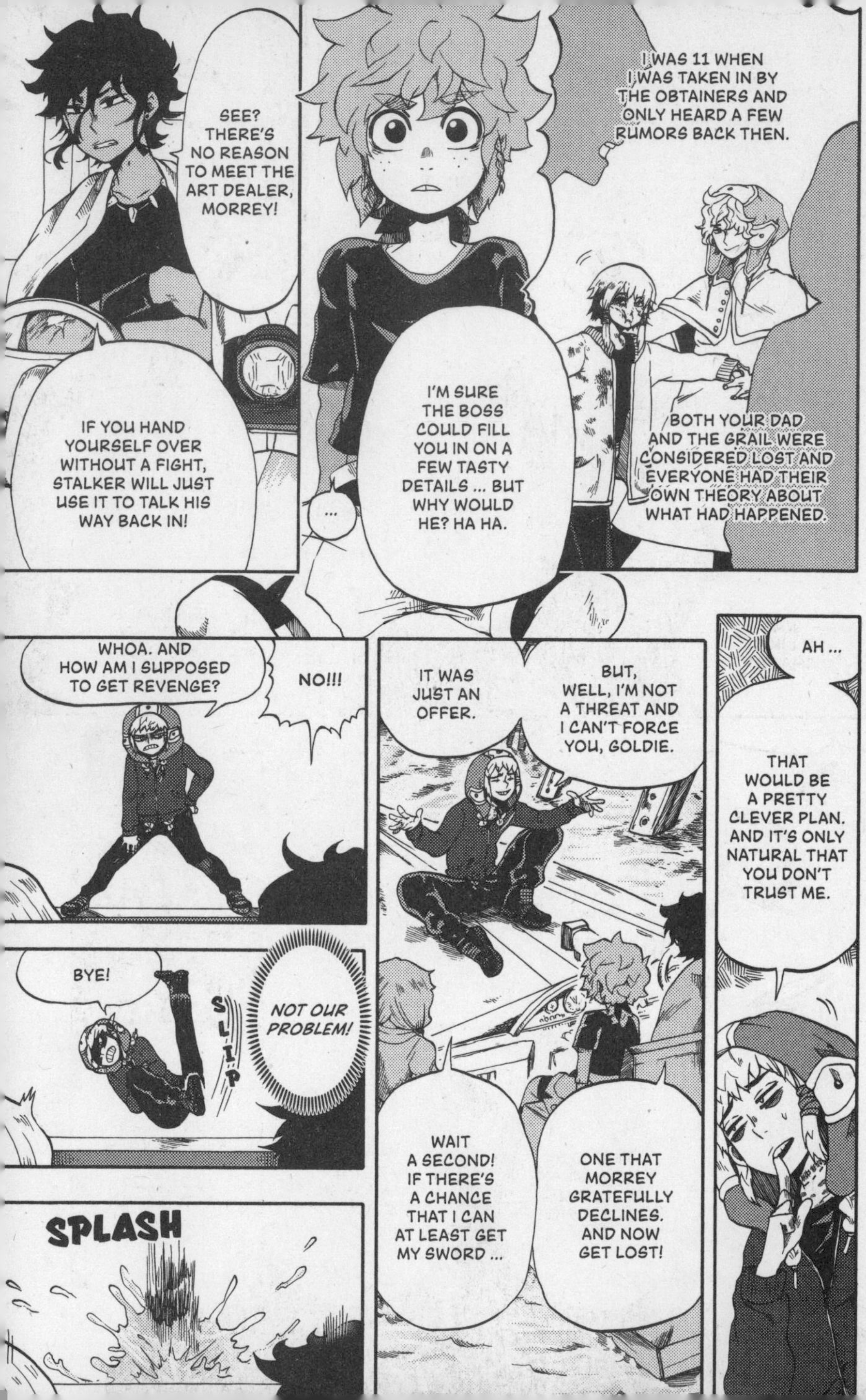
I WAS 11 WHEN I WAS TAKEN IN BY THE OBTAINERS AND ONLY HEARD A FEW RUMORS BACK THEN.
BOTH YOUR DAD AND THE GRAIL WERE CONSIDERED LOST AND EVERYONE HAD THEIR OWN THEORY ABOUT WHAT HAD HAPPENED.
I'M SURE THE BOSS COULD FILL YOU IN ON A FEW TASTY DETAILS ... BUT WHY WOULD HE? HA HA.
...
SEE? THERE'S NO REASON TO MEET THE ART DEALER, MORREY!
IF YOU HAND YOURSELF OVER WITHOUT A FIGHT, STALKER WILL JUST USE IT TO TALK HIS WAY BACK IN!
AH ...
THAT WOULD BE A PRETTY CLEVER PLAN. AND IT'S ONLY NATURAL THAT YOU DON'T TRUST ME.
BUT, WELL, I'M NOT A THREAT AND I CAN'T FORCE YOU, GOLDIE.
IT WAS JUST AN OFFER.
WAIT A SECOND! IF THERE'S A CHANCE THAT I CAN AT LEAST GET MY SWORD ...
ONE THAT MORREY GRATEFULLY DECLINES. AND NOW GET LOST!
WHOA. AND HOW AM I SUPPOSED TO GET REVENGE?
NO!!!
NOT OUR PROBLEM!
SLIP
BYE!
SPLASH

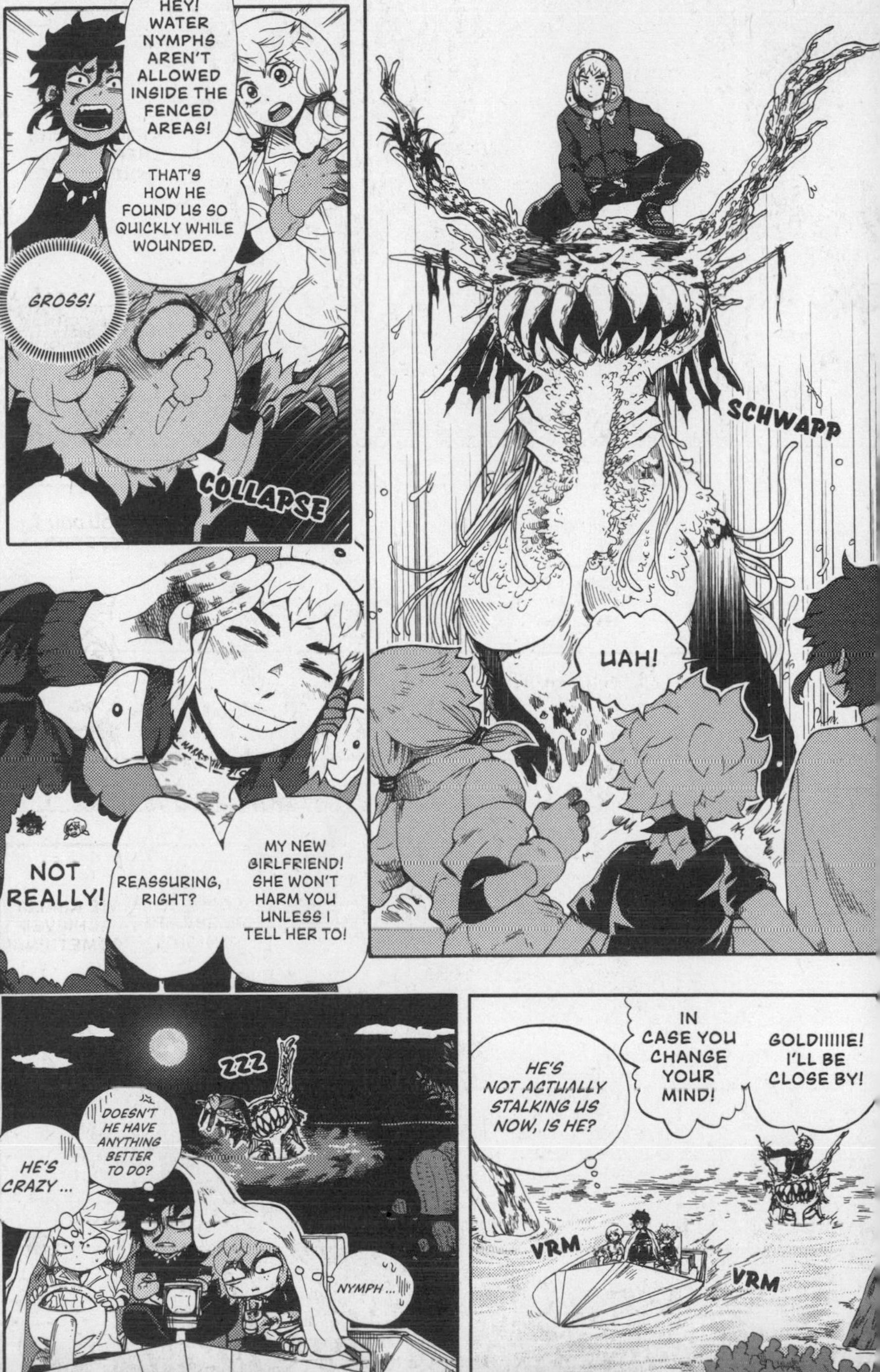
SCHWAPP
UAH!
HEY! WATER NYMPHS AREN'T ALLOWED INSIDE THE FENCED AREAS!
THAT'S HOW HE FOUND US SO QUICKLY WHILE WOUNDED.
GROSS!
COLLAPSE
MY NEW GIRLFRIEND! SHE WON'T HARM YOU UNLESS I TELL HER TO!
REASSURING, RIGHT?
NOT REALLY!
GOLDIIIIIE! I'LL BE CLOSE BY!
IN CASE YOU CHANGE YOUR MIND!
HE'S NOT ACTUALLY STALKING US NOW, IS HE?
VRM
VRM
ZZZ
DOESN'T HE HAVE ANYTHING BETTER TO DO?
HE'S CRAZY ...
NYMPH ...

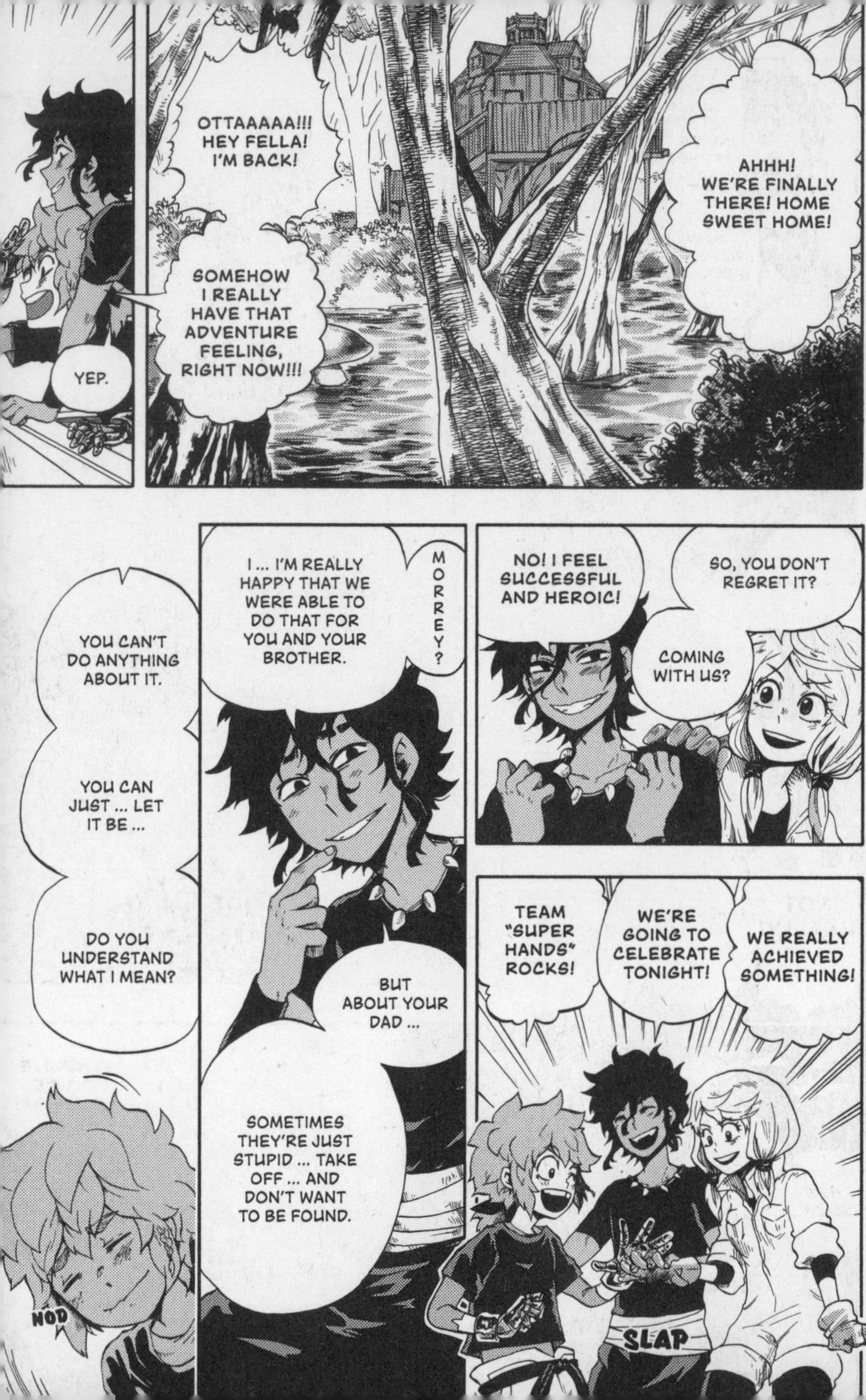
AHHH! WE'RE FINALLY THERE! HOME SWEET HOME!
OTTAAAAA!!! HEY FELLA! I'M BACK!
SOMEHOW I REALLY HAVE THAT ADVENTURE FEELING, RIGHT NOW!!!
YEP.
SO, YOU DON'T REGRET IT?
COMING WITH US?
NO! I FEEL SUCCESSFUL AND HEROIC!
WE REALLY ACHIEVED SOMETHING!
WE'RE GOING TO CELEBRATE TONIGHT!
TEAM "SUPER HANDS" ROCKS!
SLAP
MORREY?
I ... I'M REALLY HAPPY THAT WE WERE ABLE TO DO THAT FOR YOU AND YOUR BROTHER.
BUT ABOUT YOUR DAD ...
SOMETIMES THEY'RE JUST STUPID ... TAKE OFF ... AND DON'T WANT TO BE FOUND.
YOU CAN'T DO ANYTHING ABOUT IT.
YOU CAN JUST ... LET IT BE ...
DO YOU UNDERSTAND WHAT I MEAN?
NOD

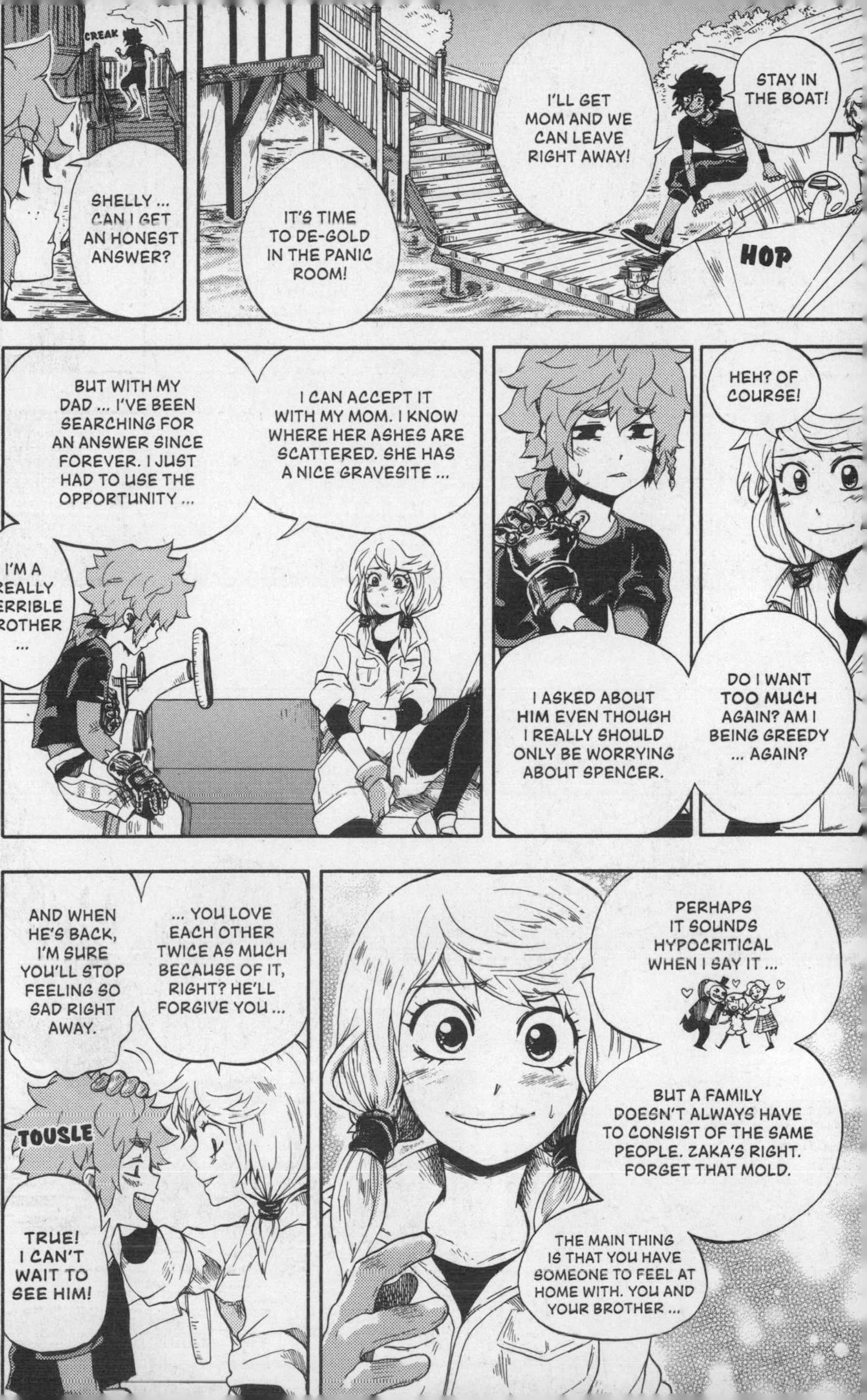
STAY IN THE BOAT!
I'LL GET MOM AND WE CAN LEAVE RIGHT AWAY!
HOP
IT'S TIME TO DE-GOLD IN THE PANIC ROOM!
CREAK
SHELLY ... CAN I GET AN HONEST ANSWER?
HEH? OF COURSE!
DO I WANT TOO MUCH AGAIN? AM I BEING GREEDY ... AGAIN?
I ASKED ABOUT HIM EVEN THOUGH I REALLY SHOULD ONLY BE WORRYING ABOUT SPENCER.
I CAN ACCEPT IT WITH MY MOM. I KNOW WHERE HER ASHES ARE SCATTERED. SHE HAS A NICE GRAVESITE ...
BUT WITH MY DAD ... I'VE BEEN SEARCHING FOR AN ANSWER SINCE FOREVER. I JUST HAD TO USE THE OPPORTUNITY ...
I'M A REALLY TERRIBLE BROTHER ...
PERHAPS IT SOUNDS HYPOCRITICAL WHEN I SAY IT ...
BUT A FAMILY DOESN'T ALWAYS HAVE TO CONSIST OF THE SAME PEOPLE. ZAKA'S RIGHT. FORGET THAT MOLD.
THE MAIN THING IS THAT YOU HAVE SOMEONE TO FEEL AT HOME WITH. YOU AND YOUR BROTHER ...
... YOU LOVE EACH OTHER TWICE AS MUCH BECAUSE OF IT, RIGHT? HE'LL FORGIVE YOU ...
AND WHEN HE'S BACK, I'M SURE YOU'LL STOP FEELING SO SAD RIGHT AWAY.
TOUSLE
TRUE! I CAN'T WAIT TO SEE HIM!

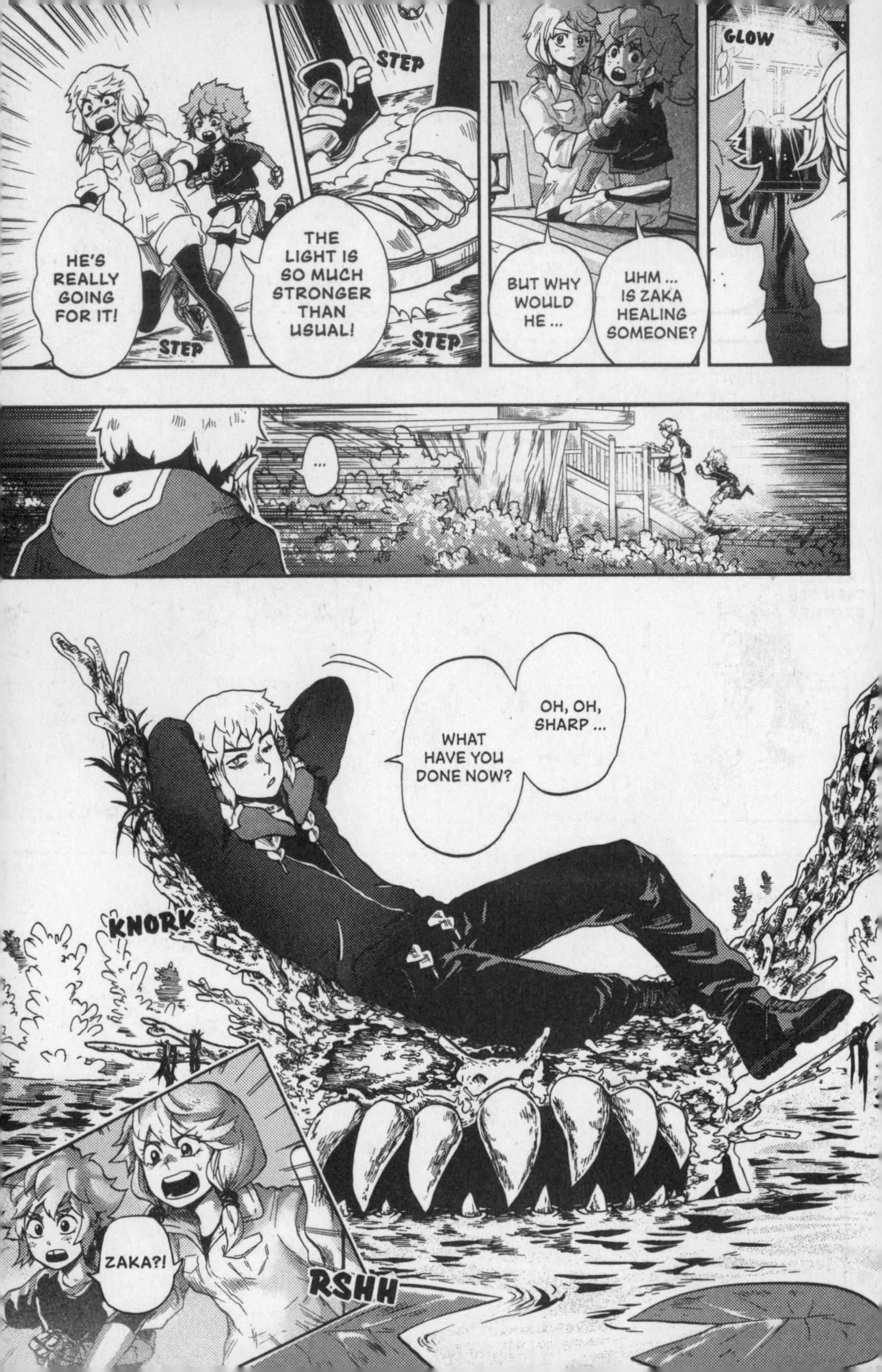
GLOW
UHM ... IS ZAKA HEALING SOMEONE?
BUT WHY WOULD HE ...
STEP
THE LIGHT IS SO MUCH STRONGER THAN USUAL!
STEP
HE'S REALLY GOING FOR IT!
STEP
...
OH, OH, SHARP ...
WHAT HAVE YOU DONE NOW?
KNORK
RSHH
ZAKA?!

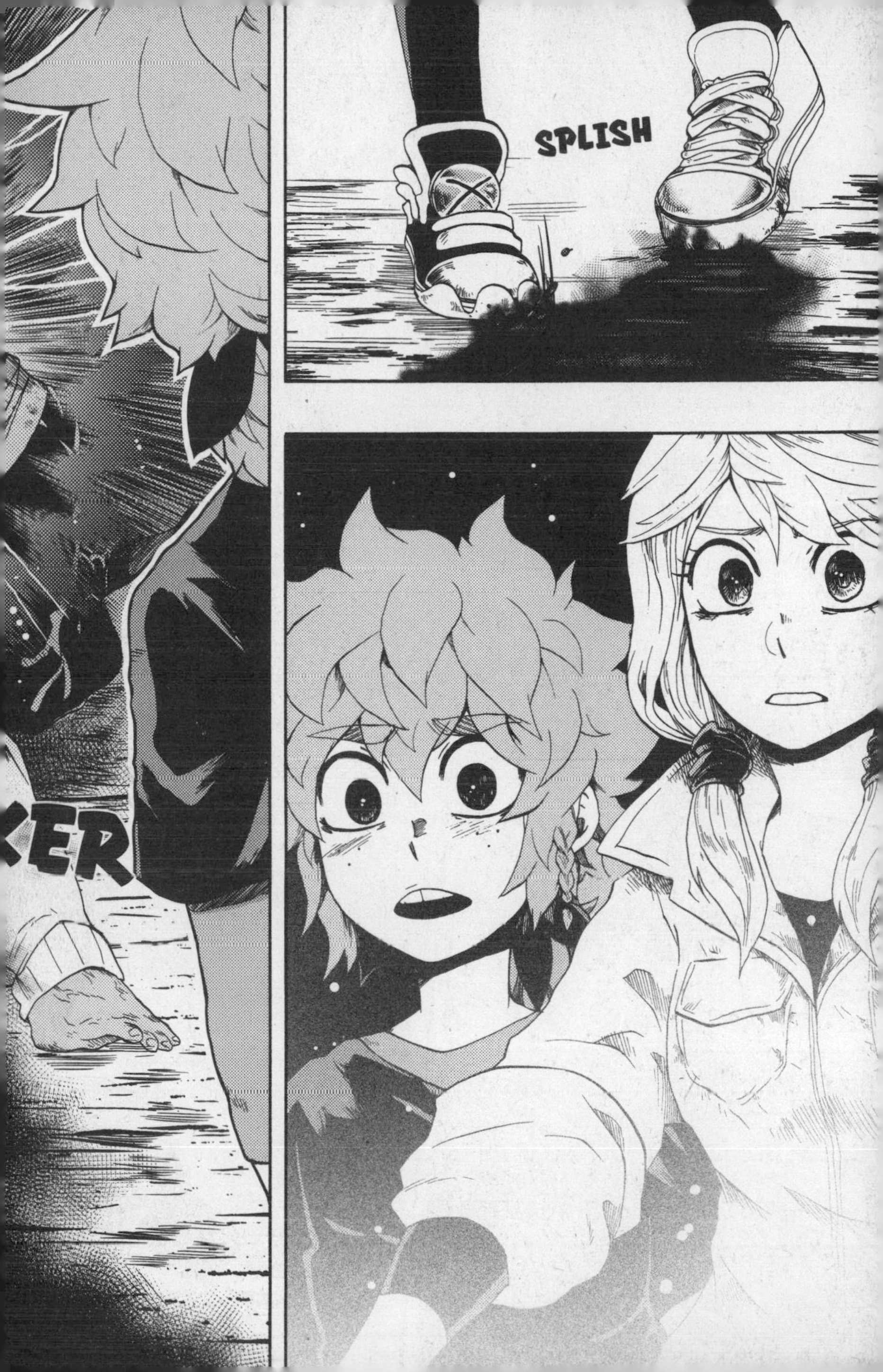
SPLISH
CER

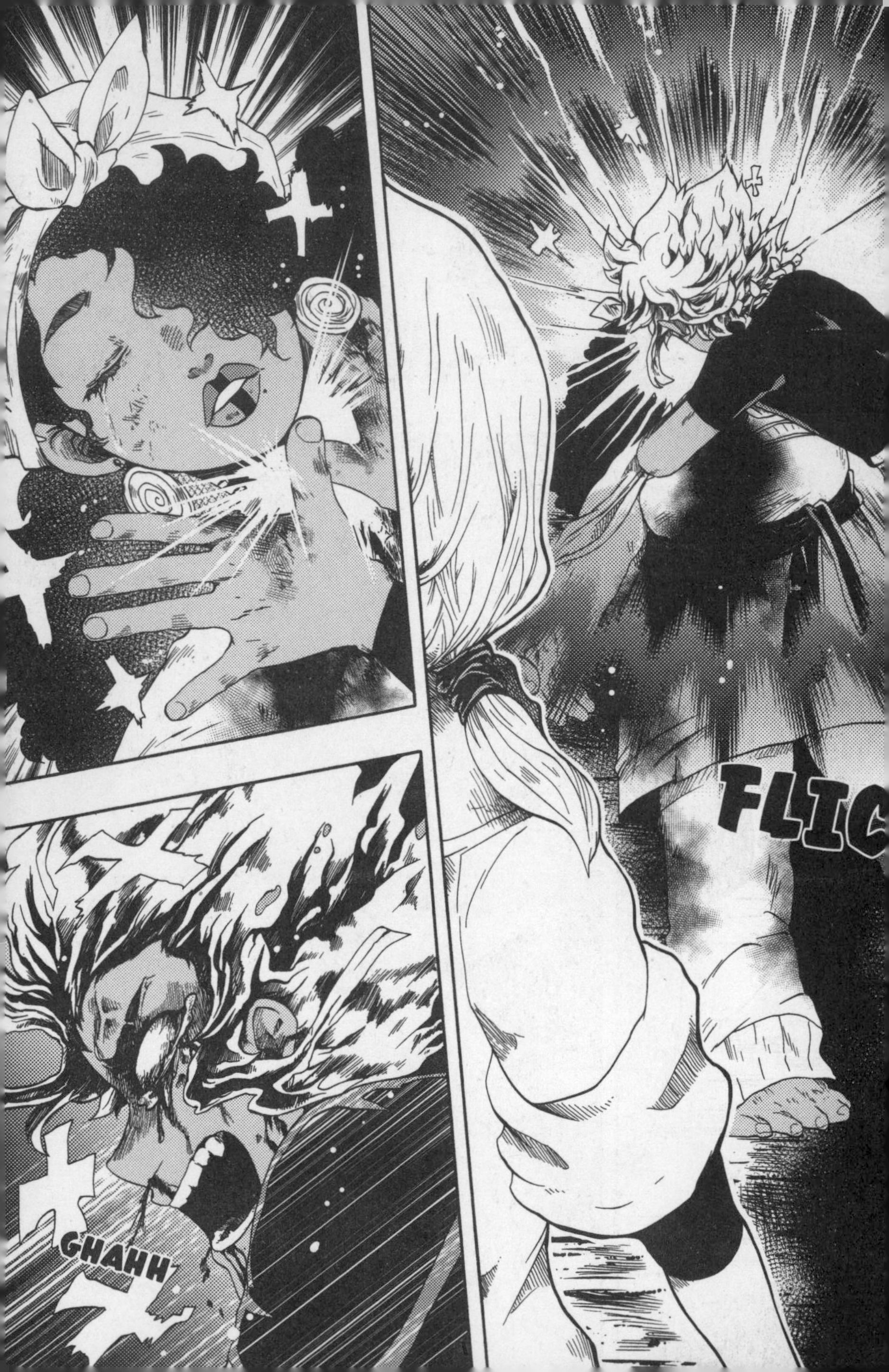
FLIC
GHAHH

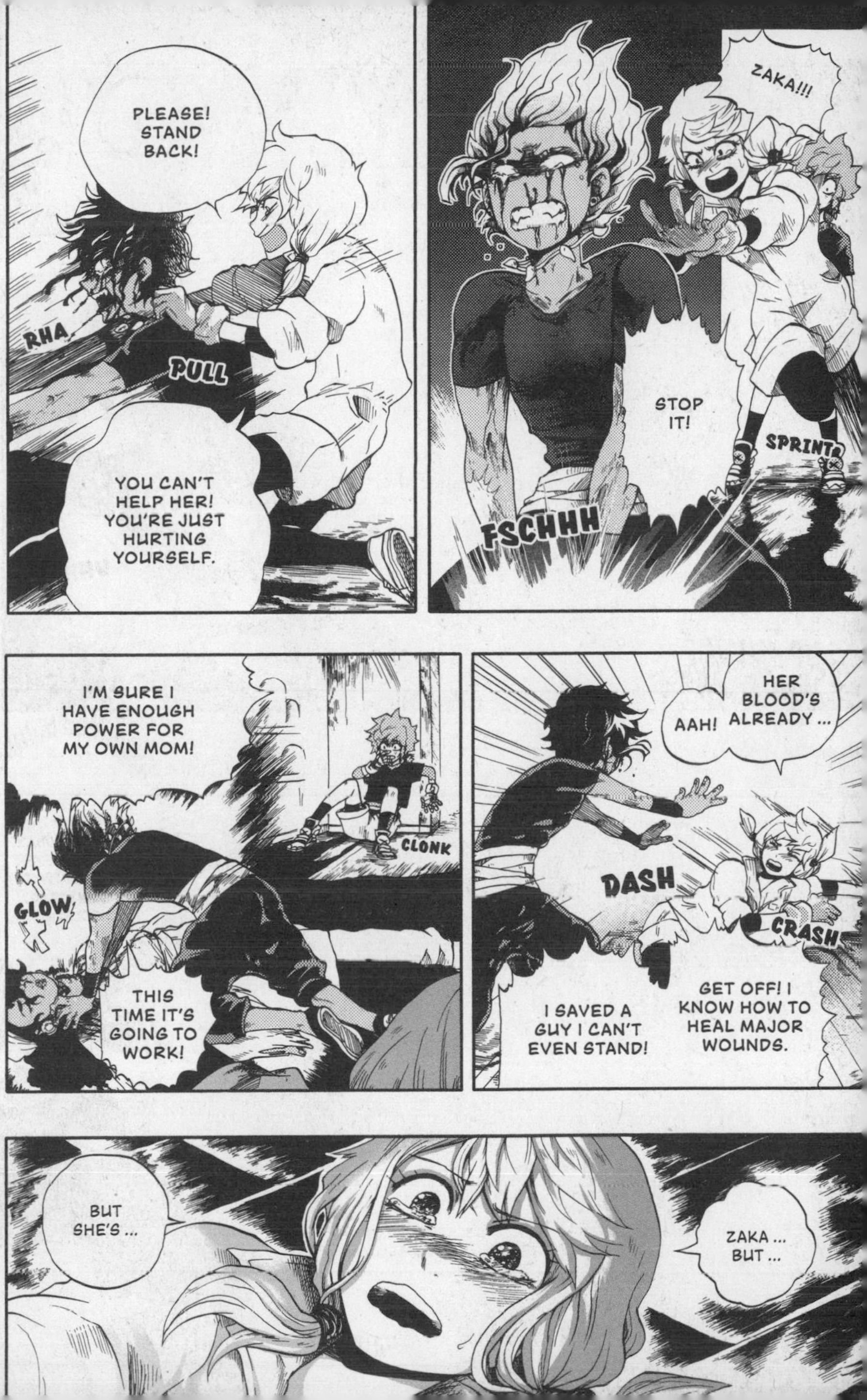
ZAKA!!!
STOP IT!
SPRINT
FSCHHH
PLEASE! STAND BACK!
RHA
PULL
YOU CAN'T HELP HER! YOU'RE JUST HURTING YOURSELF.
HER BLOOD'S ALREADY ...
AAH!
DASH
CRASH
GET OFF! I KNOW HOW TO HEAL MAJOR WOUNDS.
I SAVED A GUY I CAN'T EVEN STAND!
I'M SURE I HAVE ENOUGH POWER FOR MY OWN MOM!
CLONK
GLOW
THIS TIME IT'S GOING TO WORK!
ZAKA ... BUT ...
BUT SHE'S ...

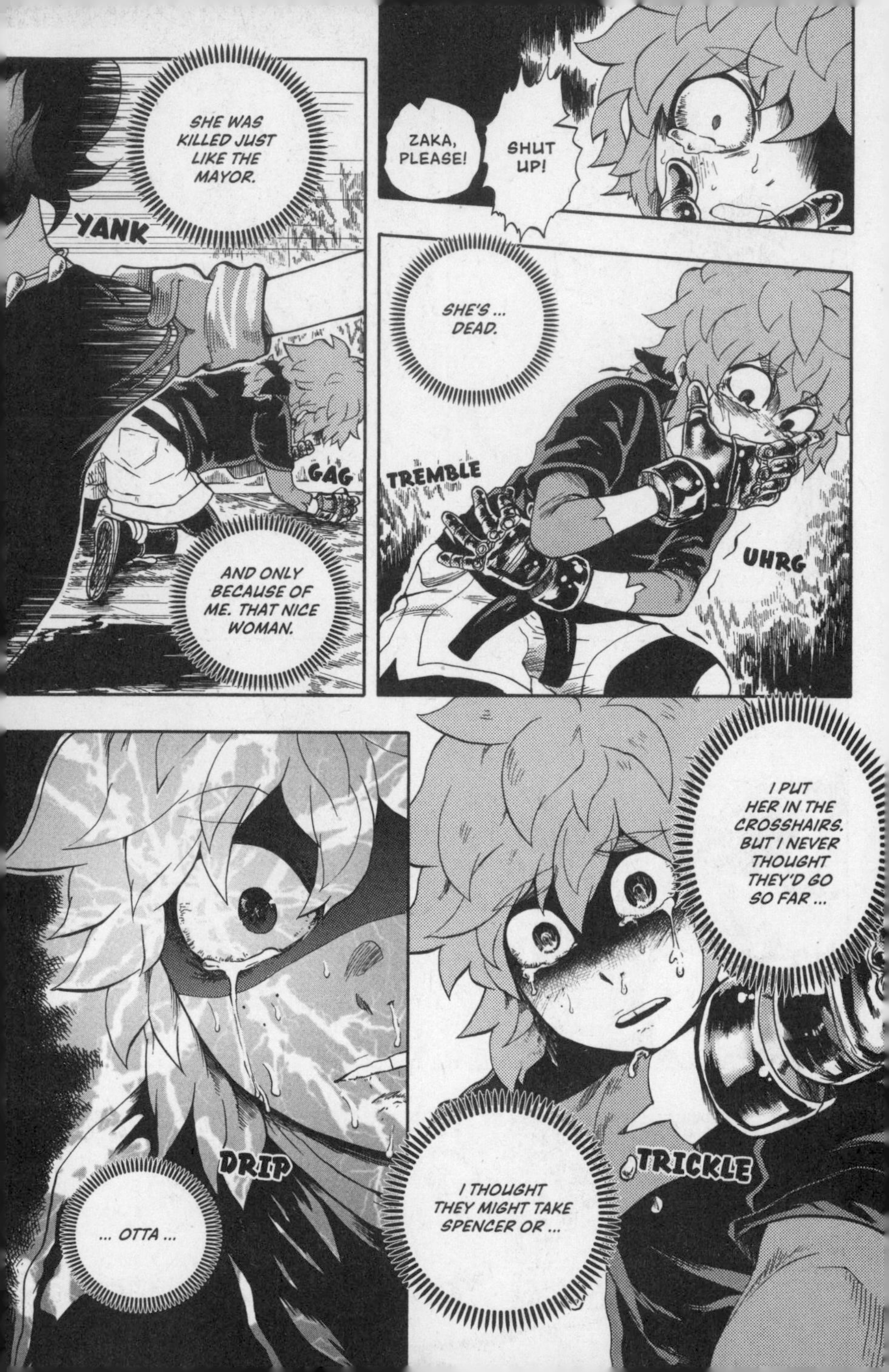
SHUT UP!
ZAKA, PLEASE!
SHE'S ... DEAD.
UHRG
TREMBLE
SHE WAS KILLED JUST LIKE THE MAYOR.
YANK
GAG
AND ONLY BECAUSE OF ME. THAT NICE WOMAN.
I PUT HER IN THE CROSSHAIRS. BUT I NEVER THOUGHT THEY'D GO SO FAR ...
TRICKLE
I THOUGHT THEY MIGHT TAKE SPENCER OR ...
DRIP
... OTTA ...

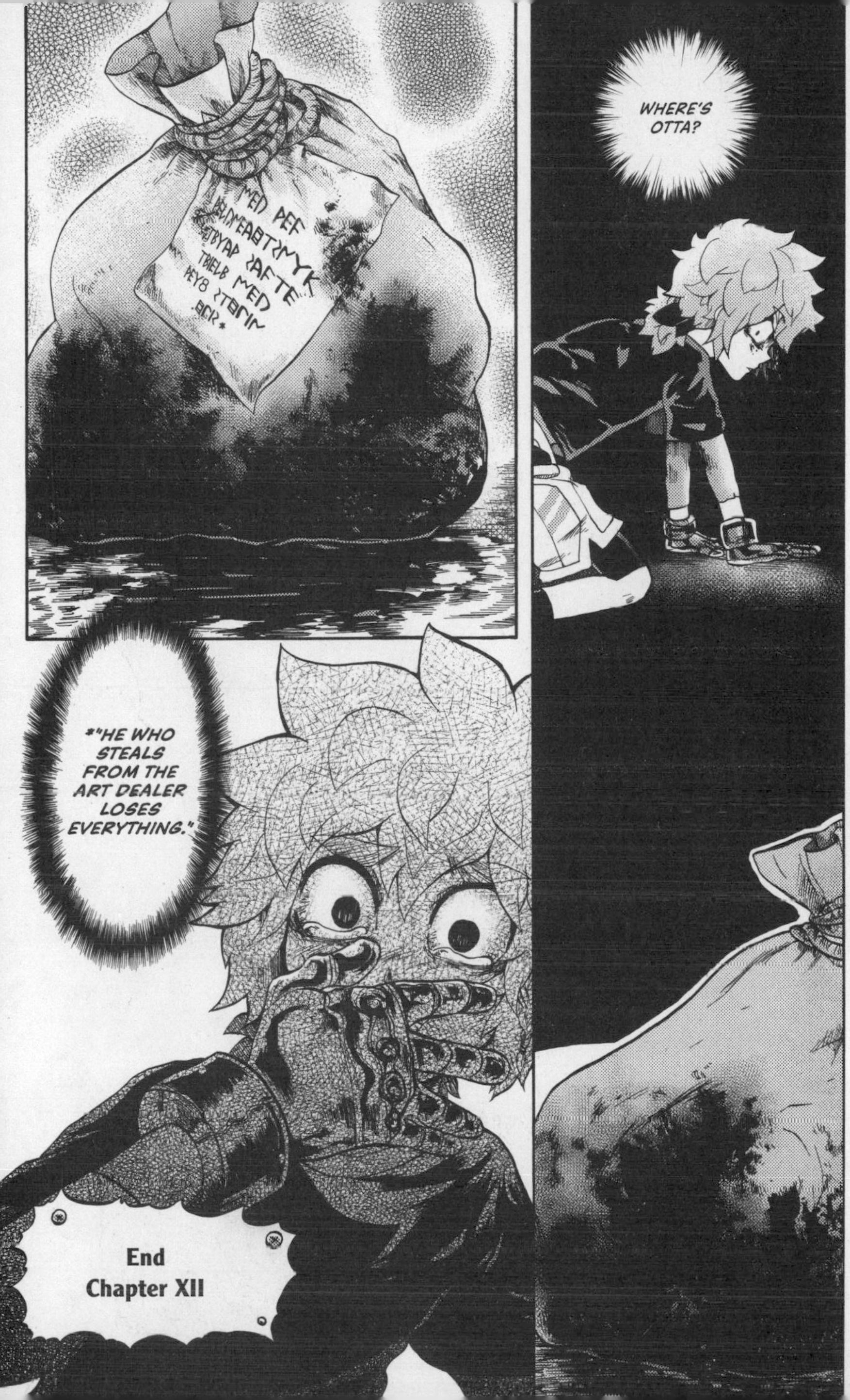
WHERE'S OTTA?
*"HE WHO STEALS FROM THE ART DEALER LOSES EVERYTHING."
End Chapter XII

In the final volume of
GOLDFISCH

When Morrey and his friends came across the shocking scene at Zaka's house, everything changed. Such a devastating loss fractures their bonds, and Morrey must go on a dangerous and painful journey to learn how to fully use his gold powers. The path ahead is fraught with difficult decisions, and he must be ready for the next confrontation with Sharp... and perhaps the mysterious Art Dealer himself.

More Artifacts, more revelations, more excitement and more gold await in the dramatic conclusion to our heroes' adventure in the final volume of *Goldfisch*!

A new legend is about to be written...

AFTERWORD

WELCOME TO THE SECOND AFTERWORD! I'M THRILLED TO SEE YOU HERE AGAIN. BECAUSE THAT MEANS THAT YOU'RE FOLLOWING *GOLDFISCH* AS A SERIES. I HOPE THAT AFTER THE SOMEWHAT *COUGH* DARKER ENDING THAT YOU DON'T GIVE UP ON THE MANGA, BECAUSE THERE'S STILL A THIRD TO GO. LIKE OSCAR WILDE SAID: "EVERYTHING IS GOING TO BE FINE IN THE END. IF IT'S NOT FINE, IT'S NOT THE END." HA HA! THE NEXT, THE THIRD BOOK, WILL CONCLUDE MORREY'S STORY FOR THE TIME BEING AND YOU DON'T WANT TO MISS OUT ON THAT!

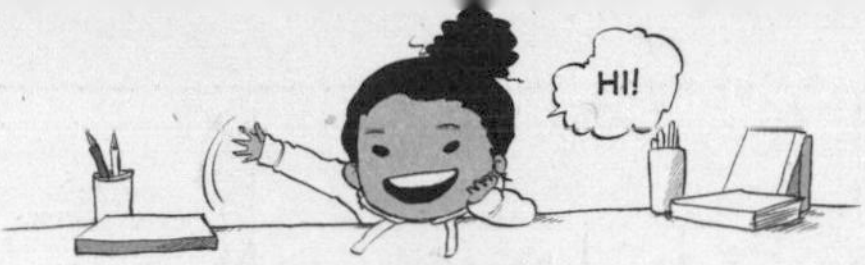
HI!

I WOULD LIKE TO USE THE FOLLOWING PAGES TO GIVE YOU SOME MORE GLIMPSES INTO THE WORK BEHIND *GOLDFISCH*. I HOPE IT'S INFORMATIVE AND A LITTLE ENTERTAINING!

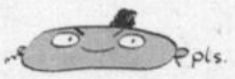
pls.

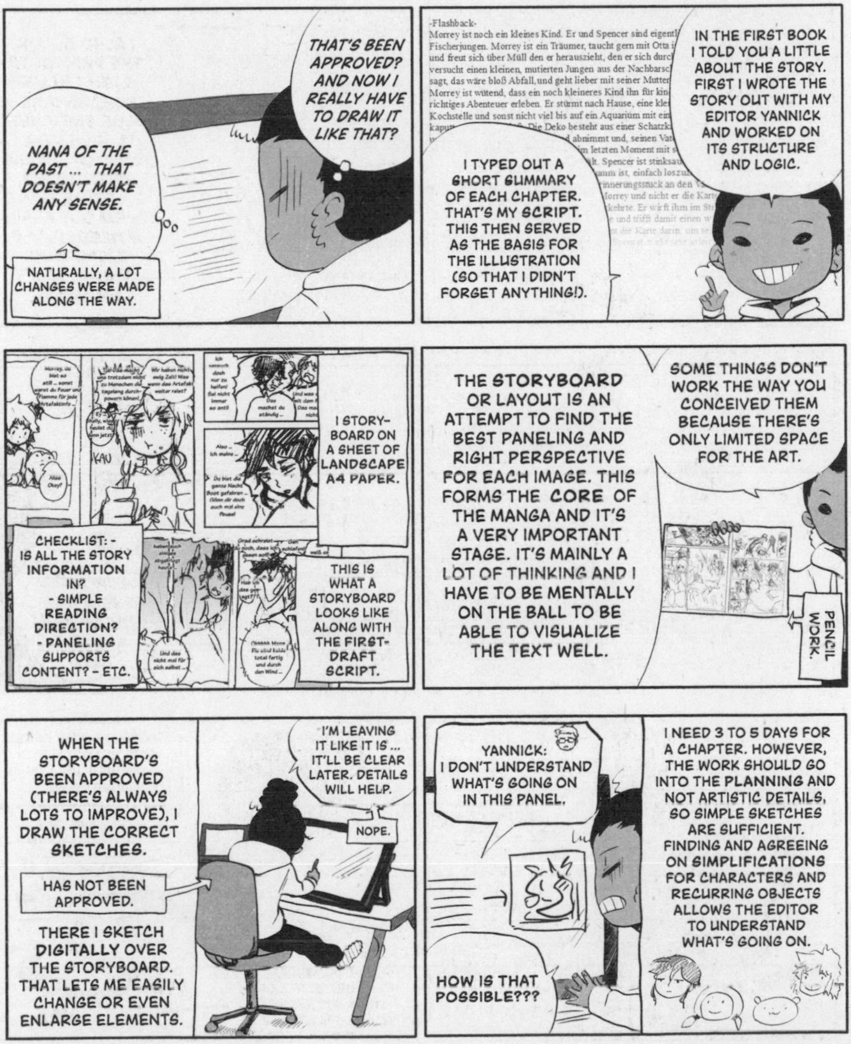
IN THE FIRST BOOK I TOLD YOU A LITTLE ABOUT THE STORY. FIRST I WROTE THE STORY OUT WITH MY EDITOR YANNICK AND WORKED ON ITS STRUCTURE AND LOGIC.
I TYPED OUT A SHORT SUMMARY OF EACH CHAPTER. THAT'S MY SCRIPT. THIS THEN SERVED AS THE BASIS FOR THE ILLUSTRATION (SO THAT I DIDN'T FORGET ANYTHING!).
THAT'S BEEN APPROVED? AND NOW I REALLY HAVE TO DRAW IT LIKE THAT?
NANA OF THE PAST ... THAT DOESN'T MAKE ANY SENSE.
NATURALLY, A LOT CHANGES WERE MADE ALONG THE WAY.
SOME THINGS DON'T WORK THE WAY YOU CONCEIVED THEM BECAUSE THERE'S ONLY LIMITED SPACE FOR THE ART.
THE STORYBOARD OR LAYOUT IS AN ATTEMPT TO FIND THE BEST PANELING AND RIGHT PERSPECTIVE FOR EACH IMAGE. THIS FORMS THE CORE OF THE MANGA AND IT'S A VERY IMPORTANT STAGE. IT'S MAINLY A LOT OF THINKING AND I HAVE TO BE MENTALLY ON THE BALL TO BE ABLE TO VISUALIZE THE TEXT WELL.
PENCIL WORK.
I STORYBOARD ON A SHEET OF LANDSCAPE A4 PAPER.
THIS IS WHAT A STORYBOARD LOOKS LIKE ALONG WITH THE FIRST-DRAFT SCRIPT.
CHECKLIST: - IS ALL THE STORY INFORMATION IN? - SIMPLE READING DIRECTION? - PANELING SUPPORTS CONTENT? - ETC.
I NEED 3 TO 5 DAYS FOR A CHAPTER. HOWEVER, THE WORK SHOULD GO INTO THE PLANNING AND NOT ARTISTIC DETAILS, SO SIMPLE SKETCHES ARE SUFFICIENT. FINDING AND AGREEING ON SIMPLIFICATIONS FOR CHARACTERS AND RECURRING OBJECTS ALLOWS THE EDITOR TO UNDERSTAND WHAT'S GOING ON.
YANNICK: I DON'T UNDERSTAND WHAT'S GOING ON IN THIS PANEL.
HOW IS THAT POSSIBLE???
I'M LEAVING IT LIKE IT IS ... IT'LL BE CLEAR LATER. DETAILS WILL HELP.
NOPE.
WHEN THE STORYBOARD'S BEEN APPROVED (THERE'S ALWAYS LOTS TO IMPROVE), I DRAW THE CORRECT SKETCHES.
HAS NOT BEEN APPROVED.
THERE I SKETCH DIGITALLY OVER THE STORYBOARD. THAT LETS ME EASILY CHANGE OR EVEN ENLARGE ELEMENTS.

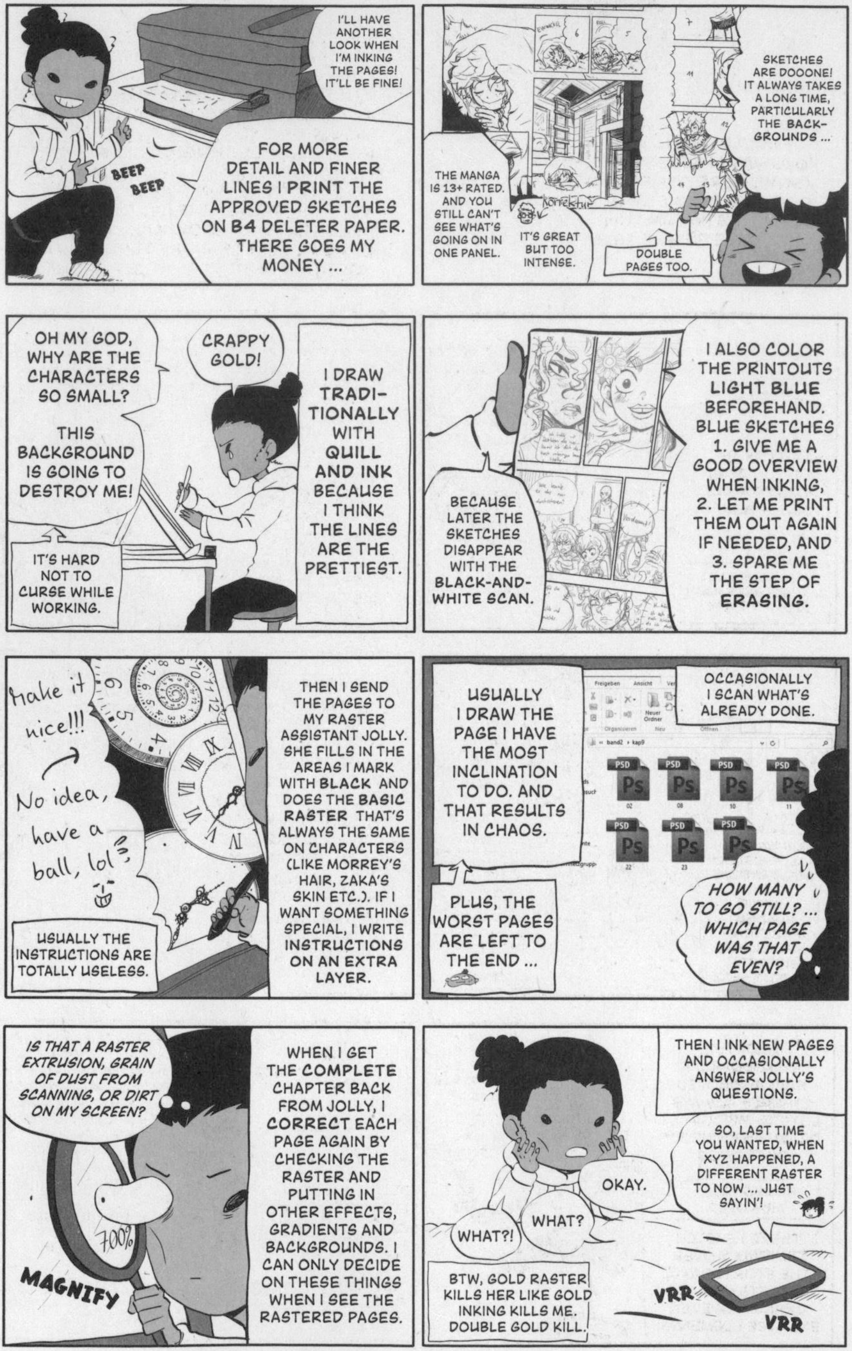

SKETCHES ARE DOOONE! IT ALWAYS TAKES A LONG TIME, PARTICULARLY THE BACK-GROUNDS ...
THE MANGA IS 13+ RATED. AND YOU STILL CAN'T SEE WHAT'S GOING ON IN ONE PANEL.
IT'S GREAT BUT TOO INTENSE.
DOUBLE PAGES TOO.
I'LL HAVE ANOTHER LOOK WHEN I'M INKING THE PAGES! IT'LL BE FINE!
FOR MORE DETAIL AND FINER LINES I PRINT THE APPROVED SKETCHES ON B4 DELETER PAPER. THERE GOES MY MONEY ...
BEEP BEEP
I ALSO COLOR THE PRINTOUTS LIGHT BLUE BEFOREHAND. BLUE SKETCHES 1. GIVE ME A GOOD OVERVIEW WHEN INKING, 2. LET ME PRINT THEM OUT AGAIN IF NEEDED, AND 3. SPARE ME THE STEP OF ERASING.
BECAUSE LATER THE SKETCHES DISAPPEAR WITH THE BLACK-AND-WHITE SCAN.
I DRAW TRADITIONALLY WITH QUILL AND INK BECAUSE I THINK THE LINES ARE THE PRETTIEST.
CRAPPY GOLD!
OH MY GOD, WHY ARE THE CHARACTERS SO SMALL?
THIS BACKGROUND IS GOING TO DESTROY ME!
IT'S HARD NOT TO CURSE WHILE WORKING.
OCCASIONALLY I SCAN WHAT'S ALREADY DONE.
USUALLY I DRAW THE PAGE I HAVE THE MOST INCLINATION TO DO. AND THAT RESULTS IN CHAOS.
HOW MANY TO GO STILL? ... WHICH PAGE WAS THAT EVEN?
PLUS, THE WORST PAGES ARE LEFT TO THE END ...
THEN I SEND THE PAGES TO MY RASTER ASSISTANT JOLLY. SHE FILLS IN THE AREAS I MARK WITH BLACK AND DOES THE BASIC RASTER THAT'S ALWAYS THE SAME ON CHARACTERS (LIKE MORREY'S HAIR, ZAKA'S SKIN ETC.). IF I WANT SOMETHING SPECIAL, I WRITE INSTRUCTIONS ON AN EXTRA LAYER.
make it nice!!!
No idea, have a ball, lol
USUALLY THE INSTRUCTIONS ARE TOTALLY USELESS.
THEN I INK NEW PAGES AND OCCASIONALLY ANSWER JOLLY'S QUESTIONS.
SO, LAST TIME YOU WANTED, WHEN XYZ HAPPENED, A DIFFERENT RASTER TO NOW ... JUST SAYIN'!
OKAY.
WHAT?
WHAT?!
BTW, GOLD RASTER KILLS HER LIKE GOLD INKING KILLS ME. DOUBLE GOLD KILL.
VRR
VRR
WHEN I GET THE COMPLETE CHAPTER BACK FROM JOLLY, I CORRECT EACH PAGE AGAIN BY CHECKING THE RASTER AND PUTTING IN OTHER EFFECTS, GRADIENTS AND BACKGROUNDS. I CAN ONLY DECIDE ON THESE THINGS WHEN I SEE THE RASTERED PAGES.
IS THAT A RASTER EXTRUSION, GRAIN OF DUST FROM SCANNING, OR DIRT ON MY SCREEN?
700%
MAGNIFY

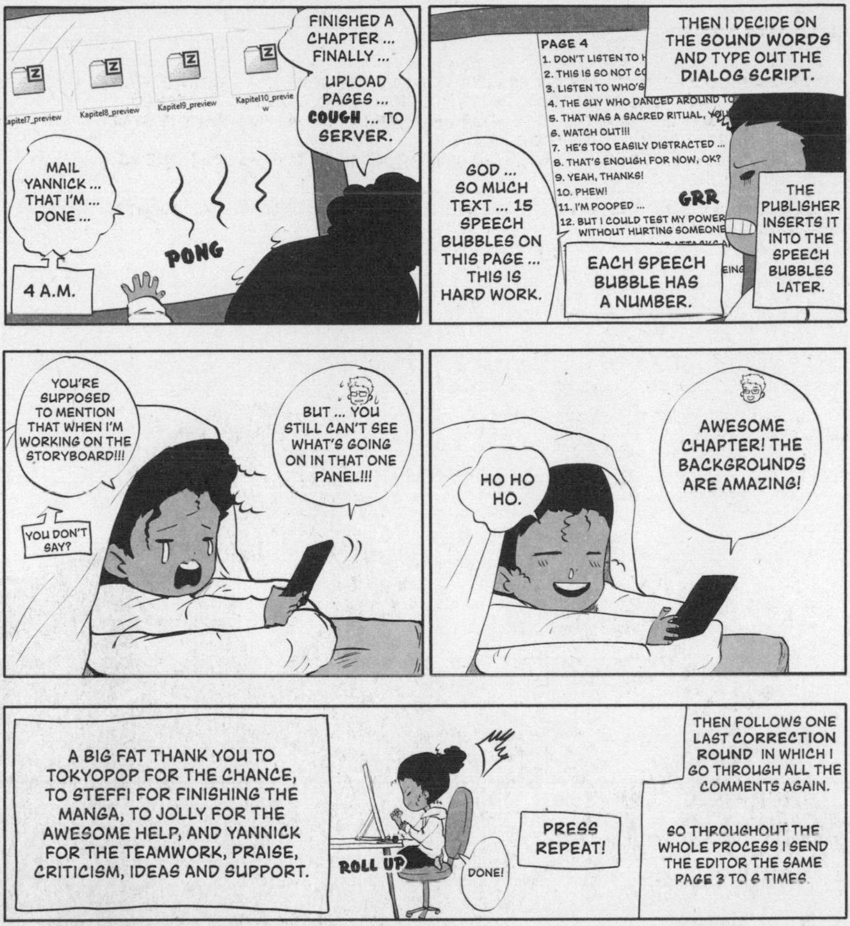
THEN I DECIDE ON THE SOUND WORDS AND TYPE OUT THE DIALOG SCRIPT.
THE PUBLISHER INSERTS IT INTO THE SPEECH BUBBLES LATER.
PAGE 4
1. DON'T LISTEN TO
2. THIS IS SO NOT
3. LISTEN TO WHO'S
4. THE GUY WHO DANCED AROUND
5. THAT WAS A SACRED RITUAL,
6. WATCH OUT!!!
7. HE'S TOO EASILY DISTRACTED ...
8. THAT'S ENOUGH FOR NOW, OK?
9. YEAH, THANKS!
10. PHEW!
11. I'M POOPED ...
12. BUT I COULD TEST MY POWER WITHOUT HURTING SOMEONE
GRR
EACH SPEECH BUBBLE HAS A NUMBER.
GOD ... SO MUCH TEXT ... 15 SPEECH BUBBLES ON THIS PAGE ... THIS IS HARD WORK.
FINISHED A CHAPTER ... FINALLY ...
UPLOAD PAGES ... COUGH ... TO SERVER.
Kapitel10_preview
Kapitel9_preview
Kapitel8_preview
Kapitel7_preview
PONG
MAIL YANNICK ... THAT I'M ... DONE ...
4 A.M.
AWESOME CHAPTER! THE BACKGROUNDS ARE AMAZING!
HO HO HO.
BUT ... YOU STILL CAN'T SEE WHAT'S GOING ON IN THAT ONE PANEL!!!
YOU'RE SUPPOSED TO MENTION THAT WHEN I'M WORKING ON THE STORYBOARD!!!
YOU DON'T SAY?
THEN FOLLOWS ONE LAST CORRECTION ROUND IN WHICH I GO THROUGH ALL THE COMMENTS AGAIN.
SO THROUGHOUT THE WHOLE PROCESS I SEND THE EDITOR THE SAME PAGE 3 TO 6 TIMES.
PRESS REPEAT!
DONE!
ROLL UP
A BIG FAT THANK YOU TO TOKYOPOP FOR THE CHANCE, TO STEFFI FOR FINISHING THE MANGA, TO JOLLY FOR THE AWESOME HELP, AND YANNICK FOR THE TEAMWORK, PRAISE, CRITICISM, IDEAS AND SUPPORT.

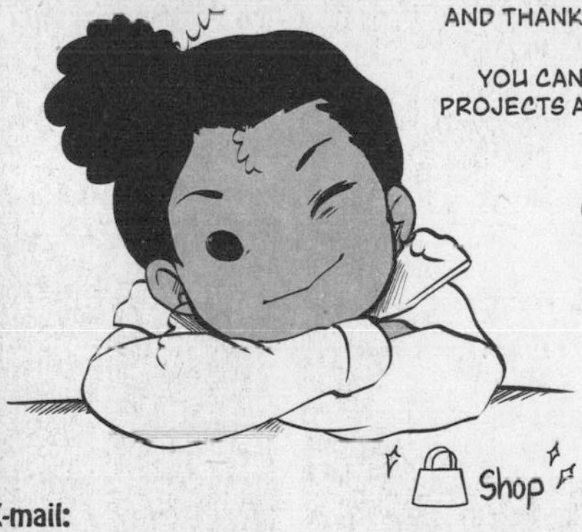

AND THANK YOU FOR BUYING AND/OR READING *GOLDFISCH!*

YOU CAN CONTACT ME, FOLLOW MY WORK OR OTHER PROJECTS AND EVEN SUPPORT ME, HERE ARE A FEW LINKS:

Online Comics:

animexx
yaa.animexx.jp

Online Gallerien:

twitter.com/Himalayaa

facebook.com/Yaatelier

instagram.com/himalaayaa

Support Links:

Shop supr.com/hon-yaa/

patreon patreon.com/NanaYaa

E-mail:

nanayaa@gmx.de

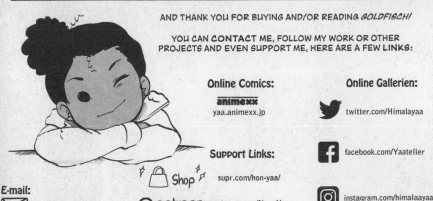

HELLO DEAR READER!

IT'S ME AGAIN, JOLLY, NANA'S RASTER ASSISTANT. A LOT WAS GOING ON IN BOOK 2, WASN'T IT? NANA DIDN'T DRAW THE SECOND BOOK CHRONOLOGICALLY AND IT ALMOST KNOCKED ME OFF MY CHAIR WHEN I GOT THE PAGES FOR CHAPTER 12 ALMOST RIGHT AT THE START. AWESOME TWIST AND DRAMA! MY POOR NERVES.
YOU'RE PROBABLY NOT DOING MUCH BETTER AFTER THAT MEAN CLIFFHANGER, ARE YOU?

IT'S CERTAINLY KEEPING THINGS EXCITING ... WE'LL SEE YOU BACK FOR BOOK 3, RIGHT? SWEAR WITH YOUR FIN?

xxx Jolly

PS: HERE ARE STALKER AND SHARP FOR YOU
(WAS A LITTLE RUSTY):

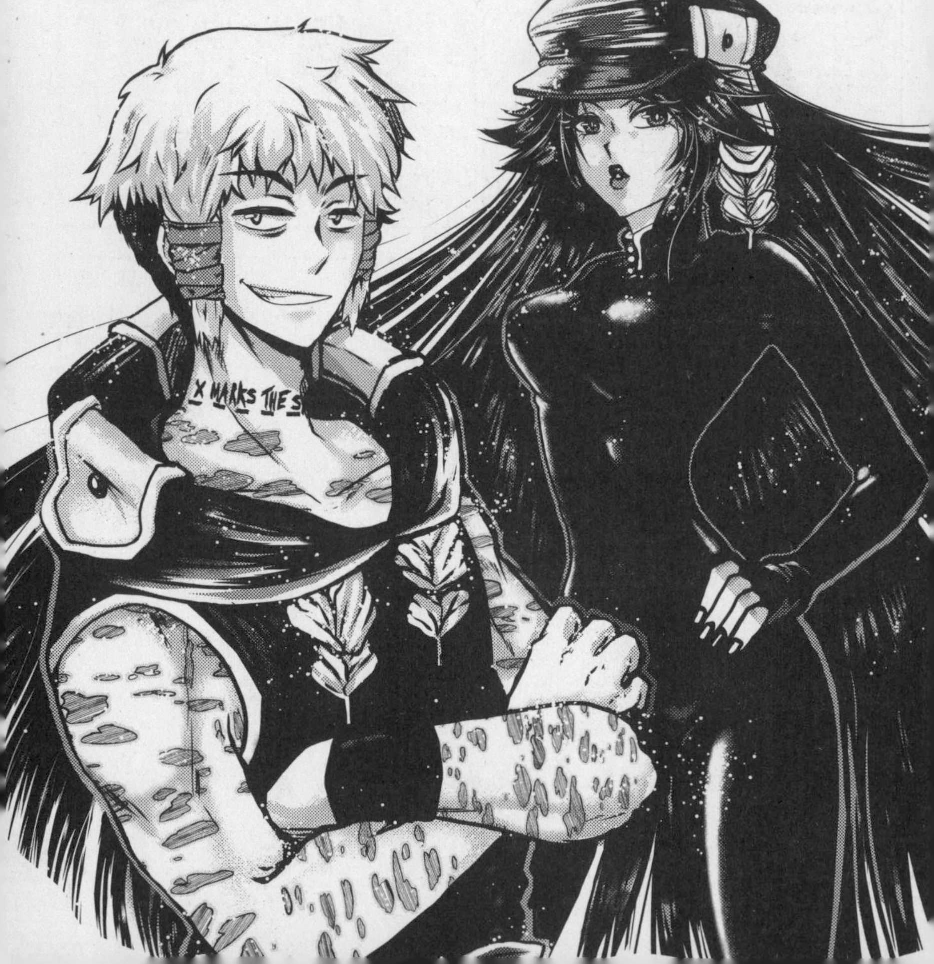
X MARKS THE S

Shelly

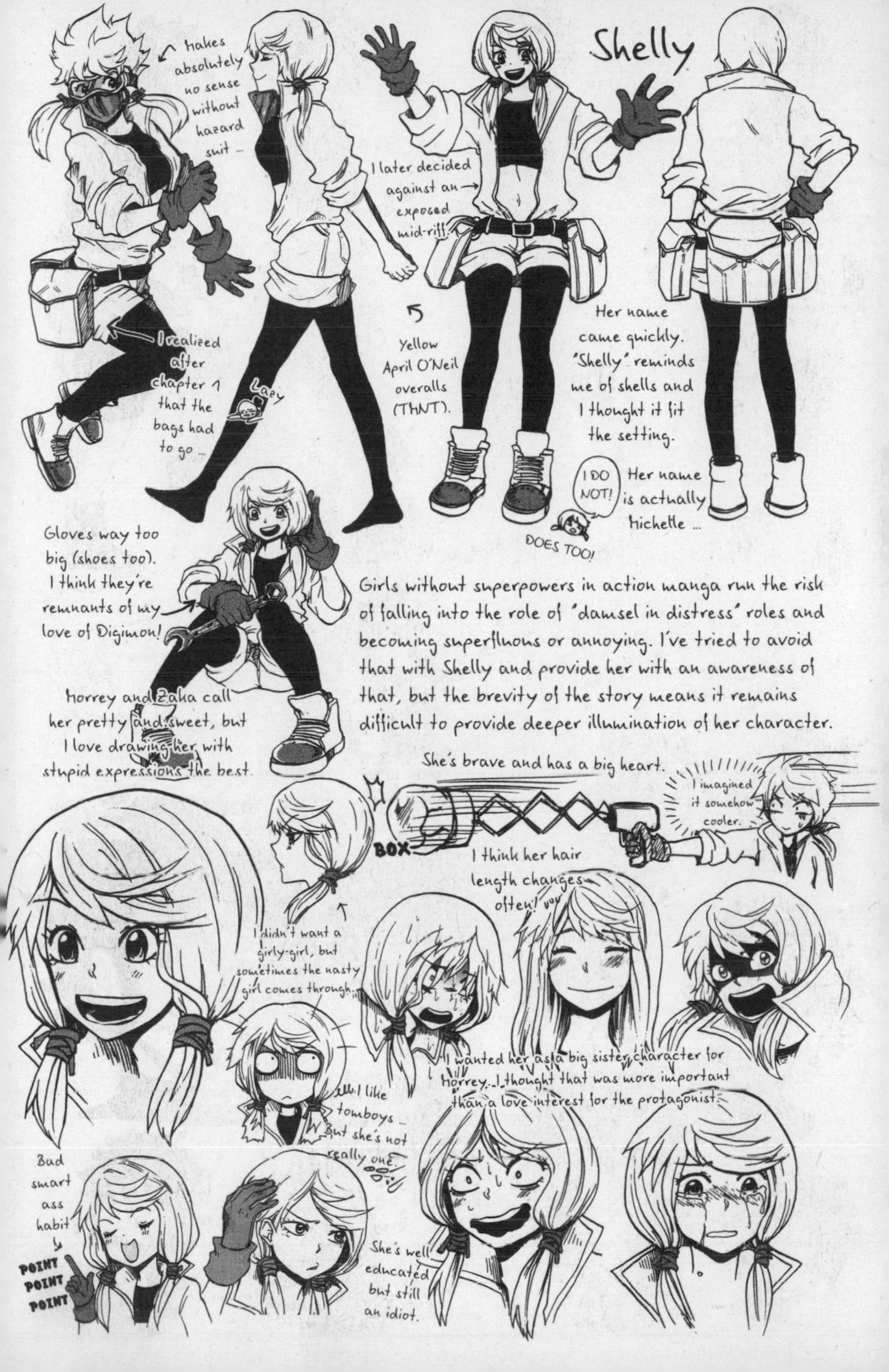

Makes absolutely no sense without hazard suit ...
I later decided against an exposed mid-riff.
I realized after chapter 1 that the bags had to go ...
Lazy
Yellow April O'Neil overalls (TMNT).
Her name came quickly. "Shelly" reminds me of shells and I thought it fit the setting.
I DO NOT!
Her name is actually Michelle ...
DOES TOO!
Gloves way too big (shoes too). I think they're remnants of my love of Digimon!
Morrey and Zaha call her pretty and sweet, but I love drawing her with stupid expressions the best.
She's brave and has a big heart.
I imagined it somehow cooler.
BOX
I think her hair length changes often!
I didn't want a girly-girl, but sometimes the nasty girl comes through.
I wanted her as a big sister character for Morrey... I thought that was more important than a love interest for the protagonist.
I like tomboys ... But she's not really one.
Bad smart ass habit
POINT POINT POINT
She's well educated but still an idiot.

Girls without superpowers in action manga run the risk of falling into the role of "damsel in distress" roles and becoming superfluous or annoying. I've tried to avoid that with Shelly and provide her with an awareness of that, but the brevity of the story means it remains difficult to provide deeper illumination of her character.

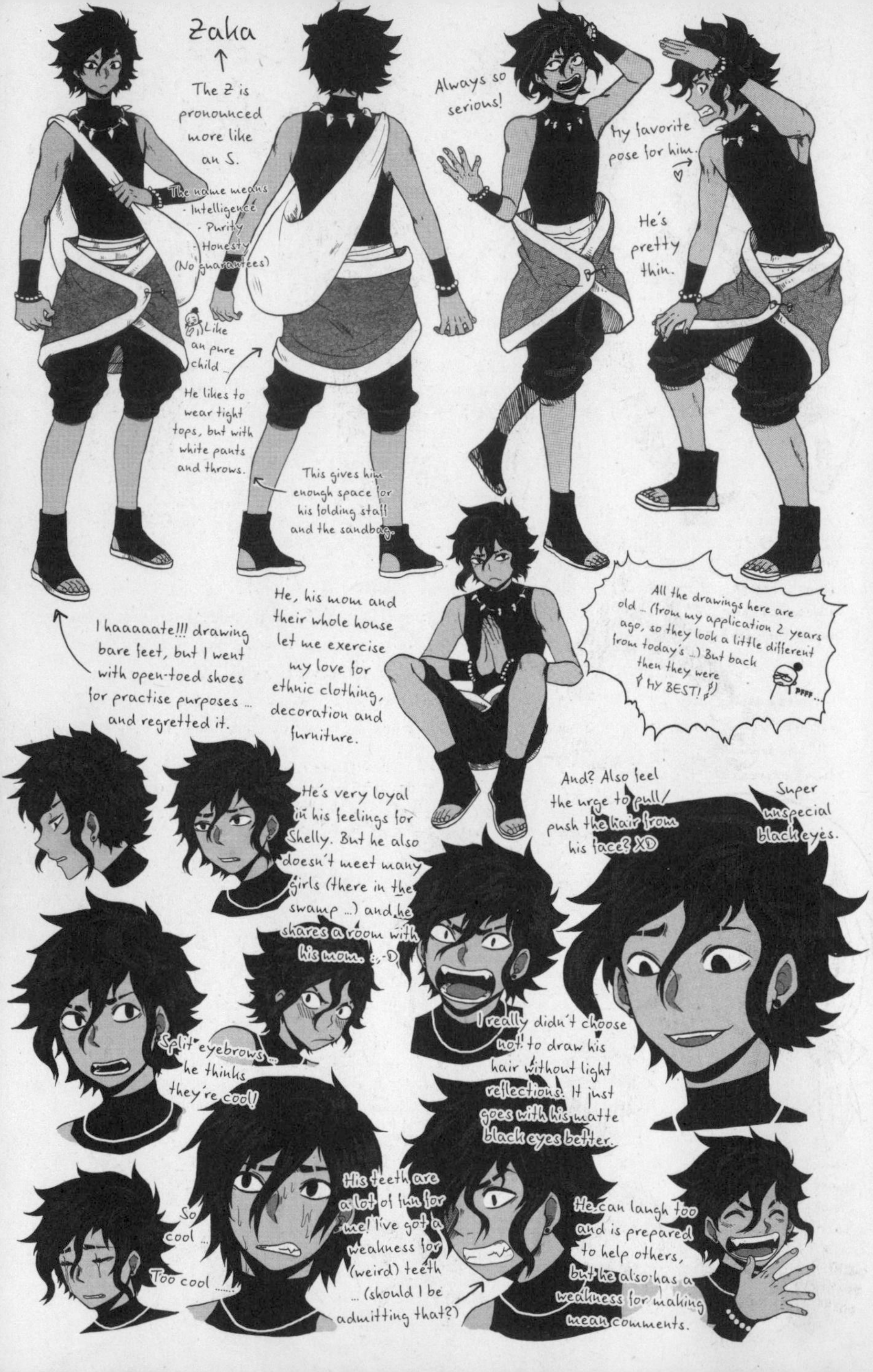
Zaka
The Z is pronounced more like an S.
The name means - Intelligence - Purity - Honesty (No guarantees)
Like an pure child ...
He likes to wear tight tops, but with white pants and throws.
This gives him enough space for his folding staff and the sandbag.
Always so serious!
My favorite pose for him.
He's pretty thin.
I haaaaate!!! drawing bare feet, but I went with open-toed shoes for practise purposes ... and regretted it.
He, his mom and their whole house let me exercise my love for ethnic clothing, decoration and furniture.
All the drawings here are old ... (from my application 2 years ago, so they look a little different from today's ...) But back then they were ♪ MY BEST! ♪)
PFFF...
And? Also feel the urge to pull/push the hair from his face? XD
Super unspecial black eyes.
He's very loyal in his feelings for Shelly. But he also doesn't meet many girls (there in the swamp ...) and he shares a room with his mom. :,-D
Split eyebrows ... he thinks they're cool!
I really didn't choose not to draw his hair without light reflections. It just goes with his matte black eyes better.
So cool ...
Too cool ......
His teeth are a lot of fun for me! I've got a weakness for (weird) teeth ... (should I be admitting that?)
He can laugh too and is prepared to help others, but he also has a weakness for making mean comments.

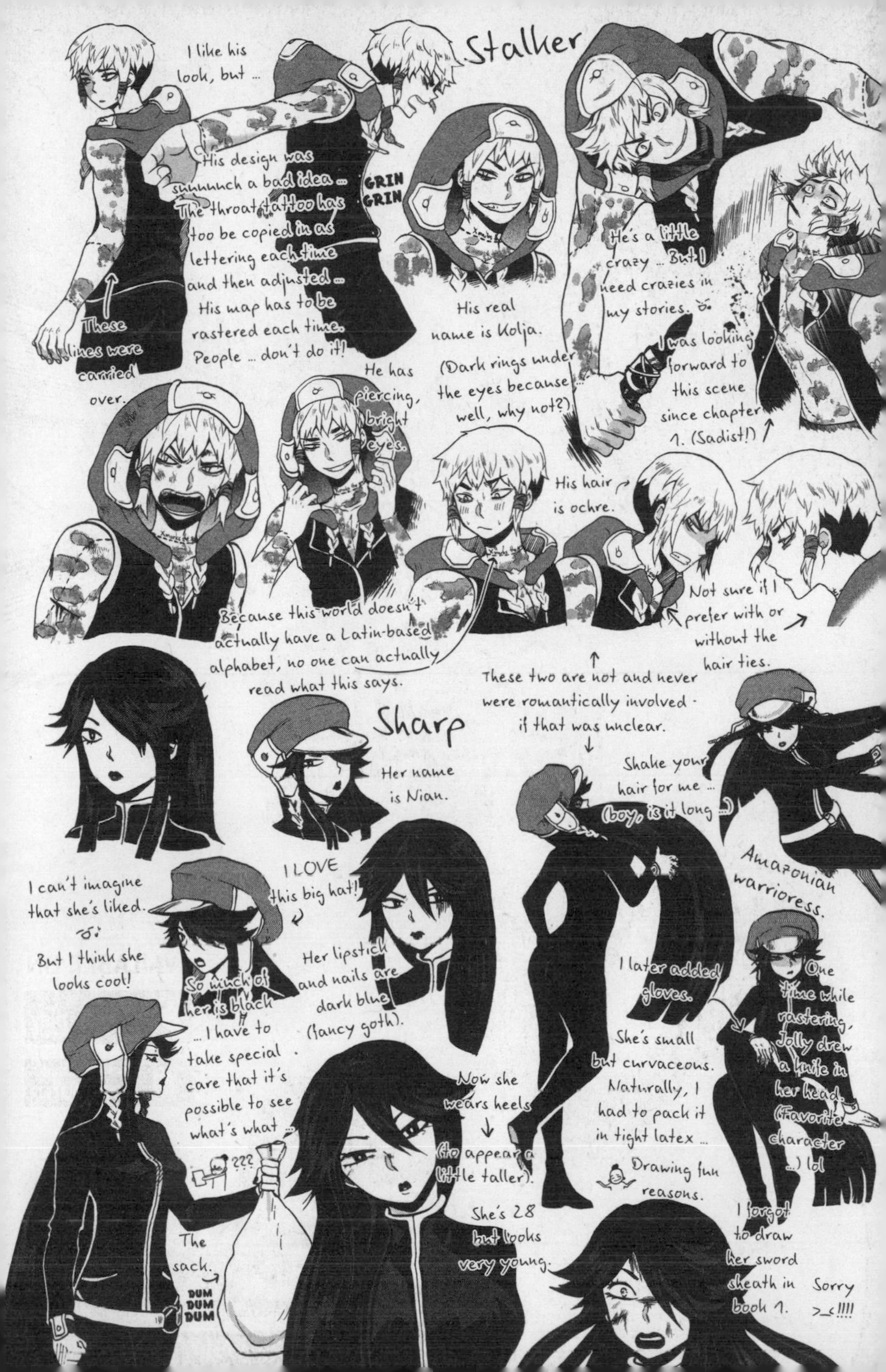
Stalker
He's a little crazy ... But I need crazies in my stories.
I was looking forward to this scene since chapter 1. (Sadist!)
His real name is Kolja.
(Dark rings under the eyes because ... well, why not?)
GRIN GRIN
I like his look, but ...
His design was suuuuuch a bad idea ... The throat tattoo has too be copied in as lettering each time and then adjusted ... His map has to be rastered each time. People ... don't do it!
These lines were carried over.
Not sure if I prefer with or without the hair ties.
His hair is ochre.
He has piercing, bright eyes.
Because this world doesn't actually have a Latin-based alphabet, no one can actually read what this says.
These two are not and never were romantically involved - if that was unclear.
Amazonian warrioress.
Shake your hair for me ... (boy, is it long ...)
Sharp
Her name is Nian.
I later added gloves.
She's small but curvaceous. Naturally, I had to pack it in tight latex ...
Drawing fun reasons.
One time while rastering, Jolly drew a knife in her head. (Favorite character ...) lol
I forgot to draw her sword sheath in book 1.
Sorry >_<!!!!
Now she wears heels (to appear a little taller).
She's 28 but looks very young.
I LOVE this big hat!
Her lipstick and nails are dark blue (fancy goth).
I can't imagine that she's liked.
But I think she looks cool!
So much of her is black ... I have to take special care that it's possible to see what's what ...
???
The sack.
DUM DUM DUM

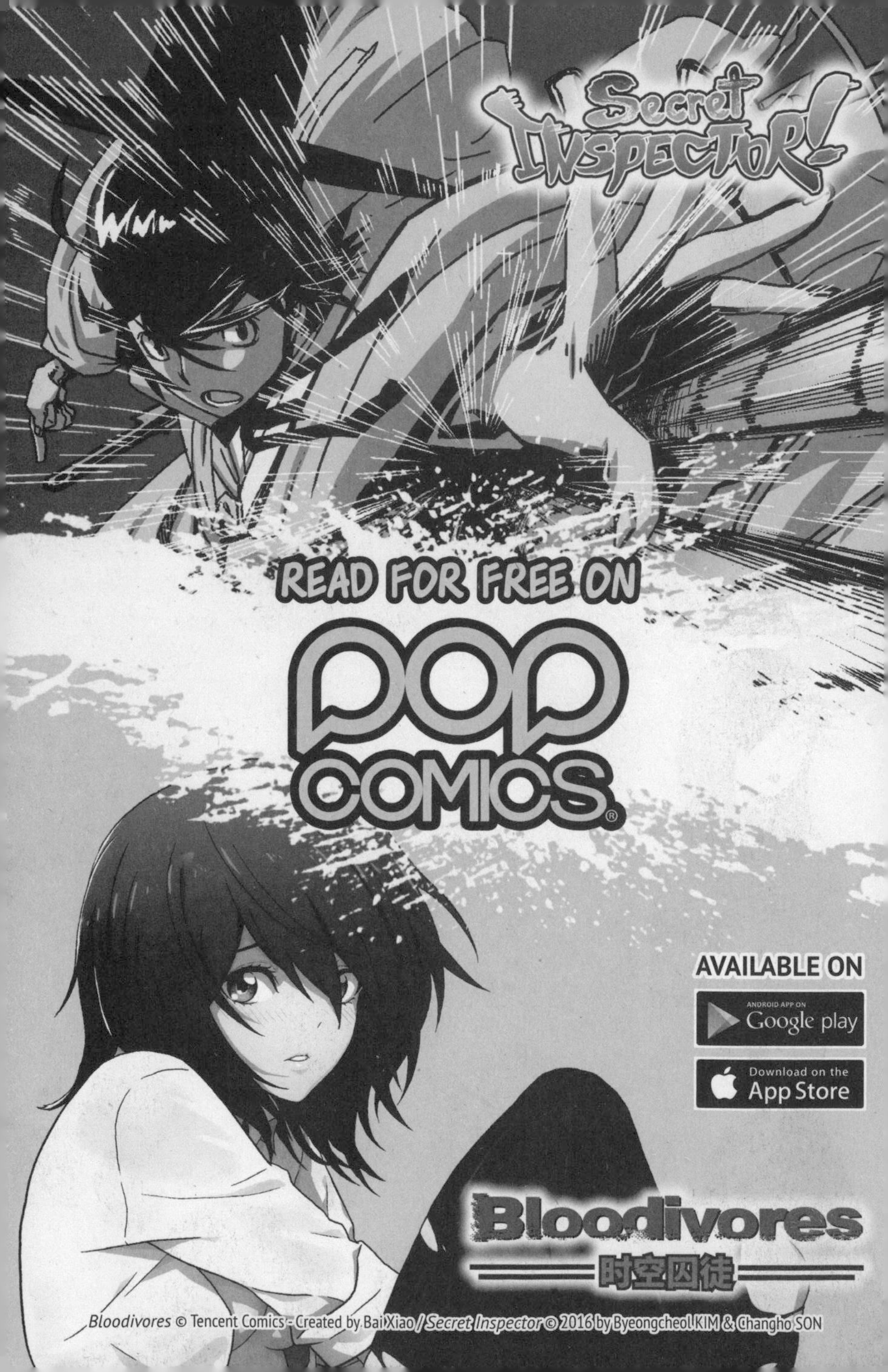
Secret INSPECTOR!
READ FOR FREE ON
POP COMICS®
AVAILABLE ON
ANDROID APP ON Google play
Download on the App Store
Bloodivores
时空囚徒
Bloodivores © Tencent Comics - Created by Bai Xiao / Secret Inspector © 2016 by Byeongcheol KIM & Changho SON

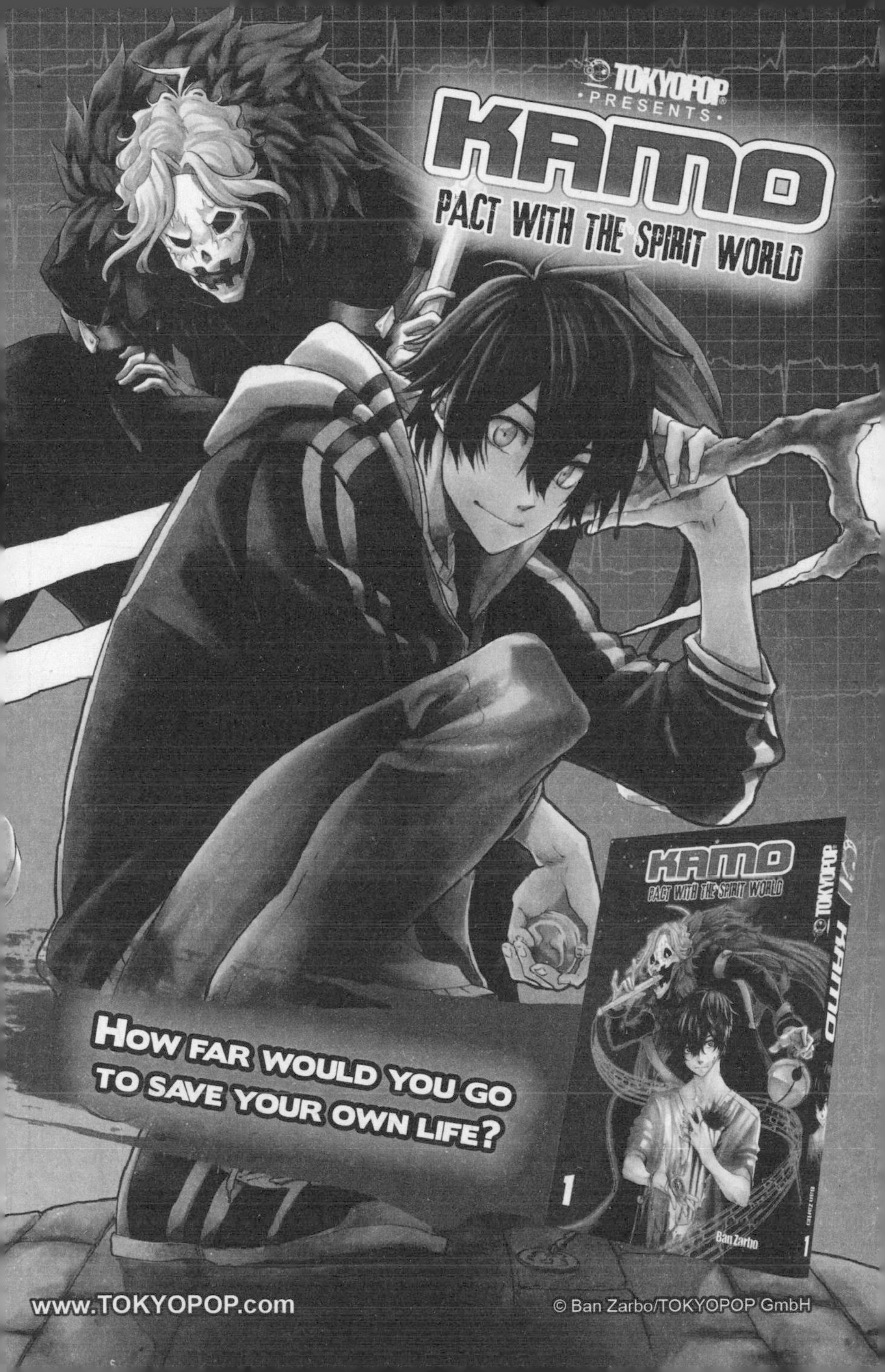
TOKYOPOP
PRESENTS
KAMO
PACT WITH THE SPIRIT WORLD
KAMO
PACT WITH THE SPIRIT WORLD
TOKYOPOP
KAMO
1
Ban Zarbo
1
HOW FAR WOULD YOU GO TO SAVE YOUR OWN LIFE?
www.TOKYOPOP.com
© Ban Zarbo/TOKYOPOP GmbH

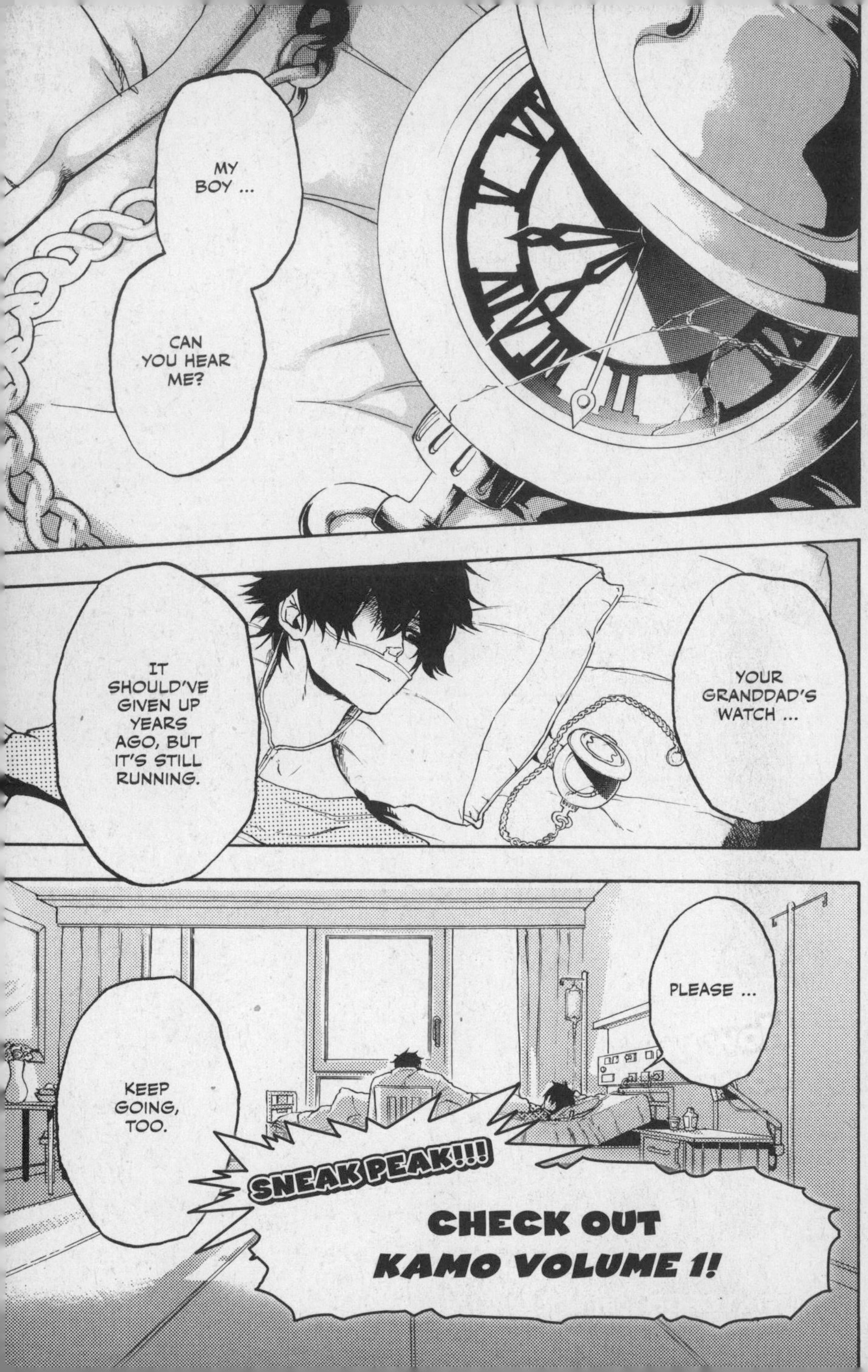
MY BOY ...
CAN YOU HEAR ME?
YOUR GRANDDAD'S WATCH ...
IT SHOULD'VE GIVEN UP YEARS AGO, BUT IT'S STILL RUNNING.
PLEASE ...
KEEP GOING, TOO.
SNEAK PEAK!!!
CHECK OUT KAMO VOLUME 1!

YOU KNOW
THERE'S NO
POINT ANYMORE.
YOUR TEARS
BETRAY YOU.

DAD ...

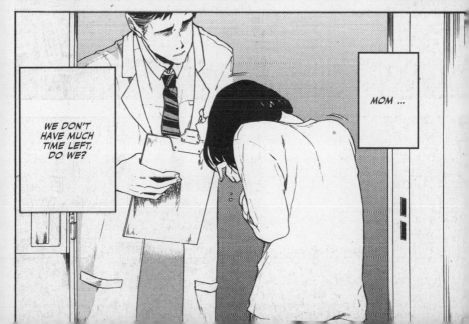

WE DON'T
HAVE MUCH
TIME LEFT,
DO WE?

MOM ...

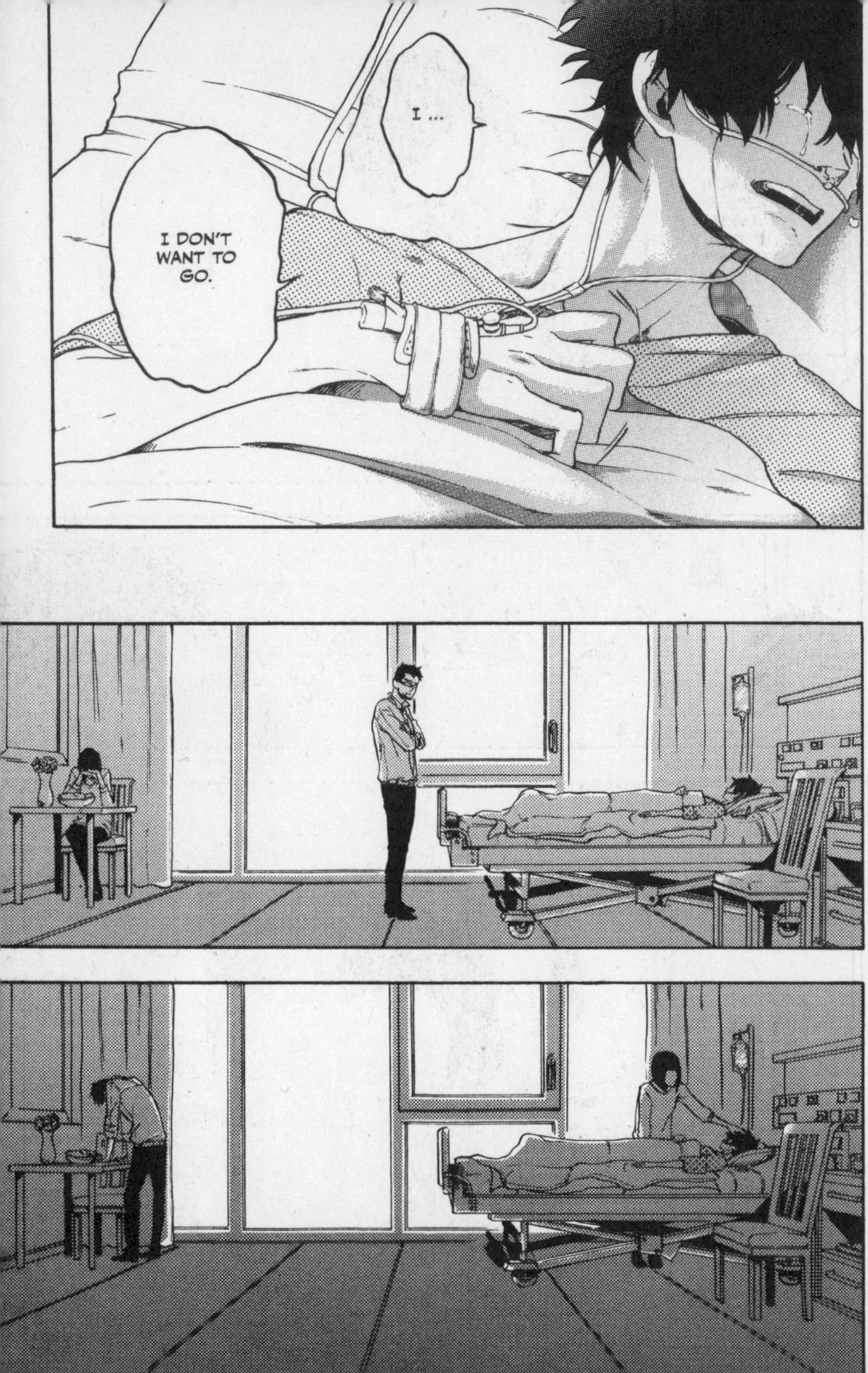
I ...
I DON'T WANT TO GO.

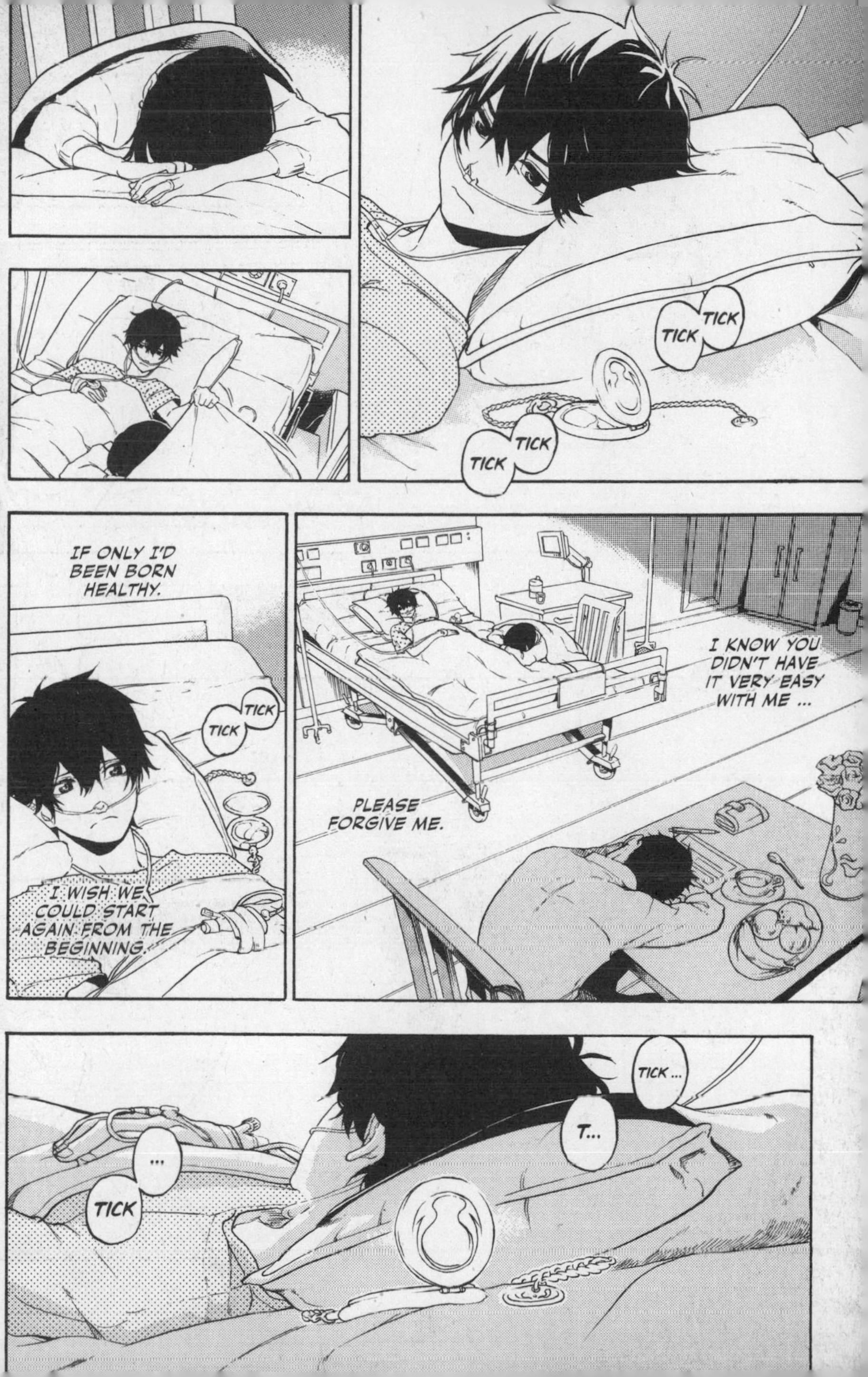
TICK
TICK
TICK
TICK
I KNOW YOU DIDN'T HAVE IT VERY EASY WITH ME ...
PLEASE FORGIVE ME.
IF ONLY I'D BEEN BORN HEALTHY.
TICK
TICK
I WISH WE COULD START AGAIN FROM THE BEGINNING.
TICK ...
T...
...
TICK

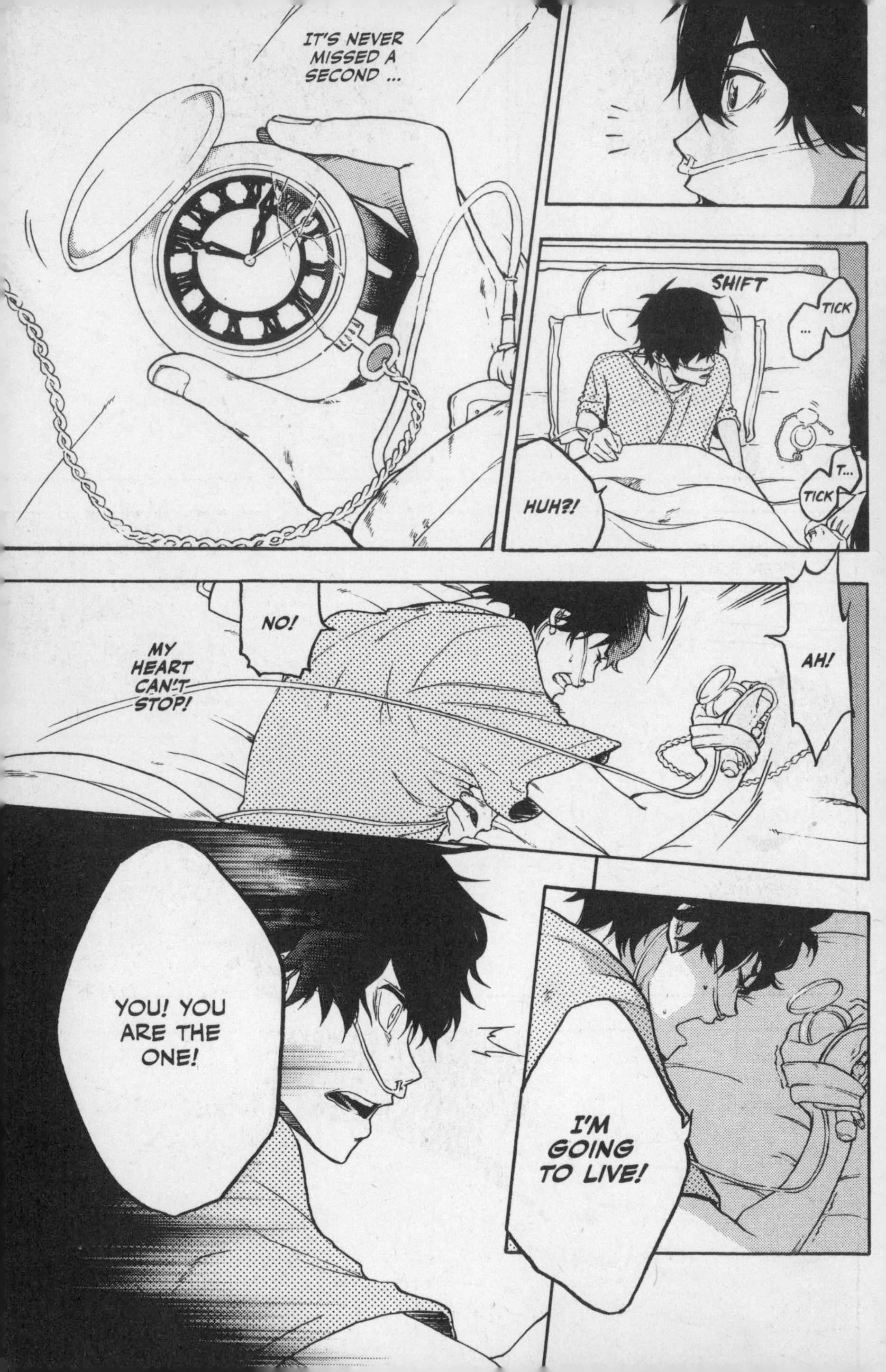
TICK ...
SHIFT
T... TICK
HUH?!
IT'S NEVER MISSED A SECOND ...
AH!
NO!
MY HEART CAN'T STOP!
I'M GOING TO LIVE!
YOU! YOU ARE THE ONE!

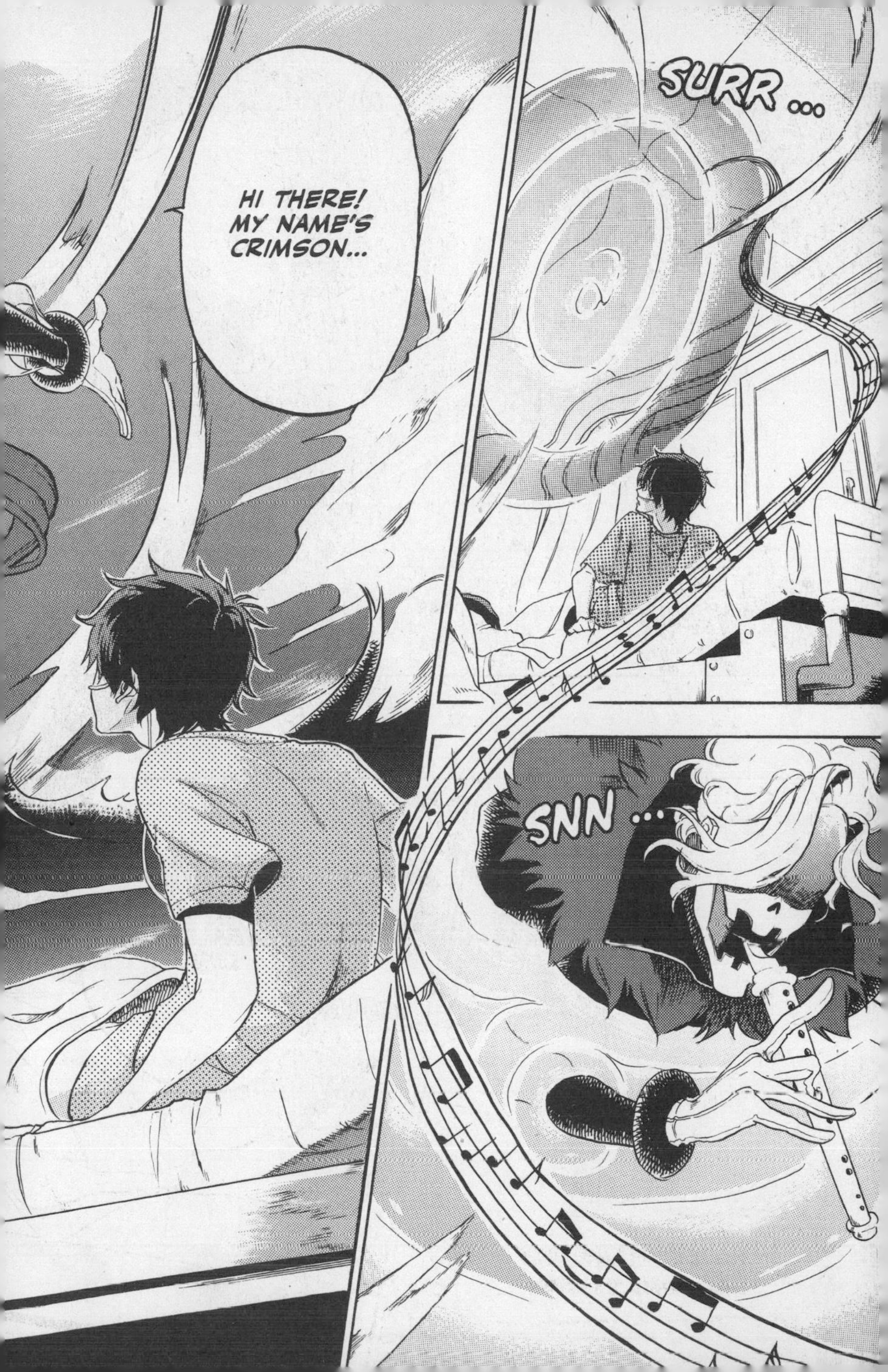
SURR ...
SNN ...
HI THERE! MY NAME'S CRIMSON...

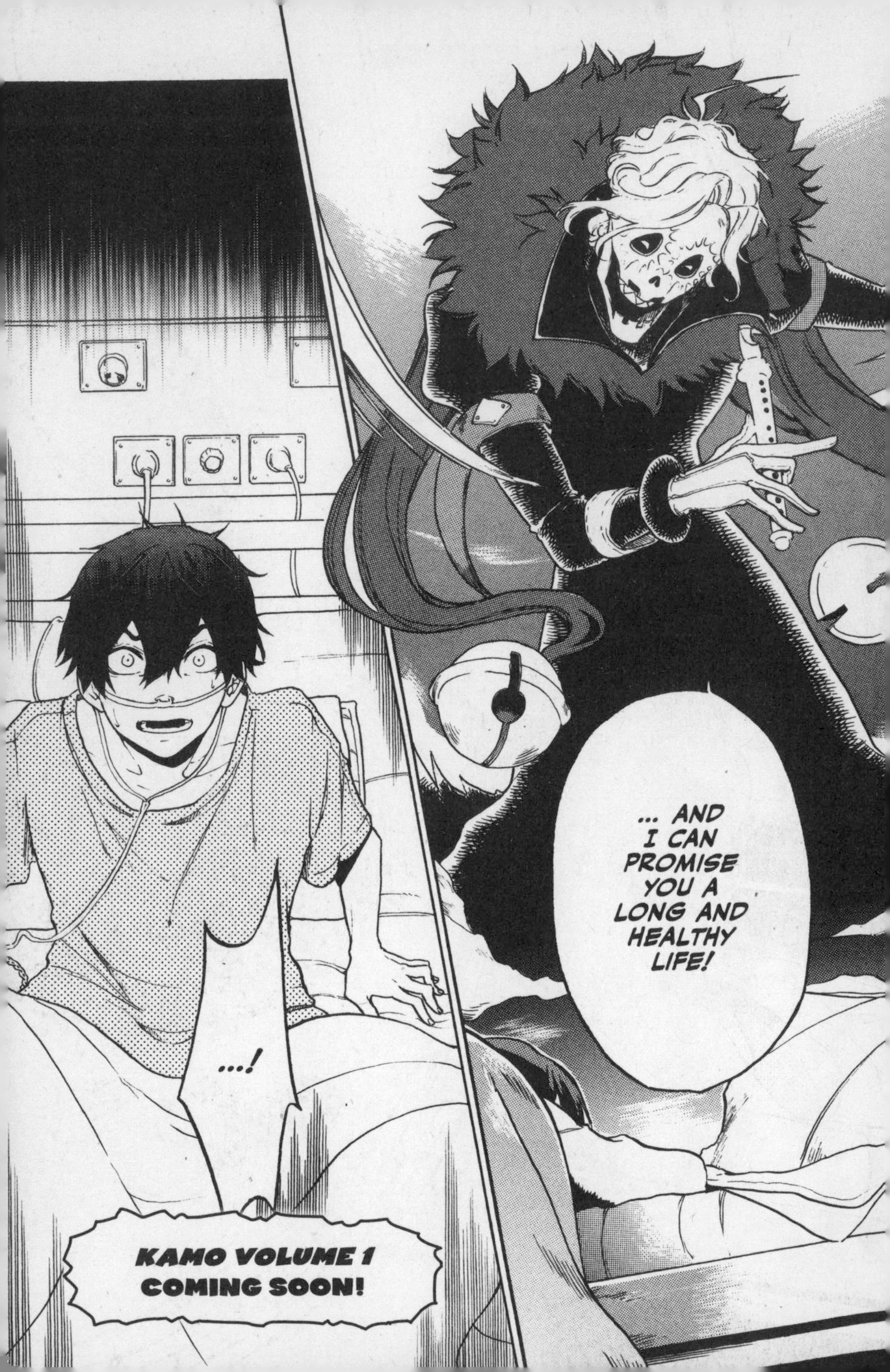
... AND I CAN PROMISE YOU A LONG AND HEALTHY LIFE!
...!
KAMO VOLUME 1 COMING SOON!

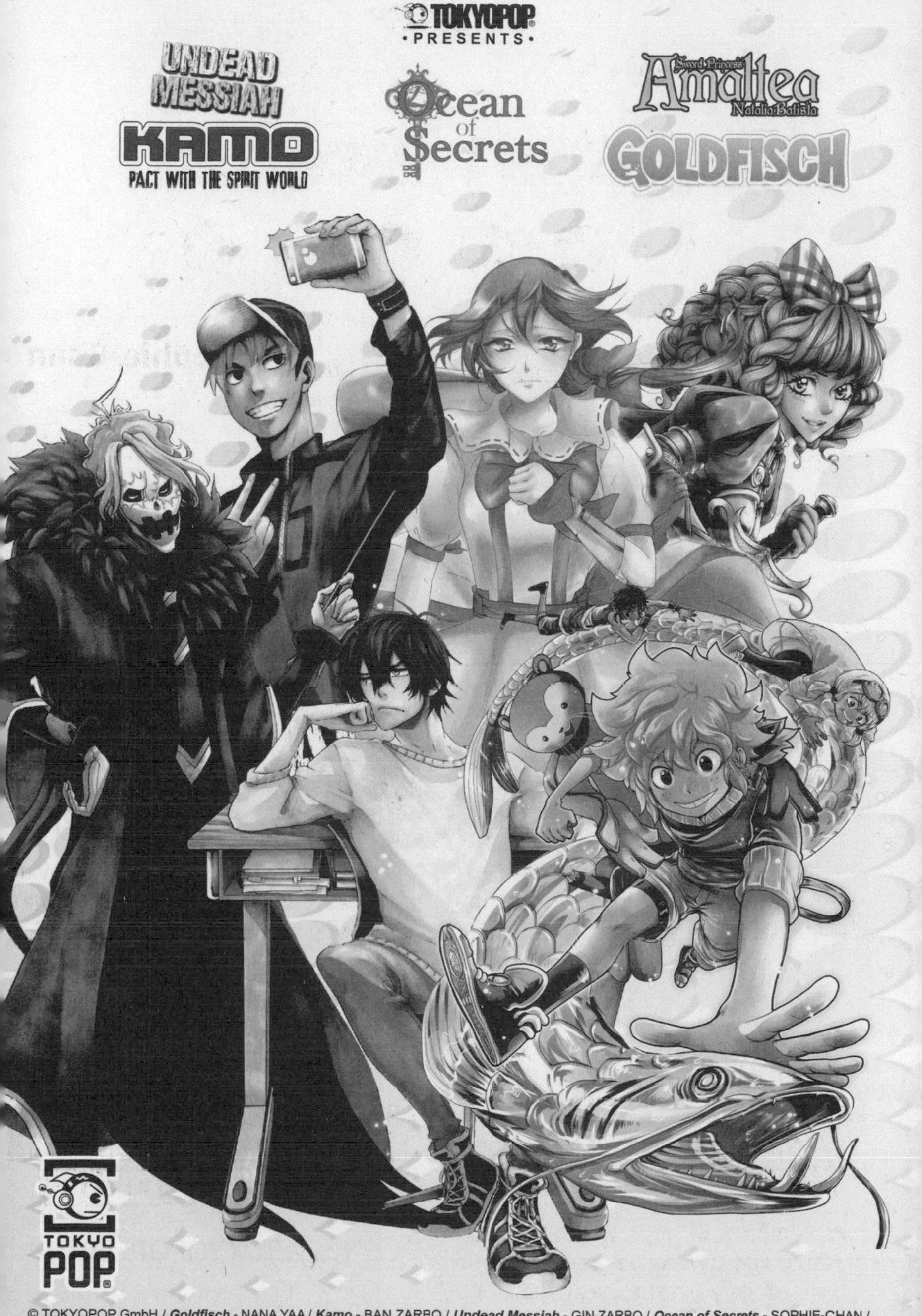
TOKYOPOP
PRESENTS
UNDEAD MESSIAH
KAMO
PACT WITH THE SPIRIT WORLD
Ocean of Secrets
Sword Princess Amaltea
Natalia Batista
GOLDFISCH
TOKYO POP

UNDEAD MESSIAH

UNDEAD MESSIAH

1

Gin Zarbo

ZOMBIE APOCALYPSES ARE SO LAST YEAR!

Goldfisch Volume 2
Manga by Nana Yaa

Editorial Associate - Janae Young
Marketing Associate - Kae Winters
Technology and Digital Media Assistant - Phillip Hong
Translator - Michael Waaler
Editor - M. Cara Carper
Graphic Designer - Phillip Hong
Retouching and Lettering - Vibrraant Publishing Studio
Editor-in-Chief & Publisher - Stu Levy
Digital Media Coordinator - Rico Brenner-Quiñonez
Licensing Specialist - Arika Yanaka

A  Manga

TOKYOPOP and 🐢 are trademarks or registered trademarks of TOKYOPOP Inc.

TOKYOPOP Inc.
5200 W. Century Blvd. Suite 705
Los Angeles, 90045

E-mail: info@TOKYOPOP.com
Come visit us online at www.TOKYOPOP.com

f www.facebook.com/TOKYOPOP
🐦 www.twitter.com/TOKYOPOP
▶ www.youtube.com/TOKYOPOPTV
📌 www.pinterest.com/TOKYOPOP
📷 www.instagram.com/TOKYOPOP
t. TOKYOPOP.tumblr.com

ISBN: 978-1-4278-5819-1

First TOKYOPOP Printing: March 2018
10 9 8 7 6 5 4 3 2 1
Printed in the CANADA

STOP

THIS IS THE BACK OF THE BOOK!

How do you read manga-style? It's simple! Let's practice -- just start in the top right panel and follow the numbers below!

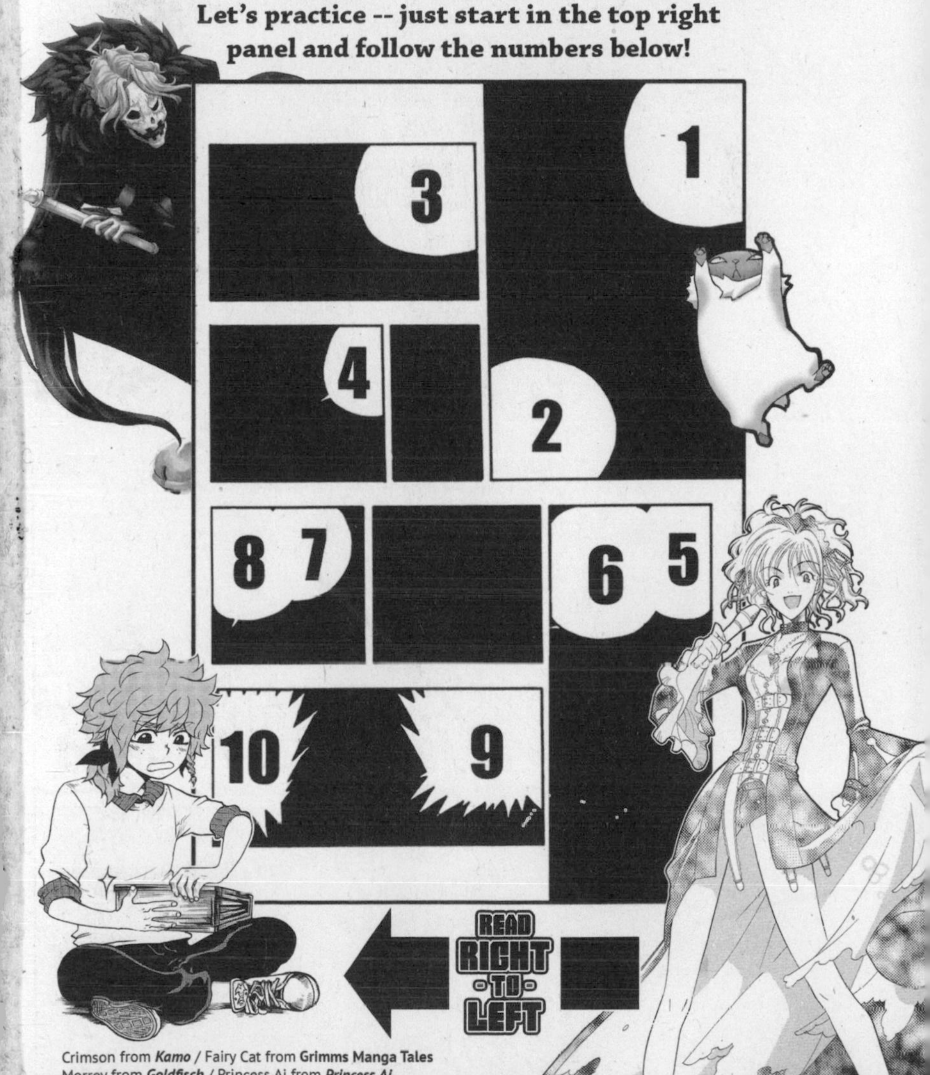
1
2
3
4
5
6
7
8
9
10
READ
RIGHT
-TO-
LEFT

Crimson from *Kamo* / Fairy Cat from **Grimms Manga Tales**
Morrey from *Goldfisch* / Princess Ai from *Princess Ai*

THE AUTHOR

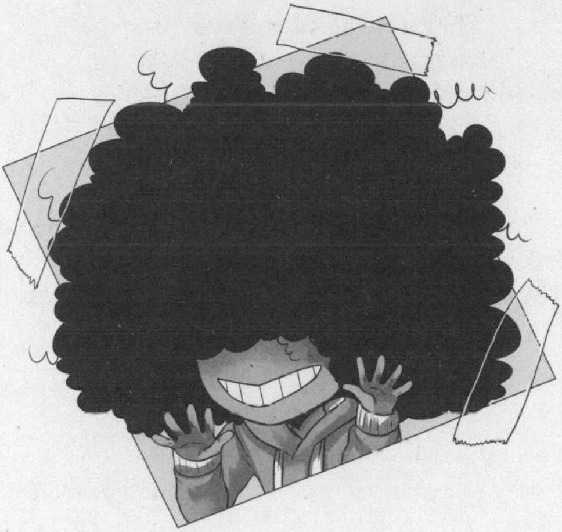

Born in 1991, Nana Yaa won first place in the manga competition *MangaMagie* at the early age of 17 and caught the attention of *TV Total* presenter Stefan Raab, who even had her on the show.

She is now among the most productive artists in the German manga scene and has already published numerous doujinshi and short stories. In addition to her contributions to anthologies by the independent publisher Schwarzer Turm, her first full-length work, *Patina*, was published by Comicstars Droemer Knaur in 2016. Her slice-of-life drama *MCS* was awarded *Doujinshi of the Year* in 2016.

Nana Yaa lives and works in Neuss and graduated with a Bachelor in Communication Design in 2015. When she's not at her work desk or thinking about a new story, she plays RPGs, drinks cocktails with friends or passes the time with her dog.